Penguin Book 2252

Pedigree

Georges Simenon was born at Liège in Belgium in 1903. At sixteen he began work as a journalist on the *Gazette de Liège*. He has published over one hundred and eighty novels in his own name, sixty-eight of which belong to the Inspector Maigret series, and his work has been published in thirty-two languages. He has had a great influence upon French cinema, and more than forty-five of his novels have been filmed.

Simenon's novels are largely psychological. He describes hidden fears, tensions, and alliances beneath the surface of bourgeois family life which suddenly explode into violence and crime. André Gide wrote to him: 'You are living on a false reputation – just like Baudelaire or Chopin. But nothing is more difficult than making the public go back on a too hasty first impression. You are still the slave of your first successes and the reader's idleness would like to put a stop to your triumphs there. . . . You are much more *important* than is commonly supposed'; and François Mauriac wrote: 'I am afraid I may not have the courage to descend right to the depths of this nightmare which Simenon describes with such unendurable art.'

Simenon has travelled a great deal and once lived on a cutter, making long journeys of exploration round the coasts of northern Europe. He is married and has four children, and lives near Lausanne in Switzerland. He enjoys swimming and golf.

Georges Simenon

Pedigree

Translated from the French
by Robert Baldick

Penguin Books
in association with Hamish Hamilton

Penguin Books Ltd, Harmondsworth,
Middlesex, England
Penguin Books Pty Ltd, Ringwood,
Victoria, Australia

Pedigree first published 1948
This translation first published by
Hamish Hamilton 1962
Published in Penguin Books 1965

Copyright © Georges Simenon, 1948
Translation copyright © Hamish Hamilton, 1962

Made and printed in Great Britain by
Cox and Wyman Ltd, London, Reading,
and Fakenham
Set in Monotype Garamond

Preface

Not so long ago, it was still fashionable for an author to introduce each of his works with a preface, a foreword, or a brief note
which put him so to speak in direct contact with the reader, to
such an extent that the formula: 'Dear Reader' was almost as
common as the pulpit introduction: 'Dear Brethren.'

Is it because nowadays the newspapers, with their interviews,
their gossip columns, and their literary inquiries, keep the
public fully informed of both the intentions and the activities
of the writing fraternity that this fashion has fallen into disuse?

On the occasion of this new edition of *Pedigree*, I am giving
in to the temptation to follow the old custom, for various
reasons which are probably not very conclusive. I have been
asked, and I am still asked, a great many questions about this
book; a great deal has been written about it, not all of it
accurate. I know too that André Parinaud has done me the
honour of devoting an important study in three volumes to
me, under the crushing title of *The Truth about Simenon,* a study
which is in the press and which I have not yet read, and that he
seeks in *Pedigree* the explanation, if not of all my writings, at
least of certain of their aspects and certain tendencies.

Shall I be accused of presumptuousness if I provide here and
now, very simply, a few first-hand details?

Pedigree was written neither in the same way, nor in the same
circumstances, nor with the same intentions as my other novels,
and that is doubtless why it forms a sort of islet in my writings.

In 1941, when I was living at Fontenay-le-Comte, a doctor, on
the basis of an inaccurate X-ray, informed me that I had at the
most two years to live and condemned me to almost total
inactivity.

At that time I had only one son, aged two, and it occurred to
me that when he grew up he would know practically nothing of
his father or of his father's family.

In order to do something to fill this gap, I bought three notebooks with mottled cardboard covers and, abandoning my

usual typewriter, I started recounting in the first person, in the form of a letter to the big boy who would read it one day, anecdotes about my childhood.

I was engaged at that time in regular correspondence with André Gide. His curiosity was aroused. About a hundred pages had been written when he expressed a desire to read them.

The letter Gide sent me shortly afterwards was in fact the starting-point of *Pedigree*. In it he advised me, even if I still intended to address myself only to my son, to start my story again, not in the first person this time, but, in order to give it more life, in the third, and to type it as I did my novels.

It was the original hundred pages or so from the notebooks which were published in 1945, in a limited edition, by the Presses de la Cité, under the title, chosen by the publisher in my absence, of *I Remember*. Even so this text had been altered so as to omit anything which might have been taken for a portrait.

As for the new text, composed after I had received Gide's letter, if it resembles the original text in its first part, it should none the less be regarded as a novel, and I would not even wish the label of autobiographical novel to be attached to it.

Parinaud questioned me at some length on this point in the course of our conversations on the radio in 1955, trying at all costs to identify me with the central character, Roger Mamelin.

I answered him with a formula which may not be my own invention, but which I shall none the less use again, to wit that, in my novel, everything is true while nothing is accurate.

I admit too that, when I had finished the book, I searched for a long time for the equivalent of the wonderful title Goethe gave to his childhood memories: *Dichtung und Wahrheit*, a title which has been translated more or less accurately as: *Poetry and Truth*.

Roger Mamelin's childhood, his environment, the settings in which he develops, are very close to reality, as are the people he observes.

The events, for the most part, are not invented.

However, particularly with regard to the characters, I used the writer's privilege to re-create reality from composite materials, keeping closer to poetic truth than to truth pure and simple.

People so completely failed to understand this that because

6

of a facial feature, a mannerism, a similarity in name or pro-fession, a good many insisted on recognizing themselves in my characters, and some had writs issued against me.

I am not, alas, the only one in this position: many of my col-leagues have had the same experience. It is difficult nowadays to give a name, a profession, an address, even a telephone number to a character in a novel without incurring the risk of a lawsuit.

The first edition of *Pedigree* concluded with the words: 'End of Volume One', and I still get letters asking me when the following volumes are going to appear.

I left Roger Mamelin at the age of sixteen. The second volume was to recount his adolescence, the third his arrival in Paris and his apprenticeship in what I have called elsewhere the business of being a man.

They have not been and never will be written, for, among the hundreds of minor characters which I should have to bring on to the scene, how many would result in my being condemned all over again to pay heavy damages? I dare not imagine.

When *Pedigree* was reprinted in 1952, in a new type, I cautiously, and perhaps somewhat ironically, left the in-criminated passages blank, keeping nothing but innocent punctuation marks, and attributing these gaps, in a brief prefatory note, to the judgement of the courts.

In the present edition, the reader will find no blanks. Not without a certain melancholy, I have renounced even irony and pruned my book of everything which could appear suspicious or offensive.

I none the less reiterate, not out of prudence but out of a concern for accuracy, that *Pedigree* is a novel, hence a work in which imagination and re-creation play the most important part, although this does not prevent me from agreeing that Roger Mamelin has a great deal in common with the child that I once was.

Georges Simenon

Noland, 16 April 1957

Part One

Chapter One

She opened her eyes and for a few moments, several seconds, a silent eternity, there was nothing changed in her, or in the kitchen around her; besides, it was no longer a kitchen, it was a mixture of shadows and pale gleams of light, without any consistency or significance, Limbo perhaps?

Was there a specific moment when the sleeping woman's eyelids parted? Or did the pupils remain fixed on the void like the lens over which a photographer has forgotten to lower the shutter of black velvet?

Somewhere outside – it was just in the rue Léopold – a strange life was flowing by, dark because night had fallen, noisy and hurried because it was five o'clock in the afternoon, wet and slimy because it had been raining for several days; and the pale globes of the arc lamps were flickering in front of the dummies in the dress shops, and the trams were passing by, extracting blue sparks, as sudden as flashes of lightning, from the ends of their trollies.

Élise, her eyes open now, was still far away, nowhere in particular; only those fantastic lights from outside came through the window and passed through the lace curtains with the white flowers whose arabesques they projected on to the walls and on to the objects in the room.

The familiar purring of the stove was the first thing to reappear, together with the little reddish disc of the opening through which tiny burning coals could sometimes be seen falling; the water began singing in the white enamel kettle which had been dented near the spout; the alarm-clock, on the black mantelpiece, resumed its gentle tick-tock.

Only then did Élise feel a vague movement in her belly, and come to, and realize that she had fallen asleep, balanced unsteadily on a chair, still holding the dishcloth in her hand. She knew where she was, on the second floor of Cession's, right in the middle of a thriving town, not far from the Pont des Arches which separated the town from the suburbs; and she was frightened. She stood up, trembling, holding her breath, and then, to reassure herself with an everyday gesture, she put some coal on the fire.

'Dear God,' she muttered.

Désiré was far away, on the other side of the town, in his office in the rue des Guillemins, and now perhaps she was going to give birth, all by herself, while hundreds and thousands of passers-by went by, bumping their umbrellas against one another in the glistening streets.

Her hand went out to pick up the matchbox next to the alarm-clock, but she had not the patience to remove the milky globe of the oil-lamp and the glass, and then to raise the wick; she was too frightened. She lacked the courage to put away in the cupboard the odd plates that were lying around, and without looking in the mirror she put on her black crape hat, the one she had worn in mourning for her mother. Then she put on her black cheviot coat which was also a mourning coat and no longer buttoned up, so that she had to hold it folded across her swollen belly.

She was thirsty. She was hungry. There was something missing within her, an empty feeling, but she did not know what to do about it and rushed out of the room, putting the key in her handbag.

It was 12 February 1903. A bat's-wing burner hissed and spat out its incandescent gas on the staircase, for there was gas laid on in the house, though not on the second floor.

On the first floor, Élise saw some light under a door; she did not dare to knock; the idea did not even occur to her. Some people of independent means lived there, the Delobels, people who speculated on the Stock Exchange, a selfish couple who coddled themselves and spent several months every year at Ostend or Nice.

There was a draught in the narrow corridor, which passed between two shops. In the windows of Cession's, there were dozens of dark hats, and inside, people looking hesitantly at themselves in mirrors and not daring to say whether they were pleased with their reflections, and Madame Cession, Élise's landlady, in black silk, with a black tucker, a cameo, and a watch on a chain round her neck.

Trams went by every minute or so, green ones going to

Trooz, Chênée, and Fléron, red and yellow ones going unendingly round the town.

Hawkers were calling out the winning numbers of the latest lottery, and others were shouting:

'The Baronne de Vaughan, ten centimes! Ask for the picture of the Baronne de Vaughan!'

She was Léopold II's mistress. There was supposed to be an underground passage connecting her house with the Château de Laeken.

'Ask for the Baronne de Vaughan . . .'

All her life, as far back as she could remember, Élise had had the same feeling of smallness; yes, she was terribly small, weak, and defenceless, in a big, indifferent world, and all she could do was mutter:

'Dear God . . .'

She had forgotten her umbrella. She had not the heart to go back for it, and tiny drops of rain settled on her round little Nordic face, on her fair, curly Flemish hair.

Everybody struck her as impressive, even the man in a frockcoat, stiff as a ramrod, with waxed moustaches and a collar as broad as a cuff, who was tramping up and down under the lamp outside a dress-shop. He was dying of cold in the feet, cold in the nose, cold in the fingers. In the crowd moving along the pavement, he was on the look-out for mothers dragging children along by the hand. His pockets were full of little colour-prints, illustrated puzzles such as: 'Find the Bulgarian'.

It was cold. It was raining. It was slushy.

She caught a whiff of hot chocolate as she passed the latticed basement windows of Hosay's from which good smells were always escaping. She walked quickly. She was not in pain, and yet she was sure that her labour had begun and that she had not much time left. Her suspender had come undone and her stocking started slipping down. Just before the place Saint-Lambert there was a narrow passage between two shops where it was always dark, and she darted into it and put her foot on a stone.

Was she talking to herself? Her lips were moving.

'Dear God, please give me enough time!'

But then, just as she was lifting up her skirts to reach the suspender, she froze: there were two men in the shadows into which a little light from the rue Léopold penetrated. Two men whose conversation she must have interrupted. Were they hiding? She could not say for certain, but she had a vague feeling that there was something suspicious about their *tête-à-tête*. No doubt they were waiting in silence for the departure of this scatter-brained woman who had rushed headlong to within a few feet of them to adjust her stocking.

She scarcely looked at them; already she was beating a retreat, and yet a name sprang to her lips:

'Léopold . . .'

She must have muttered this name in a whisper. She was sure, or almost sure, that she had recognized one of her brothers, Léopold, whom she had not seen for years: a back already bent at the age of forty-five, a dark beard, and eyes shining beneath thick brows. His companion was very young, a beardless child freezing, this February evening, in the draught blowing down the passage. He was not wearing an overcoat. His face was tense, as if he were holding back his tears. . . .

Élise plunged once more into the crowd without daring to look back. Her suspender was still undone and this gave her the impression of walking sideways.

'Dear God, please . . . And what is my brother Léopold . . . ?'

In the place Saint-Lambert there were more lamps and brighter ones: the lamps of the Grand Bazaar, which was constantly growing and had already eaten up two blocks of houses. The splendid shop windows, the brass doors which opened silently and that special hot breath of air which reached you right out on the pavement.

'Ask for the winning numbers of the Brussels lottery.'

Finally she caught sight of some shop windows of a more discreet luxury, those of L'Innovation, full of silks and woollen goods. She went in. It seemed to her that she ought to hurry. She smiled, for she always smiled when she returned to L'Innovation, and, as in a dream, scarcely able to distinguish one from the other, she greeted the shop assistants in black standing behind the counters.

'Valérie!'

Valérie was there, behind the needlework counter, serving an elderly customer and trying to match some silk, and Valérie's eyes, as they fell upon Élise's frightened face, said in their turn:

'Dear God!'

For both women were of the same sort, the sort who are afraid of everything and who always feel too small. Valérie did not dare hurry her customer. She had understood. Already she was looking in the direction of the central cash-desk, trying to catch sight of the boss, Monsieur Wilhems, with his squeaky patent-leather shoes and his carefully manicured hands.

Three or four counters further on, in the layette department, Maria Debeurre was looking at Élise and wishing she could talk to her, while the latter, standing stiff and erect in her mourning dress, was gripping the counter with the tips of her fingers. The moist heat of the shop was stifling her. The insipid smell of the linens, madapollams, and serges, the subtler smell of all these reels and bobbins, and these silky rolls in pale colours, made her feel sick, as did the oppressive silence in the alley-ways.

She felt as if hollows were forming in the sides of her nose, as if her legs were giving way, but a sad smile remained fixed to her lips and she managed to nod discreetly to some shop-girls who were very far away and of whom all she could see through a luminous fog was their black dresses and lacquered belts.

For three years she had lived behind one of these counters. When she had applied for the job . . .

But you had to go further back than that. Her life as a frightened, unhappy little mouse had begun when she was five, when her father had died and the family had left the huge house by the canal at Herstal, where timber from the north filled sheds as big as churches.

She did not understand. She scarcely knew that father of hers with the long inky moustaches who had made a mess of his affairs, signed some accommodation bills, and died as a result.

Her brothers and sisters were married or had already left home, for Élise was the thirteenth child, born when nobody expected any more.

Two little rooms, in an old house near the rue Féronstrée. She lived alone with her mother, a dignified woman, always trim and dapper, who used to put empty saucepans on the stove when somebody came, to give the impression that they were short of nothing.

One day the tousle-headed little girl went into a shop, pointed

15

to something on display, opened her mouth, but could not find the right words.

'Some . . . some . . .'

Her father was German, her mother Dutch. Élise did not know yet that she did not speak the same language as other people. She was determined to express herself, and, in front of the amused shopkeeper, she blurted out at random:

'Some . . . fricadelles . . .'

Why fricadelles? It was a word which had sprung to her lips because she had heard it at home and which, here, provoked roars of laughter. It was the first humiliation of her life. She had run home without buying anything, and she had burst into tears.

At fifteen, to make life at home a little less wretched, she had put her hair up, let her dress down, and presented herself to the polite and well-groomed Monsieur Wilhems.

'How old are you?'

'Nineteen.'

It was almost her real family that she had come to see today: Valérie Smet, Maria Debeurre, and the others who were looking at her from a distance and even from the galleries, the furniture, linoleum and toy departments.

She put a brave face on it. She smiled. She looked at little Valérie who was weighed down under an enormous mass of brown hair and whose patent-leather belt cut her figure in two like a diabolo.

'Cash-desk!'

The old lady had been served. Valérie came running up.

'You think it's due today?'

They whispered as if they were in the confessional, darting anxious glances at the central-desk and the inspectors in their tail-coats.

'Désiré?'

'He's at the office . . . I didn't dare send word to him . . .'

'Wait a minute . . . I'll ask Monsieur Wilhems . . .'

It seemed to Élise that this was taking an eternity, and yet she was not in pain; she felt nothing but a vague discomfort all over her body. Two years earlier, when they used to leave the shop arm-in-arm, she and Valérie, they invariably ran into a big, shy lad with a pointed beard and severe-looking clothes.

Valérie was always the more excited of the two.

'I'm sure it's you he comes for.'

He was very tall, about six foot, and they were each as little as the other. How had Valérie found out who he was?

'His name is Désiré ... Désiré Mamelin ... He's a clerk in Monsieur Monnoyeur's insurance office in the rue des Guillemins ...'

Now Valérie was explaining, explaining; Monsieur Wilhems glanced at his sometime shop-assistant and nodded.

'Wait for me a minute ... I'm just going for my hat and coat.'

A noise outside, as if two trams had collided ...

'Dear God,' sighed Élise.

Three times in two months there had been tram accidents under her windows in the rue Léopold. Only a few customers near the doors rushed out to see what had happened. The shop-assistants stayed in their places. A few shrill cries could be heard, then a dull murmur. Monsieur Wilhems had not so much as moved one elbow on the polished oak of the main cash-desk, and one finger was stroking his silvery moustache.

People were running past outside, in front of the screen formed by the shop windows. Valérie reappeared.

'Did you hear?'

'An accident ...'

'Can you walk?'

'Yes, of course, Valérie ... I'm sorry to have bothered you. What did he say?'

'He' was the omnipotent Monsieur Wilhems.

'Come along ... lean on my arm ...'

'I assure you I'm still capable of walking by myself ...'

The doors opened noiselessly and they went out into the damp cold where they heard a sort of stampeding noise and saw hundreds, perhaps thousands, of people making for the nearby Grand Bazaar. Already there were lines of trams immobilized one behind another.

'Come along, Élise. We'll go along the rue Gérardrie.'

But Élise was pushing up behind the crowd and lifting herself up on tiptoe.

'Look ...'

'Yes ...'

In front of the Grand Bazaar in the place Saint-Lambert there was a monumental glass canopy covering the whole pavement. Now, over a distance of ten yards or more, the panes were broken, the ironwork was twisted, the lamps were out.

'What is it, Monsieur?' Élise asked the nearest man, in a humble voice.

'How should I know? . . . I know as much as you do . . .'

'Come along, Élise . . .'

Some policemen came running up and tried to push their way through the crowd. Behind them could be heard, first a fire-engine, then an ambulance.

'Move along! . . . Move along, now!'

'The window, Valérie . . .'

Two of the Bazaar's windows were like big dark holes, and there was nothing left but a few stalactites of glass.

'What has happened?'

The policeman she asked this time was in a hurry and did not reply. An old gentleman smoking a cigar and pushing irresistibly forward answered without looking at her:

'A bomb . . . The anarchists again . . .'

'Élise, please . . .'

Élise allowed herself to be dragged away. She had forgotten her giddiness, which had suddenly been replaced by an exceptional nervousness. She would have liked to cry, but could not manage to do so. Valérie opened her umbrella, pressed up against her, and steered her towards the rue Gérardrie.

'We'll go and see the midwife . . .'

'Let's hope she's in . . .'

The streets all around were deserted. Everybody had rushed over to the place Saint-Lambert and the shopkeepers, standing on their doorsteps, were questioning passers-by.

'On the second floor, yes.'

A visiting-card bearing the midwife's name recommended ringing the bell three times. They rang. A curtain moved.

'She's in.'

The gas went on in the corridor. A fat woman tried to make out the features of her visitors in the darkness outside.

'Oh, it's you . . . You think so? . . . All right . . . Go back home, in any case . . . I'll come along after you . . . On the way I'll tell Dr Van der Donck to stand by in case he's needed . . .'

'Valérie! Look . . .'

Some gendarmes on horseback came riding along at a trot on their way towards the place Saint-Lambert . . .

'Don't think about that any more . . . Come along . . .'

And as they were going past Hosay's, Valérie pushed Élise into the shop.

'Eat something, it'll do you good. You're trembling all over.'

'You think I ought to?'

Valérie chose a cake and, somewhat embarrassed, asked for a glass of port. She thought it incumbent upon her to explain:

'It's for my friend, who . . .'

'Dear God, Valérie!'

*

At six o'clock Désiré left his office in the rue des Guillemins and set off with his long, regular stride.

'He has such a fine way of walking!'

He did not turn round, did not stop to look at the shop windows. He walked along, smoking his cigarette, looking straight ahead; he walked along as if a military band were accompanying him. His itinerary never varied. He always arrived at the same time, to a minute, in front of the pneumatic clocks, and at precisely the same spot he lit his second cigarette.

He knew nothing of what had happened in the place Saint-Lambert, and he was surprised to see four trams following one another. Probably there had been an accident . . .

At twenty-five, he had never known any other woman but Élise. Before he met her, he used to spend his evenings in a church club. He was the prompter in the dramatic society.

Walking along, he came to the rue Léopold by way of the rue de la Cathédrale, went into the passage on the ground floor, looked up, and saw wet patches on the steps, as if several people had gone that way.

Then he rushed upstairs. When he got to the first floor, he could hear a murmur of voices. The door opened before he touched the handle. Valérie's frightened little face appeared, a round face with the hair and eyelashes of a Japanese doll and two red spots on the cheekbones.

'It's you, Désiré . . . Hush . . . Élise . . .'

He wanted to go in. He went into the kitchen but the midwife stopped him.

'Whatever happens, I'm having no men in here . . . Go and wait outside . . . We'll call you when you can come in . . .'

And he heard Élise sighing in the bedroom:

'Dear God, Madame Béguin, it's Désiré already! . . . Where is he going to eat?'

'What! You haven't gone yet? . . . I tell you we'll call you . . . Look . . . I'll wave the lamp at the window . . .'

He did not notice that he had left his hat on a corner of the untidy table. His long black overcoat buttoned up almost to the collar and gave him a solemn look. He had the little brown beard of a musketeer.

*

Now the street was empty, with just a thin drizzle to give it a touch of life. The shop-windows had disappeared one after another behind their iron curtains. The men with frozen noses who distributed coloured prospectuses at the doors of the dress shops had vanished into the darkness. The trams were rarer and made more din; the monotonous noise that could be distinguished in the background was that of the muddy waves of the Meuse breaking against the piers of the Pont des Arches.

In the narrow streets all around, there were plenty of little cafés with frosted-glass windows and cream curtains, but Désiré never set foot in a café except on Sunday morning, at eleven o'clock, and then always at the Renaissance.

He was already scanning the windows inquiringly. He did not think about eating. He kept taking his watch out of his pocket and now and then he would start talking to himself.

At ten o'clock, he was the only person left on the pavement. He had scarcely so much as frowned on seeing some gendarmes' helmets over in the direction of the place Saint-Lambert.

Twice he had climbed the stairs, and strained his ears to catch some noise; twice he had fled, frightened, sick at heart.

'Excuse me . . .'

The policeman at the corner of the street, standing underneath a big dummy clock with its hands fixed, had nothing to do.

'Could you tell me the right time?'

Then with a strained, apologetic smile:

'Time seems to go so slowly when one's waiting . . . when one's waiting for such an important event . . . You see, my wife . . .'

He smiled without quite managing to conceal his pride.

'. . . Any moment now, we are going to have a child . . .'

He explained. He felt the need to explain. That they had seen Dr Van der Donck, the leading specialist. That it was he who had given them the midwife's name. That he had told them: 'She is the one I would choose for my own wife.'

'You understand . . . If a man like Dr Van der Donck . . .'

Sometimes somebody would go past, keeping close to the houses, with his coat collar turned up, and his footsteps would go on echoing for a long time through the maze of streets. Under each lamp-post, every fifty yards or so, a patch of fog and rain made a circle of yellow light.

'What are they doing over there?'

There was a lot of coming and going over in the place Saint-Lambert. Policemen's capes could be seen passing by. A horse-guard had galloped past.

'The anarchists . . .'

'What have they done?'

Désiré asked the question politely, but had he so much as understood?

'They've thrown a bomb at the shop windows of the Grand Bazaar.'

'With the children that come later, I suppose you feel used to it . . . But with the first . . . Especially seeing that my wife isn't very strong . . . and rather nervy . . .'

Désiré still had not noticed that he was bare-headed. He was wearing round celluloid sleeves which fell over his hands with every movement. He had just finished his packet of cigarettes and he would have to go too far to buy another.

'If that woman forgot to wave the lamp . . . She's got so much to do! . . .'

At midnight, the policeman himself apologized and went off. There was no longer a soul to be seen in the street, no more trams, nothing but distant footsteps, doors shutting, bolts being pushed home.

At last, the lamp . . .

It was exactly ten minutes past midnight. Désiré rushed forward like a madman. His long legs threshed through space.

'Élise . . .'

'Hush! . . . Not so loud . . .'

Then he burst into tears. He no longer knew what he was doing, nor what he was saying, nor that some women were looking at him. He did not dare touch the child who was all red. The insipid smell in the flat upset him. Valérie went to empty a bucket on the entresol.

Élise, between the sheets which had just been put on the bed, the sheets she had embroidered specially for the occasion, smiled weakly.

'It's a boy,' she stammered. As for him, with a complete lack of self-restraint, he said, crying all the while:

'I shall never, never forget that you have just given me the greatest joy a woman can give a man . . .'

'Désiré . . . Listen . . . What time is it?'

The child had been born at ten past twelve. Élise whispered:

'Listen, Désiré . . . He's come into the world on a Friday the thirteenth . . . Nobody must know . . . You must beg that woman . . .'

And that was why, the next morning, when Désiré, accompanied by his brother Arthur as a witness, went to register the child's birth at the Town Hall, he told the clerk, with an innocent expression:

'Roger Mamelin, born at Liège, at No. 18 rue Léopold, on Thursday, 12 February 1903.'

He added automatically:

'Over Cession's.'

Chapter Two

Why shouldn't it be a guardian spirit? Why was it always at the same moment that it revealed its presence and seemed to bid them good day? Most mornings, Élise bustled backwards and forwards, but today she lay motionless in the warmth of the bed, her shoulders propped up against her pillow and

Désiré's. In the cradle, the child, who had just been fed, was breathing with a slight whistling sound. Élise was wearing her morose expression, not sad, but morose, a half-smile, partly shame, partly pity, because it was not a man's work that Désiré was forcing himself to do just then.

The fire had not been alight for long in the stove. Its heat could be felt emerging in little waves into the cold of the morning; if you looked hard, you could even see a battle raging: the waves of warm, then hot air emanating from the stove collided, just beyond the table, with a belt of icy air which, all night long, had hung in front of the black panes of glass of the windows. A fire in the morning, especially very early in the morning, when you get up at an unaccustomed hour, does not smell the same as at other times of the day; it does not make the same noise either. The flames are brighter too, as Élise had often noticed.

And now, all of a sudden, it was as if the japanned iron had become distended, as if a guardian spirit inside had awoken and expanded to explode with a joyful 'boom'.

Every morning this happened. And every morning there was a thin rain of pink ash, followed shortly afterwards by the singing of the water in the kettle.

It was barely six o'clock. Out in the street they had heard only one person's footsteps, and that unknown passer-by had probably looked up inquiringly at the only lighted windows in the street. Through the window-panes nothing could be seen, not even the glow of the gas-lamps, but it was obviously pouring down, for a continuous gurgling could be heard going up and down the rain-spouts. Now and then there was a gust of wind, which showed itself by a sudden draught in the chimney and a shower of ashes falling in the tray at the bottom of the stove.

'Dear God, Désiré . . .'

She had not dared to say: 'Poor Désiré'. She was ashamed of lying there, motionless, in the bedroom, with the communicating door wide open. She was even more ashamed of the natural serenity, the glowing gaiety emanating from Désiré while he was doing the housework. Over his dark suit, he had tied a woman's apron, a little cotton apron in a faded blue check, adorned with a flounce; not caring how ridiculous he looked, he had used some safety-pins to fasten the straps, which were too short, to his shoulders.

Now and then, holding a bucket in each hand, he went down to the entresol, so quietly that she could not hear him brushing past the wall, nor the metallic noise the bucket handle always made, and could only just make out the gentle flow of water from the tap.

He had decided to scrub the floor, for a lot of people had come the day before, and since it had been raining, they had left dirt all over the place. That Saturday had been a different day from all the rest, one of those days which leave only a confused memory: Valérie, who had asked for the day off, had not left Élise's side; Maria Debeurre had come along during the lunch-hour, followed by Désiré's sisters and his brother Arthur, a gay, boisterous fellow, who was forever cracking jokes, and who had insisted on offering a drink to the clerk at the Town Hall.

Madame Cession must have been furious about all this coming and going on the stairs, and the people on the first floor had kept their door firmly shut.

Everything was clean now. It was funny how men twisted dishcloths the wrong way round, from the left to the right!

It was Sunday. That was why, while the hands of the alarm-clock went on moving, nothing could be heard outside but the timid summons of church bells ringing for the early Masses.

'Leave it, Désiré . . . Valérie will see to it . . .'

But no! Désiré had heated some water. It was he who had washed the nappies and hung them to dry on the cord over the stove. He had remembered to cover the floor, which stayed wet a long time, with the faded floral chintz which she used to put down on Saturdays to keep it clean. He had thought of everything. For instance, following Élise's example, he had slipped some old newspapers between the floorboards and the carpet so that the latter should not get wet.

Day dawned, but it was impossible to tell whether there was a thin drizzle falling or whether it was just fog that was filling the street. Big limpid drops were falling from the cornices. The first trams, with their lights still on, seemed to be drifting past.

'When I think that I can't even help you!'

They were so very much at home that morning! On the second floor of Cession's, their flat seemed to be hanging in the air at the very end of the world. Désiré hummed to himself while he was shaving. Élise tried to banish her anxiety or sadness – she did not know quite what to call the feeling which stole over her whenever she was going to be unhappy.

When she had been a little girl and had not yet begun thinking about such things, disaster had struck at her family without warning. She had found herself practically on the streets, in deep mourning, with her mother and her sister Félicie, and her brothers and sisters scattered far and wide; and since then she had always had the impression that she was subject to a special fate, that she was not like other people. She was seized with sudden, irresistible urges to cry, and she had shed a great many tears, even during the first days of her marriage.

'I've got so much into the habit of crying,' she had tried to explain to Désiré at the time. 'I just can't help it.'

Wasn't the child too red? He was breathing badly. She was sure that he was breathing badly, as if he were suffering from some obstruction, but she did not dare to say so. Soon her mother-in-law would be arriving and Élise was dreading this visit. Her mother-in-law did not like her.

'Get married if you want to, son. That's your affair, but if you want my opinion . . .'

A girl from the other side of the bridges, a girl so to speak without a family and in very poor health, a girl who, when she was with her sisters, spoke a language nobody could understand.

'Valérie's late,' sighed Élise, looking at the clock. 'You can go, Désiré. You mustn't be late. I shall be quite all right waiting by myself.'

He had put on the coarse blue uniform of the civic guard and buckled his belt. Out of a white cardboard box he had taken his peculiar cap in the shape of a top hat surmounted by a reddish-brown cock's feather, and after putting it on he climbed on to a chair – the old chair, the one on to which they always climbed – to get his Mauser rifle from the top of the wardrobe. Although the rifle was not loaded, Élise was afraid of it.

25

'Go on! I tell you I shall be all right on my own...'

He waited, standing by the window which had taken on the bluey-green whiteness of winter clouds. The shutters over the shop windows remained closed. Now and then some black silhouettes slipped past the house fronts, but very few, for people were taking advantage of the fact that it was Sunday to stay in bed.

'It's Valérie! Off you go! You're late.'

He kissed her and his moustache smelled of shaving-soap. He did not dare to touch the baby's soft skin with his spiky whiskers.

'Have I kept you waiting, Désiré?'

'Look, Valérie. He absolutely insisted on doing the house-work and washing the nappies.'

Désiré had scarcely started going downstairs when Élise got half out of bed and bent over the cradle.

'Come and look, Valérie. Feel him. Don't you think he's too hot?'

'Of course not, you silly!'

Everything seemed to be in order in the flat and yet Élise's gaze discovered something wrong.

'Valérie, put the wedge back in place, will you?'

It was a piece of wood a few inches long which had been slipped under one foot of the wardrobe to keep it steady, and which was knocked out of place every time the flat was spring-cleaned. A man, even Désiré, would never notice a little thing like that.

*

It did not matter that the streets were empty, with icy winds sweeping them from end to end, squalls of rain, and that deserted, useless look of a winter afternoon, Désiré still had the feeling that as he walked along he was being accompanied by a band which only he could hear and with which his regular stride was keeping time. Under his moustache, his thick lips were parted in a vague smile which expressed nothing but an inner satisfaction. He crossed the Meuse, came in sight of the place Ernest-de-Bavière soon afterwards, with its terreplein of powdered brick, and went towards some groups of civic guards.

'It's a boy!' he announced, making no attempt to conceal his joy.

He was happy to be chaffed, happy about everything, happy about the handshake which his captain, the little architect Snyers, thought fit to give him on this occasion before the morning's drill. The square and not particularly handsome church-tower which could be seen a hundred yards away was that of Saint-Nicolas, the church of his parish, the parish where he had been born, where he had always lived, and the narrow street which ran into the square was his street, the rue Puits-en-Sock, where his family still lived.

'Shoulder arrrrms!'

Désiré was too tall, or the others too short. He tried his hardest. He saw nothing ridiculous in playing soldiers with these men, nearly all of whom he knew in everyday life, family men, clerks, workers, and local shopkeepers.

'Stand at ease!'

In the rue Léopold, Valérie was peeling vegetables and glancing every now and then at the fire.

'Valérie, do you think I'll be able to feed him?'

'Why shouldn't you be able to feed him?'

'I don't know.'

Wasn't she the thirteenth child? Hadn't she always heard people say . . . She knew that there had been a misfortune in the family, not simply bankruptcy but something shameful: her father, towards the end at least, had taken to drink and he had died of a cancer of the tongue.

Élise's brothers and sisters had never regarded her as a normal person. A little thirteenth child whom nobody had expected, and who had turned up to complicate everything.

Louisa, the eldest, had been the only one to call the day before, and she had come empty-handed. Désiré's brothers and sisters, and mere acquaintances had all brought a present, even if it was just a bunch of grapes.

'I prefer to give him a really good present for his First Communion,' Louisa, whose hair was prematurely grey, had said. 'I knew you'd have plenty of everything. As for all these things' – she was referring to the bibs, the silver spoons, the oranges and cakes – 'you never know what to do with them and they just get lost.'

'Yes, Louisa.'

And yet Louisa was a prosperous shopkeeper at Coronmeuse.

She had stayed there half an hour, watching and shaking her head – and indeed, she must have found fault with everything. She could not stand Désiré.

'Dr Van der Donck promised to look in today,' sighed Élise. 'I'm glad he's coming. The baby still seems too hot to me.'

'Don't think about that any more, silly. Look, try and read the paper to take your mind off it.'

'What a lot of trouble I'm giving you! If I hadn't had you to help me . . . Poor Valérie!'

Valérie who was always bustling around, a tiny little thing with her round head adorned with a big bun, and who did her best to help everybody! She lived with her mother and her sister at the top of the rue Haute-Sauvenière. The three of them occupied a two-room flat, an old-maids' flat full of shadows and warmth. Marie, the elder sister, was a dressmaker and worked by the day in one of the richest houses in the town. Valérie was at L'Innovation. Her mother, Madame Smet, who had nothing to do but look after their doll's house, used to come and meet her after work, with a peculiar old woman's hat on her head, the face of a Dresden doll, and mittens from which blotchy pink fingers poked out.

'Don't forget the sugar in the carrots, Valérie. Désiré can't eat carrots without sugar.'

Élise did not know what to do with herself. It was the first time in her life that she had been immobilized in her bed, forced to feel useless. She was incapable of reading the newspaper Valérie had handed her, but she glanced automatically at the front page and suddenly felt surrounded by an oppressive silence.

She said nothing. She could not say anything, even to Valérie, for all that she confided everything to her, including things she would never talk about to Désiré.

On the front page of the paper there was a photograph of a pale young man with taut features, and she was sure that she recognized it, she was sure that it was this mysterious face that she had glimpsed with Léopold in the passage where she had gone to fasten her suspender.

She had known all morning that there was something unpleasant in the air. She did not dare to cry in front of Valérie who would not understand. What on earth had Léopold been up to?

... Yesterday, as the result of a thorough investigation, the police succeeded in identifying the person responsible for the incident in the Saint-Lambert. He is a certain Félix Marette, of the rue de Laveu, whose father is one of our best-known and most highly respected policemen. Every effort is being made to trace Félix Marette, who is on the run ...

'The poor things,' sighed Valérie, seeing that Élise was looking at the paper. 'It seems that they had no idea, that they made tremendous sacrifices to send their son to school. And when his father heard about it he said: "I'd rather see my son dead."'

But what about Léopold? What had Léopold, who was a full-grown man, been doing plotting with that boy in a dark passage?

There, now! The stove went boom, some ashes fell into the tray, the onions started browning, and the baby turned over in his cradle.

'Valérie, don't you think it's time to change him?'

Léopold, the eldest of the Peters children, had known the family in its hey-day. He had been at the University, and he had gone hunting with young men of the nobility, with armament manufacturers and notabilities.

And then, all of a sudden, he had decided that he wanted to be a soldier. At that time the only men in the army were those who had drawn an unlucky number in the conscription lottery, and Léopold, when he was twenty, had drawn a lucky number. But people had the right to sell themselves, to take the place of somebody who had been unlucky in the draw.

That was what he had done. He had donned the close-fitting uniform of the lancers. The army still employed canteen girls at that time, and the one attached to his regiment, a certain Eugénie, who had Spanish blood in her veins like the empress whose name she bore, was a magnificent specimen of womanhood.

Léopold had married her. At the same time he had cut himself off from the whole world. Somebody had seen him working as a waiter at Spa, where Eugénie had spent a season as a cook.

'Mind the pins, Valérie. I'm terrified of pins! I always think of a baby in the rue Hors-Château who ... Somebody's coming upstairs ... There's somebody knocking at the door, Valérie! ...'

It was Félicie – and Élise's eyes filled with tears, she could not say why – a furtive Félicie who announced straight away:

'I managed to get away. I simply had to come and give him a kiss.'

Félicie put some parcels on the table, a bottle of port she had taken from the bar, a breakfast-set in floral porcelain, and a purse full of money.

'No, Félicie, no money! You know perfectly well that Désiré ...'

Already they were speaking Flemish, instinctively, as they did whenever they managed to meet. Félicie was only a few years older than Élise. She had been a shop-assistant like her sister. She had married Coustou, who kept the Café du Marché near the Pont des Arches; he was so jealous that he never let her go out and forbade her to entertain any of her relatives. The two women could see each other only in secret.

Valérie came and went, without understanding anything of the two sisters' effusions. Élise could at last weep freely.

'Aren't you happy?'

'Of course, my poor little Félicie.'

Félicie's breath smelled of port. Yet before her marriage she had not been in the habit of drinking. During an attack of anaemia, the doctor had recommended stout and she had grown accustomed to it. In her café, on the quai de la Goffe, she had too many opportunities, with bottles within easy reach from morning to night.

Élise went on crying, for no particular reason, for all sorts of reasons, because the baby was hot, because she was afraid she would not be able to feed him, because the sky was gloomy and overcast.

'You haven't seen Léopold lately?'

'No. Have you?'

Élise lied. She said no.

'I must dash. If Coustou noticed I'd gone out . . .'

*

For all that Désiré had crossed the bridges, on account of the flat they had found in the town, he had never missed Mass on Sunday at Saint-Nicolas. Even on civic guard Sundays, he left his companions just when, having finished the morning's drill, they made for a little café nearby. He left his rifle with the sacristan who ran a little shop which sold candles and sweets. He arrived just in time for the eleven o'clock Mass, and, with his regular, elastic stride, and with a discreet nod to the people he knew – and he knew everybody – he went and took his place in his pew, the Mamelins' pew, the last in the row and the best, the only one with a high back of solid wood which stopped the inevitable draught every time the padded door opened.

His inner band-music merged with the voice of the organ. He remained standing, very erect, too tall to kneel down in such a narrow space. Without a word, he shook hands with his neighbours and, throughout the Mass, he gazed steadily at the high altar with the choir-boys gravitating round it.

The Mamelins' pew was the pew of the Brotherhood of St Roch, whose statue could be seen on the first pillar, with the green mantle edged with gold, the bleeding knee and the faithful hound.

'For . . . ood . . . ain . . . och . . . ease . . .'
For good St Roch, please!

At the early Masses, it was Chrétien Mamelin, with his long white moustache and his only very slightly bent shoulders, who went from pew to pew, shaking the wooden bowl attached to a long handle so as to jingle the money in it; and every time a coin dropped into it one could hear in a minor key:

' . . . ay . . . od . . . ayou . . .'
May God repay you!

After which, returning to his pew, old Mamelin slipped the coins one after another into the slot made specially for the purpose.

The Elevation . . . The Communion . . . Désiré's lips moved beneath his moustache and his steady gaze remained fixed on the tabernacle.

'*Ite missa est* . . .'

31

The organ . . . The sound of the crowd stamping across the great blue flagstones, and the rain outside, the pale daylight, the wind blowing from the place de Bavière . . .

Going along a poor little alley-way, an alley-way dating back to the days of the beggars, where the children played practically naked and the dirty water ran between your feet, he came to the rue Puits-en-Sock, the shopping street in which every house displayed a sign: a huge pair of cutler's scissors, a pale clock, a monumental civet, and finally, over the Mamelins' hat-shop, a top-hat painted bright red.

Désiré, who had recovered his rifle, went down the narrow, perpetually damp passage leading into the Mamelin house and crossed the yard. The kitchen was at the far side, with a whole wall of glass which had been made opaque with fake stained glass. He knew that a tiny patch of this colouring had been scratched away, that his mother was looking through this hole, and that she was announcing:

'It's Désiré.'

It was his hour. He recognized the smell of the stewed beef and that of the oilcloth covering the long table at which thirteen children had sat in their time.

'Good morning, Mother.'

'Good morning, son.'

'Good morning, Lucien. Good morning, Marcel.'

Steam. His mother always standing, always dressed in slate-grey, with a grey complexion and steel-grey hair.

He sat down. He let the warmth seep into him, and the smells too, without feeling the need to say anything.

'Is Élise all right?'

'She's all right.'

'And the child?'

'Yes.'

'Tell your wife that I'll be coming to see her soon.'

All the Mamelins came like this to sit for a moment in the kitchen in the rue Puits-en-Sock. In an armchair at the far end of the room, Old Papa, their mother's father, sat motionless. In the half-light one could just make out a monstrous carcass, a real bear's carcass, whose arms seemed to reach right down to the floor, and a beardless face with a stone-grey complexion, empty eyes and disproportionately large ears.

He recognized each visitor by his footsteps. Each one implanted a light kiss on a cheek as rough as sandpaper. He never spoke. At Mass time he told his beads in silence. His skin, the skin of a sometime miner, was spangled with blue dots, like encrusted fragments of coal.

*

Four-pound loaves, baked the day before, stood waiting for the whole family, for all the married offspring. Each one, every Sunday, came to collect his share.

'Is Juliette keeping well?'

'She was here just now.'

'And Françoise?'

Here the rain, falling on a zinc platform which covered the kitchen, made a noise which was so to speak a Mamelin noise. The smells were different from those in other places. The steam went on forming dirty drops which trickled down the oil-painted walls.

When it was ten to twelve, Désiré stood up, picked up his loaves and his rifle, and went off.

He did not feel embarrassed at carrying loaves of bread when he was in uniform, with a rifle slung over his shoulder. Any more than at putting a check apron over his suit to do the housework. He walked as in an apotheosis along the narrow pavements of the rue Puits-en-Sock with the trams passing dangerously close. Each shop exhaled its special breath at him: the chip-shop, the tobacconist's, the cake-shop, the dairy-shop... Heavens, he had nearly forgotten! It was Sunday! He went into Bonmersonne's to buy two tarts, an apple tart – Élise liked nothing but fruit tarts – and a rice tart for himself, since he loved sweet things.

He crossed the Pont des Arches. The rue Léopold was dead. It came to life only during the week, like all the streets in the centre, but you could never recognize anybody, because the people you saw came from far away, from anywhere and everywhere, and only passed through, whereas the rue Puits-en-Sock, for instance, was the vital centre of a district.

He walked carefully past the door on the first floor. The Delobels were always complaining about the noise and went to see the Cessions at the slightest excuse.

'Is dinner ready?'

He sniffed, smiled, clambered on to the rickety chair to put his rifle back in place.

'Well, Valérie?'

He turned to Élise.

'Have you been crying?'

She shook her head.

'Has she been crying, Valérie?'

'No, Désiré, you mustn't worry about it. You know she can't help it.'

He knew, but he did not understand. That was why Élise had said earlier to Valérie:

'You know, Désiré is the best of men, but he doesn't feel things as we do.'

What did he feel? He lived. He ate. He slept. He had a good job. Starting as the youngest at Monsieur Monnoyeur's, he had become his right-hand man and it was he who held the key to the safe.

What did it matter if he earned only 150 francs a month? Had they ever gone hungry? Well then!

'Eat up, Désiré.'

He suddenly remembered that that morning, passing Kreutz's toyshop next to his home – his home, as he still called it, was his parents' house – he had seen a whole display of masks, false noses, and rattles.

'It's the first Sunday of the Carnival,' he announced.

Élise did not understand why he should talk about that. The first Sunday was the children's carnival. Désiré was just remembering the carnivals of his childhood.

'Are the carrots sweet enough?'

'They're good. Did you cook them, Valérie?'

'Poor Valérie, if you only knew the trouble she goes to! I keep wondering what we should have done without her!'

'But seeing that we've got her!'

'Precisely! Seeing that Valérie was there, what was the point of worrying? Oh, he didn't feel things!

'Félicie came this morning.'

'Was she squiffy?'

A word they used to signify ... not exactly drunk ... not entirely sober either ...

'Désiré!'

She jerked her head towards Valérie.

'Well? Doesn't Valérie know that your sister ... Another piece of meat, Valérie? Yes do, you must keep your strength up ...'

Until three o'clock, the streets remained empty, or nearly empty. Then a few families appeared, dressed in dark clothes and dragging masked children along behind them without much enthusiasm. A little toreador went by, shivering in a ratteen overcoat and waving a rattle in one hand while he was pulled along by the other.

'What about your mother, Désiré?'

'She'll come. You know that it's an adventure for her, crossing the bridges.'

'Valérie, you don't think the baby's choking, do you?'

He was breathing badly, there was no doubt about that. You ought not to be able to hear a baby's breathing like that. What would Madame Mamelin say, she who was so fond of repeating that Élise was a sickly creature?

'Have you looked in the cupboard on the landing, Valérie? There's nothing lying around?'

For her mother-in-law was perfectly capable of opening the cupboard on the landing to prove that Élise was a poor house-keeper! Élise had taken her big Désiré away from her and that was something she would never forgive.

'You're sure we oughtn't to offer her something? A glass of liqueur? Some cakes?'

'I tell you a mother who's just had a baby never offers anything to her callers. On the contrary, it's up to them to bring something.'

He considered it natural for people to bring something! Whereas Élise would have liked to give something in return, to give more than she received, never to be obliged. She was a Peters.

'I can hear a noise.'

He opened the door and called out gaily:

'Is that you, Mother?'

The people on the first floor had gone out, and there was no longer any need to keep quiet.

'Wait a minute and I'll put on the light. These stairs are so dark.'

He was happy, so happy.

'Come in . . . Come in, Cécile . . .'

It was his youngest sister, Cécile, who was going to get married, who had come with his mother. The latter had crossed the bridges, with her grey dress and her locket, her grey gloves and her hooded cape, to see the child of the foreign woman, of that tousle-haired hoyden who had no money and no health, who was not from Outremeuse or even from Liége, and who, when she was with her sister, spoke a language she did not understand. Désiré was the only person who failed to notice that her entry into the flat produced the effect of an icy draught.

'Good day, daughter.'

She did not bend down to kiss her daughter-in-law.

'Where's your *bebby*?'

She was obviously speaking dialect on purpose. To stress the fact that *she* was a woman of Outremeuse.

Élise trembled between the sheets and Valérie stood beside her as if to protect her.

'Well, daughter, he's green, your *bebby* is!'

It wasn't true! She was just being spiteful! He wasn't green. After being too red all morning, he looked as if he had had trouble digesting his last feed. He was pale, that was undeniable. Élise herself was surprised to see how pale he was, and her hands clutched at the sheets under the blanket while her mother-in-law, shaking her head, stated once for all:

'What an ugly *bebby*!'

That was all. She sat down. She deigned to sit down while her icy gaze swept round the flat. She was sure to have seen everything. The two damp patches on the ceiling – they were there all right; the Cessions had refused to have them whitewashed – and a duster which Valérie had left lying on a chair.

She had not brought anything either. She was there because she had to be there, but not for anything in the world would she have taken off her hat.

Élise made an effort and murmured:

'A cup of coffee, Mother?'

'No thank you, daughter.'

As if her daughter-in-law's coffee was not good enough for her.

Élise was ashamed of her furniture. It was the wife who

provided the furniture when a couple married. At her home, at the time of her father's death, there had been some beautiful antique furniture. One of her brothers, Louis, Louis of Tongres as he was called because he lived at Tongres where he had made his fortune, had come and taken it all, one piece after another, under the pretext that it belonged to the Peters and had to go back to the Peters, and he had replaced it with deal furniture . . .

'Well, children . . .'

The regulation time for a call had passed.

'I still wonder whether your wife will be able to feed him.'

It was to Désiré that she spoke commiseratingly. ' You would have your way! I warned you!' These words were in the tone of her voice, in the gaze of her eyes.

'Anyway, I hope *for your sake* that all goes well!'

She went off. Cécile followed her. Désiré accompanied them downstairs and when he returned he found Élise in tears in Valérie's arms.

'She was spiteful . . . On purpose . . . She was deliberately spiteful . . .'

'But no! . . . I tell you you're wrong . . .'

He would have liked everybody to be in agreement, to like one another, to live as he did in the serenity and the joy of every passing moment. He looked at the alarm-clock.

'It's time for his feed.'

Alas, the baby vomited a murky liquid which was not milk, and which was a greenish colour.

'Valérie! He's ill . . . Dear God . . .'

Suddenly they heard the shrill noise of squeakers and rattles, and looking down from the window they saw some families who were taking advantage of a break in the rain to take their masked children on a tour of the town centre.

'Perhaps if we gave him some sugared water ? . . .'

'Look, he's all red again. Anybody would think he had done it on purpose, just when your mother . . .'

Poor Valérie. She did not lose her head for one moment. She came and went like a diligent ant, like a furtive little mouse.

'Don't start getting upset, Élise. I tell you it's nothing to worry about.'

'Why is he sick ? It's my milk, I'm sure it is. *His* mother has always said I wouldn't be able to feed him . . .'

Désiré was drumming on the window-pane with his fingers, through the lace curtain which deadened the noise, and he was delighted to be able to announce:

'Here's Dr Van der Donck.'

The doctor took an age to climb the stairs with slow, deliberate steps. He knocked on the door. He came in.

'Well, Madame Mamelin?'

She was already less frightened. Ashamed of her fears, she made an effort to smile. He had come on a Sunday and he deserved her gratitude.

'I don't know, Doctor . . . It seems to me . . . He has just thrown up his milk, and ever since this morning I've had the impression that he's so hot . . . Valérie! . . .'

Valérie, who had understood, brought the bowl of warm water and the towel, and the doctor slowly, carefully washed his white hands loaded with a gold signet-ring.

'Désiré!'

He did not understand as quickly as Valérie. The light was failing.

'The lamp . . .'

He lit it and the doctor sat down by the cradle, in the leisurely manner of somebody with plenty of time at his disposal.

'Let's have a look at the little fellow . . .'

He took a watch out of his pocket. Dr Van der Donck was fair-haired, slightly bald, with a tapering moustache and clothes in broadcloth.

'When did you feed him last?'

Respectfully she replied:

'At two o'clock, Doctor.'

'Come, now . . . Come, now . . . don't worry . . .'

He knew that she was just a nervous child frightened by all the ghosts created by an anxious mind. And yet . . . He frowned . . . He examined the child . . .

'Will you undress him for me?'

Désiré himself, whose head seemed to touch the ceiling, stood rooted to the spot behind him. More mummers went by outside. A military band passed somewhere.

'Loosen it . . . Good . . . Ssh! . . .'

He listened . . . He counted . . . He frowned. He smiled so as not to frighten the mother . . .

'Come, now, Madame, it's nothing serious . . . Don't worry . . . A touch of bronchitis, such as lots of new-born babies get at this time of year . . .'

'That's serious, isn't it, Doctor?'

She could still summon up the courage to smile so as not to annoy him with her fears, when he had come on a Sunday, a carnival Sunday.

'No, not at all . . . With a few precautions . . .'

He put on his gold pince-nez to write.

'Wipe the table, Valérie.'

He read over what he had written, and added a couple of lines.

'There you are, Madame. In a few days there won't be a sign of it left. Above all, don't get into a panic. I tell you it's nothing to worry about. Incidentally . . . Where's that milk he vomited after his last feed?'

'Valérie!'

It was Valérie who came and went. Then Désiré followed the doctor out on to the stairs.

'Doctor . . .'

'Nothing to worry about. I should just like to have an analysis of the milk.'

He held out a little phial he had in his pocket.

'If you can, without alarming her . . . Take it tomorrow morning to the Pierson laboratory . . .'

She would be the only one in the whole family whose milk wasn't good. Madame Mamelin had warned him: '*That girl* . . .'

'Come, now! Come, now! Everything will be all right, you'll see. She's rather highly strung, you understand? Get's worried about the slightest thing.'

More mummers . . . He shut the door . . .

When Désiré got back, he found Valérie trying in vain to calm Elise, who was having a fit of crying which was degenerating into a fit of hysterics.

'I knew it. I felt it. *She* said it would happen before she even knew me!'

The lamp started smoking. Désiré lowered the wick. At the same moment the stove gave its familiar 'boom', as if the guardian spirit of the house had felt that the time had come to make his benevolent presence felt.

'Hush!' whispered Valérie, when Désiré went towards the bed.

And she added in an undertone, while Élise was shaken by sob after sob:

'It does her good.'

Chapter Three

Two o'clock. Two strokes which rang out sharply in the empty air, here first, then there, at Saint-Jean, at Saint-Jacques, at the Cathedral, at Saint-Denis, two strokes which sounded early or late over the sleeping town, in a sky in which the moon was swimming. The fried-fish shops were closed. The frosted-glass globe which served as the sign for a night-club no longer attracted anybody and the doorman was inside.

An opening appeared in a wall in the rue Gérardrie, in a tiny café, a door between two shutters, and somebody gently pushed Léopold outside. In the yellow lamplight a fat blonde waitress could be seen counting the stitches in her crochet-work, the door shut again, footsteps faded into the distance.

God preserve him! And help him to find his way home through the maze of streets!

It was a relief not to see him there any more, staring at his glass, all alone, bearded, unsociable, and so still that when a traveller who was teasing the waitress stopped when he became aware of Léopold's presence, the girl motioned to him to take no notice.

He had gone. There was the noise of a shop shutter which he bumped into, then his footsteps zigzagging from pavement to pavement.

The town slept.

Élise, lying motionless, had her eyes open, and her gaze remained fixed upon the alarm-clock beside the little flame of the night-light.

Three minutes past two ... Five minutes past two ... The child did not move, Désiré was snoring, and she could feel him all warm beside her. She gave him a little push, and murmured, as if she were afraid of waking him:

'Désiré . . .'

Why this humble voice, this apologetic expression, this air of being a poor bedridden woman who would have preferred to fend for herself? He opened his eyes, swung his long hairy legs out of the bed, scratched his feet, and put on the priest's elastic-sided shoes which he used as slippers. (This was an idea of Élise's. A priest had refused to buy the shoes he had ordered, and the cobbler had sold them off cheap. They were of such good quality!)

They did not use the big lamp at night. At the slightest movement the flame of the night-light flickered and the shadow of the corner of the wardrobe started dancing on the ceiling.

Désiré lit the spirit-stove to heat the feeding-bottle in a saucepan; then, feeling cold in his nightshirt, he put on his overcoat, the only one he possessed, a black one with a velvet collar. He remained standing by the window whose panes were covered with a thin film of frost which was still transparent, and Élise's gaze said helplessly, silently:

'Dear God! Poor Désiré!'

Now Désiré was enjoying himself. He scratched at the frost-flowers, just as he used to do when he was a child – this gave his fingernails an extraordinary feeling which was quite unlike any other – and he threw a satisfied glance at the lighted window on the other side of the street exactly opposite him.

It was probably the only lighted window in the whole district. It was at Torset et Mitouron's the wholesale ironmongers, dealers in stoves, pottery, rope, and linoleum. Three floors of shops stuffed with merchandise and, on the second floor, in a little room where the buckets and brooms were stored, the night watchman. His window, like all the rest, was fitted with corrugated frosted glass bearing the inscription: 'Torset et Mitouron', and now and then Désiré caught sight of a stocky silhouette, a thick moustache, hair cut in a stubble.

'Come to bed, Désiré. I can give him the bottle.'

Why? It was always he who fed the baby, without the slightest sign of impatience. Didn't she understand that he liked it, that he liked everything about it, getting up, standing in the cold kitchen, seeing the milk go down in the bottle, carefully counting the drops of medicine, going back to bed, and dropping off to sleep straight away?

At six o'clock, when the alarm-clock went off, the light was still on across the street and his gaze greeted it. He knew that the man was making his coffee in a vessel whose shape Désiré knew only in silhouette.

He lit the fire, swept the room, went down to the entresol to empty the slops and brought up some fresh water. Even if he did not hum himself, the music was in him, a harmonious ebb and flow of thoughts similar to the flux of a calm sea, the gentle movement of a woman's breasts.

Would he see the night watchman at last? The man came downstairs at eight o'clock: Désiré knew that from seeing the light go out at that time, on the shortest days of the year. He came downstairs just as the employees arrived and threw open the groundfloor shutters. Désiré went downstairs too. But he had never met the night watchman, whom he knew only as a silhouette. Did he go out through the main door? Or before plunging into the town did he slip through a little back door which opened on to another street?

'Leave it, Désiré. Madame Smet will do it.'

That wasn't true. Madame Smet would do nothing. It was good of her to keep Élise company. It had been good of Valérie too to suggest her. It had been impossible to refuse. But old Mother Smet, who never took off either her black spangled bonnet or her mittens, and who always remained perched on the edge of her chair, as if she were paying a call, was incapable of doing anything, and she would probably have been found dead of hunger if her two daughters had not looked after her like a child.

She smiled beatifically at her daydreams while Élise fretted, blushed, coughed, and hesitated for a long time before plucking up courage to say in an imploring, apologetic voice:

'Madame Smet, could you possibly put a little coal on the fire?'

Désiré thought of everything, peeled the potatoes, got the day's bottles ready, and did everything to the best of his ability, with a sense of satisfaction, even if it was only a matter of wringing out a dishcloth.

'Don't you think the baby's looking pale, Désiré?'

42

'You're just imagining things again.'

But he was a man! Only the day before, Élise had said again to Valérie:

'You know, poor little Valérie, a man doesn't feel things as we do. Even if the baby brings up all his milk, he doesn't worry.'

Because he did what he could, all that he could, and considered that the rest would be given to him into the bargain.

Just now the night watchman on the other side of the street must be getting ready to go downstairs and would already have filled his big meerschaum pipe with the cherrywood stem. In the cold morning air, Valérie and her mother were trotting along, and in a few moments Valérie would leave Madame Smet, like a child being taken to school, outside Cession's. She had not time to come upstairs, for she had to be at L'Innovation at eight o'clock.

Désiré was ready, his hat on his head. He stood looking vaguely at the trams full of workers and clerks who had got up early in the country or the outlying suburbs and who were wearing the resigned expression of people who have been awakened too early. On Sunday they would dawdle in bed.

'Do you think they'll arrest him?'

He was astonished to discover the thought which had been occupying Élise's mind. How ridiculous to worry about that boy!

'It's dreadful for the parents . . .'

She felt sorry for them. She fretted over everybody's troubles, suffered for everybody.

'They had bled themselves white to have him educated . . .'

And she looked at the cradle, as if there were a connexion between what she was thinking and the sleeping baby, between the latter and the lanky adolescent of the place Saint-Lambert.

'Don't worry your head about that.'

Besides, it was time for him to go; he could hear the door downstairs opening, Madame Smet climbing the stairs. He brushed his moustache against his wife's forehead, then against his son's, and frowned again.

Why the devil was she thinking about that boy?

As for himself, he went into life, into this fine new day, as

43

fresh as if he were acting in a play, immaculate from head to foot, without a speck of dust on him, alert in heart and limbs.

'I wonder, Madame Smet . . .'

A word was trembling on the tip of Élise's tongue, and though she held it back now she would end up by uttering it one day, by speaking of Léopold, of the two men lurking in the dark alley-way where she had wanted to adjust her suspender.

*

While Désiré, with his regular stride, was crossing the Pont des Arches in the pink and blue light of the morning, Léopold, huddled, fully dressed, in an armchair, opened a sad pair of eyes and gazed straight in front of him at the bed on which a young man was lying curled up under a grey blanket.

It was on the quai de la Dérivation, in a new district full of little red-brick houses: an extraordinary building, an old farmhouse, dating from the time when the town did not extend that far. There remained a cock and a few hens, and some manure in the farmyard, for a cab-driver kept his horse and cab there. The building had been converted into a number of little warehouses and workshops and, as there was a fine square patch of turf left, it was hired out by the day to the women of the district who came and spread out their washing on it.

To get to the flat where Léopold and Eugénie lived, you had to go up through a ceiling by means of a miller's ladder, and there was a pulley outside the window.

Eugénie was not there. She came and went. At the moment she was probably working as a cook in some middle-class house, but she would certainly not stay there, for she loved changing.

'Get up, my boy.'

Léopold's chin was covered with stubble. His whole body was redolent with the previous night, heavy with drunkenness, heavier still with the thoughts he was turning over in his big head, and he was breathing with difficulty, groaning with every movement, as clumsy and awkward as a fairground bear.

'Get dressed!'

No affection. Not a glance for the young man who pulled his clothes on, shivering with cold and fear.

*

In another part of the town, Désiré was walking along, sweeping his hat off to the people he knew.

'He has such a stylish way of raising his hat!'

His neighbours could tell what time it was without looking at their alarm-clocks. Shopkeepers taking down their shutters knew whether they were early or late; big Désiré went by, swinging his legs along at such a regular pace that you might have thought they had been given the task of measuring the passage of time. He scarcely ever stopped on the way. People and things did not seem to interest him and yet he smiled beatifically. He was sensitive to the quality of the air, to slight changes in temperature, to distant sounds, to moving patches of sunlight. The taste of his morning cigarette varied from day to day and yet they were all cigarettes of the same brand, cork-tipped 'Louxors'.

He was wearing a jacket with four buttons, closed very high up and reaching a long way down, with no sign of the waist-line, and made of a black or very dark grey material. He had handsome, sparkling brown eyes, a big Cyrano-de-Bergerac nose, and a turned-up moustache; his hair, which was brushed back, and his bald temples gave him a high forehead.

'A poet's forehead,' Élise used to say.

It was she who chose his ties. She was afraid of colours, because they were a sign of vulgarity. What she considered distinguished were mauves, violets, purplish reds and mouse greys, with tiny designs, practically invisible arabesques.

Once the tie had been bought – one every festive occasion – it was hung on a celluloid holder and after that it did not change any more than if it had been cut out of zinc or painted on the starched shirt-front.

Crossing the Pont des Arches, Désiré spotted his cloud, a funny little pink cloud which, for the past three days, had been floating at the same time every morning a little to the left of the spire of Saint-Pholien, as if it had been tied to the weathercock. It was not the same cloud of course, but Désiré pretended that it was the same, his own special cloud, put there just to bid him good day.

It was the hour when, in the rue Puits-en-Sock, the shop-keepers arranged their window-displays and emptied bucketfuls of water over the pavement to clean it. The alley-way that ran

45

into the street gave out the smell of poverty as you passed, but it was not an unpleasant smell when you had known it since childhood.

It was also the hour when Chrétien Mamelin stood on the threshold of his hat-shop, holding a meerschaum pipe in his hand.

'Good morning, Father.'

'Good morning, son.'

They had nothing more to say to one another. Désiré stayed for a moment beside his father, the two of them standing with their backs to the old house, each as tall as the other, and both gazed at the bluish paving-stones, the tram rattling past them, the baker across the street who had come out for a breather, covered in flour and with laughter in his eyes, and the shop-assistant at Gruyelle-Marquant's who was washing her windows with a chamois leather.

The whole street knew them. They knew that Désiré no longer formed part of the rue Puits-en-Sock, that he was married, that he worked over in the rue des Guillemins, but they approved of his coming every morning, winter and summer alike.

'I'll go and give Mother a kiss.'

*

The shop next door was called the Dolls' Hospital. The window was full of dolls of all sizes. Old Kreutz, who was smoking a German pipe with a porcelain head, was standing on the door-step, like old Mamelin.

In the morning they behaved like two little boys waiting for each other outside school. Had Désiré gone into the house? Then it was time. Did they wink at each other? In any case, some signal passed between them. There was a definite moment when old Kreutz, locking the door of his shop, walked a few steps and entered the hat-shop.

In the back-shop, among the wooden heads, Chrétien Mamelin took a bottle of Dutch liqueur, a bottle of Kempenaar, out of a cupboard, and solemnly filled two tiny glasses.

Then, and only then, glass in hand, the two old men looked at one another. It was almost a ceremony. They never drank a second glass. They would not drink either wine or spirits

46

during the rest of the day. They looked at one another with a quiet satisfaction, as if they were gauging the distance they had travelled, Mamelin since the time when, in Italy, he used to sleep in barns, learning during the day how to plait straw and trying in vain to make himself understood to the Italians, and old Kreutz, whose French was intelligible only to initiates, since he had left the suburbs of Nürnberg.

Already the irons were getting hot and the hats were waiting. At Kreutz's the glue was slowly dissolving and the workshop was littered with dolls' arms and legs.

The baker across the street, wiping his white hands on his apron, came to his door for a moment and stood blinking his eyes again in the sunlight.

On the quai de la Dérivation, Léopold, sitting opposite the boy while he had his breakfast, giving a start at every noise outside, drank half a jug of gin himself, and nobody could have said what he was thinking.

*

'I'm boring you, aren't I, Madame Smet? When I think that I make you come here every day . . .'

Désiré pushed open the glazed kitchen door. His mother was alone. He kissed her. She did not kiss him back. She had not kissed anybody since her daughter had died, the daughter whose portrait was enclosed in the gold locket.

For all that it was early in the morning, her hair was sleek and shining, drawn back from her forehead, and she looked as smartly dressed in a cotton apron with a small check pattern as in her Sunday best. Nothing detracted from her serene dignity, neither peeling the vegetables, nor doing the washing-up, nor, on Fridays, cleaning the brasses. Nor was the kitchen, through which so many people passed and where so many children had lived, ever untidy.

Old Papa took advantage of Désiré's arrival to get up from his armchair and go out into the yard, for his blindness did not prevent him from moving round the house and even round the district, where everybody regarded him as if he were a big friendly dog.

'It smells good!' said Désiré, as much because it really did smell good and he liked his food as in order to please his mother.

The soup was already on the stove. It was on the stove every morning before the family got up. The stove had been made specially for the Mamelins in the days when there had been thirteen Mamelin children, thirteen insatiable stomachs, and when nobody had ever opened the door without giving the family war-cry:

'I'm hungry!'

Hungry at every hour of the day, at ten o'clock in the morning and at four o'clock in the afternoon, with every member of the family, at the beginning of every meal, cutting himself five or six slices of brown bread and stacking them beside his plate.

The cooker had ovens with revolving hot-plates on which you could bake tarts two foot wide.

From morning to night the kettle went on singing, next to the coffee-pot in white enamel with blue flowers, which had been dented near the spout, just like Élise's, since time immemorial.

'Do you want a bowl of soup?'

'No thank you, Mother.'

'That means yes.'

He had just had a meal of eggs and bacon. With his hat pushed to the back of his head, he none the less did honour first to the soup, then to a piece of cake which had been kept for him from the day before.

His mother did not sit down. She had never been seen sitting at table. She ate standing, while serving the others.

'What did the doctor say?'

From the sound of her voice, you could tell straight away that it was useless to try lying to her.

'The milk isn't rich enough.'

'Who was right?'

'She cried all night.'

'I knew all the time she was sickly. Still . . .'

This meant:

'You *would* go and marry her. So much the worse for you.'

Désiré did not take offence. She was his mother. Now and then he threw a glance at the clock. His time was calculated to a minute. At exactly a quarter to nine he crossed the Pont Neuf, where the pneumatic clock was two minutes slow. At five to nine, he turned the corner of the boulevard Piercot and the

48

boulevard d'Avroy, and this enabled him to be at his office in the rue des Guillemins at two minutes to nine, two minutes before the other employees, so that he could open the door for them.

'What did you have to eat yesterday?'

Truth to tell, Désiré's big body liked nothing but well-done meat, chipped potatoes, peas, and sugared carrots. His Flemish wife liked nothing but meat soup, red cabbage, pickled herrings, strong cheeses, and bacon.

'Does she even know how to fry chips?'

'Yes, Mother, she does.'

He did not want to hurt her. And yet he would have liked to tell her that Élise fried chips as well as she did herself.

'Haven't you brought your collars?'

He had forgotten them. Every week, all the married boys brought their mother their collars, Sunday cuffs, and shirt-fronts, for nobody else knew how to iron. Nor did anybody else know how to make sausages and white pudding, and Christmas cake and New Year waffles.

'Don't forget to bring them tomorrow. A bit more soup now, some of your mother's real soup?'

Some time in the past, the children had scratched away a bit of the multicoloured film covering the glass window-panes. Through the holes you could see parts of the yard and an outside staircase leading to the upper floors. There were some poor people living over the shop, the sort of women you always saw wearing a black shawl, without a hat, carrying a string bag, and with the heels of their shoes worn down.

On the right there was the pump, and when it was used you could hear the noise three houses away. The flagstone was always wet like an ox's muzzle, with greenish saliva on the stone sides.

There was also a zinc pipe. Now and then something would trickle down, then all of a sudden a jet of foul-smelling dirty water would spurt out, the dirty water of the people upstairs.

Finally there was the cellar. The top of the stone staircase was covered with planks which had been lined with zinc. The result was a heavy panel six foot long which had to be removed every time anybody went down. This panel had been made when the

49

children had been little because they had all ended up by falling into the cellar.

Who had gone down there that morning? Whoever it had been, the panel had been removed, and it was Old Papa whom Désiré saw emerge, steal along the wall, and slip into the passage leading to the street.

His mother had seen him at the same time. She saw everything. She heard everything. She even knew what the people upstairs ate, just by looking at the dirty water coming out of the zinc pipe.

'Old Papa! . . . Old Papa! . . .'

The old man pretended he had not heard. Back bent and arms dangling, he tried to continue on his way, but his daughter caught up with him in the narrow passage.

'What were you up to in the cellar? Show me your hands . . .'

She opened, almost by force, the big paws which had handled so much coal in the mines that now they looked like worn-out tools. Naturally, one hand was holding an onion, a huge red onion which Old Papa had been intending to munch like an apple as he walked along.

'You know perfectly well that the doctor told you not to . . . Get along with you! . . . Wait . . . You've forgotten your scarf again . . .'

And before letting him go she tied a red scarf round his neck.

In the meantime, standing in the kitchen, Désiré was setting his watch by the clock as he did every morning. A little later his brother Lucien would come and do the same thing. Arthur too. The children had left home but they knew that the brass clock in the kitchen was the only one that told the right time.

It would be Désiré's one day. That had been decided a long time ago, as far back as anybody could remember. There were not many objects of value in the house and they had already been shared out. Cécile, the youngest, whom her mother had taught how to cook and how to bake the famous tart, was to have the stove. Arthur had staked a claim to the brass candlesticks on the bedroom mantelpiece. There remained the clock and the coffee-mill. Lucien would have liked the clock, but Désiré was his senior. Besides, no coffee-mill ground as fine as this one.

'Are you going?'

50

'It's time.'

'Well, then . . .'

She said 'well, then' as if they had just had a lengthy conversation.

'Well, then . . . If she needs anything . . .'

She rarely pronounced the name of any of her daughters-in-law, of Élise, of Catherine, Lucien's wife, of Juliette, Arthur's wife, even less of Guillaume's wife who was not really his wife since she had been divorced by her first husband so that they had not been married in church.

A poke at the fire in the stove. Désiré emerged on to the pavement, set his legs striding at their usual pace, and lit his second cigarette of the day.

He had never missed his daily visit to the rue Puits-en-Sock. Lucien and Arthur had never missed it either. Only Guillaume, the deserter for all that he was the eldest of all the children, had made a bad match and had gone and opened an umbrella shop in Brussels.

*

In the ill-proportioned room overlooking the orchard where the women were spreading out their washing, Léopold, scowling fiercely, contemplated his handiwork, pulled at the painter's smock he had made young Marette put on, and pushed in the shapeless, paint-spattered felt hat.

'You've got the wallet and the sandwiches?'

When Léopold worked, it was usually as a house-painter, and his sisters turned aside in shame when they caught sight of him in the street, perched on a ladder.

'The pots . . . Drink . . . Go on, drink!'

He made him swallow some gin and the boy looked as if he were going to be sick.

'Some more!'

He spoke harshly, as if he were threatening the boy.

'Come along. Shut the door.'

The boy's teeth were practically chattering. It was the first time he had ventured out since the night of the Grand Bazaar.

Now they were out on the pavement, two house-painters with down-at-heel shoes, filthy smocks, and paint-pots in their hands.

'Keep your mouth shut.'

There was a policeman at the corner of the rue Jean-d'Outremeuse.

'Keep walking.'

The boy would have been quite capable of halting in his
tracks and bursting into tears at the sight of a policeman.

'Keep a tight grip on your bucket.'

A bucket full of dirty water with a big sponge floating in it.

Désiré was walking along too. He was walking along looking
at the sky, at the patches of sunshine on the pink bricks. He saw
the backs of two painters and passed them without knowing
who they were, without looking back at Léopold's bearded face
and the panic-stricken face of the young anarchist.

They followed the same road. All three of them went towards
the Guillemins station, crossed the Pont-Neuf, and went past the
bishopric just as a chubby canon with a blotchy complexion
was ringing the bell at the gate, as he did every morning.

There were a few yards between them; the distance increased,
on account of Désiré's great strides and Marette's stupid
hesitations.

'Keep walking!'

*

Wasn't it strange that, that particular morning, Élise should
have thought about her brother? She went on thinking about
him. The thought of him nagged at her mind, and she longed
to talk about him to Madame Smet, who was sitting there
smiling beatifically.

It was five minutes to nine when Désiré reached the corner of
the rue des Guillemins from which he could see the station
clock, and three minutes to nine when he passed Monsieur
Monnoyeur's house. It was a big, gloomy house, built of freestone. The offices were a sort of annexe to this building and
looked out on the rue Sohet. The two buildings were separated
by a garden.

Monsieur Monnoyeur was ill, had always been ill and sad
like his mother with whom he lived and who, oddly enough, was
the terror of the young ladies of L'Innovation, where she spent
her afternoons.

Monsieur Monnoyeur had bought an insurance business in

which to invest his money, so as not to look as if he did nothing to earn his living. Désiré was already in the business when he bought it.

Two big latticed windows looking out on to the peaceful rue Sohet. A door studded with iron nails.

When Désiré pushed it open, at two minutes to nine, there was undoubtedly a dignity, a special satisfaction about him which made another man of him, a second Mamelin, just as real as the first and just as important, for life at the office occupied nine hours a day. It was no ordinary job, no mere means of earning a living, no unrewarding task.

Désiré had entered this office with the latticed windows at the age of seventeen, on the very day he had left school.

A partition shut off the section reserved for the public, a partition fitted with little windows as in a post office, and just crossing to the other side of this frontier gave him a feeling of satisfaction. Thick green-painted window-panes made it impossible to see the street and created an atmosphere of supernatural calm. Before even taking off his hat and coat, Désiré wound up the clock. He had a horror of clocks which had run down. He did his best to see that they never stopped.

He performed every one of his tasks with equal pleasure. When he washed his hands, in a slow, leisurely manner, in the handbasin behind the door, it was a positive joy to him.

It was another joy to take the cover off the typewriter with the double keyboard, and to change the position of rubber, pencils, and papers.

Now the others could arrive.

First of all Daigne, the brother of Charles, the sacristan at Saint-Denis who had married one of Désiré's sisters, Daigne who smelled so bad and did not take offence when people held their noses in front of him; then Ledent-the-Sad, Ledent who had three children and an ailing wife, looked after the whole family, never got enough sleep and was perpetually red-eyed; and finally Caresmel-the-Widower who had sent his two daughters to an Ursuline boarding-school and had a mistress.

'Good morning, Monsieur Mamelin.'

'Good morning, Monsieur Daigne ... Good morning, Monsieur Ledent ...'

For everybody at the office called each other Monsieur.

Except for Mamelin and Caresmel who called each other by their names because they had started work within three days of one another.

This was the origin of the first reproaches Élise had addressed to her husband; it was to Caresmel that she referred when she spoke to Désiré about his lack of initiative.

'It's like when you had the choice between fire-insurance and life-insurance . . .'

Had Désiré really chosen the fire-insurance branch, as she asserted, because he was so attached to his little corner next to the window with the green panes?

It was possible. Yet he always denied it.

'At that time, nobody could foresee the success of life-insurance.'

When Monsieur Monnoyeur had bought the business, Mamelin had been earning 150 francs a month, Caresmel only 140.

'I'm not going to give you a rise, but I'll give you a percentage on all the new business that passes through your hands. One of you will deal with the fire policies, the other with the life policies. As you are the senior of the two, Monsieur Mamelin, it's for you to choose.'

He had chosen fire-insurance, a quiet business involving only very rare calls on clients. It was at that moment that life-insurance had started forging ahead.

To all appearances, nothing had changed. It was Désiré who, on the stroke of ten, went into Monsieur Monnoyeur's office. It was he who had the key and the powers of attorney. It was he too who had the combination of the safe and locked it every evening.

Caresmel was just a clerk, a loud-mouthed, vulgar clerk. There were often mistakes in his accounts. He was frequently obliged to ask for advice. Only he made up to two hundred francs a month in commission, while Mamelin made scarcely fifty.

'I can't understand,' Élise had protested, 'why a man who is far less intelligent than you are should earn more than you do, in your own office.'

'Good luck to him. Have we ever gone short of anything?'

'It seems he even drinks.'

'What he does outside the office is no concern of ours.'

And the word 'office', in Mamelin's mind, had a capital letter. He loved his big ledgers, and his eyes sparkled when, with his lips quivering slightly and his finger running down the columns, he did a sum, faster than anybody else, as all his colleagues agreed. They recognized too that he had never made a mistake. That was not just idle talk. It was an act of faith.

'Mamelin? He doesn't need a ready-reckoner.'

After ten years of his trade, does a juggler still experience some pleasure at bringing off all his tricks, at catching all the balls in the top-hat balanced on his wooden cigar?

*

On the stroke of ten o'clock, with that slightly familiar solemnity that sacristans display in the sanctuary, Désiré knocked on Monsieur Monnoyeur's door and disappeared inside with the post which he had just finished sorting.

At the same time, the two painters in white smocks entered the Guillemins station, like workmen on their way to do a job in the suburbs, and Marette was so pale that anyone might have thought he was going to faint.

'Two third-class tickets to Huy.'

'Returns?'

'Yes.'

Somewhere in the station there was a member of the secret police. The newspapers had said so. It was impossible to say whether it was this fat man walking up and down with his hands behind his back, or that gentleman with the attaché case who was gazing at the weighing-machine.

'Will passengers for Angleur, Ougrée, Seraing, Huy, Sprimont, Andenne and Namur please take their seats.'

'Start walking.'

*

During the quiet, leisurely hours of the morning, Valérie kept thinking about Élise who was so unlucky, who had an ailing child, and who was so upset because she had no milk.

'I'm sorry to bother you again, Madame Smet. If it isn't too much trouble for you . . . The fire!'

What a nightmare it was, that fire which might go out, and

which the old lady would be incapable of lighting again! How had she managed to be married and raise children when she wasn't even capable of keeping a fire alight?

The train moved off. The two workmen in smocks stood in the corridor and the passengers who pushed past them were afraid of getting paint on their clothes.

*

Désiré juggled with his figures. He was waiting for midday. He had set aside for himself every day an hour and a half of perfect happiness. This began on the stroke of noon, when the others went off like pigeons being released.

He stayed behind on his own, for the office remained open without a break from nine o'clock in the morning until six o'clock in the evening. It was he who had asked for this duty which he could have delegated to somebody else.

Clients were few and far between. The office really belonged to him. He had some ground coffee in his pocket. He put some water to heat on the stove, took a little enamel coffee-pot out of a cupboard as the watchman at Torset's must do every night, and then, sitting in his corner, he opened a newspaper and slowly ate a sandwich while drinking his coffee.

By way of dessert, he tackled a difficult or delicate piece of work calling for peace and quiet.

In his shirtsleeves, with a cigarette between his lips, he felt really at home, and another rare joy awaited him at half past one.

Everybody else returned to work and he went off. Everybody else had had dinner and he was going to have his. His place was laid, his place only, at the end of the table, with dishes cooked just for him, well-done meat, carrots, peas, and sweets.

His colleagues did not know this pleasure. They did not know how the town looked at three o'clock in the afternoon when everybody who worked for a living was shut up indoors.

Élise and Madame Smet watched him eat in silence. In spite of themselves, they looked at him rather as if he were a visitor from another world, and the joy he had breathed in while walking through the streets in the savoury air was foreign to them. It was like a cold draught which had disturbed the cosy calm of the flat.

It was not until Désiré had been gone for quite a while that the circle closed again, Élise resumed her morose smile and Madame Smet her interior reverie, and the slightest sound became audible once more while the two women waited patiently for the cooker's inevitable 'boom'.

He walked along. The sun was shining. But when it rained, the town looked just as delightful, and he had a way that was all his own of carrying his umbrella like a canopy. The three o'clock cigarette tasted good. Each cigarette had its special taste, the taste of a particular street, the taste of a particular time of day, of hunger or digestion, of the gay morning or the evening.

*

The slow train had stopped at Huy. The Cologne–Paris express was due to arrive. Léopold pulled his companion over to the lavatory.

'Give me your smock.'

Because nobody had ever seen a worker in a smock get on an express. It was Léopold, with his jet-black beard, who looked like a ferocious anarchist, and Marette like a frightened child.

'Hurry up.'

Such a child, and so frightened, that he felt a sudden need to relieve himself and disappeared behind one of the doors with a grating just as the train was entering the station.

'Is that my train?'

'Hurry up.'

Nobody, in this little station, was thinking about the anarchist of the place Saint-Lambert. Léopold had bought a ticket for Paris and passed it to Marette.

'You've got your wallet?'

They ran along the platform. They had no time either to shake hands or to say good-bye; the train moved off before Marette had finished buttoning his braces, and his thin, pale face disappeared into the tunnel at the first bend.

There was a train for Liège, but Léopold was thirsty. He had a drink at the station buffet. Then he crossed the square and went into a café. In a little while he would lumber out, looking for another door to push open, another café in which to sit down, and at six o'clock after losing his buckets, his paint-pots,

and his brushes all over the place, he would take off his smock
with a sigh of relief and beckon to the waiter, for want of the
strength or the courage to speak.

'The same again.'

Little grey-green glasses with thick bottoms, glasses of pale
gin which he emptied at one gulp, repeating the same gesture:

'Fill it up.'

*

Désiré locked the safe and mixed up the combination. He could
have taken the tram as far as the place Saint-Lambert. He could
have walked part of the way with Daigne or Ledent. Instead,
he set off alone, and this was another happy moment in his day,
with the streets turning purple, the passers-by seemingly gliding
along in a silent mist, the gas-lamps every few yards, the shop
windows no longer attracting anybody's attention and forming
rectangles of soft light, and finally, alongside the boulevard
d'Avroy, the deserted park and the ducks lingering on the
glistening water.

He decided to drop into Tonglet's, in the rue de la Cathédrale,
opposite the church of Saint-Denis, to buy some liver pudding.
Or some larded liver? He didn't know yet. Some larded liver?

'Give me a quarter . . . no, a quarter and a half of . . .'

Valérie was waiting for him to arrive before taking her
mother home. She had not taken her coat off, had not even sat
down.

'It isn't worth it, Élise! Désiré will be here in a minute.'

As if she were going to wear out one of the chairs; as if
sitting down constituted a sort of invasion, of vulgarity, when
she had simply dropped in to collect her mother.

Élise understood that.

Désiré did not understand.

And he came in, triumphantly, with a bit of the evening mist
clinging to the mahogany bristles of his moustache.

'Why don't you stay and have supper with us, Valérie?'

'No, Désiré, Marie's waiting for us.'

'Let her wait.'

'Our supper's ready.'

'You can eat it tomorrow.'

What was the use of insisting? Didn't he know that it was

impossible, that it just wasn't done, that the evening Élise had had the baby, Valérie had doggedly maintained that she wasn't hungry?

*

Léopold was standing, rather unsteadily, in a square he did not know, looking for the way out, and it was a miracle that he remembered that there was a station, a train to catch.

Where was Eugénie, his wife? She had been to their flat the week before, one day when he had not been there, and she had left some food which she had doubtless taken from her employers' home. But where was she working?

She would come back some day or other. He would find her there when he got home. She would say to him, in her funny accent, without losing her temper, in a matter-of-fact voice:

'You're drunk again, Léopold!'

She would have cleaned up the whole place, made the bed, and changed the sheets, which was something he never did. Perhaps it would be the next day, perhaps in a month's time. Meanwhile, little Marette was in the train, squeezed up against the partition in a third-class compartment where the lamps had just been lit, and some country folk were offering him a piece of potted head.

*

'Good-bye, Madame Smet! Good-bye, Valérie. And thank you, you know! Thank you! I feel ashamed to . . .'

They had gone. They walked very quietly across the first-floor landing, on account of the Delobels.

Arm in arm, like a couple of little dolls with outsize heads, they walked along past the shop windows on their way back to the flat where Marie was unpicking an old dress while she waited for them.

Désiré, with a sigh of pleasure, took off his jacket and his shoes, and put on his slippers, or rather his ecclesiastical shoes.

Conscious of having done a good day's work, of having accomplished all that he had to accomplish, he exclaimed happily:

'Let's have our supper!'

And yet he was not too proud of himself, for he had seen from Élise's eyes that she had noticed that he had bought a quarter and a half of larded liver instead of a quarter.

She did not dare to say anything and heaved an inward sigh.

Chapter Four

Milliards upon milliards of creatures, over the whole surface of the world, in the air, in the water, everywhere, strive continually, second by second, with their every cell, towards an evolution they do not know, like those ants which carry across precipices burdens a hundred times bigger than themselves, trudge across mountains of sand or mud, and return a dozen times to the attack on an obstacle without ever diverging from their course.

Élise, on this particular day, a fine September Sunday, as ripe and golden as a fruit, Élise the thirteenth, Élise the anaemic, Élise who had found no other weapon for herself than her timid smile, so humble that it aroused pity, Élise who was always apologizing for being there, for existing, who was always begging pardon for causing offence, begging pardon for everything and nothing, who was almost ashamed of being on earth, Élise was about to wage her first battle.

Did she know this? Did she even guess, like the ant climbing an uneven slope and constantly dropping and picking up again the same grain of corn, did she guess the importance, the object of the battle she was about to wage, and did she realize that she was waging it, not only against Désiré-the-Smiler, Désiré-with-the-Fine-Walk, but against the Mamelins of the rue Puits-en-Sock and, through them, against an entire species?

Did she already sense that she was stronger than they were, strong in her weeping eyes, in her pale, hollow cheeks, in her aching belly, in the iron prescribed for her anaemia, in her legs which kept giving way on the stairs, did she know, the little Fleming, the thirteenth-born of the Peters, what she wanted and where she was going?

She had been married for barely two years. She had always said yes to everything, but this particular Sunday, because it was necessary, because a strange force was impelling her, because she was a Peters and there were Mamelins in the world, because life was in command, she was going to fight, and fight with her own weapons.

Nobody knew this, except herself and Valérie, and Valérie, who would have liked nothing better than to obey a man, had taken fright at the idea.

'You really think so, Élise?'

There were some windows which, this particular Sunday, Élise could no longer bear to see, even though she knew that she would not be seeing them much longer. These were the twenty-eight pale windows of corrugated glass, on which, repeated over and over again, in funeral black, there were three words which looked almost obscene: *Torset et Mitouron . . . Torset et Mitouron . . . Torset et . . .*

Désiré suspected nothing. He had gone to the rue Puits-en-Sock, after hearing Mass at Saint-Nicolas in the pew of the Brotherhood of St Roch. He had brought home the brownish loaves baked by his mother as well as an apple tart. The hours flowed along at their usual pace and he was far from suspecting that their course was going to change.

When the baby was ready in his cradle, he had to be strapped in, as he was every day, while Désiré and Élise took the pram two floors down.

'Mind the walls . . .'

They could make as much noise as they liked. The Delobels were on holiday, in a villa at Ostend. Only Madame Cession did not disarm for a moment. She was lying in wait behind the door, dressed in black silk, with gold chains round her neck, ready to rush out if one of the pram wheels happened to scrape against the wall in the semi-darkness.

There was room for it at the end of the passage, under the stairs, where nothing was kept but the dustbins and nobody ever set foot.

'If you insist on having a pram, you must keep it in your flat.'

Désiré stayed downstairs. Élise went to fetch the baby. The bottles, underneath the mattress, were still warm.

'She didn't say anything,' said Désiré, stepping out and pushing the pram as he often did on Sundays.

61

You might have thought he was doing it on purpose, and Élise had all the trouble in the world to keep up with him.

It was another Mamelin Sunday, and Désiré had no idea that there were going to be Sundays of a different sort. They went by way of the back-streets. This was a habit of Élise, who always took short cuts along narrow streets and past blind alleys where she invariably felt the need to adjust her suspender.

They had not got far to go. They soon reached the church of Saint-Denis and, behind it, a little old square with a provincial look about it, shaded by chestnut-trees and enlivened by the gay song of a fountain. Every morning the cheese market was held here, and the smell lingered on, spreading far and wide through the near-by streets and growing more insipid as the day wore on.

They were going to see Daigne, or rather Charles as they were in the habit of calling him. Charles Daigne, the sacristan at Saint-Denis, had married Françoise, the eldest of the Mamelin girls; he was the brother of the Daigne who worked at Monnoyeur's and smelled so bad.

Charles did not smell bad. He smelled of the church, of the monastery. The whole house was impregnated with a sweet smell that was at once cosy and virtuous.

The heavy front door flanked by its two stones was polished like a handsome piece of furniture and adorned with gleaming brass knockers. There was not a stain, not a scratch, not the slightest speck of dirt to be seen, and the façade of the house, as an extra touch of cleanliness, had been painted with oil-paint, in a creamy white which harmonized with the cheesy smell of the square.

Nobody came to open the door. Désiré rang the bell by pulling a brass ring. There was no noise to be heard inside, but a well-oiled catch was released and the right-hand door-panel opened a fraction of an inch. Anybody who had not been told about it would not have noticed it and could have spent hours waiting on the doorstep.

The door was heavy, and opened into a solemn-looking porch with fake-marble walls and blue and white flagstones which were the same as those in the church.

The building belonged to the church council. The vast block

in front was occupied by a barrister, Monsieur Douté, the president of this church council.

Désiré had never set eyes on him, nor had Élise. To avoid marking the flagstones with the wheels, they carried the pram in silence, walking on tip-toe, and scarcely daring to look at the flights of stairs on each side, or the doors with their stained-glass window-panes.

Did Monsieur Douté have a wife and children? They never heard anything, and only now and then did they notice a maid-servant, silent and dressed all in black, who gave the impression of being a nun in mufti.

What if the baby, being carried along in his pram, started to cry? They did not dare to think of the effect this would produce in this calm, in this absolute silence where not even the smell of cooking could be distinguished.

Finally they reached the second door which separated the porch from the courtyard, a long convent yard, with tiny round paving-stones, polished like pottery. A green gate shut off that part of the yard which was reserved for Monsieur Douté, who had never set foot in it.

Élise was depressed. She was thinking about the odious twenty-eight windows, about the empty hours which were about to elapse, about what she had to do next. Would it be best to speak in the street, when they got back to the rue Léopold? Or should she wait until they were in the kitchen where the fire would be sure to have gone out?

At the far side of the courtyard there were two smart little white houses, both meticulously clean, that of the church porter at Saint-Denis, Monsieur Collard of the thick moustache, and that of Charles Daigne, the sacristan.

'Be careful how you shut the door, Désiré.'

For here a voice, an ordinary human voice, became a thunderous din, and the next day Charles received a written remonstrance in an icy style from the barrister.

'Hush!'

The gravel had crunched under Désiré's broad soles.

Nowhere else was the air as clear as it was here. Anybody might have thought he was in a world of porcelain.

The other Mamelins, used to the plebeian hurly-burly of the rue Puits-en-Sock, never ventured here. Only Désiré and Élise came every Sunday to see Françoise who was always dressed in black.

Inside the house, where the air was a blue colour with a hint of purple, the two couples kissed. Charles smelled of incense and mustiness. He was tow-haired, with fair, frizzy curls. He had a gentle sheepish face, slow gestures, and a voice so mono-tonous that nobody ever waited for the ends of his sentences.

In his house, in his kitchen, in his bedroom, everywhere, it was as if you were still in church, and Élise kept having to call Désiré, who had a loud voice, to order:

'Careful, Désiré!'

He suspected nothing. He went on blandly living his Sunday-afternoon life, but today Élise's face was more pointed, she smiled her morose smile more often, and she kept repeating for no apparent reason:

'Poor little Françoise . . .'

Françoise had a child too, a girl a year older than Roger. She was expecting another baby.

The windows had little panes as iridescent as soap-bubbles, but you could not see them, hidden as they were by two or three thicknesses of muslin curtains.

'What are you doing, Désiré? Heavens, Françoise, he's so free-and-easy . . .'

'I'm in my sister's home, aren't I?'

He made no bones about opening drawers, about changing around objects frozen in religious immobility.

Everybody would have liked to go and sit in the courtyard, in the sunshine, in front of the white wall, but what if one of the children started crying?

Désiré made himself comfortable, tilting his chair back a little on account of his long legs. At the other end of the courtyard, the barrister's windows were even more thickly lined with white curtains than Françoise's. Didn't a prisoner's hand ever push them aside, didn't an ivory-coloured face ever appear behind the window-panes?

The Mamelins had brought along an apple tart. They had it with some coffee, before Vespers and Benediction. Charles went off first, bare-headed, for he had only to cross the street to get to the narrow door of the sacristy. Monsieur Collard followed him, in full-dress uniform, and you always had the impression that his moustache smelled of spirits. People said that he drank.

'Just imagine, Élise . . .'

He did it on the sly, and never went into a café, for fear of the church council.

Who was going to look after the children, then? It was Désiré's turn. He could give a baby the bottle and tie its napkins better than any woman. When the children cried, he beat a drum to send them to sleep.

The two sisters-in-law went off to Benediction. Élise felt the need for something to soothe her heart.

'If only you knew, Françoise, how nasty Madame Cession is!'

She was frightened now at what she had done. Just as she was leaving the Daignes', she had caught sight of Désiré smiling blissfully, crossing his legs and lighting his cigarette, and it had struck her that it was an act of treachery that she had committed.

They said their prayers unthinkingly, in the shadow of a pillar. They saw Charles, holding a wax taper in one hand, coming and going around the altar, genuflecting every now and then.

Coming out of the church, they were greeted by the vague smell of the cheese and the song of the fountain.

'But yes, you must stay to supper.'

'It's so much trouble for you, Françoise!'

Élise had a congenital fear of causing people trouble. She had never dared to occupy the whole of a chair.

'I assure you it's no trouble at all, Élise.'

'Then let's go and buy some meat at Tonglet's. We'll go shares.'

It was only a few steps away, on the corner of an alley-way where decent people avoided going. In ten years' time, wherever she might be living, Élise would go on maintaining that only at Tonglet's was the pig-meat any good, especially the larded liver.

'A tenth of larded liver.'

They had brought along a china plate. In another shop, quite close, they bought fifty centimes' worth of chips which they covered with a napkin. The plate was hot to hold, hot and greasy. They walked fast in the fading daylight which was casting a blue glow over the streets.

'If only you knew, Françoise, how the rue Léopold gets on my nerves . . .'

No. She must not say anything . . . Her sifter-in-law murmured:

'Hush . . . Careful . . .'

They had come to the porch, the famous porch which had to be crossed on tip-toe and which they were defiling with the smell of chips.

Désiré had laid the table and ground the coffee. Charles had come home, still surrounded with something of the half-light of Vespers and Benediction. They had supper. A little later, Charles would show them some of his photographs. He was incredibly patient. For a whole fortnight, every morning at six o'clock – the street had to be empty – he had levelled his camera at the General Post Office, near the Passerelle, and he had obtained some unique cloud-effects, greys of wonderful delicacy.

'Next Sunday, if the weather's fine . . .'

For months he had been promising to take a photograph of the whole family. They would have to be able to leave the children naked on a sheepskin.

Nine o'clock.

'Heavens, Françoise! . . . As late as that! . . . And we're keeping you up . . . I'll help you with the washing-up . . .'

'But no . . .'

The baby, in his pram, was warm and sleepy. They covered him up and raised the hood, for fear of the cool night air.

'See you next Sunday! Come early.'

'I'll bring a Savoy cake from Bonmersonne's.'

'Careful . . . Hush . . .'

The porch.

'Really, Désiré!'

He had pulled the door shut too sharply. Élise trotted along. She had never managed to keep in step with her giant of a husband who was pushing the pram along with the satisfaction of duty done. Other families were making their way home along the pavements in the same way, and sleepy children were perched on their fathers' shoulders.

'You've got the key?'

It would be best to wait a little longer. Élise trembled.

'Listen, Désiré . . . There's something I have to tell you . . . You won't be too cross with me? . . .'

She wept as she walked backwards up the stairs, holding one end of the pram. The gas was alight on the entresol. The jet was sputtering.

She took advantage of the fact that they were jammed in the narrow staircase with the unwieldy pram.

'*I've taken another flat.*'

Désiré had not said anything. Hadn't he heard? Now they were home again. He struck a match, raised the glass of the lamp, and went over to the stove where there were a few warm, pink embers left.

'You aren't cross with me? If you only knew how unbearable Madame Cession is . . .'

Désiré took off his jacket, put on his priestly slippers, adjusted the wick of the lamp. Obviously upset, he looked around him at the kitchen, at the bedroom, at the night-watchman's window which was already lighted, at all this which was his, which formed part of him.

'Are you terribly cross? Remember there isn't a single place in this district where I can take the baby.'

He did not dare yet to ask to what part of the town, to what unfamiliar setting she was taking them.

She sniffed and blew her nose, taking heart from his silence.

'First of all, it isn't any dearer: twenty-five francs a month. There isn't any water on that floor, but there is on the landing just below, and the landlady will let us leave the pram in the passage.'

So for weeks on end, while he had thought that she was busy wheeling the child round the church of Saint-Denis, she had been pushing the pram all over the town, looking for 'to let' notices!

That was why, every morning, she had complained about Madame Cession, or about the noise of the trams which woke Roger up, or about the stairs which were so hard to climb!

Hadn't he felt anything? Was he pretending not to understand?

'If only you knew, Valérie, how he clings to his habits! Just the idea of moving . . .'

It was true. He was a Mamelin, and the Mamelins had never moved house. On his arrival at Liège, even before getting married, Chrétien Mamelin had settled in the rue Puits-en-Sock and he had never budged since. All his children, except for Guillaume, who had installed himself in Brussels, had stayed in the same district.

'Why should we be any better off somewhere else?'

Those were Désiré's words. What could one say in reply?

'What are we short of here?'

Élise had trotted all over the town, stubborn and secretive, and only Valérie had been admitted to her confidence. For Élise, one district was as good as another. Nothing attached her to any particular street. She was incapable of looking affectionately at a gleam of sunshine on the wallpaper, or the shadow of the big wardrobe on the ceiling.

She had taken a flat the day before in the rue Pasteur. She had paid a month's rent in advance. She had even . . . Yes, she had actually had the nerve to give up the flat in the rue Léopold. She had told Madame Cession that they were leaving.

'Good riddance!' the latter had retorted. 'We won't have your pram on the stairs twenty times a day any more.'

'Are you cross with me?'

He asked simply:

'Where is it?'

'In the rue Pasteur.'

Then, suddenly voluble, she listed the advantages of their new flat.

'It's a wide modern street, in a new district, close to the place du Congrès. The house is brand new and the rooms are bigger than these, with wide windows. The flat is on the second floor, but the stairs aren't hard to climb and the floor is as white as the table. Yesterday I went and rubbed it down with sand.'

Without his knowing anything about it!

'What did you do with the baby all that time?'

'The landlady, who's terribly nice, helped me to carry the pram upstairs. There isn't any dust in the district. And you won't have so far to go . . .'

68

He was not listening. He was thinking of the way he would have to go from now on, four times a day. The rue Pasteur was only five minutes' walk from the rue Puits-en-Sock. He would pass in front of the church of Saint-Nicolas. He would go down the narrow rue des Récollets, which came out right in front of the hat-shop.

He tried on his route as he would have tried on a piece of clothing, paying attention to the smallest details . . . Yes . . .

'All right.'

But then he suddenly thought of the move itself.

'We'll have to move everything . . .'

And he took fright as he looked around him at their few pieces of furniture.

'By noon tomorrow, it will all be over. I've been to see the chair-mender in the rue Jean-d'Outremeuse who has a hand-cart. He's coming at eight o'clock with a workman he knows, and in three trips they'll have taken everything.'

In that case, of course . . . All the same, he was a little sad, possibly a little distressed . . . Setting off . . . Leaving something behind . . .

'You aren't cross with me? You see, Désiré, the rue Léopold has been getting on my nerves so badly that I should fall ill if I stayed here any longer.'

He undressed in silence. She lay down beside him. Only the night-light lit the room into which the glow of the gas-lamps filtered through the curtains.

Élise did not close her eyes. She had won. He had not said anything. He was not cross.

And Valérie had been so frightened! More frightened than herself!

'You see, Valérie, with men . . .'

She did not yet add:

'He's a Mamelin, and when you're dealing with the Mamelins, you have to present them with a *fait accompli*. Otherwise they'd spend the whole of their life in the same place.'

She did not think this quite so clearly as yet. She did not fall asleep straight away, for she was vaguely aware of the importance of this day. Only the day before, when she had gone to see the chair-mender, she had scarcely been able to breathe, and yet it had all been so easy.

'Are you asleep?'

He said:

'Yes.'

She would have liked to say thank you, to squeeze the tips of his fingers. But she mustn't. He would have thought that she was sorry.

He was a man. He was a Mamelin. If you didn't push him... For instance, at Monsieur Monnoyeur's, didn't they take advantage of him? It was Désiré who organized everything and he was paid little more than young Daigne. He did not dare to complain. When Élise spoke to him about asking for a rise, he changed the subject.

He was too attached to his habits. He was always satisfied. He did not want to see that they had just enough for the bare necessities of life.

The bare necessities ... Those were the words she had used three days before to her sister Félicie, who had dropped in on her unexpectedly. Félicie had only to dip into the till when she wanted some money. Nobody ever counted. People bought their meat without looking at the scales.

Now that the Cession question had been settled, Élise kept repeating the two words: *bare necessities*. They took on a definite meaning. They became something like the programme of a new stage to be covered.

'You see, Félicie, Désiré earns just enough to pay for the bare necessities.'

At Monsieur Monnoyeur's, three years before, the work had been divided into two sections, fire-insurance on the one hand and the new life-insurance on the other. It was Désiré who had been given the choice.

He had chosen fire-insurance, as a matter of routine, because it was not much trouble, and it was Caresmel, who was far less intelligent, who had obtained the life-insurance section.

And now life-insurance paid well. Caresmel made up to two hundred francs commission a month and, when his wife had died, he had been able to send his two daughters to an Ursuline boarding-school.

'All that, Valérie, just to avoid changing his little routine. We Peters, we'd go to the ends of the world to make five francs extra.'

She fell asleep. At two o'clock, for the last time in the rue Léopold, Désiré got up to warm the bottle and he addressed a melancholy farewell to the night-watchman whom he would never see.

Chapter Five

IT was the end of March and there was still ice on the duck-pond near the boulevard d'Avroy; footsteps crackled along the paths of dark box-trees in which pale statues stood gesticulating.

The town was empty, as dull as a penny postcard; like a postcard too, it seemed all black and white, barely relieved by a sickly pink tint in the west.

People walked fast. They stopped. They set off again. They felt awkward, though they could not say why, possibly because of the extent of the pavement, of the boulevard, of this empty world, of this silence they were disturbing, and they unconsciously adopted poses as if they were at the photographer's, the men adjusting their ties, pulling their shirt-sleeves out half an inch, strutting along as if posterity were looking at them.

They said half-heartedly to their children:

'Give your bread to the swans.'

They slipped crumbling pieces of bread into their woollen gloves or mittens, and stopped them from climbing the green railings or picking up pebbles.

The swans were not hungry. It was Sunday. As soon as he was dressed in his Sunday best, Désiré was in the habit of tucking his right hand under the lapel of his black overcoat, holding his cigarette between two fingers of his left hand, lifting his bearded chin high in the air, and looking straight ahead, while Élise pushed the pram in which the child was sitting.

Around the bandstand, which was not being used this particular day, a few people, here and there, had made so bold as to occupy a dozen or so yellow chairs among the thousands of folding chairs over which no attendant had thought of mounting guard. Both men and women wore black, whether they were people of independent means, craftsmen or workers: those who went walking on Sunday along the boulevard d'Avroy were always dressed like that, with sometimes a mourning band, or a widow's veil which the wearer lifted in order to blow her nose.

Françoise's house, that is to say Charles-the-Sacristan's house, had been empty that afternoon, at the far end of the courtyard which a cold sun barely touched. Élise and Désiré had pulled the brass ring, plunged through the warm, silent canal of the porch, crossed the courtyard, and found the door locked, without any message, without any note such as Françoise usually left when she went out.

'Your sister's angry,' Élise had sighed, turning the pram round with a thrust of her belly.

Angry because Désiré and his wife had not been to see her for two Sundays in succession. Élise had warned Françoise:

'When the weather's fine, we ought to take the children out.'

'Charles has his Benediction and his Vespers.'

He would have them all his life, his Benediction and his Vespers! Was that a reason for never taking out little Loulou, who was as white as chalk? Élise had tried to insinuate as much. Perhaps she had said something about musty bedrooms? This was the result. Where could Françoise have gone? The Daignes didn't know anybody. In any case, they could have left a note to say: 'Come and join us here or there.'

'She's forgotten!' said Désiré, without really believing it.

They had pushed the pram along the boulevard de la Sauvenière and then along the boulevard d'Avroy, and they had gone round the duck-pond three times. They were not alone. Other families were circling round just as they were, the men solemn and impassive, the women in their Sunday best, turning round to look at a dress or a hat, the children not being allowed to play but forced to keep walking. The sound of footsteps echoed along the boulevard. The air was unnaturally crisp and there was an atmosphere of indefinable melancholy which made Élise want to cry.

It wasn't because of Françoise. Certainly not! If Élise went to Françoise's every Sunday it was for Désiré's sake. Not once had she failed to pay for her share of meat and chips, and every time she had offered to help with the washing-up.

It went back further than that. It was something like an inner void which she did not feel on weekdays because of all her work but which on Sunday suddenly became perceptible, as annoying as a question which nobody can answer.

A little earlier they had crossed the Pont-Neuf for a change, and they had gone along the rue des Carmes, past the Schroefs' big house with its door and shutters all closed, a house of such an impressive appearance, built of such immutable freestone, that it was like a monster crushing the street beneath it.

Élise did not envy her sister. Not for anything in the world would she have married a Hubert Schroefs who had neither heart nor breeding. All the same, that freestone, that door which, during the week, saw the wholesale grocer's wagons rolling by, those four shop windows with their iron shutters, that loggia on the first floor and those windows with the petrified curtains were an impressive sight. What were they doing inside? How did they spend their Sunday?

Désiré had been unable to refrain from reminding her:

'They treated you like a maid, less than a maid, because they took advantage of the fact that you were the little sister not to pay you anything. And you slept in the attic!'

It was true. All the same, she protested.

'Don't say that, Désiré!'

How she had wept in the days when they had been engaged and he had taken her home from L'Innovation in the falling dusk!

'They insist on me living with them on the pretext that it isn't decent for a young girl to live on her own. But it's really because when the shop-girls have gone home in the evening they need somebody to look after the children . . . Then it's Élise here, Élise there, always Élise . . . The others can go to the theatre . . . But little sister has to earn her keep . . .'

They had been the only ones, absolutely the only ones in the rue des Carmes when they had passed first the mass of ironwork and glass of the Meat Market and then the proud citadel which Schroefs, a former schoolteacher and the son of a Maeseyck peasant, had built; and yet, when Désiré had opened his mouth, Élise had said, just as if they had been in church:

'Hush!'

She had not dared to turn round. Perhaps *they* were in the loggia? They had not seen anything of each other since Élise had married a little clerk without any prospects.

'You'll understand one day, my girl! You'll be sorry!'

Because of that, for other vague reasons, and because it was terribly Sunday, she had tears in her eyes as she walked beside Désiré around the docks, pushing the pram along with her belly.

Was it because she had already exhausted the pleasure of polishing and dusting her flat in the rue Pasteur, with ist spotless windows and the floor so clean that you could eat off it? Or because she no longer enjoyed pushing the pram along the wide, level pavements towards the place du Congrès, with the magistrate's wife waving to her over the plants in her window, as she went by on her way to see Madame Pain, who had a child of the same age as Roger and was married to an important traveller in coffee? Or because, in spite of everything, this winter had already left a feeling of emptiness in her heart?

Yet they were on the threshold of a spring which you could feel approaching, and the winter had been so mild that people had scarcely noticed it. And it had been a snug, cosy winter in the two new rooms with the new wallpaper, where everything was clean – just the two of them with the baby, and Valérie for supper on Friday, Valérie whom Désiré used to accompany, teasing her and joking with her, as far as the Pont des Arches which served as a sort of frontier.

Désiré was always asking:

'What haven't we got, to make us happy?'

He held himself erect, smoking his cork-tipped cigarette and looking straight ahead, his long body tilted slightly towards the pram as if to proclaim his solidarity with the baby and Élise.

Possibly, in the wasteland of this Sunday afternoon, his thoughts went to the rue Puits-en-Sock, where all the Mamelins, the brothers, the sisters, the brothers-in-law, the daughters-in-law, were going into the yard, into the kitchen, shouting, laughing, cracking a joke, or bellowing a loud 'Hullo, everybody!'

'Have you seen Désiré?'

'He came this morning after the eleven o'clock Mass.'

'I saw them after dinner going towards the Pont-Neuf.'

There was no further mention of them. The gas was lit. It was lit earlier here than anywhere else, because of the fake stained glass which kept out the light. Old Papa solemnly filled his pipe from the tobacco jar which Arthur, the practical joker, had filled with horse-hair. Juliette, Arthur's wife, opened her immaculate tulle blouse and released a white breast which she pushed towards her baby's greedy mouth, while Catherine, Lucien's wife, made sure that her baby's bottle was not too hot.

'Poor Désiré!'

Arthur sang in a high baritone and played tricks on the others, Lucien calmly smoked his long worker's pipe, Old Papa listened to them dreamily, and while Chrétien Mamelin stood on the doorstep with old Kreutz, Madame Mamelin, cold and grey, cooked the supper, which would be eaten in shifts, the children having theirs first, the parents afterwards. Cécile would watch over the babies as they fell asleep, the tow-headed Kreutz sisters would look in to bid everybody a neighbourly good evening, and the door would go on constantly opening and shutting on other people of the rue Puits-en-Sock.

If the weather had been a little less chilly, they would have put some chairs out on the pavement, in spite of the tram which brushed past, but which, on Sunday, went by only every quarter of an hour. 'Shall we go home now?'

'You want me to push the pram?'

'No, Désiré.'

They could have gone back along the quays, where there was no longer a soul to be seen, but they returned through the town to have the benefit of a little light and warmth. Not that Désiré did not generate enough inner light and warmth for himself. He was smiling. He was walking along as erect as ever. He did not care if the lamps on the bandstand were not alight, if the remaining silhouettes, sitting on the iron chairs scattered around, looked like ghosts waiting for heaven knows what romantic performance; he did not care about the icy moon which could be seen in the sky at the same time as the setting sun.

He kept on walking. The child, sitting in his pram, fell asleep and his head started nodding.

'Give me the pram.'

'Not in town.'

They plunged into the rue du Pont d'Avroy, the liveliest street in the town, and behind all the windows, in a halo of comfortable warmth, they could see people drinking cups of coffee filtered through silver percolators, smooth half-pints of beer, and port in delicate glasses, with a golden biscuit in a saucer beside each glass, while the cloud of cigar smoke thickened, and you could sense the collision of the balls on the green billiard-tables.

They looked as if they were fleeing and it was Élise, seized with a sort of giddiness, who was walking the faster of the two.

This procession, this flood of humanity pouring out of a long porch, these people stretching their limbs, still smiling and looking surprised to find a little daylight left outside, were coming out of the Walhalla, the café-concert, and Élise looked over their heads into the auditorium which she could just distinguish, a place of mystery with its hundreds of little red and white lamps, its marble tables, its Chinese lanterns and the muffled sound of the orchestra's finale.

The glance which she darted at the impassive Désiré afterwards was not a reproach. Even if he had offered to take her to the Walhalla, she would have refused.

'It's too dear, Désiré.'

Hadn't she spent the whole of her life in mourning? Once, and only once, she had gone to the theatre with Désiré, in the early days of their marriage, right up in the gallery; she had taken off her veil, put some *Floramye* on her handkerchief, and taken some sweets along.

He never felt the need to go into a café. He was never thirsty and, when they went into the country, they took sandwiches with them which they ate by the roadside. Hundreds of people were buying waffles and, straight after coming out of the Walhalla, pushing open the glass door of a beer-hall.

The bridge over the black, icy-looking water; the boulevard

de la Constitution, to shorten the journey home, for Élise's back was beginning to ache; the tree-trunks; the massive stocky figure of a man on the kerb, obviously a drunkard, a bearded, scowling individual who had opened his overcoat and was urinating with a satisfied air, facing the passers-by.

'Quick, Désiré.'

She stole anxiously along under the trees, not looking back, and quickening her pace. She would have run if she had dared. She wondered if Désiré had recognized the drunkard.

'He's following us, isn't he?'

They had turned the corner of the rue de l'Enseignement. The rue Pasteur was the first on the left. Their house was the first in the rue Pasteur. They could hear footsteps behind them.

'I think it's him,' said Désiré.

'Dear God! Let's hope he doesn't try to come in!'

It was Léopold. The sound of his drunken footsteps echoed along the wall of the church club.

'Do you think he recognized us? Open the door quickly. Help me to carry the pram in.'

It was a positive rout, and they rushed into the house as if they were being pursued.

'I can hardly stand! Light the gas . . .'

He pulled at a little chain hanging from a wrought-iron lantern with coloured panes of glass, and the gas came on automatically. The landlady's light was on. They took the child out of the pram.

'You take him, Désiré.'

They went upstairs. Opening the door, they were met by a familiar warmth and a smell unlike that of any other home. The clock was ticking, there were pink embers in the stove, and the table, which Élise had laid before going out, was ready for supper.

'Do you think he saw where we came in?'

'What difference does it make?'

He did not feel anything. He never felt anything, as Élise was always telling Valérie and her sister Félicie. As for her, she felt all too much, she felt so much that it hurt, indeed perhaps she even felt things which did not exist.

Was that why she remained nervous, irritable, anxious after the encounter with Léopold? The next morning, when Désiré set off for the rue des Guillemins, she was still very uneasy, and she went shopping earlier than usual, with the baby on one arm and her string bag hanging down her side, hurrying into the butcher's and the greengrocer's, and looking behind her as if she were being pursued.

But when, at ten o'clock, she got back to the rue Pasteur, Léopold was there, as dark and stocky as ever, standing on the opposite pavement and gazing at the windows of the house.

She went bravely forward and took out her key, something which called for a whole series of gymnastics on account of the baby, the purse and the shopping-bag.

'Come in, Léopold. Had you already rung the bell?'

She was afraid that he had rung the bell and the landlady had answered the door. He smelled of alcohol. He muttered a few syllables which she could not understand. If only he didn't stumble on the stairs and fall headlong!

'Hold the banisters.'

He was a heavy man. He crushed the steps under his weight and he still dragged his left leg a little. He looked around him at the neat kitchen, went across to Désiré's wicker armchair by the stove, and sank into it.

'What's the matter? Wait a moment while I put the baby in his chair.'

What was the matter? Nothing. He didn't understand the question.

'I came along to say hullo.'

'I wonder if I've got a drop of something I can offer you.'

She knew that there was nothing, that the carafe in the sideboard was empty.

'Won't you have a cup of coffee?'

She poked the fire, moved the kettle and picked up the coffee-mill. She was still uneasy, she could not help it. It seemed to her that there was some significance in their meeting on the boulevard de la Constitution.

'Is Eugénie keeping well?'

'Probably. She's supposed to be in a big country house.'

'Take your coat off.'

He shook his head. She did not dare to insist. Never, however often he might come and sit down in the kitchen by the stove, would he agree to take off his coat or his bowler hat which seemed to be inseparable from his bearded face and his bushy eyebrows. Never would he meet Désiré either, or make the slightest reference to him.

He sat there, heavy and motionless. She did not know how to talk to him and spoke politely as if he were a stranger, and yet these were the two extreme links of the family chain which had come together, the eldest of the Peters and the little thirteenth child who might have been his daughter.

He watched her coming and going, always on the move, as if she were afraid of suddenly finding herself immobilized in front of him.

'You aren't too hot like that? You won't have a little milk in your coffee? A sandwich? There's a bit of cheese left.'

He did not trouble to reply. There was no way of knowing why he had come, what had impelled the vagabond to sit down in this kitchen, next to this little sister of his whom he did not know and whom he gazed at with surprise in his eyes.

Once again, without realizing that she had already asked the same question, she said:

'Is Eugénie keeping well?'

She had seen Eugénie only once, an astonishing woman who must have been very beautiful at one time, a brunette with a Parisian accent who called everybody 'dearie' and used the familiar *tu* with people.

'Have you seen Louisa lately?'

She talked about her sisters, about Louisa who lived on the quai de Coronmeuse, about Marthe, Schroets' wife, about Félicie who was extremely unhappy with her husband.

'She's married a madman. He hides in the dark at night to frighten her. He beats her too. She's shown me the marks.'

Léopold heaved a sigh and she felt more and more uneasy, yet drawn to him by a mysterious force. There were so many questions which she would have liked to ask him, so many questions which, like an augur, only he could answer!

Why was it that she felt guilty? If Désiré had come home unexpectedly, she would not have known what to say, what attitude to adopt, and she would have begged his pardon.

'You knew Father well, Léopold . . .'

He drank his coffee, with drops running down the black

hairs of his beard. His eyes sought automatically for another drink which he would have preferred, and he heaved a sigh.

'Is it true that at the end of his life? . . .'

'That what?' he asked gruffly. 'That he drank?'

Désiré's armchair creaked under Léopold. Tha latter knew everything. He had been to see his father's birthplace, at Herzogenrath, on the other side of the frontier, the vast, comfortable house of a big landowner.

The place itself remained incomprehensible to Élise, those three frontiers close to the Meuse, those low-lying meadows, that house situated in Germany whose windows overlooked Holland while from the bottom of the garden you could see Belgium.

'Mother lived in the biggest farm in Dutch Limbourg. She was a Liévens.'

The daughter of a rich farming family, a family which was still one of the richest in Limbourg.

The young couple had decided not to go far: they had crossed the Meuse and settled in Belgian Limbourg, at Neeroeteren. Peters was a dike keeper. It was he who controlled the movement of the water in the polders. From Neeroeteren, you had to walk for an hour before you saw another house.

'It's there that you were born?'

'The others too, Hubert, Louis, Marthe, Louisa, all of us except Félicie and you. And I'm not so sure about Félicie. Wait a moment . . .'

He started counting and she tried to picture that expanse of pale, spongy grass, those endless meadows divided by curtains of poplars and by irrigation canals.

'In winter, we used to go to school on skates, along the canal.'

'You aren't too hot like that, Léopold?'

It was strange that she should have met him again just now. She scarcely ever went to the rue Puits-en-Sock. She never saw her sisters, except Félicie, when the latter was able to escape for a few minutes, or when Élise went to the market and caught sight of her through the windows of the café. The day before, when they had found no note on Françoise's door, Élise had experienced a feeling of emptiness.

She circled round Léopold, not daring to look him in the eyes. She wanted to ask him so many more questions.

'How did we come to lose all our money?'

'First of all we moved to Herstal. On account of the poplars.'

She did not grasp the connexion between the poplars at Neeroeteren and the move to Herstal. Yet it was quite simple. By means of the poplars on his estate, her father had been initiated in the timber trade. He had decided that this business would be more profitable than farming, that they should go and live near the town.

Élise remembered vaguely that they had lived in what had once been the castle of Pépin d'Herstal. There were some underground passages left and an old tower which had since been destroyed, where a mysterious light could be seen every night.

'We had four barges on the water and ten horses in the stable.'

All that Élise could remember was the ewe which they used to feed on sweets and chocolate and which nobody had had the heart to kill. That was her only recollection, together with the smell of the timber and the story of the light in the tower.

'Then Father started drinking.'

'What for?'

He just looked at her.

'You know, my girl . . .'

He called her my girl. He would always call her that.

'He started drinking. At the café he made the acquaintance of a certain Brooks.'

The man who still held the contract for the emptying of the town's dustbins. So those heavy dustcarts which went through the streets in the morning had a distant connexion with Élise!

'Brooks asked him to sign some bills of exchange. He wasn't able to pay on the day. People turned against Father and he was forced to sell everything.'

She felt like asking him:

'And you, Léopold, where were you at the time?'

But she was just as timid in front of him, who could talk about the past, as she would have been in front of a witch who could predict the future.

'Poor Mother!' she sighed. 'I remember our flat in the rue Féronstrée. She never went out without her gloves. She used

to tell me time and again: "You see, daughter, it's better ̣
arouse envy than pity. People won't give us anything anyway." '

Léopold had not been at his mother's funeral. There had
been whispers, at the time, that he had gone to England with
a countess older than himself, while Eugénie had taken a job
as a cook in a middle-class house.

'Wait a moment while I put some more coal on the fire.
Move back a bit. No, don't go yet.'

She wanted to know more. She was afraid of all that Léopold
knew and yet she was also afraid of seeing him go, she needed
to question him, to feed on the Peters' past, on their history,
on their life.

How far away was the hat-shop in the rue Puits-en-Sock,
and even big Désiré sitting behind the green windows of the
insurance office!

'The next time you come, I'll have something for you to
drink.'

Yes, she would go and buy some spirits, just for him, seeing
that he probably didn't like coffee. She would hide the bottle.

'You really think that Félicie drinks? It's the doctors who
told her to start drinking stout, because she was anaemic. I'm
anaemic too. At night my back goes numb all over. Perhaps
it's because we were the last to be born?'

He shook his head, a cigarette which had gone out sticking
to his lip.

'Listen, Léopold . . .'

What was she going to add? She didn't know. A devil was
pushing her on. She felt an urge to go on talking. She circled
round him, grating some carrots on a corner of the table,
picking up the baby's celluloid doll, and shutting the window
which she had opened for a moment on account of the steam.

'*I saw you, the night of the Grand Bazaar . . .*'   ,

No! She didn't say it. She had stopped in time, afraid to go
on. She did not bear Léopold a grudge. He was what he was,
the eldest of the Peters, and he knew everything.

'What's the matter, my girl?'

Was it another Peters disease? Félicie was like that too. She
would sometimes burst out sobbing, for no apparent reason.
It was her nerves, as Élise said. Désiré, who could not understand, was forever saying:

'What are you complaining about? Are we short of anything? Aren't we happy?'

'What's the matter, my girl?'

Léopold for his part, did not wait for an answer. It was as if he knew. He gazed at the floor like a man whose thoughts are far away.

'Those poor people whose son . . . The father handed in his resignation straight away . . . He's lost so much weight you can't recognize him now . . . When he walks along the street, he keeps close to the houses, thinking that everybody's pointing at him.'

She was lying. Léopold knew that she was lying. It was not about old Marette that she was thinking. He looked at her inquisitively. Perhaps he had not recognized her when she had gone into the alley-way to adjust her suspender? He shook his head, hunted for some loose tobacco in the depths of his pocket and rolled himself a shapeless cigarette.

'How could he have done a thing like that? What good did it do? His parents had given him a good education. He could have become somebody. And now? Heaven knows where he is . . .'

Heaven and Léopold, who said nothing and heaved a sigh, because all this was pointless, it was words, nothing but words. He wished that she would stop talking and get on with her housework without bothering about him, that she would leave him in peace in his armchair to breathe in the atmosphere of hearth and home.

'It was just the day Roger was born. I was on my way to get Valérie at L'Innovation, because I was afraid of having the baby before Désiré got home. It seems there were some people killed. I didn't have the courage to read the papers.'

He could have taken out of his pocket, as well as bits of tobacco and an old pipe with the stem tied together with cotton, some letters written on poor-quality paper. There were not many of them, six or seven, undated, some unstamped, all in pencil.

. . . I am not putting a stamp because I haven't enough money to buy one . . .

As soon as he had arrived in Paris, Félix Marette had plunged

83

into the rue Montmartre district, where the streets smelled of printing ink and where, in the cafés, you could catch sight of black backs, wide-brimmed hats, loosely tied bows, prominent paunches, political pundits whose names you could see every day in the papers, whose silhouettes you could recognize as they passed, leaders of the lower classes, heralds of proletarian thought.

The thin, starved-looking boy roamed along the slimy pavements, pressing his nose against the windows behind which pipes were being smoked and proofs were being corrected on the marble-topped tables, between the beer-mugs and the sauerkrauts.

With his shoes sucking in water, he had waited with others outside dark passages, to see the bundles of freshly printed newspapers being carried out at a run towards the boulevards.

I am not putting a stamp because . . .

I can feel that I am going to achieve something, I can feel a force within me which . . .

He was ambitious to write in his turn, to see the thoughts seething inside him printed on pale sheets of paper. He prowled round the great men who went by, looking calm and busy, haloed by the glory which barely-dry ink procures.

I have made the acquaintance of a libertarian who recites poetry in a tavern at Montmartre. We argued the whole of one night walking side by side between the Central Market and the boulevard Montmartre. He too is in favour of direct action and I confessed to him that . . .

'Another cup of coffee, Léopold? Yes, do. I'll cut you a piece of cheese.'

Léopold-the-Bearded did not stop her, since she insisted on it, but he would not eat the cheese. All he needed was a little bit of courage to drag himself out of the wicker armchair, go down that new-smelling staircase, turn the door-handle, and make straight for the first café he could find. There was one in the rue de l'Enseignement; he had noticed it on his way here, and at the time he had very nearly gone in.

Since the day before yesterday, I have been earning my living, as is shown by the stamp on this letter. I eat at mealtimes . . .

84

He had had a stroke of luck. In that rue Montmartre where he sought nothing but food for his fever, next to a huge draughty building in which the offices of a score of different newspapers were superposed and intermingled, the boy had noticed, stuck on a stationer's window, an advertisement written in purple ink.

Young man wanted to serve in the shop and run errands.

He had gone, at high noon, into the semi-darkness of the shop whose window was full of indiarubber stamps, 'made to order, delivered within twenty-four hours'.

'Excuse me, Monsieur . . .'

A man as sad and gloomy as an ant, a woman who could scarcely be seen at the cash-desk, and the smell of ink, paper, indiarubber and glue, especially glue.

'I read your advertisement and would like to offer my services . . .'

He was examined through iron-rimmed spectacles.

'I can only give you sixty francs a month and a little bedroom on the sixth floor. But at least it's a shelter, a door, a roof, a bed. For your meals, you'll have to fend for yourself.'

Marette had eaten a sauerkraut with sausages. He reported to Léopold:

I went into the Brasserie du Croissant and there, at the next table to Renaudel and Jaurès, I ordered a . . .

A sauerkraut! His employer, whose name was Vétu, had not asked him for his papers and had taken him to his attic by way of endless corridors and staircases. He was afraid of waking up with a start during the night, because if he did, his head would bump against the ceiling.

. . . a sauerkraut with two sausages and a huge slice of ham. I was so excited that it would not go down: I had to make an effort and I was afraid my neighbours were going to laugh at me . . .

It was Marette's last letter. He had added:

I have started work on the indiarubber stamps. It is not as difficult as you might think. The Vétus have a daughter whom I haven't seen yet and who spends the whole day practising the piano on the entresol. The floor vibrates . . .

'Are you going already, Léopold?'

Yes, he had got to his feet. He stood a moment longer in front of the stove on which the dinner was simmering. She knew, she felt, that he would return, but she did not dare to ask him when.

I'm so happy ... If you see Eugénie, give her a kiss from me ...

He heaved a last sigh, shedding bits of tobacco from his heavy verdigrised overcoat.

'Good-bye, my girl.'

He had not looked at the baby. He had not paid the slightest attention to him. Did he even know his age?

She only hoped Léopold wouldn't fall down the stairs.

'I'll see you to the door.'

She followed him down a few steps, and heard the landlady, down below, opening the door a little way, just like Madame Cession. When she had taken the flat in the rue Pasteur, she had thought it would be different. Alas, landladies were all the same. There was trouble if you spilt a couple of drops of water on the stairs.

Trouble with the pram too ...

'I shall be glad when your son can walk by himself. Every time I have to go down to the cellar, I bump into that pram ...'

It was so much trouble to push a baby's pram a few inches to one side!

'Good-bye, Léopold. Don't forget to come again.'

Without bothering to reply, he found the handle, shut the door behind him less violently than she had feared, dived into the street, and headed for the nearest café.

*

'Don't cry like that. You know very well that your mother's tired, that her back hurts. If you're naughty, they'll have to take her to hospital and operate on her.'

The child, who was one year old, did not understand.

'You've thrown your toys on the floor again. Really, Roger! And Désiré'll be back at any moment ...'

The carrots were nearly burnt. She set to work. She still had to empty the slops, and then ... The minutes went by ... The ticking of the alarm-clock speeded up ...

And when Désiré came in, his stride was even, his face smiling, his lanky figure impregnated with the joy he had experienced at walking through the town, for all that the weather was dull. Cloudy weather had its charms too, and so did rain.

'I'm hungry.'

'It's ready, Désiré. By the way . . .'

She had to tell him.

'Léopold came. He sat down for a minute and had a cup of coffee.'

'How was he?'

'All right.'

That was all. He dropped the subject. But not entirely. A long time afterwards, he asked:

'Is he working?'

'I didn't dare to ask him.'

He ate his sweetened carrots with a well-done steak without noticing that Élise was darting furtive glances at him, as if she were hiding something from him, as if she were afraid of being found out.

'Monsieur Monnoyeur said to me this morning . . .'

She raised her eyes to the ceiling. Monsieur Monnoyeur was always saying that: 'Next year, if all goes well, I'll give you a rise.'

But today, as if to obtain his forgiveness, she pretended to share Désiré's pleasure.

'That would enable us to buy some new curtains, some twilled curtains. I've seen some at L'Innovation that weren't too dear . . .'

If he had felt things like a Peters, he would have realized that a new element had introduced itself into the house, an element so subtle that even Élise, still trembling with emotion, could not have said what it was.

*

Léopold had bought a sausage somewhere and was eating it without bread, in the half-light of a low tavern, gazing vaguely in front of him.

Chapter Six

It was the silence that morning which produced in Élise that feeling of an illness one is sickening for, which one can feel inside oneself everywhere and nowhere. The kitchen window was wide open, revealing the backs of a row of houses, the little yards, and a great stretch of bright blue sky indented by the gables; and that extraordinary, frightening silence came flooding into the room in concentric waves, travelling like the sound of a bell. It came from beyond the roofs, from behind the watercolour sky, making her long to shut the window to prevent it from invading the house.

For everybody was bound to have the impression of being the centre of that silence, everybody who, in the midst of that immense, absolute calm, set off little individual noises, with a fork, a glass, opening a door, coughing, breathing.

Outside this sonorous nucleus which each person carried around shamefacedly within him, there was nothing. The pink brick walls of the house which was being built underneath Élise's windows were deserted, indecently bare; the masons were not working and the first noise she missed was the crunching of the mortar under their trowels. In the centre of the block of houses, the forge at Halkin's, with its heavy hammer-blows and the echoing sound of sheet-iron, was dead. And at ten o'clock, in the courtyard of the Friars' school in the rue de l'Enseignement, the shrill explosion of playtime failed to occur.

The trams were not running. They had heard two when the sun had barely risen, but these had been derailed and overturned Fétinne way. On the day before this radiant First of May, all blue and white like the Virgin, Monsieur Monnoyeur had chosen to fall ill, to wrap himself up in mufflers, and to curl up in his leather armchair.

'What do we decide to do, Monsieur Mamelin?'

And Désiré had replied simply:

'We open, of course.'

It was as much as he would do, when he was reading the

paper in the evening, in his shirtsleeves, by the fireside, to tell
Élise that he might not be coming home to dinner. The paper
carried in big black disaster letters the words:

'GENERAL STRIKE DECIDED ON.'

'What's going to happen, Désiré?'

'Why should anything happen?'

*

He had gone off as usual, with a few extra sandwiches in case
the police barriers prevented him from coming home at two
o'clock, but he did not think they would.

People had laid in stocks of food. There was nobody in
the streets. Godard, the butcher in the place du Congrès, had
left the door of his shop ajar, but only a few neighbours had
slipped inside.

It was as if everybody had the plague or was afraid of catching
it. No postman. The unemptied dustbins had been left on the
kerbs. No schoolboys in their hooded cloaks, not a single
shout, not a single noise. Unless they were all dead, the inhabitants were somewhere or other, possibly lurking behind
their curtains. Now and then a door opened a fraction of an
inch, and through the gap you could sense that an eye was
studying the dramatic emptiness of the street, somebody who
was afraid of breathing the miasmas outside, the hallucinating
miasmas of silence.

Yet about ten o'clock Léopold arrived, dragging one leg
along, regardless of the fact that he was awakening the echoes
of the rue Pasteur. He looked up for a long time before
ringing the bell, for he had a horror of using the bell, on account of the landlady who pretended she had heard only one
ring instead of two and hurried to answer the door.

'Good morning, my girl.'

He looked the same as the other times he had been. He sat
down in his usual place in Désiré's wicker armchair; Élise
gave him a cup of strong coffee which she had brewed specially for him.

It was strange that he, who knew everything, gave the same
answer as Désiré, who felt nothing, who would go to his office
at the same time, by the same route, if the whole town were in
flames.

'What do you expect them to do?'

He never explained himself. He knew what he meant, uttered a few weighty, mysterious words of oracular wisdom, then, after a long silence, produced a disgraceful crackling noise from his old patched-up pipe.

'Unless *the others* open fire.'

'And what if they do?'

The oracle made no answer and plunged into his meditations which the silence of May Day failed to disturb.

Léopold had come. He had sat down. He had drunk his cup of coffee and he had gone off again.

'Good-bye, my girl.'

*

Silence once more. The clatter of a spoon on a plate. The sound of footsteps, the familiar metronome footsteps, Désiré coming home at two o'clock as if nothing had happened, just as he had prophesied.

'Well?'

'Nothing.'

'The strikers? The miners from Seraing?'

'They are staging a march. They are quite calm.'

'Dear God, Désiré!'

'But I tell you everything's quiet. People just get worried about nothing.'

He went off as he had come. The baby seized the opportunity to scream, to howl until he was blue in the face, to pierce the circles of silence with his shrieks.

It was five minutes past four, six minutes past four, by the alarm-clock ticking feverishly on the black mantelpiece, when the feeling of suffocation from which Élise had been suffering since the morning suddenly turned into panic. She could not stand another five minutes of it. She put on her outdoor clothes, not looking at her hat in the mirror, not shutting the window, not putting any coal on the fire. She picked the baby up as if she were saving him from a disaster and went downstairs.

She knew that the landlady, Madame Martin, was listening and was going to open the door. The pram was under the stairs. The door moved. The old woman looked at her tenant. What if she tried to stop Élise from going out? But no! She stared at her in terror, without saying a word, her mouth half open like a fish, looking as if she thought that Élise had gone mad, and then shut herself in again, turning the key in the lock.

Élise walked along, pushing the pram, taking the shortest way into the town, and getting excited, all by herself in the wilderness. She wanted to know what was happening, she had to know.

'Excuse me . . .'

The astonished policeman looked at her inquiringly.

'Is it still possible to cross the bridges?'

'That depends where you're going.'

She answered at random.

'To L'Innovation.'

'They'll tell you further on.'

It wasn't his sector. He didn't know. It was all one to him. She went off again, pushing the pram along with her belly. She could see some people in the distance, at the Pont des Arches, but she still could not hear any noise.

'Where are you going?'

'To L'Inno . . .'

A sudden inspiration. She corrected herself.

'Home. I live in the rue Léopold, over Cession's, the hat-shop . . .'

'Carry on . . .'

She rushed triumphantly on to the deserted bridge, envied by the onlookers. At the other end, she came up against another barrier.

'Where are you going?'

'I live in the rue Léopold, over Cession's, the . . .'

'Carry on if you can. You'll see further on.'

She was winning points. She didn't know where she was going, what she wanted. She went forward for the sake of going forward, because her instinct was impelling her, but at the corner of the rue de la Cathédrale she met a wall of human backs and stammered in vain:

'Excuse me, Monsieur . . . Excuse me . . . Excuse me . . .'

She pushed the pram against the legs of the people lining the street and they turned round angrily.

She had come as far as she could. The policemen and the gendarmes could not do any more for her, because she had reached the route of the strikers' march. All the same, she made another attempt to slip through, stood on tip-toe, hung on, bent down, but could not see anything but heads filing past. Then, beneath the silence of the town, she heard the strangest of noises, composed of footsteps, nothing but footsteps, without a single fanfare, without a single shout, without a single voice, without a single murmur, the footsteps of one hundred and twenty thousand men, women and children who had been marching along in serried ranks since daybreak, past blind windows, with the same policemen at every cross-roads, the same gendarmes with their arms at the order, who seemed to be hemming them into an ever-narrowing circle.

'Madame, with your baby, you'd be well advised . . .'

But the man who spoke to her so politely was just a little non-commissioned officer whom she could talk round if she tried. Another came running up, a captain or some such rank, with sweat beading his forehead. He had caught sight of the pram.

'Come on! Push them back! . . . Push the whole lot back! . . .'

Everybody suffered on her account. Because of her, the people who had managed to cross the Pont des Arches were forced to go back to the Outremeuse district where there was nothing to be seen.

Why did Élise suddenly feel anxious as she got nearer home? Was it because she had left the window open? Whatever the reason, she felt uneasy. She had to indulge in some complicated gymnastics to get the pram up the three steps outside the front door. On the stairs, the reason for her uneasiness became clear to her. There was somebody in the flat. Somebody was walking up and down.

Bravely, just as she had borne down upon the town, she threw open the door, and it was in a voice which astonished herself that she murmured:

'Désiré!'

It was such a shock to find Désiré in his shirtsleeves in the middle of the kitchen! As for him, he asked her, as simply as could be:

'Where have you been?'

'But what about you?'

She had already understood. The civic guard's uniform . . .

'Désiré! They've . . .'

'The town crier has been along all the streets. All the civic guards have to report to the place Ernest-de-Bavière at seven o'clock.'

'But what for?'

'They don't know themselves. Pass me my belt, will you?'

'Wait at least until I've made some coffee for your flask.'

He did not know how dramatic these little things were. For him, this was just a general strike, a May Day rather more agitated than most, but for her it was a man, her man, putting on his uniform, buckling his belt, and wiping the grease off his rifle. This amused Désiré.

'It seems they're going to issue us with cartridges.'

'Take care of yourself, Désiré.'

If only Valérie had been there! She was immobilized too, over at L'Innovation, where, about three o'clock, the police had ordered them to lower the iron shutters.

What if Élise went to see Madame Pain, fifty yards down the rue Pasteur? Alas, Madame Pain was always bemoaning her lot. She had something wrong with her liver and her womb. She was bound to be shaking with fright.

'See you tonight or tomorrow morning. Don't worry. Nothing can happen.'

Désiré's moustache when he kissed her did not taste the same as other days.

'Be careful.'

Careful of what? In the rue Jean-d'Outremeuse, he met some other civic guards, friends he had been to school with, and they sauntered along like boys on holiday.

'What are they going to make us do?'

The march was still following the route which had been marked out for it, and the strikers were respecting their leaders' instructions: they were keeping silent. What spoke for them was the flags, the trade unions' pennons, bright red for the most part, and banners stretching from one pavement to the other, swaying about at the height of the first-storey windows.

They had come a long way, from Seraing, Ougrée, Tilleur, Ans, from the collieries, from the mining villages all round the town, from the factories which you usually glimpsed only from the train, dark and mysterious, with the bloody maws of the furnaces being fed by half-naked demons.

Some had started before daybreak. They were beginning to drag their feet. Their hobnailed boots were scraping along the paving-stones or the asphalt. The men seemed to be astonished by the sight of these districts where they had never been before and where fear had blinded windows and doors.

They were eight or ten abreast. Some of them were carrying a child on their shoulders. There were women stumbling along, clutching dark shawls with thick woollen fringes to their breasts.

The miners were wearing their boiled leather helmets and some people, behind their curtains, shuddered as they watched them pass by, their eyes brighter in their hard faces than those of the other men.

Élise started praying, without knowing exactly why. She felt an urge to kneel down in a corner of the kitchen and murmur:

'Dear God, Blessed Virgin Mary, grant that . . .'

Grant that nothing may happen! And yet, she would have liked . . . No! She didn't want anything to happen, she didn't want a riot. It was more a physical need. Her nerves were raw. She would have liked to be over there. She found it unbearable being all alone in her everyday kitchen.

'Grant that Désiré . . .'

She was lying to herself. She cried a little. That calmed her down. Then she got Roger's bath ready.

What were they doing? Why was it that she still couldn't hear anything?

There were horse-guards all the way round the huge place Saint-Lambert. The iron shutters were down at the Grand Bazaar, Vaxelaire-Claes's and L'Innovation, and, when night fell, the milky globes of the arc lamps did not light up. Darker still was the north side, the bulky Palace of the Prince Bishops with the massive pillars which looked as if they were destined to support the sky. Every now and then there was a whistle, a shouted order, a soldier riding across the empty terrace.

The strikers, or rather their leaders, had promised that the place Saint-Lambert should be neutral ground. All the five or six ways into the square were guarded, including the alleys. The big Café du Phare, with its thirty billiard-tables, was closed. So was the big china-shop. Between these two buildings there was a dark, slender façade, some open windows, a balcony on which a silhouette was outlined now and then.

This was the Populaire, the official headquarters of the unions and the workers' parties.

It was surprising, coming from the dead town, to see café waiters here serving bottles of beer, red and yellow soda-waters, and ham sandwiches. The floor was dusty grey with trails of moisture here and there, the walls brown. Little tables were being used as desks, men in cloth caps were checking lists, and on the first floor papers were piling up on the secretaries' long table.

'Ougrée-Marihaye?'

'Two thousand two hundred.'

'The Sclessin wire-mills?'

Somebody went to fetch the secretary in question, who had gone out on the balcony to have a look.

'Eight hundred and fifty-two: the whole lot.'

'Vieille-Montagne! Where's the Vieille-Montagne?'

The march was not far away, moving past less than two hundred yards away as the crow flies, behind the big, shuttered shops; yet there was nothing to be heard, and now and then everybody listened anxiously to this silence; the leaders, standing near the window, talked of other things. They were all bearded men, Vandervelde who had come specially from Brussels, Demblin-the-Thunderer who had written some scholarly studies of Shakespeare and read Ovid in the original, Troclet-of-Liège, and finally a young man who was not a member of parliament yet, a young man of disquieting roughness: Flahaut.

'Telephone!'

The ringing scarcely ever stopped. This time, it was not a report from the provinces.

'It's for the chief.'

'Hullo!... Yes... What?... But no! I can assure you that orders have been given to that effect...'

The chief of police was speaking at the other end of the line. In the Town Hall offices, they were all gathered together as at the Populaire.

'There are some rather alarming movements as if...'

Yet the two sides had come to an agreement. A march, well and good, but no singing, no band, above all no *International*.

The workers were to provide relays of guards in the foundries and the factories.

'Hullo! What's that you say?'

A few yards from the telephone, you could hear the words:

'... Civic guards ...'

'That's a mistake ... What? ... Certainly not! ... But I tell you there's to be no meeting, no speeches, no ...'

The chief looked across at Flahaut and the latter turned his head away.

'Flahaut! It seems that your men ...'

The miners from Seraing ... They had apparently withdrawn from the march little by little, in small groups ... There was talk of infiltration ... Over at the Town Hall they were worried ... The civic guard had been called out ...

'I haven't given any orders,' said Flahaut, but he was capable of lying.

The gas was lit. Outside, the air was turning misty. The sound of troop movements could be heard coming from the direction of the rue Léopold. It was the civic guard, which had been mustered in the place Ernest-de-Bavière and which was coming to take up its position in the place Saint-Lambert.

As if in confirmation of the chief of police's fears, some shouts came from the other end of the square. There had been a sudden commotion on the corner of a little street. An orderly from the Populaire was sent across and came back within a few minutes.

'It's over already. A few miners who tried to force the barrier ...'

And yet they could still feel something like a threat in the air. Where, for instance, had they come from, those men who were beginning to form a group on the terrace and who were looking across towards the windows of the Populaire?

It was too dark to make out their faces. They were strikers, that was certain. How had they managed to get there?

Just as the civic guards, who, for the first time, had been issued with cartridges, came into the square from the rue Léopold, a chorus of shouts greeted them:

'Down with the civic guard!'

One solitary shout:

'Come over to our side!'

There were two hundred of them now, possibly more, who had entered the forbidden quadrilateral. A little group of officials arrived in its turn: the burgomaster wearing his sash, the chief of police, a few policemen.

Some whistles blew.

Nobody knew as yet what was happening on the other side of the barriers, in the streets where a little while ago the strikers had been marching quietly along. Everybody strained his ears. The officials had come close to the Populaire. Their eyes looked up at the balcony like a silent prayer.

There was still time to avert a clash.

No! It was too late. A whole section of the march had taken on a new life, as if an order had been given and passed on, and the direction of the march changed, the line extended, the men dispersed and formed up again in a different order, some policemen were pushed aside.

'Place Saint-Lambert!'

A shout which grew in volume, which was repeated over and over again, hurrying footsteps, piercing whistle-blasts. People almost expected the burgomaster or the chief of police to go into the Populaire and demand an explanation, but that was impossible, for they were forbidden to speak to one another in public.

Some mounted policemen had drawn their swords, over towards the place du Théâtre, where the crowd seemed to be thickest. Then, just when it was least expected, after some confused pushing, the barrier gave way, and hundreds and thousands of men and women poured into the square, jostling one another as they came.

Should the leaders go on to the balcony and try to make themselves heard? They argued the point, in low voices, among the beermugs, the ham rolls, and the paper littering the dirty floor.

'Hullo. This is the commandant of the gendarmerie speaking. Unless the strikers withdraw in good order . . .'

How could they speak to them? To whom? To what? It was a human sea, growing all the time, in which you could no longer make out any individuals. The pressure of the crowd had broken a sheet of glass behind the metal shutters of L'Innovation. This noise had excited the men, and a few stones had been thrown at the frosted-glass panes of the porch.

T – P. – D

Somebody in the group of officials sighed:

'If only it would rain!'

At L'Innovation, Monsieur Wilhems had collected the shop assistants and the inspectors together in the basement, next to the ironmongery department, and Valérie kept thinking about Élise, all alone in the rue Pasteur with the child.

Everybody was waiting for something which seemed to be inevitable and, contrary to all expectations, that thing did not happen. Time went by, and the noise of stamping feet grew louder until it seemed that the whole town was being angrily trampled underfoot, that the sound was coming from all sides without a shot being fired in reply.

The square had so to speak been divided into two. The terrace opposite the Palace of the Prince Bishops was still surrounded by the mounted gendarmes. The space in front of the Grand Bazaar was occupied by the civic guards whom the pressure of the strikers was crushing closer and closer to the shopfronts.

Night had fallen. There were no lights anywhere except in the windows of the Populaire, where the strikers tried to recognize the shadows moving around.

'Hullo!... Yes... Close your shutters... That's an order ... When they can't see any light, they'll go away...'

The augurs hesitated. If they closed the shutters, they would give the impression of weakening. They decided just to put out the lamps, and once that had been done, there was darkness inside and outside, and they could go out on the balcony without being seen.

Where did it start? It was after ten o'clock. One might have thought that the night would go by in this incoherent expectancy, or that empty stomachs and fatigue would get the better of the strikers. But then there was a vague murmur. A song, first sung softly, then growing louder, spreading from one to another, and finally intoned by thousands of voices:

'... The last fight let us face...'

At the same time, a thrust from the crowd. A few men, in the midst of the chaos, conferred in an undertone. The mayor, a tiny little man, could not see anything beyond his immediate neighbours.

The first couplet was over. A pause. You could sense that the second couplet was about to burst forth, but then, in the short silence, there came the strident call of a bugle, bringing a lump to every throat.

On horseback, standing in his stirrups with drawn sword, the commandant of the gendarmerie advanced as far as he could towards the crowd of men whose faces could no longer be distinguished, and after the third bugle-call his voice rang out, so clear that it must have been audible all over the place Saint-Lambert.

'First summons! Let law-abiding citizens go home. We are going to open fire.'

A tremor went through the crowd, which moved forward, then back. A murmur arose.

'Second summons! Let law-abiding citizens . . .'

There were shouts as everybody gave voice to his anger.

'. . . We are going to open fire!'

Another silence. The bugle.

'Let law-abiding citizens . . .'

The shot rang out; a solitary shot, absurdly faint, and yet it resounded in every heart. Nobody knew who had fired, or at what, or whether anybody had been hit.

'Present, arrrms! . . . Load, arrrms! . . .'

Women's screams, a scuffle, a breath of panic passing over the crowd, and another movement, forward this time, deliberate and full of hate.

'Fire!'

Had they fired into the air? Nobody knew. Nobody knew where he was going, everybody pushed, elbowed and punched in an effort to find a way out, and the mounted gendarmes charged into the crowd, their horses' breasts thrusting the strikers aside while their bare swords zigzagged through the air like lightning.

There was utter silence on the balcony of the Populaire, where there were a score of them crowded together, trying to understand, and peering down at the panic-stricken ebb and flow in the darkness of the square.

Who had had the idea? Who had given the order? The fact remained that all the surviving lamps of the Grand Bazaar, Vaxelaire's and L'Innovation lit up with the bluish crackling of carbon filaments.

Waves of humanity disappeared through all the outlets,

into all the streets, and the torrent flowed away little by little, interrupted by isolated barriers, by shots here and there, by charging horses.

Élise was trembling, sitting by the lamp. The door of the bedroom, where the child was asleep, was half open on to the darkness. She did not know what was happening and could not hear anything except a noise like the distant rumbling of a train. She kept trembling, getting up and sitting down again, feeling ill at ease everywhere, and wondering now and then whether she ought not to give in to temptation.

It was impossible! She could not leave the child alone. In the silence of the night, footsteps came running up. You might have thought there was a flock of panic-stricken animals outside, but as the streets grew wider and emptier, and people got further away from the place Saint-Lambert, the pace slackened, shadows called out to one another, and groups formed up, trying to find their bearings.

Some of these people came running along the rue Pasteur itself, probably on their way home to Bressoux or Jupille. Élise was at her window, in the bedroom, listening. She could make out nothing but disconnected words, and longed to go downstairs and ask questions.

Finally she made up her mind. She stole downstairs in her slippers and noiselessly opened the outside door a little way; as if on purpose, nobody came along for several long-drawn minutes.

At last a man, a woman, a child being literally dragged along.

'Excuse me, Monsieur. Has there been any shooting?'

She startled them. The man hesitated for a moment and his wife snapped at him:

'Come along!'

Élise trembled, wept, went on waiting. She thought she could hear her son crying upstairs and, since she had left the lamp alight, she went back.

She did not go to bed. She did nothing but keep the fire in and make coffee for when Désiré came home. And he returned at last, at six o'clock in the morning, with some of the dawn mist clinging to his moustache; he returned smiling, a smile that was a little forced.

'Dear God, Désiré! What happened?'

He put his rifle away on top of the wardrobe and emptied his cartridge pouch in which all the cartridges were still in place. There was a little cold coffee left in his flask in its brown cloth casing.

'We were stuck against the houses between the rue Gérardrie and the rue Léopold, next to the Grand Bazaar. We couldn't see a thing. There were some mounted gendarmes in front of us and all that we were afraid of was that the horses might back into us.'

He smiled as he remembered something.

'You know the clockmaker's next to the chemist's? It's there that we were, a whole bunch of us: Ledent, Grisard and big Martens. Grisard was the first to piddle against the shutter . . .'

'Dear God, Désiré!'

'Then everybody else did the same. It was only this morning that we noticed it was the shutter over the door. The shop is on a lower level. When they open the shop this morning . . .'

He heaved a sigh of pleasure as he unbuttoned his tunic and dipped his moustache in the hot coffee.

'As for the rest of it, we didn't see a thing. They read the riot act and they fired into the air, that's all I know. It seems that one gendarme had a bullet through his cap. They say . . .'

What was the use? It wasn't certain. The ambulance had come to the place Saint-Lambert twice over. The civic guards, immobilized against the shop fronts, had been unable to see what was happening.

'You aren't too tired?'

'I'm hungry.'

She could see that his lip was trembling in a way which was not usual with him. She pretended not to notice. She was sad, more tired than he was, and light-headed, and if it had been left to her, if it had not been time to do the housework, she would have gone to bed.

At seven o'clock, a familiar siren announced the resumption of work at Halkin's, and a few minutes later, while the builders were unloading bricks on the waste ground underneath the kitchen window, the first blows of the hammer on the sheet-iron rang out.

Chapter Seven

Five minutes before . . . Not even five minutes . . . It took so
little time for bad luck to strike and it was Élise who was right,
she knew it, she felt it, however much people might make fun
of her morose expression, her way of creeping along apolo-
getically as if to incite fate to pity. Once, speaking with exaggerated good humour so as not to annoy his wife, Désiré had
explained:

'You're a regular wet blanket!'

He would never understand, and it was all the better for
him.

Five minutes before, her life had been bright and simple.
She had been crossing the Passerelle. Roughly half-way between the Pont-Neuf and the Pont des Arches, a sort of frontier
between the suburbs and the centre of the town, the Passerelle
was a wide wooden bridge. It was quicker. It was more familiar. It was in a sense the chattel of the inhabitants of Outremeuse, the bridge they used to cross hatless, on an ordinary
errand.

You went up a few stone steps. The planks of the bridge
clattered and trembled under your feet. At the other end, you
went down and, in the early morning, this descent was like
a landing in a new world.

Everywhere, as far as the eye could see, the market spread
out, the vegetable market on the left, the fruit market on the
right; thousands of wicker baskets forming regular streets,
blind alleys, crossroads; hundreds of short-legged women
who had pockets full of change in the three thicknesses of their
petticoats and who kept catching hold of customers or insulting
them.

Élise heard them murmur as they smiled at her son:

'He's such a dear!'

Or else:

'That's the little lady with the kiddy who's so spick and
span.'

Along the quays, there were still a few old houses with high roofs, façades covered with slates, and windows with little greenish panes. There were hundreds of horses and wagons, and the horses, at that time of day – after being on the move for most of the night – had a bag of oats hung on their heads.

Élise ventured timidly into this world which had come from somewhere else, from the surrounding countryside, a world which would disappear in a little while, at the sound of a bell, leaving nothing behind it, on the cobblestones of the quays and squares, but a few cabbage-leaves and carrot-tops.

At last she had her push-chair! For months on end, they had kept on saying:

'When we can do without the pram!'

When, always *when*! *When* Roger would be down to only six bottles a day, *when* he would be able to go on to phosphatine, *when* they could sit him in his chair, *when* he began to walk, *when* it would no longer be necessary to carry him on the stairs . . .

Élise, who suffered from backache and, now that the child could walk a little, had him on her hands all the time, knew that it was all a delusion, but it was no use telling Désiré that it would always be the same. Besides, at bottom, Désiré knew it too. He just pretended to believe . . .

Just now, when she had left the rue Pasteur with the new push-chair for its first outing, he had said gaily to her:

'You see! You won't get tired any more.'

Then he had set off with his long stride to go and sit down for a moment in his mother's kitchen before going on to his office. Élise had decided to make some gooseberry jam and she was almost gay, almost determined, like Désiré, to see the world in the light of this May morning. However, try as she might, her head still hung a little to one side.

'What can you expect, Désiré? I've got used to bad luck . . .'

She could sense bad luck where it was most carefully concealed; she dug it out where nobody would have suspected its existence. The proof of that was what had happened this morning. She had just bought some red gooseberries, then some big green gooseberries enlivened by a little purple spot. She meant to drop in on Madame Pain on her way home to borrow her copper preserving pan, and then to spend the rest of the day making jam in front of the open window which the pink wall and the white masons had nearly reached, for they were building a new house behind theirs and every day the walls went up by a few rows of bricks.

Then all of a sudden, spitefully . . .

It was that, the spitefulness, the treachery of fate which upset her. She did her best. She had got up as usual at six o'clock in the morning. Anybody could come into her flat unexpectedly: everything was tidy and the soup was always simmering on a corner of the fire. Not a single child in the district was looked after as carefully as Roger. His nappies were washed more often than was necessary, and there was no insipid smell hanging about the kitchen as was so often the case in houses where there was a baby. She made all their clothes. She never bought anything ready-made. She saved money on the smallest things. And had Désiré ever come home to the rue Pasteur without finding his dinner ready?

This morning, the blow had had to come from Félicie.

To crown it all, Élise had felt it coming. She ought to have followed her instinct. But just because Félicie ran a café in the middle of the market, did that mean that she could no longer buy anything in town but had to do her shopping in the rue Puits-en-Sock like her sisters-in-law on the Mamelin side?

The stallholders knew her and smiled at her. She was so pleasant with everybody!

'You know, Valérie, if only everybody took the trouble to be pleasant!'

It hurt her when somebody failed in this elementary duty. Even Désiré sometimes! Too many people didn't feel things and this made it worse for those who did! They were the ones who suffered.

She knew. Not exactly what was going to happen to her, except that she would wish that she could sink through the floor. All the same, she had a sort of premonition.

Doing her shopping brought her gradually closer to the huge Café du Marché with its bay windows, its monumental white marble bar, its sparkling beer pulls. She had bought her gooseberries and her shopping-bag was full, hooked on to the folding push-chair which they would at last be able to take up to the flat, thus avoiding causing any annoyance to the landlady.

She had haggled over the price and the stallholder had scarcely put up any resistance.

'Ten sous?... Get along with you!... Well, just because it's you, lady...'

She never came to the market without a hat and yet nobody thought her bumptious. She knew that Félicie had seen her through the café windows. She had seen her husband, whom the two of them called Coucou between themselves, come out, dressed in black and wearing a bowler hat, and set off towards the centre of the town as if he were going to a funeral.

Although Coucou was no longer there, she did not go in. She stayed outside. She did not want Félicie to be able to reproach her one day with having come to the market without saying good day to her, but she did not want to impose herself on her either.

Wasn't it Félicie who had always been coming to see the Mamelins, when they lived in the rue Léopold, to complain about her husband? To such an extent that Désiré had prophesied:

'One fine day, we shall have trouble with Coucou.'

Yet Désiré had not known everything, for instance that one morning Félicie had arrived looking like a madwoman, afraid of being followed. She had been bare-headed, with a shawl folded across her blouse, and she had brought out a little packet.

'Élise, for the love of God you must keep this for me until I come and ask for it back. Whatever you do, don't show it to Désiré.'

The packet had remained hidden for three days on top of the wardrobe, next to the rifle.

'Poor Félicie.'

To attract her attention, Élise tapped timidly on the glass pane, and looked inside where the market women were eating eggs and bacon and rice tarts two inches thick, and drinking big bowlfuls of coffee. These women took their money out of old purses stuffed with coins and notes, without knowing exactly how much there was inside.

Félicie was standing with her elbows on the bar, wearing a pretty white blouse with a lace insertion which emphasized the rich curve of her breasts. She was chatting with a customer of whom Élise had only a back view. Near Élise, some draymen were delivering beer through a trap-door and the air reeked of it, while the two horses pissed urine the colour of ale.

Élise was on the point of going. She thought it would be best to leave. But suddenly her gaze met that of her sister. Félicie came towards her, turned round to say something to her companion, reached the door and opened it just as Élise was starting to smile.

'*Now what have you come begging for?*'

She had said that! Her eyes cold, her features motionless. Élise looked at her uncomprehendingly, unable to think of anything to say in reply. She would have given a great deal to be far away, anywhere, and never to have heard those words.

'Dear God!'

Yes, she must have stammered òut 'Dear God', while looking around her to make sure that nobody had heard. One person who had heard was the waiter, Joseph, the bald one who knew her. Élise walked away with the push-chair. She rushed along.

Listen, Désiré . . . No, Désiré wasn't there . . . He was at his office and she would never tell Désiré . . . Poor little Valérie! . . . No she wouldn't tell Valérie either . . . Valérie must never know . . .

Léopold perhaps? . . . If only Léopold could come this morning to the rue Pasteur! . . . He would understand, he who knew them all, all the Peters . . . He must still know a few things which Élise only suspected . . .

Begging!

She marched along, crossing the Pont des Arches without getting her breath back or her normal colour. She looked at the passers-by as if they were planning to hunt her down. She murmured:

'Félicie's mad.'

As she walked along this phrase kept coming back like a refrain:

'Félicie's mad.'

She longed to talk to somebody about it straight away. She knew that she would know no peace until she had got it off her chest. She crossed the place Ernest-de-Bavière and passed in front of Saint-Nicolas. She very nearly went inside with the child to throw herself before the altar of the Virgin, since it happened to be her month.

'I knew it all the time: Félicie, our Félicie, is mad . . .'

Nobody in the whole family knew Félicie better than Élise. Before her marriage, Félicie had lived with her and their mother in the little flat in the rue Féronstrée. She was already beautiful and very well developed for her age, and men used to turn round to look at her in the street; above all she had a provocative way of throwing out her chest.

Begging! Élise who always refused to take anything, who was so embarrassed every time she went to see her sister! Élise who sometimes made a big detour to avoid just that.

And besides, what use to her were all those breakfast sets in fine porcelain? Wasn't it a regular mania?

'Here, Élise, take this for little Roger . . .'

Why always breakfast sets?

'Oh, come now, Félicie! Last time too . . .'

Did Félicie remember that she had given her a breakfast set only the week before? In the end, Élise had had to hide them from Désiré. She didn't know what to do with them.

'Don't worry, dear. Take it! It's a lovely one.'

Always Limoges porcelain, with tiny pink flowers. Was it really true that Félicie drank, and in that case was it . . .

'No, Félicie, not money. You know, I can't possibly take it . . .'

'Don't be silly!'

Money which she took by the handful out of the till, and which she thrust into her sister's hand or into her bag.

'It's for the baby.'

Money which Élise was ready to return to her straight away. She had never spent it. Without saying anything to Désiré, she had opened a Savings Bank account in the child's name. After leaving Félicie, she used to drop into the General Post Office.

Now she felt like crying. It was the reaction. Her nerves were giving way. She felt tired out and started worrying about the two storeys she had to climb with Roger in her arms. Then she blushed.

Not all the money in the Savings Bank account came from Félicie. But nobody could say that she had taken the other money from Désiré. He never thought of putting anything aside. He never asked himself what would become of her and her son if anything happened to him. Why did she do her shopping at the market? To save a few centimes on this and that. At the end of the month she had several francs which she took to the Savings Bank.

The masons were in their places, scarcely six feet below the window, already silhouetted against the sky. The bean soup had got stuck to the bottom of the saucepan.

Élise did not go to Madame Pain's to borrow the copper preserving pan. She made her jam, without any enthusiasm or pleasure, thinking all the time about Félicie. Léopold did not come. As long as she had not spoken to anybody, she would not feel easy in her mind.

At two o'clock, Désiré was surprised to see her with a white face mottled with pink, as if she had been crying.

'What's the matter?'

'Don't take any notice, Désiré. It's my nerves.'

A prudent man, he never pressed the point on these occasions. He ate his meal, facing the open window. It was she who spoke up first.

'I saw Félicie this morning.'

Without thinking, Désiré asked:

'Was she squiffy?'

A family word which served for Léopold and Félicie, and which one day, alas, would serve for Marthe.

'Why do you say that, Désiré? Félicie doesn't drink.'

'Then what would she be like if she did?'

'You don't understand my family.'

He scented danger and made no reply, searching for something else to talk about.

'You just can't understand people who've had a hard time of it.'

She was on the verge of tears, and he lost no time in finishing his meal and lighting his cigarette.

'Poor Félicie! If you only knew . . .'

'Oh, yes! Coucou, I know . . . Well, if he beats her, she's only got to leave him. Good-bye, Élise.'

Roger was asleep. The sound of footsteps faded away downstairs, the street door closed again, and Élise took fright at the idea that she had come close to telling Désiré everything.

She waited for the child to wake up. She did not want to wake him herself, but the time seemed to drag, and possibly, getting dressed to go out, she made rather more noise than was necessary. With her hat already on, she fed him, made up the fire, closed the window, and went downstairs.

She simply had to speak to somebody and she had decided to go to Coronmeuse to see her sister Louisa.

'Poor Louisa! If you only knew what Félicie said to me this morning . . .'

No! She wouldn't tell her what Félicie had said.

'Louisa, poor Louisa, I do believe our Félicie is mad.'

She had forgotten the insult. Nobody would believe it, and yet it was the absolute truth. It was not for her own sake that she was hurrying like that along the interminable quai de Coronmeuse. It was in her nature. She would have run like that for anybody, for she always felt an urge to help others, only to sigh afterwards, with head bowed:

'People are so ungrateful!'

She wanted to do something for Félicie, to save her. She had noticed a great many things, but it was all so subtle, so difficult to explain to anybody who did not feel things like a Peters . . .

On certain mornings, for instance, Félicie burst into tears as soon as she saw her sister and clasped her in a long embrace, as you would after a disaster.

'Is it Coucou again?' Élise would ask.

Élise had never talked about this to anybody; indeed she had never dared to think about it, as she was doing now. Félicie might sigh:

'He'll kill me one of these days!'

But Élise felt, Élise knew that it wasn't because of her husband that her sister was crying. She even guessed the real reason. But it was even harder to believe. She guessed that Félicie wasn't really unhappy, that she was acting a part, in the brightly lit room which smelled of bacon and coffee, acting the part of the unhappy wife, and darting a furtive glance now and then at her reflection in the mirror.

Félicie gave her some money. She would have given her all that she had. She plunged her hand into the till.

'Take it! . . . Yes, do! . . .'

Who could tell whether, about ten o'clock or eleven o'clock, her mood would not have changed? Once, not long after a tearful scene of this sort, Élise has passed the café again and she had seen her sister roaring with laughter with a commercial traveller. She had been laughing like a . . .

No! She mustn't say the word, or think it.

'Listen, Louisa. Once when we were both living with Mother . . .'

Would she tell her sister Louisa about that?

She walked on and the setting changed around her. She had left behind the less pleasant part of the quay, the part which was not shaded by a single tree and beside which the Meuse flowed along, broad and shining. She had come to another quay, the quai de Coronmeuse, and with it the canal and the port in which a hundred or two hundred barges, perhaps more, lay side by side, sometimes ten abreast, with washing drying, children playing, dogs dozing, an invigorating smell of tar and resin.

Would she tell Louisa?

Here was the shop window, an old-fashioned window cluttered up with starch, candles, packets of chicory and bottles of vinegar. Here was the glazed door and its transparent advertisements: the white lion of Remy starch, the zebra of a grate polish, the other lion, the black one, of a brand of wax.

And the door-bell, which you would recognize among a thousand others.

Finally, the unique and wonderful smell of that house where there was nothing commonplace, where everything had a rare, exceptional quality, as if years had been spent on it.

Was it the smell of gin that predominated? Or was it the more insipid smell of the groceries? For the shop sold everything, barrels oozing American lamp-oil, rope, stable lanterns, whips, and tar for boats. There were jars containing sweets of a doubtful pink and glazed drawers stuffed with sticks of cinnamon and cloves.

The end of the counter was covered with zinc, three round holes had been made in it, and out of these holes there protruded bottles crowned with curved tin spouts.

And there was another smell too, the smell of wicker, which came from the end of the corridor, for Louisa's husband was a basket-maker and worked with a hunchbacked assistant in the back room overlooking the yard.

'Why, it's Élise!'

Louisa looked as if she were Élise's mother, with her grey hair, her thick waist, her black dress and her lavender-blue apron. Her features were delicate and regular, her smile as morose as her sister's.

'Poor Louisa . . .'

'Come into the kitchen.'

Louisa finished serving a bargee's wife who had three children clinging to her skirts. Élise went through the double glazed doors with their curtains embroidered with white flowers, and, in the kitchen, which was lit by a peculiar skylight, she found absolute calm, neatness, cleanliness and quiet. One of the girls, probably Anna, the eldest, was playing the piano in the drawing-room, on the other side of the corridor. Between serving two customers, Louisa came and planted herself in front of her sister, her belly thrust forward, her smile tinged with sadness.

'Is your husband keeping well?'

Louisa detested Désiré. Nobody in the Peters family liked big Désiré.

'Yes, he's keeping well, Louisa, thank you. You know that we've moved: we're living in the rue Pasteur now. It's healthier for the child, you see.'

Louisa, who knew that Élise had come for a particular reason, poured her a cup of coffee and went to get some sugar from the shop.

'Take your things off. You've got time.'

'No. I have to get back. I've been making some jam. Louisa, listen, I have to talk to you. I saw Félicie this morning. I wonder . . .'

Would she dare to say it?

'I wonder whether Félicie isn't going mad.'

'Come, come!'

Down-to-earth Louisa shook her head with a look of pity.

'Poor Élise! The ideas you get into your head!'

'It's true, Louisa. You can't understand . . .'

'You're mistaken. Félicie may not be very happy with her husband. She isn't very strong. She's always been highly strung.'

She felt like adding:

'Like you!'

For they still regarded with a certain condescension the last two children, the two nobody had expected.

'There are some days when she's so peculiar, Louisa.'

Without realizing, they had started speaking Flemish.

'I assure you Félicie isn't what you think.'

Élise had sat down on the edge of the wicker armchair, which was just like Désiré's. She had taken a handkerchief out of her bag, automatically, as if she could see tears coming which somehow failed to materialize.

'Drink your coffee while it's hot.'

The best thing would be to tell the whole story. She didn't dare, not here, in this cosy atmosphere, impregnated with the most reassuring of smells, cinnamon, wickerwork, cloves, all such everyday smells!

'How do you account for it, Louisa . . .'

'I tell you it's all imagination.'

Yet what about that night long ago, that night Élise had been thinking about since the morning, since the moment she had stopped feeling angry with her sister?

It was the time when the two of them, she and Félicie, were living with their mother. Félicie was working as a shop-assistant at a draper's in the rue Saint-Léonard. Now, to begin with, Élise knew that her sister was lying when she said that the shop closed at half past seven. It closed at seven o'clock. What did Félicie do every day during that half-hour?

'Whatever happens, don't ever tell Mother or anybody else.'

Once, in the winter, in the darkness of the rue Hors-Château, Élise had caught sight of her sister standing in a doorway, clasped in a man's arms. The silhouette was not that of a young fellow, and Élise could have sworn that he was a married man.

She had not said anything, but since then she had always regarded her sister with alarm, and, as they slept in the same bed, Élise felt a certain embarrassment at each contact.

Already, Félicie had her moods, sometimes singing gaily at the top of her voice, sometimes spending several days without uttering a single word, as tense and anxious as a cat waiting for a storm; or else she would start sobbing in bed, and whisper to Élise, who was then barely fourteen years old:

'Don't ever tell Mother about me crying. If only you knew how unhappy I am! I wish I could die.'

Who knew about all that, apart from Élise? And then there had been the most serious thing of all, during their mother's illness, a bad attack of bronchitis: her bed had been moved into the kitchen, because there was no stove in the bedroom, and every evening she was given a sleeping-draught which eased her breathing and sent her into a deep sleep.

'Aren't you going to get undressed, Félicie?'

She remembered Félicie's eyes that evening, those staring eyes which had looked at the frightened little sister like – yes, like a lunatic's eyes!

'Shut up . . . Don't say anything . . . I'll be back . . .'

Félicie had slipped out, holding her shoes in her hand, and taking the key with her. Alone in the dark, Élise had trembled for hours, jumping at every noise in the street.

'Félicie! . . . Félicie! . . .'

It was she at last. Élise had struck a match. She had seen the time by the alarm-clock. It was three o'clock.

'Félicie!'

'Shut up, you little fool. Put that light out.'

She had undressed in the dark, then slipped between the damp sheets. Élise had smelled something. First the smell of drink: Félicie had drunk something strong. Besides, she dropped off into an unnaturally deep sleep.

Then another smell, as if there had been somebody else in the room, in the bed.

Élise had never said a word about all this. In the morning, her features had been drawn. Félicie's face did not look any more rested than her own. She did not dare to say anything. She washed and dressed with weary gestures.

'What do you want me to give you?'

And the younger girl, on the verge of tears, had answered: 'Nothing! For heaven's sake, no!'

And yet Félicie was unhappy. Élise who knew nothing of life, felt vaguely that it wasn't her sister's fault, that she couldn't help it.

Hadn't she married a man of forty afterwards? And now, if he beat her, wasn't there a reason for it?

'You're all upset. Wait a minute while I get you a drop of something.'

Élise sat up and exclaimed:

'No, Louisa! *For heaven's sake, no!*'

Not like Félicie, like Léopold, like her sister Marthe who also drank!

'I don't want anything, Louisa. Thank you all the same. Thank you very much. I can't help it, you see. I'm certain that Félicie is hysterical . . .'

She had uttered the big word whose exact meaning she didn't know, but which seemed to her to express the truth. At that word, Louisa's face had frozen, her features had hardened, and she gazed sternly at foolish little Élise.

'Will you kindly refrain from using words like that in my house!'

For two pins she would have gone to make sure that her daughter Anna, who was still playing the piano, had not been touched by the dreadful syllables.

'You don't even know what it means.'

Why did her sisters insist on treating her as an insignificant little girl? Did Louisa know what she knew?

'Then how do you explain . . .'

'There's nothing to explain. You've got too much imagination. I'm beginning to wonder whether it isn't you who are what you've just said.'

There! Élise had been wrong.

'I'm sorry. But that scene this morning . . .'

'What scene?'

'Nothing. I can't remember. Don't take any notice, Louisa.'

Louisa shook her head. If Élise was forever murmuring 'Dear God!' her sister of the quai de Coronmeuse, for her part, stammered with a strong Flemish accent:

'Jesus-Mary!'

And her head wagged from one shoulder to the other as a sign of pity for all that was not the perfect order and neatness of her home.

'Aren't you happy with Désiré?'

'Of course I am, Louisa. Désiré's a dear.'

Did she want to make amends for what she had said about Félicie, that accusation which ought never to have been made by a Peters? She in her turn shook her head. It was contagious. She looked around her at this house where you only had to stretch out your hand to touch shelves and cupboards.

'He's a Mamelin, you see. He hasn't any ambition. He doesn't need anything else. I'd have liked to start a little shop, any sort of shop, and I'd have made a success of it, I can tell you that! But he has never wanted to. And do you know why? Because he says that he wouldn't be able to eat in peace any more, that he'd always be being disturbed by the shop-bell. But wouldn't that be better than living on the bare necessities of life?'

She was off on her hobby-horse. Was this what she had come for? Had she already forgotten Félicie?

She knew that she was pleasing Louisa, that anything she said against big Désiré would be well received by her sister.

'"What are we short of?" That's all he says. He doesn't have to do the shopping. When he comes home, the dinner's ready. But I know what things cost . . . If only he had a bit of initiative! There's a clerk who started at Monsieur Monnoyeur's at the same time as him, who earns twice as much already and sends his daughters to the Ursulines' boarding-school. But Désiré would think it beneath him to ask for a rise.'

'Poor Élise.'

She could whine and whimper without annoying her sister, now that it was no longer a question of Félicie, but of Désiré. Every now and then, Louisa was called away by the shop-bell and you could hear gin being poured into glasses, the timid voices of the bargees' wives who had their money in their hands, the exact amount, and the noise of the coins falling into the till.

'A little dairy-shop, for instance. I'd have opened a dairy-shop like the one in the rue de la Province . . .'

*

In the wide, quiet streets of Outremeuse, away from the rue Puits-en-Sock and the rue Entre-deux-Ponts, there were some shops which were not real shops. They were middle-class houses where the front room on the ground floor had simply been fitted out with a counter and a few shelves. The result was that the shop windows – which were not real shop windows either – were too high up. They were lit by a solitary gas-jet, and from a distance all that you could see was a yellowish halo in the dark line of the houses. The street door was open. There were two or three steps and there was no light in the corridor.

When you opened the inside door, a bell rang, or else some brass tubes knocked against one another to make a tune. Even so, you had to call out several times:

'Is there anybody there?'

There was some black pudding on a plate, two or three Hervé cheeses under a glass cover, half a dozen tins of sardines, and some biscuits. Something was cut. Something was weighed. Then the brass tubes knocked against one another again and the street resumed its absolute calm.

That was what Désiré had not wanted.

To reward her sister for her complaints, Louisa went to get a box of cakes, a box she would never be able to sell because the mice had nibbled a corner of it.

'Eat that, my girl.'

'Thank you, Louisa. But I didn't come here to eat. It's been preying on my mind for a long time . . .'

Was it true? Was it a lie? She didn't know. She could no longer find her bearings among her anxieties and complaints, among all the complicated misfortunes on which she gorged herself.

'Dear God! Five o'clock already! And Désiré'll come home and find nobody there . . .'

'Why don't you come and see us one Sunday afternoon? What do you do on Sunday afternoon? We're always here, because of the shop.'

What did they do? She didn't know. And this reminded her that they never stopped at a café for a glass of beer.

'*The bare necessities . . .*'

She wiped her eyes and smiled.

'Ah, well! Good-bye, Louisa. And thank you.'

Thank you for what? For the cakes? For the cup of coffee? For the tears?

On the pavement, while her sister was seeing her off, Élise thought to herself:

'You cat!'

For she had noticed that the box of cakes had been nibbled at. She had even refused to let the child have a cake, on the pretext that he was a little out of sorts. She turned round.

'Thank you, Louisa.'

And she blushed for shame: she had been disloyal to Désiré, for no real reason, to change the subject, because Louisa had not wanted to hear anything about Félicie and she had had to find another explanation for her tears.

She had half an hour's walk in front of her, with the push-chair, and the approach-ramp of the Pont-Maghin to climb.

She only hoped that the jam had set. Had she put enough sugar with the little gooseberries?

Chapter Eight

In the rue Montmartre, in Paris, a girl called Isabelle was playing the piano next to the window of a low-ceilinged entresol which had been built into the top of the ground-floor rooms. It was the upper part of the shop front which served as the entresol window, so that when the stationer leaned out into the window, the girl seemed to be walking on him.

*

In Liège, in the rue Jean-d'Outremeuse, Élise stopped propelling the push-chair along for a moment, picked up something white and darted a furtive glance around her. The black-bearded painter on his ladder had not noticed anything. It was Léopold: Élise had just recognized him. Taking a red handkerchief out of his smock, he had pulled the letter out with it.

'*Monsieur . . .*'

Élise had read just that one word and seen the delicate, passionate handwriting, but she was a long way from suspecting the grandeur of that simple '*Monsieur*' addressed to a man whom the police picked up every week in the gutter.

Because of Monsieur Pain, who happened to be passing just then and had noticed her action, Élise came back to the bottom of the ladder.

'Léopold.'

If she had not spoken to him, he would have pretended not to recognize her, so as not to shame her. He just blinked his eyes, without saying thank-you, and went on rinsing his big sponge in a bucket which had some acid in it, for the water dripping on to the pavement was a greenish colour.

'*Monsieur* . . .'

Élise walked on. She walked fast, as usual. Where was she going? Oh, yes, to Schuttringer's the pork-butcher's, to buy a couple of pork chops. In a few days' time, when the festivities were over, she would speak to Désiré.

It was strange that she had not spoken to him sooner and that she could not even say what had prevented her. She had been pregnant for two months now. Only this time she had the impression of an illness rather than a natural condition. She was suffering much more than she had with Roger. She had backache, like most of the women she knew, from going up and down two flights of stairs with a child who was getting heavy, from carrying buckets, from wringing the washing. At night, she felt a sharper pain between her shoulder-blades, as if the little bone there were going to pierce the skin.

*

Who could be writing to Léopold when she, his own sister, didn't know his address?

Monsieur

I keep worrying about what you are going to think of me. I am so afraid of losing your esteem, the only thing left to me in the world, and yet I do not want to go on lying to you any more, and hiding from you the terrible drama I am living through hour after hour. Will you understand me, you who understand everything? Forgive me if I doubt it! It is all so extraordinary!

I am in love! Yes, me! Oh, how sorry I am now that I did not listen to you that evening. You said things to me that made me want to cry, you looked at me like somebody who could see into the future, but you did not know that it was too late, that the parcel I had in my hand could bring our conversation to an end at any moment, you did not know that everything was already nearly over, that I was waiting for you to go, with my forehead beaded with sweat, to go and do what I could not postpone any longer.

Today, I am in love as nobody has ever been in love before. I am so much in love that I roll about in despair on the floor of my bedroom. I am not worthy to raise my eyes to look at her, to touch the hem of her dress, and it is monstrous that I, who cannot bear my own name any more, should live under the same roof as she does and that I should listen to her from morning to night. For I can hear her now, practically over my head. A thin floor separates us and that floor is vibrant with her music. At the moment she is practising one of Chopin's 'Polonaises', the most stirring of them all . . .

*

Élise was in a hurry and turned the corner of the rue de la Liberté to take a short cut. She was always taking short cuts. Her life was a constant struggle against time. She did her utmost to save a few seconds here and there, just as she did her utmost to scrounge a few centimes of the housekeeping money to put them in the Savings Bank.

She thought that the street was empty, all sunshine and shadow. It was a hot day. At the beginning of the week, the schools had closed for a couple of days on account of the heat. You could feel a storm in the air. She jumped as a voice hailed her.

'Élise!'

Unable to beat a retreat, she tried to summon up a smile.

'Good morning, Catherine.'

It was Catherine, the carpenter Lucien's wife, who had installed herself in the blue shadows of the wide pavement, opposite the girls' school, behind a trestle table covered with sweets. Léopold at least had pretended not to see his sister.

'Good morning, Élise. Good morning, little Roger. My, how nice he looks! And how he's grown! Just imagine, Élise . . .'

Catherine kissed the boy, and slipped into his hand a bright red acid drop which Élise looked at in alarm.

Catherine's mother sold chips in a back-street where she was buying the houses one after another, one of those streets which smelled bad, where the gutter ran along the middle of the roadway, bluish and nauseating, a street where, when a woman went past who was too well dressed, too obviously respectable, a voice would shout at her from the dark hole of some passage:

'Look at her, with her posh hat!'

'I must hurry, Catherine. Don't be cross with me. I'm going to Schuttringer's to buy some chops.'

As soon as she had turned the corner, she would take the red sweet away from the child, but she would not dare to throw it away for fear that Catherine would notice it on her way home.

*

Félix Marette had changed his name. Though not very radically. Used to his own name, all he had been able to think up was Félicien Miette. He was right at the back of the shop, listening to the music over his head, waiting for the moment when Isabelle would come downstairs with her music-case in her hand.

She resembled nobody, neither her father with his sad moustache, nor her mother who remained at the cash-desk all day without moving, so still that customers sometimes started when she happened to make a slight gesture.

Isabelle would come downstairs, always pale, her face angular, without any trinkets or anything feminine about her dress, her blue serge blouse buttoned high under her chin, and her hair in tight plaits forming a bun behind her neck. She would not look at anybody, would not see anybody.

'Give me some money.'

For the Métro, to go to the Conservatoire or to see her teacher, a red-haired, middle-aged man of whom Marette was bitterly jealous.

The next day, Sunday, he would not see her, he would not leave his room; he would write, for her, with a heat-hazy skylight as a horizon, the story of his life, which he would never give her to read.

The Vétus had a little country house over Corbeil way, and set off for it early every Sunday morning. Marette was left alone with his portable stove, his unmade bed, and some bread and cheese which he had bought the day before.

Tell me, I beg you, that you don't despise me, write whatever you like to me, but write, so that I may at least know that there is somebody in this world who takes a little interest in my fate.

Élise had very nearly kept this letter which she had picked up at the bottom of the ladder.

*

The next day, it was the feast-day of the parish of Saint-Nicolas, and everywhere floors were being scrubbed and you could breathe the smell of cleaning right out in the middle of the streets. In the place Delcour, and again at the end of the rue Méan, fairground people were hammering nails in, putting the finishing touches to shooting-galleries and roundabouts.

Why was it that feast-days, all feast-days, made Élise feel sad? Was it because, on those days, she felt even less at home than usual?

The next day's festivities would begin with a morning concert. The men had got the Bouquet ready. This was a huge machine, a pole several yards high, a mast rather, with yard-arms attached to it, and the whole contraption, which it took several men to hold upright, was adorned with thousands of paper flowers.

The band marched along in front and the children behind, each child holding a Chinese lantern at the end of a stick.

The procession set off from the sacristan's house, next to the church, and stopped straight away outside the café on the corner of the rue Saint-Nicolas. After that, it would stop outside every café, every shop, wherever there was a drop to drink, so that soon it would be trailing behind it an increasingly pungent smell of gin.

Léopold, as soon as he heard the band, would seize the opportunity to leave the district, crossing the bridges to start a new novena in the first quiet pub he came to in another parish.

The streets, the pavements, the stones of the houses were so clean that day that you could eat off the cobbles, and the children still smelled of the bath they had been given in the washtub and of the cosmetic used to set their unruly hair.

In the bluish calm of the crossroads, men and women were getting the altars of repose ready for the procession: every window of every house was turning into an altar, with brass candlesticks and bunches of roses and carnations.

The next morning, everybody was dressed in his Sunday best, even Élise, who was wearing a dress in thick blue material, with a lace collar and a high wimple stiffened with whalebone. Thus her head, with its bun which was always coming undone, looked bigger than it was. Her smile was more morose than ever. She had roasted a joint larded with cloves, as she did every Sunday, and she basted it every now and then and put some fat on the stove for the chips. The air started turning blue in the kitchen, in the bedroom and even on the staircase.

It was in the place Ernest-de-Bavière, where the civic guards drilled on other Sundays, that the real spectacle began. The artificer had arranged hundreds of iron pots in a line. At the end of the high Mass, a man came running up, waving his arms. That was the signal. The children were kept on one side. At the wheelwright's on the corner, a rod of red-hot iron was waiting in the forge.

The sun had never failed to shine for the feast-day. The skies were clear. It was summer.

The iron pots were filled to overflowing with black powder, and along came the artificer, dragging his red-hot rod, and leaping from one pot to the next while the whole district echoed with a sound like that of gunfire.

Before the din had finished the procession came out of the church, and in front of it, in every street, little boys and little girls in starched, embroidered dresses scattered rose petals and coloured paper lozenges which they had spent weeks cutting out.

Nothing remained of what had been the day before. The world had been transfigured. The town was no longer a town, the streets were no longer streets, and the very trams stopped respectfully at the crossroads.

The smell of the procession preceded and followed it. It would linger until the evening, and even until the following day, in the streets: the smell of the big red roses, of the leaves being trampled underfoot, and above all else of the incense, as well as the smell of the cakes and tarts being cooked in every house and that of the fair which would be opening very soon.

A sound as characteristic as, for instance, the humming of a swarm of bees, a symphony to be more precise, filled the streets: the trampling and shuffling of the thousands of people who were following the procession as it moved along, the hymns which were constantly changing in tune and tone: the little girls from the schools or from the Congregation of the Blessed Virgin had scarcely gone by before you could hear the drone of the men in black, the men of St Roch who had no eyes for anything but their hymn-books; the band was at the end of the street; it turned the corner; but even so you could suddenly hear the shrill voices of the deacons and sub-deacons heralding the arrival of the Dean, stiff and erect in his golden vestments, and carrying the Blessed Sacrament under a canopy held by the local notabilities.

Just as at the fair you would hear at one and the same time the music of ten or fifteen roundabouts, the explosions of the shooting-galleries and the shouts of the women selling chips, this procession, which was nearly two miles long and did not miss a single street or alley-way, would occasionally overlap or catch up with its own tail.

The saints had all come out, the Black Virgin of the parish, St Roch and St Joseph, on flags which kept tilting dangerously, and they were preceded by banners, little boys, little girls, men, women, old people, all grouped together in brotherhoods and sisterhoods.

Désiré was carrying a taper at the end of a stick painted red and white. Old Mamelin, for his part, gloved in white, was holding the canopy over the Blessed Sacrament.

At eleven o'clock there could be heard the high-pitched notes of the barrel-organ of a tiny roundabout for children, a round-about at two centimes a ride, and after that the first rifle shots.

The next day, or the day after that, Élise would speak to Désiré about her condition. He would be pleased without thinking of what it would involve. When he came home for dinner, she could tell from his breath that he had drunk an apéritif. He was in a merry mood. It was the parish feast-day.

Very soon now, on the stroke of two o'clock, all the Mamelin children and grandchildren would gather together, dressed in their Sunday best, in the courtyard in the rue Puits-en-Sock. Élise's head was already buzzing at the thought. When dinner was over, standing in front of the mirror, with pins between her lips, she pinned up her bun three times, four times, growing increasingly impatient as it kept falling to one side. Désiré was there behind her, doing nothing.

'Take the push-chair down, will you?'

He took it down, and then the child, for he could foresee the moment when, as so often happened on a Sunday, she would burst into tears, her nerves frayed out, or else suddenly tear something up.

When she finally joined him, he did not ask any questions. He wheeled the push-chair along. The ground was littered with flowers and pieces of coloured paper. There were children besieging the yellow carts of the Italian ice-cream vendors.

'If your mother starts getting at me . . .'

'She won't say anything to you. You mustn't take any notice.'

They greeted the passers-by who smiled at them. Désiré knew everybody, all the names you could see over the shop windows, even people who had left the district but who came back on the parish feast-day like prodigal sons, carrying babies they were proud to show to their old neighbours.

'What did I tell you, Désiré? We are too early. They are still at table.'

'What does that matter?'

A long table had been set out in the courtyard in the rue Puits-en-Sock. Another table was laid in the kitchen. Sooner or later, somebody would have the idea of counting the people gathered around impassive Old Papa: thirty-seven, including twenty-two grandchildren and Chrétien Mamelin who, together with his old friend Kreutz, would go and sit outside on the pavement, between the two shops.

Everybody was looking his best, their cheeks pinker, their eyes brighter than usual. They kept coming in and going out. The women had put on some eau-de-Cologne or scent.

'Good afternoon, Françoise.'

'Good afternoon, Élise.'

Nobody knew that it was the last time this gathering in the rue Puits-en-Sock would be complete. The mother, dressed in grey as usual, with her grey hair in bandeaux, was the only person who never sat down for a single moment, for there was always somebody who was hungry.

Exactly ten days from now, when everybody least expected it, she would suddenly feel dizzy, there, in that kitchen of hers, in front of her stove of which she was so proud.

There would be nobody there but Old Papa, sitting in his armchair.

'I don't know what's wrong with me, Papa. I'm going upstairs for a minute. If it starts to burn on the stove . . .'

'Get along with you, my girl.'

Nobody had ever thought that anything like that might happen. For the first time in her life she would go to bed at four o'clock in the afternoon, all alone, and when Cécile came home a little later, it would be her cries that would give the alarm. They would call in the doctor. They would send for Désiré, Lucien, Arthur. Only Mère Madeleine would be unable to come, for nuns were forbidden to return to their old home, even when their parents were dying.

At ten o'clock at night, however improbable it might seem to them all, it would be over.

Nobody, today, had any suspicion of this. Now a daughter, now a daughter-in-law would unbutton her blouse to feed a baby. Thirty people at least, of all ages, went to and fro in the yard and in the kitchen. The Kreutz sisters came along to have a piece of tart. There were so many tarts that people began to wonder whether they would all be eaten, and every time somebody ate a piece it meant another plate to be washed.

'Give me an apron, Cécile. I'll help you . . .'

It made your head spin to have so much happening at once, and the babies in their prams started crying because there was not always time to attend to them.

The men smoked cigars and drank liqueurs. The children were shared out among the parents. The bigger ones were taken out for a ride on the roundabouts and were bought ice-creams and cheap toys, usually paper windmills spinning round at the end of sticks or else balloons made of goldbeater's skin.

People had scarcely finished eating before it was time for them to start again and groups lost track of one another, eyes became feverish, almost wild.

'Where's Loulou?'

Loulou was Charles Daigne's daughter; she was of the same age as Roger.

'I think she's gone out with Catherine.'

There were things to see everywhere. The whole district was in holiday mood. And on all sides you could hear the music of the roundabouts and the noise of the shooting-galleries.

'Do you want me to warm the bottles?'

Then there was supper which started at six o'clock, a ham which Désiré's mother had cooked the day before and which was eaten with lettuce and mayonnaise.

The men in particular were not the same as on other days, because they had smoked cigars and drunk liqueurs. Heaven knows where they had been when they had gone out earlier.

'Get along with you, Arthur . . .'

Arthur always exaggerated.

The feast-day smell grew fainter. The dust became thicker and thicker. The sun had vanished and the world was slowly turning purple, with perspectives of frightening depth.

Eyes were smarting and bodies growing weary, especially the little children's bodies, and yet it was the children who clung to the enchantment of it all.

Élise had backache, but she said nothing. All this eating nauseated her and once she wondered if she ought not to go into a corner to be sick. Not for a single moment did she feel at home.

'Come along with us for a walk round the fair.'

'No, Cécile. It's nice of you, but really, I'd rather not.'

Cécile was married to a locksmith, a good-looking man with a waxed moustache who, on Sunday mornings, right up to the time for eleven o'clock Mass, wore a contraption to train it. His name was Marcel. He had the aggressive look of a handsome, common young man. Élise did not like him. In the whole family, in her opinion, the only person who was any good was Françoise.

When the gas had to be lit, although it was still light outside, it revealed, beneath the blue haze formed by the cigar-smoke, piles of dirty plates, coffee stains, pieces of tart, and the remains of the ham.

'Désiré.'

She tried to get him to come outside. He did not understand. He was at home here. He was talking about Monsieur Monnoyeur and everybody was listening to him because they knew he was the most intelligent and the best educated of them all.

She signalled to him. He finally noticed and asked aloud:

'What is it?'

Anywhere else he would have guessed straight away, but here he had already turned back into a Mamelin.

'Is anything wrong?'

She felt like crying. Her head was spinning. Her hand went out as if to hold on to a table.

'Come outside for a minute.'

How discreet it was! Everybody watched them going out. In the yard, next to the bronze pump, next to the children who eyed them too, she stammered:

'I don't feel very well. Listen: you can stay. I'm going home with the child.'

'Why don't you go upstairs and lie down for a while?'

How could he possibly suggest such a thing? Lie down, her, in her mother-in-law's bedroom, for instance, or in the bedroom of Cécile and Marcel who lived in the house! Why, the smell by itself would be enough to make her sick! They were clean, of course, but that didn't alter the fact that every person, every house had its particular smell. And what if she was going to be ill, and couldn't get up straight away?

Ugly little creases appeared near the sides of her nose. Désiré gave in.

'Let's go.'

'No, you stay! Yes, I insist. What will they say if you leave them on a day like this?'

'Come along. I'll explain to them.'

'No. I mean it, Désiré! I haven't the courage to go back into the kitchen. Bring me my hat and my gloves. They are by the coffee-mill. Tell them . . .'

She was tired out. She leaned against the pump and closed her eyes. Désiré, in the kitchen, tried to joke in order to conceal his embarrassment.

'Élise doesn't feel well. She's very sorry. It's fatigue. She isn't very strong, you know, she isn't used to so much noise.'

His mother remained as cold as marble.

'You aren't coming back?'

'I may do. But if she really isn't well . . .'

'Take a few slices of ham at least. What are you looking for? Her gloves?'

Élise was the only one who had come with gloves. Catherine, for all that she was wearing a black silk dress for the first time, had not even put her hat on to walk the three or four hundred yards from where she lived.

'Good night, Mother. Forgive us. Good night, everybody.'

'Good night, Désiré.'

Élise was outside in the yard. Although nobody could see her through the fake stained glass, she turned towards the kitchen, gave the ghost of a forced smile, and murmured:

'Good night. Thank you . . .'

They went along the whitewashed passage. Chrétien Mamelin, in the falling darkness, was still smoking his pipe in the company of his accomplice Kreutz. They had taken a couple of chairs out of the shop. They were at home on this pavement where, in front of the shops, there were other groups like their own watching the young people dancing.

'What's the trouble?'

'I don't know. I'm sorry.'

'But you must feel something?'

'Don't be cross with me, Désiré. If only you knew . . .'

The truth, the real truth, was that her back was not aching as much as it did on a wash-day, for instance. If for a moment she had felt like being sick, that had passed. She could have stayed.

It was rather a moral anguish that had taken hold of her in the midst of that merry family, that vulgar, cordial disorder in which they were all so happy.

In which they were wallowing, as she would say to Valérie later. They had no refinement, no feelings. Nobody had noticed that she was doing all the washing-up and, when somebody had suggested that she should go to see the fair, it was too late, the others had already gone out two or three times. She would not have gone, but she would have liked a little consideration.

The noise diminished as they came nearer to the rue Pasteur and the feast-day smell grew fainter in the dark. The gas-lamps were alight.

'Are you really ill?'

So much the worse for him! She felt the need to take her revenge. There was nothing to lead her to suppose that what she was saying was true.

'I think I'm going to have a miscarriage.'

'But . . . What? . . . You've never said anything to me about it . . .'

'I was waiting to tell you. I could feel there was something wrong . . .'

'Do you want me to go to get Doctor Matray?'

'It would be pointless. It probably won't happen for some time.'

She was being spiteful, and she knew it. She was spoiling his day, his last real Mamelin day, but a devil was urging her on.

'How long has it been?'

'Two months.'

'And you have kept quiet all that time!'

He didn't understand. *At home*, things were managed much more simply. He took out his key, opened the door, and picked up the child who was much heavier than the little push-chair. He felt sorry for his wife, of course. He was worried. All the same, he bore Élise a grudge. He could sense that she was putting on an act in which he preferred not to believe. He turned round to watch her coming upstairs, and he felt sure that it was on purpose that she walked more laboriously than was necessary, stopped on the landing and leaned against the wall.

'Élise.'

She smiled, that smile which she always put on when she wanted to say:

'Don't worry about a poor creature like me! I'm used to suffering. When I was only five years old, I was a wretched orphan . . .'

He lit the lamp, and changed the child who was wet.

'Oughtn't you to go to bed?'

'You haven't had your supper.'

Then he exclaimed:

'*And what about the ham?*'

He was right: there were the slices of ham his mother had given him. The last ham she would have cooked for the whole family, and of which, like this, he would have his share after all. He was the favourite. They were talking about him in the rue Puits-en-Sock. They were saying:

'Poor Désiré!'

Bengal lights were going up all over the district and, above the fair, there hung a thick pall of smoke of a reddish yellow colour. The firing in the shooting galleries went on. The music from the various roundabouts intermingled.

'Élise.'

'It's nothing. It's already gone.'

She had been lying earlier on. She had felt an urge to take her revenge on the rue Puits-en-Sock, on the Mamelins who exasperated her. She had been unable to think of anything better than to fall ill, to go off in the middle of the festivities, and, out-side, as she had still felt something of a grudge against Désiré, she had taken the opportunity to speak to him about her pregnancy.

She was sorry now that she had. She watched him coming and going, attending to the child, tidying everything up in the flat, and she was seized with a superstitious fear. Why had she talked about a miscarriage? What could she have been thinking about? She had thought that her pregnancy was not enough, she had made up something else, she had wanted to be utterly unhappy, utterly pitiful in face of the coarse joy of the Mamelins.

And if, now, to punish her? . . .

'Dear God, please may nothing bad happen to me. Please may what I said just now not come true.'

Suddenly humble, she called out:

'Désiré.'

Poor Désiré who flew into a panic straight away and did his best to help!

'Forgive me, Désiré. I've been wicked. I've spoilt your parish feast-day.'

'Of course you haven't.'

'Go back to them now. I insist. There's still time. I heard your mother asking if you were coming back. They must be talking about you now. They all detest me.'

'You just imagine things. Try and rest.'

And, as he had not read the paper yet, he settled down under the lamp, in his shirtsleeves. For a long time she saw him smoking his pipe, in a cloud of smoke, with a sidelong glance now and then towards the bed, then a glance towards the child's cradle. He was no longer as anxious as he had been.

She pretended to be asleep.

'Dear God, please may . . . Forgive me for what I said just now . . .'

*

She was frightened. She fell asleep frightened, and it was day-light when she suddenly opened her eyes and felt for the body lying next to hers.

'Désiré . . . Quick . . . Run and get Doctor Matray!'

Chapter Nine

François Marette was dead. It appeared that he was not an ordinary police constable but a sergeant.

Since the death of her mother-in-law, Élise had got into the habit of collecting death notifications, and announced each decease in a sorrowful voice:

'You know, Désiré, that sprightly old gentleman we always used to meet in the rue de la Commune . . '

Were there really more deaths this autumn than in previous years? Or did she think that a long death-roll would make each case of mourning less painful?

She was wearing the veil again, the one she had worn for her mother, a veil which was so thick that you could scarcely recognize her, and so long that when the wind caught it suddenly on a street-corner Élise felt as if her hair were being pulled out.

Désiré had only had to change his tie. Every year Élise bought him one for his name-day, in a distinguished colour, mauve or violet, and she fastened it once for all on a celluloid hanger. They had taken the black tie from the left-hand drawer.

'People are wondering, Désiré, if he didn't commit suicide. Ever since his son was involved in that business, he had gone all neurotic; he was just the shadow of what he'd been before.'

People said too that Marette had had a cancer of the stomach.

'Madame Pain's sister lives next door to their house in the rue du Laveu, a little house which they had built themselves and which they were paying off by annual instalments. It seems it's awful.'

Why should it have been more awful than, say, Madame Mamelin's death in the house in the rue Puits-en-Sock?

The leaves were falling. Winter overcoats had been taken out of the wardrobes. It was not All Saints' Day yet but already you met people with colds, including Madame Pain whose nose was as smooth and red as a cherry. The streets were brighter and looked dangerous, covered as they were with a fine dust which the wind blew along a few inches from the ground.

'It's because of the pension . . .'

Désiré did not understand, and was listening with only half an ear to this story of the rue du Laveu into which a pension had now been introduced. His mother was dead. It was not a dramatic happening. It was not something people talked about. It was a gap, a gap every day, every morning, for he no longer went round by the church of Saint-Nicolas and the rue des Récollets to spend a few minutes in the kitchen with the fake stained glass. He could if he wanted to. Cécile, who had married Marcel Wasselin, had stayed in the house with her father.

'If they proved that he had committed suicide, you see, who knows if his wife would get the pension?'

Was it grief after what his son had done? Was it the cancer of the stomach? Was it because of his resignation, which he had tendered very abruptly, when people had started pointing him out in the street? François Marette had got into the habit recently of going for a walk every day along the quai des Pitteurs, a long way from his home, in one of the few places where the quays of the Meuse had no parapet. For hours on end, in complete silence, puffing away at his meerschaum pipe, he would watch the anglers.

It was possible that he had had a fainting fit. It was also possible that he had committed suicide.

'Like that, his wife will have her pension all the same!'

Élise pursued her train of thought.

'It's not enough to live on. It's scarcely enough for the bare necessities. Luckily the house belongs to them.'

Mourning had made her frailer, more girlish, you might say, with her cloud of fair hair.

'Madame Pain told me . . . Are you listening? She told me that Madame Marette had decided to take in some lodgers, some students. She's already found one who's paying thirty francs a month for a room, even though the rue du Laveu is so far from the University!'

Désiré ate his supper, snuffed out the lamp, smiled at Roger. He did not understand or did not want to understand. He was endowed with an exasperating force of inertia and in a few minutes, in spite of being in mourning, he would play the drummer-boy, marking time round the room with the child on his shoulders.

He did not know Madame Marette who was a widow and was going to take in lodgers. He was not in the least interested in all the local widows he kept hearing about.

Every morning he left the rue Pasteur a quarter of an hour later, because he no longer dropped in to see his mother; he no longer took her his collars to be washed, and he ate bread from the baker's.

Was Monsieur Marette dead? Monsieur and Madame Marette owned a house in the rue du Laveu, a little way outside the town, on a hill, a house rather like the one Élise had dreamt of renting for a long time, Élise who was not a widow, who did not know if she would be one one day, but who was already tormented by the idea.

'Thirty francs for a single room, Désiré! Think what you could make out of a house by letting only three rooms.'

He was not listening, did not believe what she was saying. There were some contingencies which he would always refuse to envisage.

'Do you think he really committed suicide?'

Who? The policeman? Well, if he had committed suicide, it was because he had thought it was the best thing to do.

'. . . And do you think it was because of his cancer?'

'You have to die of something!'

One sorrow at a time. His own first of all, this gap in his life, this rue Puits-en-Sock whose corner he no longer turned, this impression that he had suddenly lost an anchor, an impression which was making him work twice as hard at the office.

'I can't help thinking about the poor woman.'

'You said just now that she had a pension.'

'It isn't enough to live on. And what if she hadn't got a pension? What if she wasn't a policeman's wife and he hadn't thought of buying a house?'

Didn't she understand that this drummer-boy hour belonged to him, that it was an hour of profound joy? The child, on his shoulders, shouted:

'Again!'

Did she want to force Désiré to reply yet again:

'What are we short of?'

It was no use her trying, he did not want to think, he never would think that she might become a widow like Madame

Marette. He sang, for the boy whom he had just put to bed, and
whose eyes were still open in the semi-darkness:

> There were two lovers
> Who dreamed of distant loves.
> There were two lovers
> Who bade their parents farewell ...

He was moved. For no particular reason. Because of his
mother. Because of himself. Because of his son. And Élise who
seemed so sure that she would be a widow one day and would
not have a pension!

> They sailed away
> In a fragile boat:
> They sailed away
> To the land of exiles ...

She had backache. She was anything but strong. She had
complained to Doctor Matray.

And yet, what was she short of, in this two-room flat which
a single fire was enough to heat, a single lamp enough to light?

> The lover said: 'Dear heart,
> I laugh at the storm.'
> The lover said: 'My heart
> Will have no fear near yours ...'

'You're getting tired, Désiré. Shut the door. Leave him.'

> The lover said: 'Dear heart,
> I laugh at ...'

There were lots of widows, that autumn, in the district, lots
of widows in the town. Madame Marette was a widow and had
already taken in lodgers to make a living, but Félix Marette, at
the back of his shop in the rue Montmartre, did not know about
this, did not know that his father was dead either.

Would it upset him to hear the news? Once, in a fit of
irritation, he had told Philippe Estévant and Doms, when they
had spent part of the night drinking in a corner of the Café de la
Bourse, behind the theatre:

'I hate them! I hate my district, my street, my home, I hate
the school I went to ...'

And yet he opened his eyes without any feeling of disgust or impatience, in his attic in the rue Montmartre. He had no need of an alarm-clock. At seven o'clock, the partition started to vibrate. It was his neighbour, a sempstress, setting to work.

The rain streamed down the sloping windows of the skylight. He pulled on a pair of trousers, put on his slippers, took his pail and went along the corridor to get some water.

Here he did not have that impression of sordid, hallucinating mediocrity – there had been times when he could have screamed at it – which used to overwhelm him when he saw his father in his nightshirt, with his hairy legs, contentedly humming to himself while he trimmed his beard and his moustache in front of the wardrobe mirror.

The sempstress was a fat creature with freckles who had a child out to nurse. Once a week, a man came to see her, and Marette heard everything, without feeling either envy or disgust, he who used to suffer from the insipid smell of his mother's room.

How he hated it, that wallpaper with its little pink flowers, the same flowers for fifteen years, with the same stains, and a dark patch on a level with the bed produced by the sleeper's breaths.

He washed. In the rue Montmartre, the whitewashed walls were anything but clean. He had just hung up a drawing to decorate them. He had no artistic pretensions, but patiently, starting over and over again, he had drawn a strange portrait of Isabelle, a long, regular oval like that of certain medieval wood-carvings of the Virgin, the two bandeaux, two concave lines, like an accent, which formed the big closed eyes, and the sinuous line of the mouth.

That was all. His gaze was enough to give life to this picture which he could now reproduce in three or four lines by dint of having traced it.

His suit was shabby and worn. When he had a bit of money, he would spend it on a new pair of shoes. He polished them himself. Going downstairs, he smoked his first cigarette. The apartment-house had four staircases A, B, C and D. His staircase D, which started under the second arch past the courtyard, was the narrowest and the dirtiest of them all; it led to countless cells in which, as you passed, you could catch sight of life being lived, precarious existences being eked out by creatures from all over the world, an Armenian, some Polish Jews, a furrier, a dealer in feathers for hats, an embroideress; and all this was summed up in a few words, black on white enamel, in the main passage near the lodge.

In the rue Montmartre, which at this time of day still smelled of the market, Félix Marette went into a little bar where he ate some croissants, dipping them in his coffee while he glanced through a newspaper.

It was his parents' kitchen which he remembered with the greatest hatred. It was tiny but new-looking, with its walls painted with oil-paint, its calendar, its cheap newspaper-holder, the pipe-rack and the two copper saucepans which were never used. In the morning, it smelled of eggs and bacon. The soup started simmering. You could sense the monotonous passage of time, the ringing of the bell by the milkwoman.

Madame Marette, wearing slippers and with her hair in pins – hair so black that some people thought it was a wig – Madame Marette opened the door, without a word, and held out her enamel saucepan. She was tiny, thin and angular; her expressionless face looked as if it had been carved out of wood and painted black and white. Without saying either good morning or thank you, she handed over her money, glanced down the street and shut the door.

Just thinking about it made Félix suffer. That sloping street with its houses which were all too new, too small, too clean, those doors opening one after another as the greengrocer came along, stopping his cart to blow a trumpet . . .

And the other streets, on the left and right, already marked out, with unfinished pavements, puny trees which froze every winter, and big holes between the houses which looked as if they had been put there temporarily.

He remembered it all with nauseating accuracy, the colour of the blocks of freestone at every hour of the day – and the smell of the freestone in summer, in August, when you were playing marbles out in the sun – the mists in winter, and the gas-lamps which were alight when, in a hooded coat, you came home, kicking a pebble along the street. The light he could see through the keyhole, at the end of the narrow passage, before knocking on the letter-box. Even the characters of that word 'Letters', engraved in copper, which he could have reproduced exactly.

The crush in the damp little bar in the rue Montmartre did not bother him. The dark shop, with part of the window taken up with rubber stamps, did not strike him as ugly. He felt no revulsion on seeing solemn Monsieur Brois arrive.

Yet what if Monsieur Brois had been his father?

'I hate them! I hate them all!' he used to say excitedly to Estévant and Doms, in the warmth of the Café de la Bourse.

Even the Jesuit Fathers of the Collège Saint-Servais where his parents had sent him at considerable sacrifice to themselves.

'The Superintendent said to me . . .' old Marette used to begin, with gentle satisfaction, when he came home at night, with a little smoke hanging about his whiskers.

His son would glare at him, hating him for that docility, for that stupid, simple-minded pride, hating him for being himself, for being his father.

Why didn't he hate Monsieur Brois, who was so ugly, so flabby, always dressed in a dirty shirt and the same stained and baggy suit, ill-shaven, and flaunting in his buttonhole the ribbon of heaven knows what shameful decoration?

'Would you be so kind, Monsieur Miette, as to fetch me two dozen Elephant rubbers, model B, from the stock-room?'

Even this affected politeness, which Monsieur Brois obviously considered the acme of scorn, failed to irritate him.

Back home, in Liège, everything had irritated him, down to the very streets, the way he went every day at fixed hours, and the shops, among others a big hosier's with three windows in the rue Saint-Gilles, which he could smell a hundred yards away.

It was out of hate that he had left school after the fifth form, out of hate for his schoolmates, and also because he no longer had any interest in studying.

'I want to work,' he had announced.

His mother had stood stock still, which was her way of showing her feelings, as at the news of a catastrophe. His father had thought fit to address a solemn speech to him, shaking his head, looking pleased with himself, and blowing smoke rings.

'Son, you'll soon be seventeen, so it's a man I'm talking to, it's as a man I'm going to talk to you.'

Félix dug his fingernails into his flesh. Oh, to get away! Anywhere! For good! To see no more of them! To see no more of what he knew *ad nauseam*!

Instead of which he went from one job to another, full of hatred and bitterness, and one day, at the Café de la Bourse, he happened to meet two extraordinary men, Philippe Estévant, with his long hair, his dark eyes and his loosely tied cravat, and the impassive, terrifying Frédéric Doms who rarely opened his mouth.

Those two understood him. Those two listened to all his excited speeches, and Estévant used to exclaim enthusiastically:

'You ought to write all that down. Don't you agree, Doms? We'll publish it as soon as we've got our printing-works. It's absolutely in line with the spirit of the moment. Absolutely!'

Why had the two men picked the peaceful Café de la Bourse, so warm and calm, where the same local speculators came and sat at the same tables, and where Jules, the waiter, knew beforehand what to serve them?

They had their own special place, in the corner formed by the double doors and the wall. They sat there without talking, just smoking their pipes. Now and then they went through the papers which Estévant brought along in a bulging briefcase.

For Félix it had become a necessity. As the hour approached, he felt nervous, his fingers started trembling like a drug addict's, and nothing on earth could have stopped him from going there. He walked fast, keeping close to the wall. The streets lost their ugliness. A fear took hold of him, the fear that the two men might not be there, or else the much more horrible fear that they might grow tired of the boy that he was.

Didn't Doms regard him with a certain contempt? What could Doms, who had travelled all over the world, who was about forty, who had met so many people, what could Doms think of him?

He was fat and clean-shaven. With his thin, fair hair, he gave the impression of an unfrocked priest, and his eyes were deformed by a pair of strange spectacles, in which a thicker disc in the middle of each lens caught the light.

Estévant too went in dread of a remark by Doms, one of those remarks which he made in a cold voice, looking somewhere else, as if his companions did not deserve so much as a glance.

Was he Dutch? Or was he Flemish, as his accent suggested? He hinted that this was a fearful secret known to him alone; he claimed that there was not a police force in the world capable of solving the enigma of his personality.

Now and then he would disappear for a few days. Estévant would tell Marette:

'He has gone to Berlin.'

Or else:

'Geneva! A group of our Russian friends is preparing an operation.'

Estévant wrote poetry, and also tracts which were to be published when the printing-works was ready, in other words when they had enough money.

For this purpose, Marette had stolen small sums of money from his parents and his employers.

'Thanks! Unfortunately it's only a drop in the ocean compared with what we need if we want to go into action.'

They had lent him some ill-printed booklets which bore no publisher's name. One of them, written in bad French, was about direct action and the importance of the gesture.

Every evening, Estévant went back to his parents' home, a comfortable house on the boulevard d'Avroy, for he was the son of a professor at the University. To what den did Doms retire? Marette had never discovered where he slept. He had just been told that it was never twice in the same place.

*

What would his feelings be now if he learnt of his father's death? Would he think about it for as much as five minutes and would not the piano, over his head, soon rouse him from his stupor?

It was the day for the Conservatoire. Isabelle would come downstairs just before ten. He was writing addresses on pale blue envelopes of rough paper which made his pen splutter. The chief clerk, Monsieur Brois, came and went round him and Monsieur Vétu bent over his rubber stamps, for he worked at a little table by the window.

Wasn't she unhappy too? Why was she always so pale? He had never seen her smile.

She would emerge from the entresol as from a bath of music with which she was still impregnated, stop in front of the cash-desk, and say in her expressionless voice:

'Give me some money.'

Nothing else. Never anything else. She wore a pair of high patent-leather boots. She did not change her hat from one end of the year to the other.

He longed to follow her into the street, to walk beside her, to surprise her gaze somewhere else than in the dark shop.

He was in love with her. He had written to Léopold, that puzzling creature for whom he had conceived a greater admiration than that which Doms inspired in him.

To begin with, he had not taken much notice of him. He was just a stocky little man with a black beard and a drunkard's breath who staggered into the café, slumped heavily on to the bench, and gazed at his glass without paying attention to anybody else.

Why had Léopold looked at him with his dark eyes with their surprisingly piercing gaze?

Was he listening to their conversation? Once Félix Marette had had the odd idea that he was an agent of the secret police in disguise and he had ventured to say so to Doms.

'Do you think he's following you?'

Doms had examined Léopold through his double lenses, then had shrugged his shoulders without saying anything.

Well, Marette had not been as mistaken as all that. Léopold was certainly not the man he seemed. He knew things of which Doms was ignorant. The proof of this was that he had followed Marette one evening, zigzagging along. He had bumped into him and had growled – possibly just because the boy was in his way:

'You ought to be more careful!'

Weeks went by without his putting in an appearance. Marette did not know that these were the weeks he spent on a house-painter's ladder.

Once, it was late in the evening. Doms and Estévant had not come. Marette was moping in his corner and drinking more than usual when Léopold, sitting at the next table, had started talking, as if to himself:

'It's disgusting, working on a kid's feelings like that.'

'Are you talking to me, Monsieur?'

'If those people have got some dirty work to do, why don't they do it themselves?'

*

The time had come. The piano had fallen silent. Footsteps. Isabelle was walking right across the entresol. She obviously did not bother to look in the mirror while putting on her coat. In winter – and winter was beginning – she put a narrow marten tie round her neck.

At the cash-desk, her mother was already getting the money ready and finally Isabelle's boots appeared on the spiral staircase, the hem of her coat, the music-case.

One day, without a word, with just a look, a single look, the last, he would hand her the story of his life, and then go away.

He already suffered at the thought, living that final minute, the steps he would take to leave the shop. He would not look back.

'You've got your gloves? There's a cold wind.'

She knew this, although she never went out, because the customers were blue when they came in and automatically warmed their hands at the stove.

Félix followed Isabelle with his eyes, and went across to the window to see her as long as he could, without realizing that he looked utterly moonstruck and that any other woman but this imbecile mother would have guessed the truth straight away.

In the street, which was an ugly November grey, Isabelle's pale face passed the window and it had scarcely disappeared before Félix Marette had a shock. On the other side of the street, on the opposite pavement, next to a draper's shop, a man in a thick overcoat was standing with his hands in his pockets, staring at him.

It was Doms. The latter did not signal to him, did not attempt to make contact with him in any other way than by his glance which scorned to express anything.

'I am here.'

That was all. Félix might plunge into the semi-darkness of the shop, but he knew that he remained tied as by a thread to those eyes enlarged by their double lenses.

He was so agitated that Monsieur Brois looked at him in astonishment and coughed. What could dusty Monsieur Brois do, where could he go, when he left the shop in the rue Montmartre? It was inconceivable that a wife, children, even a sister, could be waiting for him somewhere. Nobody could ever have kissed that colourless, ageless face which smelled

141

of paste. Monsieur Brois did not smoke, but ate cachous which he took every quarter of an hour out of a little metal box.

Marette found something to put away near the window and did not see Doms in his place; for a moment he almost felt relieved, but then he realized that he had not got rid of him.

What was he to do? He had to leave the shop. Even if it was only to go back to his attic, he had to go by way of the street.

Léopold was right. By what chance had Léopold happened to cross his path less than half an hour before the incident of the bomb? Unfortunately he knew nothing about it. He guessed the truth, but he obviously thought that it was for some other day. If only he had known, if only he had glanced at the parcel Marette was holding in one hand, how many things would have been different!

That evening, Marette had prowled in vain around the Café de la Bourse: neither Doms nor Estévant had been there. Oughtn't they to have been there to help him? Wasn't it up to them to play that part?

'Come along.'

That hairy bear Léopold was lurching along in the shadows.

'Come along, now.'

And he had led him as if by the hand. Marette would never forget that trap-door in the ceiling, the dubious-looking packet of meat which his companion had taken out of his pocket, the bed which he had given him, the fit of sobbing which had left him hot and empty with burning cheek-bones.

How had Doms managed to find him? Marette had given nobody his address; even Léopold wrote to him *poste-restante* under the name of Félicien Miette.

Seeing him out there in the street brought him as it were a breath of Liège, but it was not the breath of the Café de la Bourse, it was the breath of certain streets, especially the rue du Laveu, so empty when Marette came along it at night, with the gas-lamps at regular intervals, the light in the first-floor flat of an old lady – an officer's wife – who suffered from insomnia, and then the smell of his own house when he opened the door, the note which his father had left for him:

'*There is a cold chop in the sideboard.*'

He did not know that his father, since then, had summoned

up the patience to go walking beside the river for weeks on end, along the quai des Pitteurs, so that his death should not appear suspicious.

'Would you be so kind, Monsieur Miette, as to climb that ladder and put these blotters in the second pigeon-hole on the left, right at the top.'

He obeyed without realizing what he was doing. He was frightened. How did he know that it was not Doms who belonged to the police? There was a lot of talk of *agents provocateurs*. In the booklets he had been given to read, there was mention of them.

Time went by but he did not manage to control his excitement, even though he did not see Doms again on the opposite pavement. On Conservatoire days, he did not see Isabelle on her return, for she came home at a quarter past twelve, when he had already left, and he had never dared to wait for her in the street.

Monsieur Brois tied his knitted scarf round his neck, put on his shapeless overcoat, and opened his mouth to insert with great care a tiny cachou.

'Good morning, Monsieur Vétu. Good morning, Madame.'

He had to go out, whatever happened. Marette plunged into the street, tried to mingle with the crowd, and made for the Grands Boulevards without looking around him. He had not covered fifty yards before a quiet voice beside him said:

'How are you keeping?'

He made a blunder and pretended to be surprised. Doms simply murmured in an accusing tone of voice:

'I thought you had recognized me.'

'The fact is, I wasn't sure.'

'Where do you lunch?'

'It all depends.'

Another clumsy lie, for he was in such a panic that he took his companion to a restaurant where he had his own napkin in a pigeon-hole and where he paid with tickets.

'There's only one bed. And then, Monsieur Vétu might come upstairs . . .'

'What would he be doing up in the attic? If it came to the worst, you could tell him that I was a country cousin of yours.'

Doms looked at his watch, and picked his teeth a little longer.

'I must be going. There are some people expecting me. I'm glad I've seen you again. Incidentally, did you know that Estévant is starting a review? A real review, at a real printer's.'

A smile conveyed to the young man all the scorn Doms felt for this periodical.

'See you this evening. Don't forget. Let's say at . . . But now I come to think of it, do you have dinner here too?'

He said yes. It was not true. In the evening, to economize, he just had a bit of cheese in a dairy-shop.

'In that case, I'll wait for you outside the shop and we'll come along here. I hope I shan't be late.'

He went to the door, then turned round and came back.

'Now I come to think of it, let me have a few francs. Thank you. See you later!'

Marette was the first to return to the shop and, for the first time, the piano sounded over his head for a while without his hearing it.

*

Under the gas-jet which had just been lit, staring at Monsieur Brois's face, he was seized by sudden fits of panic, as in his childhood nightmares, with a damp sweat on his forehead, a mad terror in his chest, and a leaden weight in his legs.

Chapter Ten

It was raining and dark. Léopold, crossing streets at an angle, was already hobbling from the feebly luminous haven of one pub to another. He could sense the approach of the holidays several days ahead. The mob getting ready to enjoy itself bewildered him and he no longer knew where to put himself, feeling grumpy and ill at ease everywhere. He grumbled and drank, going anywhere in search of a corner which the others had not yet invaded.

It was 31 December. Very soon now a little ceremony would

take place at Monsieur Monnoyeur's. Every year, it was exactly the same. On the stroke of six, Désiré coughed and motioned to his colleagues. The latter, after straightening their ties, followed him into the office of their employer, who made a pretence of being surprised.

'Monsieur Monnoyeur, it is our duty and pleasure, on this last day of the year, to come and offer you our best wishes for health and prosperity in the coming year.'

Monsieur Monnoyeur, thin and weasel-faced, stood up, and shook hands all round.

'My friends . . . hum . . . my dear friends . . . I am deeply . . . deeply touched . . .'

The office smelled of old paper and old leather. On the mantelpiece, next to a bronze statuette, a bottle of port stood ready, with the requisite number of glasses.

'If you have no objection, we will drink to the New Year.'

The box of cigars was ready too. Everybody took one and lit it. A little blue smoke rose into the air. They sipped the port, and outside, in the garden stripped by winter, they could see the rain falling bleakly.

'To you and yours.'

It was all over. Monsieur Monnoyeur took the box of cigars and held it out to Désiré.

'Do me the favour of sharing these with your colleagues.'

The share-out took place in the office. Four cigars each, not counting the one which you went on smoking on the way home and which kept a sugary taste of port.

*

Élise, who had not put her veil on so that she could go faster, was running through the streets like a mouse. Holding her umbrella rolled up, she slipped past a shop window, vanished into the darkness, bobbed up again for an instant under the gas-lamp, and reappeared in front of a window-display, in such a hurry that her lips were already shaping the words she was going to say to the butcher.

Madame Pain had agreed to look after Roger for an hour. She had a son of the same age, to within a month. She was a woman who did not know how to do anything in the house, who was always tired, always complaining, one of those women of whom one is not surprised to read in the paper that their child has scalded itself or been drowned in a near-by pond.

The Meuse was swollen again, the slimy, uneven planks of the Passerelle bounced up and down, you pushed through the crowd without being able to make out any faces, and the town was just a collection of luminous dots. Place Cockerill, rue des Carmes; Élise plunged into the icy world of the meat market where the arc lamps left part of the iron girders in darkness.

'A pound of beef, Madame Mouron, and then a roast as usual, not too big, and a marrow-bone.'

On Saturdays and on the eve of holidays, she came to the market to buy her meat, but not for anything in the world would she have gone to any butcher but her own. She pitied and rather disapproved of those women who went to different shops, either out of ignorance or in order to save a few centimes. Over meat, she maintained that you should never haggle.

She held clutched in her hand the purse which she was always so afraid of losing with the key which was inside. She counted out the coins and smiled.

'Thank you, Madame Mouron. See you on Saturday.'

She would have been extremely surprised to learn that the fat butcher never recognized her and wondered why this customer greeted her and said good-bye so politely.

Opposite, there were the three windows of Schroefs' shop; Élise, who did not want to look that way, sped along the current of rainy air in the street, umbrella first, her shopping-bag swinging against her hip, and just as she was turning the corner, opposite the University, she ran straight into a man, and stammered an apology.

He, with a dead cigar-stub protruding from under his grey moustache, said simply:

'Élise!'

'Hubert!'

It was he who had behaved badly towards her, and yet it was she who felt at a loss, smiled, looked embarrassed, and wondered whether she ought not to kiss him.

'I've just been round to your flat.'

'Dear God! And you found nobody there!'

It was Schroefs, Hubert Schroefs, her brother-in-law, Marthe's husband. To think that she had spent three years in his house, after her mother's death, and now he seemed such a stranger, so impressive! Admittedly the Schroefs, at that time, were not yet living in the huge rue des Carmes building but in a humbler shop, with a single window, in the rue André-Dumont.

Élise followed her brother-in-law, wondering what he had to say to her. He took his time. Now that she thought about it, if he had gone round to her flat when they had not seen each other for two years, indeed for over two years, ever since Élise's marriage, that meant that something serious had happened.

'Dear God, Hubert! Marthe?...'

He nodded and said:

'She's locked herself in again. She must have found my revolver in the bedside table. Just now, she threatened to fire through the door.'

He was not the man to say a single word too many, or to go to the trouble of smiling to please somebody. Anybody would have thought that he was leading her along the dark street on a leash, with his hands in his pockets, knowing that she was following him. And she was indeed following him, stumbling along, she who, a little earlier, had been in such a hurry that she could not decide which short cut to take.

'You must speak to your sister.'

'She wouldn't do that, Hubert! I know Marthe.'

She could not refrain from adding:

'She's got everything she wants!'

The shop was full of goods, the shelves overflowing with luxury foods in golden tins or bearing golden labels. There were shop-assistants in white aprons bustling around and customers waiting. Hubert crossed the shop, his bowler-hat on the back of his head, his dead cigar between the grey hairs of his moustache and the thick bristles of his square-cut beard on which the nicotine had traced a brown circle.

He went up a few steps, opened the door of a glazed office, gave an order out of force of habit, and glanced into the yard where in the rain you could just make out a horse harnessed to a wagon which was being loaded, and some big white letters on the canvas cover: *Hubert Schroefs*.

Paying no attention to Élise, he went up the private staircase and asked the maid who appeared on the landing:

'Madame?'

'Still the same, Monsieur.'

The two children were in the dining-room. Jacques who was twelve and Germaine who was eight.

'How they've grown, Hubert!'

The gas radiator was giving off a stifling heat. The chairs were covered with leather fastened with brass nails.

'Try and talk to her, Élise. I can't stand any more of it.'

He was really tired, with black rings under his eyes. He was a massive man, with a paunch which was already prominent; he did not give an impression of health so much as of strength, on account of his hard features and his colourless complexion.

This evening he looked flabby, and his eyes were shifty. He sent the children out of the room, slumped into an armchair, heaved a sigh, and picked up the paper.

'Go on!'

It was almost a threat. He had done what he could. Now he was throwing in the sponge. He was as it were placing Marthe's fate in the hands of a Peters. He had not dared to go and fetch Louisa from Coronmeuse. He had gone to the rue Pasteur where he had never set foot before. Their quarrel did not matter to him.

'Go on!'

Let Élise look after her sister, seeing that they were of the same blood. He was at the end of his tether and it was not the first time that he had threatened to have his wife locked up in a nursing home.

What had the landlady said to him, in the rue Pasteur? Had he told her that he was Hubert Schroefs, the wholesale grocer?

Élise considered it natural that he should have come to fetch her, seeing that she was needed. She put her shopping-bag down.

'Where is her room?'

'Oh, of course. Léontine will show you.'

He had forgotten that Élise had never been inside the house

in the rue des Carmes. Did he even remember the causes of the quarrel? He had not wanted to see her marry Désiré because it would mean that she would not be able to look after the children in the evening. When she thought of all the piddle that had gone on her dresses!

He lit another cigar which would go out later, and sank into a silence as heavy as himself.

'If you only knew, Madame Élise!'

Léontine whispered to her, on the landing, next to the open door of the kitchen.

'This time it's really awful. It's been going on for three days now. You know how artful she is. She gets ready to take advantage of a moment when I'm away and then she comes into the kitchen to grab anything she can lay her hands on. Though heaven knows where she got the bottles.'

A door, with no light showing under it, and there was Élise, alone on the landing, in this strange house, Élise who was in a hurry, whom Madame Pain was waiting for, Élise whose fire was going out and whose supper would not be ready on time.

She called out softly:

'Marthe!'

She could sense something moving. She found it embarrassing that she could be heard in the dining-room where she could see a ray of light.

'Marthe!'

She had unconsciously adopted the Flemish accent and it was in Flemish that a voice, so close to the door that Élise jumped, asked her:

'Who is it?'

'It's me, Marthe. It's your sister Élise.'

'What are you doing here? He went to fetch you, didn't he? He's frightened.'

'No, Marthe. I was just passing by and dropped in to say hullo.'

Tears were flowing, but she was not crying. They were special tears, more fluid than the rest, with no bitterness in them, silent tears which came naturally to her eyes whenever it was a question of somebody in her family, Léopold, Louisa or Marthe, or when she spoke of Louis of Tongres who came to the Stock Exchange every week and had not called to see her once.

'Open the door, Marthe. I must talk to you.'

'Where is he?'

'Hubert? I don't know. I think he's downstairs.'

'You're lying. I heard him come upstairs. If you've come here to tell lies . . .'

'Please, Marthe. You're right, he's in the dining-room. He's reading the paper, I tell you . . .'

And suddenly, when Élise least expected it, she found herself in front of an open door. She did not realize this straight away, for the room was in total darkness and it was the light coming from the street which told her.

'Come in quick. What do you want? What have you come to complain about now? It's Désiré, isn't it?'

As if, when two Peters girls came together, it was necessarily to complain about something! Élise wanted to throw herself into her sister's arms. She could just make her out, in the orange halo of light coming from the glass roof of the meat market. Marthe, her hair falling untidily on to her shoulders, like a woman who had just got out of bed, looked fat and flabby, she who, a few years before, had had the bearing of a queen.

'Poor Marthe! If you only knew how unhappy I am . . .'

She had been unable to think of anything else and, in any case, it was exactly the right thing to say. There they were, the two of them, crying in the same way, shedding the same warm tears without a single sob.

'Poor dear! But I warned you. Men, you know . . . What has he been doing to you?'

Désiré would be coming home any time now! Roger was with Madame Pain who was quite capable of letting him play with matches. Élise had promised:

'Just half an hour, Madame Pain. The time it takes to run there and back.'

Monsieur Pain would be coming home too, and he was a difficult man.

'Dear God, Marthe! Why don't you light the lamp? Why do you lock yourself in like this?'

Already Marthe had scented the enemy.

'I *thought* your tears were just crocodile tears! What have you come for, eh? Go on, admit that it was him that sent you! You are in league with him, with that filthy brute, that miser with a stone instead of a heart.'

She went towards the bedside table on which Élise could see a revolver.

'One day I'll do it, you'll see!'

A cry.

'Marthe!'

'I mean what I say, you'll see! He treats me like a servant! He treats everybody like servants! And all men are the same! All of them!'

An unmade bed, some shapeless objects lying around, some food and a dirty glass which Élise could just make out in the reflected light from the glass cupola opposite.

'There! I knew it! He's listening at the keyhole.'

'I tell you you're wrong, Marthe.'

'There's only him that counts, him and his money. If it was in his interest to kill me, he'd do it. Do you hear? Your Désiré too! All men. They know what they want. It's disgusting, and when they've finished their filthy business, they fill their pipes and think of nothing but making money.'

She became suspicious once more.

'Why did you come here today, when other days you went along the street without coming into the shop?'

This time, Élise started sobbing, without knowing why, and with her nerves on edge implored her sister:

'Light the gas.'

She changed her mind straight away.

'Wait! I'll do it. Give me the matches.'

It was too late. Marthe had already climbed on to a chair, and her sister saw that she was swaying, that she was probably going to fall and set the house on fire.

'Mind out, Marthe.'

'If you think I'm drunk . . .'

A poof! A bright light engulfed them, a cold white light in which they scarcely recognized each other for a moment.

Marthe whispered:

'Oh, my poor girl . . . I wouldn't hurt a fly . . .'

This time Élise had heard Schroefs moving away from the

door, and, reassured, returning to his leather armchair in the dining-room.

The bed was in disorder, the table too, there was disorder everywhere in that comfortable room which had been turned upside down, and Marthe was tousle-haired like a fishwife, like those women you saw fighting and shouting filthy words in the back-streets. It was Élise who did the talking, in Flemish, blowing her nose, twisting her handkerchief, moaning and whispering, without taking her eyes off the revolver, even when the two sisters finally fell into each other's arms.

*

A quarter of an hour later, the door opened a little way and then shut again. Élise went into the dining-room after knocking. Hubert, who was at table with the children, did not invite her to join them. She motioned to him and slipped the weapon into his hand.

'Désiré's waiting for me. I have to get back. Whatever you do, don't rush her. She's quieter now. She's going to sleep. Tomorrow, all you need do is behave as if nothing had happened.'

'You wouldn't care to come here with your husband after lunch, would you? We've some people coming. I think it might be a good idea.'

'You think so, Hubert?'

As if she didn't know that, for her and Désiré to be invited, they had to have need of her!

She started running again. The lights of the shop windows had disappeared. She explained over and over again, all by herself:

'You mustn't be cross with me . . . I assure you, Désiré . . .'

There was a light in the flat in the rue Pasteur. Just as she was putting the key in the lock, the door opened. Désiré was there, huge and icy.

'Where have you been?'

'Listen, Désiré, I . . .'

'And the child?'

'What? You haven't . . .'

He had not thought that the child would be at Madame Pain's. When he had found the house empty, he had sat down at first, after putting some more coal on the stove, thinking that his wife and son would be back in a few minutes.

'It's half past seven.'

'Dear God! Wait a minute, and I'll go and fetch Roger. And there's Monsieur Pain at home!'

She had never seen Désiré looking so pale. It made her tremble as she was running to Madame Pain's and, while she was banging on the letter-box, her legs nearly gave way. The empty house, already cold, and, when she had come home without the child, Désiré, white as a sheet, opening the door!

She came back and found him sitting by the fire with his eyes shut, like a man who has had a severe shock and needs some time to recover.

'Forgive me, Désiré. If you only knew! Just imagine, my sister Marthe . . .'

Then he stood up and, for the first time, raised his voice.

'I don't care about Marthe, do you hear? I don't care about her! I don't care a damn about her!'

And he went into the bedroom to conceal his emotion, the nervous collapse which had overtaken him after his fright.

'What did you think had happened, Désiré?'

He would not say. He had thought, dammit, of the slimy streets, of the narrow pavements of the rue Puits-en-Sock, of Élise always running like a lunatic, of a tram knocking passers-by over like so many skittles.

'Come and have your supper. And forgive me.'

*

It was just then that Léopold, who had not drunk his fill, came limping home. Looking up, he saw a slit of light round the trap-door leading to his flat. He was not surprised. He climbed up the ladder, lifted the trap-door with his shoulders, felt that the room was warm, and saw that everything was tidy, the fire lit, the table laid. He just had time to take off his shoes, which had taken in water like sponges, before the trap-door opened again. Eugénie appeared, a shawl over her shoulders, a packet of meat in her hand.

'There you are, Léopold!'

She said this as if the surprising thing was to see him there, him and not her.

'You haven't had your supper, I hope?'

They did not kiss and scarcely looked at one another, merely darting furtive little glances at each other, glances full of trust and tenderness.

Eugénie had cleaned the flat from top to bottom. It was always like that when she returned. People said that she had a cameo profile, because her features were unusually regular, and she had the most beautiful dark eyes in the world.

'I wasn't happy with those people any more. They never entertained and they never knew what they were eating. I told them it was a waste of time taking a cook if you weren't capable of telling the difference between one dish and another.'

She had brought some tobacco for Léopold.

'Your overcoat's unstitched again at the collar. I wonder why it is that your overcoats always come unstitched at the collar?'

She would sew it up again later, while he was falling asleep; she would stay there maybe a week, maybe a month, as long as her money lasted; and then she would look for a new post. She would not say anything to Léopold. But one day he would find the flat empty, with a cold supper on the table.

*

Désiré had not scolded her. Thinking he would be cross, she had not dared to speak to him about Schroefs' invitation. She had got up early to go to the first Mass. She had prayed for a long time, with tears in her eyes, for Félicie, for Marthe, for herself, for all who were unhappy on earth.

She knew that Marthe was no more responsible than Félicie, perhaps less. Marthe was unhappy. It wasn't her fault. She was short of nothing, and yet no woman with a spark of feeling in her could have been happy in her place.

There were some Mamelins in church. She took the opportunity, outside, in the cold light of dawn, to wish them a happy New Year, kissing them three times.

The rain had stopped. You could feel that it was going to freeze. Already, in patches, the pavements were turning a hard grey.

'A happy New Year to you, Lucien, and lots of luck, and may all your wishes come true. Tell Catherine, in case I don't see her, that I wish her a happy New Year.'

She went home, lit the fire, and sprinkled some paraffin on it to make it burn faster. Then she ground some coffee and heard Désiré moving.

'A happy New Year, Désiré. I beg your pardon again for yesterday. I swear that I couldn't help it. Happy New Year, little Roger.'

It was too bright to light the lamp, too dark to see properly. She washed the child and dressed him, watching the breakfast at the same time, while Désiré shaved by the window.

'Listen, Désiré. Don't get cross before I've finished. I simply must go this afternoon to Schroefs' house. I've promised. Hubert insisted on you coming too.'

What she was saying was so bold that she did not dare to look at her husband. Until now, the New Year's Day ritual had been immutably fixed and it was in the rue Puits-en-Sock that they had always spent the afternoon. Mother Mamelin had been dead only a few months. Élise went on with a lump in her throat:

'I'm afraid that something might happen. When Marthe is like that, she's capable of anything.'

Did Désiré understand the importance of the game which was being played, possibly the most decisive of their life together? His face, over which he was carefully passing the razor, was reflected, motionless, in the wardrobe mirror which looked dirty in the half-light.

'You could drop in at your home this morning, I'll go with the boy to kiss your father, about ten o'clock.'

He said nothing, which meant yes. She was afraid that he might be sad, or vexed, or cross, and while she was eating her eggs and bacon she talked about Marthe, hurriedly, to avoid having a silence.

'It's partly Hubert's fault. He does nothing to make life pleasant for her. He gives her everything she wants, of course. She just has to dip into the shop. But on the other hand she never gets a compliment, a sign of affection, a delicate gesture. When he goes upstairs in the evening he slumps in his armchair with a groan and starts reading his paper . . .'

*

Désiré had left to go to Mass. He sat down in the pew of the Brotherhood of St Roch. His father took the collection. Everybody knew them and shook hands with them outside.

'Happy New Year.'

'All the best.'

They embraced, very simply, scarcely touching one another, as generals kiss officers they are decorating.

'Happy New Year, Papa.'

'Happy New Year, son.'

He accompanied his father to the rue Puits-en-Sock, kissed Cécile, Marcel, who was still wearing his moustache-fixer, then Arthur, who arrived soon afterwards.

The day remained bitterly cold. Old Kreutz came and sat down for a quarter of an hour by the fire, and Arthur, joking all the time, shaved Old Papa in the kitchen, as he was in the habit of doing five or six times a year. Mourning hung behind the window-panes, on which the geometric patterns of the coloured paper stood out more clearly than on other days. On the brown oilcloth covering the table there was the bottle of Kempenaar, glasses for everybody, and a plate of cakes which Cécile had made using her mother's recipe.

About ten o'clock, Élise came in with the child, and saw Désiré sitting in a corner, with his chair tilted back slightly and his long legs stretched out. Seeing him here, she had the impression that he looked bigger than usual, and she scarcely dared to speak to him.

'Happy New Year, Papa. Happy New Year, Arthur. Happy New Year, Cécile.'

She wondered if Désiré had already told them that they would not be coming in the afternoon. She waited a little while. The child started walking around.

'Mind the fire, Roger. And what about you, Cécile? When is it due?'

For Cécile was expecting a baby.

'I have to go to watch my dinner. Don't come home too late, Désiré.'

And Désiré, at a quarter to twelve, announced as he stood up:

'We shan't be able to come this afternoon. We have to go to see one of my wife's sisters.'

It was done. Never, during his mother's lifetime, as long as her grey, somewhat monastic silhouette had inhabited the kitchen in the rue Puits-en-Sock, would he have dared to say anything like that.

He avoided looking at his father who no longer felt really at home now that he was living with Cécile and a son-in-law.

'Good-bye, all!'

The roast, the chips and the sugared peas were waiting for him. Roger was dressed in feverish haste.

'Aren't we taking the pram?'

People, today, were not in their usual places, and they noticed inexplicable exoduses in certain streets, empty spaces in others.

'I'll carry him, Désiré.'

She knew that he would not let her. She wanted to be nice to him, to make him forget what had happened the day before, to thank him for coming to Schroefs'.

She trotted along, a little behind him as usual. At the corner of the rue des Carmes, which was empty, she felt a quiver of excitement. The house with the closed shutters impressed her, and she looked up at the loggia before ringing the bell.

'Good afternoon, Léontine. Happy New Year. Is my sister better?'

'Madame is very well, Madame Élise.'

Had they to go upstairs all the same? After all, they had only been invited because of Marthe's novena.

Hubert was standing on the stairs. He shook hands with Désiré, then with the child, whom he did not kiss.

'Come upstairs. Nobody's arrived yet.'

The table had been cleared in the dining-room. The children, in their playroom, were waiting for some little friends who were due to have coffee with them.

'Where's Marthe?' Élise asked timidly.

'She's in her room. She's getting dressed.'

'May I go and see her?'

Désiré was offered a chair by the gas fire which Hubert bent down to regulate.

'A cigar?'

They did not know how to start the conversation. They did not even know if they ought to use the familiar *tu* with each other. It was Hubert who made the first effort, with a certain awkwardness, sitting up in his armchair and relighting his cigar-stub:

'Did Élise tell you? It's always the same! This morning, she was better.'

Élise had knocked on the door.

'Is that you? Come in! How's the boy? You've brought him along, I hope.'

There was not the slightest trace left of what had happened the day before. The maid had cleaned the room and polished the furniture and the floor, and you would never have thought that for three nights Hubert had had to sleep on a camp-bed installed in the dining-room. The house was warm and comfortable. Marthe was putting the final touches to her appearance. Her dark hair was carefully arranged, she was wearing a black silk dress, trimmed with lace, which emphasized her proud bosom, and you could only just sense that she was a little absent-minded, a little vague, talking in an affected way with a hint of weariness.

'Why don't you come and do your shopping here, like Poldine? We let her have everything at cost price. She drops in once a month and gets all her groceries.'

'That's sweet of you. Thank you, Marthe!'

'When Hubert isn't there, I shove masses of things into her bag. It's nothing really. You must come too. With what Désiré earns . . .'

'Thank you, Marthe.'

It was just the same as it was with Félicie, entirely good or entirely bad, according to the day. Marthe too, if her sister were to come to the shop the next day with her bag, would be quite capable of calling her a beggar.

'When I think that I haven't seen your son yet. Go and fetch him, Élise.'

She kissed him, looked all around her, rushed into the kitchen, and returned with a huge bar of chocolate.

'Not now, Marthe. He's just had his dinner.'

'What does that matter? Eat it, darling. Don't bother about what your mother says, or her disapproving looks. It's good chocolate!'

They were all daughters of the same mother and father. You could recognize them by a particular way they had of bending their heads and smiling, that humble, resigned smile which was peculiar to the Peters girls.

Élise felt overwhelmed by the huge bedroom with its impressive furniture, and by her sister's dress.

'Look, Marthe, you're expecting some people and we'll only be in the way. Don't you think it would be better if we left you?'

She felt ill at ease, and would really have preferred to go down into the street, under the loggia, and off towards the duck-pond.

'Are you mad? If you only knew how often we've talked about you! I kept wondering what was the matter with you, your husband and you. I hope Désiré's keeping well?'

It wasn't her fault. Marthe had forgotten. She had forgotten everything she had said against Désiré when Élise had announced that she was getting married. She had forgotten that she had not even given her sister a present. There had not been a proper wedding, it was true, because Élise had still been in mourning. Nobody had been invited. But the Schroefs could have sent something, however small.

Marthe had forgotten. Perhaps she had also forgotten the scene the day before. If not, she pretended to have forgotten it.

'Roger! Roger! Mind the lovely bedspread.'

'Oh, let him be. Go on playing, darling. Don't listen to your mother.'

What did it matter? When it was torn, they would buy another. And with a conspiratorial wink she added:

'He can afford it.'

Poor Marthe, she was so kind. She would give you all that she had. She would even give you her nightdress if you asked for it. But later on she would throw it back in your teeth with hard words, words that hurt!

The worst of it all was that you never knew whether it was

.when she had had a few drinks that she was her real self or when she was sober.

Seeing that they would have to come again, now that they were no longer on bad terms, Élise decided to tell Roger:

'Whatever you do, don't accept anything from Aunt Marthe.'

But Aunt Marthe insisted on filling his pockets, just as she filled the shopping-bag of Poldine, the wife of their brother Franz, who was an inspector at the Herstal armaments factory.

The two women and the two men came together in the dining-room, which was already full of smoke. Hubert was drawing contentedly on his cigar. Peace had been restored to his house.

However there were certain details which only Élise noticed. For instance, when she had passed the drawing-room door, she had caught sight of a table laden with cakes, biscuits and bottles. The guests had not arrived. The Mamelins were not real guests and they were being kept in the dining-room until the others came.

Désiré was talking insurance. Hubert had started questioning him, for he never wasted an opportunity, and Désiré didn't understand, he thought Hubert was talking to him as he would to any one else, and he felt proud at being asked for advice.

Élise could scarcely bear it. Now and then she longed to whisper to him:

'Let's go, Désiré. You don't understand that we're out of place here.'

They were in the way! They weren't wanted any more. The guests, the real ones, were expected, and they were taking their time. They had plenty. Three o'clock. Nobody knew what to do any more. Hubert had gone downstairs to the glazed office to get a briefcase containing his fire-insurance policies, and Désiré went through them, giving his opinion, while the women stayed with the children in the playroom. The little friends, the daughter and sons of Roskam, the big dressmaker, had not arrived either.

'It would be better if we left you, Marthe.'

Dusk was falling when they heard a ring at the bell.

'I tell you, Marthe . . .' Élise repeated anxiously.

'That really would be the limit! You're my sister, aren't you?'

The lamps were lit in the drawing-room. Greetings were exchanged on the landing. The Mamelins heard the childish voice of a tiny little bald man, who was an important cheese-merchant and had the same accent as Schroefs. They both came from the same village in Limbourg. His wife's fat pink arms reminded you of their old dairy-shop, a little shop all in white marble. They had no children.

'Do sit down. A biscuit? A glass of port?'

Élise, after all the trouble she had taken to persuade Désiré to come, did not know how to tell him that they ought to go and made signs to him which he failed to understand.

After Monsieur Van Camp, the cheese-merchant, Monsieur Magis, who ran a restaurant in the rue Saint-Paul and who, like old Marette, had cancer of the stomach, arrived.

'A cigar? With pleasure!'

Legs were stretched. Désiré thought that this was his day, that he was the great man of the gathering, because people were questioning him all the time about insurance problems, and because on that subject he knew more than anybody else. He juggled with figures, answered queries, and offered advice which would save all three of them, Schroefs and Magis and Van Camp, thousands of francs.

'Your health, Monsieur Mamelin. You were saying that in the case of a fire covered by a Class B policy . . .'

Everybody in the insurance world knew that Désiré Mamelin had never made a mistake, that he had never needed to consult a ready-reckoner or the terms of a policy. He was like a conjuror who had never bungled a trick.

'You would lose twenty per cent because article eight stipulates that an extra premium is necessary for . . .'

He was the great man, that was certain! These business men who were so sure of themselves were little children compared with him and humbly asked his advice, looking knowingly at each other.

It got to the point where Hubert Schroefs, irritated by all the noise coming from the playroom, called out for the door to be shut.

'And what if the risk had increased in the meantime without an additional clause being inserted in the policy?'

The Mamelins were gathered together in the rue Puits-en-Sock, and for the first time Désiré was absent, for the first time Chrétien Mamelin, not waiting for the traditional tea and home-made cakes, had gone for a walk with his friend Kreutz.

Élise was happy and worried at the same time. She could feel things. She wished that Désiré could feel things too. He was given a third glass of port.

'Désiré!' she said imploringly.

He did not hear her. And a little later, when they were going home through the dark streets, it would be Désiré, with the boy perched on his shoulders, who would congratulate himself on his day.

'They understood what I was telling them! Their policies are as badly drawn up as they could be!'

She did not dare to say anything. What was the use? Those were things the Peters could understand, but not he.

The fire had gone out. She lit it again. They had brought home some liver pudding from Tonglet's.

'I thought your sister Marthe did everything she could to be nice.'

She could not explain to him. And what would be the point of making him share the bitterness of that empty afternoon in which they had only played walking-on parts?

'Help yourself, Désiré. I've already taken two slices. I assure you I'm not hungry any more.'

The Schroefs had not asked them to stay to dinner. Just as they were leaving – she did not dare tell Désiré – Marthe had slipped two tins of sardines into her bag, all that she had been able to pick up as they were going through the dark shop.

'Take them! You need to keep your strength up. Don't tell Hubert.'

She had felt embarrassed all the way home by those two icy tins which she did not know how to hide, and once she was in the flat, she had slipped them under the child's mattress.

Chapter Eleven

Élise and Julie Pain had installed themselves with the children on a bench in the place du Congrès, just opposite the rue Pasteur, so that by looking round every now and then they could make sure that nobody was ringing their door-bells.

It was a bright March day, the sun was shining, silvery clouds were sailing across the sky, and a clear, sharp light accentuated the details of the scene.

The children, Roger and Armand, were squatting on the ground, playing with the gravel and the fine dust as if it were sand.

The two women chatted together in low voices, speaking in little whispered phrases. Élise knitted. Julie Pain did not know how to do anything with her hands.

'If you only knew how it irritates me, Désiré, to see those two motionless hands!'

They often shook their heads, with a smile tinged with melancholy, and yet they were not sad, indeed they may have been happy, for this was what they were like – they had become friends straight away – and they waited until the children came out of the Friars' school in the rue de l'Enseignement before going to make up their fires, drink a cup of coffee and eat a slice of bread and butter.

'Don't hit Armand with your spade, Roger!'

There had been many afternoons, and there would doubtless be many more, similar to this one, more or less sunny, but just as quiet, for it was only at rare intervals that a tram crossed the place du Congrès, and you could count the passers-by in the six streets radiating from it. Now and then, for a few moments, the pavements were deserted, and you had the feeling that the first person to venture out on them was ashamed of the noise his footsteps made.

'The worst of it all, you know, Julie . . .'

Roger and Armand were just babies who were still dressed

in pinafores. Roger's pinafore was blue, for he was dedicated to the Virgin.

Armand, who was the elder of the two by only a month, was much fatter, and very placid, with the dark slit eyes of a Mongol. Wherever you put him, he stayed there as long as you left him. Once Élise had made so bold as to say:

'Do you think it's normal, Julie?'

They had nearly fallen out over that. Élise did not mention it any more. It was like the way Julie Pain had of disposing of the child by leaving him sitting on the doorstep all day, with his little bottom touching the stone. Whenever you went down the rue Pasteur, the Pains' door was open, Armand was sitting there, and you could make out Julie in the half-light of the kitchen, unless she was gossiping at a neighbour's.

'The worst of it all, you know, Julie, ever since my accident, has been the pains in my stomach. Sometimes, at night, I feel as if I was being torn up inside.'

Now this moment was to remain engraved for ever in a certain memory. Roger, who had just knocked over his bucket of gravel, had looked up at the bench. The picture he saw, the piece of life which offered itself to his gaze, the smell of the square, the fluidity of the air, the yellow bricks of the house on the corner – all the other bricks in the district were red or pink – Godard's empty butcher's shop on the opposite corner, the newly painted wall of the church club at the end of the rue Pasteur, all that constituted his first conscious vision of the world, the first scene which would accompany him, just as it was then, through life.

His mother would always be that woman he saw from below, still dressed in black, in half-mourning as from today, with a lace collar round her neck, a jabot held in place by a locket and billowing over her chest, and lace at her wrists, a bare-headed woman with fair hair which curled and quivered in the March breeze.

He gazed at her. He listened. He tried to understand and his forehead creased. Finally he spoke.

'Why does your stomach hurt?'

Startled, Élise looked furtively at Julie. They never paid sufficient attention to the children!

'Go on playing, Roger!'

'Why does your stomach hurt?'

'Because I carried a tub of washing that was too heavy for me. You know, the tub I wash you in.'

He thought for a moment and accepted the explanation. Élise heaved a sigh. Finally, as if not attaching any importance to it, in a very casual manner, the child started raking the gravel again with his wooden spade.

No doubt he would not remember everything. However, henceforth, in the rue Pasteur flat, there were two eyes and two ears more than before, and only time would make a final selection from all the sights, sounds and smells. Henceforth, when she threaded her way along the narrow pavements of the rue Puits-en-Sock where so many tram accidents happened, when she went to buy fifty centimes' worth of chips, a couple of chops or half a pound of pudding, when she complained of this or that, or when, from the fruit market, she looked through the windows of the café for Félicie's bright, slim silhouette, Élise was no longer alone.

The first picture to remain in the boy's mind was the place du Congrès on a March day, two women on a bench, an empty butcher's shop, Élise who had put on a white collar for the first time for months, and Julie Pain with her ridiculous red-tipped nose, her waist so high up that she walked like a stork.

The first problem which Roger was to turn over in his little head was this stomach which hurt, he could not understand why, this woman's stomach which had been mysteriously injured. It would become even more tragic and mysterious when Élise seized every opportunity to say:

'If you don't behave yourself, a carriage will come to fetch me.'

A cab had stopped one evening in front of a near-by house, to take to the clinic an old man who had been buried a few days later. The child had seen it.

'Where will it go, the carriage? Will it take me?'

'No, not you. It will come to take me to hospital.'

'What will you do in hospital?'

'Have an operation.'

'What for?'

'My stomach.'

He did not cry. He kept quiet. He turned his thoughts over

for a long time, and now and then he darted quick glances at that swollen stomach which his mother's princess dress accentuated.

At night, before dropping off to sleep, when, through the half-open door, the oil-lamp in the kitchen peopled the bedroom with moving shadow-figures, he sometimes asked questions from the depths of his bed.

'It isn't coming to fetch you, is it?'

'What?'

'The carriage.'

The sound of a horse's hoofs on the cobblestones of the street froze him all of a sudden. He listened in terror, not breathing again until he was sure that the carriage had not stopped, until the noise had finally faded away into the distance.

'Does your stomach hurt, Mother?'

'What on earth are you talking about?'

She was embarrassed in front of Désiré, who often reproached her with her mania for complaining.

'Just like your sisters! It's in the family! If every one of you were given a castle and a million francs you'd still fall into each other's arms and cry!'

The world would grow imperceptibly, picture by picture, street by street, question by question.

'Why don't you carry me?'

'Because I'm tired . . .'

'Why are you tired?'

'Because I'm a woman.'

'And isn't Father tired?'

'Your father's a man.'

A woman.

People stopped Élise in the street because of the child. The magistrate's housekeeper rushed out every time she passed and always had some sweets ready for him.

'It's too good of you, Madame Gérard. You're spoiling him.'

'He's so sweet, so mischievous! His eyes really talk to you, Madame Mamelin!'

'You can't imagine how tiring he's getting! It isn't so much that he's heavy to carry. There are children his age who are heavier than he is. But he asks questions from morning till night. Sometimes it's quite embarrassing. Look! He's listening to us now. He can understand everything we're saying.'

She was wrong. He wanted to understand, but what he wanted to understand was not always what people said, it was other mysteries Élise never thought of, subtle things often, which he did not dare to talk about, as if he knew that this was his personal domain, into which nobody else could penetrate.

For instance, there was something which went up and down in the sky on certain days. The kitchen window formed a big blue rectangle. He sat on the floor, on the brown blanket with the floral pattern, the blanket which was put down on Saturday afternoon when the flat was cleaned and which, folded in four or eight, was used by him during the week.

He stared at this plain blue rectangle, and all of a sudden – he had never been able to determine the precise moment when it began – something transparent, a long, curling shape, left one corner of the rectangle and zigzagged towards another, sometimes staying motionless for a moment before being swallowed up by the infinity hidden by the window-frame.

What was it? He did not dare to ask. He was convinced that even his father did not know. Perhaps he was the only one to see this living thing?

'Why don't you go on playing, Roger?'

'I *am* playing!'

When he remained motionless, Élise was always afraid that he was ill.

'Are we going to go for the chops?'

'What is it the day for?'

'It's the day for fish.'

Why was it the day for fish? And when Léopold came and sat down by the fire, why was his mother different?

'Anybody been?' Désiré asked when he came home.

'No.'

And what about Uncle Léopold? Probably she had forgotten. He reminded her.

'Uncle Léopold came.'

She blushed, and moved her saucepans about on the stove.

'Oh, yes. He just looked in for a moment. I'd completely forgotten.'

'Is he keeping well? And Eugénie?'

Why did Élise dart that glance at the child? Why did she speak in a low voice, as she did with Madame Pain?

'Just imagine, she's found a post quite near here, in the rue de la Province, in a boarding-house.'

'Who's Eugénie, Mother?'

'Nobody, Roger.'

'Who's nobody?'

He had finely drawn features and little eyes; he already creased his eyelids.

'And I should so much have liked to have a child with big eyes! They're so beautiful, big eyes are! He has to go and have the same eyes as Louis of Tongres.'

On Sunday, nowadays, they went to the Schroefs' in the rue des Carmes. Nearly every time, Élise was in a state of nerves and a quarrel broke out before they set off. For no particular reason, because of her hat which she could not manage to put on straight, because of her hair which did not stay up, because of the pins which were too long or too short, or because of the princess dress which Désiré spent ages trying to do up.

'You're hurting me, you know you are. Dear God! Why is it that you aren't capable of doing up a dress?'

She had already felt like crying, possibly before dinner, before Désiré had come home from the rue Puits-en-Sock. She had planned everything beforehand, and the scene always took place at the very last moment, when the other two thought that at last they were going to set out.

'I'd better stay behind. You go with the child!'

'What should I be doing by myself at your sister's?'

'And what about me when I have to shut myself up for hours in the rue Puits-en-Sock or at Françoise's?'

'Oh, come now, Élise! I didn't say that I don't want to go to your sister's. I just said . . .'

'No! Leave me alone! You'd better not say any more. Go on! Get out! I'll stay here with Roger.'

'You know very well they're expecting us.'

'Is it me they're expecting? No, it's you. Hubert wants to talk to you again about insurance or heaven knows what, to make you do the work he daren't give to his accountant. The last time, you stayed shut up in his office for three hours. If you think that's enjoyable.'

'You were with your sister.'

Often she undressed and threw herself on the bed, at the end of her tether and at a loss for arguments. Then, a quarter of an hour later, she washed her eyes with cold water, put her dress on again, and stuck her long hat-pins in at random.

'Can you see that I've been crying?'

They set off. They crossed the Pont-Neuf or the Passerelle. They rang the bell. They whispered while the maid came downstairs.

'You'll see, the children will have gone out again.'

Why should that matter to Élise? Did she come for the children's sake? Why did she insist that they were invited as stopgaps because the Schroefs were bored on Sundays, because they had no friends, because they were lonely in their big freestone house and Hubert dreaded being left alone with his wife?

'Listen, Désiré, if Marthe is squiffy, I'm not staying. You do what you like, I'm going.'

'Ssh!'

Footsteps. As if in obedience to a signal, Élise assumed her bent attitude and her amiable smile, expressing gratitude in advance.

Hubert came to meet them on the landing and they could tell that he had just got up with a sigh of relief from his leather armchair by the gas-fire in the dining-room. That was his corner. The dining-room smelled of cold cigar: he had a cigar-stub between his moustache and his beard.

'How are you keeping?'

He shook hands with Désiré but scarcely noticed Élise. As for the child, he had probably never spoken to him and would not recognize him in the street.

'Marthe must be in her bedroom, or in the box-room.'

'Thank you, Hubert.'

He was dressed in his weekday suit, a long, full jacket in steel-grey, which looked rather like a frock-coat, over a waist-coat crossed by a heavy watch-chain hung with charms. He was wearing his bowler-hat, which he kept on by the fire, out of force of habit, because his life, his real life, consisted of bustling about downstairs, going into the yard a dozen times to super-vise the loading of a wagon, climbing the ladders in the huge warehouses, hurrying in and out, watching his men and picking up a tool himself to open a crate which had just arrived.

'Sit down, Désiré. Have a cigar.'

The newspapers, which he had read from back to front while he had been waiting, were scattered on the table. He regulated the gas, crossed his short legs, and relit his cigar-stub.

'Well, what news?'

Élise was right, the children had gone out. They had some little friends of their own age, and each in turn gave a coffee-party on Sunday or Thursday. The maid took them, bringing them home at dusk.

Marthe was not ready. On Sundays she lacked the courage to get dressed. She took the opportunity to open cupboards, to change the contents round, to arrange and sort things, without any taste for what she was doing, without any enthusiasm, her feet in soft slippers.

'Sit down, Élise. I'll have finished in a minute.'

'Do you want me to help?'

The street itself was calculated to upset the Schroefs, that street which was so busy during the week, full of wagons un-loading quarters of various animals in the din from the meat market, and which all of a sudden, on Sunday, was utterly deserted, with not even a cat in it, so that you might have thought that the houses were empty.

*

'Is Marthe keeping well?'

Hubert heaved a sigh and looked as if he were going to touch wood.

'She's in a good period.'

Nobody took any notice of Roger. The women half disap-peared into the cupboards stuffed with linen and clothes.

'You aren't expecting anybody, are you, Marthe? I'm always so afraid of being in the way.'

'You know very well that you're never in the way, silly. Who do you think we'd be expecting? Apart from Van Camp...'

He might come along, by himself or with his fat pink wife, his infantile wife as Marthe called her.

'I assure you she's really infantile. You feel like giving her a sweet to suck.'

In a few minutes they would be sure to hear the two men leave the dining-room to go downstairs to the office where Hubert always had some papers to show Désiré. Schroefs would fall ill if he could not go downstairs to the office.

Finally, when little Monsieur Van Camp, with his shining pate, arrived, he would be shown upstairs with his wife, they would sit down in the dining-room, and Marthe would call out through the half-open door:

'I'll be with you in a minute! Excuse me, won't you?'

Léontine would make the coffee in the kitchen.

'Léontine, take the child with you. He's bored here.'

The house was like a garment too big for the wearer in which he feels more uncomfortable than in one which is too small. Nobody knew where to go. At the far end of the kitchen there was a door which led to a world which was literally infinite, the world of the warehouses where the goods were stocked.

It was a three-storeyed block, with big rectangular holes in the floors, ladders, pulleys, walls of crates, mountains of sacks and bales. There was straw lying about on the concrete floor, coffee beans and bits of cinnamon, and when you leaned out of one of the unglazed windows, you could see, in the stables at the back of the yard, behind the shed where the wagons were kept, the five horses with their strong cruppers and the groom shaping a piece of wood or repairing a whip.

'Léontine! Go and tell Monsieur that the coffee is ready.'

All this time, Élise had been trotting along behind her sister, trying to make herself useful and speaking in odd snatches.

'Talking of Eugénie, just imagine, she's working in the district, so that we risk meeting her any day in her old things and without a hat.'

Tomorrow it would be over, and a new week of real life would begin. Hubert Schroefs would be the first to go downstairs, at seven o'clock, in his frock-coat jacket, with his bowler-hat on the back of his head and his cigar in the corner of his mouth. He would walk round the office, the yard, the stables and the warehouses. He would go on living his life until the evening, and when he finally came upstairs again, he would slump into an armchair. Then, after dinner, he would stretch his legs out in front of the gas-fire and bury himself in the newspaper.

'Coffee's ready, everyone.'

Tarts. Cakes. Van Camp could scarcely speak French. In any case, he did not talk much. He was satisfied like that, breathing in the atmosphere which surrounded Schroefs, the great man of his village.

At home, he was unhappy. He had made the mistake of selling his cheese factory too soon and now, alone with his wife in a flat in the rue Neuvice, he was bored.

The two men had arrived at Liège together; the difference between them was that Schroefs was educated, a qualified schoolmaster, and that he had started work as a book-keeper at Madame Winand's, the grocer's in the rue Sainte-Marguerite, while Van Camp, in a white smock, was pushing carts loaded with cheeses through the streets.

Both men were now rich. Schroefs was the richer of the two. They were short and stocky. They had kept their accents. Now and then they exchanged a few words.

'You remember little Kees who had freckles?'

'The postman Pietke's son? What became of him?'

'I don't know.'

They enjoyed talking about those days, recalling the long journey through the mud and the snow when they went to the school in their village, in Campine, wearing clogs.

Now Schroefs had a big drawing-room which he did not bother to open for Van Camp and Désiré.

Hubert was talking about coffee, his favourite subject. He knew every kind of coffee in the world, and could identify them by biting on a single bean. Élise bent her head, watching her son.

'Now, Roger. Don't eat so much. You'll make yourself sick again.'

And Marthe said:

'Leave him alone, Élise. Let him eat, the poor little darling, seeing that he likes it. Don't look at your mother, Roger. Eat up. When you are at your Aunt Marthe's, you must never look to see if your mother's looking disapproving.'

'Incidentally, Marthe, we shan't be able to come next Sunday.

We have to go and see Désiré's sister who's an Ursuline nun at Ans.'

Out of politeness, because the Schroefs might be offended, she felt obliged to imply that she considered this visit to the convent a tedious business.

They had put a couple of cushions under the child, who looked all around him. He would not forget certain things which the others had probably never noticed. For instance, all the pictures in the house were inscribed with gilt lettering on the frames, for they were free gifts distributed by the leading manufacturers of biscuits, tinned goods or chocolate. Opposite Uncle Hubert's armchair there hung a picture which was darker than the others, showing some people in black hats standing round a naked man who was a greenish yellow colour.

Roger would have liked to ask:

'What are they doing?'

It was a reproduction in colour of *The Anatomy Lesson*. These men in black standing round a corpse were associated in the child's mind with the hard, grey silhouette of Uncle Schroefs, with his bowler-hat which he had taken off only to sit down at table, and with the spicy smell which filled the house, mixed with the smell of the rough wooden crates.

Aunt Marthe kept stuffing things into his pockets, sometimes things which he could not eat, not only chocolate or biscuits which crumbled straight away but tins of anchovy fillets.

Why did his mother take them from him? Why did she scold him when they had scarcely turned the corner of the street?

'You mustn't accept anything from Aunt Marthe. You must say: "No, thank you, Aunt." '

And this *no thank you* became a sort of proper name for him. 'Nothankyou.'

Why did he have to say: 'No thank you'? Why, when the two women were together in the bedroom or the box-room, especially the box-room, did they start crying, wiping away their tears quickly if anybody came in? And why, when they met, did they nearly always say:

'Poor Élise.'

'Poor Marthe.'

Yet it was the most beautiful house in the world. When the grown-ups wanted to be by themselves, Léontine took Roger away. She was a queer girl, very thin, very flat-chested, who had a habit of squeezing him too tightly when she kissed him. She took him round the warehouses. She let him touch everything. She had taken him to see the horses; and the man who was in the yard – or in the stables when it was raining – a shabbily-dressed old man, had made him a whip, a real one, with a string which cracked.

When the daylight began to fade, Élise looked at her husband and tried to attract his attention, making signs to him which everybody understood.

'But no! It isn't late,' Marthe or Hubert protested.

It was time to lay the table for supper. The children would be coming home soon. They were in the way. Couldn't Désiré feel that they were in the way?

For the past quarter of an hour, Schroefs had had enough. He was only just managing to restrain himself from yawning, and, now that the day was nearly over, he wanted to settle down in his corner, in front of his gas-fire, and to look through his papers, sighing all the time.

Désiré believed everything he was told. If somebody said to him: 'But no, do stay . . .' – he stayed!

At last! Van Camp had got up, though he would have liked to stay. Everybody went towards the door. They said good night two or three times, once before putting on their outdoor clothes, then on the landing, then again downstairs.

'Come this way.'

The shop door was opened a little way, revealing the violet shadows of the street, the silence outside, the trams in the distance.

'A week on Sunday, then. Thank you, Marthe. Désiré, carry the child. We'll be able to walk faster like that.'

A few steps.

'They made him eat three pieces of tart again.'

Désiré did not understand, did not manage to feel indignant or offended.

'I'm sure Hubert's going to say that you come on purpose to smoke his cigars.'

'I smoked two.'

'Let's buy a bit of ham for supper. The fire will have gone out.'

The child, on his father's shoulders, saw the gas-lamps go by almost on a level with his head. In the rue Puits-en-Sock, he saw, one after another, all the dimly lit shops which stayed open on Sunday and would stay open until ten o'clock at night, with the shopkeepers eating behind a curtain or behind the glass panes of a back room, and goods of all colours in the windows. And he saw the tram which suddenly emerged from the shadows of the place de Bavière.

'Désiré, mind the tram!'

The Mamelin hat-shop had kept a gas-jet burning as if somebody was going to come and buy a hat at that late hour.

'Father!'

Roger had to shout. He was perched too high up. Élise was carrying her husband's hat, because the child used to knock it off by clinging with both hands to Désiré's head.

'What are we going to do at home?'

Roger would have liked to stop in the rue Puits-en-Sock. He knew that once they got to the rue Pasteur, the day would be over. They would give him his supper, then he would be put to bed straight away, and for a long time he would hear the murmur of his parents' voices in the kitchen.

'We aren't going home yet, are we?'

'No, darling.'

'Where are we going?'

He asked again:

'Where are we going now?'

'We're going for a walk.'

'Where are we going for a walk?'

And he knew that it wasn't true, since they were turning into the dark rue Jean-d'Outremeuse which led to the absolute calm of the rue Pasteur.

Chapter Twelve

There was nobody in the rue Pasteur but Monsieur Lorisse, the gentleman from next door, who had just been gently pushed outside after his muffler had been tied round his neck, and who was being watched from the loggia. He was standing motionless on the kerb, his hands behind his back, with a plaited leather whip in the right one; he was looking vaguely at his dog, a Pyrenean sheep-dog with long fawn and white hair which, with its stiff hindquarters, looked as impotent as its master. The dog ran along for three yards, sniffing the ground, picked its cobblestone, and lifted its leg or squatted down, but it did nothing and went off to start again a little farther on, while Monsieur Lorisse too covered three yards and took up his former attitude, so that the two of them looked like those fretwork toys you see in the middle of sheep-pens.

From the loggia, Madame Lorisse and her daughter – who was forty years old and a very gentle soul – watched him. They were people of independent means. Monsieur Lorisse might go as far as Madame Pain's, or even as far as the place du Congrès, but he would not turn the corner, for he knew that that was forbidden.

'What an idea, Désiré, to call their dog Lorisse like themselves!'

For the dog was called Lorisse like its masters and that shocked everybody, even though it was the handsomest dog in the district.

If he had been down in the street, what would have excited Roger would have been the battle which had already begun, the battle between the shadows and the sunshine which was as mysterious as the thing which went past the kitchen window in the sky.

This battle took place in the neighbouring streets. He had never noticed it in the town, in the rue Léopold, for instance, or in the place Saint-Lambert, when they went on Thursday to say hullo to the ladies at L'Innovation.

In the rue Pasteur, it was fought minute by minute; the deserted street was always divided into two camps by a clearly defined line which advanced or retreated and which sometimes, at half past eleven, when the boys came out of the Friars' school, left only a narrow corridor of shade running along the houses.

Roger, sitting on his chair, was not paying any attention, for the moment, to what was happening in the street. Consequently nothing was happening there. The kitchen window was shut but the bedroom window was open, so that it was the air from the street which was puffing the curtains out like balloons. They were yellow. Everything was yellow at that hour of the day, because of the sun: a yellow of a delicate pinkish hue. There was nothing bluish except the kitchen window-panes; it was tomorrow, Saturday, that the kitchen was cleaned, and today the window-panes were dirty.

'What do you want me to do, Désiré? Should I ask her not to come again?'

Élise had asked that question again that morning. It was Friday. It was Madame Smet's day. Every week since Roger had been born she had spent every Friday at the Mamelins'. She sat all day by the fire without moving. In the evening, when L'Innovation closed, Valérie came and joined her, and Désiré took the opportunity, after dinner, to go and play whist at Velden's. So that Friday was to some extent his day too.

What they had not foreseen was that there would be the Universal Exhibition, that Élise would take a season ticket, that the summer would be glorious and that it would be a crime to keep a child indoors all day long.

'You go out with the boy, my dear. Don't bother about me. With my old legs . . .'

Élise sighed:

'I assure you, Désiré, that if she wanted to, she could. But she doesn't want to walk. It's a fad of hers. She'd go a quarter of an hour out of her way just to catch a tram.'

They had been pleased to have Valérie's mother when Élise had been alone, in bed, with the baby to look after.

Élise listened for the sound of the trams stopping in the place du Congrès and footsteps in the rue Pasteur, but all she could hear were the two or three measured steps Monsieur Lorisse took behind his big dog, which needed half the morning to relieve itself.

Then there was the matter of the sweets! Élise thought about it while she was shaking up the mattresses of the beds.

'Why don't you go on playing, Roger?'

'I *am* playing.'

He wasn't playing. He was gazing at the wonderful mist of fine golden dust which was coming from the bedroom and which was as it were absorbed slowly, irresistibly by the damp air of the street. When his mother beat the mattresses, it was as if there were thousands of little animals spinning around, coming together and parting again, while there were some feathers which stayed for a long time suspended in space. Just now, there was also the circle on the ceiling, another sort of animal, a luminous, impalpable animal, which trembled in one corner of the ceiling and suddenly rushed across to the other wall when somebody touched the window, for it was just a reflection of the sun.

Because it was the day for Madame Smet and Valérie, there were more saucepans than usual on the stove. Élise had not yet had time to do her hair or put her shoes on. She was busy polishing the washstand with the white marble top, and the pink china jug and basin which together looked like a big flower and were never used for fear they might be broken.

Ting-a-ling ...

One ring. It was for downstairs.

Ting-a-ling ... Ting-a-ling ...

Two rings. Élise rushed to the window and leaned out, bending double.

'Wait a moment, Léopold, I'll throw you the key.'

That key which could never be found when anybody came!

'Where did I put the key, Roger? I bet you've been playing with it again. Ah! Here it is.'

She wrapped it in a napkin which she threw out of the window.

'Mind out, Léopold.'

And there followed a curious sound, a sound which was well known in the rue Pasteur, at once soft and hard.

What had Léopold come for? He had never dropped in on Élise on a Friday before. He didn't know that it was Madame

Smet's day. His heavy footsteps on the stairs. She hoped that he wouldn't be too peculiar, that he wouldn't smell of gin.

'Come in, Léopold.'

Ting-a-ling . . . Ting-a-ling . . . Ting-a-ling . . .

She bent over the window-sill again like a puppet in a Punch-and-Judy show.

'I'm coming, Madame Smet.'

'Are you expecting somebody?' Léopold asked suspiciously.

'No, of course not.'

And as if the whole world knew Valérie's old mother with her waxy face, she added with a smile:

'It's just Madame Smet. Sit down. What have you got there?'

He had an untidily wrapped parcel under his arm, but she had to leave him to go downstairs. He could hear her in the corridor saying:

'Go up slowly, Madame Smet. Dear God! More sweets! You really shouldn't!'

Those sweets! Those horrible sweets covered with pink sugar flowers which Madame Smet bought every Friday, heaven knows where, which had probably been out on display and which couldn't possibly be given to Roger. Élise was obliged to glare warningly at him as soon as the bag was put on the table.

'Don't give him any now, Madame Smet. He's just had his breakfast. Sit down. Do you know my brother Léopold?'

Léopold wanted to go. He didn't like this and looked as if he thought it had been deliberately arranged.

'Sit down, please, Léopold. This is Valérie's mother. You know, Valérie. She was so good to me, they both were, when I had Roger.'

Roger looked at her. Élise opened the parcel.

'Did you paint that, Léopold?'

She talked and talked, trying to put them both at their ease, so as to prevent them from getting the impression that they were in the way. She did everything at once, poking the fire, grinding Léopold's coffee, putting up her hair which was falling down, and feeling about with one foot for her shoes which had slipped underneath the bed.

Now she brandished the picture Léopold had brought her. She knew perfectly well why he had come, why he had felt the need to bring something, and why he was staying on in spite of everything, he who was so unsociable, as if he were waiting for absolution.

The day before, because of Madame Smet's day, Élise had done part of her shopping in the dark while Désiré looked after the child. She had gone to the nearest shop, the pork butcher's in the rue de la Province where she never went as a rule, and had come upon Léopold unexpectedly. She had nearly stopped in her tracks but had had the presence of mind to go on, to pretend not to recognize him, although she could have wept for shame. Her brother was standing against the wall of a house, the boarding-house which took anybody in, even bad women. Then the window of the basement kitchen opened a little way, a pool of light invaded the pavement, and Eugénie passed a packet to her husband.

Although Élise had hurried on, Léopold was bound to have recognized her. Now he had brought her a picture.

'I thought you might like it, my girl.'

'It's our parents' house, isn't it, Léopold?'

'It's the *Waterringen*, yes.'

'Look, Madame Smet. This is the house my parents were living in when Léopold was born. How long did you live there, Léopold?'

'Till I was fourteen.'

'You were telling me the other day that Mother, who was expecting Félicie, couldn't manage to get into the carriage.'

Her present was a real canvas stretched on a frame. Léopold had done the picture conscientiously, like a house-painter, spreading the paint carefully, without any shadows or light or perspective, so that the house looked as if it were perched on a big piece of grass and the canal on the right were on the point of collapsing on to it.

'Excuse me for doing my hair in front of you, Léopold. Madame Smet, make yourself comfortable. Tell us what Father did, Léopold.'

'He was a *dijkmeester*.'

'If you don't explain, how do you expect people to understand? That means a dike-keeper, Madame Smet. It was his job to flood the fields or to dry them out. That's right, isn't it, Léopold? Just imagine, the boats went past higher up than the house. You explain, Léopold. You know all that better than I do.'

She went from one room to the other. She was looking for pins. She was always short of hairpins and she was in the habit of holding them between her lips while she did her hair.

'Tell us how you used to go to school.'

'It was a long way, an hour's walk away. In winter, we used to go on skates with Hubert.'

Élise had never seen the *Waterringen*, but when Léopold came to see her, she liked him to talk to her about it, and she was even happier, now that she could see from the picture what it had been like. She would have liked Madame Smet to admire it too, but good Madame Smet shook her head at everything she was told.

'And the time the doctor had to be sent for . . .'

'I went on a sledge with Father.'

'A sledge pulled by a horse, Madame Smet. Go on, Léopold . . .'

Ting-a-ling . . . Ting-a-ling . . .

Straight away, Léopold stood up.

'Don't move. I assure you I'm not expecting anybody. You know perfectly well that nobody ever comes to see us.'

Meanwhile Monsieur Lorisse and his dog, walking three yards at a time, had got as far as the place du Congrès, where they had to turn round and from which point they could vaguely see the two women in their loggia.

'I can't see who it is . . .'

She had leaned out of the window. She had not recognized the pearl-grey hat or the mastic overcoat. She coughed. The visitor raised his head and she exclaimed in unfeigned surprise:

'Dear God, it's Guillaume! But it can't be!'

Then, all of a sudden, she was bustling about, juggling with things as if she had a dozen hands.

'Stay, Léopold, do. It's Guillaume. Dear God!'

All the pins she had dropped were promptly returned to her bent head of hair. Somehow or other she laced up her shoes while looking round the flat, seeing tiny things lying about which nobody else would have noticed.

'Stay here! Just a minute, Madame Smet . . .'

It was Guillaume, Désiré's eldest brother, who had arrived

two hours before at the Guillemins station, without any warning, because he wanted to see the Exhibition, and because he had recently bought a mastic overcoat which had just been put on the market.

Coming out of the station, Guillaume could have gone to say hullo to Désiré in his office which was almost opposite. But he never did things like other people. He always had to spring a surprise. And he did not dare to go to the rue Puits-en-Sock, because of the mastic overcoat on which, as a sign of mourning, he had merely pinned an armlet.

He had decided on Élise. To while away the time, seeing that it was too early, he had gone into a barber's and he had stayed there half an hour being smartened up, powdered and perfumed. That was Guillaume all over. Downstairs, Élise could be heard saying:

'Well, I never expected . . . Isn't your wife with you? No, of course, she's got to mind the shop.'

Guillaume owned a shop in Brussels, in the rue Neuve, right in the centre of the city, a narrow shop selling umbrellas and walking-sticks.

'Go on upstairs. Won't Désiré be surprised! You didn't drop in to see him?'

Just as they were about to come in, they found Léopold already in the doorway, his back bent, his beard black, more bear-like than ever with his eyes which never smiled at anybody and still less at this peculiar character who smelled of the barber's shop and whose moustache was turned up in two sharp points.

Élise, for her part, smiled at everybody.

'I don't think you know my brother Léopold? This is Guillaume, Désiré's eldest brother. Guillaume has a business in Brussels.'

'Good-bye, my girl.'

'Léopold, stay a bit longer, just a little bit longer.'

Léopold did not listen and plunged down the staircase muttering to himself.

It had been the eldest members of the two families who had met for a moment in the rue Pasteur kitchen, the eldest of the Peters and the eldest of the Mamelins. Élise leant over the banisters.

'Thank you for the picture, Léopold. I like it a lot, you know! Come back to see me soon.'

She knew that he was not listening, that he had come along looking forward to the surprise he was going to give her and the long time they would spend quietly talking about the house at Neeroeteren. Élise had never seen the picture before but she had often heard about it for he had already refused to give it to Louisa, who would so much have liked to have it, to Marthe, and even to Schroefs, who would not have been averse to showing people his in-laws' house.

She would have liked to accompany her brother to the street door, but she did not dare to leave Guillaume alone with the old woman whom he did not know and whom he greeted with solemn politeness.

'Madame Smet, Guillaume . . . The mother of Valérie, my best friend, who helped us so much when I had Roger . . .'

'My respects, Madame.'

Just like the theatre! Then, straight away, without realizing that every syllable counted, that his words were being registered for ever, that today he was playing a well-nigh historic part, he went on:

'Now let's see my little nephew!'

He had no children and seized upon this one like a toy. The idea had occurred to him, at the station, to give Désiré's son a present he would never forget.

He obviously did not realize that Roger, sitting on his folding chair, was seeing him from below, as he so often saw his father. Above all, he could not imagine that, freshly shaven, with his moustache waxed and pointed and his cheeks powdered, smelling of lavender and brilliantine, he appeared today as a sort of demon Désiré, a Désiré played by a ham-actor who had turned up the points of his moustache too far, who had put too much bright gold, too much mocking gaiety in the brown pupils of his eyes.

Yet that was how it was. Roger was frightened and attracted at the same time. This was his father with a different accent, with more extravagant gestures, a louder voice, an extraordinary overcoat and an amazing stick with a gold knob, his father with a practically bald pate and more clearly defined features.

Élise got into a panic, opened the sideboard, and hid

something under the shawl which she had just thrown round her shoulders.

'Just a second, Guillaume. You won't mind if I slip out for a second?'

This uncle from Brussels, the one nobody ever saw, even in the rue Puits-en-Sock, because he had married a divorced woman and they had not had a church wedding, this was Guillaume, who appeared from nowhere just like the people you saw at the Exhibition coming down in a balloon, who landed in the rue Pasteur, fresh and dapper, with light-coloured spats over his patent-leather shoes.

'Take your coat off. I'll be back in a moment.'

'Yes, of course. But you aren't going out for my sake, I hope.'

He was lying. He was pleased with life. He had seen the bottle which she had taken out of the sideboard and which she was going off with under her shawl.

'You'll watch the fire, won't you, Madame Smet?'

She ran out, leaving the door ajar, because she had left her key upstairs, and rushed round to Dupeux's in the place du Congrès.

'Have you got some bitter, Monsieur Dupeux? The best, you know. It's for my husband's brother who's just arrived from Brussels.'

She explained everything, she always had to explain, as if she were in the wrong.

'Fill the bottle. No, wait a minute, just half, like that, that's enough. We never drink, you know.'

She returned out of breath, triumphant.

'Guillaume, you'll have a glass of bitter, won't you?'

'On one condition, and that is that you'll entrust your son to me till this afternoon. All right?'

He was Mephistophelian.

'We've got great plans, the two of us, haven't we, sonny? Ssh! Don't look at your mother. Don't be afraid of your mother. Have we got great plans or haven't we?'

Overawed, the child stammered:

'Yes.'

Élise turned to Madame Smet to appeal for her help, but Guillaume said airily, as if he had known her all his life:

'Come now, my dear Madame Smet, don't let me down, don't

take any notice of my sister-in-law's winks. It's all agreed, then!
Good health! And off I go with Roger. Roger's mine, let's say
till four o'clock.'

'Listen, Guillaume . . .'

'It's agreed, isn't it? Have I or haven't I come from Brussels
just to see my nephew?'

'Of course, Guillaume. Only let me change him at least.'

And she who had never entrusted her son to anybody, except
for a few minutes to Madame Pain, now found herself obliged
to give in, because Guillaume insisted and because Madame
Smet was there.

What would Désiré say? If only Léopold had stayed! She
tried to create a diversion.

'Look, Guillaume: it's my parents' house at Neeroeteren.
My father was a dike-keeper. The barges used to go past on a
level with the roof of the house. I never saw it, but all my
brothers and sisters were born there, except Félicie.'

He stroked his moustache, looking politely, without listening. It was all one to him.

'Go and piddle, Roger. You're going for a walk with your
Uncle Guillaume. You'll be nice, won't you? You'll be good?'

Everything was going wrong. Nothing, today, was happening as usual. Weeks, months went by without seeing a living
soul and then, all of a sudden, things happened in a rush.

She watched Roger go off with his uncle.

'You know, Madame Smet, he isn't used to children. I can
tell that he's got some bee in his bonnet. He is going to buy
something for Roger. I only hope it's something useful! With
Guillaume, you can never tell.'

The kitchen seemed so empty without Roger. If Madame
Smet had not been there, Élise, without saying anything, would
have followed her son at a distance.

They walked along in the dazzling sunshine and Guillaume
bent down slightly, without managing to adjust his pace to the
child's, talking to him as he would to an adult.

'You see, if your mother had come with us, she wouldn't
have let me do what I wanted. I know her. She's still dressing
you like a girl.'

He was ignorant of the rites, for instance, that you had to stop
in front of the human dummies in black frockcoats who

mounted guard outside the dress-shops in the rue Léopold and handed out prospectuses to children. He did not know that these prospectuses were puzzles, that you had to find the Bulgarian or the huntsman in a jumble of lines. He wondered why his nephew insisted on walking over the grating outside Hosay's where you could breathe in the hot chocolate air from the basement.

'Are you tired?'

'No.'

'You'd like us to take the tram?'

'No.'

He went into L'Innovation as if it were an ordinary shop, into L'Innovation where all the shopgirls knew Roger and where on Thursdays – yesterday, for instance – they passed him round like a doll as soon as Monsieur Wilhem's back was turned. He did not know Valérie. He went past her counter without stopping, and Valérie got into a panic and trotted over to another counter.

'It must be Désiré's brother.'

'What can Élise be doing to let him take the child?'

Guillaume was at home everywhere. Here he was, picking Roger up and standing him on a counter.

'Isn't your mother with you, Roger?'

'No, Mademoiselle. Today Roger is mine for the whole day. Now let's see what you can show me.'

He was in a holiday mood. He was the uncle who had arrived miraculously from Brussels and who was going to transform a boy's life completely.

'No blue, Mademoiselle. Find me something gayer.'

Valérie did not dare to approach. The assistant regretfully produced a red jersey suit which delighted Guillaume.

'Put it on him, will you?'

The assistants made signs to each other from one counter to the next. They all knew that Roger was dedicated to the Virgin, and imagined Élise's face when she saw her son come home in that gaudy red suit.

'Perfect! Leave it on him. Put his dress on one side. His mother will come and pick it up one of these days. How much?'

He was Guillaume! And with Guillaume, everything was

186

different. The boy followed him, dumbfounded, still a little frightened.

'Now let's see. What would you like to do now?'

Roger's gaze alighted on an ice-cream vendor's yellow cart. 'An ice-cream!'

He would never have dared to say that to his mother. Guillaume leaned his elbows on the little cart and spoke familiarly to the vendor, as he spoke to everybody.

'Give this little nipper an ice. A strawberry ice, Roger?'

'Yes.'

Then he plunged into the town crowds with the child, who let himself be pulled along while he sucked his cornet crowned with pink cream. If only Élise had seen him!

This was all so different from the quiet visits to L'Innovation the other days, from the silent walk between the counters, the discreet exchange of signals, the long halts in front of a piece of madapollam or merino, the words which were whispered with an eye on Monsieur Wilhem's silhouette or the Inspector's frockcoat!

Guillaume went along streets where Roger had never been. In the place Verte, they crossed a sea of sweet-smelling flowers where the flower sellers sat behind their bouquets like the women in the market behind their baskets of fruit or vegetables.

'What if we went and had dinner at the Exhibition? Would you like to go and have dinner at the Exhibition?'

They took the tram. With Élise, they took the tram only when it was absolutely necessary. The ice was still lasting. There was a bit of it left when they got off the tram outside the Exhibition gates and Guillaume paid for them to go in; he did not even know that children did not pay and bought two tickets, afterwards making straight for the restaurant section.

Usually they avoided this section where, in brightly painted houses, you could see people eating huge Brussels waffles with the holes filled with whipped cream. They went straight across to the free stands, including those where samples were given, the chocolate stand, for instance, with its machines, its huge shining wheel, the belt slipping along without a sound, and the Negro dressed as if he had come out of the Arabian Nights who distributed the drops of chocolate which had fallen from the machine.

Guillaume did not know that Élise forbade her son to eat these samples.

'It's dirty!' she would tell him, wiping the palms of his hands with her handkerchief.

He did not know that when the child was thirsty and stopped in front of the stalls on which rows of coloured bottles of soda-water were lined up, you had to pull him away and say:

'You'll have a drink when we get back home.'

Guillaume did not know either where you had to go to get the sumptuous prospectuses of which Roger already had quite a collection, the coloured pictures, the series of wild animals given by Remy starch, and above all the booklet advertising Swedish matches, with its thin, silky paper on which you could see matches of all colours, green ones, red ones, and even some with golden heads.

'What does you mother give you to eat?'

'I don't know.'

'Tell me, waiter . . .'

For they were sitting under an arbour, with a waiter in a white apron beside them, like the people they walked past so quickly the other days before going to have a snack on a bench.

'What are you going to give this little fellow?'

'You could always start with a soup. Then something light, a fried sole for instance?'

'A fried sole, then.'

He drank some wine. His eyes laughed like Désiré's. They were the same dark brown, but they did not have the same gentleness, or rather there was in their gay flame a more vulgar note which was sometimes rather aggressive.

'Are you happy? Are you enjoying yourself?'

'Yes.'

A man went past with some paper windmills fastened to coloured sticks.

'Do you want a windmill?'

'Yes.'

The child was impressed. A grown-up's napkin had been tied round his neck. Nobody had seen to it that he piddled, and he had done so in his red jersey trousers which were scratching him between the legs.

It was all too much for him. He could not stand it any longer.

His cheeks were burning. He was hard put to it not to burst out sobbing.

'Do you want to go on the water-slide?'

He pulled at the hand which was dragging him along.

'No!...No!...'

He was frightened. For hours on end, the other days, they had watched people in boats coming down the slope of the water-slide, but the idea of going on it himself had never occurred to him.

'You aren't tired, are you?'

'Yes...No...'

He would have liked it all to last a long time and yet he could feel a mounting anguish in his chest. When he looked at his Uncle Guillaume, he thought he would recognize his father, but it was such a different father that he was afraid of him and became sad.

'What do you want us to do now?'

With his mouth full and his hands full, he did not reply. The jersey was chafing his thighs which were probably all red, especially with the piddle.

'What if we went to say hullo to your papa, who's still in his office?'

The child clutched at this straw, even though the word papa, which was never uttered in the rue Pasteur, shocked him.

'Yes.'

Was his father waiting outside, at the corner of the Pont du Commerce, to the left of the entrance, as on the other evenings when they came out of the Exhibition? For Désiré had not gone to the expense of buying a permanent ticket. When he left his office, he came to wait for Élise and the child, and, since Roger was always tired by that time, he carried him home on his shoulders.

'Put him down, Désiré! He's too big now.'

'I don't want to be put down.'

Today everything was different. Time had disappeared. The Exhibition was all topsy-turvy. Nothing was in its place. You could not be certain of anything any more. He felt lost in a world which no longer had any meaning and in which people bustled about in all directions.

'Wait a moment. We'll take a carriage.'

He did not understand. Carriages were for taking people to hospital. He clung to his uncle's hand.

'No. I don't want to.'

But Guillaume had already signalled to an open cab.

'You really don't want to get in?'

'No.'

'Why not?'

'I don't want to. I want Mother.'

There was only the Pont du Commerce to cross, the square with the ducks where the flags fluttered in the sunshine. Then they were already in the rue des Guillemins. They turned the corner of the rue Sohet. A triumphant smile appeared on Guillaume's lips as he pushed open the door of the insurance office.

The child, for his part, saw only a partition with windows in it which he could not reach.

'Well, I never! Guillaume! What are you doing here in Liège?'

And Guillaume mischievously lifted Roger up in his arms and placed him on the sill of the little window.

The boy discovered a world he did not know, a stove, some furniture, a piece of bread and butter on an unfolded napkin, a bowl full of coffee, and his father, in shirtsleeves, who looked quite at home here although they had surprised him in a strange setting.

It was funny: Désiré was almost embarrassed by his son's inspection of this scene, but he smiled straight away and went to open the communicating door.

'Come in, Guillaume. Come in, son. I suppose it's you. Guillaume, who bought him that suit?'

What was the use of pressing the point? Élise would tell him herself!

'Sit down, Roger. You see, this is your father's office. And how's your wife, Guillaume? Are you here for a few days? You've had your dinner, I suppose?'

He picked up his bread and butter, next to the typewriter, while the child stared hard, as if he were making a memorable discovery, at his father eating somewhere else than at home, in his shirt-sleeves, just as he was in the evening in the rue Pasteur flat.

Chapter Thirteen

'Do you think the colour will come out, Valérie?'

Élise took out of the hot, soapy bath a blood-red, shapeless mass which was Roger's first suit. Were there any pink streaks in the bluey water? That was the vital question.

'I assure you it won't, Élise. You'll see, *they*'ll take it back all right.'

Élise was in a state of nerves. She couldn't find any other word for it. She felt just as she did when she had cried a lot and yet she had not cried at all today: her head and legs were empty, and there was a sort of hurried ticking going on all over her body, as if there were a machine driving her along, wanting to go faster than her.

Madame Smet was the same at nine o'clock in the evening as at ten o'clock in the morning, always the visitor, with her mittens on her freckled hands, wagging her head in approval of whatever was said to her, and sitting erect on her upright chair, for she had never agreed to sit in an armchair.

Valérie's fingers were fluttering over a piece of crochet-work. It was the only kind of work she could do. Her fingers were so delicate, so diaphanous, her hands so frail, that she would sprain her wrist if she had to bring up a bucket of water.

Wasn't it paradoxical that she should have become Élise's best friend? Valérie had no bones, no nerves. When you looked at her hand in front of the lamp, you could not see any bones in it, or hardly any. And her feet were so tiny that she had to buy her shoes in the little girls' department.

She did not weigh heavily on the earth. She was like a strange little princess who was neither pretty nor a princess, an unsubstantial creature with a plain face, a big head, and the hair of a Chinese doll, who, apart from her silks and laces, was unfit for everything, even for living, and there was no doubt at all that she and her mother would have allowed themselves to starve if they had not had Marie, the elder daughter, the dressmaker, to do their housework for them before going out to work.

Élise was fond of Valérie, but it made her suffer all the same to see a woman as young as that sitting impassively beside a tub full of dirty crockery. In her place, she would have stood up long ago and said:

'Give me a dishcloth, Élise.'

This evening, Élise kept asking anxiously:

'Do you really think they'll take it back?'

The door was half-open. Roger was asleep. It was nine o'clock. As happened every Friday, Désiré had gone to play whist at the Veldens'.

He was happy over there. He was the most skilful person there, just as in the rue Puits-en-Sock he was the most intelligent. He was also the gayest. He joked and smiled all round with a smile which was almost condescending.

Yet the Velden brothers, the coppersmiths, were one of the oldest families in Outremeuse and they had a score of workers whom the siren – you could hear it from the rue Pasteur – called back to work at one o'clock. There was also Émile Grisard, who was a government architect and whose brother was a traveller for a big champagne firm. And there was Monsieur Reculé, a chief clerk on North Belgian Railways, who travelled first class free of charge.

They needed Désiré so badly, people like them, that if he was a quarter of an hour late, they came ringing the bell in the rue Pasteur!

'You'll see, Élise, when it's dry and ironed, it won't show any more.'

They made up a tremendous fire. The suit started drying, the irons warmed up, red clinkers rained down into the ashtray inside the stove and all this sent Madame Smet to sleep. She dozed off, giving a start every time the whispering grew a little louder.

*

When he had come home at two o'clock, Désiré had not said anything. Élise could not forgive him for it. He had arrived delighted with his meeting with his brother, full of that good humour which she so detested in the Mamelins.

She had not noticed anything at first. He had teased Madame Smet, as usual, and had sat down to table with a merry appetite.

'You haven't seen Guillaume, have you?'

'He dropped into the office just now with Roger.'

'Where are they?'

'We came back together on the No. 4 tram.'

She could see them, she could swear she could see them, on the platform of the tram which went right round the town; they had not gone inside so as to be able to smoke, and also because it was gayer outside; Roger had remained standing between their legs while they told their stories.

'Where's Roger?'

'Guillaume left me and got off the tram in the place du Congrès. He wanted to show our son to an aunt of his wife's who lives in Bressoux or Jupille.'

Thoughtlessness! There was no other word for it!

'What were you thinking of, Désiré?'

'But Guillaume is perfectly capable of looking after a child.'

She had not cried, on account of Madame Smet. Perhaps it was because she had not cried once all day that she was in such a state of nerves.

Now it all came back to her, all that had been done to her, all that she had suffered, all that she sometimes brooded over for hours on end while looking after the child in the place du Congrès, when Madame Pain was not there.

Désiré had had his dinner. He had drunk his coffee, had wiped his moustache with an air of satisfaction, had picked up his hat and stick. He had not told her everything. She had been a long way from suspecting that at that moment he had already seen the red suit and that, like a coward, so as to enjoy his dinner in peace, he had said nothing about it.

Worse still, she remembered murmuring:

'I wonder what surprise he's going to spring on us.'

And with a vague gesture he had replied:

'With Guillaume, you've got to be ready for anything . . .'

He had known all the time! And he had gone off, as stiff as a ramrod, his conscience at peace. And Élise had been left alone with Madame Smet, with whom you always kept wondering what to say and whether she was listening.

Three o'clock . . . Four o'clock . . . Guillaume had promised to bring the child home at four o'clock and the hands of the alarm-clock on the mantelpiece already stood at twenty past.

'Listen, Madame Smet . . .'

She apologized, begged the old lady to forgive her. She did not know this relative of her sister-in-law's, a person who was said to live at Bressoux, on the other side of the Dérivation, right out in the suburbs and even outside the town.

'All I'm asking of you is a quarter of an hour. It's because of Roger . . .'

She did not know where to go looking for him. For quite a while she stood hesitating in the middle of the place du Congrès, looking at all the streets leading off the square and trembling at the approach of every tram.

Finally, without any valid excuse, she dashed off in the direction of the rue Puits-en-Sock. Generally speaking, she did not go there without a hat, just wearing a shawl. She felt embarrassed. It always made her feel queasy to breathe in that smell of saltpetre, in the whitewashed passage in which a creaking gate had been installed to stop the children from rushing out under the wheels of a tram.

She had never been able to breathe freely in that house. Everything in it shocked her, especially the stench in the yard, that smell of poverty, of slops, which you found only in certain lower-class districts. Even when she and her mother had been at their poorest, they would never have agreed to live in the midst of smells like that.

She knew that she had already been seen through the fake stained-glass windows. She knocked. She went in.

'Good evening, Cécile.'

And once again it was a mute hostility which she encountered, which struck her as being aimed personally against her, that atmosphere in the kitchen which had remained the same for all that Madame Mamelin was dead and Cécile had taken her place. To think that Désiré had lived until the age of twenty-four in that house!

The lamp was not lit until the last possible moment. All the objects in the kitchen were in the same places, where they had always been, and the least among them had gradually acquired a physiognomy like a human being, the coffee-mill for instance, the wooden chicory-pot, the matchbox, the pendulum of the clock, everything, even the warmth of the room which was not the same as anywhere else.

And Cécile! It was ironing day. As far back as anybody could remember, Friday had always been ironing day in the rue Puits-en-Sock, and Cécile was duly ironing, with her mother's heavy laundry irons in which embers were burned; the brackets were in their usual place on the blanket on which the burnt patches served as guide marks.

You felt that you were in the way, that you were disturbing an eternal harmony. Cécile had been ironing all day and would go on ironing like that until the end of time without giving any sign of surprise or impatience if, by some miracle, Friday were to last forever.

Élise had not seen Old Papa when she had come in. It was too dark and she gave a start as she caught sight of that stone statue in its armchair.

'It's only me, Old Papa.'

'I know, my girl.'

Through the windows, on the other side of the yard, Chrétien Mamelin could be seen in his workshop slowly and solemnly steaming a hat, and that ill-lit picture too had a dreadfully eternal appearance.

'I've come for my chip-dish.'

The chip-dish which they sometimes left there on Sunday on the way into town and picked up on the way back, thus avoiding the necessity of having to go and fetch it from the rue Pasteur. This was an excuse she had thought up on her arrival, because, seeing that Guillaume was not here, she could not mention him. She was very tactful.

'There it is, Élise. Next to the scales. The cloth is inside.'

Cécile was expecting a baby, but this was not noticeable, nothing was noticeable in her, not even her youthfulness, so completely had she adopted all her mother's gestures and attitudes, so serenely did she reign over that kitchen of the Mamelins in which no child, even after becoming a husband and father, would have dared to alter the position of a single tiny object.

When Élise returned to the rue Pasteur the notice had disappeared from the house in the rue Jean-d'Outremeuse, that house which she had been looking at enviously for such a long time.

TO LET.

It was too soon, she knew that. And the house was rather big. You would have to take in at least five lodgers, and for five lodgers it was necessary to have a maid, who ate all the profits.

Dear God! Where could Guillaume have gone with Roger?

She went as far as the Pont de Bressoux, running like a lunatic, and came home to find them quietly installed in the kitchen.

'Who opened the door to you, Guillaume?'

'A lady with her hair dyed like a hairdresser's sign.'

The landlady.

For Madame Smet would never have gone downstairs, even if there had been a fire in the street.

'Come here, little Roger.'

She would have given a great deal to be able to cry as much as she liked, for it was a feeling of utter disaster which took hold of her at the sight of her son, who looked at her with new eyes, who had just lived through a whole day of which she knew nothing, who had been stuffed with sensations, treats and memories, and who to cap all had been dressed from head to foot in red.

Yet her reaction expressed itself in the form of stammered thanks.

'Dear God, Guillaume, you've been far too extravagant. You shouldn't have done it! It's too good of you, Guillaume. Such an expensive suit!'

He could have bought him anything else, even a useless toy! But that red suit! The trousers were already all wet!

'Thank you, Guillaume. You'll have a glass, won't you? Yes, you will! There's some left, and we never drink. Now that you're in Liège for once . . .'

She ached all over, from sheer nerves.

'Good-bye, Guillaume. A pleasant journey home. Tell your wife . . .'

What had he to tell his wife, whom she had glimpsed only once, at her mother-in-law's funeral?

Not a single moment of relaxation, not a single second of solitude. Madame Smet was there, like an expensive doll which could only wag its head with an eternal smile.

Somebody whistled out in the street.

'It's Désiré, Madame Smet. I have to throw the key down to

him, out of the window. Just imagine, we've only one key.'

For Désiré whistled when he came home at night. Then there was Valérie's discreet ring at the door, and the whispering of the two friends on the stairs.

'Later on, when he's gone . . .'

'Oh, poor Élise, when I saw them trying that red thing on him . . . All of us . . . Even up on the third floor of the shop . . . We all thought of you, you know!'

*

Madame Smet was dozing, giving a start now and then at the distant noise of a tram, and Valérie was doing some crochet-work with her ethereal fingers, a piece of delicate lace-work destined to serve no particular purpose. Élise detested her that evening, for her nimble fingers fluttering in the yellow rays of the lamp, for her frail limbs, for her carefree life with her mother and her sister, for letting Marie make her bed and empty her slops. She detested Cécile too, who had not said anything to her, who had gone on quietly ironing in her kitchen, and she detested Madame Pain whose husband earned good money.

Rancour had entered into her and remained there like a ball inside her chest.

'If you only knew, Valérie, how my back hurts in the evening! It's my organs. I have to go every week to see the doctor who's fitted me with a special appliance.'

At the word 'organs', Valérie, who had poor health but had never been ill, and for whom the stomach was a mystery she did not want to understand, Valérie went pale.

And yet, this particular evening, Élise had neither stomach-ache nor backache. She kept talking about it and complaining to keep her fever up. Since the disappearance of the notice, she had had a vague feeling that all the day's little misfortunes had to be directed to a particular end.

She ironed the red trousers and examined them under the lamp.

'You know, Valérie, the house in the rue Jean-d'Outremeuse has been let . . .'

Valérie knew all about this plot which dated back two years, to the day when Élise had won her first victory by settling in the rue Pasteur.

Since then, without respite, as tireless as an insect driven by an age-old instinct, she had kept on making plans, saving money, carefully putting aside anything which could immediately or remotely serve her purpose.

'You know, I've already got seven hundred francs in the Savings Bank. Désiré doesn't know anything about it. It's for the furniture, you understand.'

A sou here, a franc there, sometimes a big coin. She hid them for a while in the soup-tureen with the pink flowers on it. When she went to Coronmeuse, she used to say to her sister Louisa:

'What can you expect? He's a man who would spend the whole of his life on the bare necessities.'

She complained. It all helped. And today when she was really unhappy, without meaning to be, when she had been forced to hold back her tears all day, she was going to make the most of it.

'You know those little rolls that cost three centimes each? The baker who supplies the boarding-house in the rue de la Province has told me that with just a bit of butter on them they cost the students ten centimes. And some of them eat four or five at a time. And listen to this: they have to pay fifty centimes for a bucketful of coal which you've only got to carry upstairs and which you buy for thirty centimes in the street!'

How much coming and going these few words represented at the houses where students were lodged, how many innocent questions asked here and there! These students, Russians, Poles, Rumanians and Japanese, who came to study at the University at Liège, she followed them, in the street, with a miser's eye.

'I'd only need three, Valérie, not too rich because they would expect too much, but not too poor either. They'd be so happy with me!'

Was it her fault if that was her fate in life? She had just suffered a big disappointment. Just after four o'clock, in the middle of the place du Congrès, then again at the end of the Pont de Bressoux, she had been the genuinely distressed mother who had lost her child. It was all Désiré's fault. He was Guillaume's brother. At two o'clock, when he had known everything, he had been a coward and kept quiet.

'Men, Valérie! They are so afraid of having their peace disturbed, their little habits changed!'

Désiré, who suspected nothing and who had won at whist – the money went into the kitty – left his friends at the Veldens' door. Élise recognized his footsteps, awoke Madame Smet, Valérie put her hat on, and the two friends kissed each other good night.

Désiré accompanied Valérie and Madame Smet to the tram-stop in the place du Congrès. The three of them stood waiting in the soft shadows until the tram, swaying along the rails, braked in front of them with a tremendous din.

The windows of the tram, this fine night, looked pink. The heads inside no longer looked alive, or rather they seemed to belong to a different life, as if they were in a museum.

Désiré lit a cigarette. Everything was perfectly quiet under a sky studded with stars, the cigarette was good, and he would have been quite capable of sitting down on one of the benches in the square and staying there for a long time gazing at the Milky Way.

He had enjoyed seeing Guillaume again. That faint rectangle of light in the distance was the little café on the corner of the rue Puits-en-Sock where he had learnt to play billiards. Roger had been impressed to see his father in shirtsleeves, just as he was at home, in the rue Sohet office. He had drunk from his cup. He had tapped the keys of his typewriter and they had put some bulky year-book underneath him.

Désiré walked along. His forehead creased a little as he drew nearer home, for he suspected that Élise was annoyed with him about the red suit. And now she was by herself, waiting for him. There was a faint halo of light, coming from the kitchen, in the bedroom window.

He had left the door ajar when he had gone out with Valérie and her mother. He climbed the stairs, frowning as he saw a big patch of light, the kitchen door wide open, and heard the familiar sounds of an iron bucket. He found Élise on her knees, scrubbing the floor.

'What are you doing?'

She had the pale face, the sharp features of her bad days; her chest looked flatter than ever under the apron, and her hair was falling into her eyes.

'I have to do some of tomorrow's work tonight, seeing that I've got to go to L'Innovation.'

He understood. He did not know what to do with himself. She was doing it on purpose!

'Can I give you a hand?'

'It isn't worth it. Go to bed. It only makes me later than ever, having your legs in the way.'

It was just like certain Sunday afternoons, when she was in a state of nerves and they were due to go out, only worse. She would burst into tears any minute now, but he could never foresee the exact moment, nor what would provoke the crisis. If he spoke, what he said would be too much. If he kept quiet...

'Listen, Élise.'

'No! Leave me alone! You can see I'm tired out. It's ten o'clock and I'm only just starting the cleaning. Not to mention the fact that your loud voice is going to wake the child.'

Wake the child! When it was always Désiré who sent him to sleep by playing the drummer-boy!

Who could find his way along the winding paths taken by Élise's mind? Did she even know herself by what route she was going to arrive at what she wanted?

'My back has gone all numb.'

'Let me go and empty the slops at least.'

'You'd only get your suit dirty and then I'd have to clean it!'

She scrubbed away as never before. She put a desperate strength into it, ghastly pale, a striking picture of human energy pushed to the point of paroxysm.

'The doctor told me again last week...'

She started crying. There! Not much. Not sobbing. She was snivelling rather, with something like a quiet gleam of resignation shining through her tears. She was sniffling like a little girl, drying her eyes on a wet corner of her apron with its little blue checks.

'Élise...'

'I know it doesn't matter to you, that you'll never have an affectionate word or a delicate thought for me. Have you ever once called me *darling*? You're a Mamelin, just like Guillaume! You make a good pair of brothers.'

Guillaume... The red suit...

'When I think that the baby was at the point of death, with its bronchitis, and the carnival in the rue Léopold, when I dedicated him to the Virgin! And Guillaume, the old fox, so proud of himself, goes and picks a suit in the brightest red there is! And you, you don't say a thing!'

'Oh, come, Élise . . .'

'Leave me alone. I've got to get on with my work. You, you've finished at six o'clock. It doesn't matter to you that at ten o'clock at night I'm still scrubbing the floor or peeling the vegetables: you go off to play cards at the Veldens'.'

Once a week! He never went out apart from that! And then it was only because Madame Smet and Valérie were at home on Fridays!

'Go to bed!'

Slowly she got to her feet, sat down as if she were at the end of her tether, and leant forward with both arms on the table, sobbing so that he could not see her face, and pushing away the arm which was trying to encircle her shoulders.

'No, Désiré, no! You're too selfish. All you think about is yourself, your peace of mind, your little life, and if anything happened to you tomorrow I'd have to go and work as a servant.'

Why as a servant? Had she been a servant when he had met her?

Try as she might, she could not manage to work herself up to a real crisis, to the kind of crisis in which she writhed about on the bed, clutching the blankets. Perhaps the trouble was that she had waited too long? She had better look at the red suit, then at the room all topsy-turvy around her, the bucket on the floor, half the room running with water . . .

'I'm tired out . . .'

'Well, there's only one thing to do, we'll get a charwoman in.'

'And how can we pay her? We've only got enough for the bare necessities.'

'We'll have her for two hours a day, for the rough work.'

'No, Désiré! Don't bother about me. I was saying just now to Valérie . . .'

That wounded him. What had she been saying to Valérie about their domestic affairs? Did he ever talk about her at the Veldens'?

She picked up the scrubbing-brush and the floorcloth, still snivelling without actually shedding any tears, and now she felt that the time had come, that a little later the atmosphere would have changed.

'If only Roger were at nursery school . . .'

It was so unexpected . . . And so trivial, such a little thing compared with what he had been expecting!

'I know perfectly well that for you, your son is sacred. Yet there are some younger ones than him who go to the sisters' school and Madame Pain herself decided this week . . .'

It was Élise who had persuaded Madame Pain to send Armand to nursery school. How patiently she had plotted and planned!

'We'll talk seriously about it tomorrow. I don't say no.'

'But you don't say yes either! And in the meantime, you're the one who's accustoming him to being carried, without worrying about the fact that when I'm alone with him he refuses to walk. As for Guillaume . . . He struts around with his nephew, dresses him up like a clown . . . They haven't got any children . . . The two of them live only for themselves . . .'

Without saying a word, Désiré had taken off his jacket and removed his cuffs. He picked up a bucket of dirty water and went to empty it into the sink on the landing downstairs. When he came back, the kitchen looked greyer than usual, emptier too, and Élise really tired, really pitiful. He made an effort to smile.

'All right then, it's agreed, we'll send Roger to school.'

She managed not to look triumphant, to stay weary and touching, and she soaked her floorcloth in the clean water.

'I'll go and see Sister Adonie tomorrow,' she said simply.

There was still a feeling of drying tears, of a scene which had nearly become unpleasant. The boy was tossing about in his bed. And meanwhile Valérie and her mother had arrived at their flat where Marie Smet was waiting for them, working at her sewing machine.

When Roger was going to school, Élise would be able to raise the question of lodgers again and Désiré would no longer reply:

'But what about the boy? How can you look after lodgers and the boy at the same time?'

As for her backache and stomach-ache, she would take care

of all that. That was her affair. She would get better, she would be as strong as anybody else.

Désiré suspected nothing, and when he went to bed, an hour later, after lowering the lamp and tracing a cross on his sleeping son's forehead, he did not know that the household in the rue Pasteur had already ceased to exist, that their little home was dead, that after having left the rue Puits-en-Sock for the rue des Carmes and the quai de Coronmeuse, he was going to lose that peace by which he set such store, the cosy hours by the fire, in slippers and shirtsleeves, with the child asleep behind the half-open door and the familiar sound of the potatoes which were being peeled falling one by one into the fresh water in the enamel bucket.

'Good night, Élise.'

'Good night, Désiré.'

She added, vaguely worried:

'Aren't you going to kiss me?'

'Yes . . . Sorry . . .'

She was already running, in imagination, along all the streets in the district, looking for notices; she was counting rolls and buckets of coal at fifty centimes each; and she was peopling her house with respectable Russians and Poles – she was going to pick them carefully – who would not be allowed to entertain women as they were in the rue de la Province.

Free access to her house, no, never!

Part Two

Chapter One

One morning when the milkman had not been by eight o'clock, Élise had asked Désiré:

'You wouldn't care to take Roger to school?'

And that had been enough to create a new ritual. For with Désiré the repetition of the same action took on a ritual character, and the various stages of the day followed one after another as harmoniously as the priest's gestures accompanied by the organ.

It was hard to say whether it was the boy who gave his hand to his father, or whether it was the father who took his son by the hand: every morning, at the same time, on the doorstep of the house in the rue de la Loi, the little fingers nestled inside Désiré's hand and the boy's legs tried to take three strides for every stride of the quiet giant.

With half her body hidden by the door, Élise leant out, following them with her eyes until they had turned the corner of the rue Jean-d'Outremeuse where the barber was raising his shutters. Then, before vanishing into the warm solitude of the house, she made sure that the greengrocer, whose trumpet could already be heard, had not appeared yet round the other corner.

The nursery school was quite close, at the back of a peaceful courtyard, next to the rectory, an oasis of cobblestones which were noisier and bluer, of air which was clearer; there were geraniums dozing on the window-sills, and the passage leading to the sacristy, as cool and dark as a grotto, gave off a smell of incense.

Sister Adonie, so soft and gentle that she made you think of something good to eat, welcomed into her vast skirts with their clinking rosary the awkward chicks that were brought to her from every corner of the district, keeping a special smile for that Monsieur Mamelin who greeted her with such a splendid sweep of his hat.

While the mothers clutched their shawls around them and returned to the life of the district and the day's cares at the other end of the courtyard, the door closed on a quiet, cosy little world, four white walls adorned with images, canvases, plaits and samplers, red wool on holland.

In her full black robe with its folds covering her feet, Sister Adonie did not appear to walk but to glide along a little way above the ground.

Through the two windows the Dean could be seen, short and fat and purple-cheeked, walking along the garden paths with little steps, reading his breviary and stopping in the middle of every patch of sunshine.

It was hot. The black cylinder of a monumental stove stood in the middle of the classroom, with a black pipe leading off to imbed itself far away in the glaring whiteness of the wall. The little cans of white coffee which the children had brought for their ten o'clock snack were warming side by side, and, in their oval boxes, their sandwiches were turning dry, the butter was soaking into the bread, the bars of chocolate becoming covered with tiny drops which would end up by forming a sort of lacquer.

Some of the cans were white or blue enamel. Others were iron, like those of Velden's coppersmiths who, at midday, had their dinner on the pavement after paying the greengrocer two centimes for the boiling water they needed for their coffee.

'Coloured cans are common,' Élise had stated.

She had not said that above all they were more expensive. Common too, in her opinion, were those sandwich tins decorated with scenes from *Little Red Riding Hood* or *Puss in Boots*.

On Roger's box, which was a discreet brown, there was nothing. Nor would Roger ever wear those check pinafores, pink for girls, blue for boys, which he hankered after so badly.

'It's workers' children that are dressed like that.'

Why workers' children? He was condemned to black pinafores, in sateen which would never wear out and did not dirty easily.

Bells tolled near by, in the tower which you could just see if you bent down; the Dean was going to sing a Requiem; there was a murmur of organ music, solemn echoes of a *De Profundis*; time flowed along, cheeks were red with warmth, eyes smarted, fingers mechanically plaited scarlet, yellow, green and blue ribbons of glossy paper which gave off a subtle smell.

Not long ago it had been winter, and, while Élise went round the junk-shops and the sale-rooms looking for second-hand beds and wardrobes, Sister Adonie, in the afternoon, used to light a wax-taper at the end of a pole. It always took her some time, in the twilight, to turn the taps of the two gas-jets which were high up. Looking up, the children waited with a secret anguish for the two 'plops', then the crude light, the nun's huge shadow gliding across the screen formed by the wall, and finally the end of school and that special sort of giddiness which came over them on the frontier between the overheated classroom and the wet, dark world where their mothers were waiting.

Winter was over now. In a few days' time, immediately after Easter, the stove with the pipe would stop being lit and school would be held outside, in the garden where the Dean read his breviary every morning; they would be able to watch the slow comings and goings of the old gardener as he pushed his barrow along, hoed or raked the earth, or stretched strings to sow his spinach and carrots straight.

Today was a special kind of day, neither winter nor summer, one of those days without a wrinkle or a ripple on it, which you remembered long afterwards, and while Sister Adonie was handing out the cans of coffee, while Désiré, on the stroke of ten, was knocking at Monsieur Monnoyeur's door, Élise, feeling a little feverish, was watching the street, her hand clutching the edge of the curtains.

In the house in the rue de la Loi, the new house as they called it, there was an atmosphere of expectant calm, and this calm enveloped Élise so closely that she felt imprisoned inside it, that she had the impression of being short of air, that occasionally, if she had obeyed her instincts, she would have rushed around haphazardly to avoid the anguish of immobility.

She had nothing more to do. There was not a speck of dust left in the dining-room, the furniture had been polished so brightly that the knick-knacks were reflected in it, the walls of the staircase, painted a pale green, had been washed with soap and water from top to bottom, the stairs sandpapered; there was nothing left to move, nothing to wash, polish or scrub.

At ten o'clock in the morning, Élise was dressed in her

Sunday best and, without doing it on purpose, she was smiling her rather sad, rather worried Sunday smile, the smile which went with the pleated pastel-blue blouse, with the puffed shoulders, with the skirt in navy-blue serge which touched her heels at the hem and which, fitting tightly over her corset, went up to just below her breasts. Her fair hair formed a mass as big as her head, gathered together, rather far forward, in a heavy bun.

All alone in the silent house, in the street where nobody was passing, opposite the red wall of the Friars' school where play-time had just finished, Élise felt almost frightened.

Perhaps this was because her work was over, that work which had lasted a whole winter or even longer, and which she had brought to a satisfactory conclusion alone, so tense that some-times she had wept while carrying her buckets, while scraping the dirty woodwork, while collecting heaven knows where the furniture whose price she did not dare to confess to Désiré and which she had trundled home in a handcart, under cover of darkness.

Could Valérie, with her porcelain hands, have helped her? Could Madame Pain, who was always timid and complaining? So who had whitewashed the walls of the yard? Who had climbed the ladder poised unsteadily on the stairs? And who had painted the outside door, whose colour, when they had taken the house, nobody could have specified?

It was all over. Probably it was because she had finished her work that Élise felt empty, that her knees were trembling, that her hands, which she had had to rub with pumice stone after all that rough work, shook helplessly at times.

From that window to which she kept coming back in spite of herself, and where she felt ashamed of keeping watch, she could see nothing human except two legs and two feet in red carpet slippers resting on a straw-bottomed chair.

She could not see the rest of the man who sat there day after day outside the house, but she knew that he slept in a ray of sunshine, so thin that his clothes hung on him like the old clothes which are hung on sticks in the fields to scare away the sparrows.

Two fat, common women, who kept the pub next door, an old woman and a young one, put him there like an inanimate object as soon as the weather turned fine, and moved him around as the sun moved across the sky.

Élise did not talk to those neighbours. When she went out, she tried not to look their way. It was from the woman who ran the dairy-shop that she had learnt that the man, whose name was Hosselet, had lived in the Congo, from which he had brought back the sleeping-sickness. He had become so light that either of the two women could carry him like a child.

No, Élise had no regrets, she was not afraid. She knew that she had been right, that she had had to do what she had done.

It was the street, to which she had not grown accustomed yet, that baffled her, those houses about which she knew nothing, those windowless walls of the Friars' school, that dark green door where, at half past eleven, a friar with a wooden leg would station himself to supervise the pupils' departure.

Why should she feel sorry that she had left the rue Pasteur, where she had had two flights of stairs to climb? What had she lost?

'You'll see, Valérie! Once I've found my lodgers . . .'

A student had gone past a few minutes earlier, a tall, dark young man, very smartly dressed, wearing an orange velvet cap with a long peak. He was one of Madame Corbion's lodgers, a Rumanian.

'Just imagine, Madame Élise . . .'

Why did Madame Corbion, who had a child of the same age as Roger and dyed her hair red, insist on calling her Madame Élise?

'. . . Just imagine, his parents send him three hundred francs a month and he still manages to run into debt!'

Madame Corbion used cosmetics, without even trying to disguise the fact.

'I assure you, Désiré, she's a respectable woman. Her husband was an officer.'

The rue Pasteur was less than a hundred yards away; the Mamelins' old house was the second on the left, just round the corner. Yet how far away it all seemed!

When the student had gone past, never thinking that somebody was looking at him, Élise had thought:

'That young man would take the pink room at thirty francs;

he wouldn't be particular about the price of coal or anything else, but he'd probably insist on free access, because I'm sure he spends his three hundred francs on women.'

She would have to get used to it. She would get used to it. Already, if anybody uttered the word Poles, it meant for her young men who had very little money, fifty to eighty francs a month, but who were none the less proud for all that. Soon she would be like innkeepers and restaurant proprietors for whom the world had a different meaning than for the ordinary run of mortals. If a car happens to pass, slow down and stop, it is not a car with tourists in it; it is three meals at so much a meal, wine, coffee and liqueurs, or else it is a grumpy old couple, two meals with no wine or extras.

'You see, Madame Élise, the Russians are poorer, but they don't expect so much. And there are some of them who are still a bit wild.'

There were no students in the rue Pasteur, and not a single window displayed the yellow notice which Élise could read through her own window-panes and which she had fastened there two days before with sealing-wax.

'Furnished room to let.'

She had added an *s* in ink: furnished rooms.

Three weeks before, at the same time, Élise had gone out of the house in the rue Pasteur with Roger to sit on the bench in the place du Congrès. Straight away, she had automatically looked up at the Lorisses' loggia, sure that old Madame Lorisse would be there, or her daughter, or the two of them, doing some embroidery and keeping an eye on the old man and the dog.

They were rich people, people of independent means. Well, as soon as Élise turned in their direction, smiling discreetly, Madame Lorisse would nod her head and give a little wave of the hand, and Élise knew perfectly well that that gesture meant:

'There's the young mother from next door taking her child out for a walk. She deserved credit for bringing him up in a second-floor flat and keeping him so clean! How thin she is! How tired she must be! How proud and brave she is! We must show her our esteem and smile at her son with his thin little legs. There you have an excellent person who deserves our consideration.'

Élise for her part, after stroking the dog, made a mute reply.

'You can see that I am touched by your solicitude! You understand me. I do what I can, even though I can't afford anything but the bare necessities of life. You are the richest people in the street and yet you wave to me from your loggia. The proof that I am not ungrateful and that I know my manners is that I stroke your dog, which frightens me so badly every time it goes near Roger and, with its mania for licking his face, could easily give him worms. Thank you. Thank you very much. Believe me, I do appreciate . . .'

Élise walked along. She knew who lived behind every door. The door of the magistrate's house opened a little way as she approached.

'How is the dear child? Isn't he sweet! He's got such expressive eyes, Madame Mamelin! How I envy you! How happy you must be!'

What did it matter if Madame Gérard was a sometime cook whom the magistrate now called his housekeeper but whom he seemed to be in no hurry to marry?

'The handsomest child in the district, Madame Mamelin. I keep telling Monsieur Dambois so.'

The proof that everything was a question of breeding was that in those days Élise would suddenly cross the road, if she had time, as soon as she caught sight of fat Madame Morel, although the latter was an engineer's wife, a former waitress with a shrill voice.

'Come here, little Roger. Come and get some chocolate from old Madame Morel.'

Then Élise's smile would say:

'Thank you! I thank you out of politeness, because that is the correct thing to do. But we don't belong to the same world. The Lorisse ladies would not wave to you from their loggia. Everybody knows that you were brought up in the gutter and that you are the most foul-mouthed woman in the district. I say thank you but I feel embarrassed when the neighbours see you stopping me in the street.'

Those people lived only for their stomachs, both husband and wife; they were fat and flabby, with wet lips and shining little pigs' eyes. It was Madame Morel who had shouted at the greengrocer in front of everybody:

'You're a thief, Sigismond! You've palmed off some rotten carrots on me again!'

When the greengrocer was not even called Sigismond! That was what she was like.

'Say thank you to Madame Morel, Roger. Give her your hand. Not that one. Your right hand.'

After Morel's, there was the house with the white door where Monsieur Hermann lived, the first violin at the Théâtre-Royal, who was always so well dressed and had ash-blond hair as fine as a woman's. And farther on there was Julie Pain's ever-open door.

'I'll be with you in a moment, Élise.'

For Julie was never ready!

Godard's the butcher's . . . The place du Congrès, so neat and regular, with its four corresponding terraces, its benches, and the No. 4 tram describing an harmonious curve . . .

No! Élise had no regrets and never would have any. She was not like Désiré, who had turned his head away – she knew very well why – when, in the evening, when the last piece of furniture had been taken away, he had locked up the two empty rooms in the rue Pasteur before giving the key to the landlady.

She would get used to it. She was already used to it. She was beginning to smile at her neighbours on the right, the Delcours – the eldest son was a house-painter and looked rather like Arthur. It was a pity that the house on the left was a pub, but nobody ever went into it, except an occasional carter who did not even stop his horses and came straight out wiping his moustache on the back of his hand. The fact was, those people probably lived largely on the pension Hosselet received on account of his service in the Congo and his sleeping-sickness.

Élise went to see to the fire. The same perfect order reigned in the kitchen as in the dining-room which they called the drawing-room. She felt like going upstairs to have a look at the bedrooms, but a mysterious force drew her into the front room, behind those curtains where she would not be caught watching for anything in the world. What would people think?

How wonderful it would be if, at two o'clock, when Désiré came home, she could let him eat his dinner without saying anything, and then, trying not to tremble, finally announce:

'Incidentally, I've got a lodger.'

And now, at eleven o'clock, just after a tram had gone along the rue Jean-d'Outremeuse and the sick man had been moved along the pavement – there were people who could find that upsetting and who, because of that, would hesitate to ring the bell – now here was a woman stopping in front of the house, in front of the window with the carefully draped curtains and the brass flower-pot cases which contained asparaguses from Coronmeuse.

'Dear God, how ugly she is!'

For a moment life came to a standstill. The woman had disappeared. Élise's heart had stopped beating. Finally the sound of a bell rang out, echoing through the whole house, which had never seemed so empty before; Élise had not had time to break the spell which rooted her to the floor before the bell was rung again, violently, hard enough to pull the chain off.

'Come in, Mademoiselle.'

The visitor did not smile, did not say good morning, did not apologize; she came in as if she were already at home, or in a place which belonged to nobody, and she looked uninterestedly at the spotless walls and the brass ball at the foot of the banisters.

'Where is the room?'

Roger, full of warmth and well-being, was dozing beside Sister Adonie's big stove, and Désiré was waiting for the moment when he would finally be alone in the rue Sohet office to take off his jacket and unpack his sandwiches, for, like a true Mamelin, Désiré was always hungry.

*

'Dear God, how ugly she is!'

This swallow who had come such a long way to be the first to settle in the rue de la Loi house was Frida Stavitskaïa, born on the shores of the Black Sea, in a suburb of Odessa.

Because she was the first to cross her threshold on an unusually calm morning, Élise would always see her as she appeared to her at that moment, dark and thin, with an emaciated face in which a wide, blood-red mouth and two huge eyes stood out sharply.

How could a human being, a woman who wasn't twenty-two yet, get herself up like that? Her tightly plaited hair formed a bun as hard as a stone on a neck which was yellow and probably unwashed, and a flat hat, which no servant-girl would ever be seen wearing, had been carelessly put on top of it. A shiny skirt failed to conceal either the absence of any hips or the big feet which anybody would have taken for men's feet. Not a single touch of white, not a single trinket, not the tiniest jewel or family souvenir to relieve the strict poverty of the high-necked dress which recalled the uniform of some Puritan sect.

But it was above all the absence of any smile, even the vague smile which you give to anybody, to the beggar who greets you in the street, which disappointed Élise.

She would have liked to show the visitor into the drawing-room whose door was open.

'Do sit down, Mademoiselle.'

'No.'

A very simple no, a no such as nobody would ever utter in Outremeuse, not even cold Monsieur Pain, a no which said no, because Frida Stavitskaïa had not come here to sit down, or to admire the neatness and cleanliness of a room where she had no reason to be. A no which hurt Élise and froze her blood, for she had never dared to speak like that, she was too afraid of hurting, of shocking, of causing the slightest offence.

For the sake of saying something, she asked, her lips trembling in a forced smile:

'Are you a student, Mademoiselle?'

Frida, standing in the doorway and looking towards the stairs, did not feel any need to reply, since this was nobody's business but hers. She merely repeated:

'I should like to see the room.'

'Go ahead, Mademoiselle. I'll show you the prettiest one, which looks out on the street. The furniture is as good as new.'

She was so afraid of not saying enough that she felt like adding:

'It's the bedroom suite we had when we were married.'

For they had sacrificed the handsome furniture in solid oak, the bed which had been made to measure on account of Désiré's size. Élise and Désiré now slept in an iron bed bought at an auction sale.

'Metal mattresses, Désiré, are so much healthier!'

With her heart pounding, Élise pushed open the door of the

pink room. Everything was pink, the lamp, the toilet set – a set they had had for their marriage too – and even the marble top of the washstand.

Frida Stavitskaïa, bearing down on the sharp point of her parasol, did not bother to go in.

'This is the only one you have?'

'It's the prettiest, the gayest.'

She would have liked to explain everything at once, that the house had been cleaned from top to bottom, that the water from the Artesian well was the best in the street, that there was gas laid on, that the landlord had promised to put in electricity later on, that she had put the wallpaper up herself, and that there wasn't a single bed-bug in the beds.

But Frida had opened another door, the door of the green room, which was smaller and where the sun came in only towards the evening.

'How much?'

'The big room, thirty francs a month, including light, with coal extra, as usual, but . . .'

Without offering the slightest encouragement, Frida waited for the rest.

'This one is only twenty-five francs. Mind you . . .'

'It's too dear.'

That was all. She was going to go. She was going. Her face was expressionless. Her beautiful eyes, as bright and black as certain beetles, settled nowhere; they lived their own life and had nothing to say to this woman in the liberty blouse.

'Listen, Mademoiselle, I've got another room, on the entresol . . .'

She talked fast. Whatever happened, she mustn't let her go.

'It's smaller. It's not so cheerful. The light comes from the north and the window looks out on the yard . . .'

'How much?'

'Twenty-francs.'

For the first time, something vaguely resembling a human emotion passed like a scarcely perceptible breeze over Frida Stavitskaïa's face. A regret? Not even that! She had simply paused for a moment. She accorded the room a brief glance, for a fraction of a second; perhaps she had thought that it would have been pleasant to live in, but she was already going down-stairs.

'I can't afford more than fifteen francs.'

'Listen, Mademoiselle. I'll make an exception for you. You're the first who's been . . .'

To think that she had had to put up such a struggle against Désiré, that she had saved sou by sou, cheated on the smallest expenses, and counted the lumps of sugar, only to come to this!

'If I let you have it for eighteen francs?'

'I told you I can't afford more than fifteen francs,' the other woman repeated in a flat voice.

'Well, then . . .'

Frida looked at her as if she had no inkling of the drama being played out.

'When do you want to move in?'

'Today.'

'There's something else I must tell you and it's rather delicate. I've got a child, and some sisters in business. The whole of my family is . . .'

Élise blushed, faltered, spoke faster.

'You understand; I can't allow free access.'

Frida didn't turn a hair; only her eyes had a questioning look.

'I mean that you can't receive anybody you like. It wouldn't be decent for men to come into your room.'

Élise might have been talking to an inhabitant of another planet. Frida showed no indignation. At the most a hint of contempt turned down the corner of her mouth.

'Very well. I'll pay you now.'

And she took the fifteen francs out of a bag with an artificial silver clasp.

'But come in here for a moment. You'll have a cup of coffee, won't you?'

'No.'

'There's some on the stove. I'll serve you straight away.'

'I said no. Will you give me the key, please?'

It was all over. Élise had just time to go and fetch Roger from school, give him his dinner, and take him back to Sister Adonie before Désiré came home.

'I've let a room!'

She announced the news straight away, she was so afraid of betraying her uneasiness.

'Whom to?'

'A girl . . . A Russian . . . She's moving in today . . .'

She had not mentioned the rent and she was relieved that Désiré did not ask any questions on that subject.

In the afternoon she bustled to and fro, on edge, happy and yet not happy, she didn't know why.

'I've got a woman lodger, Madame Corbion.'

'You'll find that the women aren't as easy to live with as the men. One day I'll tell you about all the dirty tricks they've played on me.'

They were at table that evening, in the kitchen with the glazed door, when the key turned in the lock, and it created a peculiar impression, the first time, to see the street-door open when it was nobody in the family. Élise rushed out of the room and pulled the little chain which lit the gas in the lantern hanging in the hall.

'Give me your suitcase, Mademoiselle Frida.'

'No, thank you.'

She carried it herself. She had not said good evening. Élise did not dare to follow her upstairs. And the lodger was no sooner in her room than she bolted the door.

They heard her coming and going overhead, for the entresol was just above the kitchen.

'She can't have had any dinner.'

Élise listened. What could the foreigner be doing? Where did she have her meals?

'Where are you going?' asked Désiré, who had settled down in his wicker armchair and opened the paper.

Élise went upstairs. Feeling rather nervous, she knocked on the door.

'It's only me, Mademoiselle Frida.'

The door did not open. Silence.

'I just came to ask you if you needed anything. The first day, you know . . .'

'No.'

Standing helplessly on the landing, Élise did not know how to say good night, and, to the syllables which she stammered out, she received no reply. For two pins, she would have wept as she went downstairs.

Désiré took his pipe out of his mouth and half raised his head.

'Well?'

'Nothing. She doesn't need anything.'

That was all. She cleared the table. Désiré, who had tilted his armchair back, puffed at his pipe, while Roger fell asleep over his bricks.

Élise opened her mouth. No. What was the use?

Soon they would be going to bed in the ground-floor room whose glazed double doors opened on to the yard. It was not a real bedroom. It was the old dining-room. They had to get used to the iron bedstead whose bars stood out as if they were drawn in Indian ink, to the hanging space which had taken the place of the mirror-fronted wardrobe which they had put in the pink room, to the deal table covered with a honeycomb towel which did service as a washstand.

Désiré did not suspect that this room itself would one day be abandoned to a medical student from Vilna, that the iron bedstead would go right up to the whitewashed attic, and that in the evening, to save on their coal, the lodgers would settle down in the kitchen, in his armchair.

He still had his corner. He sank into it, haloed in smoke and tranquillity.

'Madame Corbion was telling me this afternoon . . .'

He was obviously reading a fascinating article, for he paid no attention to what she was saying. Fortunately for her. She changed her mind. It was no use explaining to him that according to Madame Corbion, who had experience of them, women students were worse than shrews.

'You don't want to put Roger to bed?'

Soon from the next room, Désiré's voice came to her:

> There were two lovers
> Who dreamed of distant loves . . .

She cocked her head to listen, not to the murmur of the lullaby, but to the silence upstairs.

> There were two lovers
> Who bade their parents farewell . . .

Chapter Two

Élise had had her suspicions. She had even promised herself to speak about it to Léopold the next time he came.

'You've got to understand, Léopold . . . I'm sorry to have to say this to you, because what you do is none of my business . . . But next door! . . . They know who you are . . .'

She had not dared, and perhaps the real reason for her silence was not the fear of offending him. Now that she lived in the rue de la Loi and left the door ajar all the morning while she did her rooms, and now that he for his part no longer needed to ring the bell nor fear the appearance of the landlady's scowling face, Léopold came along more often to sit down in the kitchen.

The first-floor windows were wide open, and the dust was flying in the rays of sunshine which seemed to be sucking it out like smoke. Élise was tidying the pink room which she had just let to a Jewess from Warsaw, Pauline Feinstein, whom they already called Mademoiselle Pauline.

She was leaning out of the window, watching for the coal- man, when she caught sight of Léopold turning the corner and passing the hairdresser's window with his shoulders slanting sideways.

She always wondered whether Léopold knew where he was going, dragging one leg and walking obliquely with his head down and his eyes fixed on the pavement, so that it was a miracle that he had never been run over by a tram. However, he left the pavement, always at the same place, like a blind man, crossed the street diagonally and, after a moment's hesitation and a furtive glance at Élise's house, plunged into the darkness of the pub next door.

He did not stay there long, just long enough to have a drop or two, standing at the bar in silence, and there he was at the door, still hesitant and suspicious, growling like a dog sniffing at a place before venturing inside.

He crossed the threshold, touched the door, pushed it open, saw the empty passage and the glazed kitchen door standing ajar, and heard the soup on the boil. Élise finally came out of one of the upstairs rooms and leant over the banisters, holding her bun in one hand.

'Come in, Léopold. Sit down. I'll be with you in a minute.'

It was understood between them: she went on with her work, going to and fro while her brother, sitting in Désiré's wickerwork armchair, drew on his old pipe with its disgusting gurgle.

Even if she sat peeling vegetables beside him, he said nothing and, after a lapse of time fixed by some rule known to him alone, he went off as he had come, with a vague:

''Bye, my girl.'

Élise came downstairs and disappeared straight away.

'Excuse me, Léopold. It's the coalman.'

She carried her buckets out on to the pavement, came back for her purse, opened and shut a succession of doors, washed her hands, and finally settled down to strain the soup.

The conversations between Élise and her brother were completely unlike those they had with other people. It was as if they were waiting, by tacit consent, for a certain atmosphere to surround them, for a warmth to envelop them, for a contact to be made, for the silence to become profound enough for the ticktock of the alarm-clock to seem like the pulse-beats of the house itself. Then, and only then, Élise sighed:

'Oh, poor Léopold. I don't talk about this to anybody, least of all to Désiré. If you only knew how women . . .'

Was it because she did not dare to be more explicit that she left her sentence unfinished? Was it because she and her brother had no need to be explicit? Or was she still preparing the atmosphere with a preamble of vague words, words which did not tie up with one another?

'I've got three lodgers now. Well, you know, I don't mind doing Monsieur Saft's room, for all that he smokes in bed and throws his cigarette-ends all over the place. But the women! . . . Last Friday, I nearly spoke to Valérie about it. Luckily I remembered in time that she had a smell too. Once I had to sleep with her, and it turned my stomach.'

Léopold gazed at the reddening disc of the stove, and now and then you could hear the gurgle of his pipe. He let his sister go on talking. Élise did not bother to find out whether he was listening to her or whether he was thinking of something else.

'The first time I did Mademoiselle Frida's room, I didn't think I'd be able to finish it. How a woman, a girl, can have so little pride in herself is beyond me. As for me, the thought of leaving another woman to make my bed and empty my slops . . .'

Poor Élise! The day she was talking about – it was a month ago now, but she could remember the smallest details to the extent of suffering from them – that day had probably been the richest in misfortunes in the whole of her life. She had worked so hard, calculated so carefully, worked everything out to within a centime or so, and suddenly she had found herself face to face with a reality so different from her dreams that she had felt herself weakening and had wondered whether she ought not to begin all over again.

The smell of another woman, of a stranger, when she had pushed open the entresol door after Mademoiselle Frida had left for the University; the sight of that unmade bed, still warm and damp, and then, on the filthy grey surface of the soapy water in the basin, those little balls of dark hair floating about.

That time, Élise had opened the window and, since there was nobody there to see her and she did not need to smile, the corners of her mouth had dropped in a grimace of weariness and disgust.

'Mademoiselle Pauline isn't any cleaner, and I don't think she ever washes herself all over, but possibly because her room is bigger and there are two windows, the smell isn't so obvious. If you could see their powder-puffs, Léopold! Madame Corbion was right, you know, when she told me about women students, and she was right too when she said that all Russians are still savages to some extent.'

Léopold emptied his pipe by knocking it on the edge of the coal-scuttle. Élise was afraid that he was going to get up already, for he did not usually stay much longer, but this particular morning, he sank back into the armchair again and heaved a sigh.

'Am I boring you, Léopold?'

He grunted. That meant that she could go on.

'I don't understand why it's you I tell all my little troubles to, even those that only women can understand . . .'

She did not interrupt her work for a single moment, or stop looking through the glass panes at the street door, which was letting in a thin ray of sunshine. She peeled an onion and put it in a frying-pan, walking backwards and forwards between the stove and the table.

'You know, those people haven't the same reactions that we have.'

Now things were going better, and Mademoiselle Frida had been practically tamed. All the same, Élise still felt aggrieved at the memory of the Russian woman's first day in the house. She had arranged that room so lovingly and now you could scarcely recognize it! Why had her lodger removed the tablecover which was spotless and as good as new? On the deal surface there was nothing but a pile of books, and on the dressing-table a broken comb, a toothbrush reddened by an unfamiliar toothpaste, and some little bits of cotton-wool.

Élise looked up and noticed a gap: the gilt frame containing an enlarged photograph of Valérie had been taken down, and so had the two little pictures with white lacquer frames showing a lily-pond and some deer in a forest.

On the black marble mantelpiece, there was nothing left, neither the embroidered mats, nor the vases, nor the big shell from Ostend: knick-knacks of no particular value, it was true, but which brightened up the room.

A photograph had been slipped into the frame of the mirror: a single-storeyed wooden house – a real savages' house – and a family lined up in front of the door, a fat woman with grey hair, a younger, very ugly one, holding a baby and leaning to one side, two little girls and a fifteen-year-old girl who was none other than Frida.

No men. Élise did not know that old Stavitsky, a country schoolmaster, had been in a Siberian prison for the past five years.

Anxious and vexed, she hunted around for her vases, her souvenirs and the portrait of Valérie. In the wardrobe she found nothing but a dirty chemise, with no embroidery, lace or inset, a pair of stockings with holes in them, and some slippers which she would not have dared to wear to do her housework.

Anxiety engulfed her. On the landing there were two doors, the lavatory door and the door of the cupboard where she kept her buckets and brushes. It was behind this latter door that she found her possessions, thrown in anyhow.

'Would you have behaved like that, Léopold? If you'd seen that bare room!'

She had not said anything to Désiré. She had found time, before going to fetch Roger from school, to run over to the rue Puits-en-Sock and buy a few flowers, carnations they were, lovely hot-house carnations she would always remember. She had done that with a bitter taste in her mouth, as if to overcome at any price the despair which was stifling her, to push her goodwill to the limit. She had chosen the most precious vase in the dining-room, a narrow vase in iridescent crystal, and she had put it on Frida Stavitskaïa's table.

The latter had come back about half past eleven. Wouldn't she come into the kitchen to say hullo, or at least give a wave in the direction of the glazed door as she went along the hall?

She went past as if she were going along the street where nobody knew her. Did she even know that Roger existed, or wonder whether her landlady had a husband?

Mademoiselle Frida was holding a little white packet and Élise had understood why: she was going to have a cold meal in her room where there was no stove and the fire had not been lit.

'I just couldn't help it, Léopold, and I'm sure that you would have done the same . . .'

Taking advantage of the fact that Désiré was not there, she had taken up a bowl of soup. Outside the entresol door, she had stopped short at the sight of her vase, which had been put on the floor, with the flowers. She had knocked all the same.

'What is it?'

'Open the door for a minute, Mademoiselle Frida.'

She turned the handle, but the door had been bolted.

'The idea, Léopold, of locking herself in as if the house wasn't safe, or as if she had something to hide!'

The door finally opened a little way. On the table, among some open lecture-notes, there was a hunk of bread and a hard-boiled egg.

'Excuse me, Mademoiselle Frida . . . I thought . . . I ventured to . . .'

The dark eyes settled on the steaming bowl.

'What's that?'

'I thought that a bowl of hot soup . . .'

'I didn't ask you for anything.'

'At your age, especially if you are studying, you need to keep your strength up. I'm sure that if your mother were here . . .'

'I know better than anybody else what I need.'

'I put some flowers in here so that the room shouldn't look so cold.'

'I don't like flowers.'

'The portrait that was on the wall was a photo of my best friend.'

'She isn't mine.'

Élise had not betrayed herself in front of Désiré. It was the first time, after a long month, that she had spoken to somebody about it.

*

She never forgot the time. Even when she neglected to shoot a glance at the hands of the alarm-clock, she remained alive to everything which marked the passage of time: the hammer at Halkin's – which you didn't hear as clearly here as in the rue Pasteur – the boys coming out of the Friars' school, the siren at Velden's.

In twenty minutes it would be time to go and fetch Roger from the rue Jean-d'Outremeuse. Léopold was still there. It was the first time he had stayed so long. Élise frowned:

'You hadn't anything to say to me, Léopold?'

He grunted.

'Eugénie's keeping well?'

'She's at Ostend for the season.'

All the same, he had come for a particular reason, she could feel that, and he wasn't happy.

'I get on your nerves with my stories, but you know, you're the only person I can tell them to.'

'Yes, my girl.'

She made an effort to be brighter, and almost overdid it.

'You know, since then, Mademoiselle Frida has been a lot better. As for Monsieur Saft, he's so well-bred! He's a Pole. He didn't want me to carry up his coal-bucket or brush his shoes. It seems that in his country no woman would ever brush a man's shoes, even her husband's. Did you want something?'

He had opened his mouth as if to speak, but then he had put his pipe back in it straight away and had started shuffling his feet, a sign that he would be going before long.

'To finish with Mademoiselle Frida . . .'

It was no longer a drama now, or at least it was no longer Élise's drama, and she was having her revenge.

'If anybody had told me a story like that before, I wouldn't have believed it. Just imagine, one morning I didn't see her go out. To begin with I thought that she hadn't any lectures and she was taking advantage of the fact to have a morning in bed. In the afternoon, after Désiré had gone, I began to get worried; because I knew there wasn't anything to eat in her room. It was a Thursday and Roger was at home. I put him in his chair, I went upstairs, and I knocked on her door.

'"Mademoiselle Frida!"

'No answer. No noise.

'"It's me, Mademoiselle. I'm a bit worried. You aren't ill, are you?"

'"Go away."

'And the door was bolted again!

'"Mademoiselle Frida, tell me at least if you need anything and I'll put it on the landing. Don't worry, I'll go away afterwards."

'I had to go downstairs again. I wasn't able to go out to L'Innovation with Roger as I usually do on Thursdays. The child was restless and, over the kitchen, I kept hearing a sort of rattling cough.

'When Désiré finally came home, I told him about it and he shrugged his shoulders.

'"If she's ill, she's only to say so. After all, we can't break the door down."

'"She's got nothing to eat."

'"That's her affair."

'You know what Désiré's like, Léopold.'

She speeded up the telling of her story, for fear that Léopold would go before the end, and also because Sister Adonie would soon be throwing open the doors of her chicken-coop to the sunshine in the yard.

'The next day, seeing that things were just the same, I went

227

to see Doctor Matray without saying anything to anybody. Seeing how pale I was, he teased me about it.

'"Why, Madame Mamelin, your lodger is just a hysterical young woman."'

'She stayed locked in for three days, like Marthe when she's having a novena . . .'

She bit her tongue. Dear God, there she was talking about Marthe's novenas in front of Léopold who drank too! She didn't know where to look. She put some more coal on the stove. It would be time soon, it was time already.

'I'm afraid I've been boring you, poor Léopold.'

She would have liked to ask him again:

'You're sure you hadn't got something to say to me?'

For there was no deceiving her. She knew. Unfortunately she had to go.

'I'm not throwing you out. You can stay if you like. I've just got to go and fetch Roger and I'll be back straight away.'

No. He left her on the doorstep. Out of tact, so as not to force his company on her in the street, he pretended to have some business in another direction.

'By the way . . .'

There, hadn't she been right?

'You haven't had any news of Louis of Tongres?'

'You know I never see him, Léopold. Since mother died, the only time he's remembered my existence was when he came to collect our parents' furniture. Yet he's in Liège every Monday, because Hubert Schroefs meets him at the Stock Exchange. Once when I was passing with Roger, I caught sight of him in the Taverne Grüber, looking at people with those little eyes of his.'

He was a queer fellow, Léopold. He stayed at his sister's for nearly two hours. He listened to her while puffing his pipe and drinking a cup of coffee which he allowed to go cold, he waited until they were out in the street before asking a question, and now he went off without saying anything, not even good-bye; he was already far away when Élise was still talking and she could see nothing of him but his round back brushing past the houses.

She was going to be late. Monsieur Saft, so fair haired and so well dressed, turned the corner of the street and solemnly greeted his landlady as if she were a great lady. She smiled as she quickened her pace. The first day he had kissed her hand, bending in two like a puppet.

*

That day, which was a Monday in May, a man with hulking shoulders, a greenish bowler-hat and an old-fashioned overcoat, went to and fro, with a bearlike gait, among the groups of stockbrokers standing on the left-hand terrace of the place Saint-Lambert, between the Café du Phare, the Populaire and the Tavern Grüber. His black beard gave off a strong smell of alcohol, for instead of having dinner he had been drinking in every pub in the rue Gérardrie, and his walk was sometimes so unsteady that people drew back as he passed.

What did Léopold care about the contempt of these fat, shining, self-satisfied men doing business, calling out to one another, taking notes, and occasionally plunging into the cafés where the big pots were majestically enthroned while other people were standing and gesticulating between the rows of tables?

In his pocket he was crumpling a dirty piece of paper, a letter bearing a Paris postmark, and he followed the train of his ideas, mulling over his thoughts, picturing a drama which had kept him gloomy and absent-minded for two hours in Élise's kitchen.

Had he any money? Had he ever had any? Before Eugénie had left for Ostend, where she had a job in a boarding-house, hadn't they spent the odd francs she had put on one side during the last few months? For a long time now he had not had a watch, and his wife didn't possess a single jewel, not even a little gold chain.

Two or three times, scowling ferociously, he had gone up to one of the big windows of the Grüber. The first time, Louis of Tongres, whom people called the rich Peters, had been eating all by himself in front of a dazzling tablecloth, his gaze wandering over the respectful crowd, or answering a doffed hat with an imperceptible flicker of his eyelids.

Louis had tiny little eyes, or rather he had a habit of creasing his eyelids so that in the narrow slit between them you could only just distinguish the bright pupils, which were disconcertingly sharp. It had become a mannerism with him. To say yes, to express approval, to show satisfaction, he shut his eyes completely, very quickly; you had to be extremely alert to notice this sign of acquiescence, for it was as quick as the click of a camera. On other occasions, he would open his eyes a little way, and the lens remained fixed for a while, revealing a pair of cold, motionless pupils; this meant no, a no which nobody in the whole world had ever made Louis of Tongres retract.

The second time that Léopold's helot figure had approached the bay window of the Grüber, his brother had finished his meal and was slowly picking his teeth while, on a chair in front of him, a man with a servile smile was taking documents out of a leather briefcase.

The third time, Léopold had been almost afraid that Louis, who had just lit a cigar with a wide band, was going to turn towards him and recognize him. Haloed in smoke, hunting in his waistcoat for his amber cigar-holder, listening to his companion without looking at him and answering only with his eyelids, he sat there as if he were in a shop-window, as relaxed as if he had been in his own home.

He was the king of the Limbourg forests and the fertilizer business. Little by little, he had become interested in everything that was bought and sold in his fief. Hadn't he married the only daughter of the governor of the province, a nobleman?

Other men, facing the velvet-covered bench on which he sat motionless, had come to open their briefcases and hold out papers, to beg for a signature, an endorsement, an order; and still others were waiting, standing a little farther off, when Louis Peters' gaze slid over the bluish surface of the window against which a poor man's bearded face was pressed.

The eyes of the two brothers met. Léopold did not move, and nobody around him had any idea of the courage the drunkard had to summon up to stay in his place while Louis stood up, knocked the ash off his cigar and, without taking his hat or picking up his papers, went towards the door.

All the Peters were short and stocky; Louis, who was more wiry than the others, looked wellnigh thin, on account of his dried-up face, his pointed nose, and the liveliness of his movements when he suddenly emerged from his immobility.

He crossed the tavern and shot like an arrow through the

revolving doors; on the pavement he stopped short and nothing in him moved except his eyelids.

He waited; it was Léopold, the eldest brother with the hunched shoulders, who came forward with his oblique gait. There were groups of people around them, a thousand voices mingling together, and yet they were able to talk without anybody listening to them . . .

Léopold spoke, shaking slightly, his breath stinking; he said only a few words, quoted a figure: five hundred francs.

On the terrace, on the pavement, in the café, men were buying and selling boatloads of timber, trainloads of phosphates, farms complete with their flocks, whole harvests.

Léopold asked for only five hundred francs. His nose was running; he took a big red handkerchief out of his pocket and half-covered his face with it while his brother asked him two or three incisive questions.

What did he reply? That the money was not for him? That he had never needed any money? No! He did not bother to reply. He had seen the icy, wide-open eyes, and he had understood. Turning round, he plunged into the crowd, rolling from side to side.

Félix Marette could ask only Léopold for the five hundred francs, and Léopold could ask only Louis of Tongres.

Léopold bumped into passers-by without apologizing, his instinct leading him quickly to a narrow street where he found familiar smells again, to a little café where there were men leaning on the bar with the same empty, staring eyes as his.

What did the letter matter now? He would answer it later, in three days, in a week, some time or other, when his wanderings had brought him back to his ladder and the trapdoor leading to his rooms.

They were waiting and hoping in Paris. Marette had written, in a handwriting which had changed in a few months and become more deliberate: 'We *must* find a solution . . .'

He had underlined *must* with a thick stroke of the pen.

He would not be able to manage otherwise. A month before, Doms had staged one of his periodical disappearing acts. Was he really in Russia, Rumania or Barcelona, as he would pretend when he returned, as threadbare, as quiet, as silently menacing as ever?

Doms was a nobody! The truth of the matter was that Doms had no money, no friends, no means, and belonged to no group or party. He was a contemptible individual whom Marette despised, even though he was forced to put him up in his attic and to buy him a meal in his little restaurant every time he asked.

Marette had discovered that truth a long time ago, by accident, one morning when he had been lying on the floor and the other man had been asleep in his bed. Félix Marette had had his eyes open a fraction of an inch, rather like Louis Peters, and Doms, thinking that he was asleep, had been himself, in the grey atmosphere of that winter morning, with the bleak daylight falling from the skylight on to the grubby sheets and the brown blanket: a Doms without spectacles, looking fatter than usual, shining with the sweat of the night, a hulking mass of pale flesh with stupid, vulgar gestures and such miserable, empty eyes that they had given Marette a shock.

For several minutes the self-styled anarchist had scratched his dirty feet, then he had put on his threadbare socks, pulled on his trousers, and stayed there limply, not knowing what to do with himself. He had taken a few sous out of his pocket and counted them, ending up by furtively plunging his hands into his friend's pockets and extracting a few coins.

That was all. A little later, when he had put on his thick spectacles, he had become the Doms of the Café de la Bourse once more, but Marette could no longer be taken in.

He had to endure him, with impatience and disgust, and what made it worse was the knowledge that the man was nothing but a contemptible little crook, perfectly capable of denouncing a friend to the police.

Hadn't he gone so far as to follow Marette in the street, so that now he knew everything?

His smile had been enough to tarnish the only really beautiful moment Marette had experienced till then.

It was about Christmastime. One evening when Félix had been in his attic, feverishly writing the story of his life, it had started raining so hard that water had begun pouring through the roof and he had had to move his bed.

The next morning, although it was his fate that was involved, Marette had nearly failed to notice the open umbrella which was dripping in a corner of the shop, after the rain had stopped.

It was Isabelle Vétu's umbrella. He had recognized it later, and then the light had dawned; he had realized that she had gone out, probably by herself, the previous evening.

He had never thought of this simple eventuality. He had watched outside for two whole evenings. Finally he had seen a light in the shop, and Isabelle had come out on to the pavement, walking quickly in the direction of the Conservatoire where there was a concert.

While she was entering the warmth of the concert-hall, full of the smell of wet wool, he had rushed up to his room like a madman, stuffed his manuscript into his pocket, and come back to station himself between a couple of gas-lamps. A little music filtered out to him. The rain kept falling intermittently, and in between two showers the silvery light of the moon fell on him.

When the audience started coming out, he let people bump into him, trembling, afraid of missing her, standing on tip-toe. At last he caught sight of her, walking quickly; and he ran after her, finally stopping, out of breath, under a gas-lamp, in a street whose name he did not know.

'Mademoiselle . . .'

A white face before him, that face which he was now capable of drawing in three or four lines. He hunted in his pocket for his papers.

'I wanted to . . .'

And suddenly, as if a piece of flesh were being torn from him:

'I love you, Isabelle . . . I can't stand it any longer . . . I'm too unhappy . . . I love you, do you understand?'

He was crying, and felt ridiculous. He dropped his notebook and she bent down to pick it up at the same time as he did; unable to see anything, he went mad, clasped her in his arms, pressed her face against his wet cheek, brushed his lips against her mouth.

Then . . . then the most unexpected thing happened. Her mouth remained stuck to his, and looking again, he saw her face motionless against his, whiter than ever, and her open eyes close to his eyes.

'Isabelle . . .'

It was too much. He had not hoped for this. Frightened by the happiness which filled him, he let go of her suddenly with an abrupt movement and ran away, bumping into a fat, fleshy figure a few yards farther on.

Not a word. A cackle of sneering laughter. A hand falling heavily on his shoulder.

It was Doms. Marette, without knowing what he was doing, had followed him, and they had spent two hours drinking beer in a café he would have been incapable of finding again.

Since then, the winter had gone by. Doms, one fine day, had vanished without a word.

Night had fallen. At one end of the rue Montmartre, the arc-lamps had been lit between the buildings in the Central Market and, at the other end, the noisy life of the Grands Boulevards was flowing by.

Marette waited, tense and expectant, his nerves on edge. Some light filtered at last between the shutters of the Vétu shop. A silhouette brushed against the walls. After the first turning, he walked faster, passing his arm round a waist which showed no surprise.

'Well, my love?'

His eyes looked at her in a pathetic inquiry, Isabelle's eyes smiled, and their lips met, heedless of the passers-by who were merely shadows.

'Have you had a reply?'

They were walking along, crossing the Central Market as they had done nearly every evening for three months now, and soon they would come to the deserted embankment, to the Seine surging noisily past the stone walls.

'No. It must come, mustn't it? It just has to.'

'Calm yourself, my dear.'

'And your mother?'

'No. You can't see anything yet.'

He felt an urge to take some violent action, to gesticulate frantically, but then he suddenly repented and calmed down, putting his arms protectively around Isabelle as if she had become fragile.

'And to think that all we need is to find five hundred francs; to think that that horrible woman refuses to accept my word and give us credit! You know, Isabelle, there are times when ... there are times ...'

All that energy, all that despair, all that need, all that determination to be happy, meeting the tranquil emptiness of a fine night!

'Calm yourself, my dear. You know very well that when you're like that you frighten me. It doesn't do any good.'

And they walked on in silence, pressed against one another, gazing at the grey paving-stones in front of them.

Chapter Three

'Where are you going, Roger?'

'To play with Albert, Mother.'

'You've put your pinafore on?'

'Yes.'

'Mind the tram.'

She leant over the banisters while Roger took his straw hat from the hallstand, snapped the elastic round his neck, and stood motionless in the hall for a moment, like a grown-up wondering if he hasn't forgotten something. Finally he opened the letter-box and took out his marbles.

'Make sure that I can see you all the time.'

He did not reply, but went out, leaving the door ajar. The rue de la Loi was hot and empty. A solemn silence hung over the school yard, for the holidays had started the day before, and the friars could be seen going out at unusual times, in threes, with the edges of their hats turned up like wings, their black cloaks floating behind them, and one of their white bands always sticking up in the air. Brother Médard himself had come out of the green gate a little earlier, not to plant himself in the middle of the pavement as he did the other mornings to watch the boys coming in and out, but to go off towards the town. Was he taking a holiday too. In any case, he had looked to see if he could catch sight of that neat, hard-working young mother who took in lodgers.

For a long time now, Élise and Brother Médard had known each other without having exchanged a single word, separated as they had always been by the width of the street. Brother Médard looked like nobody else and defied all classification. He was extremely fat. His shiny cassock was stretched over a belly as round as a barrel. A huge head, with close-cropped hair and plump, shiny cheeks, was stuck solidly on top of this cylindrical mass; the whole massive ensemble rolled from left to right at every step, on account of the wooden leg which had to be lifted off the ground; Brother Médard sweated profusely, mopping his face with a red handkerchief like Léopold's, and you could hear his stick on the pavement long before he appeared in the frame of the green gate; yet in spite of all that, he imposed respect and confidence and it was to him that, if Élise needed advice, she would go to ask.

She was flattered by the glance which he granted her every morning, by that vague, modest greeting which you addressed to somebody you did not know but wanted to know; several times she had noticed that he hung around after the boys had gone if he had not seen her at one of her windows.

In the autumn, Roger, who was five and a half, would be going to the Friars' school.

The latter, who looked rather like crows, were greeted with shouts of: 'Caw! Caw!' by the street-urchins, those dirty, cheeky children whom Élise called filthy brats.

There were plenty of filthy brats in the district. Between Saint-Nicolas and the rue Puits-en-Sock, in the back-streets where you went only when you were in a hurry, as a short cut, you met nothing else: dirty little girls, without knickers, sitting on the kerb with their legs apart, babies with their noses running and egg-stains round their mouths, and boys who bumped into passers-by and threw stones at you with deafening yells.

A hundred yards away, in the rue de l'Enseignement, the children who went to the state school were filthy brats too.

'Behave yourself, Roger! Don't put your finger in your nose. You don't want to look like a brat from the state school!'

Now and then a gang of children from somewhere or other,

236

Bressoux or the parish of Saint-Pholien, descended on the place du Congrès; rough, common and noisy, they stood on the benches, dirtying them, climbed the trees, pulled off the leaves, swung on the lower branches and frightened the mothers, until the figure of a policeman looked up or they thought of a prank to play somewhere else.

Even at the Friars' school, in the rue de la Loi, there were some children from the back-streets, in other words more filthy brats, some of whom clattered about in clogs. For the school was divided into two parts. Opposite the Mamelins' house, the green gate which Brother Médard guarded led into a spacious yard and the pink building of the Institut Saint-André.

You never said 'the Friars' school', for people might misunderstand. The pupils of the Institut Saint-André came out in a row under the supervision of their masters, unless their mothers were waiting for them in the glass parlour on the right of the porch.

A little farther on, on the other hand, the pupils of the free school could be seen every afternoon rushing out of a sort of dirty barracks in a noisy, unruly horde. A friar followed them with some difficulty to the door, a big, fat, common-looking man, a sort of peasant in a cassock with his nose smeared with snuff, who, without bothering to arrange the children in two rows, seemed to drive them out of the peaceful middle-class street.

This invasion lasted only a few moments, but if Roger happened to be outside just then, his mother was sure to appear at the door or at one of the windows of the house:

'Come in quickly, Roger!'

Spick and span in his black pinafore with its wide folds, his Jean-Bart hat on his head, and his calves bulging out over his navy-blue socks, he wandered along, as dreamy or as thoughtful as a man, in a setting whose details were more familiar to him than to anybody else. Two houses further on, behind the panes of a window with impeccable curtains, he knew that he would catch sight of Raymonde. Raymonde, who never played in the street, not even on her own doorstep, was a girl of his age, as pink as any expensive doll, a quiet little thing with lovely golden curls. She looked at him too, but those window-panes always separated them. Raymonde lived in a quilted box into which neither the air nor the noises from outside ever penetrated, and gliding behind her you could sometimes see a governess in black with a narrow lace collar. Raymonde's father and mother, Monsieur and Madame Rousseau, were both in the teaching profession; they went off in the morning and came home in the evening, grave and dignified.

Roger turned round to watch a tram going past along the rue Jean-d'Outremeuse, then, after a moment's thought, chose a glass marble, one of the big greenish marbles used as stoppers in soda bottles, and threw it in front of him.

Wasn't he too in a sort of box, a bigger box than Raymonde's, a box whose lid was a patch of blue sky with roofs and chimneys standing out against it, and whose edge was the gentle curve described by the No. 4 tram which you saw passing along the rue Jean-d'Outremeuse and which reappeared in the place du Congrès, at the end of the rue Pasteur? In this box, he knew the colour of every house, the shape of the windows, and even certain hollows between the paving-stones which served as holes for his game of marbles.

He knew that it was Saturday because this morning his mother had not put on her cotton check apron but the apron in coarse blue cloth which was reserved for the weekly cleaning, and, looking round again before turning the corner of the rue Pasteur, he recognized the soapy water flowing along the front of the house. In the afternoon, the streets looked like a draughtboard, with big black squares in front of certain houses and white squares in front of others. The shining black squares were the wet patches, where the women had washed their stretch of pavement and roadway with bucketfuls of water and where each woman had left her little pile of dust and dung in the middle of the street.

It was scarcely a week since the policeman had rung every door-bell along the street and ordered the occupants to pull up the grass between the paving-stones; Roger had spent hours squatting on his heels with a potato peeler in his hand, digging up the narrow strips of grass or moss and trying to keep long pieces intact, his teeth set on edge by the grating of the blade on the stones. The whole district was outside, people nobody ever set eyes on; some looked embarrassed while the police-man Leroy, who lived in the rue de l'Enseignement, strolled up and down with a satisfied smile.

Armand Pain was alone outside his house. Roger did not say hullo to him. If his mother had been there, she would have scolded him.

'Say hullo to Armand.'

'I don't want to.'

'He's your friend.'

'I don't want him to be my friend any more.'

He went past looking the other way, on purpose. His friend nowadays was Albert.

'Albert who?'

'Albert.'

'Why hasn't he got another name?'

'Don't try to understand. Go and play.'

Roger stopped in front of a house in white brick, the only light-coloured house in the street, right opposite the Pains'. He banged the letter-box, and a gentle, fair-haired young woman opened the door.

'Oh, it's you, Roger. Have you come to see Albert?'

It was not a house like other houses. Everything in it was gayer and more delicate, there were flowers in the vases and scent in the air, and Albert's mother was always dressed in pale silk.

'Albert! Do you want to go to play with Roger? Don't stay too long. Remember we have to pack your things.'

Albert was not an ordinary boy either. With his hair as fine and fair as his mother's, and his white skin with a few freckles under the eyes, he looked like a girl, and he wore velvet suits with big white collars.

From the opposite pavement, Armand enviously watched them walking off towards the corner of the street, for Roger and Albert were supposed to play at the junction of the rue Pasteur and the rue de la Loi, so that their mothers could see them. On the way, they showed each other their marbles, not forgetting to turn round to look scornfully at Armand, who pretended to be enjoying himself on his own.

'I'll never play with him again,' Roger promised with a

certain solemnity, as if Albert had reproached him with their former friendship.

He was afraid of displeasing Albert. He admired his suit, his easy manner, even those little golden spots which gave a special glow to his face.

'What shall we play at?'

The corner of the street was formed by a tall yellow house and, at pavement level, there were the windows of a basement kitchen. They were wide open, showing a maidservant at work, tiled walls, and copper saucepans on a white enamel cooker. The maid was grating carrots and this made a noise like an insect. A bulldog bitch, the only one in the district, was lying on the doorstep, on its back, and now and then Roger glanced furtively between its paws, as he did with the dirty little girls in the rue des Récollets. In this connexion, there was a question he would have liked to ask Albert, but he did not dare.

They could hear the shrill voice of fat Madame Morel who, from the pavement where she was standing, was talking to a neighbour at a first-floor window.

'Can you do that?' asked Albert, interlocking the fingers of both hands and suddenly twisting his thin wrists.

'It's easy!'

However, Roger did not manage it at the first attempt.

'Wait a minute! You can do it because you've tried it before.'

Trams went by every ten minutes along the rue Jean-d'Outremeuse. Friars came back in groups of three and rang the bell outside the green gate. Roger, who watched everything, knew that there was a wire across the yard and that it was by pulling a handle attached to it that the cook worked the mechanism of the door from his kitchen.

Only a month ago, he and Albert had been hoarding cherrystones, which they managed to make white and shiny by cleaning them and by turning them over and over in their pockets, but the cherry season was over. The asparagus season too. Asparagus was what Roger liked best of all.

Albert announced:

'Tonight we're leaving for the seaside.'

'Have you seen the sea already?'

'Yes. We go there every year. You too?'

'No. Is it very big?'

Élise Mamelin was washing her part of the street, to get ahead with her work. Wearing clogs, she flung bucketfuls of water over the pavement, scrubbed away with her brush, straightened her crumbling bun. Mademoiselle Frida came home and crossed the wet patch with stork-like precautions, wearing a white blouse over her flared skirt and a flat boater on her raven hair.

'But yes, Mademoiselle Frida, you really must come with us. You'll see how good the air is on the heights. She must come and spend the day at Embourg, mustn't she, Désiré?'

Monsieur Saft had gone back to Poland. He had been so afraid of failing his examination and having to stay to prepare for the one in October! He would be coming back in the autumn. His room was being kept for him, even though he did not pay for it during the holidays, for he was not rich.

In the morning, he always came downstairs first, went into the yard, wearing a white vest showing the shape of his torso, and, for half an hour, while Élise was making the coffee and the house was gradually awakening, he did his exercises, very difficult exercises, then ran back upstairs to his room with a wet towel tied round his neck.

Mademoiselle Pauline, who had another oral examination to come, was leaving at the beginning of the next week. Her mother, a fat lady who walked with difficulty because of her bad feet, had come to see her at Christmas and had brought a smoked goose.

'I bet you've never eaten any smoked goose!' Roger said to Albert.

'It doesn't exist.'

'It does, in Poland. I know, because we've got some Poles in our house. And what about cherry soup, have you ever had that?'

'You can't make soup out of cherries.'

'You ask my mother! She made some once for Monsieur Saft and I had some. Mother! Mother! Albert doesn't believe...'

'Careful, children. Don't go where it's wet. Go and play somewhere else.'

There was only one shop in this part of the street – the other part, on the far side of the rue Pasteur, didn't count, people never went there, it was another country – and even then it was not a real shop. It was a private house in which the Venetian window had been converted into a shop-window. It was too high up. The children had to perch on tip-toe, or cling with the ends of their shoes to the freestone basement jutting out . . .

'You're spoiling your shoes, Roger!'

Behind the half-lowered blind, they gazed at the boxes of cigars whose gold bands fascinated them. There were some ordinary ones, but there were others with broad coats-of-arms bearing complicated emblems, sometimes the profile of an eminent person, Léopold II's white beard.

'When I'm bigger, I shall collect cigar bands.'

They went to and fro, serious and thoughtful, in search of a new game, the basement kitchen on the corner sent out whiffs of stew, and the bitch, rolling in a pile of steaming dung, exhibited its pink belly with the two rows of pimples and the little slit with the hair along the edges which intrigued Roger so much.

Albert's mother came towards them, sheltering her fair hair under a mauve parasol, and bent forward like a flower on its stem.

'Are you coming for your dinner, Albert?'

She never shouted from her doorstep, like the other mothers of the district.

'Good-bye, Roger. See you in a couple of months. Have a good holiday.'

Élise had taken in her bucket and brushes and Roger hopped towards the square patch of wet pavement, building another lock of mud in the gutter before going into the hall which was being invaded by blue steam from the kitchen.

It was after two o'clock. Désiré, who had just come home, was at table and Roger could hear the sound of his fork, his voice and then Élise's, for all the doors were open this Saturday, even that of Mademoiselle Frida's room, and draughts were blowing all over the house.

'Roger!'

He was expecting it. He already knew what his mother was going to say.

'If you're going to stay on the doorstep, take your cushion.'

A pity. He liked the feel of the cold stone which was a grey colour bordering on blue, and the contrast of this chilliness with the heat of the sun beating down on his face. He went to the hallstand to get the red cushion his mother had made for him with a piece of carpet.

As soon as he had sat down, he shut his eyes, to gain time, for he was playing a private game; he let a numbness come over him which you could not obtain every day or even every hour of the day; he savoured the prickling of his cheeks, of his eyelids which the golden rays were piercing; he studied the thickening of his blood in his veins, deliberately confused the sounds reaching him through the crystalline air, mixed up the pictures, created whirlpools of bright colours.

With a hand over one eye, to create a dark contrast, he spelt out from the brass plate of the school, in the limpid shade of the opposite pavement which was turning a greenish colour: 'Ins-ti-tut . . . Saint . . .' – for Sister Adonie had taught him to read on the sly: he had to keep it a secret, since he was not old enough.

'Ins-ti-tut Saint . . .' The Friars' green door was shut. The little door, which was cut out of the big one and was always left open, was shut too.

'I'm sure that Mathilde Coomans . . .'

It was his mother's voice in the vibrant coolness of the kitchen. In the rue Pasteur, Armand was sure to be sitting on his doorstep, without a cushion, with only his feet protruding beyond the shadow which, at this time of day, formed a narrow ribbon running along the fronts of the houses. Had Albert already gone? Would a motor-car come to fetch him, Monsieur Méline's motor-car which stopped every week in front of the white house and which the neighbours watched out for?

'You'll see that Mathilde won't refuse us that.'

Roger blew on the back of his hand, then breathed in the sharper smell of his skin. He gave a start as he heard the trumpet of the ice-cream vendor who had just stopped in the burning wilderness of the place du Congrès, picturing to himself his little lemon-coloured cart with the brass lids and the painted panels, one of which showed the Bay of Naples, a turquoise-blue colour, and the other a dramatic eruption of Vesuvius.

'*Git orf ze cart!*'

The funny little Italian with the waxed moustache flew into a rage when the street-urchins climbed on to the wheels of his carefully painted cart. They deliberately hung on to it as soon as he had his back turned.

'*Git orf ze cart!*'

They ran off, not very far, coming back soon, and Di Coco, with a wealth of gesture, shrieked at them in phrases in which he mixed up the Walloon dialect and that of his own country.

*

'You couldn't mention it to Victor, could you, Désiré? Tell him that Mathilde would only have to come for a quarter of an hour every morning to make Mademoiselle Frida's bed and empty her slops.'

A fly went by. A tram. Roger, when he was drunk with sunshine like this, could, if he wished, hear the fly as clearly as the tram. He could mix everything together, behind his lowered eyelashes, the spire of Saint-Nicolas, motionless against a violet background, the brass plate of the Friars' school, and the humps of the cobblestones surrounded by a trickle of water which bore witness to the morning's cleaning.

He could experience things which had already happened and other things which were still to come; Désiré was going to get up with a sigh of satisfaction and stop in front of the hallstand to put on his boater and take his stick. Then Élise would hang up a curtain – not a real curtain but an old sheet – behind the glazed door of the kitchen. He could already hear the water boiling in the washtub.

'Roger!'

No! Not again, not before his father had left, before his mother had gone up to the second floor to get the clean linen, the glycerine soap, the glove-sponge which became soft and slimy in the soapy water, and the nail-scissors.

Roger, without needing to listen to what his parents were saying, guessed what they were talking about, and there was an element of mystery in their plans which alarmed and excited him.

For three Sundays now they had not been to Ans, to the Ursuline convent, to see Mother Marie-Madeleine, who was an aunt of his and whose coif used to bump against him when he kissed her. They had not been to Coronmeuse either, where the grown-ups sat on straw-bottomed chairs outside Aunt Louisa's shop while Anna played the piano in the sitting-room with the windows open and Roger, armed with a wicker wand from the workshop, strolled along the shady embankment and looked at the boats on the canal.

He did not know why, but one Sunday, all of a sudden, they had gone into the country with some people he had never met before.

'Say good day to Aunt Mathilde and Uncle Victor.'

He had gathered later that they were not a real uncle or a real aunt. They were cousins of Uncle Charles, the sacristan at Saint Denis. If he turned his head, Roger could see their shop, on the corner of the rue de la Loi and the rue de la Commune, in the part he did not like, on the far side of the invisible frontier.

He did not like the Coomans either, or their son who was six months younger than he was and a cheeky little boy.

They had taken sandwiches, hard-boiled eggs, and coffee in the civic guard's flask. Taking the tram, they had passed through a world of factories and dark little houses which all looked the same; then, on foot, they had climbed a long slope bordered with bushes. Désiré had covered the back of his neck with his handkerchief, keeping it in position with his boater, and he had taken his jacket off.

They had picnicked on the grass, by the side of a dusty white road, and in the evening their clothes had been covered with a layer of powder.

Roger opened one eye and shut it again quickly; another smell came back to him, the smell of the prize-giving, the garden of the nursery school where they had been placed in three rows in front of the conservatory, among some evergreens, the children in the front row sitting cross-legged, to have their photograph taken. Where had his mother put the crown of gilded laurel-leaves which he had tearfully refused to keep on in the street?

Uncle Victor was a printer; he talked politics through his nose, a long narrow nose; his thin moustache which dropped over his lips looked as if it were coming out of his nostrils. Aunt Mathilde had taken it into her head to open a grocer's shop on the corner of the rue de la Commune. It was a huge room, too bright and painted beige, a room which smelled of paraffin and where nobody ever set foot.

'She hasn't got a head for business, you know, Désiré. Now if I were running that shop!'

Désiré's footsteps came nearer. He bent down slightly, brushed his lips against Roger's forehead.

'See you tonight, son.'

'Good-bye, Father.'

Élise was going to call him. She had gone upstairs to get the linen.

What were they going to ask Aunt Mathilde for?

*

'*Do you think they'd let us have a cup of milk, Désiré? We'd pay for it, of course.*'

They were on the dusty road. Beyond meadows where sluggish cows were grazing, you could see, far away, in the blue and green of the horizon, the red and white patches of some villages, a slender spire on the top of a hill.

Standing a few yards away from the three little whitewashed houses, they had discussed the point for a moment, then Élise had bravely made for the nearest open door, which was at the top of a flight of five or six steps.

'Excuse me, Madame. Forgive me for bothering you. It's because of the children, you see.'

That was how they had made the acquaintance of Madame Laude, a big, powerful woman built like a man, with a loud voice and an upper lip covered with dark brown, who had promptly picked Roger up in her strong hands.

Madame Laude had taken them underneath the Virginia creeper in the garden and a wasp had fallen into the boy's milk.

'How good the air is here!' Élise, who had semicircles of sweat under her arms, had kept remarking.

'Why don't you leave the little boy with me during the holidays? That would put some colour into his cheeks.'

Nobody had thought that Roger was listening, but he had declared:

'I don't want to stay with her.'

They had sent him to play with the Coomans boy who was as ill-mannered as the children at the state school. The green shutters on the first floor had been opened, and Roger had seen that his parents were going over the house, arguing, nodding their heads; he had caught sight of Élise making signs to Désiré behind Madame Laude's back.

On the way home, the grown-ups had gone on talking in an undertone all the time.

'You see, Mathilde, there'll be nobody left in the house but Mademoiselle Frida. Monsieur Saft is going, Mademoiselle Pauline, too. As for Monsieur Chechelowski, the engineer I told you about, who's on a course at Ougrée-Marihaye, he's waiting to hear from a fellow countryman of his whom he's supposed to be joining at Charleroi during August.'

The proof that this was what his father and mother had been talking about just now was that on Thursday Élise had bought some cream material at L'Innovation to make into smocks for Roger. They had already been cut out. In her draughty room, where both the door and the window were open, Mademoiselle Frida, probably for the first time in her life, was busy sewing.

'Roger! It's time. Roger! What are you doing?'

Nothing. He was in something of a daze. He was dawdling. In the kitchen, his mother undressed him, but not without his saying:

'Lock the door.'

For he lived in dread of being caught in his bath.

'Wash your ears well, Roger.'

His hair was brushed and combed, his toe-nails were cut, steam collected on the window-panes and, when he was ready at last, dressed in clean clothes from head to foot, a new feeling on his skin succeeded the caress of the sun: he felt at once very heavy and very light, rather empty too, and his ears stayed crimson until the evening.

'Go out for a walk. Don't get dirty.'

She gave him five centimes to buy an ice-cream and he sucked this for a long time, very seriously, in the place du Congrès, where he was all alone with the Italian.

The blue of the sky became tinged with pink, then red, puddles of water glistened on the newly washed pavement, and, on the shady side, the freestone which had been scrubbed with iron brushes was an implacable white.

Désiré came home half an hour later than usual, for he had

gone to the rue des Pitteurs to have a bath. Élise had had time to tidy the kitchen, to pack the food they would need the next day, and even to iron some linen, for a vague smell of ironing hung about the kitchen.

'What did Victor say?'

'That Mathilde would be only too pleased.'

'Tomorrow we'll tell Madame Laude, and we could leave next Sunday. Listen, Roger: we are going to spend a month in the country, at Embourg, at Madame Laude's, where father will join us every evening.'

The street door had been left open to the soft summer evening, and Désiré, in his shirtsleeves, installed his chair on the pavement, tilting it backwards, a couple of yards from the Delcours, the people next door, who were sitting like him outside their door. There was a girl of sixteen who was at the teachers' training college, a big fellow of twenty-two who was already a schoolmaster, another brother who was a draughtsman in a factory, and the eldest of the family, a thirty-five-year-old painting contractor who was always joking like Arthur and was familiar with everybody.

Farther on, other people were taking the air. Mademoiselle Pauline, all pink from the glow of the setting sun in the pink of her room, was idly looking out of her window with her elbows on the sill, and, over the wall of the Institut Saint-André, she could see some of the friars strolling round the yard.

Désiré started talking. A circle formed round him, the chairs were drawn nearer to one another, the painter who looked like Arthur answered him and everybody laughed, the girl made a show of indignation, and they all looked up now and then at Mademoiselle Pauline. Élise, who had put on a clean pinafore with little flounces, came out, smiling too, to have a look before returning to the thousand-and-one tasks waiting for her in the cool interior of the house.

The bells rang for the evening service, but there must have been only a few old bigots in the empty church. The whole parish was living its Saturday life, the shopkeepers of the rue Puits-en-Sock taking the air on their doorsteps, Chrétien Mamelin smoking his pipe in silence beside old Kreutz, and the two dolls – as people always called the tow-haired Kreutz sisters – knitting away as if their lives depended on it.

Two or three shop-windows, which the owners had obstinately left alight, threw out an artificial glow. The shops exhaled their smells, sugared sweets and gingerbread at Gruyelle-Marquant's, cardboard and paste at the Dolls' Hospital, butter and cheese, and then the tarts at Bonmersonne's which would be piled up on the shelves the following day. A woman without a hat trailed behind her, as far as the nearby cul-de-sac into which she disappeared, the greasy smell of the chips she was carrying in a dish covered with a red-edged napkin.

In the rue de la Loi, Désiré was making them laugh, on the two thresholds which had become one, and even Mademoiselle Frida, who had come to lean quietly against the door-jamb, stretched her lips in a condescending smile.

'Go and play, Roger. It's for grown-ups. Besides, it's time to go to bed.'

'Another five minutes, Father! Just another five minutes!'

'You know perfectly well that you'll have to get up early tomorrow.'

Roger was more afraid of the twilight than he was of the dark. That cold light, which struck him as the reflection of the dead sun, frightened him, and he did not like the yellow, oily colour of the flame of his night-light, or the glow which he could still make out through the blinds.

'Are you in bed, Roger?'

His mother came upstairs and tucked him up in bed

'Sleep well. Tomorrow, we are off to Embourg. Are you pleased to be going to Embourg for your holidays?'

He did not reply. The whole day, in a single moment, palpitated within him and puffed him up, his ears started buzzing, his body which smelled of Saturday evening and the bath curled up, he pulled the sheet over his head to see nothing more, and yet he could still make out, far away and at the same time very close, shrill laughter in the street, the sound of voices, his father's voice dominating the others, and a snatch of song which was promptly drowned by the noise of the tram.

'Well, Élise?'

'Just a minute . . .'

She came out smiling, a little tired, at first refusing the chair which was offered to her in the circle, then sitting on the edge of it, her hands motionless in her lap, and heaving a sigh.

The gas-lamps had been alight for a long time when, one after another, the doors shut, and suddenly it was Sunday, the seven o'clock Mass, the smell of eggs and bacon in the kitchen, Mademoiselle Frida astonished by the prospect of the day before her, Mademoiselle Pauline to whom the house was being entrusted, the coming and going, the voices, and the excitement which would die down when the door had finally shut again and they were out in the empty street.

'You haven't forgotten anything? You've put the ham in the bag?'

The tram. Roger managed to stay on the platform with his father, next to two anglers who were cluttered up with their equipment.

It was not yet ten o'clock and there they were, slowly climbing the long slope between two green hedges, with cow smells hanging in the air, Mademoiselle Frida, dressed in black and white with her boater flat on her head, holding herself as erect as in town and poking the dust with the tip of her parasol, and Désiré carrying not only their provisions, but also his jacket which he had just taken off.

'Don't dawdle, Roger, keep walking.'

And they smiled as they looked back at the town behind them, and their breath burned their throats; for want of practice, they were rather out of breath.

Chapter Four

It was on 15 August 1908 that Désiré spent half the morning trying to send a kite up from the Piedboeufs' meadow, but if a gust of wind lifted the light contraption of red and green cotton, if hope finally relaxed the features of Roger who had to stand several yards away from his father, the air promptly closed up again and you could see nothing in the atmosphere, which was humming with invisible insects, except the hot circular waves which the sun was sending out like rings.

The day before, in the bluish twilight, Roger and his mother had been waiting, as they did every day, at the top of the Thiers des Grillons; and they had seen that Désiré, who was reading his paper as he climbed the hill, was carrying an oblong parcel. It was the dismantled kite: four fragile sticks, some cross-pieces, a piece of green cloth and one of red. What Roger had not known at the time was that his father had another surprise in store.

After supper, in Madame Laude's garden, nobody had thought of putting the boy to bed, in the room where he used to go to sleep with his window open to the stars and to the croaking of the frogs in the brickworks, and where the pale light of dawn brought the lowing of the cows on Halleux's farm.

A Désiré whose moustache was quivering with impatience bustled mysteriously to and fro. He could not wait until darkness had fallen completely: a firework exploded in the road, and a rocket soared into the sky to fall slowly to the ground in a fine shower of sparks.

Roger would never forget the three houses with their white walls growing indistinct in the dusk; the mound opposite and the hedge with the red berries; a solitary, twisted tree, at the foot of which he had recently dug his canary's grave; some silent groups of faceless figures, children who had come quietly from the pump crossroads; Désiré himself, as self-important as a stage-hand in a pantomime who can only just be glimpsed in the wings; the flame sputtering at the end of a rocket; and finally the real stars lighting up in the sky. A smell he had never known before invaded this corner of the countryside as it was transformed by the Bengal lights, and, when a rocket misfired, when the green stars went out too soon in the sky, Roger held his breath, so moved that he could not answer his mother.

'Are you happy?'

He did not move, not daring to go forward or to turn round.

'You're enjoying yourself? You aren't frightened?'

He wasn't frightened. And yet the creatures moving about and whispering in the shadows struck him as unfamiliar. He did not recognize either Madame Laude or the children in clogs from the other houses. A triple windmill gave Désiré a lot of trouble. One of the windmills went out too soon and he struggled to start it up again, bending double so as not to block the light. When he finally came back towards his son, Roger looked at him differently from before, rather as if he were not his father.

He walked in his sleep that night.

'You see, Désiré, he's too sensitive.'

And the next day, he was hunting around on the road, to which the sunlight had restored its familiar appearance, for the pale blue tubes of the rockets and the twisted wires which still smelled of gunpowder, when he caught sight of his father, in his shirt-sleeves, busy assembling the kite in the Piedboeufs' meadow.

*

That same day, in a bigger meadow, two miles from Nevers, thousands of people were gathering together who had come by road from all points of the horizon, in carts, by motor-car and on foot. Fences had been put up and canvas stretched across stakes in the ground to prevent those who had not paid from seeing into the enclosure. In spite of that, there were more people outside the meadow than there were inside the barriers, families were picnicking on the grass, horses were grazing, and hawkers in white jackets were selling lemonade, liquorice water and scones.

It was hot. There were some youths perched on the fences with their legs dangling, and others were defending the top of a grassy mound or the branches of a walnut-tree as fiercely as you would defend your seat in a theatre.

For the first time in this part of France, some aeroplanes were going to give a flying display. The biplanes with their canvas wings and fragile fuselages were there, at the edge of the ground, surrounded by a few men who were fussing around and looking inquiringly at the sky where two little white clouds were hanging.

Nevers station had never been as empty as it was that morning when the train from Paris came in and the coaches moved slowly by; Félicien Miette was almost alone on the sunny platform where he had been pacing up and down for half an hour. Tense and nervous, he gazed fixedly at the few doors which opened and at the travellers picking up their suitcases and looking for the way out.

Suddenly he turned round. Isabelle was there, smiling at him, very much herself, although he had not seen her getting out of her third-class compartment.

He felt unreasonably furious at not having seen her sooner, among the thinly scattered silhouettes, furious at having given a start, at having failed to understand straight away why she was alone, at having shown it, at behaving in such an unnatural, nervous way in front of her, when after all he was expecting her, and last of all at seeing her just as she was bound to be, dressed in the usual way, calm and simple, with a gleam of affectionate mockery in her eyes.

He did not even think of kissing her.

'What's the matter, my love?'

He looked past her, worried, puzzled, and to put an end to his anguish she explained:

'My father had an attack last night. He wanted to send you a telegram. I insisted on coming, and Mother sighed:

'"When they've got to that point, Joseph!"'

He asked in a flat voice:

'You haven't any luggage?'

'What for, seeing that I'm going back tonight?'

He was going to relax. He relaxed. But he was upset, and for a moment he nearly started crying for no particular reason.

'Come along.'

Already, while she was looking for her ticket in her bag, he kissed her, and she could feel him trembling; outside, he put his arm round her waist, as he used to do in Paris, when, in the evening, they walked along the deserted embankments.

They had been apart for only a month. For a month he had written her up to three letters a day, page after page covered with closely written lines, and yet it was taking him some time to get to know her again, and he walked along in silence, looking at the ground.

He knew that with her first glance she had taken everything in, his hair which he had allowed to grow longer, something which made him look thinner – he had in fact lost weight – the loosely tied cravat and the wide-brimmed hat. His fingers linked with Isabelle's fingers, and their two bodies leaning towards one another formed a single shadow on the pavement.

She asked gently:

'Are you happy?'

*

Roger Mamelin's mother had asked the same question, the previous evening, during the firework display, and the boy had made no answer. Félicien Miette, for his part, just increased the pressure of his fingers. He had been so afraid, just now, unreasonably afraid, that she would have changed, that she would have stopped loving him, and the funny thing was that he had been even more afraid when he had not seen her parents who were supposed to be coming with her.

'Poor Papa! I do believe that he won't be easy in his mind until we're married.'

Then, as at last it occurred to her to look around her, in the shade of the avenue de la République lined with striped awnings, she asked:

'Is it far?'

He hesitated and frowned, and his features became sharper, as they always did when he fell a prey to his evil thoughts.

'No. Five minutes' walk. Do you love me, Isabelle?'

'Already?'

How often had he asked her that question, sometimes when they had been apart for scarcely an hour?

'Answer me!'

'And what if I said no?'

She could not even allow herself that innocent jest without his growing as tense as a bowstring.

'Get along with you, you big silly!'

'You haven't any regrets?'

'No.'

'You're sure you haven't any regrets, any regrets at all, that you never will have any?'

'I'm quite sure.'

'All the same . . .'

She could feel that he was turning bitter, and knew that a sudden, sharp, painful violence, springing from the very depths of his being, would follow on that bitterness; and as they walked along, holding each other round the waist, with people turning round to look at them, she murmured:

'Be quiet.'

He could not understand why anybody should love him. There were moments when he refused to believe that it was possible, when he hated Isabelle for deceiving him and looked at her with wild eyes.

'Tell me about your paper,' she said.

'Not now.'

It was about them that he always had to talk, without ever exhausting the subject, the subject of him and her, the subject of their love. How many times had he tried to elucidate the same mystery?

'The first evening, after the Conservatoire, in that back-street, when I fell on you like a madman . . .'

'Well?'

'You weren't in love with me!'

He stated it as a fact. She in her turn declared:

'Yes, I was!'

'It's impossible. You couldn't have been in love with me, yet you let me take you in my arms. If it had been any other man . . .'

'No!'

'When I told you all that I'd done . . .'

'Be quiet.'

'You see!'

'No, my poor love . . .'

He was ashamed of the past and he would go on cheating, just as he was cheating in taking her to that house whose key he kept turning over and over in his pocket.

'It's here that you live?'

A town dwelling which looked like a country dwelling, a white house with green shutters and boundary-stones at both corners, where they found silence, cool shadows, the intimate smell of a household, children's toys in the hall and fishing tackle behind the door. It was next to a stone bridge and a stream whose limpid water flowed over the flattened grass before losing itself in the Nièvre. The greengrocer in the shop on the other side of the road watched them go in and said something about them to her customer.

'Come along.'

The steps of the polished staircase creaked under their feet. The window of the room with the mahogany bed was open, but Félicien Miette, heedless of everything, had already taken Isabelle in his arms, and fiercely, spitefully, he crushed his lips against hers as if he wanted to suffocate her.

She gently disengaged herself and got her breath back, looking over his shoulder at the sunny rectangle of the window.

'There's somebody watching us.'

He felt cross with her for having noticed the patch made by an old woman's face behind the window-panes opposite.

'Close the shutters, at least!'

He obeyed her irritably, then looked at her, in the room which was now striped with light and shade.

'What's the matter?' she asked.

'You don't know? You don't want anything?'

'Yes, I do.'

It was not so much her flesh that he wanted, or sensual pleasure, as to feel that she was his, more so all the time, so much his that nothing and nobody could ever make them two distinct individuals again. He clasped her to him like somebody attempting the impossible, and when he finally lay still in the ravaged bed he felt sad, she knew that, she knew him so well, she who lay looking with tender astonishment at his thin body, the body of an unfinished man.

It was he who, in a suspicious mood, broke the silence.

'What are you thinking about?'

'About us. You still haven't told me anything.'

And if he did tell her everything, absolutely everything, she would be frightened, or indignant, or disgusted; she would get dressed with abrupt gestures and go off for ever, without a word or a look.

All the same, he wanted to talk. Often he was tortured by the urge to confess everything to her, perhaps even to tell her more than there was, to exaggerate. She thought that she knew him because he had told her about his hideous youth and the deed he had committed to put an end to it all.

She knew nothing. The truth about the five hundred francs, for instance? Every time he thought about it his forehead broke out in an unhealthy sweat. Sometimes, at night, he tossed about in his bed without being able to banish that memory. He recalled the place, at the tip of the Ile Saint-Louis, just behind the eternal mass of Notre-Dame, where he had announced one evening:

'I've received the money-order.'

They had walked along in silence, both too nervous to be pleased.

'When shall we go to see her?'

'Tomorrow if you like. Listen, Isabelle . . .'

What was the use of recalling what they had decided? What else could they have done, in the circumstances?

He had waited on the horrible old woman's landing. It had been raining and the whole house had smelled of onions. A bat's-wing gas-burner had been sputtering on the floor below. Tenants had passed him on the landing, and Miette had turned his face towards the wall, like a man surprised in a place of ill repute. When Isabelle had come out of the flat, in which he had caught sight of some armchairs upholstered in crimson velvet, she had been pale and unsteady on her legs. They had gone home keeping close to the walls, and Félicien, in the stationer's shop, had been unable to look Monsieur Brois in the face any more.

For Léopold had not sent the money. It was Monsieur Brois who had lent it. Miette had gone to see him at his home in the suburbs, where he lived by himself in a little house built of grey stone. He had told him everything, in a violent, tragic speech, and since then, every day, Isabelle had walked past Monsieur Brois.

'What's the matter, my love? What's bothering you?'

He flew into a temper with himself, with the whole world which was doing its best to curb his impatience.

'You think this room's mine, don't you? Well, it isn't. With what I earn on the *Gazette du Centre*, I can scarcely afford a sordid room in the most sinister hotel in the town.'

He was lying, cheating all the time. He could not help it. With what he earned, he could have taken a fairly decent room, and indeed he had found one in a widowed lady's house, but his cross-grained character could not put up with neatness and tranquillity, and it was on purpose that he had chosen the disreputable hotel to which, every evening, the local prostitutes brought their casual customers.

'Don't you understand? It's because your parents were

T—P.—I

257

supposed to be coming that I borrowed this room from Chapelle, an absolute fool, the assistant editor of the *Gazette*. We are in his house. He has taken his wife and children to the flying display. At this very moment, they are picnicking somewhere on the grass.'

She looked at the untidy bed; he guessed what she was thinking and felt ashamed. On his return, his friend would know what purpose the key he had lent had served, and his wife would stop short in horror at the sight of the crumpled sheets.

Isabelle, who was slowly getting dressed again, made no reproach.

'And even if he knows, what of it?' Miette asked in a truculent voice.

'Who are you talking about?'

'You know. You're ashamed of being my mistress. You're afraid that people will know.'

'No.'

There was a difference which he pretended not to see between knowing and being suddenly confronted with the crude revelation of that ravaged bed.

'You know, Isabelle, you're like all the rest. Whereas I . . .'

He put his head in his hands. He was suffering.

'I'm all alone! I've always been alone! I'll go on being alone all my life! Nobody tries to understand and yet if you only knew . . .'

She was about to say 'I know' when he bridled angrily.

'You yourself, you don't believe me when I tell you that I'll get to the top, that one day I'll hold them all in the hollow of my hand, like that, look!'

And clenching his fist until the knuckles showed white, he hit the wall in a convulsive gesture so that the bricks echoed with the noise.

'I assure you, my love, that I've got confidence in you.'

'If you really had confidence in me, if you really felt what I feel, you wouldn't start worrying whether a mediocre idiot who's lent me his bedroom and his fat fool of a wife know or don't know that we sleep together . . .'

'Forgive me . . . No, Félicien, don't cry!'

The tears were inevitable. Crying helped him to relax; she stroked his hair and talked softly to him.

'You'll see, my love, everything will work out all right. Everything is practically settled already, seeing that my father . . .'

He sneered:

'Your father!'

'You've got to admit that he has been more understanding than we could reasonably expect.'

'Because he was afraid of a scandal. He imagined . . .'

'He imagined the truth.'

He did not like seeing that shady part of their past resurrected, and later on he was determined to erase it completely from their memory. Dark streets, the winter, rain, figures gliding along in the slimy shadows, and that disreputable hotel in the rue Coquillière where he had not hesitated, one evening, to push Isabelle in front of him, past that huge woman who had been soliciting the passers-by from the next doorway.

He had had to have her at all costs. He had had her, icy, docile.

'I wonder how you can love me. No, it isn't possible.'

Who could understand that it wasn't his fault, that some strange force was driving him on, forcing him to go forward in spite of everything?

'Don't you see, it's because I love you, I love you more than everything else in the world, because I've only you, nothing but you.'

'Yes, that's it.'

He had fallen on his knees, that evening, in that sordid bedroom, and begged her forgiveness. He had cried there too, out of fury, and he had beaten on the wall with his clenched fists.

'I'd like life to be beautiful, everything to be beautiful, our love . . .'

Had Monsieur Vétu already followed them in the darkness of the streets? They had never known. One evening, when Isabelle had pushed open the door of the shop, she had been surprised by the light. Her father had been there, with his hat on, very pale, standing with his back to the shelves filled with green files.

He had looked at his daughter, then turned his eyes away and sniffed before saying:

259

'Go up to your room.'

Miette, calmer now, his eyelids rather red, was tying his cravat in front of the mirror and Isabelle murmured with a smile:

'It suits you!'

The long curly hair, the black suit, the loosely tied cravat and the sombrero gave added emphasis to the tense and fervent side of his character. Monsieur Boquélus, for his part, the editor of the *Gazette du Centre*, when he had seen his young reporter dressed like that for the first time, had shaken his head: then, with a deliberate candour more insulting than a reprimand, he had said:

'I see that you're an artist.'

Félicien preferred not to think about that any more. He asked:

'You're sure? You like it?'

She seized the opportunity to make the bed and, if he noticed, he took care not to say anything.

'Come along. Now you're going to tell me all about your paper.'

Outside they found the street again, the greengrocer dimly visible behind her shop-window, the hot sun and the stone bridge, and Miette's arm returned automatically to its place round Isabelle's waist.

'At the moment, all they pay me is a hundred francs a month, plus a commission on any advertisements I bring in.'

He was watching her unobtrusively, as if she were going to give herself away.

'It may be some time before they give me a rise, a year or more.'

She knew perfectly well what he was thinking. She had seen his ingenuous trap. She could read his thoughts without having to look at him and she was not irritated by what she discovered that was childish or deceitful.

He waited, as if he had just asked a leading question, and to avoid exasperating him any more, to avoid a fresh scene, she said, gazing at their shadows in front of them:

'We'll get married when you want to, my love.'

To begin with, Monsieur Vétu had declared:

'When he gets a job, we'll see.'

Then:

'When he's earning two hundred francs a month.'

Miette would state that he was earning two hundred francs. Isabelle would say the same. Monsieur Vétu would believe it. He believed everything. He had not come to Nevers today, to see for himself, as he had announced that he was going to, and possibly his stomach trouble was just an excuse.

In less than a year, Félicien had obtained everything he wanted. One morning, when he had gone into the shop, his employer had not given him time to put on his grey overall.

'Will you come upstairs for a moment, Monsieur Miette?'

It was the first time he had been invited to climb the spiral staircase, the first time he had entered that huge, dark, low-ceilinged room which served as both drawing-room and dining-room, and his gaze had been drawn straight away by Isabelle's piano. Madame Vétu, who had not yet gone downstairs, had disappeared as if in obedience to a silent order.

Monsieur Vétu, for his part, had opened a drawer and Félicien had had a shock on recognizing his letters which had been held out to him without a word.

'I must ask you to leave this house immediately.'

Where had Isabelle been? Probably behind a door which must have been that of her bedroom.

'I must explain to you, Monsieur . . .'

Nothing had stopped him, neither the simple dignity and sorrowful reserve of the sick man standing in front of him, nor the unfamiliar atmosphere enveloping him, nor the bell ringing in the shop.

'You can't throw me out without listening to me. I love your daughter. Isabelle loves me.'

'Go on.'

How long had he gone on talking, his throat full of suppressed sobs, his eyes shining wildly?

'I'll leave here. I'll go anywhere you like. On the other hand you must, you simply must leave me some hope, I must know that one day . . .'

He had obtained this reply:

'Perhaps.'

And he had experienced the blackest of weeks, so black that he could remember it only in outline, with aimless comings and goings, interminable waits outside the rue Montmartre house from which Isabelle no longer emerged. Sometimes he had pressed his nose against the window-pane like a poor man trying to arouse pity.

He had run after Monsieur Brois.

'She hasn't said anything to you? Please, Monsieur Brois, give her this letter. I'm capable of anything at the moment. A dozen times I've nearly thrown myself in the Seine.'

Monsieur Brois had handed the letter to Isabelle. In the evening he had brought back a reply.

'My father is very unhappy. I feel ashamed of the sorrow I have caused him. He was ill for two days. He does not speak to me any more, and does not dare to look at me. We must wait, my love, wait patiently . . .'

Then he had found pathetic words with which to counter, in Isabelle's heart, the sight of her father's unhappiness.

Unshaven, with his clothes in a pitiful state, he had hung around under her windows in all weathers.

'Have no fears. You will soon be rid of me and your father will be able to breathe again . . .'

Eight days? Ten days? He could no longer remember. It was a black hole, as black as the memory of the rue Coquillière and the five hundred francs.

And then one morning he had seen her come out of the shop, in broad daylight, and walk up to him.

'My father says it is all right for you to come to the house this evening. He makes no promises. He doesn't know you.'

They had given him a cup of coffee, a cigarette, and a biscuit, and after that, every evening, he had spent a couple of hours in the big low-ceilinged room while Madame Vétu did her house-work and Monsieur Vétu brought his invoices up to date on the table after it had been cleared of the dinner things.

'Later on, when you've found a job, we'll see.'

Monsieur Brois had sent him to the Stock Exchange Press where they were looking for a proof-reader. He spent his days in a glass cage, bent over proofs still wet with ink, with two rows of linotype machines as his horizon. Journalists came and went, looking busy and important.

'Tell me, my boy . . .'

And at night, his lower lip quivering with pride, he wrote:

'Your poor father imagines that I am going to take over his shop one day and manufacture rubber stamps!'

He used to accompany the Vétus, on Sunday, to their little country house on the banks of the Marne, feeling impatient and disgusted with their calm, empty existence.

'When we are just the two of us . . .'

He had written a long letter to Léopold.

'*It is absolutely essential* that you should get me a birth-certificate form, either from Liège or from a near-by village, preferably a small village.'

And triumphantly, without admitting that it was Doms who had taught him how to forge identity papers, he had filled in the blanks himself. As for the rubber stamps with the arms of the borough of Huy – he remembered his brief acquaintance with that town and the painter's clothes which he had taken off in the station lavatory – he had made them himself with his own hands, with the help of materials taken from Vétu's shop.

'You see! Nobody will ever write to the Huy town hall to check the authenticity of this paper. Henceforth I'm officially called Félicien Miette and I'm twenty-one years old, so that I've finished my military service.'

He had no remorse. It was *absolutely essential*, as he had written to Léopold, that his fate should be fulfilled. So much the worse for those who did not believe in it. And if the obstacle was too stubborn to be overcome, he went round it, without any false sense of shame.

'Once I get going, you'll see, Isabelle, what sort of a life I'll give you.'

One day, two journalists had been talking together at the door of the glass cage.

'I've had a letter from Boquélus to say that he's looking for a young fellow for his Nevers rag who doesn't expect too much. You don't know anybody who would do?'

'Excuse me, Monsieur. Did you say that somebody was looking for a journalist?'

'Why, do you want to be a journalist?'

Going to the police-station, reporting lectures and charity bazaars, fairs and accidents, putting on the earphones and taking the telephone calls from Paris – this had been his work for the past month.

Monsieur Vétu had promised:

'When he is earning a minimum of two hundred francs . . .'

He was earning only a hundred, but what did that matter, seeing that Isabelle was in agreement?

He had thought of everything, even of making Félicien Miette legally an orphan.

He was joking now. He had banished the memory of all the black holes of the past. They were lunching together in this bright restaurant where they were alone and where, crossing the threshold flanked with laurels in wooden boxes, they had made the sleepy-headed waiter jump.

'A table for two, sir?'

His eyes were laughing at the future, the tablecloth was white, the glasses sparkling, the light gentle with the blinds lowered, but the slightest thing was still sufficient to cast a shadow over his features.

'What are you looking at?'

'Nothing.'

He turned round quickly, jealous already, but saw nobody behind him, nothing but a row of tables with napkins placed fan-wise in the glasses and yellow chairs in curved wood.

'What were you looking at?'

Him! It was at him that she had been looking a moment earlier, at him that she was looking now, not at his face which had brightened up, but at his head with the long hair which made the neck look thinner, at his shoulders which were not yet a man's shoulders. While he talked and ate, she could see him from behind in the mirror which went all the way round the restaurant; it was strange seeing a man from in front and behind at the same time, and she smiled vaguely. He bristled up.

'You're laughing at me!'

He was so sensitive to the slightest sarcasm that she hastened to reassure him.

'No, my love, I'm happy. It's nice here, just the two of us.'

It was true. The cloud has passed, swollen and grey like those ugly summer clouds which melt so quickly into heavy streaks of rain, leaving nothing but sunshine in their eyes, and around them the wonderful tranquillity of this restaurant which they had entered at random, because of the simple laurels, the waiter who called them Monsieur and Madame, and the proprietress who looked in at them now and then through the half-open yellow door of the kitchen.

'What are you thinking about?'

'Nothing.'

About nothing and everything, about themselves, about the life which was beginning. They discussed all manner of things for hours on end, wandering haphazardly through the streets which the flying display had emptied and where they could imagine themselves to be alone, kissing each other whenever the idea entered their heads.

'You'll see. I'll start looking for somewhere to live straight away. I'll put an advertisement in the *Gazette*. When you come in a month . . .'

Now and then a breeze ruffled the pale foliage of the plane-trees and the shadows moved on the pavement.

It was four o'clock. From the terrace of the café where they had finally stopped, they could see the station clock.

'I can't go a whole month without seeing you. Next Sunday, I'll come to Paris. I'll tell Monsieur Boquélus . . .'

He would make up some tale or other. It didn't matter what it was. What he was sure of already, was that he would go.

'Do you love me?'

'It's time for me to go, my love.'

She got into her compartment too soon and he frowned as he saw a young sailor on leave inside. They said nothing more.

'See you in a month.'

'Next Sunday.'

The doors were closed. The train waited a little longer. Miette turned his head away to hide his eyes which the clouds were invading once more.

'See you on Sunday. Promise me . . .'

He saw the sailor standing behind her. The train moved off. A handkerchief disappeared round the bend.

'Give me a Pernod, waiter, and some writing materials.'

He had sat down at a table in the Café de Paris, where four musicians were playing Viennese waltzes.

My love: You have only just left, I am alone and . . .

He felt feverish, ran his fingers through his long hair, and looked vaguely at the table facing him, where there were four

265

elderly whist-players for whom real life had already ceased to exist.

I beg your forgiveness, my darling, my love, my all, I beg your forgiveness on my knees for making another scene with you, but if you only knew how unhappy I am, how often I am tormented by evil thoughts! At the last moment, when I saw that man behind you in the compartment, I felt like jumping on to the train and leaving everything to . . .

'Waiter! The same again . . .'

Four pages, six pages, of his fine, nervous handwriting. The music carried him away; and he could dimly make out the noise of the black and white discs in the backgammon boxes, the sighs of the card-players.

When, quite soon now, we are on our own, just the two of us at last, I feel sure that . . .

He was hot. His temples were throbbing. He went himself to put his letter in the box at the General Post Office. After that he did not know what to do. He was not hungry. He roamed about in the twilight, thin and restless, while in the white house by the stone bridge the Chapelle family were sitting down at table round the steaming soup-tureen, and Monsieur Vétu, in Paris, was dissolving a tablet in half a tumblerful of water.

At Embourg, swaying from side to side on his bench, in Madame Laude's garden, Roger was waiting for that oppressive day of 15 August to come to an end with the reassuring concert of the frogs.

Chapter Five

On All Saints' Day, they had been to the Robermont cemetery, on Désiré's side, as they put it, and the next day, All Souls' Day, to the Sainte-Walburge cemetery. Because for the dead as for the living, and even for inanimate objects, a distinction was made between the 'Mamelin side' and the 'Peters side'.

'She's a distant cousin of yours on your father's side,' Roger was told.

266

Or else:

'This box comes from an uncle on my side.'

The button-box! Although Roger, who was now at the Friars' school, no longer played with the buttons, the box remained in its place on the kitchen shelf, between the alarm-clock and the brass candlestick, a very old box decorated on five of its sides with scenes from *Robinson Crusoe*.

It was a box from Élise's side and its contents were even more characteristic of the Peters, since it came from the branch of the family which had remained in Germany, from relatives of whom they knew scarcely anything, of whom all that they possessed were two yellow photographs in the album with the brass corners, shiny photographs with an oval bulge in the middle of the cardboard: an ascetic-looking woman, severely dressed in black, who belonged to a third order, and a lanky young man who was so indistinct that you could no longer make out his features. Élise was incapable of explaining to Roger what a third order was. She knew only that this cousin lived all alone in a big house at Aix-la-Chapelle, and that she was a nun in a lay dress.

The buttons inside the box came from the same branch of the family. When she had been very young, Élise's parents had taken her by train to somewhere in Germany, she had forgotten where, on a hill covered with fir-trees (she really must ask Léopold about it, but she kept forgetting), and she had been shown round a button-factory which belonged to a cousin of hers.

These buttons, which Roger had played with for years, were as foreign to the house, to the district, to the town, as the photographs in the album or the cups decorated with brown squares which hung in Aunt Louisa's kitchen, at Coronmeuse, and which probably came from the same source. The prettiest and newest buttons were white with red, blue or green dots. Others were decorated with circles or crosses; some were made of brass, with figures in relief, or of bone, with real hunting scenes, stags and hounds. Finally, in the middle of some buttons, there was a white flower which did not exist in Belgium; the school-master next door had only recently told them that it was an *Edelweiss* from the mountains.

The Robermont cemetery, which was on the same side of the

bridges as the rue de la Loi, but higher up, was as it were an extension of the district where they lived. From the parish of Saint-Nicolas, they went straight into the parish of Saint-Remacle where Arthur lived. They stopped outside his house, in front of the window full of caps, they said hullo to Juliette, who always looked attractive and whose children were extremely neat and tidy, and they slowly climbed the gentle slope of the Thiers de Robermont where they would pass hearses coming away empty.

They always met the whole population of the rue Puits-en-Sock and Désiré never stopped raising his hat. On the plateau, the streets were wide and the houses new, built of bricks of a pale, fresh pink, with spaces between them surrounded by fences behind which Élise went to adjust her suspender.

'Building plot for sale. Ten francs a square yard.'

It was to one of these streets, which had no name as yet and was only half paved, that a fortnight before Roger had started coming every Thursday for violin lessons. For his parents had bought him a violin, because there had been a child's violin for sale in the district. For want of a real violin-case for such a tiny instrument, he carried it in a cardboard box, and the end of the bow, which was too long for the box, stuck out through a hole.

His teacher, the organist at Robermont, had bad breath which he insisted on blowing into his face; with the same cruelty, he pressed the child's fingers on to the strings until he cried out in pain.

'Music is such a wonderful thing!' Élise used to say ecstatically. 'It's so nice to be able to play an instrument.'

Why was it, when they went to the Robermont cemetery, that the weather was nearly always fine? It was November, admittedly, but a breezy November, with long intervals of sunshine. The cemetery was a gay sight, a new cemetery surrounded by brick walls, with a fine centre walk, a chapel, and monuments in immaculate stone.

They greeted on the way the vault of the Gruyelle-Marquants the confectioners in the rue Puits-en-Sock, that of the Velden family, and others on which they recognized the same familiar names as on the shop-signs in the district.

They never lost their way in the maze of paths. The candles, in the glass cases in front of the tombs, burnt with a bright flame, and on both sides of the cemetery railing, hawkers were selling waffles and chrysanthemums.

'Good afternoon, Lucien, good afternoon, Catherine. How the children have grown!'

'Are you still pleased with your lodgers, Élise?'

Every week, Chrétien Mamelin came to care for his wife's grave as if it were a garden, with its upright tombstone surmounted by a cross.

> Marie Demoulin, wife of Chrétien Mamelin
> born at Alleur on 5 October 1850
> died in her 61st year
> Pray for her

A medallion set in the stone showed a child with blurred features, the little girl who had died in infancy.

Désiré put a pot of flowers on the grave, Élise lit a few candles from those which were already burning, and then, taking an old tin hidden behind the tomb, she went to get a little water from a nearby tank to pour it over the pots.

'Nobody ever thinks of watering the flowers.'

A sign of the cross. Désiré stood there for a few moments with bowed head, looking at the grave and moving his lips, made the sign of the cross again, took his son's hand and walked away, putting his hat on again.

This was the day on which they wore their new winter coats which still smelled of the tailor's shop.

'Shall we go home by way of the drill-ground?'

The wind made the veils of the women in mourning flutter like flags. Going along an alley-way with uneven paving-stones, half in the town, half in the country, they came to the vast plain between Jupille and Bressoux and followed the quais de la Dérivation; everything here was familiar and reassuring, and they scarcely felt as if they had left the place du Congrès district.

The next day, the sky was invariably dark, with gusts of wind sending the dust and the dead leaves flying. Beginning with the Mass, on account of the black hangings and the catafalque, the day took on a dramatic character which, in Roger's mind, was naturally associated with the 'Peters side'.

Even the names had a different colour. Robermont conjured up the wide, airy streets of Saint-Remacle, the new district on the plateau with the building plots for sale, the freshly scrubbed tombstones and the hawkers' golden waffles.

Sainte-Walburge was first of all the dark-green tram which they took in the place Saint-Lambert, and which was always so full that they had to split up.

'Keep Roger with you, Désiré. Don't let him lean out.'

The tram smelled of All Saints' Day, chrysanthemums, and the crape and cheviot of mourning clothes. During the whole of the journey along the narrow shopping streets of the Sainte-Marquerite district, you could see the passengers' heads swaying from left to right and right to left, and their eyes staring vacantly ahead, and Roger, on the platform, was squashed between the grown-ups' legs.

After that, they walked a long way, along a road which was always muddy and from which they could see the spoil-heaps of the collieries in the midst of fields of black earth stinking of rotten beetroot.

They were high up here too, but on the other side of the Meuse, on the Peters side; the Sainte-Walburge cemetery was an old cemetery with twisting paths where they used to lose their way among the grey tombstones overgrown with ivy and moss.

'Dear God, Désiré! We've taken the wrong turning again! We'd better go back and look for the monument with the pink marble columns.'

The cold numbed their fingers, and their noses were reddened by the wind.

'Wait a minute. I think I can see my sister Louisa with her children. Yes, it's her all right.'

At Sainte-Walburge, they met a lot of people, people whom they never saw during the rest of the year yet who belonged to the family. The women spoke Flemish to each other in a whisper, without taking any notice of Désiré.

'Dear God, Poldine! Good afternoon, Franz.'

It was one of Élise's brothers who was an inspector at the national armaments factory and lived right at the end of Coronmeuse.

'Don't you think, Franz, that Poldine has grown thinner?' She added deliberately:

'I came here yesterday to tidy up Mother's grave a bit.'

She had borrowed a spade from the keeper. Her brothers and sisters never thought of doing this but just brought flowers and candles along on All Souls' Day; and if it had not been for Élise, their mother's grave would have been a tangle of weeds and dead leaves.

'Just imagine, some people . . .'

She did not say the neighbours, but she pointed to the near-by tombs.

'Just imagine, some people had thrown all their rubbish behind Mother's tombstone. I painted the little railing too, Louisa. It needed it.'

She still had some enamel paint on her fingers which pumice stone had failed to remove.

'Good afternoon, Madame Smet. Good afternoon, Valérie.'

Everybody kissed. Roger's cheeks retained the smell of all these foreign kisses; he waited in one place after another, for there were a great many graves to be visited if nobody was to be offended. Désiré followed along too, a foreigner in a world of which he did not even know the language.

'You haven't seen Marthe and Hubert Schroefs, have you?'

'They must be visiting the grave of Hubert's brother, at the far end of the cemetery, towards the colliery.'

'To think that Louis of Tongres hasn't been to see his mother's grave since the funeral! He wouldn't be able to find it again.'

At Robermont, they had stayed only a few minutes. At Sainte-Walburge, dusk started falling when they were still there, forming groups which broke up only to come together again in front of another vault.

'How is Félicie?'

'I haven't seen her for over a month. The poor girl! She's so delicate, and she has to pick a fellow like Coucou!'

They had finally met the Schroefs, and Hubert walked along behind the women with Désiré.

It was dark by the time they reached the rue Sainte-Walburge where a few shop-windows were lighted. They turned round every now and then to make sure that the others were following.

'Why, Franz and Poldine have gone off without saying good-bye!'

'You know what Poldine's like.'

Just before they reached the brightest shop-window, Élise protested:

'No, Marthe, let's not stop. It looks as if we've come for the tart. Besides, we are going to the evening service at Saint-Denis. There's such a good preacher.'

But Hubert Schroefs had stopped with Désiré in front of his sister's cake-shop. Marie Beckers had caught sight of them through the window and was already waving to them. It was too late to cross over to the other pavement.

'Good evening, Marie. Don't bother about us. We didn't want to go past without dropping in to give you a kiss, but you've got so much to do on a day like this . . .'

The door kept on opening and shutting, ringing the bell every time. Marie Beckers, helped by her eldest daughter, was shaking the sugar canister over some tarts, wrapping these up in glossy paper, and banging the keys of the cash-register whose drawer opened automatically.

'Go into the kitchen. I'll be with you in a minute.'

It was dark in there. There were tarts everywhere, even on the chairs. The windows looked out, not on a yard, but on the bakehouse with the glass roof where Beckers, bare armed, his vest white with flour, grey hairs in his armpits and powder all over his head, was working with his two apprentices.

'No, Marie, we aren't hungry. We didn't come for that. And we're in a hurry, aren't we, Désiré? Françoise is expecting us for the evening service at Saint-Denis.'

It was no use. The cups were filled with coffee, the chairs were cleared, and big slices of rice tart were cut while Marie Beckers, a thin little woman with feverish eyes, bustled to and fro between the kitchen and the shop.

As Élise used to say, it was hard to believe that she was clumsy Hubert Schroefs' sister, she was so sensitive and sad. Élise followed her into the shop to ask her in an undertone:

'And your husband?'

'He's always the same. You've seen him.'

How could she have married that vulgar man who spoke Walloon more often than French and who had the biggest nose Roger had ever seen? If he opened the bakehouse door, it was to make a coarse joke. He had no respect for anything, not even his own daughters.

'Just imagine, Élise, the other evening, when I asked him if he'd seen Germaine . . .'

Germaine was the eldest of the three Beckers girls. She was seventeen. She was fresh and sprightly, but unfortunately she had her father's coarse features. Without appearing to do so, she pricked up her ears to listen to her mother's whispering, and Marie lowered her voice even further and started talking in Flemish.

' "Your daughter," he told me, "must be coupling in a corner with her young man." It made me cry, Élise. That wasn't the way we were brought up. He makes no bones about talking crudely in front of her about certain things. "What's a girl for," he says, "if it isn't to go with a boy?" '

Nobody took any notice of Roger who was stuffing himself with sugared tart in the noisy kitchen.

'You must come and see us one Thursday afternoon with the little boy, Élise. I'm so lonely, you know. If I hadn't got the business to keep me busy, I don't know what would become of me.'

Élise promised, but it was a long way, a steep climb.

'One Thursday when it's fine.'

They went down into the town by way of the rue Pierreuse, with the soldiers from the Citadel clattering past them with a great din of hobnailed boots. They reached the cheese square late, the stained-glass windows of Saint-Denis were covered with black hangings, and when Désiré pushed open the padded door, they heard the preacher's loud, booming voice.

'Pick your feet up, Roger . . . Thank you, Monsieur, don't put yourself out . . .'

They remained standing behind the chairs which had been turned to face the pulpit. An unobtrusive sign to Françoise who was sitting near the reredos. The Dominican's voice bounced off the walls of the huge nave and the faces turned up towards him looked as if they were carved in ivory.

A cough now and then, stern looks, the legs of a chair grating on the flagstones.

'. . . In the name of the Father, and the Son, and the Holy Ghost, Amen!'

The Dominican blew out the candle burning on the edge of the pulpit and vanished down the winding staircase, all the chairs were moved at once, the organ thundered, a thousand signs of the cross were made, and the fingers of the faithful groped about on the sticky stone of the basin, searching for the cold touch of the holy water.

They waited for Françoise by the fountain and kissed Loulou, who had a cameo profile and had played the part of the Virgin in the last procession.

'You will come and have supper with us, won't you?'

'No, Françoise. We don't want to bother you. Besides, the lodgers are waiting for us.'

That was true. For fifty centimes a day, Mademoiselle Pauline and Monsieur Chechelowski now had their supper in the rue de la Loi kitchen. Élise stopped at Tonglet's to buy some ham, then in the rue Puits-en-Sock where she had left her chipdish on the way to the cemetery. They rediscovered the atmosphere of Outremeuse and brought to it from Sainte-Walburge something of a Peters flavour, still hearing the echo of laments in Flemish, the accents of Aunt Louisa and Schroefs, still seeing Aunt Poldine's Lenten silhouette and the grin of Franz who had the same mannerism as his brother Louis and kept shutting his eyes. How many women in mourning, nearly all belonging to the family, they had met! Élise often used to say that it was the fate of big families to be always in mourning.

'If I reckoned it up carefully, I do believe I'd find that I've been in mourning for three-quarters of my life.'

She lit the fire again, and spread the tablecloth with the red squares over one half of the table, the half reserved for the lodgers, for the Mamelins had their meals on an oilcloth which was rolled up on a stick afterwards.

In obedience to the daily ritual, Élise opened the glazed door a little way and called out into the darkness of the hall:

'Mademoiselle Pauline! Monsieur Chechelowski!'

There was a noise on the first floor, then in the ground-floor room. The chips were keeping hot in the oven.

Élise divided up the ham. It was a small kitchen. They were all on top of one another. The Mamelins, for their part, had some bread and butter with a little piece of cheese or some ham. Désiré waited until supper was over before burying himself in his paper, where there was talk about William II and the inevitable war.

'Hurry up, Mademoiselle Pauline, your chips are going to dry up.'

For the Polish girl always waited several minutes before coming down, wasting her time putting on powder and scent.

'What's the use?' Élise had asked her once. 'Whom are you trying to please?'

Monsieur Chechelowski, who was a real Russian, and Mademoiselle Feinstein, who was a Polish Jewess, never spoke to each other, confining themselves to a stiff greeting, even though they had supper every evening at the same table.

'Do you know what she answered, Valérie, when I asked her whom she was trying to please?

' *"Myself!"* '

She was fat and red-haired. If she wore scent, it was because she smelled bad by nature. She had a big nose and thick lips, there were folds of flesh on the back of her neck, and her ankles were so swollen that she could not lace up her boots to the full extent.

'And you, Mademoiselle Pauline, if you had the power to change yourself to suit your taste, how would you like to be?'

Élise told this story to everybody. The lodger in the pink room had answered in her calm way:

'Just as I am now!'

Mademoiselle Frida waited in her room until the others had finished. Only then did she come downstairs, take her tin from the kitchen shelf, and pour some boiling water into her little blue enamel coffee-pot.

'You understand, Mademoiselle Frida, it's a question of tidiness and cleanliness. If everybody had his meals in his room, the house would look like heaven knows what. I'll give you a tin in which you can keep your bread, your butter, your coffee, anything you like.'

Gazing vacantly into the distance, while Élise started her washing-up on a corner of the stove and Désiré read the newspaper, Mademoiselle Frida slowly ate the bread on which she had scraped her butter and made sure that there were no grounds left in her coffee-pot.

*

The days had grown even shorter. As early as three o'clock, Brother Mansuy had lit the two gas-jets, creating that murky, almost stifling, atmosphere which invaded the classroom on winter afternoons. The two blackboards above the platform looked red rather than black. The bottles on the polished shelf took on a strange life, and in the next classroom Monsieur Penders' pupils could be heard chanting in unison:

'The Belgium of old was bordered to the north and east by marshes, to the west by the sea, to the south . . .'

In the passage-ways between the light-coloured desks, Brother Mansuy moved noiselessly, without displacing any air; his cassock glided gently through space and his touch made you jump like the touch of a bat you don't hear coming.

It was always from an unexpected corner of the room that his calm, soft voice spoke out.

'What is God? Van Hamme, answer.'

The catechism lesson was for the second-year pupils who occupied the left-hand part of the classroom. The first-year pupils, of whom Roger was one, covered their slates with pot-hooks which they rubbed out with a little wet sponge.

'God is a pure spirit, infinitely perfect, eternal, and the Creator of heaven and earth.'

'Good. Ledoux. How many persons are there in God?'

One pupil sat down while another stood up.

'There are three persons in God: the Father, the Son and the Holy Ghost.'

'Is each person God? Your turn, Gallet! Van Hamme, I forbid you to prompt. Is each person God?'

Roger applied himself to his pot-hooks, holding his breath, the waves of heat sent out by the nearby stove reddening his cheeks. Brother Mansuy was not far away and perhaps, on his way past, he would take a pink sweet out of his pocket, or, better still, a violet gobstopper of a sort which you could not find at Gruyelle-Marquant's and which he kept for his favourite pupils.

For that, you had to take care not to look at him or to raise your head. It was a game which had its unwritten rules. He went past, and it was only when he reached another corner of the classroom that you knew whether he had put a pink sweet or a violet gobstopper on a corner of the desk.

Brother Mansuy was young, rosy-faced and fair-headed, and if you looked at him just then, he turned his head away to hide a smile.

It was raining. Bright pearls slid down the black window-panes and in the yard you could hear the discreet rustle of the rain. You could also hear Brother Médard, two classrooms farther on, thundering at some poor pupil and pounding the platform with his wooden leg.

The three classrooms were separated by glazed partitions. The lower part of the partitions was made of solid wood. Brother Mansuy was tall enough to see over it, but the boys could see nothing of the other classrooms but the platform.

Roger went on waiting, but the friar did not come as far as him. He had suddenly turned round, leaving Gallet to hunt for his answer on the ceiling. Somebody had knocked timidly on the door. The boys could feel the draught of damp air, but did not dare to turn round. They heard a woman's voice, and Roger gave a start, for he thought that he could recognize it.

'Mamelin! Get your things. Somebody has come for you.'

He was red in the face. The others looked at him enviously. His mother, whom he could not see, murmured in the rain:

'Thank you, Brother Mansuy. He wouldn't have found anybody at home at four o'clock, because all the lodgers are at the University, you understand? Excuse me for bothering you.'

Roger joined her, and she put up the hood of his coat.

'Come along.'

His mother's hand was quivering with impatience. She had left the door ajar, across the road; she went into the hall to put his satchel on the hallstand, then ran to the kitchen to make sure that nothing could burn on the stove.

She went off with her son, taking short cuts through the backstreets.

'A message came for me that Aunt Félicie is ill, very ill. We mustn't make any noise, Roger. You will be good, won't you?'

The rain was blurring the lights of the gas-lamps and the shop-windows. They brushed past a tram. The trees on the boulevard were dripping with rain and the planks of the Passerelle spat out a little dirty water with every step you took. The town was nothing but trembling lights and wet figures. Over on the quai de la Goffe, the big bay-windows of the Café du Marché were lit up and you could see the waiters coming and going, carrying their trays, but it was into the alley-way that Roger's mother pulled him, and she knocked on a door which opened immediately as if somebody had been waiting behind on purpose.

They promptly plunged into a chaotic world in which Roger, who only a few minutes before had been sitting snugly in the cosy warmth of the classroom, felt completely lost.

Nobody took any notice of him, not even Élise who had fallen into Louisa's arms and was crying.

There was a corridor, which the child had never seen before, lit by a skylight which opened into the café. He could hear billiard balls colliding and smell the stench of beer. The door of a cellar stood wide open and now and then a waiter rushed through it saying:

'Excuse me . . . Excuse me . . . Excuse me . . .'

A staircase. Unfamiliar faces. Louisa shaking her head despairingly and whispering:

'I've just been up there. You do what you like. Jesus-Mary! If anybody had told us something like this was going to happen!'

Everybody was waiting for something, but what? These people who did not know one another and who were standing squashed together in the narrow space avoided each other's eyes.

Élise rushed upstairs. They could hear her stop and hesitate on the first-floor landing. Somebody came down, a man in a tailcoat who spoke in an undertone to Louisa.

His head, which went gravely from left to right, said:

'There's nothing to be done.'

Sobs upstairs. It was Élise, Roger was sure of that, and started crying in his turn. A market-woman bent down and wiped his face with her handkerchief, despite his protests.

Why didn't his mother come down again? Who was that man standing with his back turned to them, at the end of the corridor, near the cellar door?

The market-woman spoke to Aunt Louisa, pointing to Roger.

'This little boy shouldn't be left here.'

Where could they put him? Perhaps they were going to take him into the café, but at that very moment a cab drew up in the street outside, the door opened, and the boy caught sight of the hood of the carriage, a lantern, a horse's glistening cruppers.

Three men clattered into the house, as much at home as undertaker's men coming to fetch a body.

But Aunt Félicie was not dead. When the men got to the first floor, she could be heard uttering piercing shrieks, struggling, shouting for help. It seemed that she was trying to bite. Élise came downstairs in a state of great distress.

'Dear God, Louisa! It's terrible. I don't want to see it. Where's Roger?'

She looked around for him. An indescribable group started coming downstairs, in which you could make out a woman, Aunt Félicie, whom two men were carrying by her shoulders and feet, and who was writhing about, her face convulsed, her hair hanging down on to the steps. Another man was following with a blanket.

Everybody had to stand back against the wall. Élise chewed her handkerchief, Louisa made the sign of the cross, and the market-woman tried to push Roger behind her so that he could not see anything.

Félicie screamed.

However what Roger was looking at, wide-eyed, his chest so tight that he could scarcely breathe, was the man at the end of the corridor. There had been a hoarse sound, a sob which must have torn the throat from which it had come, and suddenly that big, broad-shouldered man had hurled himself against the wall, his head between his arms, his body leaning forward, his shoulders shaking spasmodically.

Nobody took any notice of him, nobody gave him so much as a glance or a word, for it was Coucou, Félicie's husband, who had beaten her so hard that she had gone out of her mind.

The open door let in a little fresh air. The cab-driver was waiting calmly beside his horse, with his whip sticking out of his box-coat. Some onlookers were standing in the dark.

The most difficult problem was getting Félicie into the cab, for she was still struggling and bending backwards so far that you might have thought she was going to break in two.

'They ought to put a handkerchief between her teeth.'

Somebody had said that, but Roger would never know who.

'Come, Élise, be brave.'

Élise's face was unrecognizable, at once a child's face and an old woman's, the features were so distorted by horror. It did not occur to her to hide her emotion. She made as if to rush towards her sister who was being taken away, whose body was already half inside the cab, and whom the male nurses were pushing as if she were a parcel.

'Félicie . . . Félicie! . . .'

Aunt Louisa seized her round the waist. She resisted for a moment. Coucou's shoulders were still heaving slowly. A waiter had opened the door of the café and was watching.

'Shut the door.'

'No, Louisa. I want to see it out to the very end. I want to go with her.'

'Don't be a fool. What good would that do? And what about your son?'

Then, in her confusion, Élise remembered Roger.

'Where is he?'

'He's here, Madame,' replied the market-woman.

The cab door slammed to.

'Has she got everything she needs? Won't she catch cold? Tell me, Doctor . . .'

The man in the tail-coat was the doctor. He put on his overcoat and looked around for his hat which somebody held out to him.

'Have no fears, Madame. I'll get there before she does. I've got my carriage at the corner of the street.'

'When can I go and see her?'

'Tomorrow if she quietens down.'

Élise felt annoyed with Louisa who stood there 'like a tower'.

'You don't understand, Louisa. You didn't know her like I did. If you only knew how unhappy she was! Come along, Roger. Désiré will be coming home . . .'

The hall emptied, until nobody was left but Uncle Coucou

still groaning against the wall; and a few days later, when they passed the black ramparts of the Saint-Léonard prison, Élise would be unable to refrain from saying to her son:

'Coucou is in there. He used to beat your poor Aunt Félicie. It was him who killed her. But he isn't your uncle any more. You must never say that he's your uncle. Do you hear, Roger?'

'Yes, Mother.'

Aunt Félicie would die in the lunatic asylum, without recognizing anybody, and Élise would put on her mourning veil again. She had been right to say, the other day, at Sainte-Walburge cemetery, that in big families you came out of mourning for one person only to put it on again for another.

They would go to Coronmeuse, after four o'clock, taking the tram to save time, and go through Aunt Louisa's shop.

'Have you heard anything about the post-mortem?'

'What's a post-mortem, Mother?'

They both promptly started talking Flemish, standing, Louisa with her hands folded as usual on the blue apron which her stomach pushed out. The police doctor had found traces of blows. Two plain-clothes policemen had come for Coucou one evening, and had taken him to Saint-Léonard.

There had been a funeral, but Roger could not remember it, for only his father had gone, the women and children had not joined the procession, and Élise had remained on her knees beside a confessional in the asylum chapel.

'Six months in prison is too good for a monster like that.'

Why did Désiré avoid the subject? Sometimes, when Élise started talking indignantly or plaintively, he opened his mouth as if to say something, but prudence got the better of him and he kept quiet.

Léopold's attitude resembled his.

'She was so good, Léopold. You can't imagine. She had nothing she could call her own. She wouldn't have hurt a fly.'

Léopold kept quiet, sitting by the fire, drawing on his old pipe.

'She was the best of us all, and she's the one who's gone, so young too!'

For a long time Élise would be unable to talk about her without starting to cry. You would have thought sometimes that she felt a sort of remorse, that something was weighing on her heart.

Was it because she remembered the night when her sister, when they were girls and living in the rue Féronstrée, had come home at three o'clock in the morning with the smell of a man clinging to her clothes?

And the little packet which Félicie had brought her in the rue Léopold, over Cessions', begging Élise to hide it for a few days?

It had been money, she knew that, a great deal of money; without telling anybody, she had opened the packet. To whom had her sister intended giving it?

'You see, Léopold, Félicie wasn't responsible for her actions.'

Only then did he raise his head and look at her for a long time, without a word. What was he thinking about? Did he know himself? Had he guessed?

Was it because he wasn't responsible for his actions either?

Félicie was dead and, the next All Souls' Day, there would be another grave to visit in the Sainte-Walburge cemetery, in the new section where you could not distinguish between the paths whose freshly turned clay stuck in big lumps to the soles of your shoes.

Sometimes they would have to wait a little while at a distance.

'What are we waiting for, Mother? Why are we staying here?'

'Hush. Pretend you're not looking. It's Coucou.'

For Roger the latter would never be anything more than a silhouette; he would always see just his back, a back which struck him as bigger and broader than others, the dark back of a man who had been to prison and was not his uncle any more.

Was it because he was ashamed that he did not dare to bring any flowers?

'Come along now. He's gone. Say an Our Father and a Hail Mary for Aunt Félicie who was so fond of you.'

Élise could not talk any more. She could not help it. It was only at Félicie's grave that her heart became so full, that she felt so insignificant, that the world struck her as so wretched.

'Don't take any notice, Désiré. Take the boy away.'

She needed to remain alone, to cry until she could see

nothing but dim patches, and to stammer out, her eyes fixed on the bunch of white flowers she had brought along:

'Poor Félicie!'

Chapter Six

The universe grew bigger, people and things altered in appearance, certainties were born at the same time as anxieties, the world became peopled with questions, and a ring of chiaroscuro made contours less reassuring, extended perspectives to infinity.

Monsieur Pain had been in prison, like Coucou. Armand's father was a murderer, a real one: he had killed a woman with a revolver shot.

Sitting on the imitation-leather bench in the Café de la Renaissance, with his little legs dangling in space, Roger was looking through the stained-glass windows. On the marble-topped table, his glass of grenadine was as rich a red as the triangular panes of glass framing the diamond-shaped milky-white panes.

Désiré was playing cards. Every Sunday, starting that winter, after High Mass at Saint-Nicolas and a brief visit to the kitchen in the rue Puits-en-Sock, the father took his son by the hand to this café in the middle of the town; the waiter knew what he had to serve; Monsieur Reculé and Émile Grisard were already there, while Joseph Velden, who was not free this Sunday, had been replaced by fat Monsieur Baudon.

Through the windows, Roger was looking at the stucco façade of the Théâtre de la Renaissance and that was why he was thinking about the commercial traveller in coffee who lived in the rue Pasteur, for it was there that Monsieur Pain had killed an actress, in the days when he had been a cavalry officer.

Roger had heard his mother telling the story to Mademoiselle Pauline.

'He was reduced to the ranks. They stripped off his epaulettes in front of the whole regiment.'

A colonel of the Lancers rode along the rue de la Loi at noon every day, and every time Roger thought of the epaulettes which had been stripped off. Monsieur Pain, who was nearly as tall as Désiré, measured over six foot. Roger pictured to himself a minute bow-legged colonel standing on tip-toe and pulling with all his might at the gold bullions.

The world was becoming complicated. Not so long ago, things had existed only during the time they could be seen in the light and then had returned to nothingness or limbo. If Monsieur Pain turned the corner of the rue Jean-d'Outremeuse, or if the shadows invaded a corner of the bedrooms, there was nothing left.

Now, even when he was sitting at his desk in Brother Mansuy's classroom, Roger could follow people in imagination, and he did so in spite of himself: for instance, he saw Monsieur Pain who 'travelled in coffee' going into the grocers' shops of Chenée, Tilleur and Seraing, and he imagined him pulling samples out of his pockets, without a word, his face always expressionless.

The woman he had killed looked like the one on the poster next to the door of the Renaissance, with a dress trimmed with feathers and a diadem on her head.

It was because Monsieur Pain was a murderer that he had such a white face, grey hair and stony features; it was on account of his crime that he was always alone, that Julie, his wife, was sickly and that Armand was slit-eyed. Wasn't it extraordinary that a man who had killed somebody and who had been in prison should live in the rue Pasteur, practically opposite the magistrate's house, and that Roger should play with his son on the pavement?

Monsieur Reculé, who worked for North Belgian Railways, travelled first class, as Élise was always saying, and would have a pension when he retired. Roger tried to picture this pension, to give it a form and consistency, and he turned a gaze heavy with questions on the thin face of the head clerk whom he saw, in slippers and straw hat, ending his life in the garden of a country house.

In the days when the world had been simpler, Roger had questioned his mother unceasingly.

Nowadays, he kept quiet. When he was found with his

thoughts far away, he pretended to be playing. He listened to what the grown-ups said among themselves; certain phrases, certain words haunted him for weeks, while others translated themselves as pictures which imposed themselves on him willy-nilly and which he later tried in vain to dispel.

If he heard his mother undressing in the next room or washing in the morning, the word *organs* came to his mind, the ugliest and most frightening of all words.

'It's my organs, you see, Valérie. Doctor Matray wanted me to have them removed. I refused, for Roger's sake, because you can never tell what may happen after an operation.'

And he saw some bleeding objects like the things which hung in butchers' shops, coming out of a pale body that had been slit open from the neck to the legs.

Anxious and ashamed, he was conscious of moving towards discoveries which ought not to be mentioned to anybody, and he promised himself not to join Ledoux again in a corner of the yard, next to the tap, during playtime.

Monsieur Pain's crime was linked with this discovery he was in the process of making, and generally speaking everything grown-ups talked about in whispers, including Aunt Félicie's death.

How had Ledoux managed to find out? Roger turned away from the card-players to try to imitate his gesture, even though it was certainly a mortal sin.

Talking about his Aunt Cécile, Roger had said to Ledoux: 'She's going to buy me a new little cousin.'

Ledoux, who was in the second year, had a long, pasty, clown-like face, a mouth which he stretched and twisted as if it were made of indiarubber, and stiff hair which came forward as if it had been brushed the wrong way.

'You still think people buy babies or find them in cabbages?'

It was then that he had made the gesture. He had made a ring with the thumb and forefinger of his left hand and then, with a peculiar gleam in his eyes, he had pushed his right forefinger into this opening.

'What does that mean?'

'If you don't know, I can't explain it to you.'

A dozen times Roger had returned to the attack, following Ledoux around at playtime and turning round in class to address mute appeals to him. The other hedged, promised, took back his promise.

'I bet you don't even know who St Nicholas is!'

'He's the patron saint of schoolchildren.'

'He's your father and mother!'

Now, on that point Ledoux had been right. Roger had thought about it for a long time, and he had recalled St Nicholas's Day in previous years. A few weeks before the great day, St Nicholas looked into houses when the children were doing their homework to make sure that they were being good, and, if he was satisfied, he threw a handful of almonds or walnuts through a fanlight or a half-open door.

Roger had watched his parents. He had noticed that every time St Nicholas had manifested his presence in that way, his father had been in the yard and had come in afterwards making a show of surprise.

St Nicholas was Father and Mother. But he mustn't say so. Roger pretended not to know and, as in previous years, he would write the traditional letter listing the presents he would like to be given. He turned round and looked at Ledoux when, in class, Brother Mansuy made them sing:

> Oh, great St Nicholas,
> Please come down to us,
> Fill our baskets . . .

Seeing that Ledoux had told the truth about St Nicholas, he must know about babies too.

'Tell me and I'll give you my top.'

'I can't. You're too little.'

'I'm as big as you.'

'You know you aren't, because you're in the first year and I'm in the second. If you want to know, look at a couple of dogs. It's practically the same thing.'

Roger blushed as he recalled the dogs he had met on summer days, joined to one another and looking so unhappy. No! It couldn't be true that Aunt Félicie and Coucou . . . It would be too awful. He would not think about it any more. He would not talk about it any more to Ledoux, who lived at Bressoux and whose mother was a charwoman. He was practically a slum child.

Élise was right:

'The friars ought not to admit certain children to the Institut Saint-André. The state school is there for them. In Roger's class, there's a boy whose mother sells vegetables from a barrow in the street. Those people think that provided they pay, they can go where they like.'

It was Thioux she was referring to, a big, rugged, red-haired boy with innocent blue eyes, whose clothes were impregnated with the smell peculiar to the back-streets. His pockets were always full of food, and he chewed away from morning till night, giving a start whenever Brother Mansuy called out his name and looking around for help, for he never knew his lessons.

Roger gave a start too as he met his father's gaze, and he looked to make sure that his fingers were no longer making the gesture.

'What is it, son?'

'Nothing, Father.'

'You aren't bored?'

'No.'

The men too, like Élise when she was with her sisters or with Valérie, sometimes spoke in an undertone, making sure that Roger was not listening. But they did not speak in the same tone of complaint or anxiety. They smiled. They were merry. Every year, the whist-players at Velden's went on a trip for three or four days with the kitty. This summer they had been to Paris. In a night-club in Montmartre, when big Désiré had gone in flanked by the tiny Grisard brothers, the singer had shouted:

'A round of applause for the giant and his two clowns!'

Désiré had also told how they had spent the evening in *Paradise* and *Hell*, explaining that in the first night-club the waiters who served the beers and cherry brandies were dressed as angels while in *Hell* they were dressed as devils.

Why did his father wink at certain allusions?

'You remember that little brunette who wanted to sit on Émile's knees and swore she had a *béguin* for him?'

Although he had promised himself not to ask any more questions, Roger had none the less asked his mother:

'What is a *béguin*?'

'You know what it is, Roger. It's a bonnet that babies wear, like the one you wore yourself when you were little.'

Brother Mansuy made them sing:

> When I was a little boy,
> I slept in a little bed,
> And my mother sang to me:
> Darling, rest your little head . . .

And every time this song made him feel like crying. His mother. The organs. The carriage which was always going to come for her and take her to hospital. Tears came to his eyes when they got to the line:

> When your hair is white . . .

His eyelids started prickling, and he stopped his ears so as not to hear:

> . . . I will earn some money,
> Money so that you may lead
> A life of milk and honey.

'Off we go to dinner, son!'

The game was over. Désiré swallowed the creamy dregs of his beer, wiped his moustache and shook hands all round.

'See you on Friday!'

They met the crowd coming out of the half-past-eleven Mass at Saint-Denis. Désiré greeted people. He was happy. Footsteps were louder, because it was winter, and outlines, especially those of the freestone buildings, clearer.

They stopped at the Spaniards', whose shop with the exotic smells was painted canary-yellow. Among the piles of Brazil nuts, figs, oranges, lemons and pomegranates, they picked their Sunday dessert, a bitter orange which Roger would suck after putting a lump of sugar inside, or a pomegranate with the pips embedded in pink jelly.

The planks of the Passerelle went up and down under their feet. Désiré stopped again to buy a packet of Louxor cigarettes. What had he said to the shop girl when his son had not been paying attention? She had turned away murmuring:

'You are a one, Monsieur Mamelin!'

Everybody was walking faster, for it was time for them to go home if they did not want to arrive late at the Wintergarten.

Mayol was singing there for the first time in Liége. Élise had decided not to go, although she wanted to, because of the child.

'There'll be such a crush!'

As usual, there was roast beef, chips and stewed apples for dinner.

*

On the almond-green wall of the classroom, opposite the shelf holding the measuring-cups, there was a picture which had been stuck on canvas and varnished, a picture the colour of old ivory which represented the winter fair, probably in a Rhineland town, for all the school pictures came from Leipzig. The Gothic houses had indented gables, steep roofs and latticed windows. The town was covered in snow. The men were wearing bottle-green or rust-coloured greatcoats and fur caps; a girl in the foreground was sitting on a sledge being driven by a coachman dressed in a bearskin. In the square there were stalls loaded with food and toys; you could see a performing monkey and a flute-player with laced breeches. It was a lively scene, for Christmas was near, and the town was in a fever of excitement.

Brother Médard, in the big boys' classroom, pressed an electric bell. Straight away, in the three classrooms with their glass partitions, the boys stood up in a single movement, made the sign of the cross, and jabbered out the evening prayer before rushing for their coats and berets.

While the others filed out in the half-light, led by Monsieur Penders, Roger only had the street to cross; on the first floor of his house he could see two windows of a soft, warm pink. The windows had no shutters or Venetian blinds, and through the lace curtains which were draped across one another, he could make out the pink globe of the shade with the pearl drops and Mademoiselle Pauline's curly red hair bent over her books.

Through the keyhole, which was just the right height for a child, he could see, before knocking, the kitchen door and his mother's silhouette. He had come out of one warm, familiar atmosphere only to enter another; the water was singing in the white enamel kettle, and the oven door was half open, revealing the firebricks which would be put in the beds in the evening; but this evening he would not be sitting down at the table covered with the old oilcloth to do his homework.

'We're going into town, Roger. Don't take your coat off. Let's see if your hands are clean.'

She put some more coal on the fire. Outside, in the dark yard, there was a glow of light from another window, Mademoiselle Frida's, just above the kitchen. In Monsieur Saft's room too the light was on, for every cell in the honeycomb was occupied; only Monsieur Chechelowski would not be back until supper-time. Everywhere there was a stove purring away, flanked by its coal-bucket, poker and shovel; each person lived in the centre of a zone of silence and, when one or other of them got up to put some coal on his fire, Élise automatically looked up.

Had she remembered everything? Her bag, her purse, her key. They hurriedly crossed the wilderness of the rue Jeand'Outremeuse where there was not a single real shop and where you could feel snow in the wind; and they plunged, as if into a warm room, into the swarming crowds in the rue Puits-en-Sock.

'Hold my hand, Roger.'

The town's breath was heavy with smells peculiar to the period before St Nicholas's Day. Although it was not snowing yet, invisible particles of ice were floating in space and gathering together in the luminous halo of the shop-windows.

Everybody was outside. All the women were running along, dragging behind them children who would have liked to linger outside the shops.

'Come along, Roger. Pick up your feet.'

Thousands of mothers were uttering the same words.

'Mind the tram.'

The sweet-shops, the confectioners' and the grocers' shops were as full as the stalls in the picture at school. Two smells predominated over the others, so characteristic that no child could have mistaken them: the sweet aroma of gingerbread and the smell of chocolate figures, which was not the same as that of chocolate bars. The shop-windows were stacked from top to bottom with honey-cakes, some of them stuffed with coloured comfits. Life-size St Nicholases in gingerbread, frosted with sugar and adorned with cotton-wool beards, stood surrounded by sheep, asses and farmyard animals, all a brownish or wholemeal colour, sugared, scented and eatable. It was enough to make your head reel.

'Look, Mother.'

'Come along now.'

They went to buy some butter at Salmon's, in a little street running down from the Pont des Arches, on the other side of the river. Not for anything in the world would Élise have gone anywhere else to buy the oblong blocks wrapped in cool cabbage leaves. It was in a tin next to the soup-tureen that she kept the tickets which, at the end of the year, entitled the customer to a three-per-cent refund.

They went into the Vierge Noire, in the rue Neuvice, to buy some coffee. In the window-displays in the confectioners', which were gaudier than the rest, there were rows of marzipan cakes imitating fruit, cheese, even a cutlet with chips and green peas.

'Look.'

'Come along.'

Further on, to distract his attention from all these window-displays, she asked:

'What do you want St Nicholas to bring you?'

He thought of Ledoux, with his thin face topped with unruly hair.

'A box of paints, real paints, in tubes, with a palette.'

The pavements were crowded and you had to push your way along the middle of the street; the trams, which could move only at a walking pace, kept ringing their bells all the time; a mysterious force drew you on.

Now and then, to avoid an attack of giddiness, Élise pulled her son into an empty, icy alley-way. They took a short cut. Soon, as at the end of a tunnel, they found themselves back in the light and bustle of the shopping districts.

In every shop Roger was given something. Madame Salmon had given him a thin slice of Dutch cheese on the tip of her knife. At the Vierge Noire, he had been allowed to pick a sweet biscuit out of the box with the glass lid. For fear of losing her, he hung on to his mother's shopping-bag or her skirt.

'Aren't we going to the Bazaar?'

For they were passing it on their way to say hullo to Valérie at L'Innovation. But it was impossible to get into the Grand Bazaar. There were queues outside the brass doors which kept opening and shutting, and you had to fight to get near the windows.

'Dear God, Valérie! Six o'clock already and Désiré will be home soon.'

His cheeks on fire, trying all the time to look back, and clinging to his mother's shopping-bag, Roger was dragged along by a series of short cuts, through dark side-streets which did not smell of St Nicholas's Day.

For all that he knew that Ledoux was right, he was not in his usual state; December, with St Nicholas's Day, Christmas and then the New Year, was a month heavy with mystery, with sweet and rather disturbing impressions which followed one after another at breakneck speed.

*

The school yard was a livid colour. The big boys in the third and fourth years, in Monsieur Pender's classroom, were reciting all together a lesson as rhythmic as a song. Who noticed the first flakes? Despite the possibility of a gobstopper from Brother Mansuy, who was walking up and down with an innocent air, every head was soon turned towards the window, and to begin with you had to look hard at the roof opposite to make out the light particles of snow which were beginning to detach themselves from the sky.

The boys were in a fever of excitement. Darkness fell and the flakes became thicker and slower. In the waiting-room where the gas had been lit, the mothers could be seen around the stove, their lips moving soundlessly.

Brother Médard's electric bell, the prayer which was thrown to the echoes and came rattling back, the lines forming up, the door finally opening: it was settling! The snow was settling!

The children, whether they were in the first year or the sixth, dressed in little hooded coats or blue ratteen overcoats with gilt buttons, were promptly transformed into so many excited gnomes which Monsieur Penders had difficulty in keeping in two lines as far as the corner of the street.

A mysterious signal, and everybody rushed away through the flakes which kept sticking to your eyes and turned the street-lamps into far-away lighthouses on the ocean.

The place du Congrès, with its huge stretches of darkness, its three ill-lit shops, and a few feebly glowing windows, was too big for the noisy band of schoolboys. A tiny patch of it was enough, the bit nearest the rue Pasteur. Along the terrace, the water in the gutter had frozen; the bigger boys were already away, their satchels bumping against their backs. Some of them fell and picked themselves up again. Clogs slid best of all, after a preliminary clatter, while hob-nailed boots made white lines. Excitement mounted. Uneven patches of snow were forming on the terrace, and a light covering of snow was hemming the black branches of the elm trees. You had to pick it up in several places, in little heaps which weighed nothing, before you could make a ball out of it to throw at cold cheeks or a blue hood.

A big boy decided:

'The little boys aren't allowed to use our slide.'

And the little boys watched them sliding along, their arms outstretched, bending their knees as if they were on springs. They tried to make another slide more their own size, a little further on, but there was not enough ice, and pebbles grating under the soles of their boots stopped them half-way.

Fingers were frozen, nostrils wet, cheeks tight-skinned and burning, breath short and hot, eyes shining.

A woman's voice called out in the mysterious distance:

'Jean! . . . Jean! . . .'

'Yes, Mother.'

'Come home quick.'

'Yes, Mother.'

Another go on the slide, another two.

'If you force me to come and fetch you . . .'

One less! Grown-ups went past unnoticed, men in dark overcoats, women clutching their shawls, their hair powdered with snow. The light from the grocer's shop-window fell across the slide which was turning a bluish black.

You opened your mouth, put out your tongue and tried to catch a snowflake which left a taste of dust. You declared enthusiastically:

'It's wonderful!'

And it was indeed wonderful, this first frost, this first snow, a world which had lost its everyday appearance, roofs dimly outlined against the soft sky, lamps which shed scarcely any light and passers-by who floated through space. Even the tram became a mysterious vessel, with its windows doing service as portholes.

You did not dare to think about tomorrow. Too many hours separated the present moment from the next day, and waiting would hurt.

The Grand Bazaar, this particular evening, would stay open until midnight, perhaps even later, and when the iron shutters finally came rattling down, the shop-assistants, pale and tired, their heads as hollow and noisy as drums, would find themselves standing dazedly in the midst of the ravaged shelves.

> St Nicholas, patron saint of schoolboys,
> Please bring me nuts, apples, and toys,
> To have some sweets, I shall be as good as gold,
> I shall always do as I am told,
> Singing tra la la la,
> Singing tra . . .

Another anxious mother called out in the dark:

'Vic-tooooor! . . . Vic-tooooor . . .'

The group of boys melted away. Those from Bressoux had gone off in a bunch, still picking up snow along the quai de la Dérivation. Armand was watching the hoods bobbing up and down from his doorstep. Some little street-urchins, who had come from heaven knows where, had invaded the slide, and Roger, walking a little unsteadily, kept close to the walls of the rue Pasteur and the rue de la Loi, and looked through the keyhole at the soft light in the kitchen before knocking on the letter-box.

Surprised by the warmth, he felt his eyes smarting; he would have liked to go to sleep straight away, to go to bed without supper so as to be up earlier the next day.

Désiré, on his return from the office, did not put on his old jacket as usual and his slippers had not been put to warm on the door of the stove. Élise was dressed to go out; even Mademoiselle Pauline wore a conspiratorial smile.

In the winter, Roger undressed in the kitchen, by the fire, putting on his long dressing-gown in white flannelette and his slippers, and his mother took his brick upstairs and tucked him up after making sure that the paraffin night-light was not smoking.

'Be good. Sleep well.'

He listened. He said his prayers.

'Dear God, please may I have no bad dreams and may we all three die together.'

For he could not bear the idea of following one day the hearse carrying his father and mother.

'Dear God, please may I have no more evil thoughts. I promise.'

Shouldn't he give something in return?

'I promise not to talk to Ledoux any more.'

He would talk to him again, that was practically certain, but what counted was that he should make a resolution not to talk to him any more. If he happened to do so, he would beg pardon and promise all over again.

Further proof that Ledoux really knew: one Thursday, when they came home about five o'clock, Élise had heard voices in Monsieur Chechelowski's room and had listened hard.

'Be quiet, Roger. Don't make any noise.'

She had knocked on the door, pale and determined.

'Excuse me, Monsieur Chechelowski ... Excuse me, Mademoiselle ...'

There had been a rather ugly young woman in the room who had looked at Élise calmly while smoking a cigarette with a cardboard tip.

'You know, Valérie, she all but blew the smoke into my face. As for him, I thought he was going to take me by the throat, he was so furious.'

'This is my room, do you hear, *I pay*!'

Roger had heard his mother tell the story several times, to Aunt Louisa, to Hubert Schroefs, to Cécile.

'If you are engaged and your intentions are honourable, then you will understand and agree to move into the dining-room. It's all the same for you.'

For Monsieur Chechelowski had met a fellow-country-woman who was studying medicine like Mademoiselle Frida and whom he intended marrying as soon as he had finished his studies.

'A queer couple they'll make!' Élise prophesied.

That was of no importance. What mattered was that they had gone into the dining-room, the door of which Élise had deliberately left ajar. What mattered most of all was that she had said to Valérie, on the Friday, when Désiré had gone out to the Veldens':

'You understand, don't you? Whatever happens, I won't have them coming *to do that* in my house.'

Roger repeated to himself:

'Dear God, please may I have no more evil thoughts.'

No! He would not make that gesture with his fingers again. He did not even want to think, this evening, that St Nicholas was Father and Mother.

Yet he had heard his parents going out. If he went downstairs, he would find nobody in the kitchen but Mademoiselle Pauline, who had been asked to mind the house and who was copying out some lecture notes by the fire.

It was so rare for Désiré and Élise to find themselves out together, especially in the evening, as in the old days when Désiré used to wait for the young shop-assistant outside L'Innovation!

She held his arm, and, being too short for him, looked as if she were hanging on to it. As soon as they got to the rue Puits-en-Sock, they could scarcely move, and they in turn were gripped by the general fever of excitement and would have liked to buy everything they saw. Everything looked beautiful to them: there were rocking-horses covered with real skin and hair, electric trains, and dolls which you might have taken to be living babies and which lacked nothing but the power of speech.

'It's too dear, Désiré. It's better to have something small but good.'

It was the workers, the people who lived in the back-streets, who were the biggest spendthrifts and jostled the passers-by at the shop doors, pushing brutally with their elbows in order to be served first, carrying on their shoulders tricycles, forts, and cakes so big you could hide behind them.

'They spend all their earnings like that and they won't have enough money left to pay the rent.'

It was their wives who bought meat at the beginning of the month without asking how much it weighed, their children had holes in their socks, and, by the fifteenth of the month, they had to start taking things to the pawnshop.

For a long time Désiré and Élise stayed out in the snowy night, going from darkness to light and queuing in front of shop-counters; and Élise's hand kept returning to its place on big Désiré's arm.

Mademoiselle Pauline, her breasts pushed up under her chin by her corset, worked quietly in the kitchen where the steam was trickling slowly down the oil-paint on the walls.

Noises, voices, the sound of doors banging interrupted Roger's sleep. Two or three times he awoke and stared at the flame of the night-light, but it was not yet time.

At last he heard the familiar sounds of the stove being lit and caught the smell of paraffin which Élise insisted on pouring on the fire to hurry it up. He jumped out of bed, barefoot, his legs caught up in his nightshirt. He did not put his slippers on. The stairs were cold, the tiles in the hall icy.

The dining-room door was locked.

'Wait, Roger. Your father will open it.'

Désiré came downstairs, his trousers fastened loosely over his nightshirt with its collar embroidered with cross-stitching in red cotton.

The family had never all been up so early before and this added to the exceptional character of the day.

On the first St Nicholas's Day that Roger could remember, when they were still living in the rue Pasteur, he had burst into tears at the sight which had suddenly presented itself to him. It had been too much for him.

Even now, although he was expecting it, the smell disturbed him: the smell of the tarts, the chocolate, the oranges, the raisins. The dining-room was no longer just another room in the house. On the tablecloth there were plates full of marzipan cakes, fruit, and sweets, and you could not see everything at once. The gaslight had not been turned on, and only the dancing flame of a candle lit up this spectacle.

Why had he picked up a big orange which he held as he had seen the Infant Jesus at school holding in his hand a blue ball surmounted by a cross, a ball which represented the world?

Calm and solemn, he proceeded to carry out a methodical inspection, scarcely glancing at the hoop and the soldier's peaked cap (it was Uncle Arthur who had made it for him, who had even measured him for it), the Eureka rifle or the two picture-books, but going to sit in a corner to examine his paint-box.

'Are you happy?'

An absent-minded yes.

'Have you seen this?'

It was a Meccano outfit he had not been expecting and he granted it only a vague glance. When he looked up again, he saw Désiré who had gone over to Élise. He was giving her a little case containing a brooch. He was awkward, as he always was on these occasions, with his eyes shining and his moustache quivering. Roger had sworn not to have any more evil thoughts.

'Its' too much, Désiré, it's really too much. Thank you.'

She nearly burst out crying.

'It's much too pretty. For you, all that I've got is . . .'

A pipe, a pipe with a thin curved stem of the sort Élise liked because they looked distinguished.

'You like it, though?'

Désiré filled it straight away and lit it, even though he had had nothing to eat. Nothing mattered today. The lodgers were still asleep. The family had gathered together in the dining-room with the shutters closed, and finally they lit the gas as if it were the evening. They still smelled of the bed and they did not notice the cold.

Roger ate a chocolate, a fig, and a raisin, and cautiously nibbled the edge of a marzipan cake and the horn of a ginger-bread goat from Dinant.

'Desiré, you ought to go and get your slippers while I'm making the coffee.'

It was even more unreal than the place du Congrès in the snow. The smell of coffee came from the kitchen, and Élise's voice:

'Don't eat too much, Roger. We're just going to have breakfast.'

The first workmen's tram went by along the rue Jean-d'Outremeuse, and the bells of the parish church started ringing for the first Mass. In the church lit by only a couple of tapers, the choirboy would be ringing his bell, or rather no, there was no choirboy this morning and it was the sacristan who served Mass.

In the kitchen, they did not have eggs and bacon as they did on other days, but just sweet things they had chosen from the plates, each according to his taste; the whole house smelled sweet and sickly when Désiré finally went upstairs to wash and dress.

Next door a shrill trumpet could be heard, and at nine o'clock, sitting next to Mademoiselle Frida who was having her breakfast, Roger was still in his nightshirt, with his nose in his plate, his stomach full and his body as sluggish as when he had not had enough sleep.

They had to resign themselves to opening the shutters, revealing a fairy-tale street. The world had disappeared. The Friars' school, although it was so close, was just distinguishable in the distance, through a white fog which clung to the window-panes and which you could tell was icy cold. People went by with their coat collars turned up and their hands in their pockets, and you had scarcely glimpsed them before they had vanished into a pale nothingness. The tram kept on ringing its bell, not daring to move at more than walking pace, and the dust-cart had turned into a mysterious carriage.

It was the only day in the year when you were entitled to live as you pleased, to crawl around on the floor, to dirty yourself, to eat what you liked at any time of the day.

Mademoiselle Frida, for her part, gave just one cold glance at the enchanted dining-room and went off to the amphitheatre where she would spend the morning cutting up corpses.

Roger was washed in the kitchen, with hot water.

'Come in, Mademoiselle Pauline, it isn't important.'

Élise wetted the comb to put a parting in the child's hair.

'No, you're going to give me your gingerbread and your chocolates.'

They had to be made to last until Christmas. Then it would be the turn of the black pudding and the bouquettes, followed almost immediately by the pale cakes and waffles of New Year's Day, the little glass of Kempenaar which you drank early in the morning in the rue Puits-en-Sock, for it was there the day began, the claret or port at Schroefs', where whole boxes of biscuits were opened and the contents stuffed into the children's pockets, and finally, in the afternoon, the white wine from Touraine at Coronmeuse.

Tomorrow, at school, Brother Mansuy would already be playing on the harmonium:

> 'Come, sweet Messiah,
> To save us today.
> Thou art our desire,
> So come now, we pray . . .'

And probably Mademoiselle Pauline's mother in Warsaw would send her daughter a smoked goose, like the year before.

The brushes, when Roger rinsed them in a saucer of water, left pink and mauve streaks. The boy furtively wiped the bristles between his lips. They had a tart taste which became another St Nicholas taste.

Chapter Seven

To give herself a start, she was doing the green room, Monsieur Saft's room, thoroughly; she had already polished the bed and the feet of the table; now and then she could hear Mademoiselle Pauline moving about in her room.

The weather was neither fine nor bad; it was what she called everyday weather, more white than grey, and fairly cold; occasionally a gust of wind lifted up the dust on the zinc platforms. Yet when playtime started at the Institut Saint-André and Roger crossed the street to come to drink the egg beaten up in a glass of beer which his mother prepared for him before going up to the bedrooms and left on the stairs, Élise was reasonably happy.

'It's me!' the boy shouted, pushing open the door which stayed ajar all morning.

Élise's happiness matched the weather: a little lukewarm happiness which she had manufactured for herself while she was polishing.

'If you could only see those poor letters, Louisa!'

Élise talked a lot while she was working, as if to give a direction to her thoughts; she needed to address herself mentally to somebody and, although no sound emerged from her lips, her face none the less assumed expressions in tune with her remarks.

Her imaginary companion changed frequently, according to the subject occupying her attention. Just now, it had been Madame Corbion, because the latter had lodgers like herself and could understand certain things. Sometimes she came along in the afternoon, dressed in silk, powdered and perfumed, with a gold chain round her neck and a lace handkerchief tucked in her belt.

'Just imagine, Madame Corbion, his mother works as a doctor's housekeeper. He isn't ashamed of her. That's what I admire about him. The poor woman, killing herself with work so that her son can become somebody!'

Madame Corbion never got excited, never showed any reaction. What interested her was students like hers, preferably Rumanians or Turks, who had a lot of money and whose love affairs fascinated her. She declared that she did not allow free access to her house, but it was clear that she did not look too hard at who went in and out.

'If only you could see her letters, Louisa!'

Her sister at Coronmeuse ought to understand, seeing that she made her own children study. Évariste was at the University, training to become a lawyer; Anna, the least gifted of the three, stayed at home but studied music; and Aimée, the youngest, was still at school.

'. . . Poor, clumsy writing, the writing of somebody who didn't stay at school for long. I can't read it, because it's in Polish. There are grease spots on the paper, I'm sure it's full of mistakes. Well, I think it's wonderful, and I think it's even more wonderful that Monsieur Saft isn't ashamed of his mother. He could have told me anything, that he was the son of this or that. Because he's always so spick and span! Just imagine, at night he folds his trousers and slips them under his pillow . . .'

She went to get some water to wash the windows, and, standing in the frame of the open window, she looked down on to the yards and the little gardens shut in between the blocks of houses.

'He has his meals in the rue de la Casquette. It isn't a real restaurant, or a boarding-house either. A Polish student who hadn't enough money to go on with his studies had the idea of renting a ground-floor flat and cooking for his friends. They pay him the cost price, or just a bit more. You can say what you like, I admire those people.'

If she had been there, Louisa would have replied:

'When people haven't enough money to study, they'd be better off learning an honest trade.'

She must have made that remark once. There were a number of ready-made phrases like that which you thought you could hear as soon as you pictured her to yourself. Perhaps they had been talking about Roger, whom Élise too wanted to make into somebody. Élise had almost certainly replied, with that quivering which affected her lips whenever she said something unpleasant:

'But you make your son and your daughters study all right!'

For after all, Louisa's husband had never been anything more than a basket-maker. He worked with his hands, while Louisa served drinks to any carter who came in and spent her days standing behind a counter. Why shouldn't she want to see other people nursing the same ambitions as herself?

'Brother Mansuy has told me that, if it wasn't for his age, he'd have him moved up into the second year.

' "*I can't teach him anything this year. He's too far ahead.*" '

The two women in the pub next door, the old one and the young one, were doing the washing in their yard.

'I bet you don't even know why there are so many poor Polish students . . .'

The first time that she had brought Monsieur Saft and Monsieur Chechelowski together in her kitchen, they had bristled up so much that she had thought sparks were going to fly. Finally they had controlled themselves. Monsieur Saft, looking very pale, had sat down without a word. Since then, they had never spoken to one another.

'And that's because, for a hundred years and more, the Poles have been under the Russian jack-boot. They think of nothing and work for nothing but their liberation. Isn't it wonderful? They have holes in their socks, they don't eat enough, but they study so as to be able to rebuild their country one day, and every week Monsieur Saft practises fencing with a teacher.'

There was a portrait of him on the mantelpiece, in tight-fitting white trousers, a padded fencing-jacket, and a mask covering his face. The foils were behind the wardrobe.

The minutes went by like this, the same colour as the weather; the chamois-leather squeaked on the window-panes, setting her teeth on edge; a voice in the hall called out:

'Coal?'

Élise had not heard the coalman's trumpet. She dashed downstairs.

'Three buckets.'

While they were being filled, she ran to get her purse in the kitchen. It was Friday. Old Madame Delcour, on the next doorstep, was waiting her turn and said good morning to Élise.

'Nice and full, please, Monsieur Joseph. The price still hasn't come down?'

'It's more likely to go up one of these days. Three buckets at forty centimes each: one franc twenty, lady. You haven't the exact change, have you?'

Élise had such sharp ears! She said nothing, but her head cocked imperceptibly towards the upper storey of the house and a bitter smile appeared on her lips.

How could Mademoiselle Pauline stoop so low? It made you wonder if it wasn't on purpose that she hadn't gone to her lectures. Just as the coalman was giving her her change, Élise had heard the first-floor window being carefully shut.

Now the spell was broken. When she went back up to Monsieur Saft's room, it did not occur to her to go on with her calm monologue, and she forgot the mother's letter, the photograph in fencing clothes, the good smell of wax-polish, the rather insipid atmosphere of an ordinary morning.

Élise could sense misfortune a long way off. She could not help it. Not just real misfortunes which you could talk about and which aroused pity, but all those little vexations which made a sensitive person suffer so much.

She could think of nothing but Mademoiselle Pauline, who had not wanted her to do her room that morning because she was working. What had happened was Désiré's fault. She had told him a hundred times that it was a mistake to joke with people who had no sense of humour.

'Can't you see, Désiré, that they haven't got the same mentality as us?'

He took care not to tease Mademoiselle Frida, who remained ice-cold, showing no reaction, as if you were talking to somebody behind her. Désiré's *bête noire* was Mademoiselle Pauline, who for her part, her eyes shining, went red in the face, puffing out her breasts which her corset pushed up underneath her plump chin.

'Anybody can tell that you come from the rue Puits-en-Sock!'

She herself did not understand this game of his – if it was a game – which consisted of saying unpleasant things while pretending to be joking.

Désiré returned to the attack in season and out of season.

'He doesn't leave her in peace a single evening, Valérie. As soon as she comes into the kitchen, he starts on her. He just can't help it, and he seizes on any pretext he can think of.'

Her hands, for instance. Mademoiselle Pauline cared for her hands, which were small and plump, as if they were precious objects; she gazed at them lovingly, making no secret of it, and was fond of telling how she put cream on them every night and wore gloves in bed. When she was eating, with her elbows on the table, she moved her fingers with their polished nails delicately, as if they were precision instruments; she had a way of peeling an apple with exasperating care, or crumbling her bread as you would for a bird. There in the kitchen in the rue de la Loi, where nobody stood on ceremony, she was as dignified as if she were at a state banquet, and was not in the least embarrassed if everybody else got up while she was still at table.

'Madame Mamelin, I can't eat with a nickel fork.'

Had she gone, as it would have been so easy to do, to buy some silver cutlery in the rue de la Régence? Only somebody who did not know her would imagine that she would do that. She had written to her mother and the latter had had to send her some cutlery from Warsaw.

'If I were in your place, Mademoiselle Pauline,' Désiré had said to her, 'I'd refuse to eat off anything but gold plate. After all, when you're used to that sort of thing! And then, the food must taste so much better.'

She detested him, she hated him; as Élise used to say, if her eyes had been rifle barrels, Désiré would have been dead long ago. Few evenings went by without a skirmish. One day when she complained that she had been unable to find her usual brand of hand-cream in Liège, Désiré asked:

'Why don't you try some cheese?'

That Herve cheese which smelled so strong that it could not be put on the table except under a cover and which made Mademoiselle Pauline run a mile as soon as she saw it.

Élise could not manage to summon up a smile at this memory, nor at the thought of Désiré's description of his lodger to Hubert Schroefs:

'The fact is, her fingers look like diseased sausages.'

Suddenly she listened, then called out:

'I'm coming down, Léopold.'

She bent over, but could not hear anything more in the hall. She went down a few stairs and bent over the banisters again.

'Oh, it's you . . . I'm coming . . .'

It was the poor old man who came every Friday.

'You couldn't give me two weeks' money at once, could you? I shan't be able to come next week.'

Élise could not forget that slight noise which had made her look up when the coalman was giving her her change. She could not have been mistaken. While trying to banish that memory from her mind, she was already getting ready to defend herself.

'We may be poor, Mademoiselle Pauline, but in this family we have always been honest.'

She felt tempted to add – and would if she were driven too far:

'Our parents didn't make their fortune selling stockings and underpants in the poorest suburb of Warsaw.'

For that was the case with the Feinsteins. They were none the less proud and haughty for all that, and when Mademoiselle Pauline's mother had come to Liège the year before, she had imagined that she deserved every consideration. She had bustled round the house, giving orders as if she were speaking to servants; and not for anything in the world would she have got up if a saucepan had started boiling over, forgetting that she had spent her life behind the cash-desk in a porter's lodge converted into a shop.

T–P–M

Monsieur Saft had known them and had told Élise all about them. He seemed to hate the Jews even more than the Russians.

'They aren't Poles, Madame. You must never say that they are Poles, because it would be insulting us. In Poland, they live in special districts, where real Poles never go.'

Mademoiselle Pauline was studying to become a mathematics teacher and was incapable of boiling an egg. She mended her stockings with wool of any colour – what did it matter since it was on her feet and could not be seen? – and she would have mended them with red string if she had had nothing else to hand.

'How will you manage when you have children, Mademoiselle Pauline?'

For Élise, who scolded Désiré for poking fun at their lodger, could not restrain herself sometimes from telling her a few home truths.

'I shan't have any children.'

'Then you must be cleverer than most. Because men . . .'

'No man is ever going to have any rights over me.'

Her calm self-assurance was exasperating. She was full of love and admiration for herself. Once when Désiré asked her if she didn't sometimes kiss her reflection in the mirror, she had replied: 'Why not?'

Roger had already come home. It was time to lay the table. Élise rushed around, thinking all the time of the unpleasantness which was going to happen; she felt so impatient and annoyed that for two pins she would have gone to meet the attack half-way and knocked on the door of the pink room.

'Well, Mademoiselle Pauline, say what you have to say to me. I know that you opened your window like a thief. I know why, too. I've been expecting this for a long time. Speak up, now. I'm listening.'

For it was true that Élise had been expecting what was going to happen or some other attack. One day, she had been unable to refrain from saying to her lodger in front of everybody:

'Here are three francs sixty, Mademoiselle Pauline.'

The other woman, who had understood, had chosen to feign surprise.

'You've got a mania for leaving money around all over the place. This morning there was even a twenty-centime piece under the rug by your bed. You'd be doing me a favour if you put your money on one side.'

A word to the wise is enough! Monsieur Chechelowski had smiled behind his moustache. Mademoiselle Frida had looked hard at her landlady.

'It's true. You always seem to suspect people of being after your money. You think of nothing but your money. I'd better tell you, Mademoiselle Pauline, that there aren't any thieves in this house.'

'I never said there were.'

'But you put marks on your bottle of eau de Cologne and you weigh your bag of coffee in your hand before putting it back in your tin.'

Élise blushed to herself, for once or twice, running short of coffee and not wanting to go to the Vierge Noire, she had taken a little coffee out of each of her lodgers' tins. As for the coal . . .

'You know, Madame Corbion, what makes me angry is that she could easily afford it. To begin with, she had her meals at the boarding-house in the rue de l'Enseignement, where they charge you a franc for a meal. If it wasn't that Désiré won't let me have people here for meals, I know how much I'd make by doing the same . . .'

She bustled about, her forehead creased with worry, regretting her good day which had been ruined by Mademoiselle Pauline, and remembering all the little disappointments and the petty vexations which fate took care to reserve for her. Yet heaven knows that she did her best.

Why, from the very start, had she had only poor lodgers?

'What can I do about it? I told Mademoiselle Frida: "Give me your stockings and your linen and I'll wash them for you." I charge her scarcely anything for the soap. I charge five centimes a pair for mending Monsieur Saft's socks and I provide the wool. And when for once a lodger turns up who could pay, she has to be miserly and suspicious, forever doing her accounts in a little notebook which she always carries with her. She even goes to the extent of counting her lumps of sugar.'

When Mademoiselle Pauline had seen that the others ate in the kitchen and were given boiling water for their coffee, she had worked out that this would cost her less than having her meals outside. Her mother sent her sausages, hams, smoked goose and cakes from her own country. She had never offered anything to anybody, not even to the child. Élise had had to steal a bit of goose to find out what it tasted like. It did not matter to Mademoiselle Pauline if she made the others feel sick; on the contrary, she spread out her provisions, installed herself in the best place, stayed a whole hour at table, and, if there was nobody in the kitchen during the day, she came downstairs with her books and her lecture notes to save on the fire in her own room.

'Mademoiselle Pauline, you've let the milk boil over on to the stove. Didn't you smell it burning?'

'I'm not here to watch your saucepans.'

She was spiteful, Élise knew that, and she envied everybody, because she was ugly, because she was a Jewess, because her father had been born in a ghetto on the Russian frontier, an old Jew with a long beard who, back there, stole humbly along the streets, keeping close to the houses. That was why there was not a single portrait of her father in her room: she was ashamed of him.

She would take her revenge, that was only to be expected, for Désiré's jokes; she would take her revenge on Élise who made a distinction between her and the other lodgers, and who, for washing her linen, charged her two centimes a piece more than she charged Mademoiselle Frida.

Now here she came, sitting down without a word, and twisting her napkin while she waited until Monsieur Chechelowski and Mademoiselle Frida were at table. Tense and feverish, Élise gave her son his dinner without looking at them. She could feel the attack coming, and eventually it came, soft and sugary.

'Tell me, Madame Mamelin, how much does the dealer who comes along the street charge for a bucket of coal?'

'Forty centimes, Mademoiselle Pauline. Coal went up five centimes last month because of the strikes.'

Silence. The plump little hands delicately removed the transparent skin from a slice of garlic sausage stuck on the silver fork.

'Why do you ask? Is it because I charge you forty-five centimes a bucket? Don't forget that I have to carry it up to you, that I provide the wood and the paper, that I light the fire. If you consider that five centimes is too much to pay for my trouble, there's nothing to stop you . . .'

'I didn't say that. I've a right to ask questions, haven't I?'

'Of course, Mademoiselle Pauline, you've every right, including the right to carry the coal up to your room yourself.'

'You are getting angry.'

'I'm not getting angry. It's you who are insinuating . . .'

'I am not insinuating. I am what I am.'

You might have thought that it was all over. But no, it wasn't all over, for Élise, who had cheated again, was anxiously wondering whether Mademoiselle Pauline realized this.

It was true that she charged only five centimes more than old Joseph for the coal. What she failed to add was that the coal scuttles in the bedrooms held a good third less than the coalman's buckets.

'You understand, Valérie, it wouldn't be worth all the trouble I take if I didn't make a profit.'

That was why this was not just a mere skirmish. It was a real drama. Élise was honest. She would not take a ten-centime piece which her lodgers might leave lying around, but she cheated in all sorts of ways, for two centimes here, for three centimes there, and Mademoiselle Pauline suspected as much, perhaps more than she said.

Had the others, for their part, noticed anything? Just now, Mademoiselle Frida had darted a peculiar look at Élise, as if an idea had occurred to her.

'Me who's always looking for ways of being useful to them!'

That was true. And that was just the trouble which nobody, apart from Élise, could understand. It upset her when Mademoiselle Frida had got nothing but some bread and butter for dinner and she tried to persuade her to accept a plate of soup; it was she too, who, when she went out on Thursday afternoon with Roger, suggested:

'Come downstairs to study in the kitchen, Monsieur Saft. You'll be by yourself and it's warmer there.'

Unfortunately, afterwards, she counted the cost. Every week she had to take some money to the Savings Bank to put it into Roger's account; she hid small sums all over the place, in the soup-tureen, in her linen-drawer.

Did anybody ever give her anything for nothing? Why,

seeing that they were all students, shouldn't she be entitled to make a student out of her son?

'If only she could leave the house!'

Now Mademoiselle Pauline's presence oppressed her, as if it represented a constant threat. She could not talk about it to Désiré, because she cheated him too. She even cheated with the gas and water for he never thought of checking the meters.

'When I take in some new lodgers. I'll make sure they are Belgian,' was all that she said, while he in his turn was having his dinner in a ray of sunshine which had finally pierced the clouds. 'However nice they are, foreigners are foreigners. They don't feel things as we do.'

'Who wanted them in the first place?' he retorted, without thinking any more about it . . .

'Mind you, I'm not complaining. I'm just saying . . .'

How could such a futile incident upset her to such an extent? She was as feverish as if she were sickening for an illness. However much she reasoned with herself, she remained uneasy, waiting for some fresh misfortune. She had started to clean her brasses, the task she liked best, the one she did on Friday afternoon; all the brasses in the house were gathered together on the table: candlesticks, flower-pot cases, ashtrays, saucepans, and the oil-lamps which they kept partly in case the gas failed but chiefly because they were used to seeing them on the kitchen shelf.

Désiré went off. He could not have got as far as the rue Puits-en-Sock before there was a violent ring at the door. She gave a start, for she usually recognized people from the way they rang the bell, and this was a ring she did not know.

Just in case, she opened the dining-room door as she went past.

'Monsieur . . .'

A well-dressed man greeted her politely, came in without a word, and walked calmly into the front room, which always smelled musty even though it was aired every week. Did he notice that Élise had her hands tightly clenched on her apron, that she smiled thinly as she pushed forward an Henri II chair for him, and that she threw an anxious glance in the direction of the door of the Institut Saint-André, as if she were looking for the reassuring silhouette of Brother Médard?

'I must apologize for troubling you, Madame Mamelin.'

His voice was soft and cordial; everything about him was cordial, kindly, almost familiar; he reminded you of a family doctor or a prosperous businessman.

Élise did not suspect that soon she would be calling him Monsieur Charles and that he would walk into the house in the rue de la Loi as naturally as Léopold, sit down on this chair which she had given him today and carefully light a handsome meerschaum pipe.

'Your lodgers have all gone out, haven't they?'

While he was saying this, he turned towards the door of Monsieur Chechelowski's room, as if he were familiar with the habits of the house.

'Why do you ask?'

'Have no fear, Madame Mamelin. We have had the best possible reports about you. I'm from the police.'

She remained standing by the door which she had left open.

'I'm particularly concerned with foreigners, including of course, Russians, and I should have come here a long time ago to have a little chat with you.'

He was rather plump and pot-bellied, with a fresh complexion and thinning fair hair brushed back from the forehead, and she noticed that he was wearing a wedding-ring; this detail, for no particular reason, reassured her.

'You were probably busy, I suppose. I should be sorry to have picked my moment badly.'

'Dear God, I'm not very presentable. I was doing my brasses . . .'

She took the opportunity to take off her apron and straighten her bun.

'You have a student here, haven't you, called . . .'

He hunted for the name in his notebook, although she was certain that he knew it perfectly well.

'Let's see. Frida Stavitskaïa . . . Do you mind if I smoke? If you would sit down, that would put me entirely at my ease.'

Didn't he know that you didn't sit down on the best chairs in the dining-room in your working clothes?

'With regard to this young lady, could you tell me whether she often entertains friends here?'

'I don't allow free access.'

'Oh, I see. Yes . . . Of course . . .'

Did he understand what was meant by free access? He was a gay person. It was hard to believe that he was a real policeman. He was looking at Élise with an amused expression in which you could almost distinguish a certain tenderness, something, at any rate, which was at once affectionate and ironical. Possibly because he had encountered a good many Élises, he seemed to know just what she was like.

'Even if she doesn't entertain any men, I suppose she can receive women friends in her room?'

'I can see that you don't know her. She's much too shy to have any women friends.'

She was more at ease already. Pretending to be perplexed, he gazed at a letter which he had taken from his pocket and which, under the name of Frida Stavitskaïa, bore an address crossed out with purple pencil.

'I suppose you sometimes have to go out to do your shopping? At those times, you obviously can't tell if anybody comes in here.'

A change of tactics was indicated. Élise did not like anybody suspecting her house.

'Listen, Madame Mamelin, I'm not going to pretend with you any more. I belong to the Second Bureau. We are the people whose job it is to keep an eye on suspicious foreigners, and there's no blinking the fact that there are swarms of them in the country just now. By accident, thanks to an incomplete address, this letter, bearing a Swiss stamp, went to the dead-letter office and fell into our hands.'

He looked thoroughly at home and it was Élise who felt like a stranger in her own house, to such an extent that the quiet street whose cobbles she could see through the window seemed like a refuge to her.

'I assure you, Madame, that your lodger, no doubt without your knowing it, has received somebody here in this house and has put him up for several days.'

Blushing fiercely, Élise started talking very fast, so as not to allow suspicion time to enter her visitor's mind.

'I'm sorry, I had completely forgotten about it. It was two months ago, wasn't it? I could find the exact day for you. A

Thursday, because I had been to L'Innovation. You're talking about the "devil", I'm sure. I'll tell you what happened.

'Mademoiselle Frida had told me that a relative of hers, a cousin, was coming to Liège for two or three days. She asked me if I could make up a bed for him in this dining-room which is scarcely ever used. It was Désiré, I mean my husband, who wouldn't agree. She seemed very annoyed and sulked for a couple of days. It appeared that her cousin didn't speak French and was very shy, so that she didn't want to leave him on his own in an hotel in the town.

'She hunted around for nearly a week. I had forgotten all about it when, one Thursday, as I said at the beginning, I found her, when I got home, in the hall with a man I didn't know. They were waiting for me. It was already dark and I had to light the gas. What I remember most of all is the long overcoat the man was wearing.

' "Listen, Madame Mamelin, I've brought my cousin here. We were waiting for you to tell you. He's going to sleep in my room and I'm going to stay with a woman friend of mine."

'I couldn't refuse, could I? They didn't stay together more than a couple of minutes in the room, and during that time the door was open. Once they had put his suitcase in the room, they came out on the landing where they talked for a long time in Russian.

' "Why don't you come into the dining-room?" I called out to them.

'Because heaven knows what they looked like standing there. She didn't want to. The man – we called him the devil straight away, because of his black forelock and his goatee, though we scarcely saw anything of him – he stayed in the room all the next day. I know he was writing, because I took him up a cup of coffee and he stared hard at me.

'But tell me, Monsieur . . .'

'Monsieur Charles.'

'Tell me, Monsieur Charles . . .'

She felt a pang of remorse. Mightn't she be ruining Mademoiselle Frida's reputation?

'She hasn't done anything wrong, I hope?'

'Go on, please.'

'That's all. He stayed four days instead of two. He only went

313

out in the evening and he came back in the middle of the night, because Mademoiselle Frida had given him her key. One night, he didn't come back at all, and the next day my lodger moved back into her room. I pointed out to her that her cousin hadn't said either good-bye or thank you to us . . .'

'Would you mind terribly if I just had a look inside that room? Have no fear, Madame Mamelin. I'm used to this sort of thing and the young lady won't even suspect that I've been there.'

'What if she came back?'

He shrugged his shoulders. It was as if he knew where she was, what she was doing, when she would be back.

'Come now, Madame Mamelin, I don't want to alarm you, but, seeing that you are an intelligent woman – yes, I'm sure you are – and that you can keep a secret, I ought to tell you that the devil, as you call him, is one of the nihilists who assassinated the Grand Duke, in St Petersburg, with a bomb which killed over fifty people.'

Élise smiled incredulously.

'No, Monsieur Charles, that's impossible. You'll never persuade me that in my house . . .'

In her house, indeed! In the rue de la Loi!

'Would you like me to give you some information about your other lodgers? Then you'll realize that we don't make mistakes. Do you know, for instance, where Monsieur Saft went on Monday morning?'

She frowned. The previous Monday, she had in fact heard him go out before daybreak and, when he came back, she had noticed that he was carrying a long parcel under his overcoat.

'Monsieur Saft went to Cointe to fight a duel with a fellow countryman of his. Show me the way, will you?'

He left his hat in the dining-room, throwing a sympathetic glance into the kitchen, where the waiting brasses were being steamed up by the boiling water. For two pins he would have gone in there and sat down and asked for a cup of coffee.

'Does Mademoiselle Frida get many letters?'

'A letter from Russia every week and a money-order at the end of the month. Often the money-order is late.'

'Have you got the key to this wardrobe?'

'There isn't any need for a key; the lock doesn't work.'

The man's hands went through the linen and clothes with unexpected gentleness. He opened the drawers, and a sweet-box which contained strings of various colours and hairpins. From the landing, Élise kept an eye on the street door.

'If you knew her as well as I know her . . .'

'Has she told you that her father has been in prison in Siberia for twenty years?'

'Yes.'

With the same careful movements – she had found the comparison she was looking for: he had a dentist's hands – he leafed through the medical books without finding anything.

'Well, well. She's a smart one.'

He came downstairs again and stopped in front of the letter-box.

'Who takes the post out of this box every morning?'

'It depends. Usually each lodger collects his own post. We are having breakfast when the postman comes. As for us, we scarcely ever have anything but the paper.'

'Tell me, Madame Mamelin, I'd very much like to ask you . . .'

No. He decided to abandon the idea. It would be better to come back another day, to proceed gently.

'I was nearly forgetting my hat. Above all, don't say a word to anybody, will you, not even to your husband. I count on you. I'll be back soon. And once again, forgive me for giving you all this trouble.'

How could you describe what she felt as soon as she was alone again in the house? If she had obeyed her first impulse, she would have gone across the street to tell the whole story to Brother Médard and ask his advice. Who could tell whether that man really belonged to the Second Bureau? What if he were a thief?

She went upstairs to make sure that Monsieur Charles had not taken anything. She had scarcely come down again and was dipping her rag in the metal-polish which smelled of acid when Mademoiselle Frida came back from the University.

Whom and what could she trust now? Élise had the impression that her house had been soiled, that a vague menace had insinuated itself into it. Wouldn't she have done better to keep quiet? Instead of that, she had talked and talked, she had told all she knew. The fact of the matter was, it had been fear which had impelled her. And also, she had to admit it, she had felt a desire to win the respect of that wonderfully polite man, even though she did not know him from Adam.

'Not even to your husband!' he had told her.

Poor Désiré! She was going to have to conceal something more from him! Cheating! Always cheating! She could almost have cried at the thought! And then there was Monsieur Saft who went out on tip-toe early in the morning to fight a duel!

Suddenly her blood froze, and she sprang to her feet, facing the glazed door. She had heard somebody running along overhead, the door of the annexe had opened and slammed to as if shut by a draught, and angry footsteps were coming downstairs. Mademoiselle Frida rushed towards the kitchen so clumsily that you would have thought that she was wearing heavy men's boots. She stopped in the doorway and, under the stress of emotion, spoke in Russian first of all, then corrected herself and asked in a hissing voice:

'Who has been in my room? I want to know. I want you to tell me straight away who has been.'

A fixed smile appeared somehow or other on Élise's pale lips.

'What's the matter with you, Mademoiselle Frida?'

'I want to know, do you understand?'

'But . . . I assure you that apart from myself . . .'

The furious Russian woman looked as if she could have hit her landlady or seized her wrists to shake her.

'You're lying!' she screamed.

'I swear on Roger's head . . .'

She hadn't said that on purpose, and she tried to take it back.

'I swear on my head that . . .'

'Then it's you!'

'What are you accusing me of doing?'

'It's you who have been touching my books.'

'What should I be doing with your books?'

Frida stamped on the floor.

'I forbade you to touch my books.'

'When I'm dusting them, I may move them a bit without meaning to.'

'No.'

She was quite definite. Élise could guess why and blushed even more. But why should she have to put up with a scene like this in her own kitchen?

'You've gone through the pages of my books on purpose. You've looked through my lecture notes, opened the drawer of my table. *I know!*'

She added, her teeth set in anger:

'I make marks too.'

Despite this allusion which put her out more than ever, Élise had the presence of mind to exclaim:

'I see what it is! Dear God! Mademoiselle Frida, how can you work yourself up into such a state for such a little thing? Just now, when I took the coal up, Roger followed me into your room. A child touches everything when you've got your back turned. I'm always telling him not to go in the lodgers' rooms.'

With a sharp look which was not entirely disarmed, Frida turned her back, opened the street-door, and slammed it behind her with such violence that the house trembled with the shock. Perhaps she had gone for good?

Élise hesitated no longer; she tore off her apron, did her hair again, and washed her hands at the pump. Brother Médard was there on the opposite pavement, watching the boys going out, and darting an occasional glance at the Mamelins' house.

Why had he never struck her as ridiculous? His body, underneath his cassock, looked like a big lop-sided ball on which the other, disproportionate ball of the head was balanced. He made you think of a snowman in black, and yet it seemed to her that he was probably the only person from whom she would accept any verdict.

'Come with me, Roger. Wait while I get my key.'

If she forgot to take it out of the letter-box, as had sometimes happened, she would find herself locked out and would have to wait for Désiré or one of the lodgers to return.

'Excuse me, Brother Médard. But I don't know what to do. I need advice. Something so unexpected has just happened to me . . .'

Majestically – yes, he was truly majestic – he waved to the little door which was open in the middle of the gate, the yard with the uneven paving-stones, and his empty classroom where the newish desks and benches were a pale yellow colour.

317

'Stay in the yard, Roger.'

It was the first time that she had ever been in a classroom. It impressed her as much as when she had gone with Charles, Françoise's husband, into the sacristy at Saint-Denis to admire the chasubles.

'Sit down, Madame Mamelin.'

He could not offer her his chair, for it was a high chair, made to go with the desk planted on the edge of the platform. He gestured towards the front bench and stood there, his paunch sticking out, solemn, self-assured, his eyes so calm that you felt that the world could be turned upside down without his being in the least flurried.

She told him everything. In front of him, she felt no shame at all. An arithmetic problem had been left on the blackboard. The air smelled of chalk and the dirty water in the bucket with a towel over it in which the boys washed their hands. A painted plaster Virgin looked down at Élise who went on talking, interrupted now and then by a question from Brother Médard.

'I know that it's a lie and that people haven't any right to tell lies . . .'

He smiled. He was a man who understood.

'What comes hardest is making a child tell a lie in his turn. But what else is there to do?'

He thought. He was the very statue of thought, his wooden leg raised slightly, his eyes fixed on the empty yard where Roger, left on his own, did not know what to do.

Finally he limped over to the door and called out:

'Roger.'

This was all quite extraordinary, for none of the friars ever called a pupil by his Christian name. Surprised, Roger came running up and looked inquiringly at his mother.

'Come here, young man.'

Brother Médard sat down on the edge of a bench, moved the lever underneath his cassock which enabled him to bend his wooden leg, took the child by his shoulders and, breathing into his face, said:

'You're a big boy, aren't you? And you love your mother. Now because you love your mother and you wouldn't want anything nasty to happen to her, you're going to do what I'm going to tell you. Just now, while your mother was taking up coal to Mademoiselle Frida's room, you went in and played with the books.'

'No, dear Brother.'

His ears had turned red, he couldn't tell why. He did not dare to turn his head away, and Brother Médard's thick breath was making him choke.

'Listen to what I'm telling you. If anybody questions you, if anybody asks you what you did in Mademoiselle Frida's room, you must answer that you looked through her books and opened the drawer in the table.'

He had understood. Brother Médard released him and turned with satisfaction and a touch of pride to face Élise.

'There, Madame Mamelin. As for that Monsieur Charles, if he comes again, I would advise you to . . .'

He gave her her instructions.

'You did well to tell me all about it. Don't hesitate to come to see me whenever you have a problem or some question is bothering you.'

'Thank you, Brother.'

She did not dare to say dear Brother, like Roger. It was extraordinary, but going out of the classroom and crossing the yard, she felt lighter. It had all been so easy! Everything had become familiar and reassuring once more.

'You couldn't act in any other way, your confessor will tell you the same as I.'

Out on the pavement, he made her a deep bow which made her blush with embarrassment.

'Come along, Roger.'

She took her son by the hand to cross the street. It seemed to her that everybody was looking at her, that all of a sudden she had become very important.

'Mother, why does Brother Médard want me to . . .'

She called him to order:

'Don't ask questions. You know perfectly well that Brother Médard forbade you to. Later on, when you're grown up, you'll understand.'

She finished her brasses. Now and then a somewhat sad smile, more distinguished than her usual smile, the smile she had given Brother Médard, came back to her lips without her realizing it.

And what was most surprising was that things happened after that just as she had been told they would. Mademoiselle Frida came home as usual, came downstairs and when the others were already at table, took her tin from the shelf, cut her bread and buttered it. Anybody would have thought that nothing had happened, and only Élise could see that her lodger was slightly embarrassed.

As for Roger, his gaze kept going from his mother to Mademoiselle Frida and, when supper was over, he was rather annoyed that nobody had asked him a single question, and wondered why Brother Médard had delivered such a solemn sermon to him.

Chapter Eight

'Pick your feet up, Roger.'

Roger wondered in silence. When they had turned into the rue Neuvice instead of the rue Léopold, he had thought they were going to the Vierge Noire. It was April, the air was pure, warm and caressing on the sunny side of the street, cool and bluish in the shade, some men had already discarded their overcoats, and the windows of the flats were open above the shops whose wares were overflowing again on to the pavements.

They were not going to the Vierge Noire. Roger gave up. Although they often went along the rue Neuvice, they had never climbed this particular flight of steps where the stone was so old and worn that in certain places the steps merged together; they had never gone through this reddish double-door of which only one half was open, then this second, padded door which closed automatically like a trap. Taken aback by the contrast with the busy life outside, Roger was struck by the silence and emptiness of this little, unfamiliar church with three pencils of sunlight cutting diagonally across it.

His mother genuflected, held out to him two fingers moistened with holy water, pulled him along by the hand, like somebody who had been here already, towards a side-aisle of the chapel, and knelt down in front of a confessional.

They were in the Redemptorists' church. The confessional which Élise had picked was empty and had a name over it: Father Meeus. Next to the wooden grating which concealed the part reserved for the priest there was a bell-push.

Farther on, in front of other confessionals, some women in black were waiting; a little old woman lifted the green curtain which partly hid the penitents and came out, to have her place taken straight away by another. The silence was so profound that you could hear the whispering of a woman who was probably hard of hearing and was confessing her sins in a kind of frenzy, stopping now and then to draw breath with a long hissing noise.

Élise remained motionless, her face buried in her hands, her body bent forward. You could tell that it was not the first time she had been here and that she had not picked Father Meeus' confessional at random. An oblong patch of sunlight was trembling beside the bell-push; Roger tried to find out where it was coming from, gave up, and amused himself by obliterating with his hand another patch of sunlight on the top of his prayer-stool, whose coarse plaited straw was cutting into his knees.

For the past fortnight, Élise had been a prey to a fever of cleaning. One after another, all the rooms in the house had been emptied of their contents, which had been piled up in the yard, or on the platform on top of Mademoiselle Frida's room. The mattresses and bolsters had been unstitched and the wool inside spread out in the sun.

Was it Monsieur Chechelowski's departure which had started this mania for absolute cleanliness? No doubt that event had contributed to it, but it would have come in any case some day or other for Élise Mamelin felt as if she had reached a dead-end and her nerves were at fever-pitch.

Nearly every Sunday she complained of headaches. Just as they were on the point of setting out, when everything was ready, when Roger was already waiting on the pavement, the ritual scene occurred and an attack of hysterics threatened the projected visit to the rue des Carmes or the Ursuline convent.

'You're tiring yourself out. I knew the time would come when you wouldn't be able to stand it any more.'

Here Désiré was obviously saying something he shouldn't. What is more, he was wrong. Élise would have put up with her tiredness as she had the previous year if everything, this winter, had not conspired against her. Her sister Félicie's death, to begin with, and the ambiguous atmosphere in which the drama had come to its miserable end. Then Françoise's pleurisy, even though she was only her sister-in-law. Désiré had shown scarcely any concern about Françoise, but Élise knew that she was suffering from tuberculosis, with two lovely little children on her hands. She had talked it over with Doctor Matray, who had said that only mountain air could save her and that in any case she ought to be separated from her children. Charles Daigne knew this, but did nothing. He shuttled sheepishly backwards and forwards between the sacristy and the house at the back of the courtyard, and when Élise had tried to have a serious talk with him he had just sighed:

'What more can I do? I'm praying for her. And Monsieur le Curé says a Mass every week for her intention.'

Françoise suspected nothing, and thought that she was getting better because two red spots had lit up on her cheekbones. Her voice was already soft and distant, and when Élise saw her kissing her son who was only eighteen months old, her blood froze.

'If you want my advice, don't interfere!' Désiré kept telling her.

Mademoiselle Pauline had not changed. Élise could not stand her and yet she did not dare to throw her out; perhaps, indeed, she would have missed her, she was so used to having this enemy installed in her house, giving her material, with her daily vexations, for morose reflections or silent feelings of revolt.

Mademoiselle Frida had not gone either and Monsieur Charles came nearly every week to sit down, cordial and familiar, in the rue de la Loi dining-room. To begin with, Élise had not understood. She had thought that he was simply doing his job. When a suspicion had occurred to her, she had banished it from her mind as inconceivable, and yet it was becoming more and more flagrant; he looked at her in a way which no woman could mistake, his voice took on inflections which made her blush, and he had a habit, while he was talking to her, of putting an ostensibly fatherly hand on her knee or on her arm.

The idea! A middle-aged married man with a good job,

coming to waste his time chatting with a woman in her apron and with her hair untidy, for anybody would think that it was on purpose that he always caught her in the middle of her work.

She had nearly spoken about it to Brother Médard, who always looked at the house while he watched the boys coming out of school and who, as soon as he caught sight of Élise, made an exaggerated bow towards her. So far she had not dared to.

'Do you think it's possible, Valérie? Do you think he'll try to go any further?'

'Why don't you speak about it to Désiré?'

'Never, you silly! If Désiré knew about it . . .'

It would not be jealousy. Désiré trusted her. He would never descend to suspecting his wife. He had put up with the invasion of his house by the lodgers better than she had expected, but if he discovered that there was anything at all suspicious underneath this life surrounding him, he would be capable of driving everybody out, good and bad together.

A certain Father Blanc, who was taller than Désiré and as handsome as a saint, had preached the Lent sermons at Saint-Nicolas, in a warm voice with brassy accents which had made most of the women take their handkerchiefs out of their bags. Élise had not missed a single sermon and had wept like the rest. Lent had begun just after the scene with Monsieur Chechelowski.

Of all the lodgers, he was the least troublesome, the least difficult to live with. He came in and went out without saying a word, served himself, and paid without looking at the bill, and yet it was on him that all the rancour accumulated in Élise's soul had fallen.

'Do you know, Madame Mamelin, that my bed is full of little insects?'

'What's that you're saying, Monsieur Chechelowski? Come now, you don't mean it!'

'I do! Look at my arms.'

He pushed back his cuff and showed her some little red marks on his hairy skin.

'What makes you think those are bug-bites? This is a clean house. There have never been any insects in my beds.'

'All the same, they were bed-bugs that I killed last night.'

'You don't know what you're talking about . . .'

Mademoiselle Frida and Mademoiselle Pauline were sitting there listening.

'. . . Or rather, it's you who caught some fleas and brought them here.'

He stuck to his guns and answered back, and she could not contain herself any longer.

'Listen, if what you want is to insult me in my own home, by accusing me of being a dirty woman, I'd rather you found yourself a room somewhere else. There's no lack of them in the district. No doubt you'll even be allowed to receive your fiancée in your room, since you seem to be hankering after that.'

Yet there *were* bed-bugs there. Élise had found some. They must have been in the walls when the Mamelins had moved to the rue de la Loi. Or else they had come from the pub next door. When Monsieur Chechelowski had left, without a word of protest, Élise, feeling a certain remorse, had said:

'Even if it was true, you know, you shouldn't have shouted it out in front of everybody. You know that I do everything I can. You'll find that you won't be looked after anywhere as well as you are here.'

He had generously admitted:

'I know.'

She had nearly asked him to stay, but it was too late. And instead of that, heaven knows what devil had prevented her from mentioning the knife to him. It was such a little thing and yet it would torment her for such a long time! Two or three times already, she had been on the point of running to the rue de la Province, where he lived now, to give the wretched knife back to him. She still used it every day, always with the same uneasy feeling.

Was it worth ten francs or twenty francs? It was a knife of a different shape from those you could buy in Belgium, and probably came from Russia. It cut better than all the other knives in the house and the white metal handle was soft and smooth. It fitted Élise's hand so perfectly that even in Monsieur Chechelowski's time she used to take it out of her lodger's tin to prepare her vegetables, putting it back before he returned.

On the day he had gone, the knife had accidentally been left in a bucket with the peelings. Élise knew this. Monsieur Chechelowski, for his part, had not given the knife a thought. She had nearly reminded him about it. She had not done so. You could say, in a word, that she had stolen it.

The bed-bugs had started the great cleaning crisis. The other lodgers had realized this, and the yellow powder scattered in the corners of the bedrooms constituted an admission.

Then, while in the house with its windows open from morning till night a sort of renewal was taking place in tune with the spring, Lent had begun and this passion for cleanliness had spread. Élise had felt a need to air the depths of her soul, which she would have liked to spread out in the April sunshine as she spread out the bedding on the warm platform.

Marie, Valérie's sister, who always trailed a smell of dressmaking behind her, had come one Friday to collect her mother. She was an ardent churchgoer, forever haunting the confessionals and exhausting the religious orders one after another from the Jesuits to the Dominicans and the Oblates.

'If you only knew the Redemptorist Fathers of the rue Neuvice . . .'

The next day, as she was feeling more than usually upset, Élise had gone there, furtively and with a certain embarrassment, for she had always contented herself with performing her religious duties in her own parish church, without indulging in the excesses which she called affectations.

'Father, I confess to . . .'

On her return, she brought back in her shopping-bag some provisions she had bought at the Vierge Noire, by way of an alibi, and her eyes were all red, though Roger was the only one to notice this.

Finally, this very morning, Léopold had come to sit down in the rue de la Loi kitchen. She had not seen anything of him for a long time. He looked tired. The spring sunshine made his threadbare overcoat look greener, his complexion underneath his beard dirtier.

For the first time in her life, Élise had studied him as if he had not been her brother but a stranger, and she had felt sadder than ever. After hesitating for a long time, she had murmured in an embarrassed way:

'I sometimes wonder, Léopold, if, in our family, we aren't quite like other people.'

He had not protested, had shown no indignation over this question which would have sent Louisa of Coronmeuse into a tantrum.

'Last summer, I went to Louis's, at Tongres, for their son's first communion. It was the first time he had invited me and I still don't know what had got into him. I didn't know whether I ought to accept, especially seeing that he hadn't thought of Désiré or the child. I can still see Désiré standing there, looking terribly sad, holding Roger's hand, when the train left the station . . .'

She had even bought a first communion present, without saying anything, a mauve rosary in a leather case.

'Louis lives in a proper castle, with a park and woods. All the nobles and rich men of Limbourg, whom he invites to the hunt every autumn, were there that day. Well, Léopold, you can believe this or not as you like, it was me that Louis kept looking at. It was as if he felt the need to talk to me, as if he had something on his mind.

'"Are you happy, Louis?" I asked him.

'Instead of answering, he looked around him with a sigh, then, seeing that somebody was coming towards us, he squeezed my arm and said:

'"Hush!"

'You know, nobody'll ever convince me . . .'

What was nobody ever going to convince her? She didn't really know. She was trying to find out. She had been trying to find out for a long time now.

'It's like Franz. Last Sunday, we went to his house with Désiré and Roger. We had met Poldine at Hubert Schroefs' and she had invited us.'

They lived in a little house of blackened bricks, in a suburb full of little gardens, of hen-huts or rabbit-hutches, of wires stretched between clothes-posts. The neighbours were mostly workmen who, after the day's work, gardened in shirtsleeves or trained racing pigeons.

Why had Franz, who was an educated man, married, without saying a word about it to anybody, a girl who worked at the Linière, that huge dark factory which made the quai de Coronmeuse so ugly?

At their house, they had drunk some coffee and eaten some

tart; there was a piano in the tiny drawing-room; Poldine kept hens and spent her time talking for hours on end, standing in shops or on doorsteps; their son played in the streets with the boys of the district. Franz had scarcely opened his mouth all afternoon, and Désiré had done most of the talking.

Élise had come home feeling terribly sad. Franz had little eyes like his brother Louis; they sparkled brightly but shifted as soon as you looked at him. He didn't complain. He had not a single friend in the National Arms Factory where he worked. Nor had he any in his district.

He went walking most of the time, all by himself, at an even pace, without hurrying. He drank. Not like Léopold, nor like Marthe. He did not go on 'novenas', never got drunk. It was just that his walk included a few ports of call, which were always the same; he would go into a pub without sitting down, empty his glass, and go as he had come, his smile looking slightly more sarcastic.

'Do you understand what I'm getting at, Léopold? It's as if there was something driving us on, as if we just couldn't help it . . .'

For example in the rue de la Loi there were periods of absolute calm, days when nothing happened, empty hours, like those clear skies which give you the impression of living under a cloche. A Cécile would go on ironing her washing without noticing. Juliette, Arthur's wife, would go on pushing the pram of her latest baby, to the end of the world if the pavement led there.

Élise, for her part, on days like that, held out as best she could, with a tight feeling constricting her chest, but a time would come when she could not stand it any longer, when she stood up and shook herself, desperately looking for something to feed her anguish, when it seemed to her that there was something inside her which was going to break from the effect of revolving in a void.

She felt like doing almost anything – seizing Désiré by the shoulders, begging him to take her out, to go somewhere, to beat her if need be.

She had a morbid fear of a great many things, and above all else of poverty. That was why she had had a shock just now, looking at Léopold, who, today, reminded you of a poor man begging in the street. At the recollection of certain hours she had lived with her mother in the nearby rue Féronstrée, sweat broke out on her forehead and she would have stolen, despite the fact that she was fundamentally honest, rather than know similar hours again.

It was the fear of poverty which had led her to take in lodgers. She blushed at herself when, finding herself alone in the house, she furtively opened their tins to take out a few lumps of sugar or a slice of sausage.

'Look at Louisa, Léopold . . . She's my eldest sister. She doesn't talk much to me, because she still regards me as a little girl. But I'm sure that, for all her apparent calm, Louisa isn't happy. Otherwise why should she have married a man twenty years older than she is, a man who's got a white beard now? He looks as if he was her father. Some people think he is.'

It had been a gloomy winter, this winter which had just finished and during which her mind had travelled all alone through a frightening maze of underground passages. It was not tiredness, as Désiré thought, that made her nervy and sensitive. Désiré always explained things too simply.

Rather like Madame Laude, with whom they had spent their holidays, at Embourg. Élise envied her. She was a woman who was never embarrassed or moved by anything. She ate, drank and slept, always happy, always ready to laugh her vulgar laugh. Once when they had been walking with Roger in the woods of the Fond des Cris, they had suddenly heard the sound of water, looked all round them, and finally noticed that it was Madame Laude who was urinating, standing up, without bothering to hitch up her skirts. Her husband's job was unloading wagons in Chênée Station. At night he used to come home as black as coal. He stood stark naked in a tub at the bottom of the garden, and Madame Laude threw big bucketfuls of water over his body.

There were people who lived like that and who were happy. Mademoiselle Pauline had hurt Élise badly, too. Perhaps it wasn't her fault. But why was it that some women, who were no better than others, could live as they liked and study in comfort, accepting the services of others with a queenly air, while mothers were forced to act as their servants? If only she emptied her slops and remembered now and then to say thank you!

It was Mademoiselle Pauline that Élise detested and yet it was Mademoiselle Frida that she had tormented ever since Monsieur Charles had started coming to the rue de la Loi house! She attacked her in a sly, underhand way, but not for anything in the world would she admit that she was sly and underhand.

'Is it true, Mademoiselle Frida, that the people of your country are preparing a revolution?'

She laughed nervously, and trembled as children do when they touch something of which they are frightened.

'Tell us what you are going to put in the place of what is there now. Are all the rich going to become poor, while the poor are going to be in command?'

She did not understand her lodger's icy contempt, and gave a forced laugh when Mademoiselle Frida replied:

'The rich won't become poor. We shall kill them.'

'Would you be capable of killing somebody?'

'Yes.'

'And after the revolution, do you expect to become a person in authority?'

Frida sighed:

'In your country, people talk and talk. They don't know how to do anything but talk and laugh. You have never been sufficiently hungry.'

'And you, Mademoiselle Pauline, would you kill people too?'

To which the latter replied, from the heights of her serene paradise:

'It's too dirty!'

At night, after these conversations, Élise was like a boy who had run too fast, played too hard, breathed too much fresh air. Her temples throbbed, she could not sleep, and she tossed about restlessly beside Désiré's big body.

She did not like the rich. She detested Hubert Schroefs. She could not forgive Louis of Tongres, even though he had invited her to his son's first communion.

Of all her brothers and sisters, it was Léopold that she preferred, now that Félicie was dead.

But she respected the houses in freestone where there were servants, and for her a doctor was a doctor, a lawyer was somebody, and she tip-toed across the solemn porch leading to Françoise's little courtyard.

When Roger had misbehaved himself, she told him:

'You behave like a workman's child.'

She had gone to Poldine's once, because she could not avoid doing so, but she was determined never to set foot there again. Poldine had worked at the Linière, where in the evening you could see a crowd of slovenly girls pouring out whose language was so coarse that Élise went out of her way to avoid them when she was coming home with Roger.

Élise was kind-hearted. She wanted to be kind-hearted so badly! It was a need with her. She would give all that she had, like poor Félicie, but she suffered when people failed to give it back to her a hundredfold. She was honest and yet she cheated from morning till night; only the day before, she had put another twenty francs in the Savings Bank, unknown to Désiré, who no longer smoked his Sunday cigar because it was too dear.

Was it really true that she was not like other people? When she had presented herself at L'Innovation, at the age of sixteen, and had claimed to be nineteen, Monsieur Wilhems had looked at her in a peculiar way. There had been surprise in his eyes, amusement, and also a little bit of pity, as if he had been looking at a strange animal. He had pretended to believe her.

Now, two men looked at her in roughly the same way: Brother Médard and Monsieur Charles, especially Monsieur Charles, with another feeling too, lately.

It was impossible for them to guess what she was thinking, and she never had a smut on her nose to make them smile like that.

Did they realize that she kept on going forward, heedless of the obstacles in her way, driven on by a force over which she had no control?

Valérie did not understand her.

'I sometimes wonder where you get all your ideas. You'll end up by making me think you're all romantic.'

Romantic, her!

Mathilde Coomans, whose business was on its last legs, had told her husband, who had repeated it to his cousin who worked with Désiré at Monsieur Monnoyeur's:

'Élise is too complicated for me. She'd make me take a gloomy view of life.'

Because Élise had talked to her once about the Russians. She tried to understand them, to imagine that huge country which you could not enter without a passport and where you travelled about in sledges, and those families in which the father worked in Siberia while the children lived only for the revolution – families like Mademoiselle Frida's.

On certain evenings, Désiré's calm refusal to worry about such matters irritated her so much that she became unfair to him and said the most unpleasant things she could think of.

'I wonder why you ever married me. You'd have done much better to stay in the rue Puits-en-Sock.'

He bought her some soluble iron filings to fortify her. That was Désiré's reply. He had forced her to engage a charwoman to do the washing every Monday.

That was another unfortunate idea. Madame Catteau, the woman whom Élise had chosen without knowing anything about her, had had her husband in prison for the past six months. He had been sent to prison for interfering with his nine-year-old daughter.

While they were doing the washing in the yard, the two women chatted together.

'If you could have seen the little girl, Madame Mamelin . . .'

In a common voice which carried a long way – and the walls of the backyards were not very high – she proceeded to furnish such coarse details that Élise had to remind her of the existence of neighbours.

'Oh, I know what men are like, all right! It pays me to know. If you knew the half of what goes on in my street . . .'

She lived in the rue Grande-Bêche, one of the poorest streets in Outremeuse, a real court of miracles where Désiré, as a charity visitor, went once a month.

In the early days of their marriage, when Élise had questioned him about the poor people he helped, he had just replied:

'We aren't allowed to talk about that.'

'Not even to your wife?'

As if the others were as scrupulous as he was!

'There are some bedrooms, Madame Mamelin, which stink, saving your respect, bedrooms you couldn't go into even if you held your nose. There are ten or twelve of them to a room, boys, girls, all together, with the father and mother doing you know what in front of the boys, who watch them at it and then try it on their sisters . . .'

Fear gripped her when she went past the rue Grande-Bêche, as if she were passing an abyss which was capable of sucking her down, and she had been unable to refrain from explaining to Roger:

'Look over there! You must work hard at school. Otherwise, later on, you'll be poor and live in that street.'

She did not want to be poor. The very sight of poverty made her sick with fear and disgust. She hated the rich, but she did not like the poor.

'The best thing, you know,' Désiré had said to her once, 'is to keep to the happy mean, like us.'

The happy mean was the rue de la Loi. She knew that. Often she managed to be happy there. But she could not help it if, from time to time, she felt ill-at-ease there and longed to do almost anything to get away from it, as she had got away from Cession's and later from the rue Pasteur.

'You know, Léopold, it's rather as if we were strangers everywhere, all the members of our family.'

She talked about the Peters, the men and the women.

'Marthe is unhappy with Hubert Schroefs, in spite of all his money, because he's got no delicacy of feeling. Louisa hates serving drinks at the bar, and you'll never convince me of the contrary. Louis is ill-at-ease in his wife's noble family, and she probably makes him feel that he doesn't come out of the top drawer. My best friend, Valérie, hurts me all the time without knowing, and I can never speak freely to her.'

Franz and Poldine . . . Félicie who had died as a result . . .

And Léopold who drank, who had to drink, from the moment he woke up in the morning, otherwise he was like a sick man waiting for his medicine.

'It isn't because we're from the frontier, and practically foreigners. Mademoiselle Pauline, for instance, is happy wherever she goes. On the corner of the boulevard de la Constitution, there are some Jews who go to the synagogue and who are quite at home in the district.'

She could not get rid of the idea that it was something

personal, that there was a sort of curse, a stain perhaps on the family.

'What did father die of exactly?'

'A cancer of the tongue.'

Léopold was in a sombre mood that morning. He stared in front of him, forgetting to relight his pipe. He never said what he was thinking about, and you had to guess; sometimes Élise, who was used to him, had the impression that she could hear him thinking and she answered him quite naturally.

In the rue Puits-en-Sock, all those little shopkeepers who had been born side by side and would die side by side, next door to one another, lived together like a big family, without any worries, and that was why she had an involuntary feeling of irritation every time she saw Désiré setting off with Roger for his father's hat-shop.

Scattered all over the place, and strangers in their own district, the Peters instinctively drew towards one another, because only one of their own family could understand them; but, once they were together, they kept quiet as if they were frightened of their daemon.

Sometimes it seemed to Élise that there was more in common between herself and Mademoiselle Frida, for instance, or between herself and Monsieur Saft's mother, who worked as a servant to pay for her son's education, than between herself and her own husband.

Was there a race of human beings more sensitive than the rest, who suffered more and whom nothing could satisfy?

The other day, she had been going up the rue Haute-Sauvenière. Some miners had been coming down the same street, in groups, their eyes white in their black faces and their hobnailed boots clattering on the paving-stones; and she had started trembling nervously, drawing Roger to her in an instinctive movement.

She had never admitted this to Madame Laude, but at Embourg she had been frightened every night when Frédéric had come home from work, and she had felt reassured only when, emerging from his tub, he had once more become a quiet man with a long fair moustache and a cloth cap, who played at skittles or dug his garden.

She always had the impression that something was going to

happen, that it was impossible for the world to remain suspended in space, prolonging the present moment into infinity, and she anxiously questioned the others who noticed nothing, convinced that a catastrophe was approaching of which she was the only one to be afraid.

Léopold rose clumsily to his feet, emptied his pipe by knocking it against the coal-scuttle, and drank the last drops of cold coffee left in his cup.

'Good-bye, my girl.'

'You've nothing to say to me, Léopold?'

What could he have to say to her? Far more eloquent than any words were his heavy, uncertain footsteps, which stopped a few yards along the pavement: he had gone into the pub next door.

That was why Élise had come with her son to the chapel in the rue Neuvice; that was why she stood up with a sniff and pressed the button which would ring a bell somewhere in the confessor's cell.

He was a very old man who had said to her the last time:

'Pray, my daughter. Carry out your duties as a wife, a mother and a Christian, and you will see that the peace of God will come back to you.'

She was impatient to see that happen; for the coming spring, she would have liked everything in her to be as pure and light as in her house, which had been cleaned from top to bottom and where cool draughts played from morning till night in even the smallest corners.

'Wait for me quietly, Roger.'

She knelt down behind the green cloth which concealed only half her body, and for a long time the child heard her monotonous murmur and glimpsed, behind the wooden grating, the face of Father Meeus, who looked like a character in a missal.

A little later, when they were back in the noisy street, Élise made an effort to smile at the sun and suddenly decided in front of a confectioner's shop:

'Come and eat one of those cream cornets you like so much.'

Soon it would be Easter, he would put his straw hat on for the first time, they would change into their summer clothes, and they would go on a pilgrimage to Chèvremont, stumbling along in the thick white dust of the calvary edged with hawthorn. They would recite one Our Father and three Hail Mary's at every flower-decked altar, and up there by the dairy, they would eat on the grass beside the swings, among the communicants, the girls all in white like young brides.

Then they would come home by way of Fléron, even though it was longer, so as to stay up on the heights as long as possible.

Chapter Nine

It was 1911. The life which filled the little house in the rue de la Loi had burst the walls and spread out on the pavement. In the kitchen, where the lids trembled on the saucepans, Élise spoke of the time of Mademoiselle Pauline and Monsieur Saft as Chrétien Mamelin and his friend Kreutz spoke of a period they had known when there were no trams and motor-cars, or as Désiré spoke of his youth, when there were twelve children round the table in the rue Puits-en-Sock, and when a glance from his father at his riding-crop was enough to impose silence.

Old Papa was dead. He had not been ill. There had been no reason to expect him to die that evening rather than another, and yet, in his sleep, Roger had seen a ball of fire cross his room, from the floor to the ceiling, at the time when the old miner's soul had furtively stolen away, as if not to disturb anybody, leaving on the bed a huge carcass of no importance.

They had had no news of Monsieur Saft who, once he had finished his studies, had gone back to his country. Yet he had promised Roger that he would send him some of those Polish picture-postcards which were so beautiful. On the other hand, Mademoiselle Pauline wrote now and then from Berlin, where she had become a pupil of Professor Einstein. It seemed that the savant regarded her as one of his best disciples and that she had an extraordinary brain. Élise could not get over it.

'She may have the bump of mathematics, but all the rest was hollow. You remember, don't you, Mademoiselle Frida? She never knew what to do with her hands, and she had such a lack of tact!'

Certain remarks made by La Feinstein, certain anecdotes, her hands which she cared for as if they were precious valuables, her fits of anger when Désiré teased her, her swollen ankles for which she had to buy special boots – she had a whole wardrobe full of them! – all that now formed part of the traditions of the house, and new lodgers learned them as soon as they arrived.

Of the old lodgers, only Mademoiselle Frida remained. She had always refused to change her room, even when Élise had offered to give her the green room for the same price as her gloomy entresol.

The green room, for the past few weeks, had been occupied by Monsieur Bernard, a Belgian whose parents ran a grocery shop at Verviers. He was studying medicine. He was a young man, thin and fair-haired, always joking and teasing like Désiré, and when the two of them set about Mademoiselle Lola there was such a din in the house that Élise wondered how the poor girl could stand it.

It was true that nothing ever flustered that rather childish Caucasian.

'You've only got to see her smile, Valérie. She smiles as blissfully as a child.'

She occupied Mademoiselle Pauline's pink room, which had become more feminine – indeed almost too feminine, for Mademoiselle Lola, who was very beautiful, with the tranquil beauty of an odalisk, tended and adorned her body with loving care, spent hours at her dressing-table, and went about the house half naked, with her breasts showing in the opening of her dressing-gown, and leaving a trail of perfume behind her.

She sang and laughed and had never been seen studying. Her parents were rich, and she admitted that she had entered the University only to escape from the monotony of life at home and to see something of the world.

She'll stay a child all her life. I tell myself sometimes that she's lucky.'

She spoke French so quaintly that she gave rise to roars of laughter in and out of season, especially when a doubtful meaning could be read into her innocent words. For since Monsieur Bernard's arrival the jokes in the rue de la Loi had become spicier. Désiré had followed his example, and often Élise had to motion to the two men that Roger was listening to them without appearing to do so.

There had been grey periods during which lodgers had followed one after another so quickly that there had been no time to get to know them. There had even been one lodger who, nobody had ever known why, had gone off without a word the day after he had arrived, leaving in his room an old pair of socks and a fountain-pen. The fountain-pen was still in the kitchen drawer.

Curiously enough, Monsieur Chechelowski, the only lodger Élise had ever thrown out, had sent her news of himself. Married now, and the father of a child who was nearly three, he was an engineer in an electrical works in Antwerp and did not intend to return to his own country.

His knife too was still in the table drawer.

The back room on the ground floor was let to another Russian, Monsieur Bógdanowski, of a type which they had not seen before in the house, a sort of Oriental – he came from Astrakhan – who was fat and spruce like Mademoiselle Lola, with eyes as beautiful as hers and curly hair with bluish glints in it.

Like the Caucasian girl again, he lacked the most elementary sense of decency and wandered around in his pyjamas, going dressed like that to buy his butter at the little dairy shop in the rue Jean-d'Outremeuse. Once, when he was striding up and down the hall between the kitchen and his room, Élise had called out to him:

'Please stay still, Monsieur Bogdanowski. You're making me feel giddy!'

'The enema, Madame!'

Sure enough, a few moments later, clutching his stomach, he had rushed like a madman in the direction of the little place at the back of the yard.

He was fond of talking about his intestines, and about the enema he took every week. At ten o'clock every morning, he ate a jar of yoghourt.

'For the bowels!' he explained in his comic accent.

He was as curly haired as a Negro and wore a scent calculated to turn your stomach.

*

That day was one of the longest in the year. All the doors and windows were open, for it was necessary, when every room was occupied, for the house to extend into the street. Roger, who had had his supper at six o'clock, alone at a corner of the table, in order to make room, was sitting on the doorstep surrounded by his tubes of paint, saucers full of iridescent water, paint-brushes, rags, pencils and rubbers. Heedless of the two existences, inside the house and outside, which came together over his head, he was carefully copying a picture postcard showing a mill beside a stream.

Monsieur Bernard had been so insistent on having full board that Désiré had given in. Two Belgians, both medical students, who had a room nearby, also came every day for their midday meal.

'Eat up quickly, Roger. The lodgers will be here soon.'

The stove was covered from morning till night with saucepans with trembling lids; the table had scarcely been laid for some before it had to be cleared to make room for others; and at two o'clock it was the turn of the sugared dishes which Élise cooked for Désiré.

Mademoiselle Frida, faithful to her tin box, stole imperturbably into the room, poured boiling water into her little blue enamel coffee-pot, and spread out her bread, her butter, her egg or her cheese.

As for Mademoiselle Lola, she was disorder personified. Sometimes she ate in town, nobody knew where; sometimes she demanded the same meal as the other lodgers; sometimes she decided to cook herself one of her national dishes, asked for unknown condiments, and mixed together the most unexpected ingredients, only to discover in the end that she had forgotten the exact recipe.

There was laughter. There was shouting. You could not make yourself heard. Now and then there was the sound of a chase on the stairs, doors banged and the Caucasian girl called for help: it was Monsieur Bernard running after her, seizing her by the waist, and stopping, panting, in face of her heaving flesh, her head thrown back with her hot breath setting her dark-red lips quivering.

The week before, he had laid in Mademoiselle Lola's bed the skeleton he had bought for his studies. Uttering piercing shrieks she had come downstairs in her nightdress, and, as he had burst out laughing, she had scratched him across the face; he still bore the marks.

'You're a dirty Belgian! A dirty Belgian! You hear?'

'Do you want me to beg your forgiveness on my knees, Mademoiselle Lola?'

He had done this. Désiré had laughed too. Élise had given the nervous smile which scarcely ever left her now and in whose thin creases a thousand worries lay in wait.

For she had probably never been as worried as she was in the midst of all this noisy bustle, which she had started off and of which she alone could follow the thread. In the evening, Désiré, instead of going to read his newspaper on the doorstep, had taken to lingering in the kitchen. She got impatient with him, although she was not jealous of Mademoiselle Lola.

'The Delcours are already in the street,' she observed.

This had become a nightly rendezvous, unless there happened to be a summer shower. The young people from the house next door were waiting on the pavement where the chairs had been arranged in a semicircle. The group had been joined by the fiancé of the girl Hélène, who was now a schoolmistress.

Thus, across the hall, at the end of which Roger, sitting on the blue stone, was painting his mill, the laughs and shouts in the street joined those in the kitchen, pending the fusion of the two groups.

Roger could not even settle down somewhere else. At four o'clock he had to hurry up to finish his homework. The front room, his only remaining refuge, was now let; a bed and a washstand had been put in with the dining-room furniture and the room had become Monsieur Schascher's domain.

The latter took no part in either jokes or meals. He was a little red-haired Jew, so ugly that he frightened children, so poor that he wore neither socks inside his old shoes nor linen under his clothes. In the evening, through the window and the sharp leaves of an evergreen, he could be seen studying with his fingers dug into his ears, taking advantage of the last gleams of the setting sun to save on the gas.

Although he sometimes went all day without a meal, he never complained. It was through Mademoiselle Frida that they had learnt that a Jewish bank in his country was lending him the money he needed for his studies. Afterwards, it would keep his diplomas until he had paid all the money back. This would probably take him ten years.

'Isn't it wonderful, Louisa, people helping each other like that! Why must the Jews be the only ones to do it? What a difference from a Monsieur Bernard who thinks of nothing but having fun, so that I have to lock him in his room to force him to work! It's his poor mother who gave me permission to do that. He doesn't deserve to have parents like that.'

The spire of Saint-Nicolas stood motionless against a sky of menacing stillness. The air was heavy. While the others were lingering at table, Élise had begun her washing-up on a corner of the stove.

'Hurry up, Monsieur Bernard. You're always the last to finish eating.'

He was a child and she treated him as such.

She was impatient to be left alone with her work, which would take her until midnight. While they were amusing themselves in the street, she would be able to drop that forced smile which she kept from morning till night on a face which was becoming increasingly pointed and mobile.

Where were they all going? Where was she going? And what of the house, which she had launched at a venture, like a boat, and of which she sometimes felt that she had lost control?

In the street they were playing innocent games, even big Désiré, running after each other, pushing one another, joking, getting excited. You could hear the tinkling laugh of Mademoiselle Lola, whom somebody had taken by the waist again and who was struggling with an ardent look in her eyes and the embarrassing laugh of a girl in search of love.

Suddenly she pricked up her ears at the sound of a more distant voice and footsteps running along the rue Jean-d'Outremeuse.

'Ask for the *Meuse*! . . . Special edition! . . .'

The newspaper-man came along, bent forward, barely stopping at each group to detach a sheet of paper still wet with ink from the pile he was carrying under his left arm, and then running on.

'Ask for the *Meuse*! . . . The Agadir incident . . . Insolent provocation by the Kaiser . . . War . . .'

Had she heard aright? Had he uttered the word *war*? What had he shouted after that? She rushed out of the kitchen and leant across her son's tubes and saucers which were blocking her way.

The others had frozen. They were still in the postures in which the word had caught them and there was a pause before they automatically completed the gestures they had begun, there in the street where silence had suddenly fallen like a veil.

The laughs had petered out, except for that of Mademoiselle Lola who had not understood, a tinkling laugh which itself died away slowly while the fat girl looked around her with a surprise tinged with fear.

Désiré was the first to move, going towards the corner of the rue Jean-d'Outremeuse and feeling in his pocket for a sou. They could see him waiting there, facing the rue Puits-en-Sock. The doors of the nearby houses opened one after the other, and people looked out, calling to one another.

'What was he shouting?'

The newspaper-man finally appeared, and Désiré stood there on the kerb, looking at the sheet of printed paper. Everybody wanted to know what it was all about, and wondered why he did not come back straight away. Finally he turned round and gave a reassuring wave.

'Well?'

Here he was at last. The neighbours crowded round him. He was very calm.

'No, no! There's nothing to be alarmed about. It isn't war yet. Everything can still be settled peacefully, and you'll see, it will be settled peacefully.'

He read out the news, pointing to the question-mark which corrected the threat of a headline in huge letters:

War in Europe?
Kaiser William lands at Agadir.
Monsieur Fallières calls Cabinet meeting.
Will Mobilization be ordered?

At Nevers, in the gathering dusk, Félicien Miette was bent double outside the newspaper offices, trying to start the car he had just bought. Isabelle, dressed in kid with a veil holding her hat in place, was waiting impatiently for the engine, which kept coughing intermittently, to decide to go.

Miette mopped his forehead and took hold of the starting-handle again. The engine started running. At the same moment a window opened.

'Monsieur Miette! Monsieur Miette!'

And just as Isabelle had finally installed herself in the bucket-seat, the telephonist on duty in the office, waving his arms in the air, shouted in a shrill voice which could be heard above the din from the engine:

'War!'

*

Élise was still holding her dishcloth in her hand. Monsieur Bernard, pitifully pale in the face, suddenly looked like a sick little boy. For a moment Monsieur Schascher had stuck a colourless face crowned with red hair against the window of his room, and then he had gone back to his table as if war were nothing to do with him.

With a naïvety which made nobody laugh, Mademoiselle Lola asked:

'Do you think they'll do anything to women?'

The day refused to come to an end. The rising moon was so bright that you did not notice the transition from day to night, the groups of people becoming just a little more indistinct and the voices a little louder in a world which seemed artificial.

'We'll see tomorrow whether it's war or not,' declared the eldest of the Delcours as he went off to bed.

His sister Hélène accompanied her fiancé, hand in hand, as far as the place du Congrès. They could not find a word to say but pressed close to one another, and when he left her, she felt like calling him back.

'Désiré,' Élise whispered in bed, 'do you think the civic guards will be given marching orders?'

When everybody had fallen asleep, trying to push away the hideous nightmare of war, a scream rang through the house, a piercing shriek which recalled the cry of an animal mad with terror.

'Désiré . . . Désiré . . .'

Sitting up in bed, Élise shook him. A strangely calm voice

came from the next room, whose door was always left ajar:

'What's the matter, Mother?'

Élise slipped on the first clothes which came to hand, automatically put her hair up, and opened the door at the same time as other doors were opening in the house. Mademoiselle Lola, who had given the shriek, was on the first-floor landing, in a pale nightdress; she was babbling in Russian and darting mad glances around her.

'For heaven's sake, shut her up, Monsieur Bernard. What's the matter with her? What is she saying? What has happened?'

Everybody was up and moving round the house. All that they noticed was that it was as bright as day without a single lamp being alight. Somebody said:

'A fire!'

'Quick, Désiré! . . . The child . . . There's a fire! . . .'

She did not wait for Désiré, but picked Roger up and carried him out of his room, all warm in his white nightshirt.

War . . . Fire . . .

Her arms dropped, her legs gave way beneath her, and she was just sitting down on the stairs when she realized that the fire was not in her house, even though Mademoiselle Lola's room was lit up by a fiery glow.

'The Institut Saint-André . . .'

It was behind the school's slate roofs that the flames could be seen, crossed every now and then by black objects being hurled into the air.

Désiré was close to her; he calmed her down, saying:

'It's Déom's workshop . . . Don't move . . . I'll go and have a look . . .'

People were running along the street; windows were thrown open; the mournful bell of the fire-engine could be heard, together with the murmur of a crowd in the rue Jean-d'Outre-meuse.

It was not only Monsieur Déom's furniture workshop which was on fire, but the whole house. Although the firemen had already brought their hoses into play, the neighbours were shouting:

'A chain! . . . Everybody form a chain!'

Others had come along with jugs and buckets. Two policemen were trying in vain to keep the spectators back. On the opposite pavement, Désiré, who was not wearing a jacket but just his nightshirt with the red designs on the collar, ran into Albert Velden, and the two of them watched in silence, each lighting a cigarette.

'Go to bed, Roger. It's nothing.'

The child stayed in Mademoiselle Lola's room, which was pinker than ever. The women were leaning out of the windows, while the men were outside.

'And all that wood piled up in the workshop! He used to make such lovely furniture!'

Monsieur Déom, a tall, thin man with a straggling moustache was wandering around as if he no longer knew where he was or what he was doing. Looking at him with awed respect, some people were murmuring that he had gone out of his mind. Dazed and bewildered, he roamed about among the strangers who kept running into his house holding handkerchiefs to their noses and coming out with anything that had come to hand.

'Look! . . . There's somebody there!'

A human form, two arms, were moving in a second-floor window from which smoke was pouring. It was an old, bed-ridden lodger who had been forgotten. The firemen extended their ladder.

And all the time men, women and children were arriving from the rue de la Loi, the rue Pasteur and the rue Puits-en-Sock, in an unending procession. There were people from the back-streets, and you could recognize them straight away. Among the most active rescuers, constantly going into the house and coming out with all sorts of objects, was Monsieur Bogdanowski, his face black with smoke, his eyes white underneath his curly hair.

The pink room smelled of the eau-de-Cologne which had been sprinkled over Mademoiselle Lola. Now and then, a column of flame forced its way through the burning sky and you could hear a sound like the roar of a gigantic stove on the point of exploding.

'Dear God . . . If we ever have a war,' sighed Élise, looking at the firemen who were cautiously hoisting themselves on to the steep roofs of the Friars' school. 'The poor people! What's going to be left of their home?'

She confused in her mind the threat of war and the disaster

which had overtaken the Déom house. Her blood pounded faster in her arteries, and she rushed around to no purpose. It seemed to her that what was happening had been bound to come, that what she had feared and expected was beginning: that awful final catastrophe of which she had always had a terrible presentiment.

She prayed automatically:

'Dear God, spare us, spare our house, spare Roger and Désiré. Take me if need be, but spare them.'

She gave a start at the sight of Mademoiselle Frida, pale and erect in the dancing light, like an avenging angel.

'Will you start fires too, when you have a revolution?'

And the other woman, digging her teeth into the pulp of her lips, answered:

'It will be *terrible*!'

She rolled the *r*'s of *terrible* in a long-drawn, dramatic manner. Mattresses, chairs, saucepans, nameless objects were piling up on the flooded pavement, as pitiful as the lots in a forced sale. Madame Déom, who was expecting a baby, had been taken into a nearby house where she automatically swallowed the rum which was poured between her lips.

'My house . . .' she kept saying.

Street-urchins were running in between the legs of the grown-ups, and, quite naturally, Velden and Désiré had started talking about the Agadir incident.

'Germany wouldn't dare. Nobody would take the risk of starting a war at the present moment, with the means of destruction available to every army.'

People started going off to bed. It was three o'clock when the sky darkened and the moon disappeared while black ash was still falling into the streets.

Monsieur Schascher had locked himself in his room as soon as he had seen that it was not the rue de la Loi house that was on fire. To revive Mademoiselle Lola, Élise had gone to find the bottle of Madeira which she used for sauces and she had poured out several glasses.

'Is it all over, Désiré? Did they manage to save anything? The poor people! They must be ruined!'

'Why? The insurance will pay.'

'Will the insurance give them back the things they treasured most, the souvenirs you can't replace? But it's time to think of going to sleep. Come along, Roger.'

Roger was asleep on Mademoiselle Lola's sofa, his cheek on one of her petticoats. He did not wake up when his father carried him back to his bed and tucked him up.

An hour later, Élise, who had not yet fallen asleep, heard a soft tapping on the letter-box. She went downstairs in her bare feet, and asked:

'Who's there?'

'It's me.'

It was Monsieur Bogdanowski, whom everybody had forgotten, with his shirt torn and one ear stained with blood.

'Where have you been? What have you been doing?'

'Over there . . .'

Without saying a word, he had worked with the firemen until the very end, and he had finished up in a house he did not know, in the company of strangers who had all been given something to drink.

*

The alarm-clock, which knew nothing of the fire or the rumours of war, went off as it did on other mornings, at half past five, in Roger's room. He put out his arm in a mechanical gesture, stopped the bell, and remained for a moment hesitating in the pleasant warmth under the red blanket. He had an excuse for not getting up this morning, and he would have had no reason to be ashamed of himself for staying in bed, but precisely because it was exceptional, he got up and put on his clothes in that pale, almost unobtrusive light of dawn which he knew so well.

As he was crossing his parents' bedroom in his stockinged feet, his mother asked him from her bed, in which only her long hair was showing:

'Are you up, Roger?'

'Yes, Mother.'

'You'd have done better to have a rest.'

'I'm not tired.'

Silently closing the street door behind him, he walked down the street past the blackened house with the gaping windows and the sagging roof. A fire-engine was still standing at the edge of the pavement, and he had to step over some thick rubber pipes.

It was a quarter to six – he could see the time by the Saint-Nicolas clock – when he stopped at the corner of the rue Jean-d'Outremeuse and the rue Puits-en-Sock, next to the dark green postal sign. From that vantage point he could see four streets at once. He heard footsteps in the distance, and recognized the tread of Monsieur Pelcat who, in the rue Entre-deux-Ponts, had just opened and shut the door of his shop.

He was a huge man, who weighed over fifteen stone and whose behind recalled the hindquarters of an elephant at the circus. He ran a haberdasher's shop and trailed its rancid smell behind him, but this particular morning, the smell which predominated in the whole district was the smell of burning, the special scent of ashes drenched in water.

'Did you see the fire, sonny?'

Another door opened, in the rue Puits-en-Sock. Grandfather Mamelin came along, with his walk which was similar to Désiré's, and accepted the furtive kiss which Roger bestowed on his cheek. Then, at the end of the rue Méan, there appeared the slight, tripping figure of Monsieur Repasse, the shoemaker in the rue de la Cathédrale.

The men did not start talking about the war straight away but set off automatically, as they did every morning; for every day they met at the same time, coming from different points of the compass, as if they attracted each other like magnets, and their little band grew bigger as a band of schoolboys grows bigger as it approaches the school.

In the place du Congrès, as soon as they turned the corner, Monsieur Effantin, the police superintendent came out of his house, and the strange thing was that they scarcely greeted one another; they were happy like that, although Monsieur Repasse, who had a wrinkled face and a purple nose, always looked grumpy.

They were all between sixty and seventy years old. They had reached the top of their careers. They no longer expected any surprises from life, and, every day, they walked along with measured tread, in the cool morning air, past the shuttered houses in which people were still asleep.

Roger circled round them like a young puppy, like the puppy

belonging to Monsieur Fourneau, who was waiting by the river, making the animal jump over his stick.

It was the time of day when a scented mist rose from the glistening river, the barges coated with shining pitch slowly moved away from the banks, and the tugs hooted and shuddered with impatience outside the Coronmeuse lock. It was also the time when the nearby slaughterhouse was full of the sound of bellowing and the animals being driven along the embankment bumped into one another in the roadway.

Roger did not listen to the old men's conversation. They talked very little, relaxing in long, heavy silences. You could feel that they had a language of their own, like little children, a language which only they could understand, after the forty years or so they had known each other.

They had become friends long ago, when they were thin, ambitious young men, when Monsieur Repasse, who was now the shoemaker to high society, was still employed in a little workshop, and Monsieur Pelcat, who had not yet acquired his bulky paunch, used to tour the country fairs as a pedlar.

True, they had lost sight of one another for a time, while they were working hard and starting families. But then they had come together again on the other slope of existence, and they may well have believed that they were still the same.

Did they talk about the threat of war? Roger did not hear. He was playing with Rita, Monsieur Fourneau's Malines dog, which had won its owner several prizes, throwing a stick into the water for it to fetch.

'Fetch it, Rita . . . Fetch it! . . .'

Monsieur Fallières? . . . The Kaiser William? . . .

They were getting nearer to the baths, whose diving-stages emerged from the Meuse, right at the end of the embankment, surrounded by piles and cables. The strong smell of the water was more noticeable. Just opposite, if the trees had not been there, they could have seen Aunt Louisa's house on the quai de Coronmeuse, on the canal bank.

Roger's eyelids were rather heavy, and he had an empty feeling in his chest from not having had enough sleep. He kept picturing Mademoiselle Lola on her bed when they were dabbing her face with eau-de-Cologne, and he thought about her more than the fire.

His father had said that there would not be a war.

They went through a gate, walked along a path paved with red bricks, turned left, and arrived in front of the bathing-huts. The boy rushed towards the biggest hut, the only one which could hold a dozen people.

Then the old men undressed, all together, their thin legs, freckled or blue-veined, appearing underneath their shirts; they made jokes and indulged in boisterous horse-play, throwing towels and soap at each other, while Roger pulled on the blue-striped bathing trunks which he had brought along under his arm, rolled up in a Turkish towel with his comb and his cake of pink soap.

On the other side of the water they could hear the noise of the first trains. It was the time that Élise came downstairs to light her fire and grind the coffee. The other schoolchildren were still in bed and most of them would wake up grumbling, looking for excuses for putting off the time to get up.

Under their bare feet, the bricks were cold at this time of day, even at the height of summer. The water was cold too, as Roger found when he tested it with one toe before making for the diving-stage of the big pool. Monsieur Effantin, the police-superintendent, had a skin as white as chalk, and Roger always looked away in embarrassment from his big thin body in which you could count the bones.

The old men went on fighting and laughing on the diving boards, and in the water they jostled Monsieur Repasse, who had a sour character. Only Chrétien Mamelin walked slowly to the edge of the pool, slipped gently into the water, on his back, taking care not to get his head wet, and floated downstream like that, scarcely moving his hands at each side of his body. This was because of his heart disease. He was the first to go back to the bathing-hut, walking at an even pace, with drops of water on his skin; and Roger, swimming beyond the ropes, could see him putting on his clothes with the same meticulous gestures with which he ironed the hats on the wooden heads in the back shop in the rue Puits-en-Sock.

For hours afterwards, you kept the taste of the baths on your lips, the taste too of the mouthful of coffee laced with rum which Roger was allowed to drink from his grandfather's cup, for he always dropped into the shopkeeper's kitchen for a few minutes.

On your way home, you saw more open windows and more women sweeping their doorsteps, so that you felt that for most people life had scarcely begun and that they were still sticky with the moist warmth of their beds.

'Late again, Van Hamme!' Monsieur Penders, the schoolmaster, would be saying soon. 'Ask Mamelin how long he has been up. Ask him what he has been doing before coming to school.'

Thus Roger's day began in an exceptional way. Alone of all the pupils, he was allowed to leave the school at ten o'clock to cross the street, push open the door which had been left ajar, and drink the glass of egg-and-beer which was waiting for him on the stairs.

'It's me, Mother.'

'Wipe your feet properly. The hall has been cleaned.'

Alone, because he lived nearby, he had seen the fire. Alone, at half past eleven, he would not join the line of pupils whom Monsieur Penders led as far as the corner of the street, because his house was right opposite, and everybody knew already that he was Brother Médard's white-headed boy.

The proof of this was that his mother joined the latter on the pavement where he was standing.

'Tell me, Brother Médard, do you think we are going to have a war?'

Wasn't he afraid that, if he reassured her too quickly, he would lose some of his importance?

'Who knows, Madame Mamelin? It all depends on the French Government's attitude. No doubt we shall know this evening.'

Piles of chips were waiting by the fire, ready to go a second time into the crackling fat.

'Eat up quickly, Roger. The lodgers will be here in a minute.'

Roger, this particular midday, would have a fresh roll which Monsieur Bernard had left from his breakfast.

Chapter Ten

As usual, Élise had got up at six o'clock in the morning. There was no wardrobe or coat-rack in the little whitewashed room whose two windows looked out on to the road and a horizon of meadows. Désiré was still asleep, and Roger was asleep in the next room, which was on a lower level and fitted with red tiles like a kitchen.

How bare it all was! Clean, of course. Every year, Madame Laude covered the whole house, inside and out, with whitewash. It was a poor house for all that. The walls bulged out here, went in a little farther on; a beam crossed the room without supporting anything, and nobody knew why it had been installed; the crucifix was so vulgar that Élise would have been incapable of saying her prayers if she had looked at it; and the glass of one of the two or three colour-prints framed in black, the one showing Napoleon at Austerlitz, had been cracked for several generations.

'Isn't it queer, Doctor, that I'm even nervier in the country than I am in the town?'

Doctor Matray, whose square face was rather hard by nature, had looked at Élise with a certain tenderness, without answering.

'I've tried everything, iron, tonics, those pills you prescribed for me . . .'

Nothing did any good, and it was as if the doctor knew that nothing ever would do any good. Had he discovered that mysterious taint which Élise was more and more convinced that she had inside her and which prevented her from being like other people?

The bed was clean. She had unpicked the mattress. However, stuffed as it was with vegetable horsehair, it impregnated you, especially when you were sweating on a hot summer night, with a smell of mouldy hay. Désiré called that the smell of the countryside, like the vague scent of sour milk which you could smell all over the house even though it was a long way from the nearest dairy.

Like a conjuror, Élise picked up her underwear from the round table and the two straw-bottomed chairs; her chemise, her drawers, her corset, her camisole, and her petticoat. She had a wash and then did her hair in front of the speckled mirror in which your nose looked as if it were askew, and all this time the cows were lowing, facing the Piedboeufs' farm from which some women were coming out to milk them.

However often Élise might tell herself that the country air was good for her, she was never at her ease there, and everything shocked her, even frightened her a little. She went down the few steps leading to the kitchen, whose door was open to the cool morning air from the garden, and found Madame Laude and Frédéric sitting at table facing each other over bowls of coffee and huge slices of grey bread.

She always had the impression that she was in the way; she apologized, and made the coffee in her own coffee-pot, as Mademoiselle Frida did in the rue de la Loi, although Mademoiselle Frida never thought that she was in the way. Frédéric with his thick, fair moustache, kept his cap on from morning to night, not even taking it off at mealtimes. He was a workman. All the previous week he had been on strike, and they kept seeing him go off in his black Sunday suit to attend some meeting or other.

'Come here, Frédéric.'

Madame Laude called him like a child, and, as to a child, she handed him his pocket-money, for he gave her all that he earned.

Désiré got dressed, singing to himself, and awoke his son by tickling his nose. Frédéric went off on his bicycle, his haversack on his back, with the sandwiches and the flask of coffee. After that Madame Laude disappeared in her turn, with two buckets hanging from a sort of pack-saddle fitted with chains which she carried on her shoulders, to go to fetch some water from the pump at the crossroads.

Then Élise, who had eaten standing up, while she was working, made the beds, did the dusting and peeled the vegetables for dinner.

'Hurry up, Roger. Let me see if your shirt is still clean.'

A wet comb had put a parting into the boy's flaxen hair. He was wearing a tussore jumper his mother had made for him. They were in mourning again, but in the country she let him wear out his blue trousers. She herself was wearing a white blouse with a round collar over a black skirt – a grey serge skirt which she had dyed.

They made their way slowly towards the Thiers des Grillons, in a world where they could have imagined themselves to be alone. Élise was sad, and when she was sad she felt more than usually tired. Recently she had suffered a great deal from her prolapsus of the womb. Once again there had been talk of an operation; the specialist had insisted, but Doctor Matray, for his part, had declared:

'You've got a child, Madame Mamelin. Take care of yourself, rest as much as you can, but don't have an operation.'

For Roger's sake, he had said! That meant that she might die. They would come for her with a carriage like Félicie, and take her to hospital or to a clinic. Her family would come to see her, Désiré leading Roger by the hand along those pale corridors where the smell of sickness and death took you by the throat. There would be oranges and grapes on a painted table, next to the medicines; then they would put her to sleep, and when the child and his father came again . . .

'No! No! I don't want to!'

She dreamt about it at night and thought about it in the sunshine, even on this wonderful morning dressed in pale green and haloed with gold dust.

'Play, Roger.'

He played, that is to say he banged a stick in the thick dust which covered the road and had already whitened his boots.

Françoise had died in April. She had lingered on for a month when everybody knew that there was nothing to be done. The doctors had given her up. Élise went round to see her every time she could escape from the rue de la Loi, to find her sisters-in-law there and neighbours looking after the children. Françoise herself, alone in her bedroom, gazed at her with an expression which Élise had never seen before in anybody's eyes and which she would never forget, even if she lived to be a hundred.

The blinds were always lowered, for the daylight tired the sick woman. Very thin, with her black hair spread out on the pillow, her jaw already jutting out like that of a dead person and

353

her breath coming jerkily, all that you could see of her was her big dark eyes, eyes of a frightening stillness.

She was thinking about the children. Élise knew that. She did not reply when somebody said:

'She didn't know that she was dying.'

In that case, why did her eyes express that boundless fear every time the voice of one of her children was raised in the kitchen? Why did she refuse to see them? People took them in to her sometimes, thinking it would please her, and with a tremendous effort, she would turn away from them; everybody said that she had lost her wits.

Only Élise had understood what was happening in Françoise. That was why her sister-in-law's death had upset her more than Félicie's, even though the latter had been her favourite sister.

A few moments before she died, Françoise had sat up in bed and uttered a cry like a roar, there was no other word for it, staring so fixedly at the door that it was as if she could see through it. It was just before dawn. The baby was crying in the next room and a strange voice, that of the beadle's wife, Madame Collard, was trying to coax it back to sleep.

'You're going to tear your clothes, Roger.'

He was trying to squeeze through a gap in the hedge. Surprised by his mother's voice, he looked at her and noticed that her eyes were misty, but he said nothing and went on playing by himself.

The foliage of the trees met above the steep slope of the Thiers des Grillons and formed a dark ceiling which the sun penetrated only here and there, casting bright patches on the uneven cobblestones. The air was humming with noise. The town, down in the valley, was like a bluish lake covered with mist, with factory chimneys poking into the air and railway engines whistling spitefully. You could make out the sounds of trucks bumping into one another, dredger buckets emptying their loads into space and monstrous hammers striking white-hot metal. Shriller notes in this powerful symphony came from the bell of the tram which stopped at the bottom of the hill and from the shouts of children in a nearby school; a clumsy bee brushed against Élise's face and a bird started twittering, perched on a strand of barbed wire, its beak open and its crop puffed out.

Élise sat down on the grass after covering it with her handkerchief. Roger hunted around for nuts. The rays of the sun, which had been pale and light in the early morning, turned the dark yellow of ripe corn and were filled with buzzing life.

The lodgers were on holiday. Mademoiselle Frida herself had gone to spend a month in Geneva, which proved that Monsieur Charles was right.

'Look, Mother.'

The boy came every now and then to show Élise nuts, acorns, and strawberries he had found in the wood.

'Perhaps Uncle Charles has taken the main road?'

She was beginning to think the same, for it was eleven o'clock at least, judging by the sun, and she was on the point of going back to the house when, right at the foot of the Thiers des Grillons, she caught sight of three figures in a patch of sunshine.

'Dear God!' Élise sighed sadly.

Why did Charles Daigne make his daughter wear a veil when she was only ten years old? Loulou was in deep mourning, just like a woman, and it was only half-way up the hill that the poor little girl, who must have been extremely hot, stopped to throw back the black crêpe.

Roger had already gone running to meet them. They were holding the hands of a two-year-old child, Joseph, who, dressed in black trousers at an age when other boys still wore pinafores, was climbing the stony slope with his little legs.

Mathilde Coomans, who lived on the corner of the rue de la Loi and whose business was in a bad way, had taken charge of the youngest child whom Élise had wanted to take herself, a baby of five months who was being fed on cows' milk.

'How could you manage, with your lodgers?'

It hurt to see the baby with Mathilde who was utterly unmethodical, was never dressed before ten in the morning, and kept looking round with a dazed epxression as if she did not know her way about her own shop. If a customer asked her for a pound of flageolets or split peas, she was completely at a loss.

The little group had come to a halt, for Joseph could not go any farther. His father, trying to carry him, had to stop every few yards to get his breath back.

'Dear God, Charles, you must be dripping wet. Give him to me. Good morning, poor Loulou.'

'Good morning, Aunt.'

They were alone on the long road which went down to the town, and Charles and the children seemed to have come from another world, in their black clothes which still smelled new.

'How pale she is, Charles.'

Loulou had always been pale. Her thin face was a matt white emphasized by the crêpe of her veil which had been cut out of one of her dead mother's mourning bands.

'You ought to leave her with me too, Charles. Even if it was only for a month. The air would do her so much good.'

To which Charles simply replied:

'I need her at home.'

Élise could have cried. It hurt her to see them looking so calm and natural after the catastrophe, as if they had not understood. Charles had not changed. His face still had a gentle, sheepish expression which was positively exasperating. He had not been able to come the day before because it was Sunday and on Sunday there were the offices. Not once, since he had become the sacristan at Saint-Denis, had he had a Sunday off; not once had he seen the colour of a Sunday anywhere but in the cloister with the silent porch where he lived and in the nave lit by tapers.

'I didn't think I'd be able to come today, on account of Mademoiselle Tonglet who died on Friday. Luckily they ordered the Requiem Mass for three o'clock.'

'You'll only just have time for dinner.'

How could he still go on making arrangements for funerals and Requiem Masses? There were moments when she felt like shaking him. He was too gentle, too resigned. You would have sworn that he did not appreciate the disaster which had overtaken him and his family.

'So it's you, Loulou, who's looking after your papa?'

'Yes, Aunt.'

'You do the cooking and the washing-up?'

'Yes, Aunt. Madame Collard comes and helps me with the beds.'

Loulou was so beautiful, so delicate! She had been rigged up in skirts which were too long for her and which made her look, not like a child, but like a dwarf. Everybody turned round to look at her when, in the procession, dressed in white and sky-blue, she played the part of the Virgin.

'Take your jacket off, Charles. It's too hot.'

It did not matter. He was hot, but he would not make himself comfortable, even when there was nobody there to see him. You did not know what to say to him. It was agony getting a word or a sentence out of him. He walked along, looking neither at the countryside nor at Madame Laude's house, which he entered as he would enter any place into which you chose to push him.

'You see, I've sent for the cot Roger had when he was little.'

Joseph already took after his father. He had not opened his mouth once. He had allowed himself to be kissed by huge Madame Laude and, if he had been frightened, he had not shown it.

'You'll enjoy yourself here, won't you, Joseph?'

As if they couldn't have found a nicer name than that!

'Have you brought his clothes, Loulou?'

A tiny parcel wrapped in grey paper and tied with red string. There was practically nothing light inside for the summer.

'It doesn't matter. I'll fix him up with something.'

For two pins she would have picked up Charles Daigne like a pawn to move him into the next square. At table he kept looking at his watch, thinking of nothing but his church, his funerals, his offices. Did he even know what he had been eating? Loulou looked after him as she looked after her little brother.

When the time came for him to go, he bent down and kissed his son on both cheeks, very simply, and it was on his nose that a tear suddenly appeared.

'Will you be coming to see him, Charles?'

'As soon as I can.'

Joseph did not cry.

'Say good-bye to your father and sister, little Jojo.'

She had just found a name for him. The child did not open his mouth, and watched them go with such a gentle look in his eyes that Élise had to make an effort not to burst out sobbing. It struck her that here was a child destined to suffer in life.

'If you only knew the effect it had on me, Madame Laude!'

She still felt sad, seeing the father and daughter, dressed all in black, disappearing into the distance between the two hedges, sharply silhouetted against the whiteness of the road, Charles with his bowler hat perched on the top of his head, his sloping shoulders, his tight trousers, his hand into which Loulou had slipped her own, and his gaze which you could imagine sliding over things with a gloomy indifference. They came from somewhere else, from that smoky world which Élise had been looking at while waiting for them, so dark when you saw it from a distance, and yet so full of snug little houses, of kettles singing on well-polished stoves, of reassuring little nooks, made to measure for those who lived in them, for their needs and joys and sorrows.

'What's the matter, Mother?'

Now that Roger was a big boy, she had to be careful all the time how she behaved in front of him.

'Nothing. Don't take any notice.'

Françoise's little boy had not even cried. He did not know yet that he was an orphan, and perhaps Charles, for his part, did not realize that he was a widower.

'Come here, Jojo. You're too hot like that.'

She took off his dark jumper, revealing a pair of narrow shoulders, as white as milk, which seemed surprised by the bright sunshine.

'What could we dress him in, Madame Laude? I can't stand him all in black. Tomorrow, I'll make a little suit for him.'

Not today, for they had to go out. It was time for their walk. They weren't in the country to keep the children shut up all day.

'Get your toys, Roger. Give your hand to your little cousin.'

'Where are we going?'

'To the Marronniers.'

His mother prepared an afternoon snack which she slipped into her shopping-bag, together with some crochet-work. She picked up a folding-stool and a mauve parasol.

'Good-bye, Madame Laude. You won't forget to put the stew on the stove about five o'clock, will you? With just a drop of water?'

Try as she might, she could not get rid of the picture of Charles and his two children as it had been printed on her retina when they were slowly climbing the Thiers des Grillons. They had been so lonely! They had looked like the survivors of a cataclysm which had laid waste the world, leaving only them on earth, three odd-looking creatures dressed in black, roaming about in an empty, indifferent immensity.

And yet it was only the mother that had gone!

'Roger, you must be nice, very nice to your cousin. You see, when somebody's mother is dead, there's nothing left.'

She thought of the hospital she would go to if she listened to the specialist, of Désiré holding Roger's hand and walking with him along an endless empty street. She had dreamt about it several times and she was convinced that she knew this street; she hunted about in her memories, but in vain. She had never seen it before, and yet she was sure that it existed and that one day she would suddenly stop and exclaim:

'There it is!'

'You're making him walk too fast, Roger. Remember that he's only got tiny little legs.'

Greenery, more greenery, still more greenery, the white patches of cows lying down, then some quickset hedges, more grass in the narrow lane, and a gate they went through in September to go to pick mushrooms in the Piedboeufs' meadows.

Élise was so tired!

Just off the road, where the ground sloped gently down towards the woods, they finally came to a quadruple avenue of chestnut-trees into which you went as you would into a cathedral and where little breezes caressed your cheeks. Opening her folding-stool, she got out her nickel-plated crocheting-hook and the plain white cotton to which a bit of lace was still attached as if by an umbilical cord.

With her head bent over her work, and her lips moving as if she were talking to somebody or saying her prayers, she looked up now and then at the end of the avenue where you could see a pink building surrounded by clumps of flowers and painted railings.

She was already explaining, as if Madame Dossin were sitting beside her:

'This is the nephew I told you about, the one whose poor mother . . .'

Where they were, it was as if they were in a jewel-box, with the big trees standing around them to conceal from their gaze the alarming immensity of the horizon. Élise and Roger knew these trees as if they were human beings. Each one had its own physiognomy, its own character: the third was as hollow as a sick old man, another held out horizontally a low branch on which Roger liked swinging, and there was one right at the end of the row which had been struck by lightning and which was no longer anything but a pale skeleton of a tree.

Madame Dossin's salmon-pink scarf was floating around the garden whose perfume reached them in whiffs, alternating with smells of moss and damp earth.

She would not come straight away. She would call out first:

'Jacques! Where are you?'

She did not call her son like the women of Outremeuse who cracked the crystal of the air with their piercing voices. She chanted his name, lingering a little on the first syllable, something which gave an added charm to the word.

'Such a lovely name, Madame Laude! If I could have another son . . .'

For her, Jacques was not just a child; he was the gentle shade of the chestnut-trees and the grass which was softer here than anywhere else; he was a new villa, pretty and comfortable, where everything was neat and tidy; he was Madame Dossin who did not fall upon Élise like poverty on poor people, but went on strolling a little longer among the roses in her garden.

'Where are you, Jacques?'

The latter had joined Roger under the trees, and only now did his mother appear at the end of the avenue, wearing a light-coloured dress and carrying a parasol in one hand; she came forward unhurriedly, and looked surprised to see Élise sitting there on her folding stool.

Neither of the two women was taken in by this ritual which had gradually been established and now constituted a secret and unchanging ceremonial. Madame Dossin, who had at her disposal a luxurious veranda and a garden full of flowers which an old gardener in a huge straw hat spent the whole day watering, Madame Dossin who possessed, within the perimeter marked out by the white railings, oaks, limes and copper beeches which were artistically grouped with shaded benches placed in the best places, Madame Dossin had no reason to settle down outside, and, unlike Élise who had only a couple of rooms at Madame Laude's, she could not bring along a folding-stool to sit on.

She would have dirtied her dress if she had sat down on the grass, and she accordingly remained standing, looking around for her son.

'Take my folding-stool, Madame Dossin. I assure you that I prefer the grass.'

In that case, why did she bring along a folding-stool?

'I'm not tired.'

She was young and pretty, rather ·melancholy but with sudden flashes of good humour. For two winters now the doctors had sent her to the mountains. Élise knew what that meant.

'Such a distinguished, simple person, Madame Laude! Her son is so well brought up!'

How was it that you could tell at a glance that he was a rich couple's child? He took after his mother. The oval of his face was extremely long, his complexion diaphanous, and long eye-lashes gave a languorous quality to a gaze full of charm. It was impossible to say in what way he was differently dressed from other children, and yet no other child was like him. He had been born to live in that new villa with a young and graceful mother.

'This is the son of my sister-in-law who is dead, Madame Dossin, the one I told you about. His father brought him this morning, because he's going to spend his holidays with us. Don't climb so high, Roger. Stay near Jacques. But do me the pleasure of taking the folding-stool, Madame Dossin.'

Madame Dossin was tired. She was probably bored. One fine day she would go off as Françoise had gone off, but would there be the same terror in her eye? She knew that her son would never go short of anything. He already had a governess, for he was considered too delicate to go to school.

'His little brother is with one of his aunts. The eldest child, a girl of ten, is staying with her father and keeping house for him like a little woman. If you'd seen her with her veil!'

Did Madame Dossin sometimes think that she would die soon, that it was perhaps her last summer in the house which her husband had made as bright and colourful as a new toy?

Élise did not envy her. She was sorry for her. And yet, today, she bore her a grudge, and evil thoughts started fermenting

361

inside her which she tried to conceal but which came to the surface in spite of everything.

'For the rich, don't you agree, a misfortune is never an absolute disaster. You understand what I mean?'

She had noticed the collar of genuine Flanders lace, the gold brooch, the heavy ear-rings.

'Do you think, for instance, that the death of a husband is as tragic for somebody who has got money as for those poor women at Souverain-Wandre?'

The newspapers had been full, the last few weeks, of the pit disaster at Souverain-Wandre, where eighty-five miners had been buried by a fire-damp explosion; the covers of the illustrated Sunday papers had shown their wives and children waiting among the gendarmes around the shaft down which teams of rescue-workers in leather helmets were going.

Funds had been opened. But what good did that do? The women were none the less widows, with children to feed. Many of them were pregnant. They would go to work as charwomen in the town or else they would become scavengers and you would see them, with handkerchiefs tied round their hair, sacks on their backs and iron hooks in their hands, climbing the spoil-heaps of the blast furnaces to look for a few lumps of coal among the smoking cinders.

This hurt Élise. She suffered when, in the evening, she accompanied somebody to the top of the Thiers des Grillons and saw the chimneys belching fire with a terrifying gasping sound.

She was sorry for Madame Dossin who had tuberculosis. She behaved humbly in front of her, instinctively, because Madame Dossin was rich, but she disliked her on account of this humility, she disliked her because she had offered her her folding stool, because she had insisted, because she herself had sat on the ground. She could not help it. She had been brought up like that.

She said things which could appear quite ordinary:

'It seems to me that Jacques has already got more colour in his cheeks.'

She was tempted to be really spiteful. Because she felt ill. It was not just her back and her stomach that were hurting. In the oppressive peace of the countryside, the feeling of her impotence in the face of destiny affected her more painfully than in the haven of the rue de la Loi.

At Saint-Denis they were celebrating a Requiem Mass for Mademoiselle Tonglet, the daughter of the pork-butcher in the rue de la Cathédrale. She had suffered from a bone-disease. People died every day. Who wasn't ill in one way or another?

'Roger! If the branch breaks, you'll fall and hurt yourself badly. He's so lively, Madame Dossin. It's true that I'd rather see him like that than too quiet.'

She had better stop talking. Jacques, for his part, was always quiet, timid and awkward in his movements, and although he was bigger and taller than Roger, he watched his friend climbing trees with admiration in his eyes. The previous winter, he had broken an arm falling off a chair.

'Are you happy, Jojo, to be in the country?'

She would make no more allusions. She even decided to win Madame Dossin's forgiveness and forced herself to smile her friendliest and humblest smile.

'What pretty lace you've got there, Madame Dossin! How delicate it is!'

The shadows of the trees lengthened, the cool of the evening fell on the women's shoulders, and Jacques' mother shivered.

'You ought to have brought a shawl.'

'I must go, Madame Mamelin. It's time.'

They retraced their steps in the disquieting light, the inhuman calm of the declining day. On the main road they joined Désiré, who was walking along at an even pace, reading his paper; and while Roger threw himself against his long legs, Élise thought about Charles Daigne who a little earlier had followed the same road in the opposite direction, about the women whom the gendarmes had been forced to push away from the pit-head of the stricken mine, and about the interminable funeral which the King had attended.

They sat down at table, in the garden where you could feel the shadows hemming you in. The frogs were croaking in the ponds, and unseen crickets were beginning their irritating concert.

From the tangled skein of her thoughts, Élise had retained only one thread, one idea which became more precise while she was helping Madame Laude to clear the table and listening to Désiré putting the two children to bed.

Some soldiers went by along the road, on their way back to the fortress of Embourg whose glacis extended to within eight hundred yards of the pump. Frédéric, who had come home and gone round the house without showing himself, was washing noisily and doubtless stark naked behind a screen of old planks.

It was the time when, every evening, Élise and Désiré walked up and down the road, coming and going between one point and another, invariably turning round when they got to the gnarled tree growing out of the bank where Roger had once buried his canary.

Désiré was smoking his pipe, whose smell mingled with the smell of the night. When he had finished his meal, Frédéric, still wearing his cap, would come to sit outside the house and gaze vacantly into space, deaf to his lodgers' murmured conversation.

Élise had taken Désiré's arm. Even if they had looked at each other, they would scarcely have seen one another. Feeling her tremble all of a sudden, he asked:

'Are you cold?'

'Listen, Désiré . . .'

She had to say it. She could not keep quiet any longer.

'Don't you think you ought to take out a life-insurance policy?'

She believed, she had always believed, that he had no antennae. She had said so countless times to Valérie, to Louisa, to poor Félicie. He went on walking along in silence and she was a long way from suspecting that this question, which she had finally put after a long shudder of her whole body, was a question which he had been expecting for a long time, for months, perhaps for years, and that his blood had frozen in his veins.

All the same, he managed to say in a normal voice, with scarcely any sign of strain in it:

'Why are you asking me about that today?'

'I wanted to talk to you about it before.'

How could she explain that it was the sight of Charles in mourning, the memory of Françoise's eyes, and her conversation with Madame Dossin who was suffering from tuberculosis, which had given her, by means of heaven knows what circuitous associations, an unbearable longing for security? It all went much further back, in fact, to the years spent in a dirty back-street with her mother, to the empty saucepans they used to put on the stove, to Monsieur Marette's suicide, to the hours spent with Madame Pain on the bench in the place du Congrès. Even the newspapers, which no longer talked of anything but war and catastrophes, had helped to crystallize her fears; even Mademoiselle Frida and Monsieur Charles' visits.

Her back hurt this evening. Her flesh was sick.

'I always hoped you would think of it yourself. You never know what may happen. What would I do, if I were left alone with Roger?'

Her husband's arm had stiffened. Désiré had gone rigid, as if he wanted to walk by himself.

'You'd work.'

He had said that in such an expressionless voice that she wondered whether it was really he who had spoken.

'But, Désiré, what if I wasn't strong enough to work?'

They were five paces from the twisted tree which formed a dark, almost human patch against the sky, a wounded body with its arms stretched out in despair. The stars were shining above them, a light breeze was playing in Élise's, hair a train whistled in the valley.

How could she have known that Désiré's eyes were fixed in a stare, that his teeth were clenching the stem of his pipe, that he would have given anything, yes, literally anything, for her never to speak about that? And yet he found a gay tone of voice in which to answer:

'Oh, knowing you, I know you'll always manage!'

She had detached her arm from his. She remained standing in the same place, while he took another couple of steps, but he did not dare to turn round for fear of showing his face, even in the dark.

'Are you coming?'

'Never, Désiré, never, do you hear, would I have thought that a man would be capable of saying to his wife . . .'

She would have liked to twist her arms like the branches of the tree, to roll about in the dust, to be beaten black and blue; she would have liked almost anything to happen, and she stood motionless in the darkness, with nothing to help her, nothing to support her, longing to collapse all of a piece and stay there for ever.

'And you go on smoking your pipe! You're pleased with yourself!'

'Come along.'

He would never be able to say anything more on the subject. It was years since he had applied for a life-insurance policy, since he had had the necessary medical examination, conducted, ironically enough, by the doctor of his own company, Doctor Fischer, who was practically a friend of his.

'You're a man, aren't you, Mamelin? . . .'

The heart. He had already understood.

'If you take precautions, avoid fatigue and emotion, you can still . . .'

He stood there near the crucified tree, big and strong in appearance, but he had had to put one hand on his chest, to press an organ which was beating so fast that he needed to restrain it.

'How can a man be so coldblooded as to say to his wife what you've just said to me? No, Désiré, you know, I . . .'

She went back to the house. She preferred to go back, walking unsteadily, and stepping over Frédéric who was still sitting in the doorway. He looked up at her and out of habit she stammered:

'Excuse me.'

She ran. She had only a few seconds left to herself, and she threw herself on to the bed without lighting the lamp, sinking her teeth into the counterpane. She would háve liked to die straight away, whereas Désiré, she felt sure, was calmly finishing his pipe outside under the starry sky.

Soon he would come and sit down, without a word, on one of the straw-bottomed chairs. And Roger would have to start talking in his sleep to rouse Élise from her prostration.

Feeling empty inside, with the taste of despair on her lips, she would be obliged to say:

'Have you got the matches?'

She undressed. There she was in her baggy knickers and her camisole, in the reddish light of the unshaded lamp. The bed was like a big sick animal, the crimson eiderdown taking on the shape of a whale.

Désiré went to bed first and turned his face to the wall, so that he could see nothing but the stain made by a squashed fly; then the lamp was turned out and the mattress creaked.

A long time afterwards, he cautiously put out his hand, but the arm he touched drew away sharply.

'Good night, Élise.'

Silence.

'Good night, Élise.'

Never, even after their most violent quarrels, had they gone to sleep side by side without saying good night to one another. Death could take him in his sleep, as had happened to others, and he would go off without a last farewell from his wife.

He waited, chewing his moustache which still smelled of tobacco, while Élise, whose features had grown hard and pointed, thought coldly, furiously, of putting an end to it all.

Chapter Eleven

Nearly a whole year had gone by since Embourg and life went on; indeed you might have thought that nothing had changed in the rue de la Loi. Élise cooked sugared dishes for Désiré when he came home at two o'clock and, in the fine spring evenings, in order to have a little peace in her kitchen, she sent him to chat with the lodgers outside on the pavement.

At the time, it had been thanks to Roger's mumps that life, to begin with at least, had not been more difficult. With Élise, impressions lasted. Like her sister Marthe's novenas or Léopold's plunges into the pubs in the back-streets. The slightest quarrel on a Sunday affected the whole week. To take only one example, although Roger was now eleven and in the sixth year at school, in Brother Médard's class, his mother still reproached him with the pain he had caused her at the time of his first private communion. Yet he had been seven years old at the time. He could remember the occasion too, for another reason, a particularly private reason. The day before that day, which was supposed to be the most wonderful day in his life, after a bath which had been even more meticulous than on other Saturdays, he had been walking along the newly washed

367

pavements when he had met Lucile, the daughter of the green-grocer in the rue Jean-d'Outremeuse, a girl who had a slight squint and was always hiding in corners with boys.

Roger had practically just come out of the confessional; his soul, like his body, was clean for the next day; and yet off he went after Lucile, like a dog, a prey to a nagging curiosity, talking to her shamefacedly, devising a squatting game so as to see between her legs, and finally, unable to stand it any longer and as red as the comb of a young cock, begging her:

'Let me touch.'

For several weeks, his mother had kept telling him:

'Don't forget that on the day of their first communion children must beg their parents' forgiveness for all the pain they have caused them.'

In the morning, while getting dressed for Mass, she had waited. Several times she had said:

'Roger.'

'What is it?'

'You haven't forgotten anything?'

'No.'

He knew perfectly well what she was waiting for. Taking advantage of a moment when Désiré was on his own, he had gone to ask his forgiveness in a faltering voice, but he would not ask his mother's forgiveness, he could not, precisely because she was waiting for him to do so. It was not out of spite on his part. It was just impossible. The words would not come out of his mouth.

Élise had made a tragedy out of it. She had left the house with her eyes red and her head empty from crying, and, even now, after all these years, every time she was angry with her son, she took care to remind him:

'When I think that you made me cry my eyes out the day you took your first communion.'

What would have happened if, after that evening at Embourg, Roger had not providentially fallen ill? His temperature had risen at an alarming speed. At midday, it had been 103·1°. Madame Laude had gone to fetch a doctor from Chênée. For a whole week, the bedroom walls around Roger had been made of a material at once soft and threatening, the same material as the crimson eiderdown which had swollen until it had touched the ceiling, while Roger had had the impression that his head was so monstrously big that he had felt it all over in terror.

When Désiré had come home, the first evening, Élise had said, as if nothing had happened between them:

'You must go to have the prescription made up at Chênée.'

Then, later on, when her husband had wanted to stay up to watch over the child:

'No! You have to go to work tomorrow morning. I've got nothing to do here.'

She had not forgotten, as he might have imagined. When he tried to kiss her as usual, she turned her head away and his lips touched nothing but hair.

Frédéric who, sitting on the doorstep, had practically been present at the scene on the main road, must have told Madame Laude about it. The latter glanced at Élise now and then, trying to guess what had happened, but thanks to Roger's illness, Élise had a good reason for crying when she felt like it and for showing the world the face of a *Mater Dolorosa*.

That was how things had happened. People cannot live all their lives in an atmosphere of drama. Human forces have their limits, and the most violent sorrows ebb away, however much energy you may expend on stopping them. Élise happened to smile at a joke of Madame Laude's and then to speak to Désiré on other subjects than the child's health. Thus Madame Laude was able to announce to Frédéric:

'They've patched it up.'

Désiré had been taken in for a moment, for he had a habit of taking his desires for realities, and there was no malice or rancour in him.

A glance, every now and then, as sharp as an invisible needle of ice shooting out of Élise's transparent pupils, was enough to proclaim:

'Don't have any illusions. True, I'm not dead. I come and go, and I look after the lodgers as I did before, but I shall never be the same again. There's a broken spring in me now which nobody will ever be able to repair.'

He pretended not to notice, and was merry and gay. A little spot of sunshine on his cheek, when he was shaving, was enough to set him humming to himself; every morning he awoke his son by tweaking his nose.

When a quarrel started now, Élise darted her icy glance at him and it was enough for her to murmur with pursed lips:

'Be quiet. You know very well that you're utterly selfish.'

He said nothing, made no attempt to defend himself. 'Selfish' had become the key-word. Utterly abashed, he turned away or hurriedly changed the subject, so that people might almost have imagined that there was some dreadful secret between them.

Even Roger, who on bad days, when his mother brought up the matter of his first communion, was told:

'You're no better than your father.'

And yet she had a vague feeling that this masculine selfishness which had hurt her so badly was involuntary, that it was probably a law of Nature. Désiré did not see what he did not want to see. He imagined almost sincerely that things were as he would have liked them to be. He had arranged his days so that they were a harmonious succession of little joys, and the absence of the least of these joys threatened the whole edifice. A cup of coffee and a slice of bread and butter, a dish of bright-green peas, reading the paper beside the fire, a maidservant standing on a pair of steps and washing a window, a thousand quiet pleasures which were waiting for him at every turning of life, which he had foreseen and looked forward to, were as necessary to him as the air he breathed, and it was thanks to them that he was incapable of feeling any real suffering.

'If you knew what men are like, poor Valérie!'

Since Embourg, Élise had stopped uttering these words in a resigned tone. She had broken free. There was an aggressive force in her which sometimes bordered on frenzy.

'They're not going to make a fool of me any more, oh no! I'm going to *clip* them, I'm going to *clip* them all, whoever they are.'

That simple little word was more revealing than anything else about the change which had taken place in her. She had always loathed the local dialect for its vulgarity. That was what used to irritate her most of all in the house in the rue Puits-en-Sock, where a Lucien, a Catherine, an Arthur, often tended to talk in Walloon.

To clip, in that dialect, was to steal, but not to steal openly: it was to take something in little doses, surreptitiously, to cheat, to watch for an opportunity to appropriate things. Henceforth Élise clipped unceasingly and unscrupulously, she clipped Désiré, she clipped her lodgers, she clipped Mademoiselle Frida. The house in the rue de la Loi had never been so full of life, with people coming in, going out, drinking, eating, and shouting, and Élise spent her energies freely, without counting the cost, without sparing her strength, without worrying about her back or her stomach, because every minute of the day she was clipping, every minute of the day she was taking money from one or another and slipping it into her petticoat pocket or into the soup tureen with the pink flowers, before going to the Savings Bank on Thursday afternoon, to put it into Roger's account.

Thanks to this untiring activity, this passion which she satisfied with furious determination, she was scarcely ever to be seen looking sad or melancholy as she used to; it was as if she had a fever which made her livelier and prettier, like consumptive people with their bright eyes and red cheeks.

Only she had to take care not to stop, not to relax for a single moment, for if she did, a fit of dizziness might come over her.

Madame Corbion had been right. Élise had been wrong not to believe her. You hadn't to have too many scruples. Did other people have any about you?

Few people noticed the transformation which had occurred in her. She was still as neat as ever, still as busy as ever. She had kept her humble smile, and her head still bent a little to one side as if to avoid the blows of fate; but what people failed to see was that she had an aim in life which she admitted only to herself; she had a passion, just as Léopold and Marthe had theirs; she clipped, calculated, collected sou after sou, franc after franc, always complaining that she had only just enough to live on, and determined never to touch her nest-egg for anything.

Externally, that year marked the zenith of the house in the rue de la Loi. Monsieur Bernard's two friends, Monsieur Jacques and Monsieur Dollent, took all their meals there, Monsieur Bogdanowski and Mademoiselle Lola had ended up by joining them, and, since the kitchen had become too small for them all, especially as they often brought along friends for dinner or supper, the dining-room had been reclaimed from

371

Monsieur Schascher who had had to find a room somewhere else. Considering what he paid, this was fair enough.

There was no end to the frying of chips and the grilling of chops, and the charwoman came three times a week for the whole day. Élise would have liked the house to be bigger; she would willingly have served twenty, thirty meals; nothing deterred her, and she no longer had time even to drop in on her sisters.

Old Madame Smet no longer came to spend Friday with her. Out of tact, she explained that her legs were too old to come so far, but the tram was a stone's throw away, and the truth was she was frightened by the frantic activity around Élise, and by those men from all over the world who spoke all sorts of languages and behaved as if they were in their own homes.

Élise was well aware that she could not always go on living at this pace and that a time would probably come when she would grow sick of clipping. Well, she copied Désiré; she avoided thinking about it, she refused to stay talking to herself, and for some time now, it had been in a cross voice that she had called out from the first floor, on hearing certain heavy, clumsy footsteps in the hall:

'Come in, Léopold. I'll be down in a minute.'

Had Léopold felt that he was in the way? Probably. But he was mistaken if he thought that it was because he was badly dressed and looked like a poor old beggar, or because he went afterwards to the pub next door for a drink. Élise did not care. She did not care about anything. What worried her was that in front of Léopold she became herself again. She tried in vain to deceive herself.

'In life, you know, Léopold, it's a mistake to expect people to give you anything, even if it's only the consideration you wouldn't refuse to a dog.'

Léopold's gaze was disapproving. Perhaps he had never expected to be given anything? He was tempted to push away the ritual cup of coffee, it was so obvious that Élise's life was no longer anything but a passionate calculation.

Once Désiré made the mistake of murmuring:

'You don't think you're working too hard?'

She had darted her familiar look at him.

'You dare to say that to me – you! Must I remind you of what you said to me a certain evening?'

They lived in the same house and slept in the same bed, as in the past. She looked after him to the best of her ability. Often she was gay, even when they were alone together. She dressed smartly. They all three went out together on Sundays. Thanks to Roger's scholarship – or so she said, for she was answerable to nobody – they would be able to send him to grammar school.

And yet sometimes she had the impression that she was living in a void, making gestures which meant nothing, moving her lips to produce sounds without any significance. On Sundays especially. Élise had taken a dislike to Sundays, those empty streets in which the three of them walked along as if they did not know where to put themselves, the long insipid progress towards Coronmeuse, the Ursuline convent, or some other objective. She used to come home with a heavy head, and nothing more urgent to do than to revive her fire, take off her Sunday dress and make sure that the lodgers were back.

She had two thousand francs in the Savings Bank and Désiré knew nothing about it. She wanted much more, she wanted so much that it seemed to her that she would have to slave away all her life to fill that little book whose pages were slowly being covered with pink and blue stamps representing money.

Like Madame Marette, like so many widows whom she knew, whom she collected so to speak, she wanted to have her own house; she would never feel secure until she had a house all to herself . . . Like that, when something happened to Désiré . . .

Why did she suddenly feel an urge to burst out sobbing, all by herself in her kitchen, as if the thing which was eating away at her inside had already destroyed her equilibrium, as if a big bubble of air, trying to force its way through her constricted throat, were lifting her up bodily?

Her features had just begun wrinkling up in preparation for tears when the street door opened: like a flash she pinned on her smile and straightened her bun.

'Come in, Monsieur Jacques. Monsieur Bernard had to go out. He asked if you would wait for him in his room. He'll be back soon.'

She just had time to lay the table. She would cry another time,

373

later on. Sometimes she wished that the time would come quickly when she would be able to cry to her heart's content and give way to her fatigue.

This was something nobody knew, nobody suspected. She lived very few hours by herself; the moments of crisis were brief, interspersed, so that she could stand them, with long periods of everyday life. When the lodgers were finally gathered together in the dining-room, Élise, fresher than ever, her complexion coloured by the heat of the stove, and wearing a pretty flared apron over her skirt, came in to put the soup-tureen in the middle of the tablecloth and to make sure that there was nothing missing from the table, neither a glass nor a fork, nor the salt-cellar nor the jar of pickled onions.

*

Never had Roger known a more radiant summer, lived such a long succession of grave and delicious hours, of a fullness which recalled the perfect fullness of an egg, of a depth which was equalled only by certain night skies peopled with stars to the very bounds of infinity.

Everything partook of everything else, things were transfigured, gestures were transposed, and the pink room which Mademoiselle Lola had left two days before to go on her holidays was so hot and colourful, so palpitating in every nook and cranny, that the child found himself being lulled to sleep by it, suspended between dream and reality, and filtering what he absorbed of the outside world through the grating of his lowered eyelashes.

Noises reached him, the smallest familiar sounds, the secret whispering of things, but for the past fortnight he had escaped from the ordinary rules of life; alone among the members of the household he was not obliged to submit to the discipline of the passing hours; he was living on the fringe of everyday life, which slipped around him with the fluidity of water.

The day before, the Institut Saint-André had had its solemn prize-giving, an event all the more memorable in that Roger had finished his sixth year and that in the autumn he would be going to the Jesuit college. He was first. He had been first in his class every year, except in the fifth, when he had been beaten by Van Hamme, a pale boy with a stubborn forehead, the son of a Bressoux wood-carver, who spent his life studying, with his head in his hands, and whom nobody had ever seen at play.

Perhaps, this year, Brother Médard had cheated a little so that Madame Mamelin's son should be first in spite of Van Hamme? In any case the headmaster had certainly cheated.

Roger was in the hall, among the parents, on account of the leg he had in plaster. He had had to be carried in.

'Ladies and gentlemen, my dear children,' the headmaster had said, 'I must now pay a well-deserved tribute to the exceptional conduct of one of our pupils . . .'

A shiver. Roger waited, and an eternity went by before his name was finally uttered, before the other heads turned in the direction of his blushing face.

'. . . one of our pupils, Roger Mamelin, whom an injury has prevented from taking his place among his fellow pupils, but whom I am delighted to see, loaded with prizes, in the front row of the audience . . .'

The headmaster read out the report which Brother Médard had written.

'One morning at the beginning of this month, when the stifling heat forced us to close our schools . . .'

That was true. All the schools in the town had been closed for three days, and it was on the third day that Roger had gone to play on the drill-ground with some friends from the place du Congrès. In the blazing sunshine, next to the shining torrent of the Meuse and the thundering weir whose foam was scattered into bright specks of spray, the soldiers were drilling, and guns and artillery wagons drawn by four horses were bumping up and down among the ruts and hillocks of the plain.

'. . . Frightened by a rearing horse,' the headmaster went on.

That wasn't true. The truth was simpler, so simple that it was impossible to tell it on a day like this, when the children were wearing golden crowns on their heads. There had been four of them, their cheeks flushed with excitement, throwing stones into the river like filthy little brats, when one of the boys had shouted:

'Étienne! . . . There! . . . There! . . .'

And they saw a straw hat sailing by, floating farther away

375

from the bank, swept along by the swift current from which an arm emerged now and then.

Roger had jumped into the Meuse, almost without realizing. He had swum after the other boy. Twice he had nearly given up, because Étienne had clutched hold of him and he had been frightened.

Finally he had saved him, heaven knows how, and he had pushed the dripping, twitching body on to the stones on the bank. Afterwards, they had walked over to the only house near by, a peculiar pink building standing by itself on the drill-ground, a café for the troops, and there they had been made to drink some rum. Roger had gone home by himself, talking in a whisper, a pitiful sight in the clothes which the people in the café had lent him and which were far too big for him.

It was the first time in his life that he had worn men's trousers, which were so long that huge turn-ups had had to be made in the legs and kept in place with safety-pins.

The headmaster avoided giving these details.

'As a consequence of his bravery, Roger Mamelin is confined to his chair today, when he had been looking forward so much to playing the part of the Month of May in *The Round of the Months* which we have just presented to you. . . .'

How could a friar of the Christian Schools, and a headmaster too, lie like that?

The real and the false were so confused in the stifling heat that soon Roger would end up by thinking that he had sprained his knee while rescuing his friend.

In fact, it had been the next day that he had fallen, over a line of bricks bordering a flowerbed in the friars' garden. He had been running along with one foot on each side of the bricks, like a little street-urchin; he had had a premonition of the accident but he had continued all the same.

He had been alone in the kitchen-garden. Brother Médard, during the rehearsal of *The Round of the Months*, had sent his pet to fetch something from the classroom, giving him the key.

What did it matter? It was much prettier the way the head-master told it and it was best not to admit that pupils of the Institut Saint-André amused themselves throwing stones into the water.

Everybody was nice to him. He had been solemnly presented

with a Bayard in gilded zinc. Most of the pupils' mothers came and kissed him.

At home, there were three medical students to look after him, to bring dressings and plaster bandages which they scrounged from the Bavière hospital where they worked as assistants.

Was Roger still in pain? Was his knee still swollen?

He was so comfortable like this, on a chaise-longue in Mademoiselle Lola's pink room, his legs stretched out, his arms on padded elbow-rests, and on a chair within easy reach his egg-and-beer, some coloured sweets, and a collection of illustrated papers which smelled pleasantly of printers' ink.

He read a little, looked at the pictures, lazily followed the progress of a fly or the patterns of light and shade on the weird floral wallpaper, and listened to his mother's comings and goings, the trumpet of the greengrocer turning the corner of the rue Pasteur, the hammers at Halkin's, the silence of the school which had closed for two long months.

Wasn't it extraordinary that he should already have covered this first stage of his school life, which had seemed so long to him when he had set foot for the first time in Brother Mansuy's classroom? That classroom had been gloomy on that far-away autumn morning, and yet his memories of school were nearly all sunny memories, except for one perhaps, or rather two which cast a grey shadow over the bright light of his reverie: first his perverse whisperings in corners with the clownlike Ledoux about the difference between boys and girls; then the business of the new catechism.

Ever since that business he had hated Brother Mansuy, or at least avoided him, because Brother Mansuy knew. His mother had bought Roger a second-hand catechism and its cardboard cover was a faded blue, the corners were broken, and you could see the threads of the binding and reddish stains on certain pages. Roger wanted a new catechism with a shining cover so badly that one day he had gone to see Brother Mansuy.

'My mother says you are to give me a new catechism.'

How little he must have been at that time! He could not get over having been so bold. He had had his catechism. He had enjoyed it in secret, for he did not dare to show it at home, and every night, in his bed, he was tormented by the thought of the inevitable catastrophe. Before the Easter holidays, his parents would be sent, together with his marks, a list of books and stationery supplied during the term. It was a matter of urgency for him to speak to his mother. A dozen times he nearly did so, but in the end he did not dare. He had gone into the classroom at playtime, his catechism in his hand, and it was to the friar that he had spoken, heaven knows how, so nervous that his eyes had seen nothing.

'My mother has told me to give it back to you. She has found the old one.'

Brother Mansuy had not looked surprised. It was as if he had guessed the truth. He had kept his gentle smile and perhaps he had given the child a sweet.

Even now Roger still bore him a grudge, precisely because, having guessed the truth, he had been generous enough to keep quiet, to avoid humiliating a child.

That did not matter any more, since it was all over and Roger would never go through the big green gate as a pupil again. Except for Mademoiselle Lola, who did not take her studies seriously and had gone home, the lodgers still had one or two examinations to sit for. After that they too would go home for the holidays and the Mamelins would go to Embourg.

Roger sucked a sweet, and read the story of *Onésime Pourceau, sportsman*, which every week occupied the two centre pages of the *Petit Illustré*. He breathed in the smell of the tomato soup, looking forward to going downstairs for dinner, with one leg in the air, hopping from one step to the next and holding on to the banisters. Every minute of life was good, and yet he wondered if his knee would go on hurting much longer or if he would go to play in the street for a while.

It was already eleven o'clock. A tram went along the rue Jean-d'Outremeuse, Élise started laying the table, you could hear the clatter of the plates, and a draught slammed the kitchen door shut. Mademoiselle Frida was studying in her room, with the window and the door open, facing the white wall of the yard where for some days a column of ants had been crawling around, whose nest had been deluged in vain with boiling water.

Could anybody suspect that, from one second to the next, this peaceful state of affairs would be shattered? Did Élise herself guess that the anxious frenzy driving her forward was suddenly going to reach its fermata?

The street door opened. She looked through the glass pane. Why, it was Monsieur Bernard coming home early! What was the matter with him? He seemed to be in a hurry, rushed upstairs, leant over the banisters and shouted:

'War, Madame Mamelin! It's war! The Germans have invaded Belgium. There's fighting going on around Visé.'

Visé, where they sometimes went on a Sunday to eat waffles with Aunt Louisa's family? Élise smiled incredulously.

'Impossible, Monsieur Bernard!'

Under a sky so vast and blue that, from the spire of Saint-Nicolas, you could almost see the green plain round Visé where the Meuse broadened out!

Mademoiselle Frida, stiff and erect, was standing at the door of her room.

'Do you know if the trains are still running?'

After that, everything became confused; there was no telling who was coming and who was going, what had happened before and what happened after. Élise had not taken time off to cry. She had just knocked on the door of the next house, and old Madame Delcour had appeared, bent double, the face under her black bonnet wearing a surprised expression.

'It's war, Madame Delcour! Monsieur Bernard has just come home from the hospital. He's already putting on his uniform.'

A skeletal figure half lying on a couple of chairs, the man with the sleeping-sickness looked at Élise with his empty eyes, and nothing in him moved but his fingertips.

'What are you going to do, Mademoiselle Frida?'

'I'm leaving.'

'You're going back to your country? But you won't be able to go through Germany.'

'I'll go through France and Switzerland.'

She packed her bags. Monsieur Bogdanowski arrived in his turn, in a state of feverish excitement. More cautious in his ways, he had already been to the station to reserve a seat in a train.

'You have to fight to get a ticket. If you could see the crowd . . .'

379

Monsieur Bernard came downstairs, in the bottle-green uniform of a rifleman.

'Are we having dinner all the same?' he joked without much gaiety.

'What I'm wondering, Monsieur Bernard, is why my husband hasn't come home. I don't suppose they're going to keep the office open. Dear God, Roger! Why have you come downstairs? Mind your leg. What do you want?'

'I want the plaster taken off.'

'What ought we to do, Monsieur Bernard?'

Here came Monsieur Jacques Dollent with his fine black beard, looking rather awkward in uniform, for he had already been to the Bavière hospital, where he was an intern, to change his clothes.

'You couldn't sew a button on for me, could you, Madame Mamelin?'

She thought, automatically, for it was Monsieur Dollent's favourite phrase, which he used to say half in jest, half in earnest:

'My gratitude will die only with my last breath . . .'

She did not say it. She would think of it later on; she would think of it often.

'Are you going to fight?'

'I don't know. I've got to join my regiment at the Fort of Boncelles. I'm trying to get hold of a bike so that I can travel faster.'

'Listen . . .'

They listened. They could not hear anything.

'Gunfire . . . A dull noise . . . Don't move your feet about, Roger . . .'

They listened again and this time they made out a distant rumble. Monsieur Bernard ate his dinner. Monsieur Jacques, as calm as ever, with astonishingly delicate gestures for a man, loosened the contraption imprisoning Roger's knee.

'My gratitude will die only with my last breath . . .'

Alas, it would not be long in coming! That very evening, Monsieur Dollent, who had red hair, Monsieur Dollent, who was trying to get hold of a bike so that he could travel faster, would be killed in that forest of Sart-Tilmant, near Boncelles, where they had so often gone picnicking and where two regiments of riflemen would wipe each other out, each mistaking the other for the enemy.

They did not even know how the Germans were dressed. They were not made for war. It was all a ghastly mistake.

Élise served dinner, anywhere, anyhow, all the time keeping an eye on the bright rectangle of the street door which had been left open. Everybody was still joking, especially young Bernard who, finding his medical studies too long and too arduous, had decided to make do with a diploma in dentistry.

'Have a good trip, Mademoiselle Frida. Perhaps we'll meet again in Berlin, seeing that the Russians are on our side.'

They came and went, not listening to one another, not thinking. They knew that it was war, because everybody said so and those who had come from the centre of the town had seen the posters, but an optimistic fever was buoying them all up, and it was as if they had been expecting it, expecting to be freed at last from the everyday routine, from the pile of accumulated worries which everybody trailed behind him.

Little by little the house emptied, the doors left open as after a house-moving, and things lying about on the bedroom floors: a broken comb, an empty tube of toothpaste, some cardboard boxes, a few balls of crumpled paper. When at last Désiré's footsteps could be heard, he came walking in as usual and bent down automatically to kiss his son on the forehead.

'Well, Désiré?'

Gravely, simply, he said:

'It's war.'

'Have they called out the civic guard?'

He nodded, then smiled quickly.

'We've got to guard the public monuments. They're probably afraid that the Town Hall or the Law Courts are going to run away. Don't worry. They aren't entitled to send us to the front.'

He changed into uniform, put on the strange hat with the reddish-brown plumes which he had worn so many times at reviews, or to go to the communal shooting-gallery where the best shot of the year won a silver place-set. Désiré had already won two sets. They had decided not to use them until they had one for each member of the family.

Élise accompanied him to the door, made an effort to smile. 'Come back quickly, won't you?'

He would not go very far. With a few others from his company, including little Grisard, he would be sent to guard the slaughterhouse, which the people from the back-streets had started looting. It was there, at the end of the quai des Pêcheurs, that Roger used to go every morning with his grandfather, Monsieur Pelcat, Monsieur Repasse and Monsieur Fourneau, when they went to swim in the Meuse at half past six.

Now Roger was playing marbles, all by himself, in front of the door; twice he went to the end of the street, but his friend Albert did not put in an appearance.

Élise finally sat down in her kitchen and her whole body relaxed. There was no fever left in her and no thoughts. With one elbow on the table and a hand on her forehead, she ate some cold food which she took from any plate which was to hand – it didn't matter any more – and when she stood up, she looked around without knowing what to do next. She tidied up out of habit, even though it no longer served any purpose, and she felt as tired as if she had just done a fortnight's washing.

Part Three

Chapter One

The voice of Father Renchon, who was giving his history lesson, was flowing along, as monotonous and fluid as the rain which had been falling for days and days from a twilight sky. Everything in the classroom was damp and grey – the whitewashed walls, the black desks which had been wiped with wet sleeves, the concrete floor which showed every footprint – and when Roger, in his corner by the window, moved his head, it touched the coats hanging on the hooks, with cold drops clinging to the woollen hairs.

Sitting on a bench without a back, with his shoulders hunched, he was pretending to be writing in a notebook spread out in front of him, but it was farther down that his gaze was directed, at the book with the cloth covers lying open on his knees, hidden by the desk.

The book smelled of the lending library, the coats hanging from the hooks smelled of wet wool, the classroom smelled of foul ink and stale chalk; everything was dull, everything seemed old and dirty, with excessively bold forms, excessively harsh outlines against a vague background, like the glistening roofs which could be seen beyond the huge courtyard of the college, or like that distant window, already lit up, behind which somebody came and went without your being able to tell whether it was a man or a woman, or what mysterious task it was performing.

Roger Mamelin drank in this atmosphere every time that he turned a page and raised his eyes for a moment, before looking down again at *La Dame de Monsoreau*, for which he had imagined a setting in black and grey, with patches of dull white, like nineteenth-century engravings.

Everything tied up, connected, harmonized; everything, including Father Renchon's voice, melted into his little world, to such an extent that he started when the tone of that voice altered. Then, hurriedly shutting his book, he lost no time in coming to the surface.

With a gentle courtesy which underlined every word, the voice said:

'Monsieur Neef, if what I am saying has not the good fortune to interest you, may I ask you at least to make a pretence of listening politely?'

Roger, like the rest, turned to look at first one Neef, then the other, for there were two in the class, two Neefs with no family connexion, Neef-the-aristocrat, who lived in a château and came to school every morning on horseback, followed by a flunkey, and Neef-the-peasant, the son of a country brewer, who started and blushed every time a master spoke to his namesake.

Curiously enough, despite their dissimilarities, the two Neefs had one thing in common: they were both far too old to be in the third year, among boys of fifteen. They were already men, the brewer's son with his upper lip darkened by brown hairs and his deep bass voice, and the other with his lop-sided, thoroughbred face and his mincing, foppish manners.

'Didn't you hear me, Monsieur Neef? Yes, you. It's to you that I'm talking.'

Father Renchon imperceptibly quickened his delivery, this being the only outward sign he ever gave of being angry.

'Seeing that your presence is no more agreeable to me than my lesson seems to be to you, I gladly give you permission to go for a walk until the latter comes to an end.'

Without any sign of emotion, the Neef in riding-breeches and boots stood up, bowed as he passed the rostrum as if in gratitude for some favour, made for the door, and turned round, just as he was going out, to wink at his fellow pupils.

Roger lowered his head, promptly found his page and the thread of his story, read a phrase here and picked out a word there, skipping whole passages and remarks which he had guessed in advance; everything returned to normal around him, including the voice of the master, who resumed his lesson in an uncertain tone as if he were tuning a violin.

Yet there was something wrong. Roger could feel it, since he looked up again at the precise moment that Father Renchon stopped talking. He saw every face turned towards the windows and outside, in a gallery which served a whole row of classrooms and looked like a gigantic ship's gangway, a Neef who appeared to be acting for his own amusement, gravely miming a drawing-room scene, kissing the hand of an invisible lady, gracefully refusing a cup or tea, chatting, playing the sweetheart, and finally inviting his companion to dance.

Behind him, the hard lines, drawn in Indian ink, of the iron balustrade, the slender pillars, and the uniform, dreary sky which looked like a photographer's backcloth.

Neef did not seem to be aware of this setting. He was playing his part with such conviction that he created invisible presences around himself; and he was taking the first steps of a tango, his body tense, his eyes half shut, when a monstrous silhouette entered the scene, as dark and hard as reality, slow and implacable, the big chief himself, the bogy-man of the school, Father Van Bambeek, the master in charge of discipline.

Then laughs started in tight throats, eyes smarted, the boys felt like shouting, and Father Renchon himself did not succeed straight away in turning his smile into an austere grimace; but a glance from Father Van Bambeek through the windowpanes was sufficient to freeze every face, and the master began droning away again, after a sharp tap of the ruler on his rostrum.

Roger had lowered his eyes again on to his book, which could not be seen from outside, but the spell was broken, and he read uncomprehendingly, attentive to the two silhouettes which for ten minutes would go on passing slowly backwards and forwards in front of the windows, appearing and disappearing at regular intervals, the huge Jesuit father who had once been a cavalry officer flanked by the puny Neef who had lost nothing of his self-assurance.

Just now, to amuse his friends, he had acted a part for them, and now he was making practically the same gestures, or rather he was the same man. For the two men, the Jesuit father and the squire's son, were chatting on an equal social footing, far removed from the school and its classes, the courses and impositions; and, when they parted, beyond the window through which only Roger, from his privileged position, could see them, they shook hands, and Neef came back to his bench as naturally as he had left a little earlier, while a slight flush, Roger was sure of that, coloured Father Renchon's forehead.

The minutes passed, the rain fell, and other windows lit up in the distant block of houses. Suddenly footsteps rang out in the gallery, and this time Roger, who had recognized the usher, knew that it was for him; everybody knew it, everybody looked at him, and the other Neef, the peasant with the hobnailed boots, tried to encourage him with a sad, kindly, dog-like glance.

'Monsieur Mamelin, will you kindly come with me to see the director of studies.'

For all that he was expecting it, it came as a shock. Roger stood up, crossed the classroom, and followed the usher along the cold gallery, catching sight of pupils in their classrooms, masters on their rostrums, equations on a blackboard. The usher walked in front and seemed to be pulling him along on the end of an invisible chain. He knocked on a glazed door and stood to one side. Not a sound, nothing but a scratching on paper, and darkness everywhere, except on the desk, which was lit by a lamp with a green shade. A face grotesquely sculpted by this light, a bulbous nose surrounded by deep, flabby folds, an imperceptible sliver of a glance under the lowered eyelids.

The director of studies, who was deputizing for the headmaster, went on writing in a fluid, regular script, and long minutes went by without his appearing to suspect that anybody was there. Then his hand picked up a blotter, he carefully blotted what he had been writing, and he reached out, not without disgust, for a piece of paper of which Roger had been so proud only the day before and which suddenly disappointed him with its indecent vulgarity.

It was a newspaper which he had written on his own and reproduced himself with some hectograph jelly. The front page was adorned with a caricature of the director of studies.

The latter, who had picked up the document between two fingers, as if it were something dirty, held it for a moment suspended in the light from the lamp and finally looked up at the guilty schoolboy.

For Roger, this lasted an eternity. Dry-mouthed, and with sweat moistening the palms of his hands, he could not take his eyes off the glossy paper on which the purple ink had printed its dirty marks. Was it out of pity that the Jesuit father finally dropped the document in the waste-paper basket to the left of his foot?

'I suppose, Monsieur Mamelin, that you are familiar with the school regulations?'

Even if he had wanted to, even if he had angrily decided to keep quiet, with the director's eyes upon him he could not have prevented himself from stammering:

'Yes, Father.'

'Then you know that you have rendered yourself liable to expulsion.'

A picture emerged from the chaos of light and shade which surrounded him, or rather a succession of pictures: an embankment in the rain, a bridge which spanned a swollen river and which a tram with a yellow headlamp was crossing, a boulevard lined with low houses, and himself, Mamelin, walking along, approaching the corner of the rue des Maraîchers, reaching the corner-house which had been his home for some time, and stopping as he saw a chink of warm light behind the kitchen blind and heard or thought he heard the familiar sound of the fire being poked. He had his key in his pocket, but he did not use it; he did not want to go in, and turned round, walking to and fro. A dozen times he reached the Pont d'Amercoeur, and he had to wander in the rain for a long time before he caught sight of the impassive figure of his father coming home from his office.

'Father, I have been . . .'

Even in his imagination, the word would not come out.

'I have been expelled . . .'

Of all the nightmares which had made him scream with fright, sitting up in his bed, this was the most terrifying, and yet he had not moved. He awoke, astonished to find himself standing motionless in front of a lamp with a green shade while the director of studies gently stroked the crucifix stuck in his black silk belt.

'Your act of indiscipline, Monsieur Mamelin, is all the more serious, all the more inexplicable in that you are here, are you not, on special terms. I will not dwell on the gratitude which we might expect from you or on the amazement and distress which . . .'

Oh! How he hated his mother for what he was suffering now! How certain he felt that he would go on hating her for the rest of his life! How he hated Aunt Louisa, as he remembered her in

389

her back-shop in Coronmeuse with its smell of spices and gin, her hands on her stomach, her head bent to one side, lecturing a humble and docile Élise in Flemish!

For it was there, in that lair of hypocritical kindness and bigotry, that the idea had originated.

'Why don't you make a priest of him? When the ecclesiastical authorities discover a sense of vocation in a child from a poor home, they don't hesitate to pay for his studies, and later on . . .'

Yes, later on! It was about later on that Élise had thought, about the famous question of her widowhood which was always haunting her and which Louisa had solved as if by magic. There was a line of verse on the subject which buzzed about in Roger's head:

. . . When you become a priest, I shall be your servant.

'Brother Médard, do you think that Roger would make a good priest?'

Because he served Mass every morning!

'Your act of indiscipline, Monsieur Mamelin, is all the more serious, all the more inexplicable in that you are here, are you not, on special terms . . .'

Setting his teeth, he bent his head to conceal his hatred. There was a recollection which he would have liked to erase from his memory, just as he would have liked to forget the affair of the catechism, or that of the greengrocer's daughter whom he had begged, on the eve of his first communion, to let him touch her.

'Just once . . . With one finger . . .'

How much uglier it had been, that call he had paid with his mother, who had pulled him along by the hand to the house of the Dean of Saint-Nicolas, in the little courtyard at the end of the cul-de-sac, next to Sister Adonie's nursery school! It had been in the evening, a soft bluish evening in autumn; there were some blood-red geraniums in the window-boxes. The lamps had not been lit. They had waited for a long time in a parlour, on chairs upholstered with black horsehair, and there had been an unpleasant smell in the air, a smell which Roger was now capable of recognizing among a thousand others, the smell of houses in which men live on their own, the smell which had turned his stomach in the Institut Saint-André whenever he had been sent on an errand to the kitchens, and which he met again, only slightly attenuated, in the Jesuit fathers' private quarters.

'Now behave yourself, Roger. Above all, say what I say. Don't start contradicting me again, like you usually do!'

And when the fat little dean without a neck, as common as a tobacco-jar, his face a purplish red, had finally received them, she had talked. She had talked as she knew how to when she wanted something passionately, humble and proud at the same time. The 'bare necessities' had been brought into it, and her backache at night, and her organs, and Désiré who was the best of men but who, like all the Mamelins, had no initiative or ambition.

The dean looked at her with his big protruding eyes, doubtless thinking that it was time for his dinner, but the whole family had to be mentioned, a Peters cousin who was the parish priest of a Limbourg village, another cousin, on the Mamelin side, who was a professor at the grand seminary of Louvain, Désiré's sister in the Ursuline convent at Ans . . .

'He never thinks of anything but studying. I've all the trouble in the world taking his notebooks away so as to make him play a bit. Monsieur Jacques, one of my former lodgers who's only got his final examination to pass to be a doctor, says he's never seen a child so advanced for his age . . .'

She had won. She had obtained her letter, which the dean had written with the same dazed expression on his face.

And Roger had been admitted to the Jesuit college at half the usual fee.

Now he was being expelled, but first of all they were taking care to make him pay his debts.

'. . . The most elementary gratitude . . .'

'Well, Monsieur Mamelin, do you realize the gravity of your offence?'

'Yes, Father.'

No, no, and no! It wasn't true. He felt like shouting this out at the top of his voice. He was not ashamed of himself. And if his name had been Neef, Neef-of-the-Château of course and not Neef-the-peasant who was just an embarrassment to the school, he would probably be strolling up and down the gallery with Father Van Bambeek, chatting about the last charity bazaar.

'Think carefully about the question I am going to put to you. Have you the sincere intention, the firm resolve to mend your ways, by which I mean to abandon once for all a certain attitude of mind which is out of place in this house?'

'Yes, Father!'

What a tremendous *no* would have echoed round the study if his inner voice could have been heard!

'Your case has been discussed at some length. I must tell you straight away that I explained your parents' situation. It is out of consideration for them, Monsieur Mamelin, and particularly out of consideration for your mother, whose courage and self-abnegation are well known to us, that the school has decided to exercise clemency in your case.'

Not expelled!

Roger, all of a sudden, was not so much relieved as disappointed. The priest stood up and pressed an electric bell, and the usher's face appeared behind the glazed door.

Another brief sentence, which came out so dryly and said so much:

'I hope that we shan't have to bring this up again.'

That was all. It was over. He would go on coming to the college. But he hated the director of studies for his menacing indulgence, as icy as the draught which met him in the gallery. When he went back into the classroom the lamps were on and he was suddenly afraid of the harsh light, of the eyes fixed on him, for he felt that his face was expressing, not contrition and gratitude, but ill-will.

Father Renchon must have known, for he did not even look at the boy while he was sitting down again on his bench. Perhaps he had been consulted? Would Roger have to hate him too?

A note was slipped on to his desk which had been passed from hand to hand, and Neef-the-peasant gave him to understand, with much twisting and turning, that it was he who had sent it, begging him with his eyes to answer.

The big fool with the voice which was breaking had written in his childish handwriting:

'*What did he say?*'

And Roger angrily scrawled a single word across the paper: '*Merde*.'

The note went back the way it had come, but this time Father Renchon, without interrupting what he was saying, followed its progress with his malicious little eyes. Just as the recipient was unfolding it he said:

'Monsieur Neef.'

Both of them stood up at the same time, both the Neefs, as usual.

'For once, it is not you who is concerned,' the master said with exquisite politeness to Neef-of-the-Château.

Then, turning to the other Neef:

'Monsieur Neef, would you be so kind as to bring me that paper which you seem to find so passionately interesting.'

The poor booby crossed the classroom, dragging his hobnailed boots along the cement floor where they struck sparks here and there. Blushing, he put the note on a corner of the rostrum and stood there in despair, begging Roger's forgiveness with his eyes.

'Thank you. You may return to your place.'

Father Renchon's thin lips had stretched slightly. Only Roger had noticed this. Neef, from his seat was still begging his forgiveness.

'Monsieur Neef, you will do me the favour of writing five hundred lines for Thursday.'

Neef-of-the-Château had the misguided idea of playing once too often on the ambiguity.

'Me?' he asked, standing up.

'You too, of course, since you insist.'

Had he looked at Roger? His glance had passed very quickly. But the boy was convinced that in all this there had been something deliberate, a subtle, gentle contact, a sort of benevolent message.

'Let us continue, gentlemen.'

And taking his watch from his broad belt:

'Monsieur Mamelin, it is half past three.'

Chapter Two

It was towards the end of August 1915, on one of those mornings when the air buzzes and things are so to speak haloed with a quivering smoke. Roger was at Embourg all by himself, in the new house which Madame Laude had rented on the main road and in which she was at last fulfilling her dream of running a café.

In the rue de la Loi, Élise was doing the rooms, with all the windows open and all the bedding outside, leaning out as soon as she heard a tradesman's trumpet, as she used to do in the good old days, for although she no longer had any lodgers and the bedrooms had remained empty for several months, they had just been requisitioned by the German Army.

The rooms had a name and a smell again. Désiré was alone in treating his guests coldly, while Élise bustled around from morning till night, chattering away in a peculiar German which had come back to her from her childhood.

Once again she could scrub the floors, turn the mattresses, polish the furniture, clean the brasses; packets of foreign cigarettes lay about on the tables with letters and bars of bitter-tasting chocolate. In one of the drawers of Major Schorr, a handsome, red-faced man who always smelled of eau-de-Cologne, she had found a box of chemical phials which she had mentioned to Doctor Matray.

'Just imagine, Désiré, he's got a dirty disease.'

'So much the better.'

'Such a handsome man! When you remember that he takes his pick of the Offenstadt girls, you know, the girls whose parents own the big riding-school . . .'

Mademoiselle Pauline's room – for Mademoiselle Lola had passed through without leaving her mark – was occupied by another major, one of those who wore a floating cape and trailed their sword along the pavement, an aristocratic figure, buttoned up tight in a uniform under which he was obviously wearing a corset, and with a monocle always in one eye. It appeared that in civilian life he was a banker.

As for Mademoiselle Frida's room, it was good enough for a lieutenant in the Landsturm, Monsieur Kramp, a tubby little Bavarian, all pink and fat, a champagne dealer before the war, who had already had his wife to see him twice on the sly. Needless to say, the latter had spent hours in the kitchen with Élise.

'I assure you, Désiré, they are ordinary people like anybody else. It's because you don't understand them.'

But Désiré would not even allow the subject to be brought up. His face assumed such a furious expression that you felt that it would be better to keep quiet. One day, scarcely a month after the Germans had entered the town, Élise had actually thought that he was going to beat her, and, for the first time in their married life, she had been really frightened of him.

Coming home from his office at two o'clock, he had halted in his tracks in front of a notice stuck behind a window in his own house, a notice which could be seen all over the district, with its crude lettering carelessly done with a paint-brush:

Wein, gute Qualität
1 Mark 50

Instead of going straight into the kitchen, he had gone to take the notice down, and when he had finally approached Élise, he had been so pale and wooden-faced that she had recoiled.

'Listen, Désiré, it isn't my fault ... Everybody's selling it ... Schroefs advised me to, and it was him who did the notice ... His cellar is full of wine and he's afraid it might be confiscated one of these days ... He lets me have it for a mark ...'

Désiré had not eaten his dinner, had not opened his mouth. Élise had not pressed the point, and for a long time the name of Hubert Schroefs had not been spoken in the house.

While Élise was bustling about the house in the rue de la Loi, Roger, at Embourg, was running along the burning main road, his feet half buried in the dust.

He was twelve and a half. He had just finished his first year at the Collège Saint-Louis and had won several prizes. He was wearing very short trousers which revealed a pair of legs scratched by brambles, and an open-necked tussore shirt. His hair, in summer, looked fairer than ever in contrast to his sunburnt face.

He was running along at top speed, pushing a wheelbarrow in which a big girl of fifteen was roaring with laughter.

The road was deserted and a glaring white. They had already left the village behind, and at a bend where the wheelbarrow started pitching dangerously, Roger caught sight of a shapely figure, a young woman in a lace blouse and a skirt trailing in the dust, walking slowly along in the shade of a flowery parasol.

Try as he might, the obstacle attracted him, the wheelbarrow dragged him along, and it was at the feet of the startled young woman, who stepped back with a cry, that the vehicle overturned, tipping its load into the white dust.

In spite of the joy which filled him, he was going to stammer out an apology when a voice which seemed to be coming from far away, from a world which he had long ago forgotten, exclaimed in a tone of shocked indignation:

'Roger! Dear God! . . .'

He stood in amazement. The young woman was his cousin Aimée, the youngest daughter of Aunt Louisa of Coronmeuse who had passed her examination at the training college and was now teaching at the Filles de la Croix.

All the pallor and delicacy of Romanticism were to be found in her long face, which was so narrow that it was nothing but a profile. Aimée was an ethereal creature so insubstantial that she suffered agonies when circumstances obliged her to eat in front of a stranger.

And now another voice, in which deference was fighting with a violent urge to burst out laughing, said:

'Mademoiselle!'

'Renée! . . . What is the explanation of this? . . . You, here, dressed like that! . . . You in a wheelbarrow!'

They stood there, in the dazzling sunshine, in the middle of the graceful curve of the road.

'I hope that your parents do not know you indulge in this sort of amusement?'

'They've left me at Embourg for four days, Mademoiselle.

They're coming to fetch me on Sunday. I'm staying at Madame Laude's, with Roger.'

It was one of those moments when, for no particular reason, your heart leaps in your breast, when nothing else exists but the joy of living, which lifts you up, makes your eyes sparkle, burns your eyelids.

'Are you coming, Roger?'

Cousin Aimée tried to intervene.

'Where are you going?'

'To the wood!'

'Listen a moment . . .'

They both burst out laughing together as if they had given each other the cue. They could not help it. With her school dress covered with dust, Renée threw herself into the wheelbarrow, and as Roger pushed it along, his strength increased tenfold by pleasure, she lay back with her legs up in the air.

'Did you see her, Roger, did you see her?'

'She's your teacher, is she?'

'You know what we call her at the Filles de la Croix? Mademoiselle Modesty. It suits her, doesn't it? But how can she possibly be your cousin?'

They were mad. The world was theirs, the sun shone only for them, it was for them that the birds were singing, and they laughed as they looked at one another, bursting with gaiety while the shapely figure with the parasol made its undulating way towards the village church.

Leaving the wheelbarrow at the side of the ditch, they went into the wood which covered the slope along the road and connected it to the Thiers des Grillons. They ran about and played hide-and-seek. They cupped their hands and drank water from the spring, from their spring, for although they had found it only the day before, it already belonged to them. Then they noticed a big holly bush with red berries.

'Do you want some?'

'You'll prick yourself.'

'What do I care?'

To reach the biggest branches, he plunged bravely into the bush, hoisting himself up and wriggling about while Renée, her lovely lips half open and as red as holly berries, watched him, breathing hard.

397

'Come down. You've got enough.'

He wanted more, and went higher up and farther into the prickly bush. When he finally managed to disentangle himself, his legs and hands were streaked with blood and there was a long crimson gash across one cheek.

'Let me wipe you. Yes, do. Women were made to look after men.'

She was a splendid creature, a golden-skinned brunette, already mature at fifteen. Her shining black hair fell in untidy curls on to her shoulders.

'Lie down here. . . . Keep still . . .'

And, kneeling beside him, she mopped up the blood with her handkerchief, which she had soaked in the spring.

'Am I hurting you?'

'No.'

'Just a bit?'

'No.'

'It doesn't sting?'

'No.'

'You're just saying that to be brave.'

'I say it because it's true. I can't feel anything.'

'Why did you do that?'

'To get you some holly.'

'You like me?'

He blushed, felt embarrassed, made no reply. It was only inside, with his eyes shut, that he said:

'I love you.'

And then, for the first time in his life, he felt a pair of lips press against his mouth. It was so unexpected, so wonderful that tears filled his eyes, while an indistinct voice whispered in his ear:

'You like me?'

His only reply was to hold Renée's head against his with both hands, stroking her cheek with his cheek, nuzzling her black hair and breathing in its scent.

'Are you happy?'

He did not understand why she was breathing hard, why she was enveloping him so tightly with her firm body. She pressed against him from head to foot, lying on top of him, and he could feel her cool legs intertwined with his. He did not move, and blushed again, feeling ashamed. He no longer knew exactly what was happening but he would have liked it to last for a long time, for ever. An unfamiliar warmth filled him, his hands shook, above all else he was afraid that she would say something or look at him, for he felt that all the strange and wonderful things taking place within him must be visible on his face.

It was a dream. As in a dream, the sense of time disappeared, the sense of place too, and yet he could still hear the spring flowing and now and then there was a crackling sound in the undergrowth, an animal probably, a squirrel or a weasel coming to look at them. He felt hot, he was impregnated with a smell of saliva and wet skin, hair was tickling him and for a moment he had his mouth full of it, then all of a sudden he went tense, perhaps intending to cry out or to free himself. She restrained him with the pressure of her hand on his arm, biting his lip savagely as if to order him to stay still, and seconds went by, minutes perhaps, of a life which had no connexion with the life he had known before. He was frightened. He was ashamed. His lip hurt. He felt dizzy. It was too violent. It could not last another second without his going mad, and sure enough, he suddenly went stiff and lay there as if he were dead.

When at last he summoned up the courage to open his eyes, Renée, satisfied, smiled at him with her bleeding lips, and he hid his head against her chest and burst out sobbing.

How long did he stay like that? A voice murmured in his ear:

'Are you happy?'

He could only squeeze her in reply. He tried to nod his head.

'You're a little boy, aren't you? You're my own little boy.'

And it was like a little boy that, with his lip swollen from crying and a great joy, a mad pride shining through his tears, he finally said yes.

*

It was on account of those four days at Embourg, on account of the wheelbarrow, on account of that scorching morning when they had laughed so much at the prudish dismay of Cousin Aimée who had come to pay a call and been so ill rewarded, on account of Renée that, one morning, abandoning the Collège Saint-Louis and the classics, Roger had walked up the rue Saint-Gilles with the awkwardness and nervousness of a new boy, looking for the Collège Saint-Servais.

The rue Sainte-Véronique, where the institution of the Filles de la Croix was to be found, was quite close to the rue Saint-Gilles. Renée had said to him, during the last night at Embourg, when he had gone to her bedroom by climbing from one window to the other along the narrow zinc ledge over Madame Laude's café:

'Come to see me after school outside the Filles de la Croix. The maid meets me every day, but she's a girl we can fix. We'll go along the boulevard d'Avroy. In winter, it's as dark as anything along there.'

'You're sure the maid won't say anything?'

Oh yes, she was sure, all too sure, alas! But he did not know about that yet.

What a task he had had to perform in one month, before October and the beginning of term! In order to change schools, he had to give up the classics, for, while it was true that there were two colleges in the town, each was reserved for boys from one bank of the Meuse.

'Mother, I don't want to be a priest any more.'

'What's that you're saying? I bet it's Madame Laude who's put that idea into your head.'

For Madame Laude did not believe in God and was fond of making coarse jokes about the priesthood.

'It isn't Madame Laude. It isn't anybody. I just don't want to be a priest any more, I want to become an officer.'

For, like that, he would have to study science, and science was taught only at the Collège Saint-Servais. He had thought it over for a long time. He had carefully chosen a profession which did not require a costly outlay, nor a long period at university which his parents would not be able to afford.

Finally, there was the glamour of uniform and rank to which, he was well aware, his mother was extremely susceptible.

'You know perfectly well, Roger, that it isn't possible. If you don't want to be a priest any more, you won't be allowed the fifty-per-cent reduction in fees.'

'It appears that other boys have had it.'

'Who told you that?'

'Friends of mine.'

They had been to see Brother Médard and Roger had held his ground. They had paid another visit to the Dean, then to the Headmaster of the Collège Saint-Louis, then to the Collège Saint-Servais.

For a whole month, he had lived in anguish, all his energies directed towards a single objective, without ever seeing Renée, whose parents had taken her to Ostend.

The miracle had happened. He had won. The Jesuits of the rue Saint-Gilles had reduced his fees, not by half, but by a third, possibly to get rid of Élise.

'You understand, Louisa, if he hasn't got the vocation, we can't force him. There's nothing worse than a bad priest. As an officer, he'll have a safe career, and once they've won their epaulettes they've got nothing to worry about.'

The rue Saint-Gilles, at the other end of the town, was a narrow shopping street like the rue Puits-en-Sock, with the same tram rolling along between the pavements. And yet, right from the start, Roger had felt out of place there.

The first day, he had tried to go into the huge stone building flanked by a chapel where he had gone with his mother. He had lifted the bronze knocker and the noise had reverberated as if in an empty house; a long time afterwards, the door had been opened a little way into a grim corridor, and a bewildered lay brother had looked at the boy without understanding what he wanted. Then, when he had explained, the man had pointed up the street.

'The pupils' entrance is up there.'

Roger had spent a long time looking for it, refusing to believe that it was that common, badly painted door squashed between a couple of shops, which he had taken to be the entrance of a stable or a shed.

What did he care about the hostility of the setting and of all those schoolboys to whom he was a stranger? At four o'clock, he would run off towards the rue Sainte-Véronique – for she came out of school at four o'clock too, but he would take care to be one of the first out and catch up with her. He would see Renée, and all he was worried about was the maid who had to be won over; he wondered how much money would be necessary to do that.

Renée did not come home from her holidays until about 15 October. Roger had been unable to refrain from talking about her to his new schoolmates, and he refused to believe them when they all claimed to know her, clenching his fists when, at the mere mention of her name, the bigger boys exchanged winks and dug each other in the ribs.

One evening when he was galloping along behind the girls coming out of the Filles de la Croix, he felt his heart beating wildly, for it was Renée, who, in front of him, accompanied by a maid carrying her books, had just passed under a gas lamp.

She was wearing her school dress with the wide pleats, and a round, shining, uniform hat with a hard brim; there was something different about her, he could not say what, and he had been following her for some time before he realized that she had her hair up, coiled in thick plaits at the back of her neck.

She turned left, into a dark, empty street. He quickened his pace, already opening his mouth to speak to her, and trembling at the knees. When he turned the corner, the maid was walking along the kerb by herself, a little way ahead, while Renée, clinging to a man's arm, was keeping close to the houses.

*

Two years had passed since then, two years that he had been a pupil at Saint-Servais. Father Renchon had just reminded him that it was half past three, and there he was, leaving the classroom, the light from which followed him for a moment while he opened and shut the door.

He could not have said why the school, just then, reminded him so vividly of the Linière, why a whiff of his early childhood came back to him, why his head felt heavy, his limbs numb, his mind half-way between dream and reality, as when, on Thursday afternoons, he used to come home with his mother from Aunt Louisa's.

It was a winter memory for, just as they were leaving the shop with its warm, almost syrupy light, Roger always felt a certain anguish on the threshold of the dark embankment, where a fine, icy rain hung in the air like a fog.

They turned round to say a last good-bye to Aunt Louisa, who stood framed in the doorway, and perhaps also to have a last look at the reddish rectangle of the shop-window, for afterwards there was nothing but a huge, wet, mysterious world in which gas lamps surrounded by a misty halo flickered here and there. As for what there was on their left, on the far side of the terrace with the four rows of bare trees, where you could hear the waves of the swollen Meuse, that was absolute darkness, chaos, the end of the world.

They walked fast, for Élise too was in a hurry to reach the Pont Maghin and the rows of reassuring shops. Half-way home, they came to those walls of blackened brick, soaring to dizzy heights, and perforated with high, narrow windows like cathedral windows. They were not real windows with curtains and the kindly appearance of houses that are lived in; they were grey-green holes, the window-panes were made of dirty frosted glass, some of them were missing, and behind you could sense an emptiness as vast as in a church.

In that inhuman emptiness, where the light of arc-lamps swung from side to side, you could hear the noise of machines, of metals making contact, of steam hissing; Roger knew, from having seen them come out on the stroke of six, when the siren sounded, that there were thousands of girls inside, dirty, common, hatless girls from the back-streets, who bustled about endlessly, tiny creatures at the bottom of the abyss, crushed by the space above them and surrounded by mechanical monsters.

He had almost the same hard, hostile impression of the world from which he was emerging now, from which he seemed to be escaping by himself, and which a few minutes earlier, in the director of studies' office, he had thought he was leaving for good.

Wearing his wet overcoat and holding his satchel, he walked along the endless gallery in which identical windows revealed to him the same sight of bare walls, of dark coats hanging in a row, of black benches, of pupils sitting uncomfortably but motionless in the harsh light.

Beyond the iron balustrade there was the darkness of a courtyard so huge, so bare that you hesitated to venture out into it, and to reach it you had to go down a steep iron stair-case which had a factory sound.

From the staircase, and from the yard which he walked across diagonally, you could see nothing of the ordinary world. On one side there were the blank walls of the festival hall which was only rarely opened. At the far end, there was a wall as implacable as that of any prison, and on the left, the gigantic building which he had just left and which reminded him of the Linière, with its three storeys of classrooms connected by iron staircases and galleries.

How many windows could you see at once, all as bare as one another, all emitting the same cold light? Perhaps a score on each floor; he had never counted them. There was nothing to distinguish one classroom from the next, and occasionally he still made a mistake, as all the pupils did.

There were too many of the latter, over a thousand. You could not get to know all the faces, indeed you could scarcely know all the masters by sight; the pupils formed a vast crowd in which little boys in sailor suits darted in and out of the legs of young men with moustaches.

At playtime, every class, every group was obliged to find a corner somewhere for itself, so that in that strictly geometric yard, without a single tree in it or a single handful of earth, enclosed by thousands of identical bricks all carefully cemented together, there were places where Roger had never set foot, zones surrounded by an invisible frontier which were, so to speak, forbidden territory for him.

While he was walking along, hypnotized by the disheartening sight of the windows, he bumped into somebody, no, he just avoided him, a man standing all by himself in the middle of the wilderness. Roger froze, filled with an instinctive fear, but at last the usher's voice reassured him.

'Good evening, Monsieur Mamelin.'

'Good evening, Monsieur Sacré.'

There were bicycles lined up on the right, under a shed, hundreds of bicycles at rest; but Roger did not possess one and never would, for a bicycle cost far too much. He plunged into a sort of passage which grew narrower with every step. The yard finished in the form of a funnel, with two walls coming closer together, an icy archway, and finally a door, the one to which he had taken a dislike on his very first day.

Out in the street, his step became lighter; a tram was going downhill, another was coming up, and they stopped for each other at the crossroads; the shop windows were dimly lit, for fear of air-raids; in the very centre of the town, you might have thought you were in a dreary suburban street, and from a distance the big stores all looked like those poor little shops in working-class districts in which you see a few withered vegetables next to some candles, sweets and cakes of soap.

It was raining, the pavement was wet, and his shoes started taking in water; there were no shoes to be bought in the shops any more; most boys wore shoes with wooden soles, but you could not go to the Collège Saint-Servais like that, whatever Élise might say.

'At least your feet would be dry, and you needn't take any notice of what the other boys say.'

The war had been going on for three years now and for three years the glass panes of the street-lamps had been painted blue, so that they shed scarcely any light; and when, at six o'clock, the shops closed their shutters, you wandered along the streets like a ghost, pointing the dancing ray of a torch in front of you. Now and then there would be a burst of laughter, girlish laughter particularly. You would come across a couple pressed against a door or in a corner, and try your best to light up a patch of bare thigh.

Roger's face was still burning with the warmth which had invaded it in the director of studies' room. He turned right into an alleyway, to take a short cut. It was an alley-way which was out of bounds to the schoolboys, but he had never taken any notice of the ban. They were forbidden to smoke too, and it was on purpose that he filled his pipe as soon as he was out of the door.

This particular evening he was full of a vague feeling of rancour, and now and then he kicked the kerb of the pavement like a street-urchin.

He hated school. He had been almost relieved that afternoon at the prospect, frightening though it was, of being expelled, of never having to go back there; and yet now, coming out of the alley-way and crossing the boulevard d'Avroy, he envied the pupils in his class whom he had left sitting on their benches, waiting for four o'clock and listening to Father Renchon's monotonous voice.

Above all he envied the way they went off in groups, for they nearly all lived in the same districts, the rich districts of the town; their parents knew each other, had their names on brass plates, were doctors, barristers, solicitors, magistrates, industrialists; the boys talked about their maids and the seaside resorts where they went every year; they had sisters who were already young women.

In summer especially they gave an impression of radiant life when, riding nickel-plated bicycles and casually holding the handlebars with only one hand, they went off in a group, waiting for one another as they sneaked in and out of the crowds in the rue Saint-Gilles before regrouping on the shady boulevard.

No other pupil went Mamelin's way, and if by chance he heard hurried footsteps behind him, if somebody caught up with him, panting for breath, it was Neef, Neef-the-peasant of course, who accompanied him as far as the Pont d'Amercoeur where he had to catch the tram to Chênée. Roger avoided him, shook him off. However humbly poor Neef might offer him his friendship and devotion, he spurned them; he felt guilty about it sometimes, but he could not help it, he preferred his solitude to the company of the yokel in his corduroy velvet clothes.

He went along the rue Hazinelle. Already, in the shadow of the pavements, on both sides of the Girls' High School, youths and men were waiting for the girls to come out. There was a little square there with two alley-ways leading into it, and because of those figures lying in wait, because of the stories which went the rounds, because of certain scandals which the papers had reported, you felt a special sort of fever there; the walls, the doors, the few bare trees, and above all the patches of shadow did not look the same and did not smell the same as they did elsewhere.

It was rumoured that a certain number of girls from Hazinelle – some said three, others more – had been found by the police in a furnished room in the rue de la Casquette in the company of some German officers.

Every time he passed the school, Roger visualized the same

picture which he had built up out of nothing, or rather which had formed itself in his mind almost without his knowing and which he always rediscovered unchanged, with some indistinct parts, patches of shadow, and, on the other hand, excessively sharp details, as in certain photographs which schoolmates had shown him and which always produced the same feeling of uneasiness in him.

The bedroom in the rue de la Casquette looked like Mademoiselle Lola's room, but the light was green as it was in Monsieur Saft's room, and what is more the leather armchair from the drawing-room was there. One of the officers looked like Major Schorr who had a shameful disease, while the other looked like the caricatures of the Kronprinz which were circulated secretly. Of the girls, all he could see was thin, pale faces, tired eyes, pinched nostrils, and milky patches of flesh under hitched-up skirts.

He quickened his pace, crossing the busier streets as if they were rivers with fords, and constantly taking short cuts like Élise, not so much in order to save time as out of a liking for those narrow alley-ways with their lop-sided houses where tilting stones flanked the doorways and dark passages led off heaven knows where.

Now and then the sound of footsteps made him start. He was frightened, but his fear was a pleasurable fear, as when he went to serve Mass at the Bavière hospital at six o'clock in the morning. Invariably, in the winter-morning darkness, there would be somebody walking along a hundred yards behind him, and after keeping his nerves under control for a while, Roger could not restrain himself from running as fast as he could, until he finally came to a stop in the pale light of the doorway, panting for breath and clinging to the knocker.

Nearly all his memories were blurred, with ambiguous lights and mysterious glows in settings plunged in shadow. The war itself was something dark, heavy and oppressive: the cellar where they had cowered with unknown neighbours during the bombardment; the charred paper floating in the air like an infernal snow, which they had seen through the ventilators gradually covering the pavements when the municipal library in the rue des Pitteurs had gone up in flames;

then the Uhlans, the first to enter the town – it was said that they had come to parley – whom they had anxiously watched going by, seeing nothing of them but their boots; and the lamps or candles which they had had to keep alight in all the windows of every house while the troops had marched past night after night . . .

*

The rue Puits-en-Sock and the rue Jean-d'Outremeuse had changed colour, and the house in the rue de la Loi which the Mamelins had left six months before and which he scarcely recognized, struck him as narrow and dirty, without any life or personality. He was rather ashamed of it, and felt a certain malaise at the idea that it was there that he had spent the greater part of his childhood. Indeed, he blushed over his childhood itself, and it was with a feeling of repugnance that once again – he had just decided it would be the last time – he went through the green door, heedless of the brass plate on which, from his doorstep, half-shutting his sunbaked eyelids, he had once spelt out the words 'Institut Saint-André'.

The waiting-room on the right of the porch was no longer lit, to save on gas; as he went past, Roger could only just make out the mothers sitting in the damp darkness, clutching their shawls round their shoulders.

He could have sworn that there was less light in the class-room. He crossed the courtyard. He was no longer a pupil. For those sitting on the polished wooden benches, he was a big boy, almost a man. He went straight to the kitchens; the big vat of gruel had just arrived from the food-kitchens, yellow, sugary, and with a basis of maize sent by the American Red Cross.

Roger felt sick at the sight of it, and decided that he would not even eat any today. This evening, for the last time, he had not a single word or smile for the cook with the big, pear-shaped belly, common face and soiled cassock. He knew that his mother would insist that he should go on leaving school at half past three and coming to serve their extra meal to the pupils of the Institut Saint-André.

This was another idea of hers. She was obsessed by her desire to keep his strength up. Food had become so short that it had become necessary to provide supplementary rations in the schools.

In the higher classes and in the colleges, all that the pupils were given was a tiny white roll, but the little children in the primary schools were also entitled to a bowl of that gruel which Roger, with the cook's help, was carrying across to Brother Mansuy's classroom.

On the platform, it was he who filled the bowls which the queue of children held out to him one after another; he too who kept an eye on the rolls which they took afterwards from a basket.

In return for this service, when he had finished doling out the rations in every classroom, he was entitled to as much gruel as he could eat and to three or four rolls, for there were always a few children absent and ill.

Never again would he taste that warm, sticky, ugly yellow paste with which he had sometimes filled his stomach until he could not breathe. It was a sort of revenge he was taking.

He would never come back to the rue de la Loi. He would come out of school at the same time as the others. He was going to tell his mother so straight away. He had already told Brother Médard, blushing as he did whenever he told a lie.

'Father Renchon is afraid that my missing lessons, sometimes important lessons, may affect my studies.'

Lord, how dark the school was, and on the green walls, on the shelves, on the desks, how old-fashioned things looked: the measuring-jars for instance, and the maps which had turned almost brown, and the glossy pictures, printed in Leipzig, which showed the seasons. Roger felt a pang as he looked at the one of winter, with the fair in a little town, the man in the bottle-green coat and the girl with the sledge, which had remained in the same position ever since he had left school.

He would have liked to be sure that it was really over, that he would never come back. In the yard he breathed in for the last time the smell of the slate-roofed lavatories, and in one corner he caught sight of the pale sink and the tap to which, in his capacity as Brother Médard's pet, he had held the key.

It was no longer his street, or his district. He crossed the Pont d'Amercoeur, which they had never crossed in the old days except to go once a year to the Robermont cemetery, turned left, and went along a shabby boulevard lined with little houses, warehouses and strips of waste ground.

The district humiliated him. It was almost on a par with Bressoux, where the little street-urchins came from who used to invade the place du Congrès and whom the mothers tried in vain to drive away. And if their house on the corner of the rue des Maraîchers was a handsome one, too handsome and too big for them, it was by chance, almost by charity that they were in it.

Anybody would think that Élise was unable to live like other people, that there was a spell on her. How had she come by this house which had previously been an important post office? She never gave a satisfactory answer to this sort of question, and you always felt there was something suspicious behind it all. In this case an old doctor, who lived by himself in the house opposite and had been given the task of finding a tenant, had accepted a derisory rent for the duration of the war.

There would be a scene, on account of the rolls. For seeing that Roger could eat as much maize gruel as he liked, Brother Médard's rolls were shared out among the family.

As was his habit, Roger repeated as he walked along the phrases he was going to use.

'I'm not going to help any more at the Institut Saint-André.'

And when his mother asked why not? Would he lie as he had done to Brother Médard? Instead he felt a spiteful urge to state flatly:

'Because I don't want to.'

'Why don't you want to?'

'Because I want to stay at school until four o'clock like the others.'

If his mother insisted too much, he would tell her that he was tired of being a beggar.

He was impatient to be home, imagining that he could already breathe the scent of battle which was going to invade the kitchen whose light he could glimpse as he came round the corner.

He turned the key in the lock, put his satchel down and hung his overcoat on the hallstand. Hullo, there was somebody there!

Hanging on one of the brass hooks he saw a woman's coat which he had never seen before and, on top of it, a little old woman's hat with a purple flower.

He frowned, suspicious, jealous of their tranquillity. Pushing open the kitchen door, his mouth already half open to ask a question, he bumped into his mother, who had got up suddenly with a smile which he knew very well, the sweetest smile she could summon up.

'May I introduce my son, Mademoiselle Rinquet. My Roger who's just come home from the Collège Saint-Servais, where he's studying to become an officer. Come in, Roger. Just imagine, Mademoiselle Rinquet, who is a retired postmistress, is going to live here with us.'

And she smiled more than ever, turning towards Désiré's armchair where a sharp-eyed little old woman was sitting darning a black woollen stocking.

'Well, aren't you going to say good evening to Mademoiselle Rinquet? It's a surprise for him, Mademoiselle. I hadn't mentioned it to either my husband or my son. But you'll see, you'll be one of the family straight away.'

Chapter Three

They had come together accidentally, as they did every now and then, on Sunday morning at Aunt Cécile's. In the old days Désiré used to say:

'I'm going home.'

Or else they went to the rue Puits-en-Sock. Nowadays, they went to Cécile's, even though Chrétien Mamelin was still there. He took up less space than he used to, his tall figure seemed to have shrunk, and people sometimes started when he appeared in front of them, he made so little noise.

Out of habit, everybody still dropped into the kitchen for a moment, where the smell had changed slightly, had gone sour, on account of Cécile's three little children. It was for their sake too, in order to keep an eye on them in summer when they were playing in the yard, that the coloured paper had been scratched from one of the window-panes.

Cécile was ill. For the first time, that morning, they had found a stranger doing the housework and the cooking, a strapping girl who was a maid at Gruyelle-Marquant's, and all the Mamelin sons were shocked to see her cooking the Sunday stew.

Cécile, wrapped in a shawl, was sitting by the cooker, and when Lucien came in, or Arthur, or Désiré, she explained all over again how it had come over her, lifting her dress up to show her swollen ankles, which were an unhealthy white.

She was disconsolate rather than worried. It was her enforced inactivity which was undermining her and making her feel ashamed. She kept an eye and an ear on everything and followed all the maid's movements; but it seemed to her that everything was going wrong, and she suffered physically at seeing a strapping girl of twenty-two incapable of dressing children properly.

To cheer her up, everybody teased her, Désiré like the others, in his booming voice.

'Hullo, all! Well, Cécile, how are you? Admit that you just wanted to have a little rest. Hullo, so you're here, Roger!'

Désiré, who had just come out of High Mass at Saint-Nicolas, warmed his hands over the saucepans, breathing in their aroma.

'I say, everybody, guess what we're going to have for dinner. You first, Cécile . . . No, you'll never guess. Will she, Roger? Chips, yes, chips! Just imagine, yesterday, at the office, a country client for whom I'd performed a few little services brought me a couple of pounds of potatoes. You can't find them even at fifteen francs a pound in the shops. When I opened the parcel at home, Roger nearly cried. Then I said to Élise:

' "We're going to do something silly, but never mind! It will take our ration of lard, but tomorrow we must have chips for dinner." '

They had gone on chattering a little longer, about this and that, each in his corner, warm and snug, and finally Cécile ended up by forgetting that all the housework was going wrong.

'Coming, son?'

They went home together, walking at the same pace. It was

bitterly cold. That morning, they had had to use the handle of a hammer to break the layer of ice which had formed during the night in the china jugs.

'Cécile doesn't look at all well,' observed Désiré, who had a marked predilection for his younger sister. 'When you've a minute to spare during the week, you ought to drop in on her to say hullo.'

He spoke to his son as man to man. They understood one another. They both knew that Cécile's husband, Marcel, was a brute of a man, bursting with health, who could not imagine that his wife might be seriously ill.

'A cigarette, son?'

The gesture touched Roger, that familiar gesture of the father offering his cigarette-case quite naturally to his son as he would to a friend. Then, walking along side by side, they both thought about something else, the same thing; they wanted to talk about it but hesitated.

It was a grey morning, a hard, biting grey. They both felt the same repugnance for the Pont d'Amercoeur which would always remain unfamiliar to them, and for the shabby boulevard which led to their new house and to which they found it hard to get accustomed.

Mademoiselle Rinquet had spoilt their Sunday morning, the first she had spent in their house. Admittedly it was very cold indeed. The thermometer, when they had got up, had been several degrees below freezing. They had gone downstairs before washing, as they did every Sunday. Standing at the foot of the stairs, Élise had called out:

'Mademoiselle Rinquet! Breakfast is ready!'

However much they poked the fire, you had to stand right up against it to feel a little heat.

'She doesn't answer. I hope she isn't ill.'

Élise had gone upstairs, and they had heard her talking through the door.

'She doesn't want to come downstairs. She says she isn't going to get up until I've lit a fire in her room.'

'I trust you're not going to do anything of the sort?'

Élise had hesitated. If she had been on her own, she would undoubtedly have given in.

'Come now. As it is we haven't enough coal for the kitchen,

heaven knows when they're going to issue any more, and you'd go and light a fire in that woman's room?'

'She's an old woman, Désiré.'

'That isn't a reason for using up all our stocks.'

They had eaten in silence. They had cut the bread into four parts and weighed them on the scales, and, as happened every morning, each person had received his ration for the day.

'Take the biggest piece, Désiré. Yes, do. You go out to work. You need it most.'

'No, I don't. Roger does, because he's still growing.'

They had still been at table when Mademoiselle Rinquet had come downstairs. They had scarcely been able to believe their eyes, the sight had been so unexpected. It must have been on purpose that she had not put her false teeth in, so that she had no mouth and the lower part of her face was just something slack and ugly; on the top of her head, which was practically bald, there was a tiny bun, aggressively black, and, to cap all, she was wrapped in a flannelette dressing-gown of a hideous purple colour.

'Come and warm yourself by the fire, Mademoiselle Rinquet.'

'I've never been in a house as cold as this. If I'd known . . .'

'No, Mademoiselle. It's cold everywhere. Just look at the thermometer outside. You know perfectly well that nobody has had any coal for three months.'

'You've got some in the cellar. I've seen it.'

'We've got very little, the bare minimum, and I won't tell you all the trouble we had getting it.'

They had given her Désiré's place by the fire. She had examined her piece of bread, and had got up to weigh it suspiciously.

It had been the same for everything. The stove, for instance, held only three firebricks. The night before, she had taken two of them just for herself, as if she had been entitled to them: Élise and Désiré had had to go without.

Even when she was not hungry any more, when it was obvious that she had had enough, she went on eating spitefully, down to the very last mouthful, to be absolutely certain that she had had the whole of her share.

And Élise had gone on pressing her!

'A bit more soup, Mademoiselle Rinquet. Yes, go on. I assure you there's enough. I'm not hungry any more.'

They would have to give her some chips, some of those miraculous chips which they had not had for a year and which they had been thinking about all the time since the previous day. At the very idea, Roger went pale with anger.

Meanwhile, all morning, nobody had known where to settle. Without washing, without giving herself even a cat's lick, without putting in her false teeth, and smelling horrible in her purple flannelette, the old woman had stayed glued to the cooker, so that Élise had found it difficult to reach her saucepans and keep an eye on her fire.

Usually it was the best time in the week. You hung about; you waited for some hot water to have a wash; you wandered aimlessly round the house until it was time to go to Mass; Désiré hammered in a nail or mended something.

Roger had preferred to go out and roam through the cold and practically deserted streets. He had heard a bit of Mass at Saint-Remacle, he had wandered round the market in the place Delcour, and then he had gone to sit down at Aunt Cécile's.

His father, now that they were on their way home, knew so well what he was thinking that he murmured:

'You'd better not say anything, for your mother's sake.'

Then he added – and this touched Roger much more:

'She thinks she's doing the right thing.'

That was all. There must be no more talk about that subject.

'What are you doing this afternoon?'

'I don't know yet.'

'Is there anything to read at home?'

'Some Eugène Sue.'

For Roger went twice a week to borrow some books from the municipal library in the rue des Chiroux (the one in the rue des Pitteurs had gone up in flames the day the Germans had shot three hundred people) and from a lending library in the rue Saint-Paul. He chose books he liked. In the evening, or on Sunday, Désiré would read one of these books, haphazardly, and if his son took it back before he had finished it, he might never know the end.

That was what the two of them were like.

'You'll see,' Roger could not help sighing when they reached the door, 'the old hag will fill her plate with chips. And Mother will say to her' (here he imitated Élise's sugary servility):

' "Take a bigger helping than that, Mademoiselle Rinquet. Help yourself. I'm not very fond of chips." '

He could have wept at the thought and Désiré, letting him go in front after opening the door, put his hand on his shoulder for a moment as if to remind him:

'She thinks she's doing the right thing.'

The air was a bluish colour inside the house, as it used to be on Sundays before the war, and they could hear the fat singing in the heavy iron saucepan which they had not seen for such a long time. Élise, her cheeks burning hot, shouted:

'Leave the door open for a minute, to let the smoke out!'

Then she went to the foot of the stairs to call out:

'Mademoiselle Rinquet! You can come down now. It's ready.'

*

There had been no avoiding the usual wretched discussion.

'What do you want to do, Désiré?'

'You decide. We'll do whatever you like.'

'You really want to go out?'

And Mademoiselle Rinquet was there, motionless, silent, her eyes popping out of her head, the head of a bird of ill-omen. She had eaten as many chips as she could swallow, looking as if she were defying Roger who could not take his eyes off her plate. While Élise was doing the washing-up, she was more in the way than ever; everything would have gone more smoothly if only she had moved back a few inches, and they tried discreetly to make her understand this; she obviously understood all right, but she would stay where she was just to annoy them, especially Désiré and Roger whom she could not stand.

'Where should we go? To Louisa's at Coronmeuse?'

The truth was that Désiré wanted to stay and read beside the fire, in his usual place, in his armchair which the lodger had taken over, and he wondered, without daring to ask her, whether she intended to stay there the whole afternoon.

'Are you going out, Roger?'

'Yes, Mother.'

'Would you come with us if we went to say hullo to Aunt Louisa?'

'No.'

This would go on for an hour at least and he preferred to make his escape before he was utterly disgusted. He went up to his room and started washing all over again, in spite of the cold. That morning, looking at himself in a shop-window in the rue Entre-deux-Ponts, he had had the impression that his collar did not suit him. He changed his tie three times, and tip-toed into his parents' bedroom to get the bottle of 'Floramye', with which he drenched his handkerchief. He even passed his perfumed fingers over his cheeks and round his lips. He was ready. A cold sun had pierced the blanket of white clouds. Roger went downstairs and, on account of the scent, just opened the kitchen door a little way.

'See you this evening.'

'Roger, listen . . .'

He took care not to listen and slammed the street door behind him so that the noise echoed right through the house. He had caught a glimpse of his father in slippers, his pipe alight, an Eugène Sue in one hand, looking for somewhere to sit. Their eyes had met and Désiré, no doubt with a heavy heart, had murmured:

'Enjoy yourself.'

Roger knew that he would not enjoy himself. How and why should he enjoy himself? With whom? He had already crossed the Pont d'Amercoeur and walked along the rue Puits-en-Sock, and he was crossing the Meuse by the Passerelle when most people were still lingering at table. He was always too early, wherever he went, as if he were afraid of missing the tiniest morsel of a potential pleasure. For what pleasure could he find, with nothing in his pocket but his Sunday fifty centimes, plus his grandfather's ritual ten centimes?

Though he had eaten very little, the chips weighed heavily on his stomach, because they were no longer used to them and because he had been tense with irritation while eating them. He stopped in front of the shop-windows, not so much to look at the packets of cigarettes as to make sure there was nothing wrong with his appearance. He was obsessed by the idea of looking ridiculous. Often he eyed passers-by, trying to discover what effect he was producing on them.

Youths of his age, especially if they were at college, wore breeches which were tight at the knee and laced or buttoned down the side of the leg like riding-breeches. To look smart, your stockings had to be made of thick mottled wool and have a wide border with a coloured pattern. But his stockings, which Élise had had made for him by the old Chaineux sisters because they would never wear out, were a dull grey with two stripes of a darker grey. His breeches were grey too, and his jacket black.

'It's the loveliest cloth there is!' declared his mother.

Perhaps it was. He was dressed in remnants bought in the sales. Cortleven, Élise's cousin, who was a cutter in a dress-shop, had never managed to make him a suit which looked like other people's suits; there was always something skimpy and amateurish about his work.

It irritated Roger. Twice that day he had polished his shiny-toed shoes and rearranged the parting in his hair; and in front of every shop-window he changed the slant of his hat slightly, put a glove on, then took it off, and asked himself whether they were not too yellow for the season. They were glacé kid gloves which he had found in one of his father's drawers and which the latter had worn before his marriage.

It was half past one and naturally there was nobody yet at the Carré. That was what people called the rue de la Cathédrale, the busiest and smartest shopping-street in the town, or rather one end of it, between the rue de l'Université and the boulevard d'Avroy, where, in the evening and on Sunday afternoons, the crowd moved slowly backwards and forwards like a procession.

Everything was ugly in his eyes; for things as much as for people he had a hard, hostile look which held a threat in it; and sometimes he formulated that threat in an undertone, while looking at himself in a shop window to judge the expression on his face.

'I shall run away.'

Whom was he going to punish by setting off for heaven knows what fate? Was it the shop-window in which he was studying his reflection, probably the ugliest and most depressing shop-window in the town, that of a photographer who specialized in identity-card photographs? In the acid-yellow frame of the shop, you could see hundreds of strips of proofs in grey and black, and on every strip the same face was repeated a dozen times, the same lop-sided noses, the same weak or stubborn chins, the same frightened eyes, a horrifying world, a nightmarish race which you never saw in the street and which seemed unbelievable.

'People are ugly, life is stupid. Lord, how stupid it is!'

It was fantastic to think, for instance, that at home his father and mother would still be discussing what they would do with their afternoon, under Mademoiselle Rinquet's poisonous gaze. They knew perfectly well what they would do. They would do precisely nothing. They would go on talking about it for another hour. Élise would start becoming irritable. At a certain moment, Désiré, deep in his book, would fail to answer her, she would reproach him with having no consideration for her feelings, with being nothing but a man, and, if it was one of her bad days, there would be a scene, tears, nervous spasms, Élise would go up to her icy room and throw herself on the bed, and Désiré would go to fetch her.

'No, leave me alone, will you? And all that in front of other people! Somebody who's only just arrived and who has to be treated to scenes like that . . .'

She would end up by rinsing her eyes, and going downstairs, and making an effort to smile at Mademoiselle Rinquet.

'You don't feel cold, Mademoiselle? You wouldn't like a cup of malt to warm you up? I can make you some in a few minutes . . .'

The three of them would stay there, each one encrusted in his little parcel of space, with every now and then a 'poof' from the stove, the rustle of a page of Désiré's book, the clatter of a knitting needle falling on the floor.

'Leave it, Mademoiselle, I'll pick it up for you.'

And they called that living! Roger was living too. He walked along between the rows of shops, most of which had their shutters up, glaring angrily at the shop-signs, at certain all-too-familiar names in big black and brown letters, and looking at the shivering figures disappearing into the theatres. Since he had noticed a fortnight before that his thick overcoat fitted him badly, he had worn it open, with one hand in his trousers pocket, for he was proud of his riding-breeches which nobody would see otherwise.

It did not matter greatly that there was nobody there to see him. He needed to make an impression on himself. He didn't succeed. He knew that there were a hundred little details wrong; he had stuck in his tie-pin too high up; he changed its position, but now it was askew, and the street was still empty, with the waiters standing dreaming behind the steamy panes of the cafés and taverns.

He would run away and never, never would he live like his father and mother, he promised himself that; nothing would be allowed into his existence which might remind him of his childhood.

He hated that childhood. He hated the rue de la Loi, the rue Pasteur, the Institut Saint-André and the Collegè Saint-Servais; he hated Brother Médard and Madame Laude, and all the ugly, petty little things in everyday life which hurt him. He was determined to get his revenge, he did not know how as yet, but he would get it, he was certain of that; and he was thinking about it while his hand, in his pocket, was turning over the dozen sous whose destination he knew in advance.

In a narrow side-street, the rue Lulay, he could hear the bell of a cinema, the first cinema which had been opened in the town a few years before. Roger had been to look at the col-oured posters showing pictures of cowboys, but it was not to that cinema that he intended to go a little later, for it too brought back humiliating memories.

When he was smaller, he used to go there on Thursday after-noons. He had not enough money to pay for a seat, but the lessee, in return for a couple of sous, and sometimes just one, used to let a few little boys in to fill up the front row, where nobody wanted to sit and which, if it was left empty, made a bad impression. If too many people came along, then of course he turned the boys out!

He was going to go to the Mondain in the rue de la Régence, where a wave of hot air met you at the door and there were armchairs upholstered in pearl-grey and boxes as well. There again he would suffer; all he could afford would be a seat in the front rows. The last time he had been there, his cousin

Germaine Schroefs, who had her father's thick features, had gone past him in a grey coat; he had recognized her in the light of the usherette's torch as she was being shown to the reserved seats.

The atmosphere of the cinema, the darkness crossed by a pencil of white light, the pictures jumping about on the screen, the strumming of the piano accompaniment, and the warm, invisible crowd which you could feel around you, always produced a sort of fever in him. All his desires and ambitions were exacerbated and multiplied tenfold or a hundredfold; he longed to experience everything at once; and this immense appetite finally took the form of anxious, furtive glances at the boxes. He knew what happened inside them, because some of the boys at school had told him; in any case, you only had to walk past them as if you were looking for a seat to catch a glimpse of curiously contorted couples, to make out skirts hitched up and hands feeling around. He could have sworn that the boxes in which these furtive embraces took place gave off a special smell which reminded him of the smell of the Carré at a certain stage of the evening.

For soon the Carré would be living its real life, or at least the life for which Roger was there hours in advance. When the last shutters had been put up, when night had fallen, when the street-lamps were nothing but vague landmarks, the shadows would gradually come to life, peopled with loud or furtive footsteps, with half-glimpsed silhouettes, with laughs and whispers.

Groups of girls came along on purpose, to walk arm-in-arm in the propitious darkness, and bands of students teased them, pursued them and sometimes went off with them.

Other women walked by themselves, very slowly, close to the walls, stopping frequently; as they passed, you could catch a whiff of scent, and in their wake there was nearly always a man with his coat-collar turned up.

Roger brushed past them, heavy hearted. He did not know exactly what he wanted. It was not always the same thing. He felt hot all over just at the sight of the milky globes which, in the back-streets, served as signs for certain hotels into which couples slipped furtively. The door, more often than not, opened into a stinking corridor, but this very vulgarity made him giddy; he pictured to himself the grubby beds, the tattered wallpaper, and a broken-down, stained divan; he saw, he wanted to see a woman with ringed eyes, tired lips, and a frail body gradually undressing, sadly and disgustedly, in the ambiguous light.

How happy he would be to weep with her, to writhe in despair, flesh against flesh, before plunging into pleasure!

But no! What he would really like would be to push open the well-oiled revolving doors of one of those cafés from which you could always hear music coming, an elegant, nonchalant figure with a woman on his arm, to look around disdainfully for a free table, and to summon the waiter with a blasé gesture.

'What would you like, Monsieur?'

Then to hold out to his companion, who would be busy slipping her fur coat off her shoulders, a cigarette-case, a handsome cigarette-case in gold or silver, to look at people from a great distance, from a great height, as if he could not see them, to smile imperceptibly, to place his hand casually on his mistress's knee, to behave towards her in such a manner – lovers had a special way of smiling at each other which was at once tender, grateful and affectionate – to behave towards her in such a manner that everybody could tell by looking at them that they had just left the damp sheets where they had exhausted all the joys which the flesh could give.

Why, to put it bluntly, wasn't it he who was standing in that dark doorway, mouth to mouth with a woman of whom all he could see as he passed was a vague profile, a fixed gaze.

One evening, perhaps, he would pluck up the courage to speak to Sidonie. For weeks now he had been haunting the Carré in the hope of meeting her by herself. He knew her Christian name because everybody knew it; youths murmured it in the darkness when she went by arm-in-arm with a girl-friend, recognizable by her toque and her imitation ermine muff; others, street-urchins this time, sang it to the music of popular tunes.

She was only sixteen, a slim girl with a diaphanous face; her eyes were so bright that you could have sworn that the pupils were transparent, and for him she was the incarnation of all that was fragile and feminine in humanity. She had had lovers, he wanted her to have had lovers. He had seen her with her girl-friend and some men walking gaily into a restaurant. They had been men and not youths. Everybody knew what men expected. He had met her in the company of German officers with long capes, trailing their swords along the pavements.

Yet he felt that she was pure, he wanted her to be pure, while imagining her frail white body being soiled by friends of a day; he for his part would love her, love her with his very soul, and they would walk along side by side, clasped together, cheek to cheek, without saying a word, listening to an inner music; now and then their lips would meet and a new life would begin.

'What are you doing here, Mamelin?'

He was not doing anything. He was thinking, while looking at the cigars in a window-display; no doubt he was looking at his own reflection too. Brought suddenly face to face with Gouin, he had a certain difficulty in removing the fierce expression from his face.

'I'm not doing anything, you can see that. I was waiting until it was time to go to the cinema.'

Gouin was a year or two older than he. They had not met for years, not since they had been at the Institut Saint-André together.

Now he was wearing long trousers, yellow shoes such as only flashy businessmen wore, a pearl-grey hat and a big, comfortable coat, and one hand was toying with a Malacca cane. Roger envied his self-assurance. He was a big fellow, with firm flesh and tight, pink skin.

'You remember the rue de la Loi? Incidentally, what are you doing these days?'

'I'm at the Collège Saint-Servais. And you?'

'I'm helping my father in the business.'

Gouin senior was a pork-butcher at Bressoux. Since the beginning of the war, this had become the most profitable trade there was.

'Look here, Mamelin, I'm meeting a couple of tarts at three o'clock. I'm on my own. Why don't you come along with us? You could look after the girl-friend.'

'Where are you going?'

'To the cinema for a start. What do you say? In a box, you can begin having a bit of fun.'

A flush had spread right over Roger's face.

'The trouble is . . .'

'What?'

'I've come out without bringing enough money.'

At that, Gouin burst out laughing, slapped him hard on the back, and took a handful of banknotes out of his pocket, marks and francs, both large and small denominations.

'Look! If that's all that's worrying you, I'll pay for everything. Or rather, take this . . .'

He thrust some banknotes into his hand, without counting them.

'It's easy for me, you see; I scrounge a ham from the shop every now and then and sell it. I took one only yesterday, a lovely ham that weighed twenty-four pounds.'

He did not notice that Roger, who had been red in the face a moment earlier, had gone pale, more taken aback by the good-natured simplicity with which the words had been spoken than by the words themselves.

'You're sure I wouldn't be in the way?'

'Idiot! I tell you, they're just a couple of tarts! Afterwards, we'll find somewhere to do them up and that'll be that. Let's go. They must be waiting for us already on the corner of the rue du Pont-d'Ile.'

*

He had gone with Gouin. For a moment, in the rue du Pont-d'Ile, he had nearly backed out when he had recognized one of the girls waiting there, for it was Sidonie's girl-friend. The other one, whom he could see from behind, was tall and fat. She was the one Gouin had picked for himself.

'My pal Roger, Mesdemoiselles Jeanne and Camille . . . That's how to do it, isn't it?'

Gouin had added in front of them, quite naturally:

'Camille's yours. And now, let's go and have some fun!'

He had walked in front with the fat girl while Roger had followed silently beside the short little thing with the round, common face. She was really tiny. What is more, she was too

developed for her age, and this helped to make her look like
a dwarf.

'Where are we going?' she had asked, just to say something,
seeing how shy he looked.

'I think we're going to the Mondain.'

'Is he a friend of yours?'

Embarrassed by the question, he had answered:

'I went to school with him.'

'I live behind their house. It's my mother who does their
washing.'

The sun had already disappeared, the streets were a cold
grey, and the cinema bell was ringing. They went in, and had
to wait some time before an empty box could be found for
them.

Not for a moment did Roger feel at ease. In front
of him, Gouin and his companion whispered, talked and
laughed so loud that people turned round and hushed
them.

'All right, back there?'

He replied:

'All right.'

But he was thinking about the stolen ham, and about Camille's mother who did people's washing like the woman who
came to the rue de la Loi every week. It was Camille who ended
up by timidly putting her hand, which was already moist, on
his.

'Don't you like me?'

He reassured her, at the same time thinking of what Gouin
had said.

'Afterwards, we'll find somewhere to do them up . . .'

And the little thing, doing all she could to break the ice,
murmured:

'I know you already. I know where you live: that lovely
house on the corner of the rue des Maraîchers. I go past it nearly
every day. In summer I used to see you reading in your room,
smoking your pipe, with your feet on the window-sill, and I
used to call you the young man who was always reading. Then
when I was out with Sidonie, we used to see you at the Carré.
But you're such a proud one. You never talk to anybody. You're
always so smart and well dressed! The other day you nearly

knocked us over and Sidonie was ever so annoyed that you didn't even look at us.'

'Was she really?'

In spite of the piano accompaniment, you could still hear the shrill ringing of the bell outside, you thought of the blue light over the padded door, and you could also hear the insect noise being made by the film as it unwound. People came in and others went out. Roger could feel sweat under his armpits and Camille's hand lying soft and moist in his. The dwarf cuddled up to him, and for the sake of appearances, so as not to hurt her, for he could feel that she would like it, he put his arm round her waist.

It embarrassed him that she should smell of poverty. For a long time he wondered whether to kiss her or not. He did not want to, indeed he felt a certain repugnance at the thought, but she placed one hand on his thigh and then contact was established. His hands moved too, searching for the bare skin above the stockings, then moving imperceptibly upwards into the warmth.

The other two were doing the same in front of them; you could see that from their positions, from a certain sort of tense immobility which suddenly came over them. Roger was awkwardly placed. His shoulder became stiff, his arm got tired, and when he turned towards his companion he saw, in the pale halo of the screen, a little round, attentive head, with a pair of eyes following the incidents in the film as if nothing were happening nearer to her.

Finally he asked a question.

'Why isn't Sidonie with you today?'

'What! You mean to say you don't know? I bet you're the only one at the Carré who hasn't heard. The police have been looking into it. It was the night before last, and Sidonie couldn't come out today because her dress was torn and her sister's mending it. She's a dressmaker, you know.'

She broke off for a moment to whisper:

'Careful. You're hurting me a bit.'

Then she went on, quite naturally:

'A couple of chaps had asked us to supper in a fried-fish shop, in the rue Lulay, profiteers they were, country types all dressed up, like you see on Mondays at the Stock Exchange with their pockets full of money. We'd decided to make fun of them. We began by having a good blow-out, ordering the best there was, Russian salad, lobster, steak. We were on the first floor, in the little private room, you know . . .'

No, he didn't know, he had never suspected that there were private rooms in fried-fish shops.

'We drank a lot, English beer, champagne, wine, then some more English beer. The fellows with us were drunk. Sidonie was sick. Then, instead of looking after her, they decided to have some fun and they took it into their heads to undress Sidonie who didn't want them to and swore at them and struggled. The bigger of the two, a man as red-faced as a butcher, with big fishy eyes, had already undone his buttons and started trying to . . .'

Her girl-friend, without turning round, remarked:

'Don't talk so loud, Camille. The people in the next box are listening.'

And to Gouin, who asked her what she was talking about, she said:

'I'll tell you. I wasn't there, but Sidonie told me all about it.'

In defending herself, Sidonie had cut her elbow on a broken bottle. Camille, seeing the blood, had lost her head and rushed down stairs, calling for help. The proprietor had intervened, trying in vain to calm down the two frantic girls.

'No scandal now, girls! I'll see to it all. In any case, if you came here, you must have known that it wasn't for a knitting-party.'

They were drunk and went on shouting for the police at the top of their voices. Some customers on the ground floor became alarmed and sent for a policeman.

Gouin promptly hit upon the idea of going to have supper after the film in the same private room.

'That would be fun, eh, Mamelin?'

But Camille objected.

'The proprietor won't let me in. He was livid. He even went so far as to offer us some money to keep quiet.'

'You were a couple of idiots!' said her girl-friend.

'I told you we were *schlass*. And then, after all, not with brutes like that!'

It made Roger feel ill. Try as he might, he could not banish from his eyes the picture of the private room as he imagined it, Sidonie half-naked and bleeding, the man with the face like a butcher's, and finally the policeman who did not know what to do and took them away.

He wanted to go home. If he had not been there on Gouin's money – the ham money! – and if he had not had some of that money in his pocket, he would have found some sort of excuse and gone off.

'I say, you kids, I think this is the film we saw when we came in. Let's go!'

They went. Some worthy people, who must have heard more than enough, raised a murmur of protest as they passed. They were swallowed up, still warm, by the icy darkness, and it took them a little while to find their bearings, to remember that they were in the rue de la Régence, that the place Verte was on the right and the Passerelle on the left.

'What are we going to do now?'

Just as at the Mamelins' when they argued for hours on end how they were going to spend Sunday afternoon! They walked along, without knowing where they were going, Gouin in front with his girl, Roger with Camille hanging on to his arm.

'Let's decide what we're going to do. You're sure they won't let you into the rue Lulay shop?'

'In any case, I'm not going to try. You go ahead if you want to.'

'And you, Mamelin, what do you suggest?'

The fact of the matter, Roger suspected, was that his companion no longer wanted anything, that the pleasures taken in the darkness of the cinema had satisfied him. He had lost the noisy gaiety he had displayed a little earlier. It was without any great conviction that he suggested having fun, because he had promised this to himself and to the others. It was only six o'clock.

'What if we started by having a drink?'

But Roger was reluctant to show himself in a café in the company of his little badly dressed dwarf who was wearing round her neck a flabbergasting boa with dirty feathers.

It was Jeanne, the fat girl, who saved him by whispering to Gouin. He could not hear what she said, but he guessed what it was.

'Let 'em go off on their own. He's no fun, your pal isn't. We can't do nothing with him.'

Of the two couples, probably only Gouin and Camille envisaged the projected foursome without any embarrassment. For Roger, the story of the evening in the rue Lulay had been enough. With the best will in the world, he couldn't have managed.

'She says you might perhaps like to . . .'

'She's right. Besides, I've got to get home early. My parents are expecting me.'

'See you next Sunday?'

'Right.'

They did not specify where they were going to meet. It was better that way. They shook hands. Gouin asked in a whisper:

'Fixed it?'

Roger nodded, even though both of them knew that it was not true. Then he came back and thrust into his friend's pocket the banknotes Gouin had given him.

'What are you doing?'

'Nothing . . . Have a good time . . .'

Camille went with him, hanging on to his arm, and trying in vain to keep in step with him. In the darkness they walked through the streets like the couples he had envied so much, and because of that, just as they were starting to cross the Passerelle, the idea occurred to him of taking his companion to the deserted embankment and there, in a dark corner, possessing her completely.

'What are you stopping for?'

Yes? No? Should he? If he took her, he would have to kiss her on the mouth and the idea disgusted him. He was frightened too of the cold, and of the complicated movements he would have to make. And what if, the next day, in broad daylight, she spoke familiarly to him in the street and perhaps kissed him in front of everybody? What is more, she would be sure to tell Sidonie all about it.

No.

'I have to go home. They really are expecting me.'

'You don't mind if I go with you as far as your house, do you? It's on my way.'

In the rue Puits-en-Sock, they went past his grandfather's

429

shop, but the shutters were up and everything was dark.

'Anyone can see straight away that you aren't the same sort as your friend. I bet you haven't been out very often with him.'

'Why?'

'Oh, nothing. They must have gone to an hotel. Jeanne felt embarrassed, I could see that, even though it wouldn't have been the first time she'd done that in front of me. It was you that was embarrassing her.'

He pretended to laugh. He felt flattered.

'Am I as terrifying as all that?'

'No. But if anybody had told me yesterday that the two of us would be getting together, I wouldn't have believed them. Neither would Sidonie.'

'Are you going to tell her?'

'Not if you ask me not to.'

'Then don't tell her.'

'You're in love with her, aren't you?'

He did not answer.

'Go on, admit that you're in love with her. All the men are in love with Sidonie. I'm not jealous. I can tell the difference, you know, and if you wanted . . .'

'You think so?'

'I'm sure you'd get on well together. Do you want me to speak to her?'

This time, he clasped her to him without needing to make any effort, bent down and kissed her on her cheek.

'You think I've got a chance?'

'You realize that that's the first time you've kissed me?'

'Ah!'

'Just because I spoke to you about Sidonie. Come to the Carré on Thursday.'

'What time?'

'Between five and six, as usual. I'll signal to you. If I flash my torch at you several times when you come near us, then it's yes . . .'

'And what if it's no?'

'I tell you it's sure to be yes.'

Had he even said good night to her? He could not remember how he had left her, but now he was back home again. Here, in the few cubic feet of warmth and light of the kitchen, he had found each person in his place, frozen and set in the immobility of the atmosphere like the inhabitants of Pompeii in the lava, his father sitting reading with his chair tilted back, Mademoiselle Rinquet knitting and counting the stitches with soundlessly moving lips, and his mother doing her mending, her head bent forward.

Just to say something, and despite the fact that the table was laid for supper, he asked the traditional question:

'Supper ready?'

And for a few moments he felt the palpitations of an insubstantial life which was that of the house, of that house and no other; he became conscious of something like the nibbling of time – and it was not simply the tick-tock of the alarm-clock on the mantelpiece: the stove had a breath all its own and so had the big white enamel kettle with the dent in its swan-necked spout. The air enveloped him, touched him; he felt it as if it were something with its own density, its own temperature, its own sweetness, perhaps its own intentions; it closed over him and gleams of light flickered like signals on the candlestick, on a cup decorated with flowers, on the red copper saucepan. To begin with, it was rather painful when you came from outside, but then Roger gently adjusted himself to this mysterious rhythm and regained his calm.

Chapter Four

'And for Monsieur Mamelin,' said Raoul jokingly, 'I suppose it will be a Titus cut?'

'I wonder,' Roger replied seriously, looking in the mirror, over the bottles of lotion, at his face stuck like a dummy head on top of the soft pyramid of the white wrapper.

Raoul, who had been the Mamelins' barber ever since there had been Mamelins in the rue Puits-en-Sock, had been cutting his hair now for twelve years. It was he who had sliced off with one slash of the scissors the baby's forelock which Élise had piously preserved in tissue paper, and since then the perpetual joke had been repeated every fortnight.

'A Titus cut?'

And now Roger, who for his part didn't make jokes, who had never made jokes when his hair was concerned, and who had been known to fly into a temper in the barber's chair when his hair had been left a fraction of an inch too long – now Roger looked as if he were hesitating, was really hesitating, and hid the top of his forehead for a moment with both hands as if to see how he would look once he had been shorn.

'I wonder, Raoul, if it wouldn't be the simplest thing to do.'

Raoul looked rather like Désiré; he had the same musketeer's beard, but a fiery red, the same receding forehead, bald at the temples, and the same mischievous eyes in a face which remained imperturbable while he reeled off a string of jokes from morning till night. He was a more insipid Désiré, with the face stretched to make it a little longer.

From one of the countless little drawers whose secrets Roger had studied so many times as a child, he took a clipper which he tossed in his hand.

'Then the answer's yes?'

Roger thought it over, still hesitating, but feeling scarcely any excitement. If Raoul took him at his word and started the operation, he would let him finish it. The clipper was already brushing against the back of his neck, and he could feel the cold touch of the metal, but it was the barber who funked it.

'You aren't serious, are you?'

How could Raoul have failed to notice that Roger, who was always so particular about his appearance, had dirty finger-nails and was wearing an old suit, a carelessly knotted tie and filthy shoes. Instead of his fine briar pipe, he had taken to smoking one of those coarse imitation meerschaums with a long cherry-wood stem which you could see hanging down the chests of old men taking the air on the doorsteps of their shops. Like them, he pressed down the ashes by thrusting his forefinger into the bowl, and just now, on the way to Raoul's, he had bought himself some snuff which he had ostentatiously stuffed into his nostrils in the open street.

It was the middle of March. The Easter holidays had just begun. The day before, in driving spring rain, Roger had gone in his clogs to queue at the food centre with a shopping-bag. Élise had not yet recovered from the shock.

'No, Monsieur Mamelin. I'm not going to take the responsibility for shearing you. I've no desire to have my eyes scratched out or to see you burst out sobbing. Let's be serious. What sort of a haircut do you want?'

Roger, with the smile of a misunderstood man, puffed at his pipe.

'Just as you like, Raoul.'

'The parting in the middle or on the side?'

'No parting at all. So leave it long.'

'Artist-style?'

He would have his hair cropped short later on, for he would do it one day, he had been thinking about it for over a week now. It was the radical method of putting himself once for all above all the petty trifles he despised.

Oughtn't people to understand at a glance that he had changed completely? The proof of that was that he was happy in this shop which he used to hate before, and that instead of looking in the mirror for the reflection of a tense face with a contemptuous, distant expression, he gave his features all the kindliness of which they were capable, puffing his chest out and wishing that he were fat and round like a worthy bourgeois of the district.

This morning there was a pale sun shining. Once he had crossed the Pond d'Amercoeur, with his hands in his pockets and some books under his arm, Roger had the impression that he was living in a stage-set. His eyes smiled at everything they saw: a little earlier, he had taken pleasure in watching a fat girl washing down the white tiles of a fish-shop with pailfuls of clean water; then he had looked at the fish, the spiky gurnets, the pale rays, and the distinguished soles, and he had bent over the barrels of herrings lined up along the pavement to breathe in their powerful smell.

Raoul's shop was even more of a stage-set than the rest. Besides, it already partook of the theatre whose portico could be seen a little farther on in the rue Surlet. Its narrow, lop-sided shop window contained nothing but wigs. It was hard to find the door at first, for it was in the next house; the hairdressing saloon itself was a sort of triangular nook, with an opening in one wall which contained a stove, and on the other side of this stove, in an even smaller nook which seemed to have no way out, you could see Raoul's father pinning long tow-like hair on a wooden head.

Raoul and his father were the accredited wigmakers and make-up men of the Pavillon de Flore, where operettas alternated with melodramas. The walls were covered with autographed photographs, the talk was all of baritones, singing basses and tenorinos, and everything evoked a world which was invisible yet present, a world dressed in costumes of olden times. The air seemed to smell of scenery and tours, of gas-jets and Bengal lights, the glass-fronted cupboards were full of greasepaint, and the years did not count here as they did elsewhere.

'It was the season Mercoeur put on *The Merry Widow* for the first time at the Pavillon de Flore. What a voice! What a presence! What a brilliant performance in the duet! I maintain that nobody has ever played Danilo properly since.'

The door was left open in all weathers, for otherwise there would have been neither enough air nor enough space. You were in the street. The life of the street entered the shop freely, the noises, the voices, the smells, the sunshine. And the neighbours came in to sit down for a little while as they would in a public place.

'Well, Raoul, what's new?'

'Everything's old, especially us, alas!'

'You couldn't do my beard in a minute, could you? I'm going to the funeral.'

'Narquet's?'

'I can't understand how that chap could go off so quickly. Why, only a fortnight ago, he was fishing next to me at the Grosses-Battes dam. Incidentally, this morning I saw big Henry going fishing. He won't catch anything. The river's too swollen.'

Roger listened to them, drawing gently on his pipe. It struck him that here he was breathing in the life of the whole district, and this district of the rue Puits-en-Sock, of which the rue Surlet, which went off at an acute angle, was just a sort of extension, was something which he had suddenly started to love.

He too would have liked to know everybody by his Christian name, to be able to say like Raoul and his customers:

'Wasn't it his sister-in-law – you remember, the little thing who limped a bit and was such a hot piece – who went off with the singer with the bad teeth one night they were playing *La Tour de Nesle*? I can still see her in this chair when she came to have her hair curled for her first communion.'

Roger would have liked the houses to be even narrower and more lop-sided, with sharp corners, twisting passages, mysterious nooks and corners, and smells which varied with every step. He liked people who wore the costume of their trade and spoke to each other from doorstep to doorstep, people who had been born in the house in which they lived and had always known each other, who, when they were old men and grandfathers, still tussled with one another as they used to do when they were at school together or when they served Mass in the parish church.

*

Camille was dead. She had died in January, about dawn one Monday morning. A few hours before, in a box at the Mondain cinema, behind Gouin and his girl friend, Roger had been fumbling about under her skirts.

That Monday evening, when he had been thinking about nothing but the rendezvous on Thursday and the signal Camille was going to give him with her torch to tell him what Sidonie had decided, Élise, talking to the inevitable Mademoiselle Rinquet, had suddenly said in a mournful voice:

'As if we hadn't enough with our own troubles, we've got epidemics starting now.'

It had been right in the middle of the black period, the period of the Carré and the endless walks in the dark, in search of heaven knows what ambiguous pleasures, a period when, for Roger, everything had been dismal and frightening. Élise had talked while peeling turnips and Mademoiselle Rinquet had listened, as dark as the darkest of streets.

'Why, only today, there have been three cases of cholerine, including a girl who went home last night, healthy and happy, and who had to be buried this afternoon, she was decomposing so fast. They say her mother followed the coffin screaming. She's a poor woman who does people's washing.'

Roger, looking down at his book, had felt his blood run cold.

'I've been told that if the doctors talk about cholerine, so as not to alarm the population, it's really cholera for all that. It appears that it happens in every war. Think of the thousands and thousands of corpses that lie on the battlefields day after day, sometimes for weeks on end, without being buried!'

He had managed to ask in a toneless voice:

'You don't know what she's called, do you?'

'They told me her name when I was getting the rations, but I've forgotten it. Her mother worked most of the time at the home of one of your old schoolmates at Saint-André, the pork-butcher in the rue Dorchain. That's a chap who can't complain about the war, but I hope that one of these days people like that will be made to pay. When you think of all the poor little children there are with nothing to eat!'

Roger had lived for a week in fear, a subdued fear, so to speak, a hidden fear. He had not gone to the Carré. He had not been there once. He had not seen Sidonie again. He had lived on his own, not knowing where to settle down, curling up with a book in any corner he could find, for evening after evening and whole Sundays. If necessary, when his mother and Mademoiselle Rinquet were murmuring their laments, he dug his fingers into his ears and fiercely went on reading, only going out, except for school, to change his books in the rue Saint-Paul and at the Chiroux library.

He had started neglecting his appearance, had taken a fancy to casual clothes, and had seriously considered having his hair cut short.

'Why don't you come and sit by the fire, Roger? What are you going up there again for? You'll get pleurisy, like my brother-in-law Hubert, staying in an icy room like that.'

He shut himself up in his room for all that, wrapping himself up in a dressing-gown which his mother had cut out of an old counterpane with a pink floral design. There was no gas on the first floor. He lit a candle. He felt cold, his fingers went numb, his chilblains hurt. He smoked, paced up and down, looked out of the window, with a strange emotion, at the dark, wet boulevard along which shadows were passing, and finally, with tears puffing out his eyelids, he suddenly began writing.

Sadness of the tall spire, so tall, so lonely . . .

This was the cold, hard spire of Saint-Nicolas, which he used to see from the doorstep in the rue de la Loi for days on end when he was a child. He would have liked to describe it, frozen in the cruel immensity of a moonlight night, that spire which people might consider stiff with pride, yet which gazed enviously, without ever being able to come down to their level, at the roofs of the little houses nestling below it, all those hunchbacked, ramshackle roofs, slate or tile, flat or pointed, planted with smoking chimneys or pierced with glowing sky-lights, standing fraternally shoulder to shoulder, trying to join each other across the narrow, teeming streets, and preventing one another from falling down.

*

Cécile's illness had grown worse. She sat motionless from morning till night with her feet in an enamel bucket, for water kept oozing all the time from her swollen legs.

Roger had got into the habit of going to see her. He went to the rue Puits-en-Sock every day. It was he who took his aunt the books she read in her solitude, and little by little a new life had begun, Roger's walk had become slower and more solemn, and he had taken to wandering aimlessly and without any rancour in his heart through the back-streets, under the tangle of roofs dominated by the spire of Saint-Nicolas.

He had been almost sincere when Raoul had suggested giving his hair a Titus cut and he had replied:

'Why not?'

The most he had felt had been a slight tremor of anxiety. He would have allowed Raoul to do it. But now he was satisfied with his artist style. He must let his hair grow a lot longer. All or nothing. The skull superbly shaven or an untidy mop which you shook with a jerk of the head and through which you passed your fingers like a comb.

'A little brilliantine?'

'No.'

'Shall I wet your hair?'

'No.'

He wanted his hair to look as bushy as possible. He felt sorry that he had not come in clogs, that he was not an apprentice in one of the medieval workshops in the district.

'Thanks, Raoul.'

He was pleased with life. He enjoyed to the full the ray of sunshine playing in the mirrors, and all the images jostling together there in a chaos where you could scarcely find your bearings, where he had been unable to find his bearings at all when he was little; he stroked the big, smooth, warm bowl of his pipe and, giving a final glance at his reflection in the mirror, he tried to give himself the good-natured appearance of an old Outremeuse craftsman.

There was no transition between the shop and the street, but the same life, vulgar, noisy and colourful, a life with a strong savour of the lower classes. His nostrils dilated, his eyes opened wide, and he felt no repugnance whatever; even the smell of the bluish water flowing along the gutter seemed sweet to him.

He had only a few steps to take to reach the bookshop window and, at any other time, the mere sight of the window-display would have caused him positive pain, for it was practically the last word in the sordid and the ugly. Probably because of the proximity of the flea-market, the rue Surlet had a higgledy-piggledy look with the most improbable things placed next to one another.

Witness this shop-window, where there was a row of popular novels at sixty-four centimes each, soiled, torn for the most part, as dirty as old pipes, and where next to these books you could see some electric batteries among some second-hand shoes, some celluloid combs and a fantastic dressmaker's dummy.

On the dirty floor of the shop there were always three or four brats, the youngest of them showing his bottom; once Roger had found him calmly ensconced on his chamber-pot next to the counter. A mousy-haired woman, her arms covered with soap-suds, appeared for a moment in the doorway.

'Oh, it's you. I can leave you to help yourself, can't I?'

This familiarity pleased him. He felt almost proud of being at home here, of going behind the counter, rummaging along the shelves and leaning out into the shop-window. You could hear footsteps, shouts and volleys of oaths on the next floor, for the house was full of children and low women who joked with one another through the windows or across the neutral zone of the staircase. There was no private entrance and all these people went through the shop. Roger had once seen a girl there with a

438

heavily made-up face and flashy clothes, and it had been a revelation to him to hear her call down the staircase well:

'Don't forget my chemises, Mum!'

So these women, whom he used to follow hopelessly at the Carré, lived in houses like this; they had a mother and perhaps little brothers and sisters too; and nobody was embarrassed by them, everybody considered it perfectly natural that they should go out on the streets when the time came, just as the men went to their workshops.

He looked through the books before making his choice. In the early days, he had taken Cécile the books he usually read himself, those he borrowed from the municipal library or the lending library, bound in black cloth and smelling musty. But Cécile never finished them.

'I don't enjoy them, Roger. I may be a fool, but I can't see what pleasure anybody can get out of reading that sort of thing.'

'What would you prefer, Aunt?'

She had, so to speak, never read anything. She had not had the time.

'I don't know. I remember one book I was lent a long time ago that was fascinating. I think it was called: *Chaste and Sullied*. That's the sort of novel I'd like.'

This had moved him. It was strange to see what a little girl Cécile had become since she had fallen ill. She spoke in a faint, monotonous voice. Her black hair fell over her shoulders and down her back. She felt no embarrassment in his presence, and once her blouse had opened and he had caught sight of a poor withered breast.

'I'm thin, aren't I?' she had said, without any false modesty, intercepting his glance.

It was for her sake that he had discovered this shop in the rue Surlet. The shopkeeper, who could scarcely read and recognized books chiefly by their covers, had shown him what to do. First of all, you had to pay the price of a new book as a sort of surety, then every time you came to change a book, pay twenty centimes.

One day, he had taken two books instead of one. One had been for his aunt and one for himself, because, as the result of seeing the whole series of the Rocambole stories, his curiosity had been aroused.

For fear of being laughed at, he had not dared to show that book to his father. Now he had read them all, Désiré too. Unfortunately, they could never find the complete series.

'Number sixteen hasn't come back, has it, Madame Pissier?'

'The one with the vampire on the cover? I've asked myself that question a dozen times this week. If I knew who the blighter was who's taken it and kept it over a month . . . I only hope it isn't somebody who's died since then!'

For his aunt, going by the title and the picture on the cover, he picked a sad, sentimental story of the sort she liked.

'I've left forty centimes on the counter. See you tomorrow, Madame Pissier.'

He read a book a day easily, sometimes two when he was not going to school. He started reading as soon as he was outside in the street, shutting the book only when he entered the passage leading to his grandfather's house. He crossed the yard. He was no longer a visitor but almost at home here. He greeted Thérèse, Marcel's sister, who had moved into the house to look after the children and who had a consumptive's rosy cheek bones.

'Is Aunt Cécile any better?'

'Just the same. She's already asked after you twice.'

Never, in the old days, had he gone any farther than this kitchen, where people automatically tip-toed past the corner where Old Papa used to sit. Now he went through the door at the back and it was the very mystery of the rue Puits-en-Sock which he discovered. He found himself to begin with in an airless, unlit passage along which he groped his way. He went down a couple of stone steps, his hand found a cord which worked a latch, and there he was in a bright kitchen filled with the sickly smell of sweets.

There were sweets on every piece of furniture, on the table covered with an oilcloth, on the sideboard, on a chest of drawers, and on the chairs, for Roger was no longer in the Mamelin house, but in Gruyelle-Marquant's, the confectioners next door. Through the window he could see a little yard with the workshop where the sweets were made at the far end; and he knew that if he went round the blank wall he could get to the house of the Kreutz sisters, the old maids who ran the Dolls'

Hospital, and even, farther on, the bakehouse of the cake-shop which was almost at the end of the street.

The fact was that these were in the back-streets of old; the name of one of them was still carved in the stone. There had once been a whole network of alley-ways and culs-de-sac where the craftsmen had had their workshops and which no longer had any way out, so that the houses in the rue Puits-en-Sock, with their separate façades, had kept up, as it were, clandestine connexions behind.

It gave him pleasure too to enter into the familiarity of things, to be at home here, to call out, so that nobody should stop working because of him:

'It's me!'

He could have gone in by way of the shop where he was standing now, but he preferred this detour through the wings. His Uncle Marcel was sorting invoices behind one of the counters. The shop-assistant whom everybody called 'Pipi' – he had never dared to ask why – was serving a customer, a country shopkeeper who had put a huge black straw basket down in front of her.

'Is Aunt Cécile upstairs?'

As if poor Cécile were still capable of going out! They told him again:

'She's already asked after you twice.'

The two houses were now one. At the first rumour of war, back in 1914, the Gruyelle-Marquants had taken refuge in Holland, where they were waiting for the end of hostilities. The house had remained shut for several months, then, by a round-about method, by means of a ferryman as they were called, Marcel Wasselin had received a letter asking him if he would run the shop until the owners came back.

Pipi, who had been employed in the shop before the war, had come back. She was a short, strapping girl with solid buttocks and flesh so firm that you could not pinch her. They got on well together, she and Marcel, for they belonged to the same type. In front of people, Wasselin gave her resounding slaps on her bottom, or else grabbed her breasts in both hands; and behind the shop, in the kitchen littered with pink sweets, between serving two customers, he calmly laid her out on a corner of the table. Roger had caught them in the act. They had scarcely even looked embarrassed, and his uncle, buttoning his trousers, had simply given him a conspiratorial wink.

It was this same, huge shop, with its two vast windows which had been so awe-inspiring in the past, especially just before St Nicholas's Day, when there were so many customers you could only just squeeze in. Roger could still remember Monsieur Gruyelle, who always looked rather solemn, with white side-whiskers framing a face as pink as his fondants, and with his hands behind his back, keeping an eye on his shop-assistants; and he recalled the Gruyelle-Marquant sisters, plump, fresh-faced creatures who used to kiss him and slip two or three sugared almonds into his pocket or the hollow of his hand.

Now Marcel Wasselin reigned over the shop with Pipi, the shelves were overflowing once more with sweets and chocolates of every kind, the till was stuffed with banknotes which were pushed in anyhow, francs and marks together, and upstairs Cécile was alone, with her feet in her tub, in the middle of the Gruyelle-Marquants' bedroom.

Élise had sighed when somebody had raised the subject:

'Dear God, Désiré, don't you think Marcel is a bit too free-and-easy? If Monsieur Gruyelle, who's so strict, found out what was happening! And he's bound to find out one day.'

'That's his look-out, isn't it?'

'I don't know how he could entrust a business like his, such a solid concern, which has been in existence for over a hundred years, to somebody like Marcel. You know, I can't get rid of the idea that he's making money out of it, that he isn't over-scrupulous. And Pipi isn't likely to put a curb on him. All that money going through her hands without any check on it!'

Roger darted a glance at the last counter, the one at the back, which was protected up to a certain height by a trellis, for it was there that the more expensive sweets and chocolates were displayed in glass dishes.

If, when he came down again, there was nobody in the shop, as was often the case, he would put his arm quickly over the trellis. He had already chosen the exact spot, for he had a weakness for the big chocolates wrapped in gold paper which cost fifty centimes each.

Did the others ever miss an opportunity of doing the same? Hadn't his mother herself said that Marcel and Pipi weren't over-scrupulous people? With what he earned as manager and with the hat-shop where Grandfather Mamelin did all the work, could his uncle have given his children the St Nicholas's Day he had given them this last year, with among other things a life-size doll such as you never saw in the shops and which had been adorned – this had shocked Élise to the core – with Aunt Madeleine's hair, the hair which had been ceremoniously cut off her head when she had taken her vows?

It was not for the chocolates that Roger came. It really was for his aunt's sake. He enjoyed climbing the spiral staircase which started right in the middle of the shop and disappeared into the ceiling. He gaily pushed open the door which had become familiar to him.

'Hullo, Aunt! Here I am!'

It was another joy for him to see the rue Puits-en-Sock from a first-floor window, especially on a sunny morning. He made sure that his aunt had hidden her legs under the blanket spread over her knees, for the sight of them made him feel rather sick; she did not seem to realize this, and she showed them to everybody at the slightest opportunity.

'You promised to come early.'

'Yes, but I've been to the barber's. Just imagine, Aunt, I wanted to have my hair close-cropped and Raoul wouldn't do it.'

'What a silly you are, Roger. When you're lucky enough to have such lovely hair! Sit down.'

With her, he did not feel that he was with an aunt. She was a woman. She had three children. She knew life. And yet they behaved together as if they were of the same age; indeed, since she had fallen ill, she had been the more childlike of the two. She looked like a little girl, and occasionally Roger had inadvertently used the familiar *tu* with her.

'How do you feel today?'

'Just the same. The doctor says that I'll feel better when summer comes, but I wonder if he knows anything about it. At night, it's in the heart that it affects me. I've told him so, but he says that I'm just imagining things. As if Mother didn't die of heart disease – and she never complained of anything!'

443

'The doctor's right, Aunt. You think about it too much.'

'What have you brought me to read? Is Thérèse at home? The children aren't being naughty? How tiring she must find them, and she isn't any too healthy to begin with! Quite apart from the fact that she doesn't know how to handle them. I don't dare to say anything to her, because she's Marcel's sister and she does what she can. As for me, when they come to see me and they've been here ten minutes, I feel tired out. Why, now, just talking . . .'

'Don't talk, Aunt. You know perfectly well that you don't need to stand on ceremony with me.'

'Is it true that you can hear gunfire again from the heights?'

'So they say. It depends on the wind.'

'If only the war could come to an end! I feel that if it did, I'd be able to get up. You wouldn't like a grape? Go on. Do me the pleasure of eating a few. Everybody brings me grapes and I don't know what to do with them. It's Pipi who eats them every time she comes up here.'

Roger was afraid of showing his repugnance for these fat hot-house grapes which had spent some time in the sick woman's bedroom and which Cécile had touched with her moist hands, possibly after stroking her legs as she often did with a mechanical movement. The portraits of Monsieur and Madame Gruyelle-Marquant looked down at them. On the other side of the street, in the narrow houses, you could see people moving to and fro behind the windows. Cécile knew the life which unfolded hour by hour in each household. She had only to stretch out her thin arm to push aside the curtains, and the others presumably studied her from their side of the street as she studied them. Hadn't this promiscuity something reassuring about it? Faces became familiar, life was prolonged.

'What are you looking at, Roger?'

He gave a start. Noticing this, she in her turn looked at one of the windows and smiled a smile devoid of irony. Over the grocer's shop, to the left of the baker's, a dressmaker lived who had just finished her housework, as she did every morning at this time, and who was calmly making up. She was in her underskirt. Her blouse, which was a crude white, decorated with tiny scallops, left her buxom shoulders bare; her muscular arms, which she held up in the air while she was arranging her

444

bun, pushed out her bosom, and her lips, which were obviously holding her hairpins, were pursed in a fleshy pout.

'Have you got a sweetheart yet?'

He did not reply straight away, but waited to be pressed.

'You know, you can tell me everything. I'm not the sort to tell your mother.'

'Especially seeing that my mother keeps offering up novenas that I may remain pure, as she calls it, until I get married. She tells everybody about it. The other day, she told that old cat Mademoiselle Rinquet who hates me and hates Father almost as much as me.'

'You don't want her novena to be effective?'

He bent his head and blushed, a prey to complicated feelings. After all, she was his aunt; he derived more pleasure from talking to her about these things than to a schoolmate, for instance. She was a woman. And he trusted her. He was convinced that she would keep his secret.

'You don't reply?'

He just gave a mysterious smile.

'Does that mean it's already happened? Tell me, Roger.'

He fluttered his eyelids by way of an affirmative.

'A long time ago?'

'Yes.'

'Last year?'

'No.'

'Further back than that?'

'Three years ago, at Embourg.'

'Oh, come now, Roger, you were only twelve and a half! It isn't possible.'

'I swear I'm telling the truth.'

'Dear God! And your mother keeps on praying for you ...'

He was already sorry he had spoken, for Cécile had turned thoughtful. When she mentioned Élise you had the impression that she pitied her.

'And now?'

'It depends.'

He could not tell her the truth. The truth on this subject was something he could not admit to anybody, even to those who did the same.

'I hope at least that you take precautions, Roger?'

'Yes, of course, Aunt.'

That was not true. He had not taken any precautions. He did not even know exactly what was meant by taking precautions. After the Sunday at the Mondain cinema, a longing had haunted him like an obsession, and if, on his way home from school, he had continued to sneak along the back-streets, it had not been in order to save time; on the contrary, he went a long way out of his way so as to pass, his heart beating wildly, along the narrow streets where, behind the curtains of each house, you could see a woman in a chemise knitting or crocheting.

He knew that these women, who took him for a man in the darkness, tapped on the window-pane as he went by, giving him a smile or making an obscene gesture. But he was incapable of turning round to look at them, and the stench of these streets clung to his body, accompanying him for a long time as he fled home without succeeding in calming his fever.

One evening he had found a less repulsive street near the Passerelle, a street which looked almost as respectable as the rue de la Loi or the rue Pasteur, with clean, well-built houses, and women who had struck him as more middle class, even though they lay in wait like the others behind their lace curtains.

He had not dared to ask anybody how much he would have to pay. One evening when he had a couple of marks in his pocket, he had stumbled into one of the houses, his legs aching from having gone round the block at least a dozen times. He could hear the nearby Meuse flowing along between its stone embankments, and the planks of the Passerelle echoing with the sound of footsteps.

A hand had locked the door behind him, and a thick curtain had been drawn across the transparent curtain.

'Do you want something to drink?'

He had shaken his head. Making a tremendous effort, with his ears buzzing so loudly that he had been unable to recognize his own voice, he had managed to say:

'I've only got two marks. Is that enough?'

'Show me.'

She had slipped the two marks into her black stocking, pushed open a door, and poured some water into a china bowl, next to a double bed covered with a counterpane like those in

446

the lodgers' bedrooms, exactly the same in fact as the one that used to be in Monsieur Saft's room.

'Come and wash. What's the matter? Come along.'

Then she had looked at him and understood.

'Oh, so that's it . . .'

She had thought that it was the first time and she had not been far wrong.

'Don't be frightened. Come along.'

He had left the house five minutes later and rushed towards the embankment, where he had started to stride along, trying to curb his longing to run as fast as he could. All the same, he meant to go back there. Already, two or three times since then, he had gone roaming along the street and the woman had beckoned to him; perhaps she had even recognized him; but he had never happened to have two marks in his pocket again, and one evening – a Monday, he remembered it had been – his desire had been so keen that he had nearly gone in, held out his watch and stammered:

'I haven't any money on me, but I'll leave you my watch.'

He had not dared.

'Boys are funny,' murmured Cécile, who was watching him closely.

And she confessed, as to a grown-up, as if Roger had not been her nephew:

'I've never had any pleasure out of it. And yet I've had three children. Poor Élise! When I think about her novenas . . . Incidentally, I nearly forgot to pay you for my book. Hand me my purse from the table, will you?'

She gave him the twenty centimes lending fee. Then she held out a fifty-centime piece.

'Here, buy yourself some tobacco with this.'

'No, Aunt, no thank you.'

'Come along, take it! I know that tobacco is dear. Papa scarcely dares to smoke his pipe and he keeps on letting it go out to make it last longer.'

He regretfully accepted, so as not to hurt her, for he did not like money matters to come between himself and Cécile.

'What's the sweetheart you've got now like? Because I suppose you've got another one? But tell me, how do you get to know them? You meet them in the street?'

447

'Yes.'

'And you speak to them, just like that, straight out?'

Although he had never dared to do that, he said yes.

'And they listen to you? That's what I've never been able to understand. How girls can let a man accost them when they don't know him from Adam . . .'

She had said 'a man' and he felt it incumbent on him to declare:

'They even like it.'

'And they let you . . .?'

'Not all of them. Most of them.'

'The same day?'

'It all depends.'

'When I think that I've lived all this time without knowing anything about all this! Your mother too, I bet, if I know her. Take care all the same, Roger.'

'Yes, Aunt.'

'You know what I mean?'

She was referring to the diseases you risked catching.

'Yes, I know.'

'Are you going already?'

'I promised Mother I'd go and get the bread at the food-centre.'

'Do you still have to queue as long as you used to? I don't know what things are like outside any more.'

'You have to wait about an hour, sometimes more. I always take a book with me. Good-bye, Aunt. See you tomorrow. If you don't like your novel, I'll go and get you another one.'

He had a vague feeling that this was a morning which mattered, but as yet he did not know why. He paid greater attention to details, as if he had a presentiment that later on he would need to remember them.

The armchair Cécile was sitting in was Old Papa's armchair which had been brought over from the Mamelins'. The wallpaper was a faded blue. In the middle of each curtain, a stork had been crocheted. The old floorboards had been given a coat of reddish paint which had then been polished and on which three little grey rugs had been placed. The baker on the other side of the street was standing on his doorstep, covered with flour, his hands on his hips and sunshine in his hair; and Roger waited for him to go back into his shop, for he had not forgotten the chocolates he wanted to take on the way out and he was afraid of being seen from across the street.

The shop bell had not rung for a long time, so there was a good chance that he would not meet anybody downstairs. It was the time when Marcel was usually busy in the kitchen.

'Right. See you tomorrow, Aunt.'

'See you tomorrow, Roger. Don't come too late. If you only knew how bored I get, all alone! That reminds me, on your way out can you tell Thérèse to bring up my broth? And remind her, if she leaves the children alone in the kitchen, to make sure there's nothing on the stove for them to knock over. I'm always so afraid of that!'

There. The door was shut. He went downstairs, making as little noise as possible, and little by little the whole shop became visible. The baker across the street had presumably gone back to his bakehouse, the passers-by took no notice of Roger, and he was just about to make for the trellis protecting the expensive chocolates when his eyes fell on the half-open till stuffed with banknotes.

It was too short a time since he had conjured up the picture of a certain window, of a hand drawing aside a curtain, of a woman waiting; this picture leapt to his mind, a wave of heat swept over him, he took a few quick steps, leant across the counter, and plunged into the banknotes a hand which he promptly thrust deep into his pocket.

Red-faced, his eyes shining, he made his way towards the kitchen and suddenly gave a start, for Pipi was there, silent and motionless. He stood there for a moment trying to recover his composure, not realizing at first that she had her back towards him and that, moistening a pencil with her saliva, she was too absorbed in searching for something to say in her letter to have noticed anything.

She was scarcely aware of his presence and looked at him unseeingly, murmuring in a far-away voice:

'Are you going?'

'I have to go and get our bread at the food-centre.'

Why did he linger in the kitchen where there was nothing for him to do?

'I'm going. Yes, it's time for me to go.'

449

'Your aunt doesn't need anything?'

'No. I mean yes. I've a message for Thérèse.'

He finally managed to tear himself away and went over to the Mamelin side, where the water was singing in the kettle and the children were crawling about on the floor. If Cécile could have seen them!

'Aunt Cécile wants her broth taken up.'

He went off with the memory of the multicoloured patches which the sun scattered everywhere after passing through the fake stained glass, and of the figure of his grandfather whom he could see from the courtyard, bending over the felt blocks in the back-shop. He had not the heart to go to kiss him. Running along, he swerved suddenly to avoid a tram which he had not heard approaching, and bumped into Marcel Wasselin, who was coming out of the café on the corner, wiping his moustache. Without thinking, he said:

'I'm late.'

He had the impression that his uncle had turned round to look at him, but he ran on, feeling quite giddy, and it was only after crossing the Pont d'Amercoeur, a hundred yards from the school where the bread ration was distributed, that he finally came to a stop, his legs trembling. Then he took out of his pocket the banknotes which he had been clutching all the way from the Gruyelle-Marquants' shop, and which had turned soggy with perspiration.

There were three of them, two one-mark notes as he had intended, but also a fifty-mark note which he looked at in horror, not knowing where to put it, where to hide it, and the thought of which haunted him all the time he was queuing among the house-wives and trying in vain to work up an interest in Rocambole.

For a long time, that day, he went to and fro in the house as if he were searching for something which could not be found. Finally, at four o'clock, Élise went out to buy some vegetables, the inevitable Mademoiselle Rinquet remained like an evil spider in the kitchen, while he locked himself in his room, climbed on to a chair, and removed one of the wooden balls adorning the corners of his wardrobe.

These balls were fixed on dowel-pins, and it was round one of these that Roger carefully wrapped his banknote before thrusting it into its hole.

It was all over. He gave a sigh of relief. He swore to himself that he would never touch the note again. Perhaps he would not even use the two marks which he had hidden, folded very small, at the bottom of his tobacco-pouch. Yes, he promised himself not to use them, but to give them to a poor man, for instance, although he was not yet sure that that was what he would do.

He went downstairs, put on his clogs and, without going into the kitchen where the old cat was ensconced, he went off with his hands in his pockets. He did not know where he was going. He set off in the direction of Bressoux through a humble district, passing rows of poor houses. Children were playing on the doorsteps and pavements, dust-carts went by looking as if they were trying to grind the cobblestones with their iron wheels, and everything was dirty and dreary. The sun was already going down, and big white clouds were drifting slowly past which would end up by covering the sky. The grass alongside the patches of waste ground was a dull green colour; a goat was browsing on it, tied to a fence, and breaking off now and then to bleat; a woman shouted for her son; there were sheds, stables, and workshops where there was hammering going on; hens and cocks were pecking away in the poultry-yards; it was a district half-way between town and country. Roger walked slowly along with his hands in his pockets, thinking that he would go to attend the evening service in the crypt at Le Bouhay, where some monks had built a grotto in imitation of Lourdes.

He pressed down the ashes in his pipe with one finger, spat as the workers did, dragged his clogs along like them, and beneath a sky which was growing ever paler, he looked disgustedly at the cheerless world which surrounded him and which he felt was in his own image.

Chapter Five

There was only half a minute left before the bell, ringing for half past nine, would give the signal for the change of classes. The bricks, that morning, in the huge yard, were a soft pink in the sunshine; the usher, with one arm raised, was already swinging the chain which he was going to pull jerkily. Roger saw him and shut his German grammar so sharply, without meaning to do so, that it made a noise like a clapper in the classroom.

Without a moment's hesitation, as if he had been waiting for this opportunity for a long time, the German master broke off the sentence he had begun to say:

'Monsieur Mamelin, you will write out twice for me the list of separable and inseparable verbs.'

The other boys turned round to look at Roger, who smiled in a ray of sunshine. Like that everybody saw his new suit, and Neef-the-peasant tried to express his admiration with some big, clumsy gestures which could have cost him dear.

'What do you say to that, Monsieur Mamelin?'

'I don't say anything, sir.'

'In that case, you . . .'

The bell rang out, setting off a familiar din in all the class-rooms, doors opened, the masters went from one classroom to another. The air smelled of spring. Everybody was saturated with spring. You carried the smell of spring about with you, in you. And it was in that heady atmosphere that the German master, going on talking, as if with the impetus he had gained, picked up his books with an automaton's gestures and furiously rolling eyes, and took down his bowler hat which – Roger was waiting for this ritual gesture – he would wipe with the back of one sleeve before putting on.

'. . . will write it out four times.'

He was not a Jesuit father. He was a layman. He was a poor man too, so poor that he felt it necessary to play the bogy-man to delude himself. Mamelin was the only one who had under-stood him. He had never met him out of school, but he was

452

certain that he lived in a poky house like the one in the rue de la Loi, and that he had a wife who complained about her back on washdays and was tormented by the fear of being left a widow without either money or a pension.

As he had a complicated name, Roger had christened him J.P.G., for those were the initials he put on his pupils' exercises. He corrected these in red ink, except for Mamelin's, which he did not even take the trouble to read, simply scrawling a vengeful cross over every page.

How much could the Jesuits pay him? Probably not much more than Monsieur Monnoyeur gave Désiré. He never felt at ease in the huge rue Saint-Gilles school – that was why he had adopted such a stiff bearing – and as he walked along he must have had the impression of hearing a contemptuous murmur:

'That's J.P.G., a poor fool of a German master who was starving to death before the Fathers got hold of him.'

He dressed all in black, without a single touch of colour, and with a collar so high that it prevented him from turning his head. He always looked as if he had just been to a wedding or a funeral, more probably a funeral. He waxed his black moustache, turning it up in two rigid spikes, and rolled his dark, bulbous eyes ferociously in his waxlike face.

All the boys were afraid of him except Roger, who did not take him seriously, found his jerky automaton gestures amusing, and, indifferent to the lesson, smiled at his own thoughts.

Everybody thought that they hated one another, he and the master. A good pupil on the whole, and first in certain subjects, such as French composition, Roger was bottom of the class in German, so far behind the others that he no longer took the trouble to study any more. He gave the whole of his attention to J.P.G.'s doings, watching him as he would watch a beetle.

The master had noticed this and suffered, as he pushed the classroom door open, from the awareness of this curiosity which he believed to be ironic. He did not blush, because he had no blood under his skin, but he got flustered and treated his pupils to a stern glare which did not dare to linger on Mamelin.

'It is understood as usual,' he often said just for his benefit, 'that those whom the lesson doesn't interest don't interest me either. I would merely ask them to preserve a decent attitude, that being the least I can demand from them.'

Was it possible that he felt that Roger had discovered every-thing, the thin cracks in his shoes which he blackened with ink, the ragged edges of his sleeves, all those shameful trifles which the boy knew so well, and also the terror with which the master was filled by those smartly dressed, well-fed youths whose parents were influential people who could have him dismissed?

They were the only two in the classroom, the master and the pupil, who belonged to the same social class and suffered from it, yet instead of feeling sorry for one another they bristled up, as if each were furious at seeing his own reflection in the other, they had taken a dislike to one another at sight, and they waged a merciless war on each other.

Who knows? Perhaps it was partly on account of J.P.G. that Roger was showing less and less interest in his studies? Bottom of the class in German, he had become familiar with that type of humiliation, the stigma of the bad pupil no longer impressed him, he had made no attempt in the last few months to master trigonometry, and he simply copied a neighbour's homework in algebra.

What did he care about that list of verbs which he had to write out four times? He had some money in his pocket. All he needed to do, when he left school at midday, was to go into the stationer's shop in the rue Saint-Gilles, and a seedy little pater-familias would do his imposition for him for five or six francs.

Father Renchon had come into the classroom in his turn, thin and gentle, red-haired, his face pitted with smallpox. His eyes, a purple-blue colour, would soon come to rest on Roger; the latter knew this and was filled with impatience; he was afraid of that first glance of the Jesuit, as J.P.G. was afraid of his, and he wished that the contact had already taken place so as to have done with it.

This first Thursday after the Easter holidays was not an ordinary day. Term had begun for everybody on the Monday, for Roger too to all appearances, but for him it had not been the real beginning of term, and he had tried to go unnoticed. The intervening days did not count, and he would have liked to remain invisible until this Thursday morning when, at long last, he had walked into the school with his head held high, trying in vain to restrain the proud quivering of his lips.

Some of the boys had pretended not to notice the transformation which had taken place in him, had looked at him on the sly, and then had buried their noses in their books; but Neef (Neef-the-peasant, of course) had made no mistake about it and, all the way through the German lesson, had endeavoured to make Mamelin understand his enthusiastic gestures.

J.P.G. had given a start too. He could not have understood anything about the miracle, for it was not just the suit which had changed. From one day to the next, Mamelin had been transfigured, had become like the others down to the smallest details of his appearance; or rather he was slightly superior to the others, with a more emphatic elegance, so that it was impossible not to notice him.

For the first time, just like the older boys, he was wearing long trousers. His suit was beige, a delicate beige; and was obviously made of soft English wool. His yellow shoes were dazzling, slender and pointed, with heels which tapped sharply on the pavement. He was wearing a thick knitted tie of red silk, and an immaculate handkerchief bearing his monogram protruded from his pocket. His hair, divided by a parting, shone with brilliantine, and anybody would have sworn – correctly, as it happened – that he had applied pink varnish to his fingernails.

Why, when the sun itself smiled on the transfigured Mamelin, had J.P.G. assumed an expression into which he had tried to infuse disgust? To take his revenge for that grimace, Roger, all the way through his lesson, had fixed a provocative gaze on the master which had dwelt insistently on the celluloid cuffs, on the worn edges of the sleeves, on the old shoes.

He waited for the riposte, knowing that it would come. He would have been disappointed if, missing the opportunity offered by the shutting of a grammar a few seconds before the ringing of the bell, J.P.G. had not finally allowed his rancour to explode.

'*Monsieur Mamelin, you will write out twice for me the list of separable and inseparable verbs.*'

The very way in which he said 'Monsieur', pronouncing the word with heavy sarcasm, reeked of vengeance!

Father Renchon, for his part, would show no contempt, for he liked Roger. If the one had not been a Jesuit of thirty-two and the other a pupil of fifteen and a half, they would probably have been friends. Yes, Father Renchon could have been the friend whom Roger had never had, whom he would probably never have. In the classroom their gazes sometimes sought each other out and stayed for a moment in suspense as if each were attempting some impossible exchange.

'We shall now continue our study of the influence of Lamartine and Victor Hugo on the Romantic movement.'

Father Renchon was going to turn towards him, that was certain. For the literature classes were more often than not a sort of controversy between the master and Mamelin. Lamartine and Hugo had already served as a pretext for a fierce discussion, the Father standing up for the elegance and purity of the former, Mamelin for the power and passion of the latter. The day before the lesson, each prepared the weapons he would brandish in battle.

But now Roger waited fearfully for that gaze which finally reached him across the classroom. He longed to turn away, but he could not, and he raised his head. He would have given a great deal, perhaps even his yellow shoes which he had had so much trouble obtaining, for what he feared not to happen.

It happened, almost exactly as he had foreseen it. First of all there was an amused smile, or rather a furtive merriment which appeared in the Jesuit's pale eyes at the sight of the new Mamelin. Had the latter really plastered his hair down too flat, as his mother had maintained? Could it be seen, at that distance, that he had put a little rice-powder on his cheeks? A shadow followed the smile, and Father Renchon looked thoughtful, no, sad, rather discouraged. It was already over. Nobody except Roger had noticed, but when the Jesuit opened the book in front of him, it was as if he knew that his voice, to-day, would find no echo.

'Tell us, Monsieur Chabot, what you think of the Battle of *Hernani*.'

It was not an insult, it was not an opinion, it was worse than that. Chabot-the-diplomat, as Roger called him, a tall aristocratic boy with delicate features and exquisite manners, was the only boy in the third year who could be compared with Mamelin in literature. He was in any case the most brilliant pupil in the class and he played that part with well-bred discretion; a shy boy, he seemed to be forever apologizing for his success which he accepted unconcernedly.

Why, when it was up to Roger to talk about Victor Hugo, and particularly about the stormy Battle of *Hernani*, had Father Renchon turned to his rival? Chabot, who had not been expecting this to happen, turned towards Mamelin as if in apology, and started hunting for his ideas and words.

Well, it was better that way. In any case, Roger had not prepared anything: instead of spending his Easter holidays studying the Romantics, he had read the whole series of the Rocambole adventure-stories. He did not listen to what his friend was saying. With a defiant smile on his lips, he thought ostentatiously of other things, looking out of the window, which was open for the first time that year, at a woman ironing nappies in a distant room.

This woman of the people reminded him of the dressmaker getting dressed in the rue Puits-en-Sock, opposite Gruyelle-Marquant's, and his Aunt Cécile with her feet in an enamel bucket. Something like a rancid, repugnant memory struck him and he recalled a Mamelin in wooden clogs, with a shaggy mop of hair and dirty fingernails, who, smoking the juicy pipe of an old man, had wandered with his hands in his pockets through the poorer districts of the town, on his way to the Crypt at Le Bouhay.

His face hardened, his lips tightened, his eyes narrowed until they were nothing but bright points of light between his eyelids, like the eyes of his Uncle Louis of Tongres, and his fingers contracted in their unconscious longing to crush something.

Was that how they had spent their Easter holidays, the boys around him? He was not thinking of the odd peasants, like Neef, who did not count, who got off their tram in the morning and went home in the evening without having understood anything, without having tried to understand anything of a world in which nobody had so much as noticed their presence. Those boys, stubborn, obstinate, pale with an effort too great for their simple minds, lived, blind, deaf and dumb, in a sort of tunnel at the end of which the coveted diploma awaited them.

What did it matter if they were badly dressed, if they smelled of the stables, if their breath reeked of the sausage-meat which they brought to school, together with some slices of coarse bread, in a piece of oilcloth? Did they suffer, at playtime or at the end of school, at not belonging to any group?

But what of the others, all those who, like Chabot, lived in big houses with basement kitchens and marble staircases, in the Fragnée district, with maidservants with starched aprons? Had they, only the day before, had to endure an ignoble scene with a furious Élise to obtain the two hundred francs for these shoes without which the suit would have failed to make any impression?

Every day of their lives they had been properly washed, they had been well dressed, they had eaten their fill in spite of the war, and there was no need for them to go to the rue Surlet to change the sickening novels of an Aunt Cécile in order to obtain access afterwards, after heaven knows what terrible fears, to the Gruyelle-Marquant till.

J.P.G. had never understood Roger's looks. Or perhaps he had understood, and his pride had made him turn in revulsion against the pity he had read in them.

Father Renchon had understood, and he was sad and disappointed. It was Roger's turn to feel ashamed, to bristle up against that feeling of shame, to go stiff in furious protest.

There. Today he looked like *them*. He was as well dressed as Chabot, as Leclerc, as Neef-of-the-Château, as fat Lourtie whose father was the richest brewer in the town and who was so stupid that at the age of nineteen, an obese creature already, he was sitting on the third-year benches, which were far too small for him.

Later in the day, instead of making straight for the Outremeuse district, keeping close to the houses and slinking down alley-ways, Roger would drop into Mariette's with the others to eat an ice-cream. For three years now he had wanted to; for three years he had turned his head away as he passed the confectioner's shop which fresh-faced Mariette had opened two hundred yards from the school, a shop so white, so spotlessly clean, so sweet-smelling that it made your mouth water, especially when you saw a band of schoolmates elbowing their way in.

What did he care about Hugo or Lamartine or Théophile Gautier and his red waistcoat? There was only one person in that Battle of *Hernani* who interested him, and that was Dumas, a poor nonentity, a pen-pusher in an office where he had been taken on out of charity, who had queued for hours to obtain standing room right at the back of the theatre.

Hadn't Dumas looked at the crowd around him in the same way as Roger was looking at his classmates today, and hadn't his hand, unknown to himself, contracted too as if on an invisible prey?

What did Father Renchon want of him? Why did he seem to be silently questioning him? Did he hope that he was going to raise his hand to interrupt Chabot's monotonous and over-elaborate account?

What was Father Van Bambeek doing in the gallery? He had stopped. Through the glass panes of the door, he was looking into the classroom as if he were waiting for somebody. Chabot, who had finally caught sight of him, went up to Father Renchon spoke to him in an undertone, and went out to join the master in charge of discipline.

But it was not with a matter of discipline that they were concerned, for if it had been, things would have happened differently. It was a meeting between grown men, Roger knew this, and this too put him in a fury, for nobody ever spoke to him like that, least of all Father Van Bambeek.

Their only encounter, which had been a brief one, had left Mamelin such a bitter memory that his ears reddened at the thought. It had been during playtime, on a fine day like today. Roger had been running along when a dry voice had halted him in his tracks.

'Monsieur Mamelin.'

He had gone up to Father Van Bambeek, trying to get his breath back and wondering what offence he had committed, while the latter, six foot tall and puffing his chest out like a fairground wrestler, had stood still for quite a long time without looking at him. Finally he had appeared to remember that he was there. His hand had stretched out, and two fingers had siezed the pipe whose stem was poking out of Roger's pocket, pulled it half-way out, then pushed it back.

Nothing else. Not a word. An imperceptible shrug of the shoulders, but a look of such utter contempt . . .

'Run along now.'

Not even a punishment. Now he and Chabot were talking about the latter's elder brother, whom the Jesuits had smuggled across the frontier to join the army by way of Holland and England. Roger had not got a brother at the front, nor, like Neef-of-the-Château, parents who organized charity events. He was nothing. He did not interest Father Van Bambeek, who had disdainfully returned his pipe to him.

'You have nothing to say on the subject, Monsieur Mamelin?'

'No, Father.'

'I suppose it is superfluous to ask Monsieur Stievens what he thinks of the question?'

It was Roger's turn to show his scorn, and this attained its object, bringing a flush to the master's cheeks, for it was far too easy to make a class laugh by poking fun at the most stupid pupil, who in any case had long ago become aware of the role of fool which he was supposed to play and, out of a desire to please, pretended to be more stupid than he was.

That was somebody Roger could go out with this afternoon. For that was what he had been thinking about all morning, for several days, to be precise ever since he had had his new suit. It was a suit belonging to his cousin Jacques Schroefs. The latter, like Chabot's brother, as soon as he had reached the age of eighteen, had crossed the frontier, through the barbed-wire entanglements and the electrified wire, in order to join the army.

'You see, Roger, you always think the worst and get the wrong idea about people. You were wrong to imagine that Hubert Schroefs hadn't any feelings. He said yes straight away when my sister Marthe suggested giving you two of her son's suits.'

It had been in vain that his mother had tried to get a word of gratitude out of him.

'If he thinks that I'm going to go and lick his boots, he's mistaken.'

'It isn't a question of licking his boots, Roger. It seems to me that you could at least go and thank him. They are practically new suits, made to measure at Roskam's.'

'They weren't made to measure for me, at any rate!'

There had been a scene, and one by one she had reminded her son of all her past sorrows, including the inevitable story of his

460

first communion, when he had been seven years old and had stubbornly refused to beg his mother's forgiveness.

There could be nothing more horrible than those scenes, in the narrow, overheated kitchen where they seemed to collide with one another, red in the face, their eyes shining. Usually Roger managed to restrain himself for a while and promised himself to keep calm, but soon the two of them were like lunatics. They would have felt ashamed of themselves if they could have seen themselves in such a fury, incapable of the slightest self-control; and afterwards, with throbbing nerves and empty heads, they tried in vain to forget the things they had said, the monstrous words they had uttered.

Roger knew that his mother detested Schroefs almost as much as he did. He knew too by what miracle she had finally got hold of those famous suits she had been talking about for so long without any hope, Schroefs remaining deaf to all his sister-in-law's hints. Wasn't it Élise who had said only a few days before:

'That man would let a dog starve to death in front of his door, and if it were a poor man instead of a dog, I dare say he would calmly watch him die.'

They had had to wait until Brother Médard had summoned Élise to the rue de la Loi; she had wondered what for at first.

'Dear God, Désiré, I hope they aren't in trouble with the Germans again!'

For all the friars of the Institut Saint-André had been arrested by the Germans one fine day and shut up in the Chartreuse fortress where spies were shot. It had been rumoured that Brother Médard and Brother Maxime were in solitary confinement, each in a windowless cell. People had kept an eye on the walls for the red posters which announced executions.

Without saying anything to Désiré, who would probably have forbidden her to do it, Élise had gone to the Chartreuse, all by herself, taking a big parcel of food. Nobody knew what she had said, in her bad German, to the sentries, who had finally let her in. For a whole month she had gone round the rue de la Loi and their old district collecting delicacies which she had taken to the prisoners.

Well, that was indirectly the origin of the two suits. The

461

friars had been released. When Brother Médard had sent for Élise, it had been to hand her a letter from Jacques Schroefs. So the Germans had not been mistaken, as everybody maintained, and the friar with the wooden leg was indeed an important figure in the traffic in letters across the frontier.

'Just imagine, Désiré, there was a letter from Jacques. A letter four pages long! And his father hadn't opened his mouth for the three months he'd been without any news of him. I ran like mad. I don't know how I didn't get myself run over by a tram. As soon as I was inside the shop I started shouting: "Hubert! Hubert!" He just stood at the door of his office and looked at me coldly. I'd lost the use of my legs and my voice out of sheer joy. "Hubert!" I said. "It's . . . It's from Jacques!"'

She started crying again as she told the tale.

'He went so white I thought he was going to faint. He didn't dare to read it. He went upstairs and sat down in his armchair without a word. The paper was trembling in his hand and he couldn't find his glasses. There were tears in his eyes, the only tears I've ever seen him shed. That man, you know, loves nothing in the world apart from his son. His wife and daughter could die and he wouldn't turn a hair.'

' "Read it aloud," said my sister, who was in one of her good days.

'He didn't read the letter just once, but a dozen times. Then he went to find his friend Magis, and in the meantime Monsieur Van Camp turned up unexpectedly. Hubert had an old bottle brought up. He'd forgotten all about me. It was Marthe who ended up by asking me:

' "And how's Roger, my girl?"

' "He's very well, thank you. He's still at college. He's growing so fast that I don't know how to dress him . . ." '

Élise must have added:

'On what Désiré earns!'

That was the origin of the two suits. Indeed, it was even more complicated than that. In his letter, Jacques had mentioned Louisa's son Évariste, who was also at the front, an officer already, for he had been a student before the war.

'I looked a mess in my uniform, and when I rushed up to him to embrace him, I realized straight away that he was not pleased. He gave me to understand that between an officer and a private, even if they were cousins, relations had to remain dignified. That was the word he used. He was very dignified, even icy. I left him feeling disappointed and heavy-hearted, for I have no friends in my company where I am the only intellectual and therefore anything but popular.'

Then, in front of Monsieur Magis and Monsieur Van Camp, Marthe had suggested giving her sister, for Roger, the practically new suits 'which after all will be too small for Jacques when he comes home'. Schroefs had not dared to refuse. He had taken the opportunity to make a handsome gesture.

'I'll never, do you hear, never go to thank him. I hate him. He's a repulsive character.'

'Shut up, Roger. At least show a little respect for your family.'

'What a family! Oh, yes, you can be proud of it . . .'

Their voices grew louder, the two of them lost their tempers, and his mother started snivelling. He hated her for her tears, which he called crocodile tears.

'Do you know what Hubert Schroefs said about you behind your back? He said that you were a beggar!'

'Roger!'

'It wasn't the first time either. Félicie had said the same thing before him.'

'I forbid you to talk about Félicie.'

'Because it's the truth. Yes, you are a beggar. It's in your blood. Even when you don't need anything, you look as if you're asking for something. You have to talk about the bare necessities, preferably to Aunt Louisa, because you know that anything that humiliates Father pleases her . . .'

'Aren't you ashamed of yourself, Roger, for saying things like that after all that I've done for you?'

'You're going to remind me of your prolapsus of the womb again, aren't you? Is it my fault if you have trouble with your organs, as you put it so delicately? Did I ask to come into the world? Perhaps it would have been better if I hadn't been born, considering the life that's waiting for me . . .'

'Roger . . . If you don't shut up, I . . .'

Why couldn't he be quiet?

'I suppose you think I'm proud of the life we lead?'

She took her hair in both hands and her face became convulsed. An attack was starting.

'Roger, for God's sake shut up, shut up, shut up!'

She screamed and shook him as hard as she could. He felt frightened, for he had his back to the wall. She tried to scratch his face and he made as if to reply in kind. Finally she threw herself at full length on to the tile kitchen floor, crying bitterly, and he started crying too, begging her to get up and kneeling down to ask her forgiveness, alarmed by that face of hers which was no longer that of a mother but of a poor girl who was suffering and looked young and old at the same time.

'Forgive me! Get up quickly! I'm begging you on my knees to get up. Remember that Mademoiselle Rinquet might come in . . .'

'I don't care. I'll tell her about all that you've made me suffer. Yes, I need to get it off my chest, seeing that your father lets you do as you like. I can't stand it any more. I wish I was dead.

'Mother, I forbid you . . .'

You wondered, at moments like that, if you were in your right mind, and you were astonished to see through the window, as if in another world, people walking along the pavements, houses, carts, life going on.

And yet it was after touching the depths of degradation, when the two of them had been dazedly wiping away their last tears, that he had succeeded in getting the two hundred francs for the shoes out of her. He preferred not to think of the way he had set about it. He had been obliged to represent himself as the victim of the mockery of his classmates and masters.

'You see, Mother, you thought you were acting for the best, but the mistake you made was in sending me to the Jesuit college. In any case, I know that I'm not going to stay there. I'm going to start working. I'm going to go into a workshop as an apprentice.'

Did they have any suspicion of that, all these fine gentlemen? And did Father Renchon, shrewd as he was, suspect even a quarter of the truth? The two hundred francs which he had obtained in that way? Well, they had not been enough. There had been another bit of cheating, for he cheated as much as his mother. The shoes, which he had seen in a shop window in the rue de la Cathédrale, cost exactly two hundred and eight francs, but he had realized that a price like that would scare Élise. The difference had been made up from the Gruyelle-Marquant till.

For this afternoon, a Stievens, whose mother and sister went with the Germans and dealt in heaven knows what, was not good enough for him. An effort such as he had just made deserved better than that, and when Chabot came back into the classroom, slipping discreetly between the benches as if unaware of the curiosity he had aroused, Roger took a decision.

Playtime had scarcely begun, and the groups were just beginning to form up at the foot of the iron staircase, when, avoiding Father Renchon to whom he usually talked, Mamelin went up to his classmate. Big Chabot was walking slowly along with Leclerc. He avoided showing his surprise at seeing Roger come towards him.

'I'd like to ask you something. What are you doing this afternoon?'

'But . . . I don't know yet . . .'

They had had time, he and Leclerc, to exchange glances.

'In that case, come to see the revue at the Renaissance with me. I'll have a box. If Leclerc wants to come with you, he's welcome too, of course.'

'The trouble is that on Thursday afternoons we always go to play tennis at Cointe . . . Don't we, Leclerc?'

'Yes. You're calling for my sister at two o'clock. You promised her you would.'

'Good. That's that. Sorry!'

Once Chabot had refused, the others would refuse, for the whole Fragnée group followed his lead. Why, if he had known that he was going to play tennis, had he said at first that he did not know what he was going to do? Simply for fear of seeing Mamelin invite himself along. They wanted to keep themselves to themselves. It was all very well being friends in the school yard. But once they were outside, they kept to people of their own class.

Would he fall back on Stievens, who had money too and was probably the most expensively dressed of them all? Stievens was almost as isolated as he was. He was even an undesirable. At the Carré, the boys nudged each other as they pointed to his mother and sister who looked like a couple of tarts.

Father Renchon was standing by himself next to the sunny wall. Perhaps he had guessed what had just happened. It was so as not to embarrass Roger that he pretended to be watching a game of prisoners' base when the latter unconsciously turned towards him.

Roger decided to go to the theatre by himself. He had already gone there on Sunday, but he had just taken a seat in the stalls, for he had not had his suit, which Cortleven had had to alter to fit him. He had marked out the box where he was going to sit, the first one, practically on the stage. He would sit with his arm on the crimson velvet ledge, his hand dangling in space, and he would be one of the first to applaud every couplet, with a hint of nonchalant condescension and knowing glances at the actors.

'I say, Mamelin . . .'

Verger, who had run up to him, stood there getting his breath back. He was a thin boy, with a pale, bony face, who looked older than he was and had the reputation of being immoral. He was not exactly rich, but he was not poor either, or the son of a clerk. His father was an important house-painting contractor.

'Is it true that you've got a box at the Renaissance and that you're looking for somebody to go with you?'

'Who told you that?'

'Leclerc. He's just told me that if I wanted to go to the theatre this afternoon, you'd got some seats you didn't know what to do with. Will you take me along?'

It was as if every word had been carefully chosen to wound him. With a bitter taste in his mouth, Roger stood silent and motionless, looking at the swarming yard through his half-lowered lashes. He sensed that somewhere Chabot and Leclerc were watching him, that perhaps Father Renchon too was looking at him, and he had to make an effort to keep his face impassive and then to say in a natural voice:

'If you like.'

Who could tell who would be sent him if he were foolish enough to refuse Verger?

'What time is it?'

'Two o'clock.'

'Have you got the tickets already?'

He said yes, but it was not true. It did not matter. He would get them at the box-office. Perhaps they had thought that he had got hold of some complimentary tickets? Soon they would be stopping boys at random and saying:

'Would you like to go to the theatre? If so, go and ask Mamelin.'

He was disgusted, with himself and the others, and he longed to be in his bedroom so that he could cry. Because he could not, he tensed himself, and his face became pointed like Élise's at certain times, his smile aggressive. He had nothing to say to Verger, who was no friend of his.

Once, only once, over a year ago now, they had gone together one Thursday afternoon to the home of Lafont, a boy who was already seventeen and whose father ran a big shoe-shop. Lafont had taken them up to his bedroom. His face flushed and his eyes shining, he had promptly shown them some obscene photographs on which he had commented in the coarsest possible language. He had got the maid to bring up some wine. They had heard his mother and sisters moving around the flat and the shop bell ringing every five minutes.

Why, when Lafont had brushed against his back, had he put himself on the defensive, as if he had scented a trap? He remembered the faces of his two classmates. Lafont sickly and excited, with shining eyes which had revolted him, Verger pale and apparently a prey to an obsession.

Suddenly Lafont had started indulging in exhibitionism; for all that Roger had turned away, he had kept on finding him stubbornly planted in front of him.

What excuse had he found for going away? He could remember only that he had left with the distinct impression that after his departure the other two were going to go on with their disgusting games.

'Have you seen the revue already?'

'Yes.'

'Is it good? Are there some tarts in it?'

'You'll see.'

'Where shall we meet?'

'Outside the theatre, at two o'clock.'

Luckily the bell went then, for he would have been unable to find anything else to say. He felt a pang of remorse as he caught sight of poor Neef dragging his hobnailed boots along as he took his place in the line after spending the break circling round Roger. The poor fool probably imagined that now that Mamelin was dressed like the others he would not deign to speak to him any more.

It was another of Father Renchon's lessons, a geography lesson this time. It was of no importance. Roger looked out of the open window and his gaze, lost in the distant chaos of the rooftops, grew harder and harder. That morning, his father had said nothing when he had seen him dressed in new clothes from head to foot. The day before, when Roger had displayed his red silk tie which he had just bought, Désiré had felt it for a moment.

'It was a cut-price bargain, you see. Otherwise, I couldn't have had it for six francs. It seems there's a flaw in it, but it doesn't show.'

Élise, who was always on the look-out for bargains, had believed him. She had even asked:

'You didn't see a darker one for your father?'

The tie, which he had bought in the smartest shirt-shop in the rue du Pont-d'Ile, had cost forty-five francs. During the past week, in francs as well as marks, and notes of both low and high denominations, Roger had taken about two hundred francs out of the till in the rue Puits-en-Sock.

On Sunday morning, he had nearly been caught. The shop had been empty. Roger was coming away from the till and thrusting his hand in his pocket when he had a feeling that somebody was watching him. Looking up, he had seen his grandfather standing at the kitchen door. For perhaps a tenth, a hundredth of a second, he had thought that all was lost, and he had been on the point of throwing himself on his knees when he had remembered the chocolates. He had passed his left hand over the trellis and had somehow managed to say with a little nervous laugh:

'I think I should be able to treat myself to one on a Sunday, shouldn't I, Grandfather?'

Had old Mamelin been taken in? Had he seen the boy's first movement? Had he suspected the truth? He had said

468

nothing, but had bent down to make the ritual sign of the cross on his grandson's forehead and then gone slowly upstairs to see Cécile.

Since he had handed over his business to Marcel in return for board and lodging and five francs' pocket-money a week, he had withdrawn further and further into the background, avoiding the kitchen where everybody gathered, and living from morning till night among the wooden heads in the back-shop. When he went out, it was to take the air with his friend Kreutz.

Roger had promised himself not to take any more money out of the till, and this time he meant it. He had been too frightened. Fear was the most appalling and the most degrading feeling there was. He had just over a hundred francs left. He would go to the Renaissance with Verger. He would buy some expensive cigarettes he had hankered after when he had still been at the Collège Saint-Louis and which you could find only in a shop in the rue de la Régence, delicate ladies' cigarettes which you could see, with their gold tips, through the red cellophane wrapping.

If Chabot had gone with him, or somebody else from the Fragnée group, he had promised himself to send the box-attendant to buy some flowers. After the ballet which concluded the second act, he had planned to throw them, as if it were the most natural gesture in the world, to a little dancer in the second row who had the touching face of a sickly street-urchin.

Would he do the same for Verger? Perhaps. Not so much for Verger's sake as because the latter would not fail to tell the others about it.

He had promised himself too much from that afternoon. Now he was in a hurry to be living it, indifferent to everything around him. At last the bell rang, and once again he avoided Father Renchon, although it was rarely that a day went by without his exchanging a few words with him. In the yard he waited for Neef, the only one who went his way, Neef-the-peasant who could not get over his classmate's yellow shoes.

'Where did you find those shoes?'

'In the rue de la Cathédrale.'

'They must have cost a lot.'

'Two hundred and eighty francs.'

'Your suit's jolly smart! Who made it for you?'

'Roskam . . . Let's go into Mariette's and have some ice-cream . . . Yes, I'll pay . . .'

Chabot and Leclerc went past on their bicycles without stopping. Anybody might have thought it was on purpose that there was not a single pupil from the third form in Mariette's that day. The elder Neef must have had money, but he did not give any to his son. The tall young man stood there, ill-at-ease, working out the price of the ice-cream he was licking with a respectful tongue while Roger affected an off-hand manner, saying 'Mariette' like an old customer, and sampling sweets which he took here and there from the bowls.

'How much do I owe you, Mariette? The chocolate-almond ice was terrific.'

He pulled all the notes out of his pocket at once, pretended to select one at random, and picked up his change with an indifferent air.

'See you tomorrow, Mariette.'

On the way out, he looked at his reflection in a mirror and made an effort to smile at himself.

'You're sure she gave you the right change? You didn't even look. I don't know how to pay you back, but if you'd come to Beaufays one Sunday my sisters would be delighted. I talk to them about you so often that they know all about you and keep asking me when you're going to come to see them.'

His sisters probably looked like him. They were all three older than he, none of them was married, and one of them, the eldest, Laurence, had a slight squint. Neef had already told him all this, and also that since his mother had died, his father had taken to drink.

Roger went along the rue de la Cathédrale on purpose to see the posters of the Théâtre de la Renaissance at the corner of the rue Lulay.

'That's funny! I'm going there this afternoon.'

'They say it's very good.'

'I know. I've been already.'

'And you're going again?'

Come now! He had to. He could not help it. He knew that

it was ridiculous, but he started talking about the little dancer, whom he had seen only from a distance, as if she had already granted him her favours, mentioning the second-act flowers and the box which was practically on the stage.

While he was talking away like that, in front of an admiring and envious Neef, there was not a single moment that he did not feel unbearably sad.

Chapter Six

It must have been between three o'clock and four, about the time when the rain was falling so hard that they had heard all the traffic come to a stop in the street and they had had to light the gas. Roger had a very clear recollection of what had preceded the rain. The sun was shining, but its bright rays, of a deep reddish yellow, boded no good; you could feel a menace in the air, and now and then a big, fast-moving cloud intercepted the light for a few seconds, casting a great, shifting shadow over the town.

He could recall in all its sordid details his cousin Gaston's room, on the second floor of a house in the rue Gérardrie. He was sitting at the table, from which they had removed the cover, and the mirror on the wardrobe door showed him his reflection, without his jacket, his shirtsleeves rolled up, his hair already untidy. His gaze was rather set, his movements, brusque and jerky, but you could not say that he was drunk.

He had never been drunk in his life. The only memories of his which bore a vague resemblance to memories of drunkenness were those of New Year's Day, when, at his grandfather's, he had been entitled, like the men, to a drop of Kempenaar. At the beginning of the afternoon, you hurried over to Coronmeuse, where, in Aunt Louisa's drawing-room, next to the open piano, you drank some sweet Touraine wine and ate some crescent-shaped biscuits. Sometimes you had to stop again, on the way home, at the house of some distant relative. It depended on whether you managed to slip past without being seen. It was already dark. You drank quickly, standing

471

up; you ran for the tram, whose light, travelling through the darkness of the town, struck Roger as sicklier than usual; and then, in the Schroefs' drawing-room, you still had to sip the warm wine with a sparkling ruby trembling in the middle of the glass.

Coming back to Outremeuse, he was heavy with a feeling of well-being. He had hardly any supper and soon sank into the infinite softness of his bed.

It was entirely different this time. He had begun by being pale, tense and aggressive, and putting the exaggerated confidence of a music-hall juggler into his gestures, he had first of all smashed a glass, and then stamped on the pieces on the floor.

'Pass me the Chartreuse, Gaston, so that I can taste the difference between that and the Benedictine.'

There was madness in the air; he could feel it and it excited him. There they were, Gaston Van de Waele and he, in a furnished room in the rue Gérardrie, a room rather like those in the rue de la Loi, but shabbier and not so clean. Lined up on the table were the oddly shaped bottles and glasses which they had just bought; on the floor there was a demi-john in a wickerwork casing.

The air was saturated with alcohol, but they did not dare to open the window, for fear that the people across the street would see what they were doing. The door was locked and bolted, and they gave a start when they heard footsteps on the stairs; but the callers invariably knocked on the door of the fortune-teller who lived on the other side of the landing.

One after the other, using the same glass, they sipped a greenish drink, smacked their lips, and looked unsmilingly at one another.

'Is there any difference?'

'Of course there is! This one has a smell of toothpaste the other hasn't got, but the taste is the same.'

'What if we added a few drops of essence?'

So far, Roger was aware, even distinctly aware, of the place where he was. The rue Gérardrie was a peculiar street which he did not know very well. Right in the centre of the town, a stone's-throw from the rue Léopold where he had been born, it attracted only country people, principally on account of its restaurants furnished with bare tables where you could bring your own food and buxom waitresses served eggs and bacon and tarts as big as cart-wheels. The shops sold material for farms and poultry-yards, and in the windows you could see plaster eggs, packets of powdered pig-food, and strange-looking baskets whose purpose was a mystery to the townsfolk.

It was here, very naturally, that this Fleming, Gaston Van de Waele, had settled on his arrival from Neeroeteren. Although he had money, pretensions to smartness, bought the most expensive suits and wore patent-leather shoes, it was only here that he felt at ease.

Unlike Roger, who grew steadily paler, he became redder and shinier in the face as the afternoon wore on. He began to look positively repulsive. Though he was only eighteen, he looked older; he was already a man, a sort of bull so full of sap that it oozed out of every pore. His highly-coloured skin was stretched over bloated flesh, his thick lips looked like freshly cut meat, and he had protruding eyes and a big, shapeless nose with flared nostrils under a low forehead where the hair practically met the eyebrows.

An animal tormented by crude instincts. And when, dressed in his navy-blue suit, with an excessively white collar round his neck, he capped everything by putting on kid gloves, it seemed that this civilized shell was bound to crack under the pressure of his muscles.

It was he who lived with his mother and his brothers and sisters in the house at Neeroeteren where Élise's parents had lived and of which Léopold had done an oil-painting. His father had been deported to Germany for doing some smuggling at the beginning of the war, because you only had to cross the canal in front of the house to find yourself on Dutch soil.

Was everything already beginning to get confused? There was a clap of thunder, just one. There would be no more. As if it were some sort of signal, the hail started falling, hailstones bouncing on the window-sill and the sky growing so dark all of a sudden that in every house people rushed to light the gas. The proof that Roger still had all his wits about him was that he said:

'Pull the blind down, Gaston. With the light on, they can see us from across the street.'

After that, however, he lost track of time and began to get the succession of events mixed up. He was living in an increasingly incoherent world, and now and then, seeing himself all of a sudden in the mirror, in the midst of a chaos of glasses, he burst into frenzied laughter.

'I say, do you think the chap will want to try all the bottles?'

His cousin Gaston had brought in from Neeroeteren, in the course of several tram-rides, one hundred and fifty litres of alcohol which they had made out there by distilling rotten potatoes and corn, instead of selling it fairly cheap as industrial alcohol, he had had the idea of turning it into brandy and liqueurs.

They had gone together into a shop in the rue de la Casquette where an Armenian sold essence which, so he declared, made it possible to manufacture at home, without any special apparatus, brandy or rum, Benedictine, Chartreuse, bitters and curaçao.

Luckily Roger was there, for Gaston would have been incapable of making head or tail of the leaflet which they had been given together with the tiny bottles; and now they were making liqueurs as fast as they could, trying out all the various essences, moving about in a fog of alcoholic fumes, taking a sip here and there, and discovering in all their concoctions the same underlying taste of rectified alcohol.

What did that matter? Roger had already found a buyer, for Gaston, who showed plenty of confidence in other respects, was afraid of approaching people. He had stayed outside in the street. It was Roger who had gone into a dozen little cafés.

'Excuse me, Monsieur. You wouldn't be interested in buying some brandy, rum or liqueurs, would you?'

Since the beginning of the German occupation, spirits had been strictly prohibited, and they were served only to trusted customers in back-rooms, at the bottom of a Bovril cup.

'How much?'

He made only one mistake. For fear of bungling the sale, or of being taken for a profiteer, he always quoted a price which was too low and which he promptly regretted.

'Fifty francs a bottle.'

Most of the café proprietors had been suspicious of this youth who was too well dressed and too polite. Others had haggled, asking for time to think it over. This evening, the two cousins were due to deliver ten bottles to a bar in the arcade near the Pont des Arches, next to the shop where, when he was a child, Roger used to go with his mother every week to buy butter.

What could Gaston have done without him? Why was he giving him only a third of the profits, instead of half?

He thought about that and about various other things which got jumbled up in his mind, and he remained fully aware only of the strange place where he was, hanging as it were above the town whose noises could be heard down below. On the other side of the lowered blind, he could sense a dark expanse of swarming activity, hundreds of little cafés and shops, people walking fast and others sheltering in doorways, their shoulders hunched, looking like wet dogs.

'You aren't feeling ill, are you, Roger?'

'No.'

'You look pale. Perhaps you ought to be sick.'

'I don't want to be sick.'

He knew one thing, and that was that he hated Gaston. He hated Verger too, and Father Van Bambeek. They were cowards. Verger was a coward. Roger remembered his pale face, with a deep crease across the forehead, in the box at the Renaissance. He had not laughed once. He never laughed. Only his lips moved, stretching like indiarubber. To think that all the way through the show, and during the intervals when they had gone to have a drink in the bar, he had been turning the same idea over and over in his head! It had had to come out, afterwards, in the darkness of the Carré.

'I thought you'd been given complimentary tickets.'

'Well?'

'I saw the tickets. You got them at the box-office.'

'What's that got to do with you?'

'How did you get hold of the money?'

'Mind your own business.'

'I could lay my hands on some money too.'

'What are you waiting for?'

'I know where I can find some old accumulator jars for

next to nothing. I can get hold of some lead plates and acids too.'

Roger had blurted out:

'At your father's!'

'Never you mind. Just now, accumulators are worth a lot of money, anything up to a hundred and eighty francs. I've heard there's somebody in the rue de la Madeleine who buys them at that price.'

'Why don't you go there?'

'I don't dare. I'm afraid of being recognized. If you like, we could come to an arrangement.'

'What sort of arrangement?'

'We'd carry them together, and you'd go into the shop.'

'While you waited outside in the street!'

'I'd give you twenty-five per cent. I've enough material for at least ten batteries. At forty-five francs each, that would give you four hundred and fifty francs.'

That had been three weeks ago and they had sold the ten batteries. They had taken two at a time, because they were heavy. Verger had stayed in the street, paralysed with fear, casting worried glances at Monsieur Gugenheim's shop.

Roger had not been frightened, not even the first time. Now, on the other hand, possibly on account of the alcohol he had drunk, it all seemed a nightmare to him and he bore a dreadful grudge against Verger. He would not go out with him again; in any case, he had nothing left to sell and Roger did not enjoy his company, for he always looked as if he were being tormented by shameful ideas, took fright easily, and thought he was being followed in the street.

'Look behind you.'

'Well?'

'Don't you think that fellow looks like a plain-clothes detective? Have you spent all your money already?'

'What about you?'

'I'm keeping it to buy a motor-bike for the holidays. I'll hide it somewhere in the town. My parents won't know anything about it.'

'And what if they meet you on it?'

'I'll say it belongs to a friend who's lent it to me.'

Verger was a miser. Before going into a café, he worked out

how much it was going to cost him, doing sums in his head, hesitating, torn between contrary desires.

'You pay for us both. I'll settle up with you later.'

He was a rotter, and that was a fact! Gaston Van de Waele spent freely, extravagantly, with a sort of frenzy, but he was a rotter too in his way. Roger would tell him so one day. And young Gugenheim was even more of a rotter, with his lopsided face, his Jewish nose, his big, lecherous mouth, and the heavy eyelids which fell half-way over his eyes.

Roger wanted to be sick, but he knew that he would not be able to. His eyes were haggard and worried, his mouth bitter. The room was ugly and he felt as if he were suffocating in it, for the walls were closing in on him like the walls of the room at Embourg when he had had mumps. He wondered if he had not dreamt about the huge Gugenheim shop, if a place like that really existed without anybody knowing it. For he had never heard of it before, and never noticed the narrow door with the frosted-glass window, although it was next to Ramaekers' where his mother had had a pair of shoes made to measure for him when he had started going to the Collège Saint-Louis.

Inside, though, you might have thought you were in the Grand Bazaar. There were rows of counters and two floors of galleries. In the dirty light falling from the glazed roof there was nobody to be seen, not a single customer or shop-assistant; and you gave a start when there loomed up in the echoing void the disproportionate figure of a boy of fourteen who was the only living creature among all the grotesque merchandise piled up or spread out. Hundreds of carnival masks, for instance, were lined up along one wall, with false noses in cardboard, beards and moustaches. In other parts of the shop you could see heaps of blue, green or pink combs studded with imitation diamonds, bundles of multicoloured shawls, toys, clay pipes, clothes, shirts of a kind nobody ever wore, and improbable household articles. Everything was incredibly ugly and vulgar.

Why did the boy, whose black overall covered his feet like a choirboy's skirt, press an electric bell? Was he afraid that somebody was going to murder him and steal the masks or the combs, or was he hoping to bring to life the dead world around him? The bell rang far away; a long time afterwards there came the sound of soft footsteps accompanied by the regular tapping of a stick, and an old man with a white beard, a caricature of Father Christmas, appeared from heaven knows where, wearing a ghetto skull-cap on his head.

This was the elder Monsieur Gugenheim, who was hard to understand when he spoke, on account of his accent. Accumulators? Perhaps. He did not say no. They did not interest him personally. He sold nothing but articles for hawkers and pedlars, and his business had enjoyed a high reputation ever since his father had founded it sixty years before. But perhaps one of his friends would be interested. How much did the young man want? One hundred and eighty francs? He would never dare to quote a figure like that to his friend.

Well, well! Another person, who could not have been more than twenty, had suddenly appeared without anybody hearing him coming. Standing beside old Gugenheim, he looked just like a tailor's dummy, a dummy whose yellow eyes seemed to be trying to say something to Roger.

'Bring the goods along, anyway, and we'll see. I mean that my friend will see, eh, Max? At a hundred and fifty francs, who knows if we couldn't come to an arrangement? You're starting young, aren't you? I wouldn't mind betting that your father's in business and that he sells accumulators.'

Nobody showed Mamelin out. He opened the wrong door and found himself in a yard which made him think of the bottom of a factory chimney. Then, when he finally got to the street, Max Gugenheim came running after him.

'Wait a minute. I've something to say to you. It's no use bringing the stuff to the old man, who's rich enough as it is. I'll take it off you at a hundred and eighty. Come along, and I'll show you where you can find me. You see this passage? Don't be frightened. At the far end, on the right, there's a staircase. You go up to the third floor. Don't get it wrong. Not the second, but the third. It's an attic. You've only to tell me when you're coming and I'll wait for you there.'

He looked suspiciously at Verger, who had decided to come up to them and was standing there saying nothing.

'Who's this?'

'A friend of mine. We're partners.'

'You haven't anything else to sell, have you?'

Then Verger, who was always full of ideas, spoke up.

'What do you want to buy?'

'Anything: butter, tinned food, sugar, flour, bicycle tyres, shoes . . .'

What was Roger drinking now? Brandy, rum, green Chartreuse?

'I tell you,' he shouted, banging on the table with his fist, 'I tell you they're rotters.'

'Yes, of course they are,' his cousin agreed. 'Who are you talking about?'

'About Gugenheim.'

Wasn't it peculiar that it should have been through Max Gugenheim that the two cousins had met again? One fine day, or rather one evening, in the candle-lit attic which you reached by way of a staircase with no banisters, Mamelin had found himself face to face with Gaston Van de Waele, whom he had not seen for a year.

'What are you doing here?'

'Business. And you?'

Now Roger stated categorically, hoping to be contradicted:

'And we're rotters too. As rotten as can be! So much the worse for those who haven't the courage to be rotters!'

Was it still raining? He did not know. His mind kept playing with this idea of rotters. If you weren't a rotter, so much the worse for you! His father, for instance, wasn't a rotter. And where was his father now? In an office in the rue Sohet, under a lamp with a green shade, trembling in front of a Monsieur Monnoyeur who was a hundred time less intelligent than he was. When he went home to the rue des Maraîchers, that old cat Mademoiselle Rinquet would have taken his armchair. On purpose, even if it made her sick, she would eat most of the dinner, knowing that Désiré had always had a big appetite. She had made some biscuits, using white flour, or rather it was Élise who had done all the work. She had promptly put them in a tin which they had had to lend her and they had never been seen again; the disgusting woman kept them locked up in her wardrobe, with her linen, and always carried the key around with her. Élise had not managed to scrounge a single biscuit.

'You understand, Gaston? If you aren't a rotter, you might

just as well kick the bucket. You, for instance, you're a crook. That's right, a crook.'

'You ought to try to be sick.'

'You think I'm drunk, do you? Because I say you're a crook? And what about your father? Why did he smuggle people across the frontier if it wasn't to get as much money as he could out of the young men going to enlist? And what's he doing in Germany now? He's found another way of making money, even though he's a deportee, by running a bathing establishment while there are prisoners dying of hunger. Do you want me to tell you what he is, that father of yours? He's a syphilitic! When Doctor Matray came to see your sister at home, he told my mother so, I heard him, though I pretended not to be listening.'

There was a gap in his memory at this point. All he could remember was stumbling down the stairs and pressing against the wall to let a young woman pass who smelled good and glanced inquisitively at his cousin and himself. He had looked up in an attempt to see under her dress while she was going upstairs.

He had been surprised to find some daylight left outside. The blue-painted gas-lamps were only just being lit. It had stopped raining, and a strong wind was beginning to dry patches of the road.

'You see, if the fellow insists on tasting the stuff, I'll say to him: "Excuse me, Monsieur . . ." Yes, I'll say to him . . .'

He waved his arms about. He could not recognize the streets where he was being taken. He went where his cousin pushed him, through an extraordinary town swarming with thousands of rotters, and he turned round to look at all the women with a violent desire to see them naked, disgustingly naked, their flesh pale in the twilight. Later on, he would go to see some. Where were the bottles? Had they forgotten the bottles? No. Gaston was carrying them in a parcel done up with string.

'You've got the Chartreuse, haven't you, Gaston? You see, if the fellow wants to taste something, I'll uncork the Chartreuse. On account of the colour, it's the most striking of the lot.'

'Listen, Roger . . .'

'Yes.'

'We've arrived. Do you feel capable of going in?'

'Give me the parcel! Give it me, I tell you!'

He had gone down two or three steps. There were some men there, four at least, in one corner of a low-ceilinged room. He had crossed this room without looking at them, had opened the wrong door as he had done at Gugenheim's, and had nearly fallen into a damp cellar. Finally he had found himself in the middle of a kitchen where there was an enamel coffee-pot with blue flowers on it standing on the stove.

'Here you are. I promised you ten bottles and I've brought the ten bottles along.'

There was an old woman there too, in a wicker armchair like Désiré's – or rather like Mademoiselle Rinquet's, seeing that the old cat . . . What a bitch Mademoiselle Rinquet was! But then, Élise simply had to go and take in people like that. She'd go and look for them in the street if necessary. If she hadn't somebody to truckle to all day, she'd fall ill!

'You don't want to taste them?'

He would have liked to uncork a bottle himself, to drink another glass. The proprietor of the café did not want to. He was small and round, like Monsieur Van Camp, and he looked like a cheese-merchant too. He examined Roger furtively, as if the latter was an impenetrable mystery to him. Did things happen like this in the case of Gouin's hams? Roger did not count the notes which were handed to him. What was the use? He only hoped that he would not start being sick while he was crossing the café! What would Father Van Bambeek say if he met him coming out? And where was Gaston? There was nobody to be seen in the little street. It was dark. The Meuse was flowing along somewhere.

'Gaston! Ga-aston!'

'Ssh! Well? . . .'

'Where were you?'

He had been piddling in a corner.

'Have you got the money?'

'Yes. I can't remember which pocket I put it in. Look for it yourself. Search me. Yes, search me, I said!'

He would never know where they had eaten some cheese sandwiches, but it must have been in one of those restaurants for country people where his cousin felt at home.

Was Gaston drunk too?

'Are you drunk, Gaston? What time is it? I must be off home.'

Another dark street with the wind blowing along it, a patrol with which Roger nearly collided, the heavy, regular footsteps of the three German soldiers who went off smoking their pipes. They were 'good ones', Bavarians, with an orange ribbon on their caps.

'What if we went to a night-club? I say, Gaston, let's go to the Gai-Moulin.'

He did not know that it was only eight o'clock. The darkness was enough for him. He wanted to hear some music, buy champagne for some dancing-girls, sit on a red plush bench.

'I say, Gaston . . .'

What had he been going to say? He could not remember. The whole of this black, slimy town, through which they were wandering as if in a maze, was . . . He could not manage to follow his idea through to the end, and this was a pity, for it was an important idea, indeed an idea of capital importance. He felt sad, disgusted. Everything was hideous. It was dirty. That was the word! It was dirty! And he wanted it to be even dirtier, dirty enough to make you cry with pity or disgust, to make you roll on the ground, moaning and groaning!

'What's the matter?'

He had stopped in front of a door and was pointing solemnly at the shutter, saying:

'It's Gugenheim's.'

'What of it?'

'Nothing. It's Gugenhein's. Shall we ring the bell?'

Where had they drunk a glass of beer? It did not matter. In any case, they had gone behind the Town Hall, at the foot of the spiral staircase where you went to watch weddings.

And now everything was getting mixed up again, the various pictures were being superimposed, and he made an effort to wake up, for he could feel that he was asleep. He was wedged in the corner of a bench, not far from a cylindrical stove in front of which a black and white cat was purring on a chair.

'Feeling better?' Gaston asked in a thick voice.

The rotter!

Funny! The word had come back to him. Hadn't his mind toyed for a long time with that idea of the rotter which he had unconsciously rediscovered on awakening? But when? And why? And which rotter?

'I gave you the money, I hope? You found it all right?'

For he remembered standing on the kerb of a pavement with his hands in the air while Gaston went through his pockets.

Gaston's face had never been so red before or his skin so tight. You had the unpleasant impression that he needed a bleeding. He was lying back on the leather-covered bench with his tie undone and his shirt open at the neck, and one of his hands was squeezing the breasts of a fat blonde sitting beside him.

She laughed. They both burst out laughing, Roger could not tell why, and then started talking in Flemish, only to burst out laughing even louder.

'You can help yourself too, you know,' Gaston said, jerking his head towards the woman. 'There's enough for two. Move up. Don't be frightened, it's solid stuff.'

He pawed her with his big hands, and insisted on his cousin's feeling her too. Roger had to follow his example. The woman smelled of beer, rice-powder, and hot armpits.

The two of them thought that he had gone back to sleep, but that wasn't true. His eyelashes fluttered every now and then. He looked all round him, bit by bit. He saw everything. The café was dimly lit. The tables were made of polished wood and spotlessly clean, and the sawdust formed patterns on the floor.

By the window, which was hung with an embroidered curtain, two Germans were sitting at a table with a woman who was the exact opposite of Gaston's, dark and thin, with a serious face. Sitting with her chin in one hand, she was gravely and patiently listening to what a massive Feldwebel was trying to tell her, a red-haired man who must have been in his forties and was wearing that peculiar grey cap without a peak, with a bottle-green ribbon and a cockade of black, white and red enamel.

The other German, who was even older, was puny and almost hunchbacked, unless it was his outsize greatcoat which was deforming him. His head was bowed, and he was sunk in gloom.

The red-haired giant had taken from his wallet a whole batch of photographs which he spread out on the table, among the glasses of beer standing side by side with glasses of gin. Perhaps he was drunk too? He tried to explain something, searched for words which would not come, persisted, frowning, and smiled broadly when at last the woman made a show of understanding and spoke to him in her turn in pidgin German. Without taking his eyes off the photographs of his wife and children, he happily thrust his hand under her skirt, humming a sentimental song and rocking from side to side.

It was all very far away and at the same time very close. Between Roger and the rest of the world, there floated a yellow fog which deadened the sounds and gave a soft, mysterious quality to the pictures; he closed his eyes, still hearing the song, which was soon accompanied by the noise of a horse's muffled hooves on the hardened snow.

It was probably on account of Gaston's voice, the Flemish words which he could hear being whispered, the waves of heat reaching him from the stove. He was in a sleigh, with Cécile, the second of the Van de Waele daughters, and Alice, the youngest, the one who looked like a grasshopper or some other insect. The sleigh was not a big one. Jef had taken his place on the seat and was driving. All you could see of him was his bearlike back. On Roger's right, Alice kept fidgeting all the time, but on the left Cécile, who was roughly of the same age as he was, snuggled up against him.

He had put one arm round her waist. His right hand was in hers, in her lap; a thick blanket, which had a good stable smell about it, covered them up to their chins.

Although the moon had disappeared, you could make out the black pot-hooks of the poplars on the sparkling snow. The wind buffeted their blue faces, but their hands were burning, an intimate warmth prevailed under the blanket, and from the centre of Cécile's body, whose forms Roger could feel through her dress, there came a more penetrating warmth.

He did not move. He wanted this to last a long time, and wished they would never get to the village church where they were going to hear Midnight Mass.

He had spent only about ten days at Neeroeteren. First of all Mia, Gaston's sister, the eldest of the girls, had come to Liège to obtain treatment for the sores which she had all over her body and which festered instead of healing. When the

doctors had spoken of the need for regular and delicate attention, Élise, as was only to be expected, had offered her help, and
Mia had come to stay in the house in the rue de la Loi where they
were still living. If Désiré complained about the smell of the
ointments and the unpleasant dressings which were left about
even in the kitchen, Élise retorted:

'You forget that they send us food!'

Roger had been invited to spend the Christmas holidays at
Neeroeteren. He recalled the big kitchen in which Gaston, at
the head of the table, solemnly played the part of the pater-
familias, saying grace and filling his plate first of all, while his
mother fussed around him like a servant-girl and his sisters
maintained a respectful silence.

Nowhere else had he ever been filled with such reassuring
warmth as in that room where hams and sides of bacon hung
from the ceiling and where you scratched away the frost on the
window-panes to see the cattle moving slowly across the
farmyard.

Jef, Gaston's brother, was a monster with a huge head and a
giant's hands. He had taken Roger into the pine woods to hunt
squirrels, killing two with stones and cutting them up while
they were still warm. Under a roof where the pig-food was
cooked, he had lit a log-fire and grilled the carcasses on the end
of a stick, with the blood dripping into the flames.

'Don't you want any? It's good.'

He also killed and ate cats, field-mice, all kinds of animals. He
ate anything and everything, all day long. Roger, for his part,
took along some potatoes in his pockets and baked them under
the ashes.

Mother Van de Waele, whose skirts hung round a body like a
broomstick, had, just like Élise, the timid face of a slave. Only
men counted in her house, or rather only one man, the master,
and, in his father's absence, Gaston was that master. The girls
huddled in a corner when he came in, and silence fell straight
away; he sat down, and they rushed forward to take his boots
off and put his slippers on; then they brought him his pipe
already filled and a brand picked out of the fire with a pair of
tongs.

Perhaps Roger had felt tempted to live like that in the
immensity of those fields intersected by the frozen canals and

the curtains of poplars leaning towards the east. He would have married Cécile with her smooth, rather soft skin, who looked at him with submissive eyes.

He stirred restlessly in his corner. A fit of anger took hold of him. He was going to grow excited again. What had he said to Gaston earlier on? The truth! That they were all syphilitic. It was the father who had started it all, early in his married life. His wife had had to have treatment almost straight away, and now her hair was falling out and she had scarcely any teeth left. Jef, their second son, was a mental defective who could have been put on show in a fair as a wild man of the woods. He sometimes started circling round children skating on the canals as he circled round cats and squirrels, and who could tell whether one day he might not strangle one?

'Rotters!' shouted Roger, jumping to his feet.

'What's the matter with your pal?' the blonde asked in surprise. 'Does he often get like that?'

'Sit down, Roger. You ought to have a cup of coffee, you know.'

'I don't want any coffee. I want some spirits.'

For fear that he would not be given any, he drained the two glasses on the table, one after the other, and then went and planted himself in front of the German, glaring at him fiercely.

'Why haven't *I* got a woman?'

'Ssh! Don't shout like that. Why don't you come and sit with us?'

'And what if I want to make love?'

'Not so loud, young fellow my lad,' said the manageress, whom he had not seen before, hidden as she was by her bar, behind which she had been having a little doze. 'I don't mind you having fun, but you mustn't shout silly things like that. Look how your friend's enjoying himself nice and quietly.'

'He's a rotter.'

'Now, now.'

'And I'm a rotter, too. And that fellow there's another.'

The German, who did not understand, raised his glass as if he were clinking it against another, and said:

'*Prosit.*'

'Give me a drink!' yelled Roger, wondering what he could do to feel better. 'Give me a drink right away, or I'll smash everything. And first of all, I want to piss. Where do you piss here?'

The old woman led him through the kitchen to a little backyard oozing with damp. When he came back to the café, he found the two groups together: Gaston, the German soldiers and the two women at the same table.

For a moment he was on the point of sobering up, and his eyes narrowed angrily, but putting a glass into his hand was enough to make him sit down quietly.

'You see, Gaston, what makes me mad is that it could be so stunning . . .'

What could be stunning? That was what he was incapable of putting into words. He just felt it. It seemed to him that all that was needed was an effort made once for all, and then there would be no rotters any more, life would be beautiful and clean, as harmonious as certain memories, and you would no longer have the impression of constantly floundering about in filth.

'Listen! Here's an example. One example and you'll understand. The money I've got here,' – and he slapped his breast-pocket where his wallet was – 'well, it's more than we make in a couple of months with Mademoiselle Rinquet. And what am I going to do with it, eh? Try to guess what I'm going to do with it. For a start, there . . .'

He took a note at random and thrust it into the dark woman's hand.

'Go on, take it! Don't be frightened! I may be drunk, but I know what I'm doing, and I shan't come along tomorrow to ask for it back. As for going to bed with you, no thank you.'

'Ssh . . .'

It was not a brothel, but a café such as you could find in the quiet streets around the Town Hall. True, you were entitled to sit in a corner with a waitress and to play about with her. In the daytime there was a convenient chiaroscuro, and at night the lighting was as discreet as could be.

'Why are you all looking at me like that? Have I got a smut on my nose? Well? Don't you dare answer me?'

The Feldwebel stood up and spoke to him in his language, coming up to him and making as if to embrace him.

'Keep calm, Roger. Mind how you behave. He isn't dangerous.

He says you remind him of his young brother who was killed in August 1914.'

'*Prosit.*'

The old woman had filled the glasses. She appeared only when she was needed and disappeared straight away. The hunchback, who had an unexpected bass voice, stood up in his turn, climbed on to his chair, and started bellowing a mournful song at the top of his voice.

'Come and sit here. Come, now. Don't be a fool. You aren't going to cry now, are you?'

'Why should I cry?'

He obeyed the fat woman who enveloped him in a maternal caress.

Later on, he must have sung too. He had got on to the bench, gesticulating wildly. In a corner, Gaston, blue in the face, was begging the old woman to let him go up to one of the bedrooms with his woman – for half an hour, ten minutes, just five minutes, not even that!

'I'd like nothing better, young man. You must realize that I'd be only too happy to please a nice young fellow like you. But the police are very strict. And then there are the patrols that go past nearly every night. They'd close my café. I'd be out on the streets. Be a good boy, now. Take your friend home and go to bed. You can come back tomorrow.'

What else had happened? They had forced Roger to drink some boiling coffee, which he had spilt over his new suit. They had washed the stains with warm water, with the corner of a napkin. He despised them all, while they were fussing over him.

*

They didn't understand! A month earlier, for instance, hadn't he wanted Raoul to crop his hair short? He had gone around in wooden clogs, smoking an old man's pipe and ambling over to the Crypt at Le Bouhay to attend Benediction.

And what if his father saw him now, sitting at the same table as the German soldiers? However much Roger might try to explain, Désiré would not understand either. He was not a rotter. He went through the streets without seeing the filth around him. He had never been tempted, like his son, to explore the shady side of the town. He believed what he was told to believe, and during High Mass he stood erect in his pew, as calm as a saint in a stained-glass window, while Chrétien Mamelin went from pew to pew, collecting for St Roch.

Did St Roch need money too?

*

Roger had had a rendezvous with the little dancer at the Renaissance. In the street, she was an ordinary-looking girl, timid, very poor. When he had given her the gilt powder-compact which he had just bought for thirty-two francs, she had looked at him with more alarm than gratitude, the present struck her as so magnificent.

'It's far too much,' she had stammered, in the same tone of voice as Élise when her sister Marthe slipped some chocolate or some tins of sardines into her shopping-bag.

He had tried to kiss her. She had let him do so, while staring over his shoulder.

'You mustn't send me any more flowers like you did the other day. The other girls wonder why. They think I'm putting on side.'

'What do the other girls say about me?'

'That you look nice and you're well dressed.'

'And the actors?'

'I don't know. They don't talk to us.'

*

Father Renchon pretended to take no notice of him and avoided asking him questions, for he remembered nothing of his lessons and scamped his homework anyhow, sometimes while he was walking along the street. At home, he just came and went.

'Supper ready?'

He sat down at table and went off when the meal was scarcely finished, going out or shutting himself up in his room, above all taking care not to find himself alone with his father. Sometimes he had the impression that the latter was holding him as it were at the end of a line, that he knew everything, that he was afraid of intervening and was waiting anxiously.

*

He was dead drunk. The proof of that was that he did not know how he left the snug little café. Hadn't they walked for some time in the company of the two Germans with whom Gaston had kept up an interminable conversation?

Yet he noticed that he was crossing the Passerelle, for he recognized its springy and always rather slimy planks under his feet. He had even wanted to lean on the parapet and weep as he gazed at the reflection of the moon on the water. His cousin had pulled him away. He was holding him by one arm and forcing him to keep walking.

'Don't be so rough, Gaston.'

'Then hurry up. The tart promised to come round to my room as soon as the old woman had gone to sleep.'

'And what if you catch syphilis? I say, Gaston . . . Look . . . We're in the rue Puits-en-Sock . . . I may be drunk, but I can recognize it, because it's the Mamelins' street and over there, where there's a big red crush-hat over the door, that's my grandfather's . . . Next door, that's Gruyelle-Marquant's . . . You think you know a lot, but you don't know anything at all . . . Do you want me to tell you something?'

He had nearly spoken, but his face had suddenly frozen as if he had become aware of the gulf separating him from a Gaston Van de Waele.

'It's none of your business. Go to bed with that fat girl. She smells of beer and whey.'

Why whey? He didn't know. It went with her flesh, which was as white and soft as a cow's udder.

'Listen, Roger, there's no need to tell your parents you've been out with me. If I know your mother, she'd tell the whole family.'

It was true that at Neeroeteren Gaston said grace before every meal!

'Have no fear! You can leave me now. I'm nearly there.'

And he zigzagged away from his cousin, who went on watching him, turned the corner of the rue des Maraîchers, and noticed straight away a little light filtering underneath the shutters. He did not need to take his key out of his pocket, or to tap on the letter-box, for the light had already gone on in the hall. The door opened. It wasn't his father. It was Élise.

'Where have you been at this time of night, Roger? Aren't you ashamed of yourself?'

The first thing which struck him was the familiar disc of the alarm-clock on the black marble mantelpiece. It gave the time as ten to two. At this revelation, panic seized him, but immediately afterwards he noticed Mademoiselle Rinquet lying in wait as it were in his father's armchair.

Then anger swept over him again, like blood going to his head. Red in the face a moment before, he turned deathly pale, his nostrils twitched, his eyes narrowed, and it was obvious that nothing was going to stop him now.

'What's the old cat waiting for?'

'Roger, be quiet, will you? Why, you've been drinking! Mademoiselle Rinquet has been kind enough to wait up with me. We've been up to the Pont d'Amercoeur a score of times and I even asked at the police-station, thinking that you might have had an accident.'

'She'd have been delighted!'

'Roger! Go straight to bed. Tomorrow you'll beg her pardon.'

'Me? Not likely! I hate her. I despise her. She's a spiteful woman who doesn't deserve to live, and you know it. If there were any justice in this world, it's rubbish like her they'd send on to the battlefields instead of killing poor soldiers.'

Élise grew hysterical, trying in vain to silence him and finding no better way than shouting louder than him.

'You're mad! You're absolutely mad! Mademoiselle Rinquet, my son has gone mad! It's a scandal! What have I done to deserve this? And all this time, his father's been so sick with anxiety that he's had to go to bed . . .'

At the word *father*, Roger had rushed out of the kitchen. He went up the stairs four at a time and stopped for a moment on the landing to calm down a little. While he was standing there, motionless, with one hand on his pounding heart, a voice said softly:

'Is that you, son?'

The door was ajar, and the night-light which he had had when he was a little boy was burning. It was all so unusual that Roger shivered, seized by a mortal fear.

'Is it true that you're ill?'

The worst of it was that drunkenness was still clogging his mouth and he stumbled over the syllables.

'Your mother always exaggerates. You've come home, that's the main thing. Hurry off to bed now.'

On a sudden impulse, Roger threw himself on the bed with his head on his father's chest. Sobbing, he tried to stammer out an apology, but he had a lump in his throat. A hand stroked his wet hair – he didn't know why his hair was wet – and then he heard Élise's voice, and the kitchen door opening.

And his father murmured, as if there were no need of any further explanations between them:

'Hurry off to bed. Good night, son.'

*

The next morning, at the bottom of one of his pockets, he had found a little crackled photograph showing a boy between fourteen and fifteen, in a Tyrolean costume, standing on a mountain covered with fir-trees. The boy was holding the hand of a little girl in a short skirt who must have been his sister.

He remained perplexed for a long time, until at last there came back to his memory the picture of a Feldwebel with a red moustache who was humming a song of his own country and swaying from side to side on a bench, his hand under a skinny woman's skirts.

Mademoiselle Rinquet had rushed around all day to find a room, and in the evening she had come for her things with a carrier.

Then Élise, who had cried all the time she was doing her housework, had said with a sigh of relief, after shutting the door on the old shrew:

'Good riddance!'

Chapter Seven

'Give me your arm, will you, Roger. If you only knew how often, when you were little, I told my friends at L'Innovation: "You wait until I go out on my son's arm and people take him for my sweetheart!"'

Élise made an effort to smile, to rid that smile of anything which might resemble melancholy. Arm-in-arm, they walked along the quai de Coronmeuse. The next day, Roger would take to school a note from Désiré saying that his son had been ill, although Father Renchon already knew the truth. Roger had told him the day before:

'I'm going with my mother and some cousins of mine to collect some food about twelve miles away, the other side of Visé, just by the Dutch frontier.'

It was nine o'clock in the morning, the time of day he liked best, when the streets primmed themselves up and the sun still had all its promising brightness. True, as soon as evening came, Roger was drawn by the ambiguous atmosphere of the ill-lit town, and even if he had promised himself not to go out, he only had to see through his window the bluish halo of a gas-lamp or an anonymous couple brushing past the houses to set off for unavowable walks lasting hours at a time.

In spite of all that, he remained essentially a man of the morning. Of all his memories, the best were those of spring mornings, the Passerelle spanning the sparkling Meuse, a thin mist still clinging to things, the noise of the vegetable market in the place Cockerill, and then, on the river-bank, La Goffe, littered with baskets of sweet-smelling fruit and crowded with big-buttocked women.

'You tell everybody that I cry and complain because I like it, but it isn't true, Roger. You see, I've had so few good moments in my life! You yourself, you've often hurt me. But we're happy together, aren't we?'

Yes, they were happy together. It touched Roger to sense her trembling on his arm, such a little girl and so vulnerable that he felt he had become a man as a result.

'If I've taken in lodgers, and if I've clipped them as much as I could, it's been for your sake, so that one day you'd be somebody. And you hurt me so badly when you heap reproaches on me! My only joy in life is to see you healthy and well dressed, to know that you want for nothing.'

'Yes, Mother.'

And he honestly wondered if he was not going to fulfil Élise's dream. There were several men in embryo inside him and there was still time for him to make a choice. His mother's ideal was Monsieur Herman, the first violin at the Théâtre Royal, who had never married so as to stay with his old mother. She was a dainty little thing, so fresh-faced and so neatly dressed that Élise could not suppress a pang of envy when she looked at their house with the white door in the rue Pasteur where mother and son doted on one another like sweethearts.

Roger was not a musician. He could probably follow a career like that of Vriens, the Walloon poet whom he met every morning on the embankment, wearing a huge black hat and a loosely tied bow, his eyes dreamy, his smile kindly. He wrote love songs in dialect which everybody hummed, and there was nobody who did not know him, nobody who did not turn round to look at him as he went by, drawing calmly and greedily on his pipe, on his way to work at the municipal library at Les Chiroux.

He knew Roger, who was his most regular customer, or had been until a few weeks earlier. He had been encouraging him to write poetry for a long time now.

Élise also dreamt of a cake-shop where a sturdy, good-natured Roger would toil away in the scented warmth of the bakehouse while she herself, neat and trim in an embroidered white apron crackling with starch, would serve tarts across a marble counter.

'It's such a fine trade, Roger! Have you ever seen a confectioner who was poor? Besides, all businesses that sell food do well. Just look at the butchers. I wouldn't like you to be a butcher, but there isn't a single one that isn't well-off.'

On mornings like this, it seemed as if the town, in order to win him over, was trying to show him a simple, cordial face.

Over there, on the other side of the river crowded with rows of barges, there were the baths where he went every morning with his grandfather and his old cronies. Hadn't a Monsieur Fourneau, for example, always accompanied by his dog Rita, which he sent diving for pebbles, discovered the secret of perfect happiness?

It was sufficient to create for each and every day a certain number of habits, rites, little pleasures, and life flowed along gently, uneventfully, almost without your noticing the passage of time.

In the Saint-Léonard district, people said of Monsieur Fourneau, as they said of Chrétien Mamelin in the rue Puits-en-Sock:

'He's such a good fellow!'

Roger had taken another road and occasionally he felt rather frightened, for he did not know where it led. On this road, along which a mysterious force was driving him – his mother would say that it was his evil instincts – there would be nobody to give him approval or assistance, nobody to comfort him in case of failure.

'It's like my sister Louisa, Roger. I know you can't stand her. I admit she doesn't do anything to make people love her. But one day I'll tell you her life-story and you'll forgive her, I'm sure of that. In the meantime, try to be a little nicer to her, even if it's only to please me.'

He promised. What wouldn't he have promised today? The slightest thing was capable of making him cry. Part of his childhood was smiling at him and timidly trying to hold him back, while he could feel that he was being dragged along in a course on which he had embarked almost without knowing it.

'You're going to see my friend Éléonore Dafnet, whom you don't know yet. But she knows you well. At L'Innovation, she was on the next counter to mine. She wasn't happy, because her father drank. When you were born, it was she who gave you the little silver bell that bears the mark of your first teeth. She's married a Lanaeken farmer. It must have been awful for a girl as delicate and sensitive as Éléonore. I met her one evening last week in the rue Neuvice and we fell into each other's arms. Straight away, she said to me:

'"You know, Élise, if you're short of food, don't hesitate to

495

come to us. We live rather far away, but you've got a big son now who must be a great help to you.''

He registered the reproach – an involuntary reproach, for his mother too wanted there to be no more unpleasantness between them. For two months now, he had not once offered to go for the rations. Élise spent her days queueing, now for bread, now for bacon from America, rice, potatoes or coal. On Monday she had hired a handcart which she had pushed through the streets, loaded with a couple of bags of coal, and she had had to ask a passer-by to help her to take them down to the cellar.

'If it wasn't for the war, we'd be so happy, the three of us!'

He could feel himself being sucked down into warmth and sunshine and reassurance. A few more yards and they had arrived at Aunt Louisa's shop, the glazed door with the transparent advertisements which had never changed, the smell of gin and spices, and the calendar with the two girls on it, the brunette and the blonde.

'Anna will be ready in a minute. The little Duchêne girls have gone to get some bread. Come in, Élise. Come in, Roger. Dear God, how he's grown! Anna! Anna! Hurry up. Élise is down here.'

They could hear Anna, the eldest of the Jusseaume girls, getting dressed on the first floor, where Roger had never been. They found Monique Duchêne standing in the kitchen, wearing a long, light-coloured dress with a floral pattern and an Italian straw hat with a pale blue ribbon. She had been crying and was still dabbing her eyes with a handkerchief rolled into a ball.

'Poor Monique,' sighed Élise as she kissed her. 'You're coming with us, then? You're sure it won't be too tiring for you?'

Tall and slim, she made you think of a frail flower whose stem bent in the slightest breath of air. Everything about her was as delicate and misty as a pastel drawing.

Aunt Louisa broke in:

'It's no use me telling her that everything will work out all right, that God can't want Évariste to be unhappy, she just goes on tormenting herself. This morning, some neighbours told her that he'd written again to that woman.'

Not long ago, they would never have broached this subject

in front of Roger. Probably they considered that he was big enough now to understand.

'Who knows what lies she may be telling him? But I've written a long letter too, a letter I sent off yesterday with a bargee. When Évariste gets it, he'll realize on which side the truth lies.'

Why was it that on a morning like this, when he was feeling quite relaxed and wanted nothing more than to feel even more relaxed, he had to be bothered with this disgusting family matter?

Monique was a cousin, not of his, although he called her that, but of Évariste who was at the front and had given such an unpleasant reception to poor Jacques Schroefs.

She had two younger sisters, the girls who had gone to get some bread and were going to accompany them to Lanaeken. They lived in the same district, in the rue Sainte-Foi, just behind the quai de Coronmeuse. Their father was a doctor, but he had scarcely any patients. He was rarely to be seen and people talked about him as little as possible, for he was a strange man who had a vice: he was addicted to ether. Roger had caught sight of him twice: a bearded man with grey hair and a grey complexion, always dirty and shabbily dressed, with dandruff on the collar of his jacket and eyes as dull as those of the rue de la Loi neighbour who had died of the sleeping-sickness.

How could a man like that be the father of the poetic Monique whose feet scarcely touched the ground?

Évariste and Monique had been engaged. There had not been an official engagement, but it had always been understood that they would get married one day and that they would make a handsome couple. Évariste was tall and thin, with a rather grim face, for he was a conscientious young man who took life seriously. He had had only a year left to complete his studies for the Bar when the war had broken out.

Another catastrophe, for him, had occurred before the war. A local girl had had a child by him, a working-class girl, whose father, a sturdy little man, was night-watchman in a factory. This man, a stubborn, obstinate fellow, had come to see Louisa, and to all her objections had simply replied:

'Only marriage will do.'

Louisa had tried everything. She had offered money. She had

consulted a famous lawyer. She had even tried to find proof that the Prunier girl had had relations with other men, to show that Évariste was not necessarily the child's father.

It had all been in vain. A dozen times a day, Prunier had returned to the attack, truculent and abusive, shouting and gesticulating in the shop and even outside on the pavement where he threatened to stir up the passers-by, and constantly returning to his perpetual refrain:

'Only marriage will do.'

They had been married two months before the war, when Thérèse Prunier was four months pregnant. She was a non-descript little thing, puny and pretty like so many others, a girl of the people who worked in a dressmaker's workshop.

Désiré had been the first to know, for it had been to him that Évariste, right from the start, had confided his troubles. Désiré had told nobody, not even Élise. She had wondered why Évariste, whom they never used to see before, came nearly every evening to the rue de la Loi.

He was given to seeing life in a tragic light. It was in his nature. He liked taking up attitudes and watched himself living. On his wedding-day, in the quai de Coronmeuse kitchen, pale and red-eyed, he had declared to his mother, who repeated his words as if they were a sacred text:

'I am going to my wedding as I would to the funeral of my youthful hopes.'

The couple had not lived together. It had been decided that Thérèse should go on living at her parents' home and Évariste with his family until he had completed his studies.

The war had broken out, and Évariste had gone away before the birth of his son, who was a puny, highly strung child. He had had convulsions, and his mother had nearly died in childbirth. Who could say whether Louisa did not pray for things to work out that way?

Since then, Monique Duchêne had got into the habit of coming every day to the quai de Coronmeuse, where she was treated as a daughter-in-law.

'You haven't any news, have you, Aunt?'

She did not say mother yet, but the word was implied, and the two women behaved to one another as daughter-in-law and mother-in-law; they did not doubt for a moment that the matter

498

would end like that, because it could not be otherwise, God would not allow it. They went to Mass together and could be seen together at Vespers and Benediction, praying, as Désiré put it, 'to God at the foot of the Cross'. They burnt candles. Monique took part in all the charitable activities of the parish. She wrote to Évariste nearly every day, even though the opportunities of sending post by way of Holland were somewhat rare.

To begin with, the Pruniers had refused to allow the child to go to spend a day now and then at his paternal grandmother's home.

'If the mother isn't good enough for them, they don't need the son either.'

The lawyers had been called in once more. The case had been taken to court. Louisa had won. Once a week, Thérèse's mother, who put a hat on only on this occasion, brought the child to the door of the shop, then went away, without a greeting, without a word. And in the evening it was Anna who took the child back to the little working-class house, ringing the bell, but hurrying away before anybody opened the door.

The whole family felt sorry for Monique and admired her heroism.

'If you saw her with the child, Désiré, it would bring tears to your eyes. Though she's every reason to hate it, she loves it like a real mother because, as she says, it's Évariste's child. The day the little boy comes to Louisa's, she spends the whole day there. It's her that takes him out for a walk. She dressed him up from head to foot and do you know what those people did? They sent all the clothes back in a parcel that they left on the doorstep like thieves.'

Thérèse went on writing to Évariste. As if she could possibly love him!

'You see, Élise, they've got only one thing in their heads: the idea that we've got money. The fact that Évariste is at the front doesn't stop that girl from running after men. I heard that she'd been seen with some Germans. I wrote to Évariste and told him so. I saw the lawyer again, and he told me that if Évariste wrote a letter that he drafted for me, I'd be given custody of the child. Monique would be so happy!'

And the latter sighed:

'Évariste won't do it.'

'Why not, seeing that he doesn't love that woman?'

'He's too scrupulous. He wants to do his duty in spite of everything, to drain the cup to its dregs. I know that Thérèse has written to him telling the most awful lies about us. He must be so unhappy over there, all alone, and pulled this way and that!'

Anna had come downstairs, solidly built like her mother, with a mannish face. She put on her gloves and started looking for her parasol.

'Haven't your sisters arrived yet, Monique? And I thought I was late. Good morning, Aunt. Isn't Roger with you?'

Roger had preferred to slip into the workshop which looked out on to the sunny yard, where his uncle, in the blue shadows, was plaiting scented wands in the company of the hunchbacked workman. It felt like another world. You could hear the hammers at Sauveur's, the trams going along the embankment and the rue Sainte-Foi, the sirens of the tugs, and the buzzing of flies. Roger would have liked to be back in the far-away days when he used to come to choose a willow-wand which he would patiently peel afterwards, or the still more distant time when, a little short-legged fellow, he circled round his uncle, whom he did not know, finally asking anxiously:

'Tell me, workman, don't people eat in this house?'

The yard had been bigger, the wall higher, the solitary tree enormous – that tree which sprang from between the uneven paving-stones and whose velvet leaves he stroked today scarcely needing to stand on tip-toe to do so.

'Roger! Where are you, Roger? We're going!'

He was full of goodwill this morning, as he gave his arm to his mother and tried to imagine her as a young girl lost in the immensity of L'Innovation. He was looking forward to going to Lanaeken with his cousins.

One of them, Colette, who was only a little older than he, was a pretty girl with bold eyes. Her fair hair hung down her back in two heavy plaits. She wore shorter skirts than other girls of her age and she had the gestures of a boy; several times they had pretended to fight so as to have an excuse for rolling about in the grass or the cornfields together.

The year before, when they had got into the habit of going

picnicking all together on Moncin Island, two miles from Coronmeuse, he had been in love with Colette, in the right way, without any unhealthy curiosity or any thoughts which could make him blush.

He had admired her sister Monique who had walked nonchalantly behind them with the grown-ups, holding a parasol tilted to one side. Monique had reminded him of the mother of his little friend Jacques at Embourg, under the firs, and the pretty villa among the roses in the park.

Colette, who was still rather dry and angular, would become, he had thought, the image of her elder sister, for she had the same long face and pale blue eyes.

Now, he knew. Colette was like the girls you followed in the shadows of the Carré. She went with boys, let them pull her skirts up, and did dirty things in corners. She was well known in the district. Her other sister, who was not quite fifteen, was even more dissolute than she was. People said:

'. . . The little Duchêne girls.'

That was enough. They provoked men, even married men. Respectable girls were forbidden to go out with 'the doctor's girls'.

If Roger told his mother that, she would not believe it. She never believed anything that was ugly, especially if it had some connexion with the family.

'Will you be quiet, Roger. I don't know where you get ideas like that.'

Simply by keeping his eyes and ears open. Even now, walking beside the canal along the tow-path where the trees cast a diagonal shadow every few yards, he was listening without wanting to. He would have preferred to amble along, daydreaming as he went, for of all the landscapes of his childhood, this was the one he loved best.

With a knapsack on his back and a stick in his hand, bareheaded and open-necked, he was walking in front with his two cousins. Élise, Anna and Monique followed, talking in an undertone, and stopping from time to time because Monique got out of breath easily.

Now and then they passed a barge gliding with a slight rippling of the water along the canal where, for no apparent reason, bubbles kept rising to the surface. They brushed past the tight cable and climbed the bank to avoid the slow-moving horse, which was followed by a carter or sometimes a child brandishing a switch.

The foliage over their heads formed a fresh, motionless canopy of a dark green colour which was reflected in the water, and less than a hundred yards to the right the Meuse flowed freely, without hindrance, towards the sea, spreading out between low banks and sparkling in the sunshine; there was an angler here and there, motionless under his straw hat, in a flat boat which stakes held in midstream. Everything was so quiet that you could hear the machinery of a lock creaking a mile away; a big bumble-bee went by, or else, far away, at the foot of the hills which were veiled for a moment by a long plume of white smoke, a train whistled frantically.

'She went to the cinema with young Sauveur. Knowing how dumb he is, even worse than his father, you can imagine what fun she had! I said to her: "My dear girl, if you're going to pick a man . . ."'

They talked without stopping, breaking off only to burst out laughing.

'Since Simone broke it off with Georges, she's been going with old men. You remember the one who wears white spats and followed us the whole of one Sunday afternoon? It seems that he's got a bachelor apartment not far from Hazinelle's school. He's a nobleman, but he hasn't got a penny to his name, and his family keeps him on a tight rein. Well, she went along with him. You'll never guess what he asked her to do . . .'

They whispered together, face to face, darting provocative glances at their cousin.

'What would you have done in her place?'

Why, for heaven's sake, did Roger descend to asking them, crimson-faced:

'What did he ask her to do?'

'I can't tell you.'

'Why not?'

'Yolande! He wants to know why not!'

They burst out laughing, and went on keeping him in suspense.

'Shall I tell him?'

'Are you mad? If you tell him something like that, I won't stay another minute with you.'

'Tell me, Colette.'

'Guess. If you guess right, I'll tell you.'

There he was again with his fever in the blood and his shifty look. There were certain words which he did not dare to utter, even before a schoolmate. He tried to express himself by means of periphrases and vague gestures.

'Was it that?'

'You are a silly! If it had been that, Simone would have been only too pleased. Anybody can see that you don't know her.'

'Then was it with the mouth?'

'Did you hear that, Yolande? . . . He wants to know if it was . . . Say it again, Roger! . . . If you could see your face now! . . . Have you tried? . . . Who with? . . . Tell us . . . Where was it?'

He fixed his attention on the pure sight of the canal, longing to shake off the fever which had taken hold of him. He despised his cousins and all the girls they talked about.

'Tell me what he asked her to do.'

'Who said he asked her to do something?'

'Then he asked her to let him do something to her?'

'He's getting warm, isn't he, Yolande? Shall I tell him?'

'If you do, I'll tell Monique where you went last night.',

'Where did you go, Colette?'

They kept him on tenterhooks, playing with him and exchanging conspiratorial glances.

'Do I ask you what you do with girls?'

He heard, closer to them, the voices of the three women following them.

'I know that Évariste will never divorce her. Besides, Louisa would never agree to it. She's too much of a Catholic. One case in the family is enough. If you only knew how much it hurt my sister to marry a man who'd been divorced! And yet it wasn't his fault. It was his wife who had gone off with one of his workmen.'

Roger pricked up his ears, realizing that it was Aunt Louisa's husband, that quiet old man with a patriarchal beard, who was a divorced man. So from the religious point of view his aunt was not married; for all that she went to church morning and evening, she was living in a permanent state of mortal sin.

'Believe me, poor Monique, as my sister says, everything will work out all right, for there's a God in heaven.'

Couldn't Roger, by means of a superhuman effort, manage to shake off this oppressive atmosphere with a tremendous roar of laughter? Were they mad? Were they monsters? Could they possibly be being sincere with themselves?

Aunt Louisa prayed to God to 'work things out' without a divorce. What could that mean if not that God, in order that Évariste might be happy and marry his cousin, should call to rest the poor little sempstress who had not known how to avoid having a child?

And Monique prayed to God too, took part in charitable activities, sang at High Mass! They were all perfectly capable of joining together to offer up a novena:

'Jesus and Mary, summon to Heaven that girl who is preventing the world from being happy!'

He heard Élise murmuring:

'Besides, she's a sickly little thing. Anna was telling me just now that she knows, from the woman who does their washing, that she started spitting blood not so long ago. She's got something wrong with her womb too. She wasn't strong enough for a normal delivery and she had to have a Caesarean operation.'

It was shameful. It was ignoble. And yet nothing cracked, the sky was a magnificent blue which enveloped you in serenity, thousands of daisies pushed their innocent little heads between velvety blades of grass, and the very fish which an angler was pulling out of the water seemed to be wriggling happily at the end of his line.

When the poetic Monique had been a girl, had she allowed men to paw her about on dark patches of waste ground or in public lavatories? Had she taken pleasure like her sisters in conjuring up erotic scenes before a boy?

His skin was baking in the sun. He could hear the staccato laughter of the two Duchêne girls. He turned round and saw the three women in a row; Monique's innocent parasol, the black parasol of Anna, who was not very particular about her appearance, and the bent head of Élise, who wanted everybody to be happy and who, for that reason, hoped without any malice that Thérèse would die.

On the canal, a tow-haired woman was using her buttocks to push the tiller of a barge which was moving silently along; a little girl in red, thin and naked under her dress, was playing at her feet on the deck, which was still wet from being washed down. The woman was feeding a baby at her breast, and that breast was the only white patch in the whole scene. In the distance, in the shadow of the trees, the husband was walking along, bent forward, harnessed to a steel hawser; it was he who, by dint of a slow, continuous effort, was making the barge glide along between the canal banks.

Why had the Duchêne girls suddenly burst out laughing? He had not said anything or done anything. He realized that he was looking at them inquiringly with a stupid expression on his face, and it was some time before he guessed the ignoble truth: they had started laughing because they had thought that he could not take his eyes off the bargee's milky-white breast!

*

They picnicked at Visé, which was known as the Martyred Town because most of its inhabitants had been shot by the Germans in August 1914 and the town itself burnt down.

Sitting on a grassy mound, they unpacked their provisions while looking vaguely at what remained of the town. Of the houses, churches and public buildings, nothing was left. The few walls which had been left standing had long since been demolished, and now stones and bricks were arranged in regular heaps. The streets and pavements were intact and stood out with astonishing clarity, so that it was still a town, but a town where the blocks of houses had been replaced by piles of stones up to six foot high.

Facing them, a wooden café had sprung up, flanked by a sort of arbour.

'No need to go and spend our money there. What would they give us to drink? Nothing good, I'll tell you that. I've brought some coffee for everybody.'

The bridge had been broken in two like a toy. In the distance, on one bank of the Meuse, they could see the frontier post and make out, in spite of the dazzling sunshine, the cable stretched across the river. The flashes they noticed now and then came from the light catching the sentries' bayonets.

In the first winter of the war, two hundred youths had piled into the hull of a tug without arousing the Germans' attention. They had had to wait for several days until the river had risen high enough to allow the boat to pass over the dams; and finally, one night, the tug had pulled away from the bank and forged downstream at full steam, without navigation lights, while rifle shots had crackled from the banks.

The Germans had already stretched a cable across the river, but the captain, counting on the force of the current, had gone straight ahead; the cable had given way and the tug had spun round slightly in the same place while the youths, free at last, had rushed on deck, shouting for joy.

Roger had been too young. He still was. His jaw set as he gazed at the frontier. What could he do to make life beautiful and clean, above all clean?

Head down, he walked along behind the others.

'What's the matter, Roger?'

'Nothing, Mother.'

'Aren't you enjoying yourself?'

His cousins were laughing at him. He did not care. They went along some secluded lanes, and Élise started to explain:

'The most dangerous place will be the level-crossing. You've seen the sentry. Luckily he's a Bavarian. If anything happens, we may be able to come to terms with him. You'll go first, Monique. Smart and pretty as you are, he'll just look at you and we'll take the opportunity to slip across.'

*

They finally arrived at Éléonore Dafnet's farm. She was waiting for them and exclaimed:

'What! You've had something to eat already! That's Élise all over. And I'd got a good dinner ready for you!'

She was a thin woman, of the same type as Élise, one of those women who look as if they have no stamina at all but are really tougher than men. Why did Roger suddenly think that they seemed to have been born to become widows?

'Is that your son? Dear God! I would never dare to kiss him!'

She was dressed in black like a woman of the middle classes. The farm was well kept, the kitchen as clean as a new pin. An accordion could be heard somewhere, and Élise, who was easily worried, looked inquiringly at her old friend.

'Don't take any notice. It's my lodgers. Because just imagine, Élise, I've got some lodgers too. But these came without me having to go and look for them. They are four Germans, three of them old men. I've got them well trained, and when they're not on guard duty they help me to milk the cows.'

She opened a door a little way.

'Hey, Franz . . . Come and say hullo to my friends . . .'

As he was wearing neither his tunic nor his boots, and had clogs full of straw on his feet, they did not have the impression of being in front of a German soldier.

'You must still be able to talk to them, I suppose, Élise. They're very nice, you know. I'm looking forward to them going and my husband coming back, but I can't say that this lot have been a nuisance. Go and get me a bottle from the cellar, Franz . . . *Flasche, ja . . . Wein . . .* That's right . . . You see, he's understood! . . . You'll have a glass too, you fat pig! . . . Believe it or not, nothing amuses him more than being called a fat pig . . .'

'You aren't frightened?'

'What of? . . . His father is burgomaster of his village . . . I've told him that yours was too . . . But what are you going to carry the food in?'

'I say, Éléonore, you're sure they don't understand everything you say?'

'What if they do? They know what you've come for. I give them plenty of butter to send to Germany, where everybody's starving to death . . . Where you'll have to be careful is at the level-crossing . . . Especially if you see a sergeant-major . . . He's a brute of a man who wouldn't hesitate to have you stripped in the middle of the road to make sure you're not hiding anything . . . Last week, he ordered his men to fire at a poor devil who was doing a bit of smuggling . . .'

*

Roger looked hard at Élise, marvelling that his mother could once have been the friend of this woman in front of him. At the time of L'Innovation, had they been like one another, and had life been sufficient to make them different?

Élise said something in an undertone. The other woman replied in an audible voice.

'Don't worry, my girl! I take good care not to lose on the deal. If I told you how much I charge them for washing their shirts and socks, you wouldn't believe me. But you haven't seen my favourite yet. Wait a minute . . . Ethel! . . . Ethel! . . . Come here, my lad, so we admire your pretty face . . . Well, wouldn't you say he was just like a child? . . . I don't know why they've put him with the old men, instead of sending him to the front . . . He's got the soft skin of a girl and he blushes at the slightest thing . . . These are friends of mine, Ethel, from the days when I was a girl . . . *Fräulein*, yes . . Me, *Fräulein* . . . You see! He doesn't know what to do with himself . . . His father's a solicitor at Mainz . . . He's got a sister who's married to a baron . . . A glass of wine, Ethel? . . . *Ja* . . . Get the glasses out of the cupboard . . . Try to make yourself useful . . . You see how I make them work?'

'You still haven't any news of your husband?'

'No. I haven't had a single letter for a year now.'

She heaved a sigh, but went on filling the glasses.

'What are you going to put the corn in?'

'You'll see. I'll show you when they've gone. I've made myself a double petticoat with vertical seams every couple of inches . . .'

*

They had eaten some tart with the Germans. Only Monique had remained somewhat aloof. Then all of a sudden they had noticed that time was passing fast. In the granary, they had had to hunt for a funnel with which to pour corn into the narrow pockets of which Élise's petticoat was composed. They had weighed the butter and bacon.

Roger had understood what Colette was up to when, after looking him in the eyes, she had wandered casually into a dimly lit barn. He had followed her. In a rather nervous voice she had asked him:

'What do you want?'

She must have been frightened, for he really hated her, and it was out of hatred that he had pushed her down on the floor, that his teeth had pressed against hers, that his hands had torn angrily at her underclothes. If her sister Yolande had not come in just then, he would probably have gone the whole way, to soil her.

'Well, you two believe in having fun, don't you?'

'Brute. Filthy brute!' Colette had muttered, trying to tidy herself up.

She no longer laughed at him. She respected him. It was she who, the whole of the way home, would go running after him.

*

Élise, who was slightly disappointed, did not show it.

'How much has she charged us for the corn?'

'Twenty-five francs a kilo.'

'That's five francs cheaper than in town. Her butter has a good nutty taste. It isn't like the butter you get on the ration, which is always rancid and watery.'

Had she been hoping that Éléonore would let her have all that for nothing, or at the pre-war prices?

Monique Duchêne was sent ahead to go over the dangerous level-crossing. Roger and his cousins climbed the bank and crossed the railway-line a hundred yards away from the sentries. Élise, in her wheat-filled petticoat which was puffed out like a crinoline, looked as if she were pregnant; she bore a certain resemblance to those Louis Quinze figurines in porcelain, and her face seemed delicate and fine.

'Let me carry something, Aunt.'

'No, Monique, your hands are too delicate.'

They avoided the tow-path and went along a path between the rushes beside the Meuse. They talked less and less. They ended up by not talking at all, while the sky turned pale green and the breeze covered the river with little white waves.

*

Roger envied the young soldier whom he had seen back at the farm and whom Éléonore Dafnet looked at so tenderly. Wasn't that young man lucky to have escaped from everyday life, from his family, from the never-changing houses which he had seen ever since childhood, standing around him like prison walls?

In a whitewashed scullery, four mattresses had been laid side by side on the floor. There were helmets and belts lying around on some straw-bottomed chairs, a razor and a shaving-brush on the window-sill, a piece of looking-glass fixed with some nails to the wall. On the other side of the wall you could hear the cows and horses. Sitting on his bed, barefooted, his open shirt revealing a hairy torso, a forty-year-old soldier who was a dentist in civilian life was playing the accordion.

And Aunt Louisa wrote to Évariste, who was at the front, to tell him all the tittle-tattle she had heard about his wife. Monique for her part wrote to him to hint, for she was extremely tactful, that she was waiting for him and that whatever happened he would find her on his return.

Éléonore Dafnet did not worry about her husband of whom she had no news and who was probably dead. For her name-day, she had treated herself to a brooch costing two thousand francs. She had shown it to Élise.

Désiré, that evening, would have to get his own supper when he came home from the office, for they would not get back to the rue des Maraîchers before dark. There were still a few dangerous places to pass. Not only were they running the risk of several years' imprisonment, but the sentries had orders to shoot.

*

'What do you do on Sundays?' Colette asked Roger.

He knew what she was getting at, but he would not grant her the rendezvous she was hoping for. He was glad that Yolande had turned up to prevent him from going the whole way, for Colette would probably have hung on to him.

Was it his family that weighed heavily on Roger? There were moments when he wondered whether, as Élise maintained when she was having one of her fits of hysterics, he was a monster. It was not his fault. That morning, he had been full of goodwill. Why had they had to stir up all their filth in front of him?

Solitude frightened him sometimes. But what could he do to avoid being alone?

*

They ended up by walking in Indian file. Their feet kept stumbling, the grass had turned grey, and the evening had as it were a taste of cold embers. Éléonore Dafnet's stodgy tart – the pastry had not been properly baked – still weighed heavily on their stomachs.

What was left to him of his day? A few minutes of gaiety and hope when, in the morning, on the quai de Coronmeuse, his mother had asked him with touching timidity to give her his arm, and he had had the impression of breathing the air of a period which he had not known, which he could reconstruct only with the help of Valérie and a few scattered friends of his mother's.

A little girl in red; a woman feeding her baby while at the same time pressing against the tiller; a man in the distance, in the shadow of the trees, working patiently like a horse.

Then those mattresses, those grey blankets, that barrack-room smell, those four brothers-in-arms living apart from the world and wandering about the Lanaeken farm.

*

'You're walking too fast, children. Monique can't keep up with you. It's you, Roger, hurrying along like a madman!'

He slowed down. He would do whatever they asked. It did not matter to him. He had nothing in common with them. He would obediently grind the corn in the coffee-mill and sift it through the sieve.

His life was somewhere else, he did not yet know where. He was looking for it outside and he would go on looking for it.

*

Élise felt that she had to keep it from him. She imagined that he had not heard. At a certain moment, just as Éléonore Dafnet had been beginning a sentence, she had motioned to her to be quiet, glancing at Roger. The two women had gone on talking in Flemish, and he had understood without wanting to.

Éléonore had asked Élise if she still took in lodgers, because two farmers' daughters of the neighbourhood, who were attending classes at the Pigier Institute, were looking for a room in town.

Now his mother was explaining in an undertone to Anna:

'You understand, I didn't say no. Farmers' daughters will always bring us something to eat. I haven't spoken to Roger about it yet, because he's getting even more difficult than his father. You'd think he was jealous of everything that came into the house. And then he's never there.'

He showed no reaction. Let her take in as many lodgers as she liked, let her fill the house with them, let her make him sleep in the attic again as in the rue de la Loi, it was all the same to him. As his mother put it so well, he was never there.

They got to the quai de Coronmeuse in the dark, went into Aunt Louisa's for a moment, exchanged packets and did some complicated calculations.

Then there were only two of them left to carry their load past the dark houses. Élise was tired. She made an effort to follow her son without complaining. They did not talk to one another any more. They had nothing more to say to each other.

They crossed the Pont Maghin and the place du Congrès, and automatically glanced down the rue Pasteur, where there was not a soul to be seen and everything seemed dead.

They had only to cross the Dérivation by the Pont d'Amercoeur and they would be home again; they would go into the kitchen where Désiré, in his shirtsleeves, had laid the table and was waiting for them, reading the paper in his reconquered armchair.

'Well, Élise? Well, son? Was the expedition a success?'

The two of them took off their harness. Élise chattered away, as she always did when she had something to hide, and Roger stole a glance at his father, feeling sad at heart.

Élise had brought him back a piece of tart which made a sorry sight on the table, with its paper sticking to it and the fruit soaking into the pastry.

Chapter Eight

It was four o'clock. The usher, after opening the double doors, went to station himself in the middle of the rue Saint-Gilles in order to stem the flood of schoolboys when a tram came by.

It was June 1918. On the heights, the sound of gunfire could be heard coming nearer and nearer. The Germans you met in town were old soldiers of the Landsturm, bearded, bald, too small or too tall or deformed. They no longer emptied the excess contents of their mess-tins into the gutter. You saw little groups of them trailing their short boots along the pavements and stopping to stare with childlike longing at the window-displays.

The other day, when Élise had come out of the American food-centre after spending over three hours waiting in a queue, she had seen one who had aroused her pity and she had been unable to refrain from talking about him at supper-time. He was standing on the kerb, facing the door. In his big porcelain pipe he was smoking something which was not tobacco, and which smelled like the bonfires you lit in the country, hay probably, or oak-leaves. He must have been a grandfather. You could tell that from the way in which he looked at children of a certain age. He had been fat at one time but now his uniform was too big for him, and the buckle of his belt hung down on his shrivelled belly.

'If you'd seen the look, Désiré, that he shot at the piece of bacon he could see in my shopping-bag! It made his mouth water.'

If they were hungry, the population was hungry too, and for some time now it had been possible to recognize well-to-do people who came rather awkwardly to join the queue at the working-class soup-kitchens.

People were wearing boaters made of rustic straw, 'rock-straw' as hat-makers called it. The centre of the hat had to be extremely high, the rim as narrow as possible, the ribbon non-existent. It was the latest thing, together with wide trousers and yellow shoes with American toe-caps. Another new fashion was for soft collars in piqué whose points were held in position, on both sides of the tie, by a little bar with a metal ball at each end.

Roger was fashionably dressed, except for his trousers which were of medium width. Coming out of the door, he looked round for somebody, and, when he saw Stievens, fell into step with him.

'Shall we go and have a game of billiards?'

For he had come to that: to looking out for a Stievens and going down the rue Saint-Gilles with him, with exaggerated self-assurance in his eyes and walk. He no longer used his oilcloth satchel but instead, like the students at the university, carried his books and exercise books in one hand, tied together with a strap. He cluttered himself up as little as possible. Everybody knew that now, for instance, they were not going home to study, but that a life entirely foreign to school was waiting for them.

Stievens, like Mamelin, was wearing one of those straw hats that you saw most of all on flashy businessmen. It was as if they had both broken with the rest of the class. They still came to school, sat down on their bench, and opened an exercise book as a matter of form, but it was obvious that they were no longer taking any part in the common life. Nor were they getting ready for the approaching examinations.

Neef-the-peasant was nonplussed. His eyes expressed amazement and despair at seeing Roger, who was one of the best pupils in the school, deliberately placing himself, of his own free will, on the same level as Stievens.

The two of them walked along, disdainful of the friends who passed them. In spite of the regulations, and without any attempt at concealment, they went into the porch of the Palace. There was a glass cage on the right where people bought their tickets, but they did not stop; with a familiar, patronizing good day, they walked past the doorman, who lifted the velvet curtain for them.

The auditorium was full of people sitting around tables drinking beer or grenadine. A serial film was unfolding on the screen and the two youths remained standing for a moment. Then the lights went on for a variety act, the musicians returned to their places in the orchestra pit, a net was stretched over the audience's heads, and some acrobats wearing plaster-coloured tights hoisted themselves up to the ceiling along taut ropes.

'Shall we go?'

They walked past, apparently indifferent to the amusements of the mob. At the far end of the room, next to the bar where a few prostitutes were hanging about, they lifted a curtain and went up a staircase where they could hear, at the same time as the music from the auditorium, the sound of billiard balls colliding.

Roger was not yet sixteen. Stievens was his senior by some months. Solemn, very conscious of the importance of every gesture, they walked slowly into the over-decorated rooms of the billiards saloon.

'Is Number 9 free, Albert?'

'Yes, gentlemen. The usual?'

The light of day did not penetrate into the billiard rooms. You could only just hear the music from the Palace, chiefly when a roll on the drums emphasized an acrobat's somersault.

Here everything was austere and elegant. The lamps lit up nothing but the green billiard-cloths, and the players' heads were like waxwork figures in the half-light. Each person, whether he was playing or waiting his turn, studied his attitudes, looking inquiringly at the wall-mirrors; there was a special degree of nonchalance which was difficult to acquire, a superior smile which was as it were the hallmark of the accomplished player.

The calm was so profound that a loud voice would have arrested every gesture. And yet, moving stiffly to and fro in the depths of this silence, Roger was conscious of an inner force which was carrying him along at breathtaking speed and knew that nothing but a catastrophe could stop him.

He needed Stievens. It humiliated him to be reduced to waiting for him after school, but what else could he do at four o'clock in the afternoon, seeing that he could not go home? He had already seen the films showing at the three cinemas in the town. There were no afternoon performances at the theatres. He had seen the show at the Palace the day before;

he had even watched part of it twice over. And when he was alone like that, sitting in the middle of the crowd, he was sometimes seized with an intolerable fear. He was afraid, he did not know why. He needed somebody's presence to re-assure him and so he went to Gaston's or to Stievens', for he had sometimes gone to pick up the latter at his home.

If you did not know people, you got the wrong idea about them. The Stievens, for instance, lived in a very simple house, not much smarter than the one in the rue des Maraîchers. The real difference, apart from a few knick-knacks, was that they had a drawing-room and took their meals in the dining-room. The father, who had died not long before the war, had been a broker. The mother kept his business going.

The two women, the mother and the daughter, who looked so startling when you met them at the Carré, covered in furs and feathers, were utterly nondescript at home, neither of them more desirable than the other. The girl had the same heavy features, the same coarse flesh as her brother. She and her mother loafed around at home in slippers and dressing-gowns. The Stievens, who were very careful with their money, spent it on nothing but clothes.

'I know perfectly well that I shan't get my diploma,' Stievens said without any regret. 'I don't care. I'll go into some business or other as a clerk in order to learn the ropes, and then I'll set up on my own.'

'Will you have enough money to start your own business?'

'I'll marry a girl who'll bring me some.'

Usually, when he came home, there was nobody there. He ate whatever he could find, opening a tin, if necessary, and went to bed. If he met his mother and sister in town he greeted them from a distance, whether they were by themselves or in company, and each went his own way.

*

Playing billiards brought back memories to Roger. It was such a short while back and yet it was already so long ago! At the time when he used to comb his hair with his fingers and went out in clogs, he had gone two or three times in the evening to play billiards with his father in a café in Outremeuse.

Everybody recognized Désiré and knew that it was the

Mamelins, father and son, who were playing together like equals.

'Your turn, son.'

'How would you tackle that one? A follow-through stroke?'

'Play it off two cushions, putting bottom on the ball.'

The atmosphere was heavy and familiar. Their glasses of beer stood on a little table where they went now and then to drink a mouthful. They wiped their lips with the back of one hand. There too, Roger stole an occasional glance at himself in the mirrors, but this was to make sure of the plebeian joviality of his face.

People came up to watch them playing.

'So you're teaching your boy to play billiards, Désiré?'

'Ready for the time when he'll have to give me points.'

Now they scarcely dared to look at one another, he and his father. Roger fled from the house with his mouth still full, and remorse haunted him at the idea that he was leaving Désiré alone with his mother.

*

Cécile was dead. She had stayed in bed for a whole week. Nobody had ever seen so many flies about as there were then, and the atmosphere had rarely been so stormy. His aunt's voice was so faint that you had to put your ear up against her mouth, and even then you had to guess what she was trying to say. Yet she did not realize the gravity of her condition.

'If you only knew how thin I am, Roger! Look. There's nothing left. The bones themselves have melted away . . .'

She lifted the blanket. It was horrible. A smell, which struck Roger as the smell of the death-agony, took him by the throat. He refused to go to see her any more. His aunt kept asking for him. She wanted him to read her the rest of a romantic novel which she had started and could no longer read herself.

'You're not being very nice, Roger,' Élise told him reproachfully. 'You were always going to see Cécile, and now you don't set foot there any more just when she needs you so badly.'

Was that his fault? He felt himself going pale just from looking at her, his temples became damp and his head started spinning. When she had squeezed his hand with her sticky fingers, he avoided touching anything until he had soaped his hands two or three times under a tap.

It was only at the very end that she had realized that she was dying. Instead of fighting and rebelling like Félicie, she had been surprisingly calm, almost cheerful. She had said to him:

'Heavens, Roger, but I shall make an ugly corpse! If you could only see my portrait when I was a girl! You ask Marcel for it if he comes across it. There's only my hair that has stayed beautiful. At school, they used to call me the girl with the beautiful hair.'

They had had to promise to put flowers on her head, once she was dead, as when she had taken part in the procession; and she had gone gently into the final coma, which had lasted twenty-four hours.

The whole family had agreed not to go into mourning, on account of the war. The women still had their mourning veils in their wardrobes and they could have put them on. But as Catherine, Lucien's wife, had said:

'Can you see us, Élise, queueing at the food-centre or pushing a cartful of potatoes through the streets with mourning veils on our heads?'

Désiré's suit was black. He had always dressed in dark clothes. Roger wore a mourning band on his fawn suit. Henceforth Chrétien Mamelin felt a stranger in his own home, since it now belonged to his son-in-law.

'Poor Papa! And he's never cared much for Marcel! If only he'd followed the advice we all gave him and handed the hat-shop over to Arthur, who's in the trade! He didn't want to leave Cécile and now Cécile has left him . . .'

It would not be long before Marcel married again: everybody was agreed about that. Désiré was the only one who had nothing to say. He had been badly shaken by the death of his favourite sister. When Élise started talking about it, you could feel that he was suffering and it was not long before he left the kitchen.

How had Élise managed to keep a secret for at least ten days when it must have been suffocating her? All that time, she had kissed her son as if there were nothing wrong, but she had watched him constantly; he had realized that, without being able to guess the reason. Several times, he had had a definite impression that she had something on her mind. He had not worried about it, for it had always been like that with his mother; you might say that it was like the novenas of Marthe or Léopold, whom nobody had seen for months. For several weeks she was gay, even merry, and full of attentions for everybody. Then, little by little, her face became more pointed and she started heaving sighs and darting furtive glances at people.

'No, Désiré! I tell you there's nothing wrong. Why should there be anything wrong? You give me everything I need, don't you?'

This was a sign that the storm was close. It went on brewing for some time, waiting for an opportunity to break, a pretext which more often than not was utterly futile, without any connexion with the real cause. And then came the scene: the tears, the endless reproaches, the fit of hysterics.

This time, it had come in connexion with cheeses, the little Herve cheeses which they had brought back from Éléonore Dafnet's and put in the cellar where, so it was said, they could be kept for months. One afternoon when he had been alone in the house, Roger had eaten two of these cheeses, and he had said nothing about it, convinced that nobody would notice that two were missing out of so many.

This cheese incident was something else that Élise had kept to herself for two or three days.

'Where are you going, Roger?'

'Out.'

'You'd do better to do your homework.'

'I've done it already.'

'Who are you going to meet?'

'Nobody. Friends of mine.'

'Don't you think it would be nicer of you to offer to go to the food-centre for me?'

He said nothing, determined not to do anything of the sort, for he had a rendezvous with Gaston Van de Waele.

'But no! I know you! You prefer to wait until I'm spending the afternoon queueing in the sun to steal cheese from the cellar. No, don't go. I haven't finished yet. It's disgraceful, when a big strong man like your father has the same ration as us . . .'

'Listen, Mother . . .'

'No, Roger. You see, you've upset me too much and I've got to talk to you once for all. Your father's too good to you. It's stupid, the way he treats you. If I talk to him about you, he always takes your side.'

'Please, Mother. Once we start, you know very well how it'll finish.'

'I was telling my sister Louisa about it yesterday . . .'

It was a bad sign that, for some time now, she had kept rushing off to Coronmeuse. But he did not realize as yet how serious it was. Élise herself did not know how to get to the point.

'Let's leave Aunt Louisa out of it,' he suggested. 'I'd rather go to the food-centre and have done with it. Give me the cards and the shopping-bag.'

'Aren't you ashamed of yourself, Roger?'

'I did wrong eating the cheeses, I admit that. There now. Are you satisfied?'

'I'm not talking about the cheeses. I'm talking about you. And all the prayers I've said for you to grow up a decent man.'

He went pale, and his heart missed a beat. He suddenly felt sure that his thefts from the till at Gruyelle-Marquant's had been discovered, that his grandfather had seen him and talked. He stood there, rigid, like a condemned man.

'Cécile told me everything before she died. Poor thing! On her death-bed, she was still worrying about you and she begged me to keep an eye on your behaviour.'

'What was she interfering about?'

'Don't play the innocent, Roger. You know very well what it was. And to think that I pinched and scraped so that, in spite of the war, you should enjoy the country air at Embourg! Your poor cousin went to see you, without ever suspecting what you were doing with one of her pupils. When I heard about that, I thought I was going to go mad. I didn't want to believe it. And you boasted about it to Cécile while I was praying that my son . . .'

'. . . should remain pure until he married, I know.'

'You've still got the heart to laugh at me?'

'No, Mother, I'm not laughing. Let's just try not to be ridiculous. I tell you there's still time for us to stop. But soon you'll be rolling on the floor and saying things you'll regret afterwards.'

That had happened, of course. He in his turn had lost his temper. Why had he brought up Aunt Louisa, Évariste, Monique? He felt so bitter about the act of treachery committed by Cécile, who was dead, that he had rapidly become hateful. He preferred not to remember what he had said. Things had gone so far that a frantic Élise had ended up by screaming:

'I curse you, Roger, do you hear?'

She had thrown something at him, one of Désiré's shoes which she had just brought back from the cobbler's. He had rushed out of the house. It was just five o'clock. He had gone to meet his father, who had understood as soon as he had seen his face.

'What is it now, son?'

'A scene with Mother.'

'Why do you always rub her up the wrong way? You know how nervy she is, and yet you insist on answering her back.'

'This time it's worse than that. Aunt Cécile told her things I had told her in confidence as I would a friend. About girls. She was always asking me questions.'

He found it more embarrassing to broach this subject with his father than with his mother.

'You've got a sweetheart? Is that it?'

'Not exactly. You know those novenas Mother and Aunt Louisa insist on offering up for me. Well, when Mother found out that they'd been useless . . .'

Désiré had not asked any more questions.

'Come along. Above all, if your mother talks about it again, don't answer her whatever you do, don't try to prove that you're right.'

'She's in a dreadful state. You'll see.'

But nothing had happened that evening, thanks to the two lodgers sent by Éléonore Dafnet who had arrived providentially. They were two girls who were as different from one another as the blonde and the brunette on the calendar at Aunt Louisa's. Élise made an effort to smile, in spite of her red eyes and the furious glances she shot at her son as soon as the others had their backs turned.

'Excuse me, Mesdemoiselles. I wasn't expecting you today and the house is at sixes and sevens. We've just lost one of my husband's sisters who has left three little children . . .'

Since then, they had been living in a tense, incoherent atmosphere. Why hadn't Roger had the courage to follow the advice which his father had given him?

'Don't go out for a few days. Do your best to help your mother. She appreciates little kindnesses so much. If you tackle her the right way, she'll have forgotten everything in a week.'

He did exactly the opposite, almost in spite of himself.

Then Désiré spoke severely to him.

'Your mother's right, Roger. At your age, you haven't any right to come home at midnight, or even two o'clock in the morning. You've dropped your studies. You're never to be seen with a book in your hand. You're out all the time, with unsuitable friends . . .'

But didn't Désiré seem to be telling him with a wink:

'I'm saying all this to have a little peace. I understand you. Isn't it enough for her that I stay at home every evening? I've stayed at home ever since I got married. But you are young. You have the whole of your life in front of you . . .'

Élise felt this and watched them like a hawk, trying to find some proof of their complicity.

'Ask him where he went yesterday. He must have been drinking and he brought up all his dinner. He can't deny it, because I found his suit covered with bits of vomit and I've have had all the trouble in the world cleaning it.'

'Answer, Roger. Where were you?'

'With Gaston. It was the students' day.'

Gaston Van de Waele, who had enrolled at a commercial school where he rarely set foot, none the less regarded himself as a student, and every Friday evening he put on a green velvet cap with a long peak such as the university students wore. There were hundreds of them who met at the Pavillon de Flore where the performance was reserved for them.

Roger went with them. They made a rumpus. After the show, they formed up in crocodiles and went through the streets singing, climbing gas-lamps, ringing doorbells, and storming noisily into cafés and night-clubs. The evening nearly always finished in some place of ill-repute, with a riotous drinking session accompanied by animal noises and obscene army songs.

'Then ask him where he gets the money to go out like that.'

Roger blushed and replied rather too quickly:

'It's Gaston who pays.'

'And you aren't ashamed to go on accepting your cousin's invitations? You aren't as proud as I thought you were. In any case, I'll have a word with Gaston. I'll forbid him to take you out.'

He avoided staying at home. He avoided his mother. He was afraid of the sad, anxious gaze of his father, who sometimes looked as if he were silently appealing to him. Did Désiré understand that if he thwarted his son, the result would be quicker and more disastrous than ever?

Meanwhile, it was on him that Élise's anger fell, and Roger knew it. The only respite his father had was when the two lodgers were in the kitchen, but they did not stay there long after their meals. They went up to their room or out to the cinema, never suspecting that their departure marked the end of Désiré's tranquillity.

Roger was as ashamed of this as if he had committed an act of treachery. The only thing which restrained him was the thought of his father alone with Élise in the kitchen, but a devil impelled him in spite of everything to do what he should have avoided.

'I hope that you will at least respect my lodgers?'

They were not exactly alluring. They were homespun country girls, and Roger would not have turned round to look at them in the street. One of them, Marie, who had a moon-shaped face and big vacant eyes, was in love with Roger, stupidly, hopelessly in love. The other, a skinny girl with red hair and her face plastered with make-up, played the coquette with disarming naïvety.

Out of defiance, he had made a rendezvous with them outside. He had waited for them on the corner of the street, a stone's-throw from the house. They had gone out together and had spent the whole evening poking fun at Élise and her novenas. Now, at dinner, they darted conspiratorial glances at one another and were hard put to it not to burst out laughing as they kicked each other under the table.

The catastrophe was inevitable. Roger had got to the point

of hoping for it. He was constantly short of money. The last time he had gone out with the two lodgers, the redhead had slipped a note into his hand to pay for the cinema seats. He had paid her back the next day, but to do that he had had to borrow some money from Gaston, who had no more liqueurs to sell.

He had already sold half his school books to a bookseller in the rue Saint-Paul. He had also sold the silver watch which his father had given him when he had started going to college.

Anything was preferable to the atmosphere at home, even the billiard saloon where, looking at himself in the mirrors, he gave himself the illusion of being a man. Hadn't he come to envy Stievens, who could not be said to be afraid of his mother's reproaches and who, one day when they were quarrelling, had calmly called her a whore?

It was the height of summer, and yet it seemed to him that everything around him was dark and menacing. He avoided the sunshine in the streets, and like Gaston Van de Waele sought the ambiguous chiaroscuro of certain disreputable cafés.

It often happened that he had no dinner. An economical restaurant had been set up for the undernourished population, where for one franc you were entitled to a substantial meal. It was a huge room in the old Palais de Glace, on the boulevard de la Sauvenière, lit by the crude light coming through a glass ceiling. You queued in front of a succession of counters, receiving a plate here, a set of table utensils there, and passing cooking-pots from which girls ladled out soup, vegetables, meat, and bread. After that, all that remained for you to do was to find a place in which to sit down at one of the deal tables.

Everything had the same insipid taste and, whatever the dish for the day might be, the same smell of rancid bacon and dishwater; but it was food all the same and there was plenty of fat in it.

Often Roger kept the franc and wandered through the streets with an empty stomach, in the midday sun, until it was time to go back to school.

Élise went to Le Bouhay every evening. She told her troubles to a confessor before whom she probably cried her eyes out and who must have formed a wonderful idea of Roger. As soon as she had a moment free, she rushed over to Coronmeuse, coming back with her unpleasant expression.

The lodgers lived in the same room, the handsome corner room which had been Mademoiselle Rinquet's. Roger had the room on the right, looking out on the boulevard, and his parents the one on the left, on the rue des Maraîchers side.

The communicating doors between the three rooms were all bolted. What is more, in the girls' room, a wardrobe blocked Roger's door.

The latter had not been able to go out the day before, for want of money. He had not wanted to stay in the kitchen and had gone upstairs straight after supper, a prey to angry thoughts. He had stayed for a long time stretched out on his bed in the dark, his eyes open, his gaze fixed on the lace curtains whose complicated pattern stood out sharply in the moonlight.

Then he had heard Marie and Alice coming upstairs and whispering in their room. One of them had started tapping on the wall while they had tried to bottle up their laughter.

'Are you asleep?'

At first he had maintained a sulky silence, but he had ended up by replying:

'No.'

'What are you doing?'

'Nothing.'

They were in high spirits. He could still hear their voices and their laughter. Then he had heard a dull rumble and realized that they were trying to move the wardrobe.

He had been frightened, really frightened, sensing that nothing would stop them and that, for his part, he was ready to take any risks.

'Are you there, Roger? Can you hear me?'

'Yes.'

'Would you like to come and eat some chocolates with us?'

They nudged each other, on the point of bursting out laughing, as girls always were. The bolt was pulled back and the door opened; he could only just make out the two figures in the dark room, which had a different smell from his own room, and he had the impression that the girls were as frightened as he was.

It was a gesture of defiance. Downstairs, just below them, Élise and Désiré were sitting in the sluggish atmosphere of the kitchen, and the house was so quiet that now and then you could hear the 'poof' of the stove and you had the impression of hearing Désiré turning the pages of his newspaper.

Was it conceivable that Élise was not cocking her ears at the furtive movements of Roger and the two girls?

'Where are the chocolates?' he asked, with a lump in his throat.

'There aren't any. It was a trick to make you come.'

Why were they laughing like that? They were mad. Anybody would have thought that they had been drinking or that they had an idea up their sleeves.

'Well, Marie, are you happy now?' asked Alice. 'Don't take any notice of me, you two. I'm going to sleep.'

And the redhead lay down on the bed while fat Marie protested, probably going red in the face.

'What are you talking about, Alice? You mustn't believe her, Roger. I didn't say anything.'

'Are you pretending that you didn't tell me that you'd give a lot to have him kiss you?'

'Shut up!'

'What are you waiting for, Roger? I swear it's true. She's mad about you. She talks about you from morning till night. The other day, she tried to pinch your picture from your mother's album.'

There was still time. Roger had only to go away, but he did not dare to, restrained by self-respect and perhaps also a more complicated feeling. Not for anything in the world did he want to show that he was afraid of his mother, and yet, just now, he really was afraid of her. She was busy peeling carrots, he knew that; he had the impression that he could see her using the paring-knife, and his father sitting in the wickerwork armchair, holding his newspaper in front of him.

'Wait a minute, Roger. If she's going to pretend she doesn't want to, I'll hold her for you.'

And Alice sprang to her feet and ran after her, the two girls rushing from one corner of the room to another on tip-toe, hushing each other and finally rolling on to the bed.

'You can come now. I'm holding her. Don't scratch me, you big silly! Seeing that you want to! You know, Roger I do believe that she's never been kissed by a boy, and I've known her a long time.'

Roger had found himself lying between them in the dark. His lips had pressed against the lips of the amorous Marie while his hands were searching for the other girl's hands, and their fingers had intertwined as if to say:

'It's all a joke. We're making fun of the poor girl. She's such a ninny!'

'Are you happy, Marie? Is it good?'

And Roger's hands let go of hers to slip into her bodice. He bore down on them with his full weight. The laughing stopped. Perhaps all three of them felt rather ashamed, but their faces were invisible and they did not know how to extricate themselves from the situation they had got into. Now and then the springs creaked and then Roger cocked his ears, holding his breath, convinced that he was going to hear the kitchen door open at any moment.

Alice's hands were as bold as his. He stayed face to face with Marie, but it was on to her friend that he gradually slipped his body.

Earlier on, when he had come into the room, he had not meant to do anything whatever. Even now there was no desire in him. Why then did he insist on undressing the fat girl, whom he ended up by stripping to the waist and who, as her only defence, kept her hand desperately over her sex?

'Go on!' Alice whispered to him. 'Do her up!'

Then, impelled by heaven knows what complicated desire of vengeance, it was on Alice that he did a mime of love. He did not make love to her. The idea did not occur to him. But he exaggerated the pretence, and Marie lay there beside them, her belly bare, not understanding and suffering while the other girl, to complete the illusion, started heaving sighs.

The kitchen door had opened. There had been a silence. They could imagine Élise standing in the hall, her face turned towards the staircase well, listening. All three held their breaths while she finally came upstairs and put her ear to the door.

'Did you call me, Mesdemoiselles?'

It was Alice who managed to reply in a toneless voice:

'No, Madame.'

Then Élise had opened Roger's door. There was nothing separating them, since the communicating door was open. They could distinctly hear her breathing. She had hesitated, obviously tempted to go in.

Finally she had gone downstairs, and after a long period of silent immobility Alice had given a hysterical laugh.

'What's she going to say? You don't think she'll throw us out, do you?'

'No fear. She's far too keen on her lodgers!'

He was ashamed of this uncalled-for piece of spite, but he had to say something. Marie started crying and finally got up, pulling her dress down.

'I think I'd better leave you two by yourselves.'

'There's no need to now,' the other girl replied. 'We've finished. All you had to do was let him get on with it. Isn't that so, Roger?'

'Of course.'

All this set your nerves on edge. Roger was keyed up and he would have liked to have a fit of hysterics like his mother to ease the tension.

'Where are you going?'

'To bed.'

Marie was fool enough to light the oil-lamp and the three of them looked like ghosts. Downstairs, they could hear Élise's monotonous voice and, now and then, Désiré's bass trying to calm her down in a murmur.

Roger had not gone downstairs. He had slept badly. He had walked in his sleep twice, something which often happened to him now, just as it had when he was little. He must have called out, for his parents had got up. He remembered his father, in his nightshirt and barefoot, gently taking him back to bed. His night-light had been left burning on a corner of the mantelpiece.

In the morning, he had deliberately gone downstairs when everybody was already at table. Marie was as red as a tomato, incapable of swallowing a single mouthful. Alice, on the other hand, was chattering away, and Élise was answering her while trying to assume a friendly expression.

He had kissed his mother as he did every morning. She had not returned his kiss. All the same, she had given him his breakfast and a franc for his dinner. She had announced that she was going to spend the afternoon at Aunt Louisa's and asked the lodgers to have a look at the fire when they came home.

He had scarcely seen his father. He had preferred not to see him. If he had been only a year older, he would have crossed the frontier to enlist, for youths had been accepted who were under seventeen. What was he going to do in two months' time, when the results of the examinations were announced? He did not want to pass. It was a futile humiliation, if only with regard to Father Renchon who pretended to have forgotten that he existed.

Now he was playing billiards with Stievens whose ambition it was to look like a fashion-plate. He circled round the green cloth with a mechanical walk, envying the others in the room, all those placid men who were not forced to face problems like his.

They were notabilities of the town, solicitors, big business men. Nearly all of them were fifty or more, and they had not a single glance to spare for those two adolescents carefully copying their gestures and attitudes.

'What are you doing tonight?'

'I'm going to bed,' replied Stievens, who was a great sleeper.

Gaston Van de Waele had gone off for a few days to Neeroeteren, where soon he would be saying grace, in all seriousness, at the head of the table.

Roger had rarely felt his solitude so keenly. It seemed to him that his fate was like no other and that consequently nobody in the whole world was capable of understanding him.

'Shall we have another game?'

'No. My mother has some guests this evening and I promised to be home early.'

Even Stievens was deserting him! They crossed the auditorium of the Palace just as the orchestra was playing its finale and a thousand people were all hurrying at once towards the door with the same sound of shuffling feet as at the end of a High Mass.

Outside, it was still light. The sun, although it was no longer visible, was still filling the streets with that uniform light which comes from nowhere. A red gable became as bright as a fire, and an attic window in the middle of a slate roof blazed with a thousand flames which hurt the eyes.

T – P. – T

'You're coming my way?' asked the surprised Stievens, who lived in the opposite direction from Roger.

'I'll walk with you part of the way.'

When he left his friend at his door, he was even more at a loss, not knowing what to do or where to go, and putting off the moment of pushing open the kitchen door in the rue des Maraîchers.

He had not a single centime left. He had not dared to ask Stievens to pay for him and had just had a glass of beer. He was not really hungry, despite the fact that he had had nothing to eat since the morning. It was a heavy feeling, an uneasiness which he could not place.

Surprised to find himself back in the middle of the Passerelle, he gazed at the Meuse, which was taking on a metallic colour, and at the pink faces of the passers-by, flushed by the setting sun.

At home, everybody would be at table. It had been a mistake to dawdle. In front of the lodgers, Élise would probably not have dared to say anything and that would have given him time to eat. He quickened his step and ended up by almost running. There was no doubt about that, and later on he would be tempted to believe that it was a presentiment.

He opened the door with his key. Straight away, he felt there was something unusual about the house. He could not see anybody through the curtain hanging over the glazed kitchen door, and the table was not laid. As panic-stricken as a child, he shouted:

'Mother!'

There was some movement up above, and he rushed upstairs. A door opened, the door of his parents' room, but it was his cousin Anna who appeared, very upright, very stiff, one finger at her lips, and said:

'Ssh, Roger.'

Some misfortune had occurred. The mere presence of Anna on the threshold of that room was a sign of misfortune. Roger's first idea was that his mother had committed a desperate act. He pushed his cousin to one side and stood motionless, a prey to a terrible feeling at the sight of the bedroom filled with the pink light of evening.

Désiré was lying on the bed, his head supported by several

pillows. On the bedside table there were some medicine bottles, and a strong hospital smell was floating in the air. Élise was standing by the bed, snivelling, and trying to smile so as not to cry.

'Come in, Roger. Shut the door, Anna. Don't make any noise. Come here very quietly and kiss your father.'

Désiré looked at him and there was such happiness in his brown eyes at the sight of his son that you could tell straight away that he had thought that he would never see him again.

Roger kissed him, close to the stiff moustache which still smelled of tobacco.

'It's nothing, son. Don't cry.'

'No, it's nothing,' Élise hurriedly declared. 'An attack of intercostal neuralgia, that's what the doctor told us, isn't it, Anna? It's frightening when it happens, but a week from now there won't be any sign of it.'

She was talking as people talk to the sick, to reassure them. Roger could feel that his father did not believe her. He would have liked to stay alone with him. Désiré was in a feeble condition, and his voice sounded like Cécile's.

'Go and have your supper, son. They've given me something to make me sleep. Above all, you must have enough to eat.'

It was Anna who went down to the kitchen with him and served him on a corner of the table, while at the same time telling him what had happened.

'Just imagine, your mother was at our house when they came from Sauveur's to say that she was wanted on the telephone. We'd just sat down at table to have some coffee. Monique, who was there too, had a feeling straight away that something had happened and she wouldn't let your mother go by herself. It was one of your lodgers, I don't know which, who was telephoning from the doctor's across the street from here.'

Roger ate his supper without being aware of it. He ate, but he was not hungry, and he listened attentively to the words his cousin pronounced, words which were promptly translated into pictures.

The quai de Coronmeuse was familiar enough. He could see Monsieur Sauveur's house too. And Alice, panic-stricken, at the doctor's across the way. For it was Alice. Marie would not have thought of telephoning. She would not have known how to set about it.

'It was another stroke of luck that they were at home. They'd just come back when the doorbell rang. They looked out of the window and saw an ambulance outside. It was your father whom they were bringing home from the rue Sohet. He'd had an attack at the office. They did what they could for him there, and then Doctor Fischer, a specialist Monsieur Monnoyeur had sent for, brought him here himself. Just when your mother wasn't at home! We ran here as fast as our legs could carry us. I do believe we got here quicker than the tram. The doctor was still here when we arrived.'

'What did he say?'

'Eat up, Roger.'

'I want to know exactly what he said.'

'You understand, he can't say anything definite yet, but he thinks it won't be serious this time. The worst is over.'

'Why do you say this time?'

'Because there may be other attacks.'

'Attacks of what?'

'Your father's got a weak heart. Doctor Fischer's coming again tomorrow. He knew what it was beforehand, because Désiré had already consulted him several times. You're a man now, Roger. You must be a man, because your mother has to be able to count on you, whatever happens. Your father needs to take it easy. He must have a quiet life, without any excitement.'

Élise's voice, up above, called softly:

'Can you come upstairs, Anna?'

His mother came down and slumped on to a chair as if her legs would no longer carry her. With her head in her hands, she started crying soundlessly. Roger went over to her and put an arm round her shoulders.

'Don't cry, Mother.'

He murmured anything that came into his head. The words did not matter. He stroked her hair. Then, kneeling in front of her like the little boy of old, he put his head in her lap.

'We'll take care of him and you'll see, we'll cure him all right. Don't cry. I'll be a man, I promise. I'll work. You see . . .'

How could he express what he felt, when he did not even dare to think it? And yet there was within him so to speak the

532

certainty that this had been bound to happen. Nobody had known this, but it was something which had been decided beforehand. It was a horrible thing to say. There were no words to express an idea like that. It was inconceivable that it should be true. And yet, just now, when he had gone into the bedroom, it had seemed to him that his father could have murmured to him:

'You see, son, I've set you free . . .'

For Roger was saved now. He was sure of that. He squeezed his mother's hands in his and gazed intently at her tear-stained face.

'Anna says it isn't a serious attack . . .'

'There'll be more of them. I know that. Doctor Fischer told me. He asked me if I was strong enough to bear the truth. He isn't one of those doctors who go on lying to a family to the very end. Désiré has been suffering for a long time from angina pectoris, but he kept it from us so as not to frighten us. And I was so cruel to him!'

'What are you saying, Mother?'

'You can't know. I'll never forgive myself. When I think that I reproached him for not worrying what would become of me if something happened to him! Now I know, from Doctor Fischer, that he applied for a life-insurance policy a long time ago and that his application was turned down.'

She glanced automatically at the alarm-clock.

'I must give my lodgers their supper all the same. It's too late for Anna to go back home. You'll let her have your bed and sleep on the chaise-longue in the dining-room. It seems he'll be able to get up in two or three days. He may go on for years without another attack, but on the other hand he may be carried off from one minute to the next. It really is the most horrible disease there is. To think that from now on I've got to live with the idea that I may be called to the telephone at any time to be told . . .'

She laid the table, performed the usual everyday gestures, made up the fire, poured the boiling water on the coffee.

'Where are you going, Roger?'

He did not know where he was going, possibly into the dining-room where nobody ever set foot and the shutters stayed closed from one year's end to the other. He wanted to be alone. His head was spinning. He thought that he had detected a reproach in his mother's voice and he stayed to reassure her.

'You'll see, I'll help you. I'll go and find a job tomorrow.'

But no, it wasn't possible! Was it true that he felt a sort of relief at his father's illness? He experienced a need to protest and the protest itself hurt him. He would do anything for his father to be well again and for the threat hanging over his life to disappear for ever.

Yet now, from one minute to the next, everything had been settled of what had previously been so heavy with potential misfortune. Nobody had said anything about the horrible scene the day before. Perhaps nobody would ever say anything about it again, at least for a long time to come. He was going to leave school. He would not have to sit for his examinations, or suffer the humiliation of the inevitable failure.

His mother called out automatically at the foot of the stairs: 'Mademoiselle Alice! Mademoiselle Marie!'

They came and sat down at table, rather self-consciously. Élise tried to look on the cheerful side of things.

'You'll see, it won't be anything serious. The doctor says that a week from now, it will be just a bad memory. You must have been frightened, Mesdemoiselles. It would have to happen when you were alone in the house! It's a good thing that you knew where I was and that you thought of telephoning me.'

All that time, Roger had been playing billiards, over the Palace, circling with other dummies round tables lit by reflectors. Then he had accompanied Stievens to his house and had wandered interminably through the streets.

'I'm going upstairs to relieve Anna,' he announced. 'Are there any drops to be given?'

'Nothing more until eleven o'clock. What he needs now is absolute rest. He must sleep too.'

It was Roger's night-light which was being used again. Walking on tiptoe, he motioned to Anna, who got up to give him her seat. The door-hinges creaked slightly, then there was nothing to be heard but a gentle murmur of voices and the sound of plates clattering in the kitchen. With his chin in his hands, Roger gazed intently at his father, who was sleeping and whose moustache quivered with every breath.

Chapter Nine

Contrary to what he would have imagined in the past, it was the passers-by who were in the aquarium and it was he who, through the bookshop window, watched them with a curiosity tinged with pity.

The most astonishing thing was the serious, not to say solemn expressions which people's faces assumed, just as they were indulging in their most ridiculous gestures.

The frame – the aquarium – was bigger or smaller depending on whether Roger was standing near the window or at the back of the bookshop. When he was in the back-room, which was known as the office, this field of vision, framed in the communicating hatch lined with books, was reduced to the proportions of a cinema screen.

Well, in spite of what you imagined when you were in the street yourself, the passers-by had exactly the same jerky walk as the characters on the screen, particularly the comic characters, those who gesticulated more wildly than the rest.

Whether they came in from the left or the right, they looked as if they had been hurled by a catapult into this piece of world which was barely sixty feet long, and as if they were racing each other across it, their eyes set, their jaws jutting fiercely, to disappear again into nothingness.

All day long, Roger could read on the window, the wrong way round, the words: *Germain's Bookshop*, and, in smaller enamel letters: *Lending Library*. All day long, on the other side of this frontier, people stopped short, as if a spring had broken inside them.

You could then see them from the front, in close-up. They did not move, but stayed there side by side, sometimes five or six in a row, not knowing one another, lost in the contemplation of the yellow-backed books in the window-display.

It was inconceivable that they should be thinking, in spite of their tense features and the often dramatic expression on their faces. They were simply waiting for the reverse switch to work which would send them back into their jerky walk and carry them off the stage.

The yellow trams, which went past minute by minute making a tremendous din, were not to be taken any more seriously, with the driver rigid on the platform in front, the conductor on the one at the back, and two rows of wobbling heads inside; and it would be no surprise if, like a toy which was out of order, they went hurtling against a real wall.

The patterns of light and shade changed from hour to hour, almost from minute to minute. Over the way, there was a shoe-shop with two elegant windows and a door which was open all the time. The shop-girls, who wore white collars over black dresses, went to and fro in the half-light, and now and then one of them, showing a customer to the door, leant outside, on the point of crossing the frontier into the street. She was within an ace of being caught up in the mechanism, but she sensed the danger and plunged nimbly back into her world of white boxes piled up like bricks.

All that was tiny and unreal. The solid world began near the window of the bookshop with Mademoiselle Georgette sitting behind a high desk. Roger, perched on a bamboo ladder, coughed to attract her attention and said in a voice which he had not known he possessed before, a voice which he had acquired in this shop:

'843.'

At her cash-desk, Mademoiselle Georgette, the bookseller's niece, turned the pages of a register in search of the figure 843, which was the number of a customer's subscription. When she stopped going through the book and lowered her pen on to one page, he knew that he could go on:

'Returned: 2656.'

She repeated in an undertone, without looking up:

'2656.'

That was the catalogue number of a book. The books in the lending library were distinguished from those which were for sale by being bound in black cloth, with a tiny label at the bottom of the spine bearing a number in purple ink.

'Borrowed: 4562.'

Who could say why this was a pleasure? For it was a pleasure for him, just as it must be a pleasure for a juggler to see his white balls fall into his hand at the right moment like obedient, well-trained, living creatures. A customer asked for a book? In the twinkling of an eye Roger had reached the special catalogue which hung between two sets of shelves. O . . . O . . . Here was O . . . *Le Maître des Forges* . . . 4562. That pleased him, for he had remembered that it was in the four thousands . . . The third set of shelves on the left, going from the corner of the counter . . . *Le Maître des Forges* had been brought back the day before, he was sure of that . . . Two shelves down from the ceiling . . . He slid the bamboo ladder along on its rod and climbed up, scarcely touching the rungs and not touching the uprights at all . . . He balanced up there, without holding on with his hands, and took the opportunity, by means of an acrobatic feat, to put 2656 back in its place. An Halévy probably . . . He could have sworn it was an Halévy . . .

The proof that it was a pleasure was that Monsieur Germain had come out of his den.

'Why don't you come down?'

'I am coming down, Monsieur.'

'Make sure it isn't a new book, Georgette.'

Roger said:

'No, Monsieur. It's a Georges Ohnet.'

He was in the wrong. Try as he might, he was always in the wrong, and Monsieur Germain made that clear to him with an angry glare.

'Have you finished cutting those pages?'

'Yes, Monsieur.'

'Have you stuck on the new labels?'

'Yes, Monsieur.'

How could an old man like Monsieur Germain, who was over seventy and was considered the most serious bookseller in the town, get up to tricks like that? There he was, exasperated, annoyed, unhappy, because he could not find anything to give Roger to do in order to keep him away from the customers. And that simply because he could feel that Roger enjoyed serving them.

People were not in this world, still less in Germain's Bookshop, to enjoy themselves. Work was a punishment from Heaven.

'Go and write out a new set of labels, from 1 to 10,000.'

There were already three sets ready for use, and the labels on the spines of the books were changed only when they came unstuck. Never mind! Roger would be deprived of the pleasure of serving subscribers and balancing like a monkey on the ladders.

'Why, Monsieur Hiquet, didn't *you* serve that lady?'

'I beg your pardon, Monsieur . . .'

Well done! Unlike Roger, the chief assistant got suitably flustered, looked even unhappier than usual, and ended up by stammering like a criminal caught in the act:

'I was in the smallest room.'

Everybody knew that he had to go there twenty times a day on account of his faulty bladder, that it was sheer torture for him, and that he always came back looking ill. Now, Monsieur Germain also had trouble with his bladder, like most men of his age. Seeing Hiquet go pale, he could constantly assure himself that his complaint was mild in comparison with his employee's sufferings.

All this was true. Roger had discovered it long ago. Outwardly, Monsieur Germain was a grave, impressive figure. His thick white hair was cut short. All the white hairs on his face grew horizontally and his eyebrows were as long and as thick as his moustache. You never heard him coming, and he obviously wore special shoes which made no noise. Broadshouldered though he was, you had the impression that inside his ample clothes there was just a body with no bones or muscles, floating silently in space.

He had nothing to do. He had an office at the back of the second room, but that was simply to impress people, for his only work consisted of pinning together the bills which arrived by post so as to give them to the accountant who came two evenings a week.

The rest of the time, he watched. It was impossible to tell what he had watched before engaging Roger. Possibly his, niece and poor Hiquet? During the two months that Roger had been there, it had been on *his* track that the old bookseller with the shaggy eyebrows had been from morning till night. He guessed everything with diabolical skill. As soon as Roger started enjoying a particular task, he noticed it. It hurt him. He was literally in agony until he had found something else for him to do, even if it was something which was obviously futile.

This war had been declared as soon as they had met. There was a notice stuck to the window with sealing-wax: 'Young man required.'

It was about ten o'clock on a bright, sunny morning. Désiré was feeling better. He still kept to his room, but he was no longer confined to bed and spent his time reading by the window. Roger, who was looking for a job, had honestly thought that fate was smiling on him, and, smiling himself, as fresh and innocent as that gay morning, he had gone into the shop.

'Can I help you?'

'It's about the job. It hasn't been taken yet, has it?'

It was to Mademoiselle Georgette that he had spoken, with such obvious anxiety, such passionate hope that the miraculous job had not been taken, that she had smiled sympathetically at him straight away.

Now, Monsieur Germain was there, lurking in a corner. He had seen his niece's smile, and that in itself had been a sort of catastrophe.

'What is it, young man?'

Roger, that particular day, was incapable of bristling up, even in the face of the most obvious hostility.

'I beg your pardon, Monsieur. I hadn't seen you. I saw your advertisement and took the liberty of presenting myself. I should be only too happy if I could serve your purpose, because my father is ill and I have to start earning my living as soon as I can.'

'What sort of education have you had?'

'I'm still at college. That is, I was at college until four days ago, when my father had a heart-attack. I've nearly finished my third year.'

'This isn't a post for you. I need somebody to do the odd jobs and run errands.'

'That's all right, Monsieur, I'm ready to do anything you like.'

In the space of a few seconds, looking at the window-display before coming into the shop, he had created a new ideal for himself, and now he felt sure that he could not fulfil that ideal anywhere else but in the Germain's Bookshop. He could see the resistance facing him but he refused to be discouraged.

'I can't pay you more than fifty francs a month.'

Monsieur Germain said this on purpose in order to get rid of the boy, for his previous assistant, who had not been as well-educated as Roger and had been dismissed for stealing stamps, had earned seventy-five francs a month.

'That will be enough for me, Monsieur.'

He would have worked for nothing if necessary, he was in such a hurry to tell his parents that he had found a job. He was also eager to finish with the college, where he had not been for four days, but where nothing was known yet of his decision.

'Have you any references?'

'I haven't had a job before.'

'I mean letters from people who can testify to your honesty.'

'I'll bring you some, Monsieur. All I ask of you is one hour. Please don't engage anybody else during that time.'

He had run to Schroefs'. Everything paled into insignificance in the face of this job which he had to obtain at all costs.

'Monsieur Germain? I know him very well. We're on the board of directors of the same bank. Germaine subscribes to his lending-library. I hope you won't give me cause to regret recommending you?'

'I promise you that, Uncle.'

He went off with his letter. The streets were like a heady bath. He sped towards the Botanical Gardens, where a cousin of his mother's lived whom they saw only very rarely and who was a justice of the peace.

'Listen, cousin: Father is very ill, something may happen to him any day, and I've got to go out to work. I've nearly found a job, at the Germain's Bookshop in the rue de la Cathédrale.'

Everybody was on his side. He was determined to be so pleasant that the whole world would love him. His ideal had changed. No more yellow shoes or loosely tied cravats. No more cosmetics or centre partings. He was sorry that his suit was fawn. He would have preferred it to be a dark, neutral shade. He would have liked to have the discreet bearing and manners of the clerks who went past at fixed times like Désiré and were pointed out as models of diligence and respectability.

He had said that he would be back in an hour? It had taken

him no more than forty-five minutes to obtain his two letters. He had run all the way. He rushed into the bookshop, panting for breath, his eyes shining triumphantly.

'Here you are, Monsieur. This letter from my uncle Hubert Schroefs, the wholesale grocer in the rue des Carmes. The other one is from my cousin Lievens, the justice of the peace.'

'You told them it was a very humble post?'

'Yes, Monsieur.'

What could Monsieur Germain do? Furious, he gave in.

'When can you start work?'

'Straight away, if you wish.'

'Let's say tomorrow morning. Be here at half past eight sharp.'

That had been over two months ago and the bookseller had not forgiven him yet. It was the first time that anybody had opposed him and had won his way, smilingly, almost playfully.

The director of studies at the Collège Saint-Servais had done something astonishing. Although Roger had not sat for his examinations – and everybody knew that he would not sit for them – he had given him a diploma as if he had finished his third year in the normal fashion.

At bottom, wasn't this excessive generosity just a trifle contemptuous? Roger refused to believe this. Not only was he modelling his dress and his walk on those of ordinary folk, but he wanted to adopt their way of thinking.

He was not in the least unhappy. He lived in a reassuring world. He liked going through his old district where accountants and bank-clerks lived, and this summer the new little houses, with their windows open to air the bedrooms, struck him as cosy and inviting. He was thinking seriously of joining the Catholic Club where Désiré had once been the prompter in the dramatic society. He was going to become a member of the Old Boys' Association of the Friars' school.

Désiré had gone back to his office. He was obliged to set off earlier and to take the No. 4 tram at the corner of the rue Puits-en-Sock and the rue Jean-d'Outremeuse, for he could no longer make the long journey to the rue Sohet on foot. Roger lingered in the kitchen with his mother. It was the fruit season and she had begun making jam. He looked at the alarm-clock, stood up, put on his straw hat and picked up his walking-stick, for he considered that with a walking-stick he looked more like a 'man going to the office'.

Often, before he got to the Pont d'Amercoeur, he caught sight of his father standing in front of a shop-window. Désiré had set off a quarter of an hour before. With his long legs, he should have been far away. But he was forced to stop practically every hundred yards, to wait for the spasm which was immobilizing him to pass.

He was ashamed of being ill. As often as possible, he stopped in front of a window-display and pretended to be taking an interest in the goods on show, even the wilting vegetables in a shabby little shop. Some good soul had already found an opportunity to say to Élise:

'It's funny, Madame Mamelin. Your husband, who used to be such a serious man, has started making eyes at girls.'

'What are you talking about?'

'He stops in front of shop-windows and sometimes stays there for a quarter of an hour flirting with the shop-assistants.'

Poor Désiré. He smiled a somewhat embarrassed smile when his son caught up with him. Roger had thought of going round by way of the Pont de Bressoux, but his father would not have been taken in.

'Well, son?'

'Well, Father? A bit out of breath?'

'It's finished now. Don't wait for me. You walk faster than I do and it's time you were away. Everything still going well at your office?'

He said *office* on purpose, just as they spoke of the office in the rue Sohet, because this created another link between them, a sort of equality.

'Very well indeed. I know all the ropes now. I could take Monsieur Hiquet's place at a moment's notice if necessary. There are customers who prefer to deal with me because I'm more familiar with the books. Some of them ask my advice. Instead of asking for such-and-such a title, they say to me:

'"Give me a novel of the same sort as the last. That was a good one."'

Unfortunately Monsieur Germain was watching. His hatred expressed itself in childish ways. For wasn't it childish to take away from his employee all the jobs which he did willingly and well?

It was Roger who, every morning, went into the corridor to get a pole with a hook on the end, with which he raised the shutters. During this time, Hiquet, who in the morning was invariably pale and red-eyed as if he had not slept a wink all night, took off his jacket in a small box-room and put on his black cotton overall.

Roger, for all that he took a pride in his appearance, had suggested ordering a similar overall for himself. Instead of being pleased at this sign of zeal, the fierce old man had growled:

'There's no point in doing that.'

Because he did not intend to keep him on, that was clear! He had been forced to take on this exuberant young fellow who seemed to find his work child's-play, and he had not managed to catch him out so far; but he was patient and stubborn, and he knew that that would come sooner or later. The main thing was not to let the opportunity slip.

Local deliveries, which were fairly rare, naturally fell to the newcomer. Mamelin came back with his face flushed from these errands in the open air, as if he had been playing a game. Monsieur Germain had been unable to tolerate this. It was a difficult problem to solve, since if Hiquet ran the errands, Roger would have to be allowed to serve the customers in the meantime.

Henceforth the parcels to be delivered were put together on one side. In the evening, before shutting the shop, Monsieur Germain murmured:

'Incidentally . . . Would you be so kind, Monsieur Hiquet, as to deliver these two or three parcels on your way home . . . Monsieur Mamelin will deal with the others . . .'

After the day's work! The old man rubbed his hands. He would have been even happier if Roger had protested at this supplementary work.

Roger had promised himself to do his utmost to disarm this undeserved hatred. How often had Élise reproached him with being incapable of showing respect to others? If only she could see him now, and hear him replying in an angelic voice which she did not know he possessed, with a slight nod of the head:

'Yes, Monsieur . . . No, Monsieur . . . Straight away, Monsieur . . .'

Mademoiselle Georgette was disappointed. Seeing him come into the bookshop one sunny morning, she must have hoped that this young man with the bold eyes would at last dare to do what nobody had dared before: to speak up loud and clear and challenge the tyranny of her finicky old uncle.

But nobody had ever been more docile than Mamelin.

A good many times, school friends of his had come in, including Chabot, who was a subscriber to the lending-library. If Roger had taken a single step forward, they would have shaken hands with him. He could even have used the familiar *tu* in speaking to them. Who knows whether this was not what Monsieur Germain was hoping for?

He had done nothing of the sort. He had stayed 'in his place', as they put it at Aunt Louisa's, without any feeling of rancour, indeed even taking a secret pleasure in it.

That was how you had to look at life when you had been brought up in the place du Congrès district and were destined to end your days there.

His cousin Germaine Schroefs also came in to change her novels. He could feel that she was embarrassed. She asked with a condescending smile:

'Are you still satisfied with my young cousin, Monsieur Germain?'

And the latter just replied with his bearlike growl.

Another young woman, of remarkable elegance, had come into the shop one afternoon, followed by her companion. The bookseller had rushed up to her as if she were an important person. She had bought all the latest books, touching them one after another with her fingers gloved in pale kid.

'Put it with the others . . . And this one . . . This one too, if you will . . .'

'Shall I send them to you as usual?'

She had not paid. The best people did not pay, and you sent them their bill at the end of the year. Just as she was going out, she had turned back.

'Get your assistant to cut the pages, won't you. I detest cutting the pages of books.'

A moment later, Monsieur Germain was dictating to his niece:

'Sold to Mademoiselle Estelle Peters, of Tongres . . .'

He had looked at Roger, and Roger had not flinched.

'As a matter of interest, Monsieur Mamelin, isn't she a relative of yours?'

'I suppose she's my cousin, Monsieur.'

'Why do you say that you suppose?'

The old man had scented a piece of impertinence. That was the great word! He was always suspecting Roger of impertinence, and that was something he detested as much as Estelle Peters detested cutting the pages of her books.

'I say I suppose, Monsieur, because I've never seen her.'

He scarcely knew his Uncle Louis of Tongres, whom he had caught sight of at a funeral. He knew that he had two children, a son and a daughter, that the son was a doctor and that it was to his first communion that Élise had gone the day she had cried so much and his father and he had taken her to the station.

Years had gone by since then, and now, in the back-room of Germain's Bookshop, Élise's son was cutting pages for Louis' daughter. Without any feeling of rebellion. His mind was made up once for all. He would not rebel again. Life was not unpleasant like this. There was sweetness in resignation. He suspected that some people, like his mother, derived a somewhat perverse pleasure from it. If a catastrophe occurred, nobody would be able to say that it was his fault.

The holidays were over. Although it was not as dense as in the narrow rue Saint-Gilles, the procession of pupils coming from the Collège Saint-Servais at the end of the day changed the street's appearance. Roger saw some of the boys in the morning, hurrying up the street separately. He saw them going past again in groups on their way home, and the idea that they had been shut up in those white cages hanging above the yard struck him as no less incongruous than the untidy agitation of the passers-by.

He guessed what they were talking about, looking very self-important, and he smiled pityingly. Now and then he saw the pale, anguished face of Verger, who had grown even taller and was scouring the town in search of some shady business, some traffic in accumulators or other goods. Stievens went past too, as serious as a man of forty, convinced that everybody was admiring the shine on his shoes and the crease in his trousers.

Roger saw nothing more of Gaston Van de Waele who, so he heard, had gone into business and went to the Stock Exchange on Mondays, like a Louis of Tongres.

All that, in the light and shade in the street, in the din which in the long run formed an indispensable background of music, was unreal and rather grotesque, like a world seen through the wrong end of a telescope.

People recovered their real size and density only when they crossed the threshold and came forward between the shelves filled with black volumes – except for the shelves behind the counter, which held the new books in their yellow covers. This was what counted, this was what was tangible and important: the catalogue hanging on a string, the stamp-box, the drawer for the labels, and even the towel hung behind a door.

'Returned: 1267.'

That was a Dumas. Nobody knew better than he did Alexandre Dumas' works, which he had read from the first line to the last, including the travel notes and the memoirs. He knew which volumes were out and which were available. He reached for them even more casually than for the others, like a conjuror whose hands draw objects towards them.

'*Le Capitaine Pamphile*? Just a moment, please, Madame.'

It was an October afternoon, one of the last fine afternoons in the year. The streets were unusually crowded, because during the last few days the Germans had been releasing their Russian prisoners. Men could be seen wandering around who had come on foot from some German province where there was not enough food for them. They were dressed in unfamiliar uniforms and greatcoats which were too big for them, too wide above all, for they were extremely thin and for the most part in the last stages of physical collapse.

The townspeople had started taking them in. Committees were being formed. Already individual families were trying to accommodate one or two Russians each. And if, in the poor districts, they were taken in at random, at the Carré you could see ladies and girls examining the ex-prisoners before picking one to their liking.

They knew this. They had an amazingly sure instinct. They roamed around looking like mangy dogs, and now and then, meeting a prosperous-looking woman, they bared their pointed white teeth in an inviting smile.

The bookshop was full of people The bad-tempered lady in black astrakhan who had spoken to Roger was the wife of a magistrate. Monsieur Germain had not seen her, for he would have rushed forward to serve her in person.

'Let's see . . . *Acté* . . . *Amaury* . . . *Ange Pitou* . . . *Aventures de John Davis* . . .'

Roger's finger sped down the list.

'*Les Blancs et les Bleus* . . . *Boule de Neige* . . . *Cadet de Famille* . . . *Le Capitaine Richard* . . .'

That was funny! Surprised, he went back to the beginning and read through the whole list of Dumas' works again. Perhaps somebody had forgotten to enter *Le Capitaine Pamphile* into the catalogue? He clambered up the ladder, took the books from the shelf one after another, and checked the titles.

'What are you looking for up there, Monsieur Mamelin?'

'*Le Capitaine Pamphile*, Monsieur.'

'Why are you looking for it among the Dumas, if you please?'

He scented disaster, and took on his humblest and most timid voice to murmur:

'Because it's by Dumas.'

'Who told you that *Le Capitaine Pamphile* was by Alexandre Dumas? Let me tell you, Monsieur, that Dumas *père* never wrote *Le Capitaine Pamphile*. Look for it under Théophile Gautier and you will find it. That is what you would have done straight away if you were not so muddle-headed and sure of yourself.'

Roger obeyed. He knew that he would not find anything under Gautier. He knew that all the better in that he had read *Le Capitaine Pamphile* not more than six months ago.

'Well, Monsieur, have you finally found it?'

'No, Monsieur.'

With an abrupt gesture, the catalogue hanging on its string was snatched out of his hands. Why did the customer, whom the bookseller had annoyed, look encouragingly at Roger?

He murmured in an undertone, so that only Monsieur Germain could hear him:

'I assure you, Monsieur, that *Le Capitaine Pamphile* is by

Alexandre Dumas. We haven't got it, but it's definitely by him.'

'What are you saying, young man? I don't think I can have heard correctly. Are you trying to teach me my own business?'

'I've read it.'

'Well then, you read it wrong, as indeed you do everything. Who asked for *Le Capitaine Pamphile*?'

'This lady.'

He was angrier than ever when he recognized the important and difficult customer.

'Excuse this young man, Madame, who imagines that he knows everything.'

To which she retorted:

'*Le Capitaine Pamphile* is indeed by Alexandre Dumas.'

The old man's ears went red and every hair on his head bristled up. Without a word, he went over to the counter and with a trembling hand opened the booksellers' manual. He going to brandish the avenging page, the proof that he had not made a mistake, that he had never made a mistake, and that *Le Capitaine Pamphile* . . .

But there, in the list of Alexandre Dumas' complete works, he was obliged, in spite of the anger blurring his sight, to read: *Cadet de Famille* . . . *Capitaine Arena* . . . *Capitaine Pamphile* . . .'

He raised his shaggy eyebrows and pretended to catch Mamelin out.

'Monsieur Mamelin, I cannot allow one of my employees, however highly recommended he may be, to take up an insolent attitude in my shop. Kindly wait for me in my office.'

Roger had not said anything, had not done anything, had not smiled. What was insolent was obviously his equanimity, his confidence in himself and in Dumas.

He did not know how the old man had managed with his customer. Slightly relieved by his castigation of the young man, he had probably indulged in a great deal of bowing and scraping, but all his anger returned as soon as he entered the office.

'I imagine that this incident, which I had been expecting for a long time, has been sufficient to convince you that you are out of place in this establishment.'

Roger was going to apologize. He had made up his mind. He

was ready to swear that Alexandre Dumas had never written *Le Capitaine Pamphile*, but already the office till had been opened and the hands with the prominent veins, an old man's hands, were counting out notes and coins.

'Here are fifty francs. And here are another twenty-five francs in lieu of notice. I should be justified in not giving you this latter sum, in view of your impertinent attitude. I want your uncle to know that I have behaved more correctly towards you than you have towards me. Good-bye, Monsieur. I wish you good luck and a little more respect for your elders.'

Hiquet, who saw him go out, did not know that he was leaving for good.

And that was how Roger found himself back in the aquarium. After a moment's hesitation, the spring was released, his eyebrows puckered up, his forehead hardened, and he started walking at the same pace as the passers-by, moving his arms and legs faster and faster as if a task of capital importance were waiting for him at the other side of the stage.

The oddest thing was that he was aware of all this. He could feel himself shrinking, returning to the proportions of the big-headed puppets which he used to see through the bookshop window, endlessly strutting about the fishbowl.

Chapter Ten

Sections of the serial film were alternating with the music-hall turns and with orchestral pieces which were played while the waiters were replenishing the customers' glasses. The Palace was full to overflowing. Outside, it was still raining, as you could see from the drops on the coats of the people coming in. Again, every time somebody lifted the curtain in the doorway, you could see the progress made by the darkness on the bit of pavement where the festoons of electric lamps were casting a puddle of red light.

The place was warm with human heat. Elbows were touching on both sides of the marble tables placed end to end. There was a smell of beer, wet wool, and cigars. The presence of the Russians in their grey uniforms added an exotic note.

It was not exactly a sense of uneasiness which people had been feeling for some days, but rather the strain of waiting.

Everybody was waiting, without knowing what for. The confectioner at the Pont de Longdoz, whom Roger had been to see a week ago, had looked embarrassed.

'I'm not saying no. It's true that I need somebody. Yes, I could take on an apprentice. I know your grandfather well. Come back to see me in about ten days. We'll talk about it again.'

Élise was waiting too in order to rejoice at the news. As for Roger, he had done everything he was supposed to do, but in his heart of hearts he did not believe in it.

They were living through an interval during which things were of no importance. The weather was bad. Rain and wind followed one another without a pause. It grew dark early on, and often the lamps had to be lit during the day. The Russians were arriving in increasing numbers. Nobody knew where to put them. Élise had taken in two who slept in the dining-room, and Roger spent most of his time showing them round the town.

At the Palace, as in the cinemas, they were allowed in free. It appeared that in certain camps they had been reduced to eating dung.

The German troops in the town were said to be confined to barracks. In any case there were scarcely any officers to be seen in the streets, with their pointed helmets on their heads, their jackets flapping behind them and their swords trailing along the ground.

Roger and the two Russians were smoking mildewed cigarettes which were sold in the rue du Pont-Neuf at twenty centimes a packet instead of one franc.

The canvas screen had rolled up under the frieze, the stage lit up, and a comic private came forward, a ludicrous figure in a red wig.

> 'Caroline, tumpty-tum,
> Is sick, tumpety-tum;
> She is sick
> With the sickness of love.'

He was wearing the pre-war French uniform, the red breeches and black leggings of the dragoons. With his eyes rolling and his arms waving in great epileptic gestures, he got the whole audience singing in chorus.

> 'To make her better,
> Tumpety-tum,
> She needs a stick,
> Tumpety-tum . . .'

Little by little the murmur in the auditorium, hesitant at first, became a vast roar accompanied by the orchestra, applause broke out, and the private skipped off behind a flat, coming back to take his bow.

What happened then? They had caught a glimpse of a figure dressed in black standing in the wings. The comic, still half on the stage, started talking to him without taking any notice of the audience.

They called for him. He came back to the footlights and bent down to speak to the conductor of the orchestra, who stood up, put his elbows on the stage, and, surprised, visibly hesitating, looked inquiringly at the man in black in the wings . . .

. . . and finally sat down again, said a few words to the musicians, raised his baton . . .

Then . . .

> 'Allons enfants de la Patrie . . .'

For a moment, nobody could believe his eyes or ears. With a magniloquent gesture, the soldier had snatched off his red wig and tossed back his brown hair. With the back of his sleeve he wiped away his silly mask. It was a young man with an intelligent face who roared at the top of his voice:

> 'Aux armes, citoyens,
> Formez vos bataillons . . .'

Nobody stayed where he was. Everybody stood up without knowing why, because it was impossible to remain seated, because something carried you away. Eyes smarted. Trembling voices repeated the words of the *Marseillaise*:

> 'Qu'un sang impur
> Abreuve nos sillons . . .'

The singer dashed over to the wings. Somebody handed him something which he brandished with a sweeping gesture, and a huge French flag unfurled in the glare of the floodlights.

Something else was handed to him, and the same gesture revealed the Belgian flag: black, yellow and red.

Then, while the orchestra struck up the *Brabançonne*, the man who was still wearing the costume of a music-hall soldier shouted to the two thousand people in the audience:

'It's the armistice! . . . The war is over!'

After that everything was chaos. Everybody was crying, laughing, embracing, pushing. There were some who rushed outside, to shout the news to the passers-by, but the latter knew it already, the whole town had heard it within a few moments. The shopkeepers were on their doorsteps, women were leaning out of the windows, and some people, seeing the growing crowds, wondered whether it would not be advisable to lower the iron shutters.

The war was over! In spite of the rain, the streets were filling with an increasingly excited mob, singing could be heard, and then suddenly, like a signal, the sound of a window shivering into pieces.

It was a pork-butcher's shop whose owner had worked with the Germans. Men disappeared into the shop and started throwing out hams and black puddings. The furniture followed, hurled out of the first-floor and second-floor windows: wardrobes, beds, a bedside table, a piano. The police did not know what to to and looters ran off down the street with their booty.

'Destroy if you like, but don't take anything!' a police sergeant shouted.

Ten, twenty, fifty butchers' shops suffered the same fate and the crowd continued to become increasingly varied. In the rue de la Cathédrale itself you could see whole groups of people from the poorer districts, certain cafés had begun serving free drinks and the others were forced to follow suit, for soon the mob insisted on it.

In a patch of shadow, a human figure was struggling with half a dozen determined men and Roger looked on uncomprehendingly. They were stripping a woman, tearing off every piece of clothing she was wearing. She was naked now, on her knees on the slimy pavement, and one of the men slashed her hair off with a pair of scissors.

'She can go now. We're going to do the same to all the

women who've slept with the Huns. Like that, when their husbands come back from the front, they'll know what's what.'

She ran off to an accompaniment of hisses and jeers, pale and frozen in the windy night air. Some street-urchins followed her and the same scene was repeated all over the town, so that you gave a sudden start, in the darkness, on catching sight of a white, naked body keeping close to the houses.

Roger had lost his two Russians. He had been caught up in a procession and accompanied it from one café to the next, singing with the rest, without recognizing the districts which they filled with their noisy, aggressive joy.

He drank like everybody else. When the beer ran out, it was gin which was served in full glasses, and one group would break up to join another. On his left he had a lovely working-girl who had found time to put on a dress of pale green satin.

For the first time in his life, he had gone right down the most secret alley-ways in Outremeuse and walked in single file through taverns whose existence he had never suspected. At one point a woman who looked like a costermonger had come up to his companion and, darting a suspicious glance at Roger, had taken her rings off her fingers.

He also remembered standing for a moment with his elbows on the bar of the café where he used to play billiards with his father.

A dozen times, perhaps, he had come close to his home, and every time a surge of the crowd had pushed him back. He had had nothing to eat. He could not remember having anything to eat. What stood out in his memory was hundreds and thousands of strange faces which he had never seen before at such close quarters, cheeks which you kissed, mouths which opened wide to howl a song or a shout of triumph, eyes in which you could see a dangerous frenzy. Then more cafés, dark, shining pavements, pieces of broken glass, drops of rain.

If he had been drunk, he was perfectly sober when, just as dawn was turning the sky pale and chilling the air, he crossed the Pont d'Amercoeur. He knew that his parents would not say anything, that they had probably not been worried about him. It was the armistice. His sodden clothes were clinging to his body. His shoes had taken in water. He was cold all over and he had a raging headache.

Yet it struck him that he had never been as calm or clear-headed in his life as he was this morning.

Had he really shouted with the rest? Perhaps he had tried. Yes, now he came to think about it, he had behaved that night as he had behaved during the two months he had spent at Germain's Bookshop. He had taken pains to do what was expected of him, to avoid drawing attention to himself, to behave like everybody else.

He had failed. As far as he was concerned, he succeeded by dint of trying. But the others were not taken in. It was they who looked at him as if he were a foreigner and drew away. Witness that working-class woman who had taken away her daughter's rings!

For the rest of his life, he would remember the comic singer with his sickening mask of imbecility. If it had not been for the armistice, Roger would have been returning in exactly two days – that had been agreed – to see the confectioner at the Pont de Longdoz. The latter would probably have taken him on. Roger would have become a confectioner, although he was not born to be a confectioner any more than he was born to be a bookseller's assistant.

He was not sad. It was a different feeling which made him bow his head as he walked along. Armistice night was over, the war was over, and with it a whole period of his life which he would like to forget completely.

The day which was dawning was a greyish day. It was still raining. The houses were black.

There was not the smallest spark of excitement left in him. He opened the door with his key and went straight upstairs to see his parents, who were still in bed.

'Is that you, Roger?'

'Yes . . . it's me. I hope you didn't get worried about me. I'd have liked to let you know I was all right and come home earlier, but I kept getting swept away by the crowds.'

He had the impression that his mother was looking at him in astonishment. It was probably his calm manner which surprised her.

'You didn't drink too much?'

'Not too much, no. I haven't been sick.'

He spoke in level tones, not like a man who had spent the night singing and drinking, but like a man who had been thinking deeply and carefully.

'Anybody'd think you weren't pleased.'

'But I am pleased, Mother, very pleased. I haven't kissed you yet. Forgive me.'

He kissed her and then his father, breathing in the smell of their bed with some embarrassment.

'There now. I'm off to bed. Wake me when you like.'

The two girls, Alice and Marie, were not back yet. One of the Russians had come back by himself early in the evening, already sick from over-drinking. Roger had stepped over his vomit in the hall.

Now that he came to think of it, they would have to leave the house soon, seeing that they had taken it only for the duration of the war.

'Good night.'

He was alone in his room, and on the boulevard he saw files of defeated troops beginning to go by, their heads bent, following the guns and the field-kitchens in the monotonous rain.

When he closed his eyes he could still hear them. He had the impression that he could see them too, marching endlessly along, and he suddenly remembered a Polish picture-postcard which Mademoiselle Feinstein had once received. He probably still had it in his album, for she had given it to him. It showed an old man sitting on a pavement kerb, his arms dangling, next to a child in rags who was snuggling up against him. He was gazing into space with eyes full of a pathetic inquiry.

Mademoiselle Feinstein had translated for him the caption printed in Polish underneath the picture: '*Where are we to go?*'

The line of men filed past beneath his window and would go on filing past at the same dreary pace for day after day. Roger tossed about in his sleep in the cold dawn of the unshuttered room.

He slept so soundly that when he awoke, with his eyes still shut, his first feeling was a feeling of weariness. Then he sat up with a start and rubbed his eyes, puzzled by the unaccustomed light.

555

The war was over, he remembered that. The gas-lamp across the street was lit and its glass panes had been stripped of their coat of blue paint. The clear rays, of a brightness which nobody had known for a long time, were piercing the lace curtains and drawing strange patterns on the walls.

Downstairs, he could hear a buzz of voices and the rattle of crockery. His mother poked the fire. Everybody was probably at table.

He was hungry. And yet he remained standing barefoot at the window, until the kitchen door opened and Élise's voice came up the staircase well.

'Are you awake, Roger? Aren't you coming down?'

'I'm coming, Mother.'

The time it took to get dressed without lighting the lamp, then down he went.

Some other Penguin books are listed
on the following pages

Memoirs of a Dutiful Daughter

Simone de Beauvoir

In this autobiography the author of *The Mandarins* describes her childhood in a kindly but stifling atmosphere of Catholic respectability, her revolt against those standards, and the beginning, at the Sorbonne, of her decisive friendship with Jean-Paul Sartre. Reviewing the book in the *New Statesman*, V. S. Pritchett wrote:

'The emancipation of women has been slower to come in France [than in England]. . . . Mlle de Beauvoir is clear, honest, an excellent psychologist, and the central part of her book, which carefully takes the years between thirteen and seventeen to pieces, is admirable. . . . I do not remember having read a girl's adolescent life being done before with anything like Mlle de Beauvoir's pleasant precision. . . .

'To the severely brought-up girl, whose letters were opened, whose reading was censored, and who had to fight for knowledge inch by inch, it seemed that both her parents were punishing her for their own failure, or the failure of the gloomy code they lived by. . . . She is out to expose self-mutilating and stupid aspects of bourgeois niceness.'

Simenon

André Gide, François Mauriac, and other famous French writers have been among the admirers of Georges Simenon, who is not only one of the most talented novelists but also one of the most prolific. English critics, too, for many years have been lavish in their praises:

'Simenon seems to me a man of genius' – Raymond Mortimer in the *Sunday Times*

'One of the great writers of our time' – Ralph Partridge in the *New Statesman*

'The best living detective-writer ... Maigret is the very bloodhound of heaven' – C. Day Lewis (Nicholas Blake) in a broadcast

This is one of ten new Simenons that are being added to the Penguin list, which already includes over twenty of his fiction and crime titles.

Fiction
    BLACK RAIN
    IN CASE OF EMERGENCY*
    THE WIDOWER*
    PEDIGREE
    ACT OF PASSION

Crime
    MAIGRET'S FAILURE
    MAIGRET AFRAID*
    MAIGRET IN COURT
    MAIGRET TAKES A ROOM*
    MAIGRET IN SOCIETY

*Not for sale in the U.S.A. or Canada
Remainder not for sale in the U.S.A.

For a complete list of books available please write to Penguin Books whose address can be found on the back of the title page